To Alli
From [ ]
Thank for everything

/2016

GRYPHONS.

By Alyx Jae Shaw

Text and Cover Artwork
Copyright Alyx J Shaw 2016

© 2016 Alyx Jae Shaw. All rights reserved.
ISBN: 978-1-329-88712-1

Dedication;

To Wulff H; *who had sense enough not to accept a cameo.*

To Caz M; *fan, friend, keeper of the music.*

And to my special friend **J. Loveys,** *the finest proof-reader I ever met, and companion on many literary adventures. Such as -*

Me: "That line doesn't say 'chocolate'."

J: "It should."

And let us not forget -

"I'm confused."

"Have I read this?"

"Really? ....REALLY?"

"...and J. was sick in the corner."

"COOKIES!"

"POTATOES!"

"Am I a fish again?"

"I'd rather watch 50 Shades of Grey while eating mushrooms."

And, of course – "When are you going to finish Even Fall? Because I really liked that one..."

Gryphons – Book I
'The Kids Are All Right'.

Throughout this book you will notice there are a few Sferkkaan words and phrases used. There is a handy guide to the translation and pronunciation for these located at the back.

part of Sferkkaan life and culture, and for the last five hundred years had been prohibited by the inhabiting Kryphisian government. Especially the dangerous new stuff that provoked wild excitement and reaction; the stuff that Satellite Base Four now cheerfully broadcasted to the stars as it wheeled in its orbit high above the planet's surface, looking down upon its haze.

The origin of the music was near impossible to place. It had been discovered roughly thirty years ago by a man named Enston Legri, who spent his days creating musical instruments of near-magical ability, as well as designing and redesigning complex monitoring systems. What he had been constructing the systems for no one had ever found out. Those who had known the man before he had been executed said that he had been a bit unstable, and had an obsession with finding new sounds. And, in the middle of a dead still winter night, he did.

Calling in his few friends, the small group sat and listened to what emerged from the complex speakers, faint at best, decaying into a bare whisper at worst. Alien voices sang alien songs, and more alien voices spoke between the songs. The aliens called their music Ra Khan Roll, and after a few hours of rapt attention the group began finding ways to record what they were hearing. Finally they had one full song, faint but clear. They ran it through an enhancing process, and eventually had a decently audible copy of the song. They ran off copies and distributed them by the bagful. The bootlegging went on at a shameful rate, until Enston Legri was shot for distributing material for the purposes of disrupting the peace.

The Beatles had officially invaded Sferkkaa.

The alien music provoked much feeling from the spirited Sferkkaans, and the Kryphisians wanted none of it. Anyone caught playing this new music would be shot, or worse. But despite the death of the music's finder, and the confiscation of his equipment, the music didn't go away. Instead, the music slid underground, into the darker recesses of Sferkkaan life. The music was regarded as dangerous by the Kryphisians, therefore it had to be of some value. Ra Khan Roll made its way by degrees into a place known as The Cylinder.

The Cylinder had originally been built as a city unto itself, a refuge for the highest ranking officers in the Kryphisian army; a great glass tower erected to their might. The underground of the Cylinder was literally and figuratively the lowest a person could go on the planet. South Continent drug dealers, chased out of their jungle market, congregated there, along with dissidents and rebels. Exotic whores roamed the corridors, hawkers set up strange shops and sold whatever the buyer wanted, while in the mushroom dens, the political and intellectual minds of the time gathered and plotted. Some were caught and taken away to the prisons on the Kryphisian moon, others simply grew old and cynical, writing political literature and strange poetry as they had all of their lives, smoking and injecting the illegal mushroom drug.

Those who were not yet dead or too jaded began to play Ra Khan Roll. It became a voice for the people, a way to let themselves know that they were still alive. Those who dared to play it were held in awe by those not brave enough to do so. To be a musician was a fast way to die young, but the musicians hung in, and formed groups. Many of them were politically involved intellects, not a few were working within the groups of rebels that appeared to make life miserable for the oppressors, the `Grey Boys,' as the pale, grey-eyed oppressors were known.

Musicians had always been held in awe by the Sferkkaans: suddenly they had become revered. When the war finally ended, many of the music groups had trouble with the concept of being able to play openly, and disbanded. A few stayed around, and enjoyed the adulation and financial reward. The Emperor would have been happier without them, but had no desire to do anything about the groups. In quiet moments, which were few and far between, he often had the depressing feeling that he was the only man on the planet who hated Ra Khan Roll. He was also not thrilled about being Emperor, but did not see any point in arguing the situation at the moment. He was, after all, quite likely the descendant of the last Emperor. He was also wildly popular, and the fact that he hated Ra Khan Roll only served to make him more so.

Sferkkaan humour was like that.

Chapter One

Gemma Mayfield sat on a broad leather couch aboard the enormous interstellar craft, watching her destination slowly grow larger through the observation deck window. Four months ago, when she first boarded the space craft, she had been so excited she couldn't sit still for a moment. But four months gave her plenty of time to think. She was so far from home, so far from everyone she cared about. Of course this was the opportunity of a lifetime, but… well… she hadn't realized just how far four months in space was. But an invitation from Earth's first interstellar neighbour, Sferkkaa, to participate in the Year End Festival was an enormous honour and opportunity. It would go on for five days, and according to the photos she had seen of last year's event, it was a lot like Burning Man meets Woodstock. The best bands on the planet would be there, and they had requested a wide variety of Earth bands to come play as well. Everything from Pop to Punk to Classical to Death Metal.

Gemma was there to bring Pop Music to the masses. She was intimidated, but excited. She couldn't wait to hear the Sferkkaan bands.

A large friendly presence came to stand beside her; a big man with a deep voice like warm caramel.

"You been practicing your language skills? We're gonna need them in a few days."

"Not as much as I should," she admitted, and looked up at the enormous man. When she had first met Cliff Robertson, aka K-Shot, she'd been scared to death of him. For starters he was well over six and a half feet tall and probably three hundred pounds, most of which was muscle. Then there was his police record. Not a man who was afraid to express his opinion. But during the time she had known him, she had bonded to him as a foster brother. He wasn't perfect, but whatever his flaws may be, he was overall a good and kind man.

"Me either," he said, grinning. "Man this is too much – me, on another planet, bringin' my music to a whole new place!"

"I keep having nightmares about being booed off the stage," said Gemma.

"Never happen," said K-Shot, reassuring the fifteen year old girl. "They invited a whole variety of different talent. They wanna see you, me…"

"And me," said a teen male voice in the background. K-Shot completely disregarded him.

"…that British band, those guys from Norway, the group from Japan…"

"And me."

K-Shot rolled his eyes. "And you. I suppose. Not sure *why*, since this is supposed to be a *music* festival."

Mickie Pastors walked over to the pair. Actually a more apt description would be "swaggered", but at age seventeen, scrawny, and dressed in all the most high-end "gear", he looked like what he was – a cheap corporate-made poser. The problem was Mickie thought he had real talent. Sadly tens of thousands of teen girls thought he did as well. Gemma found it fascinating that she trusted the rapper with the record from the bad part of town over little Mr. Private School Boy. But K-Shot seemed far less sleazy and far more trustworthy. For one thing, K-Shot had never showed up at her bedroom door at two in the morning holding a rope and a pillow case and wanting in. Mickie was about to say something to K-Shot, when Mickie was run over by nearly six feet of skinny guitar player with long brown hair. As the newcomer glued himself to the window like some strange insect, a weary, admonishing voice could be heard.

"Ah, Vidar, don'ts be runningks arounds likes… ah why I am bothers, even."

Vidar looked over his shoulder to the tall bony blonde behind him. "Buts whole new planets, Sigge! You gots to come sees!"

Gemma had *no* idea who had taught the pair of Scandinavians their English, but she hoped their Sferkkaan was better.

"Excited?" she asked Vidar, smiling.

"Ja!" he said, brown eyes bright. "Can'ts waits to gets on stage."

Sigge made a derisive snort. "You can'ts waits to stinks on dis planet as well as home?"

Vidar looked over his shoulder at his friend, smiling. "You loves me, admits it."

"Likes da crotch-crabs I loves you."

Vidar was completely undaunted. "Dats much?!" he said, grinning. "Yay! I goes tells da other guys we gettingks nears da planet, and you loves me likes crotch-crabs."

Vidar left the window, kissing Sigge in passing as he scampered to the main living area of the ship. Gemma, K-Shot, and Mickie just stared at Sigge. The tall blonde stared back with eyes the colour of polar ice and crossed his arms.

"Is old Scandinavian tradition," said Sigge.

"Uh huh," said K-Shot. "Started on those lonely ocean voyages in the longboats. Why don't you just come out and admit you two love each other?"

Sigge strolled to the window with a grace and majesty Mickie desperately coveted and could never manage, because Mickie would never be as comfortable in his own skin as Sigge was. But then again, Mickie was not descended from a long line of Viking warriors.

"We will," said Sigge. "Buts we nots really gets together until we starts da journey here, and he is wantings to tells his family befores we is tellings whole world. Or whole *two* worlds."

"Bet they'll be surprised," said Mickie. "I mean, finding out their son is a homo."

Gemma glanced to Sigge, but the lean blonde showed no reaction as he gazed through the great window at the planet they were approaching.

"No dey is knowings dat. Da surprise is beings what is takings us so long."

"So they're cool with him being gay," said K-Shot.

In the background there was a loud crash, and the annoyed roar of a Finnish lead vocalist. Moments later Vidar tore by, covered in black hair dye and hotly pursued by the afore-mentioned Finnish singer, who was now a lovely shade of pinto. Sigge smiled faintly.

"I think they is beings relieved he nots breed."

"So then who cares who you tell?" asked Mickie.

Sigge was showing signs of irritation. "I promised Vidar. Is importants to him."

"So who cares? He's a fucking idiot."

Gemma glanced to Sigge once more, but the lanky Swede gave no indication he heard Mickie. After a few moments, he slowly turned from the window and walked away, moving like a lord in his hall. Gemma had a funny feeling that, at some point, Sigge was going to get Mickie for that comment. As she looked to K-Shot, she could tell he was thinking the same thing.

"How long until we land?" she asked K-Shot.

"'Bout another four days," he said, gazing at the distant large white dot that was their destination. "Looks like a big ol' pearl in the blackness, don't it?"

Gemma smiled faintly, and nodded, but was still nervous about reaching their journey's end. She was distracted from her fears by Mickie.

"Can't wait to land and get me some alien *PU-SSAY!*"

He hissed the last word in her ear. She shoved him away.

"God you are such a pig, you're gross."

"Well since you're such an uptight bitch I have to find someone else to grease my pole, don't I?"

K-Shot raised an eyebrow, turning his attention to the brat. "Wait wait wait – you think you are going to find pussy…. *there*?" He indicated the still-distant planet to which they were heading.

"Well yeah! I mean they invited us to come play in that big festival, that means girls! Aw screw the both of you, I'm going to my room."

Mickie left. K-Shot and Gemma snickered and snorted with amusement.

"Do you get the impression that Mickie hasn't been doing his studying?" asked K-Shot.

"He is going to be one very disappointed pig," said Gemma.

K-Shot just grinned, shaking his head. "Hey I'll catch you later, I wanna get in some rehearsal time."

Gemma watched him go, then moved to one of the large couches closer to the observation window to gaze at the planet. In four short days she would be landing there, along with a wide assortment of musicians from all over the world – everything from children's music to classical, metal to Celtic, rockabilly to folk. Music was an enormous part of the culture of many of the different peoples on the planet of Sferkkaa; small wonder they had wanted to see how Earth rocked after making contact.

Gemma sat on the couch, finding her sketch pad under one of the cushions. How it had ended up there was a question for the ages, but she was happy to have found it. She checked her pockets, and found she had a pencil with her. Turning to a clean page, she began to idly draw the distant planet as she thought about the place to which she was going.

The fact that Mickie thought he was going to get off the space ship and have girls throwing themselves at him was funny and sad at the same time. For the last eight hundred years, the people of Sferkkaa had been at war with invaders from another world; invaders determined to wipe out everyone on the planet and take it over. They had robbed Sferkkaa of her resources, gods, history, her way of life, even the names given the days and months of the calendar and the lands in which the Sferkkaans lived. As a final parting shot, when they were at last driven off the planet, they had dumped a toxin into the water specifically designed to attach itself to female DNA, causing major organs to shut down, killing a huge majority of women and female children. The ratio of men to women on Sferkkaa currently was eight hundred to one, and of those few remaining women, only two out of ten could conceive and bear children.

There would likely be no girls waiting for the great Mickie Pastors to get off the ship.

Gemma may have been negligent in learning their language, but she had taken advantage of the information stored on the ship's computers. She had learned that, in many respects, Sferkkaan culture resembled a mish-mash of various Earth cultures. This was because, without any real idea of who they were as a whole anymore, they had taken to adopting some of the ways of their new Earth friends. These customs became blended with the few the Sferkkaans still had, so those visiting would find a bizarre combination of the familiar and utterly alien when they landed. For one thing, makeup was primarily a male thing, as were elaborate clothing and high heels. But the makeup they wore was not simply to enhance their features; colours, lines, and patterns told whole stories about the person wearing it. Gold, Gemma lad learned, was the colour of the highest imperial houses, and no one who could not prove they had an imperial bloodline was permitted to wear it. This had been distressing because it meant she couldn't wear her usual pink-and-gold eye shadow, and she felt oddly nude without it.

Another thing they had borrowed from Earth was livestock; cows, chickens, pigs, sheep, goats and turkeys had been imported to bolster dwindling food supplies, as had assorted carefully selected wild animals to help fill in massive breaks in the eco system. Crops, too, had been imported; different varieties for a wide range of climates, and the fastest growing ones to be found. The Sferkkaans were hanging on by their nails, doing their best not to go extinct, but it would be a long hard fight.

With fertile women in even shorter supply than food, it was up to the men to bear the burden of creating children, sometimes literally. Great tanks hooked up to elaborate machinery in newly-built hospitals could create a baby with donated DNA, but Sferkkaan babies who developed exclusively in those tanks almost invariably emerged eleven months later to grow into children with serious emotional problems. It seemed that the sounds associated with being in the mother's womb were a key part to healthy emotional development. Recordings played to the developing infants helped, but not enough. The solution was to create a device that could be implanted into a man to act as an artificial uterus. Children born this way came out far more healthy and stable, and while Earth men may have been horrified at the concept of finding themselves pregnant, Sferkkaan men were rather open to the idea. After all – they had endured eight hundred years of murder and warfare. Some painfully stretched abdominal muscles, loss of balance, and severe hormonal issues were a walk in the park after having to use a stack of rotting corpses as a barrier against rain and cold. The problem was many of the men were too loaded with alien viruses engineered by the invaders to qualify for an artificial uterus. Being willing to have one's anatomy rearranged was simply not enough – one needed to be free of viral contagions.

Gemma often wondered what exactly the Sferkkaans were struggling for at this point. Maybe just to save themselves. Maybe just to make sure tomorrow followed today. She didn't really understand it, personally. But she had grown up in a safe stable Canadian city in a safe stable Canadian neighbourhood. No one was dropping bombs on her, killing her sisters and friends, forcing male babies through genetic engineering to become freaks to serve the invaders, and dumping toxins into the water to make the population easier to control. Her life consisted of what was euphemistically termed "First World Problems", such as how to update her Facebook status while seventeen light years from home. Fortunately Sferkkaan technology gave her the ability, but in her opinion it stunk that it took a day and a half for the servers to get the signal stating what she had for dinner. She drew out her phone and sent an update.

"Four more days til I land on Sferkkaa! Well two and a half by the time this reaches Earth. Hope I meet someone nice, kinda

grossed out by the idea of boys in makeup and high heels but I guess it's their planet, they can dress like it's the 80s if they want."

****

As Gemma and her travelling companions slowly approached the pearl-grey planet, on Sferkkaa the cloud cover glowed softly overhead, giving away the presence of the Sferkkaan sun; a star most Sferkkaans had never seen. The perpetual cloud cover protected them from its deadly heat and glare, releasing the soft misty rain that now fell and scented the spring air. It always rained on Sferkkaa; sometimes in a faint, delicate mist, sometimes in deadly torrents, but never did it stop, and almost never did the sun shine through the clouds, save for on very rare days.

Warplanes flashed by overhead, brilliant white with gold-edged wings, silent save for the rush of air as they passed, then banked like seabirds and were gone. The young girl on the battered streets far below paused to watch the planes, smiling as they rolled, then shot straight up, disappearing into the cloud cover, out of its protective sheath and into the light. There the sun would turn them into creatures of light, showing them up on radar as birds of fire. The girl waited to see if the planes would come back. However they did not, and she continued on down the cracked and pitted paved road, clutching a thin metal cylinder. Her boots clipped quietly on the sidewalk, making tiny splashing sounds in the small shallow puddles.

She passed some tall and ragged hedges, then turned up the narrow, mossy walkway that led to her destination; an old house with a long set of stone steps leading to its bright red door. Someone had gone through a great deal of trouble to make the house look warm and inviting, and for the most part had succeeded. The fact that the back wall of the house was missing was unfortunate, but it was still one of the better structures on the block. Many of the others were little more than charred pits.

Grasping the tarnished gold door handle, the girl turned it, then poked her head inside.

"Any about?" she called.

A tall woman of indeterminate age greeted her. It was hard to guess ages – nearly everyone looked ten years older than they were. "Diza, have you heard of knocking?"

"I think I read about it once. Is Dahli home?"

"She's in her room. Stay and have supper with us."

"You mean with real food and everything?"

Teirra, who was Dahli's older sister and guardian, smiled a little wearily. "Technically it's food, I suppose. I woke up from a nap and it was trying to drag me away by my ankle. So I hit it with my text book and now it's roasting in the oven."

Diza blinked at Teirra, her facial expression rather wary. "What was it?"

"It was a something-hairy-and-bitey. All I know is it saved us about four days of rations. Come down for a piece when it's done."

Diza shrugged. "All right, thank you. I've never had hairy-and-bitey before."

"Well if it's tasty I'll make it a family recipe."

Diza laughed, then headed up the stairs. Dahli's house, like many in this area, was a surreal combination of Newly Remodelled and Bomb Crater. The neighbourhood was being rebuilt, and the trade arrangements with Earth had provided some much appreciated supplies and a few luxuries. But it was still creepy to walk up the stairs to the second floor and suddenly find a giant hole where a wall used to be, that led to a bomb crater beyond. Diza reached a room with a sign on it reading; "Warning: Kryphisian Biological Experiment lurking within." She opened the door, and paused.

Dahli Sandiniti lay on her stomach, stretched out on her bed with a look of intense concentration on her face. Before her on the floor sat a youth of sixteen years, a good friend of theirs called Czamkiar. He was perfectly still, his shining white hair pulled back from his equally pale face as Dahli carefully applied a layer of paint to his cheeks. He did indeed look like a Kryphisian biological experiment. Diza pulled down the sign and showed it to Dahli.

"Not funny," she drawled, tossing the sign onto the floor.

"Not meant to be," Dahli drawled back in perfect mimicry. Czamkiar turned his head to see who was behind him.

"Diza!" he exclaimed happily.

"Czamki!" said Dahli, sitting up. "You just made me mess your make-up. How are you supposed to impress your girlfriend if your lips are on crooked?"

"Girlfriend, she says. She doesn't even know I'm on the planet."

"Well, how is she supposed to find out if all she ever sees is some beaker who can't get his makeup on?"

"I *can't* get my makeup on, that's why I'm here, remember?"

Diza smiled at the two, then strolled casually over to where Dahli sat. She drew the silver cylinder out from beneath her arm and showed it to her friend. Dahli stared at the length of metal, then said questioningly, "You got it?"

"I got it," Diza confirmed, her tone triumphant.

Dahli made a grab for the cylinder, Diza snatching it away. "Don't wrinkle it!"

"How am I supposed to do that when it's in a metal tube? Let's see."

Diza uncapped the cylinder slowly, watching her friend squirm in delight. She withdrew a roll of shiny paper and solemnly passed Dahli one end. Then she took a single step back, unrolling the paper. Dahli let out a thin screech.

"Aren't they beautiful?" said Diza. "They get better looking all the time."

Dahli nodded. "Except the drummer."

"I agree," said Diza. "I think rumours that he's alive are greatly exaggerated."

"No way, he can't get better looking because he's perfect."

"GET LOST! He's ancient. I bet he's thirty, and he's got a face like he didn't survive his last drug binge."

"Well he's my favourite, so you can just leave him alone."

"Fine. Let's hang them up."

Czamkiar climbed onto the bed, collapsing dramatically onto his back. "You're not finished painting my face," he complained loudly, clearly upset at the interference caused by the poster. Diza and Dahli ignored him as the poster went up in its place of worship. Then the two stepped back to view it as it held reign over the head of the bed. They eyed it critically. Finally Dahli proclaimed her judgement.

"Another bad picture," she stated.

"Definitely," agreed Diza.

Czamkiar turned his head to gaze at the poster, images etched onto paper by laser lights of the five people who formed Sferkkaa's most famous and popular music group; the Mortified Gryphons. Five weird-looking people with a bad name, as far as he was concerned, and he had certainly told Dahli and Diza often enough.

"The drummer does look pretty bad, Dahli. But the little one with the white hair… she's pretty cute."

"She?" said Dahli, "She who? What one are you looking at?"

"The little blonde with the big blue eyes. Her."

"That's Khandid Stracona. He's a guy."

"That does it," said Czamkiar. "I now have absolutely *no* interest in that band."

"Oh, poor Czamki," said Dahli as she sat before him, reaching for the make-up kit once more. "Khandid wouldn't be interested in you anyway. He's married."

"Yeah? To what?"

Dahli pointed to another member to the band. "Yuri Stracona."

"Just paint my face so I can get out of here, will you?" He sighed. He then noticed the sign that Diza had tossed to the floor. "'Kryphisian biological experiment'? I don't look like a biological experiment. What do you mean by putting that on your door?"

"I am morally opposed to High Northerners wearing make-up," said Dahli. "It ruins their looks."

"I'll put anything on my face I like, or don't like." he grumped. "There are seven girls in the whole school, and the only three my age are you two, or Atania Nightwing."

All three sucked in a lungful of air and yelled; "EEEEEEEEYEEEEEEWWW!"

"Anyway," continued Czamkiar, "dating one of you would be like dating my sister, if I had a sister. So it's the new girl arriving from Avalair, or nobody. Unless I want to start dating other boys."

"Gee, Czamki, we're really sorry that females were practically wiped off the planet and ruined your social life," said Diza.

"That's not what I mean and you know it," he said, gazing at her from behind a delicate mask of pale blue lines. "It's just… I don't know. Hard. The reasons I'm pissed off are selfish ones, I know, I just hate being forced into this situation."

"You and hundreds of thousands of other guys," said Dahli. "Hey, did you hear about that visiting ship full of musicians from Earth, come to play with us at the Year End Festival?"

"Yeah," said Czamkiar. "Heard some of them are cute girls. Wonder if I can get a date with an alien?"

Dahli giggled. "Depends on if she can speak the language."

"Maybe we can communicate in obscene gestures," said

Czamkiar. "They'll be here in four days. It's exciting. Our very first invaders that we actually invited!"

"Let's hope they're better behaved than the Kryphisian ones," said Diza.

Dahli finished Czamkiar's makeup. It was a long, drawn-out ritual, the dramatic lines having to be just right. A boy's make-up had to be more than perfect; it had to be art, or no girl would be caught dead with him, and Czamkiar's options were already sorely limited. Dahli had a light touch and an artistic eye, which made her an invaluable friend to the fashion-conscious youths in her school. To paint a friend's face, she charged three trinta an hour. If she didn't like the boy, the price went up to twelve. Czamkiar had the honour of not having to pay.

"There you go," she finally said to him, "you're beautiful." The words were slightly sarcastic.

He hopped up and went to the small cracked mirror that hung on her wall to survey his make-up. "Hey, what's this orange line right here?"

"What orange line?" asked Dahli innocently.

"This orange one! I know what the others mean, here's my family history, and my name, and accomplishments, which is three blue dots for passing my first year training as a Whip. But what's that orange line?"

"Oh I made that one up just for you," said Dahli. "It lets everyone know that if your homework piles much higher you'll be able to make a hovel out of it."

"Hilarious."

He turned from the mirror to pick up and pull on his long, heavily ruffled black coat. Next came on the thigh high black boots with the very high heels. Because Czamkiar was not fully trained yet as a Whip, there was no blade down the back. A black belt circled his small waist, holding captive the blood red ruffled shirt. He pulled on his black gloves, picked up his black and silver walking stick, then struck a pose. His heavily lined eyes peered at Dahli and Diza from behind small round rimmed glasses. "How do I look?"

"Really good, Czamki," said Diza. She cocked her head and eyed him critically. "Bit short, though."

"Short? You really think I'm too short?" There was panic in his voice as he looked down at himself. "I knew I should have bought the boots with the six-inch heels!"

"You couldn't walk in six-inch heels, your feet aren't long enough," said Dahli. "Besides, you look great."

"Yeah," said Diza. "Lots of girls would love to be seen with you. I mean, if they were alive."

"Find a planet," said the thin youth, flashing her a rude gesture. He then smiled at Dahli. "Thanks for the paint on my face."

Dahli returned the smile. "Anytime. Have fun."

Czamkiar left the room, thundering downstairs in his boots with the four-inch heels, hitting the bottom step with a thump. Left on their own, the two girls had gone back to their favourite obsession.

"Concert shots are always better than studio ones," remarked Dahli, studying the new poster.

It was one of at least thirty; the walls of Dahli's bedroom were lined in them. Overlapping the posters in many places were articles regarding the band, and on the closet door was a map of all the cities the band had played on their last tour. The Gryphons had done two since Sferkkaa had become a free planet, and Dahli had managed to see one of the concerts by stealing ticket money from her now-absent mother and sneaking out of the window the night of the show. Dahli had been madly in love with the Gryphons ever since, especially the theoretically-living drummer. This was something Diza never quite understood, especially since the other band members were so attractive.

"My word, but that man is ugly," breathed Diza shaking her head. But `ugly' was not really the right word for Draephus CZimcocious. He was tall and rangy, a little too thin, and what he looked like without that long, beat-up rag of a coat, nobody knew. When he smiled, on rare occasion, he showed a row of badly chipped teeth. His large hands were scarred, the knuckles misshapen. He wore ugly, baggy clothes that always looked in need of a wash, and he apparently shaved on a very irregular basis. The sandy hair was either uncombed or hidden by a hat. His posture was bad, his facial expressions ranged from wary to defensive, and he always had a cigarette in his mouth.

"He's not ugly, he's beautiful," defended Dahli.

"If I ever saw Draephus walking toward me, I'd cross the street. Yuri is beautiful."

"Oh, sure, Yuri, the seven foot one who probably weighs all of thirty pounds, fifteen of which is hair."

"Leave him alone."

"Then leave Draephus. Look, there's a better picture of him, you can't tell me he's not cute."

"He looks like he wants to bite someone."

"He does not, he's perfect."

"He's strange," said Diza. "I read that the LEO's are so used to him doing crazy stuff, that one time when he rolled his conni into a ditch, a Legal Enforcement Officer stuck his head in the window, took one look at him, and said, "Oh it's just you, Donsa CZimcocious." Then the LEO went on his way and left him there."

"He is NOT strange."

"He is, too!"

"That's your opinion, and only yours," said Dahli, as Diza peered more closely at a portion of an article on the wall. She began to read it aloud.

"Kaisa (pr: KAY-sa) Noun. A long green vegetable rather like a cucumber. It is a hardy plant that grows well in temperate regions, often eaten only after everything else is gone, including footwear and the family pet. Has a taste and smell reminiscent of partly fermented cabbage and the approximate texture of a loofah. Immortalized by The Mortified Gryphons in their song 'Things to Do with a Kaisa.' Many people objected to the song as it only covered how to cook the things, not eradicate them.

The Mortified Gryphons have categorically denied their lead vocalist Mars David not only eats them, but LIKES them."

Dahli giggled. "I found that on an Earth site about Sferkkaan life and couldn't resist." She tugged her friend's sleeve. "Come on, let's go eat."

"Are you sure I should? Teirra invited me, but…"

"We've got the hairy thing in the oven, and our neighbour has been raising redhir in his attic. He butchered a few today and gave us two. And I went all over the neighbourhood earlier and found a whole patch of mushrooms. So we get meat and mushrooms and everything."

"I feel so mean eating redhir! They're so cute!"

"Well the good news is, once they hit the plate, they don't look like redhir anymore."

The pair went downstairs, just as the front door opened, and Teirra raised her head, seeing her husband come through the opening. She smiled at him. "Heia, handsome."

"GAG!" said Dahli, taking a couple plates out of the rickety cupboards.

Atterick Cruze ignored her as he smiled at Teirra, dropping his coat onto a chair that had seen better days, as had the coat. He walked over to her, seating himself wearily on the floor next to the chair she occupied.

"Heia," he said as he rested his head against her leg. Teirra reached down to touch his soft, blond hair.

"How was your day?"

"Wonderful. I think we found the quinticord player for our band. Here, I've a laser print of him."

Atterick reached into his back pocket and pulled out a picture, passing it to Teirra. She accepted it, then drew her breath in at the sight of the man.

"Show!" said Dahli. Teirra obliged. The man in the picture was tall and slender. Intense blue eyes burned out of a pale, delicately shaped face. Fine black stripes spread in a careful array over his cheeks, jaw and forehead, disappearing into his mane of black hair and the collar of his shirt.

"He's beautiful," said Dahli. "What planet is he from?"

"He's not," said Atterick, taking the picture back, "he's a Breed, something the Kryphisians came up with in their labs. He's got a quiet personality, which is good, and he plays incredibly well. The only problem I have with him is I keep wanting to ask him how far down those stripes go."

"You're married to me, remember?" said Teirra. "You're not allowed to go asking young men how far down their stripes go."

Atterick stared at his wife amusedly for a moment, then said, "I think I'll go get something to eat." He gave her a quick kiss, then rose and walked into the kitchen area.

"So what's new and exciting in your lives?" he asked as he grabbed a couple plates for himself and Teirra.

"Gryphons poster," said Dahli, although with her mouth full it came out, "`ryphn pfter'."

"I see," said Atterick, "and the fact that my own band finally found a quinticord player means nothing?"

"That's nice, Atterick," said Diza.

"You'd better drum up more enthusiasm than that," he said, "or I won't tell you what time those five losers you two are so in love with are on the Visual tonight."

"Twentyhour," said Dahli, mouth still full, "station line 6, the Astellis Monct Show."

"Okay," said Atterick, nodding.

He left the kitchen and walked over to the Visual, a huge square of seemingly featureless convex glass. It hung menacingly on one wall, freakishly out of place in the battered house. Atterick had looted it from an abandoned Kryphisian base, along with plates, linens, blankets, a rug, and other odds and ends to help improve life for his family. Once used to broadcast messages to the invaders, it now played the small handful of news and entertainment programmes available. Teirra and Atterick were only too happy to have the neighbours in for the more pertinent news broadcasts, and the occasional entertainment programme. Atterick reached up one hand and felt along its cool edge until he found the on/off switch, and carefully detached it. With the small square button in hand, he returned to the kitchen.

He watched the two girls eat, occasionally snatching and grabbing at attractive-looking morsels they'd arranged on a platter, growling and giggling at each other. He looked down at the knob in his hand, its black finish slightly chipped. He tossed it up in the air, catching it, tossing it once more. He attempted to balance it on his nose, and failing this tossed it into the air once again. Diza glanced up with mild curiosity, then froze.

"Dahli," she said, "he's got the on/off button."

"Oh Atterick," said Dahli, "you wouldn't."

"I might."

"We'd be emotionally scarred for life."

"I wouldn't be."

Dahli and Diza exchanged glances. "Gee, Atterick, tell us about your new quinticord player. We're really enthused."

Atterick reached over to tear off a small piece of Dahli's redhir, stuffing it into his mouth. "Much better."

Dahli made a rude gesture at him behind his back. "Put that button back or I'm gonna have to hurt you," she yelled, hearing him laugh.

The two did eventually clean up the debris of their snack, even going so far as to wash the dishes, leaving them in the rack to dry. Then, with hours to go before the show started, the two donned coats and boots and set out for Diza's house. Using the telecom would have been faster, and there would have been no need to get wet, but Diza's father refused to have one in the house. Like many older people, he was leery of the devices, and five years of peace had not been enough after a lifetime of fear to convince him that they were safe. He also refused to have a Visual, the Kryphisians having had listening beams that could be projected through such devices, as well as windows, in order to spy on suspected Revolutionaries. So any Gryphon-watching had to be done at Dahli's house in secret. It was not a pastime Diza's father would have approved of. He didn't want his daughter seeing anything on the Visual, for fear something may be seeing her in return. After losing his wife and four other daughters, he had reason to be afraid.

The air was warm, and the rain was the faintest mist. The sky was still dark, however, promising heavier rains to come. Dahli and Diza ambled along, too old now to splash in puddles but unable to resist stepping in them. They walked in silence, but Dahli had the feeling her long-time friend was about to spring something on her.

"Parents sure are bizarre," Diza announced.

"I wouldn't know," said Dahli.

"I met this guy," said Diza, "but if Dad ever met him, he'd have a fit."

Dahli smiled. "What's he like?"

"Well, he's older than me..."

"Uh-oh."

"He lives in the Lower Cylinder..."

"Oh, Diza."

"And he's from Sirius."

"Crime of the century. They'll have you shot. Is he nice?"

"He's really sweet."

Dahli grinned, shaking her head. "Well I won't tell your dad, you know that."

Diza smiled in return. "Thanks." She kicked at a stone. "He's really nice."

"Do I get to meet him sometime?"

"Yeah," said Diza. "I'd like you to. Funny how hard it is to meet a guy and talk to him. I mean actually talk as opposed to watching him wriggle around like a baby animal with a full bladder because he's so happy to meet someone with a vagina."

"Only one person in eight hundred has one of those now," said Dahli softly. "I don't know how the guys cope. I mean I like you and all but I don't think I'd want to marry you."

Diza glanced at a small group of boys across the street, all primped and preened, watching the two girls as if they were not quite certain what they were looking at. She smiled.

"Well the good news is you won't have to. Check out the pretty one in black."

Dahli did, casting a casual glance at the five youths. "Oh he is nice. I like the one in green better though. Green feathers in his hair, too. What do green feathers mean? I should know this."

"Green feathers mean his ancestors were scribes in the Imperial courts."

"Right. Wonder what would happen if I offered to show him my inkwell?"

The pair snorted and giggled, continuing on their way.

The rain had begun again by the time they reached Diza's house. They entered the silent building, the only sound within being that of the rain striking the windows. They removed their boots and coats by the door, setting these in their respective places before walking down the hallway to the living room. Diza peered around the corner of the doorway to see her father in a chair, reading a book. His feet rested on a padded stool as he turned the pages of the large tome, eyes fixed before him. Diza tapped her knuckles on the doorframe.

"Dad?"

"Hmmm?"

"Can I spend the night at Dahli's? There's no school tomorrow."

The man glanced up at Diza, staring at her. "Is Dahli here?"

"Hi," said Dahli, stepping around the corner to confirm her presence. He stared at the two of them for a long moment as though certain they were up to something, but he wasn't sure what. Diza stood in apprehension, then almost heaved a sigh of relief when her father nodded and returned his gaze to his book. Diza tugged Dahli's sleeve as a sign for her to follow, and the two went down the hall to Diza's room.

"Wow," said Dahli as she shut the door. "For a moment I thought he wasn't going to let you go. You would have missed the show."

"Never," said Diza as she pulled a bag out of her closet. "I would have sneaked out the window."

"No you wouldn't," said Dahli as she sat on the bed.

"No, I probably wouldn't," admitted Diza. "If he checked and I was gone I think he'd die on the spot of fear."

She packed her bag, stuffing into it a pair of pyjamas, a change of clothes, her make-up, a half pack of cigarettes, and her good luck charm. This was a bizarre contraption of feathers, a bird skull, bits of fur, teeth, and some small polished shells and bits of wood all strung together on thin leather strips. As she was about to drop it into the bag, Dahli grabbed it.

"What's this?"

"A lucky charm. Randish gave it to me."

"Is that your boy from Sirius?"

"Yeah."

"How long was it kicking around in his cave before he gave it to you?"

Diza snatched it from Dahli. "You're such a clart."

"Yeah and you hang around with me so what does that make you? Oh! I almost forgot. Atterick and Teirra are going out tonight."

"Yeah, so?"

"So..." Dahli grinned. "They're going to be gone for hours. We can go down to my grandfather's and get his conni. We'll go for a ride. Hey we can go to that fancy inn. Of course we'll have to park away from the place just in case Atterick and Teirra go by."

"Okay, I know the place you mean. There are lots of places to hide a conni." Diza closed her bag. "Let's go."

They walked back to Dahli's, smoking, discussing plans to do in the science duone, *(a known clart)* what they would do with a million trinta, *(get the Gryphons to play at their next party)* and Randish's body. Diza lit a cigarette as she talked about how strange he was, his large, long hands, his blue-white eyes, and the ridge of black, stiff hair that ran halfway down his back.

"It's really strange," Diza said, "it feels just like a brush."

"Brush," muttered Dahli. "I'm not sure I'd want someone who had a brush on his back. I have a hard enough time looking at facial hair."

"Well this is different. I don't have to kiss his back."

Dahli agreed that this was true, though she was well aware of just how strange the average Siriusian could be, and wasn't certain she could find one attractive. Cute perhaps, even humorous, but not something she would want to curl up next to.

"He's from Sirius, he wasn't born here," said Diza.

Dahli groaned. The ones who had been born on Sferkkaa were odd enough, but the ones from their native planet were too bizarre.

"Dizaaa...they eat...little crawly fuzzy things."

"Says she who served me a plate of the thing her sister killed!"

"You won't have babies you'll have litters."

"That's silly, Sferkkaans and Siriusians can't reproduce."

"THAT SHOULD TELL YOU SOMETHING!"

"I thought you'd be happy for me," Diza flicked away the remains of her cigarette.

"I am, as long as you're happy."

"Thank you. You're the only person I've told, so please don't mention this to anyone."

"Sure."

The two girls arrived back at Dahli's to find the house silent, Atterick and Teirra having left by now. There was half an hour before the show started, and much to do. As Dahli put a few special treats on a small plate for them to savour during the show, Diza began heating water to strain through crushed shooberries. This was a fairly popular drink, one Dahli and Diza were not supposed to have. It was a dark red tea, lightly sweet to the taste, which produced a mild high. Most households had shooberries, as they could be used for a variety of things, including antiseptic for small burns and cuts, treatment for muscle pain, backache and headache, and a remedy for fever.

Mostly people got stoned on them.

With mere minutes to spare, they made it to the Visual after having turned off all the lights in the house so there would be no distraction from the objects of their adulation. Dahli turned on the huge sheet of glass, then raised volume up to an appropriate level. Shivers of anticipation went through them like cold tickles as they waited and watched. The programme prior to the Astellis Monct Show took forever to end. After an agonizing time the show started, finding both girls nearly sick with anticipation. The live audience was of a different calibre than usual; they were louder, more aggressive. When Astellis Monct stepped out there was a roar of enthusiasm, though obviously not for him. Monct himself seemed calm and rather pleased, with good reason. The Mortified Gryphons were not an easy group to contact. It was even less easy to get them to agree to come on a show. But he had them, all five of them, and virtually no household with a Visual would be watching anything else.

"Why is he just standing there and smiling?" Diza demanded.

"Come on, clartblossom," said Dahli, annoyed. "Nobody wants to see *you,* even if you think they do."

****

Gemma's watch beeped, informing her that a Sferkkaan TV show was about to come on. Unaware her Sferkkaan counterparts were also intent on viewing the programme, she sought the remote to the wall-sized flat screen TV. She wanted to watch it mainly because it would feature the band that would be the ruler by which they would be all measured. It also gave her an excuse to use her Sferkkaan. She found the remote, drew out her electronic dictionary and turned it on, then turned on the TV.

She jumped at the sound of screaming that assaulted her ears, and the remote briefly escaped her hand, leaping into the air as she started. Gemma caught it and fought to turn the volume down, but not before it attracted several of her ship mates.

"What the fuck is that?" asked K-Shot, looking annoyed.

Gemma pointed to the screen. K-Shot and the several other people who had emerged from various parts of the ship, Mickie included, looked. Standing beside K-Shot, holding his hand, was his girlfriend Mystique. Gemma was intimidated by the statuesque beauty. Not many women could carry a name like Mystique and make it work, but she certainly could.

"Oh it's that band you're all supposed to be scared of," she said. "What's their name?"

"Arucadda Dannatti," said Brian Taylor, lead vocalist of Blacklight, a harmonic metal band.

"What's that mean?" asked Sigge.

Gemma consulted her dictionary, as on the TV a curtain pulled back and revealed a set of drums that would have struck terror into even the most experienced drummer. Terror, or possibly a spontaneous orgasm if one was to judge by the noise Brian's drummer Billy Waters, made.

"Billy want!" he yowled.

"What's that on the bass drum?" asked K-Shot.

Mickie just rolled his eyes as Billy stepped forward to look.

"Some sort of fantasy creature, with wings and a really freaky bird head…"

"It's an Imperial Gryphon," said Gemma. "The name of the band translates into…. Mortified Gryphons?!"

The group before the TV exchanged glances.

"Who the fuck came up with that?!" demanded K-Shot. "Mortified Gryphons?! And people take them seriously with a name like that?"

Brian cleared his throat. "Who here named his first band 'Atomic Glue Gun'?"

"Hey, Atomic Glue Gun is a rockin' name," said K-Shot.

The debate was halted when someone walked onto stage; a tall man with a heavy mane of black hair that hung down to the small of his back. His skin was black as well, but not a shade those gathered in the room had ever seen. There were no undertones of golden caramel to warm it, just black with an almost silvery overtone, and he truly looked like what he was; a man from another world. Then he looked to the camera, and eyes that were almost luminously blue-white stared at them.

"Okies, dey is winning," said Vidar. "I is beings scared now."

Sigge nudged him fondly. The man on the TV turned his head to watch his bandmates walk out. The next person was tiny, with delicate bones, skin like white velvet, hair like a stallion's mane, and enormous blue eyes. Dressed entirely in pale pink, it was impossible to say if it was male or female, unless one knew anything about the band. Which Mickie clearly didn't.

"Oh yeah!" he said. "I'm gonna be getting stuck up her in a couple days."

"Him," corrected Gemma.

"No way, shut the fuck up, you're just jealous."

"Whatever," muttered Gemma.

"That's a man?" asked Corey Hillman, there to bring Country-Western music to Sferkkaa. His expression was dubious.

"That's what the band bio says," said Gemma. "Hey am I the only person reading this stuff?"

"I'm with Corey," said Billy. "That tiny little thing is not a man."

"Khandid Stracona, male," said Gemma, pointing at entry in her smartphone.

"He's a cute little thing!" said Mystique. She moved closer to the TV screen to get a better look at him. She touched him with one carefully-manicured fingernail, tracing the markings on his face. "What does the thin black line under his eyes mean?"

"That he's a fag," sneered Mickie.

Sigge growled something at Mickie in Swedish. Gemma consulted her phone.

"Single black line under the eye means he was an assassin during the war."

"And what do the high heels mean?" asked Brian.

"That he's a fag," said Mickie. This apparently was going to be his stock answer to everything.

"They're not heels, they're boot blades," said Gemma. "They mean he's a Whip, a type of warrior from the Northern Continent. They mean he can leap straight up and cut your throat with them."

"They were all soldiers in the war, weren't they?" asked K-Shot.

"Partisans, mostly," said Sigge. "Da only one actuallies in da military is Mr. Scary Blue Eyes, dere. Was fighter pilot."

Gemma consulted her phone. "Raski Jervyas, pilot in the Imperial air force. Flew dozens of missions, shot down three times, decorated numerous times. Has been awarded both the Order of the Empire and an Imperial Gryphon, the latter of which was given…posthumously? What's posthumously mean?"

"Means he was dead when they gave it to him," said Mystique.

The group stared at Raski Jervyas, who was awaiting his band mates on stage, clearly very much alive.

"Okay," said K-Shot. "I have got to find out how he died long enough to get a medal than came back to play in a band."

Three more band members walked out, bringing the total to five. The microphone was taken by a very small male with wavy hair to his backside, held more or less in place by an old slouch hat. His boots had four inch heels on them, and he walked in them as if he did it daily. Beside him stood a very tall man with long black curling hair. He was model-thin, with almost freakishly long legs. He kept his head down while he played, and looked like he would much prefer to be someplace else. Then there was the drummer. Gemma thought Billy was probably dying to see who held claim to the imposing set, but he couldn't seem to make up his mind whether he was impressed or not. The drummer was tall, rangy, and lean – *too* lean, as if he spent more time high than was good for him, not that any of the Gryphons looked like they ate too often. He had clearly been in a fight, and recently. He was clad in some sort of full-length duster, which may have once been white, or pale grey. It looked like he'd been born wearing it, and how he played with it on was anyone's guess. But he did, and as Billy watched, the lanky man in the ratty coat proceeded to shame both power and speed drummers the whole Earth over.

"I think I wanna go home now," said Billy. "Is he using sticks?"

Something snapped off in the man's hand. Without missing a beat he threw away the remains of the drum stick and grabbed up another.

"He's *fast*," said Brian with quiet awe.

K-Shot suddenly darted forward to stare at something on the screen, then pointed. "THERE! Motherfucker I *knew* there was a reason we couldn't figure out the lead guitar player's moves – son of a bitch has six fingers on his left hand! And he uses *all* of them!"

"So these are the boys to beat, huh?" said Mystique.

"We nots be beatings dem no times soon," said Sigge. "What's beings dat t'ing he is playings? Is nots no guitar."

"Kannikort," said Gemma, having the sneaking suspicion she may be the only person doing any studying at all. "More commonly called a quinticord. Literally 'five-string'. Like a guitar but with a longer neck and lower range."

The band on screen was inspected thoroughly, K-Shot pointing out both of the quinticords to himself. "Okay, one, two quinticords, drums… what's the dude with the freaky blue eyes got?"

"Ulchirkort," said Gemma, struggling with the strange pronunciation. "Which translates into 'sepulchord', which is a word derived from the Sferkkaan words for 'sepulchre' and 'string'. Effectively, 'death note', so named for its deep, earthy tones."

"Like from a crypt," said Brian.

"I wants one," said Vidar.

"Jesus Christ they're ripping the damned stage apart!" exclaimed Billy suddenly.

"Who?" asked Mystique.

"The audience, look! God damn! What is *with* these people?!"

"It's a sign of respect," said Gemma softly.

"Respect?!" exclaimed K-Shot. "What kind of respect is that?!"

"It's so no band can follow them," she said. "Bands came before them, but none can come after."

"I'm gettin' the shivers," said Brian.

"Sferkkaans take their music seriously," said Mystique, showing that she too had done some studying. "It's one of the last things they have left of who they used to be."

The group stood in silence, and watched the greatest band on Sferkkaa beat them into submission before they had even set foot on the planet.

****

On the planet's surface, Dahli and Diza watched as well, taking in the entire spectacle. The noise was at a mad pitch, and there seemed little hope of controlling it.

"I can't hear them!" complained Diza, bouncing up and down from her seated position in agitation.

"The audience will calm down," said Dahli hopefully. She watched the lead singer, Mars David, stroll to the front of the precariously groaning stage. He smiled, then softly sang the first words of their latest song, 'Nightfall'. Both girls recognised it instantaneously, clutched each other and added their own shrieking to the noise.

The song ended, the screaming causing the microphones to shut down, protecting themselves from the roar. The Gryphons moved over to where Astellis Monct sat, and almost miraculously, the audience began to quieten. Not quickly, but eventually the wall of sound died down to a level with which the host and his guests could compete.

"I LOVE YOU, MARS!" someone shouted. Mars perked up

and looked in the direction of the call, but Khandid caught him and dragged him towards the sitting area where Monct was.

"Think he would have gone into the audience?" asked Diza.

"Do feralykes sniff their own butts? It wouldn't be the first time. Remember when they were touring in Trae Dae Mu and he leapt off a train through the window and into a crowd of about thirty thousand, and they didn't find him for a week?"

"Was that Mars? I thought that was Raski."

The girls pondered, then Dahli shook her head. "We'll check the Gryphon's Roost after the show, they'll know. Pretty sure it was Mars, though."

"They like you," understated Monct, and the audience bellowed its agreement. Raski laughed his strange, crazy laugh, not that anyone could really hear it.

"I wish those people would shut up," said Diza.

"They will," said Dahli, sipping her tea. She felt a mild itching on her scalp, an indication that the tea was beginning to affect her. She then lit a cigarette, eyes focused critically on the five. She took in every detail about them, their appearances, their movements, the scene burning into her mind. It was Diza who put a small dark mark on the entire thing.

"What's wrong with the drummer's face?"

"There is nothing wrong with Draephus' face!" Dahli defended. "He's got a cute face!"

"I don't know about *cute*, but somebody sure thumped him a good one."

Dahli searched the shaggy figure seated furthest from the host. He was wrapped as he always was in that hideous full-length coat which looked as though it had survived innumerable trips to the South Continent. The other Gryphons always seemed animate and conversational.

`Except,' thought Dahli, `for Yuri, who looks to be just slightly less alert than the average kiska nut, though I would never say that to Diza.'

On the Visual, Draephus watched, but made no attempt to get involved in the conversation, surveying the scene coolly from behind his opaque glasses. Then as he turned his head, Dahli saw what Diza had been talking about. The bruise wasn't very noticeable from behind the glasses, but at certain angles as the camera drew in for a closer look, it glared into view. The camera operator must have also noticed the bruise, and for a time the lens rested on his face, revealing now a row of stitches in his brow line. There was no eyebrow to speak of; it had been shaved off before the stitches were put in. Dahli's searching eyes now also noticed a thin slice cutting through his upper and lower lip, extending a ways down his chin. This was also stitched. The knuckles on the broad hand that now reached for a pack of cigarettes were scraped and raw. The hand trembled slightly as he lit the cigarette, the movements stiff and slow.

"Wow," said Diza. "Wonder what he's been up to?"

Chapter Two.

      Draephus CZimcocious awoke with a bad taste in his mouth; a combination of cigarettes, mushroom distillation, and a tooth he had been neglecting to have fixed. He had a dull headache, and the stitches above his eye were beginning to itch. The flesh around it felt a little warm, and he could feel dried blood crusted around the wound. His eyes were sore; in fact his whole upper face hurt, not to mention his ribs and neck. As he reached for a cigarette, he heard the telecom downstairs begin to ring. Šukat it, he wasn't running to get it. He lit a cigarette and ignored the telecom, feeling mild relief when it fell silent once more. It was probably Raski anyway, calling to make certain he was alive. Draephus felt a pang of guilt about not answering the 'com, but mentally he was not up to dealing with anyone, or anything. Outside his window the rain fell, tapping against the warped antique glass. He lay listening to it, his eyes slipping shut once again. They seemed too heavy to stay open. His neck screamed in protest as he slowly rolled onto his back, and he decided he had probably hurt himself more badly than he had thought. He still had to wonder if he had meant to drive his conni into that stone pillar or not. He had bled all over himself, but, apart from some stitches and the pain in his bones, he had assumed he was fine.

      He had been in the Lower Cylinder when he had done it, a place not unfamiliar to him. He had left the shattered conni where it was, slobbering green coolant onto the filthy concrete floor. The level was dark and quiet, but Draephus knew there were things lurking in the shadows, things that watched him hungrily with cold eyes. Drunk and injured, he seemed an easy target, and all that saved him were the long memories of the predators lurking in the gloom. They knew him. They had seen him before. They knew he was no easy kill, even in his current state. The predators slunk off, looking for softer meat, and Draephus found himself someone who claimed to be a doctor. Draephus supposed he could have been, he certainly had enough drugs in his apartment. He tried to recall how he had ended up in the man's home, or even his name, but couldn't. Various parts of the evening were wrapped in a fog. He knew he hadn't got the cut on his lip in the accident, but couldn't recall how he had got it. Probably from whomever he had broken his knuckles on.

He stubbed out the half-finished cigarette when a coughing fit gripped him, making him squirm in pain. He must have cracked a rib. By the time he finished coughing he was limp with agony. He would have groaned, but he couldn't seem to make any sound. His throat was raw and dry from smoke. At the foot of his bed, two slender, red-skinned creatures raised their heads and watched him with concern in their vibrant green eyes, making small worried noises in their throats.

"I'm all right," he said to them, and the creatures lowered their heads once more. They did not look convinced by his words, and they continued to watch him, trilling softly with bird-like voices to one another.

Eventually Draephus rolled gingerly out of bed, rising slowly on shaky legs. He had slept in his clothes, which were blood-spattered and smelled of three days' constant use. The stubble on his face was also three days old, too long for Draephus' liking, but he was pretty sure he wasn't going to bother with it for at least another day or two. He did not want to risk tearing open his numerous small wounds.

He made it halfway across the room before he had to rest, seating himself gingerly in an elegant antique chair next to the marble-fronted fireplace. At the time he had acquired the place, living in a castle had seemed like a great idea. It had been a ruined castle, with no heat, no lights, hand-pumped water, and power in only a few select areas. Now it was a perfectly restored castle, with no heat, no lights, hand-pumped water, and power in only a few select areas. Sometimes Draephus thought the only thing he liked anymore was his castle. At this moment, however, with no fire in the hearth and no strength to make one, he thought a castle was a pretty stupid place to live. He mused about finding another place. Perhaps a nice old people's home. Sure, he'd start his own. The Draephus CZimcocious Home for Down-and-Out Musicians and Detox Centre.

Draephus sat in the chair, feeling sore and old. The expensive woven rug beneath his chair did little to keep the cool of the red stone floor from his feet. He stunk, he needed a bath. He'd have to build a fire and pump the water, a task that usually did not bother him. He had loved the castle from the first time he had seen it, and keeping it as close to authentic as possible had always been of utmost importance. But clart, would it kill him to get some hot running water in the place? People lived in places with no hot water *before* they got rich, not after.

He gazed about the room, taking weary delight in its beauty; its huge windows boasting their intricate stained glass design, the delicately carved window seats before them. The bed, still occupied by his two guardians, sat alone on the red floor, noble and ancient, the bed of a deceased Emperor. It had black velvet drapes around it, embossed with a design in red of running stags, which could be drawn for privacy. Or, he mused, for lunatics like himself who slept all day. Everything in the room was so big he felt like an insect. The ceiling, with its depiction of a battle from centuries past, seemed miles above his head. The portraits on the walls of the castle's past owners were twice the height of Draephus, encased in heavy, gilded-wood frames. Even the fireplace he now sat before was of great height and width, the fire it could contain large enough to consume whole trees. However it was dark and empty now, and he sat before his icy hearth and gazed about his room.

He wished Vesper was there with him.

He felt ill, right to the core of his being, as he thought about him. Vesper, now off somewhere on one of his many trips to the South Continent, not due back until the seasons began to turn cold. He seemed healthy enough, fit and active, but that was the lie. He was sick, had been ever since Draephus had met him five years ago. It wasn't anyone's fault Vesper was ill. For once it was not even the fault of the bloody Grey Boys and their nightmare experiments. He had been born with the virus that lodged in his heart. According to the doctors who had been present at Vesper's birth, too much of anything would kill the baby, and he was not expected to live beyond a few days. Twenty-four years later, Vesper Anterick was still going. Despite being undersized due to his health, he had survived the Revolution, and was one of the most intimidating people Draephus knew. Vesper knew his life would be short, and he filled his days questing for knowledge of his home world, knowledge the Grey Boys tried to erase. He was determined not to waste a day of his existence, especially now that the virus had become active and he could feel his strength beginning to leave him. It was time for one last trip to the South, then back to spend his days with the people he loved.

Draephus hadn't wanted anything from Vesper when he first met him, except for him to stop showing up in the same places he was. But at every underground performance, there he was, a little thin fellow, whose eyes were just a bit too intense from behind his heavy-rimmed glasses. Raski had wanted him in the worst way, and Draephus told Raski to please feel free, anything to get the little pain out of his life. But Vesper didn't want Raski, and on more than one occasion Draephus would awake in the middle of the night to look questioningly at the small figure in bed next to him. He had always believed in fate, and, after he met Vesper, he learned to believe that there were no certainties in life. Vesper had long ago tossed some of Draephus' favourite concrete beliefs about himself out the stained glass windows.

  He could recall their first night together so vividly that he couldn't believe it happened five years ago. Five years was a bloody long time in his life; so much had changed so fast. He still had the damaged weapons in the underground safe-room beneath the castle, still had the mild tremor in his right hand from trying to use a laser pistol with a faulty mechanism that made it hum and vibrate every time it was fired. He even recalled the feelings of that time, and the ball of sick emotion that had sat in his stomach. Uncertainty, fear, and, maybe, somewhere in that mire if he thought about it, was a bit of love for the little creepy guy with the glasses.

  He had been sharing some miserable flat with Raski in the Lower Cylinder when he finally broke down and invited the little creep over. A faint smile crossed Draephus' face as he thought about it. He could see it all so clearly. He had been fixing an incendiary, partly with which to annoy the Grey Boys, and mostly keep his mind off the fact that Vesper was coming over. This distraction proved to be of little avail, and finally he dropped the thing to the floor, wincing as he did so and hoping Raski didn't notice he was tossing explosives around. He looked over at Raski, seeing his friend's eerie blue-white eyes staring back at him.

  "Draephus, don't toss things that could potentially explode into a ball of flaming matter where it can damage us."

  "Sorry." Draephus slumped back against a dirty wooden crate.

  "What's the matter?" Raski asked.

  "Vesper," said Draephus, rising to his feet and pacing about the small, dark apartment, cluttered with guns, drums, explosives, and one rather weary red sepulchord, which was missing half its tone-lights. "He's driving me crazy!" He turned sharply, spilling an overflowing ashtray. "Clart," he muttered, looking at the mess.

"So why are you having him over?" Something in Raski's tone suggested he would have been happier not to have Vesper there anyway. Draephus chose to ignore this.

"I don't know," he crabbed quietly. He shuffled his feet, looking like a huge, uncomfortable, and heavily-armed kid. He sighed, then tossed his head back, looking once more at Raski.

"Hey Rask?"

Raski was sitting on the floor, intent upon fixing the computer of a laser pistol. "Yeah?"

"How..." Draephus began, then fell silent. Raski looked up, curious, a faintly evil glint in his eye.

"Yes?"

"Never mind."

"WHAT?"

"If I do decide to advance this relationship," said Draephus, pausing as he tried to think how best to phrase his question. "What do I do with him?"

"What do you mean?"

"What I mean," said Draephus, mildly annoyed, "is what do I do with him if I take him to bed?"

The two stared at each other, Raski holding the broken pistol. "You're twenty-three and you want me to tell you what you should do with a man in your bed?"

"Just forget I asked, I'm not good at dating men."

"Men are all we have, now, thanks to the Grey Boys." Raski slipped the chamber of the pistol closed with a satisfying 'clack'. "So, you can wait the rest of your life, hoping to hook up with a woman, of which there is one to every eight hundred men, or you can date Vesper."

"I'll date Vesper," grumbled Draephus.

Draephus walked into the kitchen and picked up a knife to prepare the meat he had managed to acquire. It was only feralyke, but it was meat, a very rare commodity. There came a knock at the door, and Draephus tossed down his knife. "Great, he's on time. Who is ever on time?" He walked out of the kitchen, seeing Raski quietly skulk off to his room with some of the equipment.

"You'll do okay," Raski whispered as he walked past him.

Draephus snorted and walked over to the door. Opening it, he saw Vesper standing there, holding a bottle of wine. Draephus shifted uncomfortably. Vesper stared back at him, then finally said, "Heia."

"Heia, come on in. Please ignore the mess."

Vesper stepped into the room and slowly surveyed the flood of weapons and explosives that covered most of the flat. "I like the decor," he said dryly, "very revolutionary."

"Yeah, ha ha," said Draephus, grinning. He dragged a shoulder-firing laser cannon and an assortment of ammunition belts off of the one and only chair. "Have a seat."

Vesper did, passing him the wine. Draephus took it, reading the label. "Cardilis. I'm impressed. Well I managed to get some meat, only feralyke, but one can't be too choosy."

"Meat?" said Vesper.

"Yeah," said Draephus. Suddenly he felt a little worried. "Why?"

Vesper shifted in his seat, looking sheepish. "I can't eat meat, something about it reacts negatively with my heart medication. Sorry."

Draephus stared at Vesper, thinking about all he had been through to get the steaks, wishing he could just fall over and be swallowed by the floor. Then, from the next room, Raski yelled, "I'll eat it!"

Draephus winced, and set the wine down onto the table. "Wine and salad, then?"

Vesper nodded, and Draephus turned and went into the kitchen, pausing to stare at the two large, attractive pieces of meat sitting oh-so-pleasantly in spices and marinade that represented a lot of time and trinta he really did not have. Well there was a week of his life he'd never get back.

"Scruffin' lovely," he grumbled quietly as he put the meat in the cold box. He and Raski would eat them later.

He dished up the salads and returned to the sitting room with them. He set these down on the low table, then fetched glasses for the wine. The food he had acquired for their dinner had taken him days of scavenging and bartering to get, and he had no plans of wasting a crumb of it. He sat on the floor next to the small table, letting Vesper have the one chair. They began to eat, both mildly uncomfortable. They ate in silence, no other sound save for the crunching of vegetables, and the occasional scrape of a fork across the bottom of a bowl.

"How do you like the salad?" Draephus finally asked.

"It's very good. What are the..." Vesper poked at something in a bowl, finally spearing it with a fork and holding it aloft, using his free hand to push his glasses up his nose as he squinted at the item.

"The brown things?"

"I wasn't going to put it that way, but, yes, the brown things."

"I don't know. I mean, I know what they are, I just don't know what they are called."

Silence fell again for a time, then Vesper leaned forward, studying Draephus as he sat on the floor.

"Are you uncomfortable?"

"Oh yes."

"I meant on the floor."

"That too."

Vesper laughed softly. Draephus squirmed a little. "I'm sorry, it's just that..." he hesitated for a moment, then said, "I like you, and I don't know how to deal with it."

"Why don't you just relax and we'll take it from there," said Vesper, smiling as he slipped off the chair and sat down on the floor next to Draephus.

The two finished their meal in silence, then Draephus put the dishes in the small, stained sink. He returned to the living room and sat next to Vesper, who poured them each some more wine.

"So how goes the fight?" asked Vesper.

Draephus shrugged. "We've pretty much won at this point. If you can call it winning. The Kryphisians are leaving but… well after the garbage they dumped that killed almost every woman on the planet, and the destruction they left in their wake…"

"But they are leaving?" said Vesper softly.

"They're leaving, slowly. But how far they will go and how long they will stay away, I don't know."

"And the rumours they killed the women..?"

"They're true," said Draephus quietly. "It's not the first time they did this; they dumped the same poisons in different areas over the course of the last twenty years. First in the Southern regions. Raski and I have seen… look I don't want to talk about this. The Kryphisians are leaving, we'll have a new emperor on the throne for the first time in about eight hundred years, and you and I are having wine and salad with brown things."

Vesper smiled, then moved closer to Draephus, looking up at him with dark blue eyes. They were the eerie twilight sea colour that was particular to the Eastern Continent. Draephus swallowed.

"I'm afraid of you," he said softly.

"Why?"

"Because I don't understand why I feel for you the way I do."

"Draephus," said Vesper softly, "that applies to most relationships."

Draephus sipped his wine, looking uncomfortable. The warmth of Vesper's body was like fire; the scent of him was distracting. It was getting harder to concentrate on the wine. Vesper edged slightly closer, and he nearly dropped the glass. He felt Vesper's small slender hand slip up his thigh, but Draephus stared determinedly at his wine.

"Look at me," said Vesper softly.

He did, and Vesper moved towards him. Draephus edged back, leaning further and further over until he suddenly found himself on his back, Vesper poised over him. Gently Vesper took the wine from Draephus' hand, sipping from it before setting it on the table. He removed his glasses, placing them next to the wine. A bemused smile crossed his pretty face as he positioned himself on all fours over Draephus, his knees between Draephus' parted legs. An evil glint sparkled in his blue eyes.

"I promise to be gentle," Vesper whispered as he reached down with one hand, opening Draephus' belt with a snap.

"Vesper!"

"Just relax."

He bent and kissed Draephus' throat. He nipped at the flesh, then proceeded to move down his body, opening the metal clasps on the military-style jacket with his teeth. Draephus let his head fall back onto the dirty rug. As he stared up at the ceiling, he decided that he didn't have to know what to do with a man, because Vesper certainly seemed to.

Vesper opened the functional, heavy garment, pushing it away from the powerful body beneath it. He traced his fingers over the scarred and thin body. Draephus was muscular, but there was no spare. In fact, he was far too lean. Like most Sferkkaans, Draephus' meals were few and far between. The muscles were starkly defined; the sinews standing out like the cables on a machine.

Technological advances they had – food was another thing entirely.

"You better eat both of those steaks," Vesper said, and lowered his head to kiss Draephus' stomach.

His small, thin hand made its way down to the front of Draephus' grey combat pants, the worn clasp pulling open listlessly. Draephus flinched nervously, and swallowed hard as he felt Vesper's tongue upon him, tasting him as his hands roamed roughly over his body. He trembled as Vesper moved down lower, and then cried out, his hands fisting at his side, as the smaller man took him deep in his mouth.

Draephus flinched again, but relaxed a little. He could deal with this. He could definitely deal with this. Then, suddenly, "HEY! OW! What the hell are you doing down there?"

He felt a finger enter into him, and heard Vesper chuckle. "Just relax Draephus, it'll get better."

Draephus had serious doubts about that as he grit his teeth and felt another finger enter him. He was about to call the whole thing off, when suddenly a light exploded behind his eyes. He shoved Vesper off and pulled away from him.

"What's wrong?" Vesper asked, surprised.

"What's wrong?! You hurt me, I thought this was supposed to feel good!"

Vesper cocked his head. "Have you never… done this before?"

"No," snapped Draephus. "Believe it or not I have not found a moment between blowing up Grey Boys, hauling bodies out of houses, and trying to find my next meal to have sex."

Vesper's eyes took on a predatory gleam, and he reached out to catch Draephus' forearm. "Really. That's very interesting." The eyes softened a little. "Look, it will be all right, I promise. I won't hurt you. Trust me."

"Trust you to do what? Rip me open?"

"Trust me," Vesper whispered.

Draephus didn't, but neither did he pull away. He permitted Vesper to gently push him down to the floor again, tense and uncertain.

"You hurt me, and I'll kill you," he said.

Vesper's eyes glinted. "I know," he said.

Draephus awoke the next morning to find Vesper next to him in bed. He looked tiny and harmless, almost frail. His lips were parted, making him look soft, childlike, and he had one arm cast about a long-muzzled Night Stalker gun, six feet of deadly firepower. Draephus kicked the gun out of bed, then got up slowly, his body aching. His legs felt weak, and there was a nasty bite on his shoulder muscle, just next to his neck.

"Little creep," he muttered quietly as he rubbed the muscle. He pulled on a pair of loose-fitting pants, then paused by the bed, gazing down at the small, pretty man. He gently stroked the soft hair back from Vesper's face. Vesper shifted in his sleep, then opened his eyes, rolling onto his back. He stretched and yawned. "Heia," he said, looking small and innocent.

"Heia," said Draephus, touching his cheek lightly. "Hungry?"

Vesper blinked sleepily, nodding. Draephus smiled. "I'll see if there is anything for breakfast." He bent and kissed his face, then slowly, stiffly, left the room. He walked into the kitchen, stopping as he saw Raski. His friend stared hard at him, looking him up and down, raising one eyebrow.

"Really worked you over, didn't he?"

"Yeah he did, and where were you while I was getting raped?"

Raski pulled a gun and held it up. "Fixing the laser pistol. Wow, he bites, doesn't he?"

"Yes. He bites. What's for breakfast?"

Raski grinned. "I don't know about you, man, but I'm having steak."

****

Draephus smiled faintly. He opened his eyes and wearily looked around his bedroom. The castle seemed colder, quieter than it ever had before. He felt tired, and a dull, sick hate rested in the pit of his stomach, directed at nothing and everything. Stuff always happened to him, stuff always would. Vesper's illness was not the first piece of clart to happen to him, and he wasn't even certain it was the worst. He was a little numb by now to all the things that had occurred to him in life, though occasionally blinding rages bled up through the numbness. He'd fought, vomited, and bled all of his rage out over the last three days; it would take awhile to escalate to a dangerous level once more. His only comfort right then was that Vesper had no idea what he had done after seeing him off at the flight terminal. Draephus was exhausted, he had slept little over the past three days, and, without knowing he was about to do so, he suddenly fell asleep where he sat. His head slipped forward onto his chest, his breathing becoming slow and regular. He dreamed nothing.

The 'com awoke him a few hours later, and he made no attempt to get it. Somehow he could tell just by the ring that it was Raski, wanting to know where the šukat he was. They had to make an appearance on the Astellis Monct Show. Draephus had never pulled a no-show before; he thought his friends would trust him enough by now to know he wouldn't. Of course, given that it was Astellis Monct, who was an inane idiot as well as a daghuwai, if the rumours were true, Raski may be worried that Draephus would decide to make this his first failed appearance.

He finished the long hike to the bathroom, the red beings bounding along at his side, lighting the torches and candles for their master in the dark, tomb-like marble chamber. He peered into the grand, antique mirror above the stone water basin at himself. The swelling around his nose had gone down, though it was still sore. He didn't know how he had managed to blacken his eyes so badly. The stitches in his brow line wove erratically from the edge of his eyebrow to a little above the top of his nose, promising a scar. The cuts on his lips and chin were smaller, finer, the wound having been thin and neat. He didn't scar easily, and he couldn't see this cut leaving much of a mark. The one in his eyebrow, however, that one he would have to explain to Vesper...

His stomach did a slow roll, and he wandered towards the huge, free-standing bathtub. Sometime in a previous century, some ingenious nobleman had his servants rig up a pump so he could draw his own baths. Likewise, he had also had a simple drainage system installed that funnelled the water out into the duck pond. When Vesper discovered this, he had immediately thrown out anything deemed unsafe for the ducks, and Draephus had to get used to some pretty unusual types of 'non-harmful' soap. A few of these caused serious allergic reactions, and once he had to perform on-stage looking as though he had just suffered the world's most catastrophic case of acne. All for a bunch of ducks. He could hear them now, quacking fit to wake the dead. Stupid ducks.

He had his bath cold, washing the stench of three days in the Cylinder off of his body and out of his hair. He found a tender spot on his scalp, but it seemed only to be a bruise. He gently cleaned off the stitches, and cooled his swollen eyelids by placing a washcloth over them. He was aware of a sensation in his stomach, but wasn't certain if it was hunger or illness: perhaps a combination of both.

He heard the splash of one of his two companions getting into the tub. He knew which one it was without even looking.

"Bacca, this is my bath."

"Arf!"

"No, get out. I don't have the strength to argue with you."

"Arf!" The creature ducked himself in the cold water, then bounded out in an explosion of wetness, covering much of the bathroom floor in water. Draephus sighed heavily from under his cloth.

"Oh scruffin' lovely. You're dead as soon as I feel better."

"Arf!"

He heard Bacca pause, falling silent, then he and his companion tore off down the hall, barking their fool heads off at the 'com as it began to ring again. He ignored it. Unfortunately Bacca did not, and Draephus heard the faelin knock the receiver out of the cradle and begin barking furiously at it. He sighed loudly and heavily with aggravation.

"I just want a bath!" he yelled at the bathroom.

'Poor Raski,' thought Draephus. He'd call him when he got out of the bath. He was probably on the edge of his seat with anxiety.

Draephus loved Raski fiercely, and the emotion was returned fivefold by his friend. Raski was a clown, with a lecherous enthusiasm for all the things in life that were bad for him. The war had left him high-strung and paranoid, which made him perfect for looking after the business side of the colossal undertaking that was now the Gryphons. He was a ball of over-activity, taking it upon himself to tend to all of the band's needs, refusing to let anyone help. Which was fine by the other Gryphons, although what they would do if he dropped dead, no one knew. Nobody really knew what Raski was up to at any given moment, but the band was always carefully guarded from any dirty dealings. Not that a lot of people tried to take advantage of a band of musicians whose sepulchord player had rigged the engines of enemy aircraft to detonate upon ignition. But whatever his larger dealings may have been, Raski's smaller ambitions were on the board for anyone to see. His current aspiration was to go to bed with Delaes Randerick, the lead vocalist from a group called Bad Influence. Draephus would like to have a moving laser-image of that momentous occasion. Delaes had the body of a god, the grace of a panther, and the intellect of cheese. Mars once commented that he was beautiful until he opened his mouth.

    Draephus got out of the tub, sending the water off to the ducks, and ambled stiffly into the hallway to check the enormous clock. He was not late, but he had little time to spare. He returned to his room and began selecting clothes. He pulled out a ratted pair of combat pants that had literally survived the Revolution, though not by much. He put these on, then chose a grey sleeveless shirt. Next came on his favourite boots, low and flat soled, with large scuff marks all over them. He tied an exotic-coloured scrap of silk about one ankle, because Vesper had given it to him, then grabbed his crusty, fingerless gloves and put them on. Standing before a mirror, he scruffed up his damp, shortish, blondish hair, and left it at odd angles. Stubble still grew all over his face, and the opaque glasses he put on made him look sinister at best. Then he pulled on his filthy, blood, mud, puke and booze-spattered full-length coat, flipping up the collar.

    He had to check something before he left for the studio, but he would have to do it quickly.

    He left his room, heading along the walkway to the stairs that led to the lower level, going down as quickly as he was able to a long stone box beneath the great window in the main gathering area. He opened it, drawing out three items. The first was a knife with a strange shaped blade that looked a great deal as if someone had made a half-circle, then curved the back to make it almost but not quite crescent shaped. The handle was black bone, carved with the images of strange animals like humanoid deer. The next item was a red bag tied up with a thin black ribbon. The third was a walking stick of a dark golden-brown wood. The head was set with a silver bird skull, and had strips of leather hung with beads, feathers, bits of bone, and red cloth. Putting the dagger and the bag in his pocket, he left the castle, accompanied by his two faelins who raced ahead, barking loudly.

    They travelled down a narrow path that led from the castle and into the tall grass and trees that grew around it. They walked deeper and deeper into the grass, making their way to a very shallow natural pond, in which small fish darted about. Here he paused, carefully examining the area for anything out of the ordinary. Seeing nothing, he called aloud; "Mind yourselves, my family!"

There was a soft rustle in the grass, as if a faint breeze had blown, but there was no wind. The faelins yipped softly and briefly hid behind their master until the grass grew still once more. Draephus started forward, walking past the statue of a small figure reaching out to touch the surface of the water, following the path deeper into the woods, half singing to himself; "I creep, I creep, so the carn-crow does not see me…"

He came suddenly into a small clearing, in which a silver cage was set upon a stump. Beside it, driven partly into the ground, was a black twig. Within the silver cage was a bird, and before the creature could make a sound, Draephus raised one hand and spoke to it.

"Yes, yes, yes, I see you, Brother Bird. What news have you for me today?"

The bird hopped about in the cage, obviously anxious to be free of its confines. In the cage with it was a large, black beetle, looking fat, and clearly disgruntled at the antics of the bird. Draephus approached the cage and looked inside.

"Well that's not good," he grumbled. "Bird, you disappoint me."

He opened the cage door and left the bird to find its own way out, which it did rather quickly. Soon the beetle followed, trundling off to other business. Draephus next walked to the twig and studied it, noting sourly that it was clearly dying.

"It's not working," he said to the faelins. "Why is this not working? The bird did not eat the beetle, the twig is not drawing strength from the ground… why is this not working?"

Bacca made a quiet trill. Draephus carefully examined the twig, but already knew that it was not growing, it was dying, and even the closest examination would not show otherwise. Maybe he should try a stronger magic? But this one had always worked before, even if it was just a simple spell. The wild bird broke the beetle, piercing the shell to destroy the illness within, and the twig would draw life from the ground to renew the body. It should work! But why had it not…?

"I'll have to try a stronger magic is all," said Draephus. "I'll make Vesper well if I have to stick a twig in every inch of swamp there is on the whole island."

But not now. He had places to be. Raski and the others would be waiting. He drew the bag out of his pocket and opened it, then carefully set it on the ground and secured it to the earth with the dagger. From within the bag he drew a handful of red and black beans, and as he began walking away from the stump and twig, he threw a few over his shoulder with every step, singing very softly to himself.

"Carn crow no follow me, carn crow no follow me, I creep and creep whilst you sleep, and your eyes they no see me…"

Draephus moved stealthily, head down, keeping a furtive eye upon the tangled serpentine roots of the black trees that grew all around. His heart jumped as he did spy a carn-crow, but he quickly realized it was indeed asleep. The massive heavy black beak that could dig up bodies buried too shallow in the soft earth was tucked under one huge black wing, and it paid no attention to Draephus and the faelins as they crept past. Once they had left the clearing behind, Draephus breathed a sigh of relief, and he and the faelins moved more quickly as he tossed away the last of the beans.

They entered the castle just in time to hear the 'com ring once more. Hurrying over to it, Draephus snatched it up.

"Yeah." His voice was quiet and hoarse.

"DRAEPHUS!"

"Hi Rask."

"ŠUKAT, MAN!"

"I'm on my way," he said softly, and hung up before Raski could continue, then departed the castle and went to get Vesper's black conni. His own conni wasn't going anywhere for at least a few days.

He arrived a few minutes before show time, finding the other Gryphons in the dressing room. Raski was all over him like a new suit when he came in, wanting to know where he had been for the last three days. Draephus ignored him, lighting a cigarette and easing his pained body into a chair. Astellis Monct came charging in a moment later and nearly collapsed in relief when he saw Draephus, who was feeling rather distant from all the excitement and commotion happening around him. He scarcely noticed when Mars lifted the glasses from his face to stare at the damage. Faded blue eyes stared dully out of swollen slits, gazing into Mars' clear green orbs.

"What happened to you?" that eloquent East Continent accent inquired. Draephus shrugged, drawing on his cigarette.

"Did you win?" Mars asked, smiling. Draephus stared at him, blowing smoke in response.

"Hello Draephus," chirped a voice just off to his left. "Come to join us, did you? Very nice of you. Look, I'm wearing pink, your favourite colour. You look like clart."

Draephus shifted his lacklustre gaze towards Khandid, the quinticord player. He was indeed wearing pink. Bright, shiny, happy pink. Pink shoes, pink shirt, pink pants, setting off his big blue eyes and white-blond hair. The first time Draephus had met Khandid he couldn't tell if he was male or female, and had been afraid to ask. Much as he had tried to hate Khandid, he found him just too funny to loathe.

"What the šukat are you wearing?" Draephus snarled.

"Do you like it?"

"No."

"Too bad, I do. Been beating your face against rocks, or chasing parked connis?"

"I introduced my conni to a stone pillar, then introduced my face to the steering wheel."

"Oh. Did it feel good?"

"What do you think, beaker?"

"Just asking. Want some perfume? You don't just look like clart, you smell like it."

Draephus managed a smile, the stitches pulling at his lip. He definitely liked Khandid; he always managed to make him smile.

"CLART, MAN!" Raski went on in the background. "YOU HAD ME WORRIED!"

"Shut up Raski," chirped Khandid.

"Are you going to be able to handle this?" Mars asked Draephus softly, long thick hair, tinted fuchsia, spilling out from under the hat he was wearing.

"I'm fine," mumbled Draephus.

Astellis Monct ran out of the room to make his cue, finding himself confronted with a screaming crowd of Gryphons fans, none of whom had any interest in what he had to say. Khandid himself bounced out of the dressing room briefly, returning quickly.

"There's billions of them," he announced, "and they're all

screaming."

"Nice to be popular," said Yuri Stracona musingly, the first words he had said all evening.

"Hey don't be going off by yourself!" snapped Draephus, then coughed and clutched his ribs.

"It's fine," said Mars, "we had the area checked for triggers before we even let Khandi in here. What is wrong with you?"

"NOTHING! I might have broken a rib, no big deal, I'm fine."

Mars had put more than his fair share of broken, bleeding bodies back together, and he tried to look at his friend's ribs, but stopped, putting his hands in the air in surrender and walking away when Draephus snarled at him. They had known each other too long to argue the point. A stagehand appeared in the doorway.

"You'll have to go on now," said the man, looking frantic. "They're trying to pull the stage apart."

"Impudent little buggers, aren't they?" said Raski, hanging his sepulchord around his neck. "Well, let's go, people."

****

By the time the song ended, Draephus' abused body was so sore he was almost in tears. His neck and shoulders were flaming; it was a struggle to move at all. He crossed the stage as though he was centuries old, instead of twenty-eight. When he was finally able to sit down he hoped he never had to move again.

He sat in his usual position, as far from the host as possible. Let the others do the talking, Draephus didn't talk if he didn't have to. He was vaguely aware of Astellis Monct's comment about the audience liking them, of the roar of approval and Raski's crazy laugh. For the most part he was not there, off in a fog of his own thoughts. He noticed an ashtray close at hand, and he reached into his pockets for his cigarettes. He lit one with a shaking hand, then settled himself as comfortably as possible, switching the cigarette to his left to hide the tremor in his right. He ached, he was sleepy, and his stomach was still not certain as to what it wanted to do. At the moment it was more sick than anything. Draephus mused upon this, then began to wonder when he had eaten last. He couldn't recall. His years of living as a revolutionary had made eating seem so unimportant.

Astellis Monct droned on in the background, and Draephus

had to fight to stay awake. Twice his head jerked up sharply. He shifted his position and stubbed out his dead cigarette. The other Gryphons talked on, discussing the last tour, the coming recording, and the time they were taking off now. He could almost lip-sync the questions and answers. He lit another cigarette, then, through the smoke and mental lethargy, heard his own name. He looked up, smoke curling around his face, and his upper lip drawing into a slight snarl. What did this clart want? He rarely got spoken to during these things, but then, recalling what he had done to his face, supposed Monct couldn't resist.

"You've got an attractive set of matching bruises," said Monct.

Khandid intervened, knowing Draephus would not want to talk. "Yes, they're lovely aren't they? If they become fashionable we'll have an epidemic of people smashing themselves in the face."

"Oh I'd be glad to hit you in the face, Khandi," said Raski. "Really, no trouble."

"Oh. Thank you. You're such a šukat."

Monct's face became a little strained at the obscenity that came out of Khandid's mouth. The other Gryphons smiled like the proud parents of an idiot child, while the audience howled its approval. It was universally known that interviewing the Gryphons was not easy. The five of them had a collective attention span of ten seconds, and they were notorious for running interference for one another. Finally, after the audience quieted a little, Monct tried to plough through with another question.

"So how did you manage to get them?"

The audience reacted with obvious horror when Draephus removed the glasses and revealed the injuries.

"Quite a mess," commented Monct.

"Yeah," said Draephus, a vague, nasty smile crossing his lips. "I walked into a door."

Nobody in their right mind could have mistaken the mess for anything as ridiculous as walking into a door, especially the thin slash across his lips. Monct smiled at the beaten-looking figure.

"Pretty nasty door."

"Yes it was a big stone one," chirped Khandid.

"A stone door," said Monct. "What did it lead to?"

"A grave or something, wasn't it Draephus?" said Khandid. "Raski wanted to sacrifice a virgin to the solstice, but we needed the rib of a..."

"SSHHHHHHH!" hissed Raski loudly.

"All right," said Monct, visibly aggravated. "I can see this is leading nowhere. And I'm not certain I want to know what you people were doing out in a cemetery."

"Well Astellis," said Draephus in his soft voice, "if you really like what I've done to my face I'm sure I could do yours to match."

Monct gaped at Draephus, apparently not certain as to what he had just heard. If his ears were working properly, then he had just been threatened with physical harm.

"So you'll be working on your castle's torture chamber during your time off, I take it," Monct said in an attempt to lighten things. Pleased to have an opportunity to talk about his castle, Draephus relaxed a little.

"Actually it does have a torture chamber," he said. "And a dungeon."

"Great for band image," said Mars dryly.

"I didn't hear you complaining at the time," said Raski, grinning. Mars walloped him with his hat.

"Sounds like a nice place," said Monct. "Anything lurking in the moat?"

"Ducks," said Yuri, the second thing he had said all evening.

"Nasty ducks," said Khandid.

"Nasty fanged ducks," Raski threw in.

"Torture chambers and fanged ducks," said Monct. "Well put me down for a tour."

"Sure," said Draephus, exhaling smoke. "I'll show you the catacombs."

"Oh and what do you keep down there?" asked Monct.

"Mars," said Raski. Mars clobbered him with his hat once more.

"Dead icky former lords and dead icky former ladies," said Khandid, trying to avoid being crushed by his much-larger bandmates and their nonsense. "I've seen them, they're dead and icky."

Monct blinked. "Really?"

"Yes ickiness frequently follows death," said Khandid.

"They're enormous catacombs," said Mars, allowing Raski to give him an apologetic cuddle. He leaned back against his friend, putting his booted feet and on Khandid, who gave little reaction.

"There's almost a thousand years of history down there. There's numerous generations of the former landowners, their possessions…"

"Books," said Raski, "tapestries, furnishings, jewellery…"

"It was tradition to bring some of your favourite belongings with you," said Khandid. "There's a little baby girl down there holding a…."

Khandid stopped talking abruptly as his voice caught, his tiny body vibrating as he fought to keep his emotions controlled. Yuri drew him close to comfort him, while Mars kept talking.

"It's really an amazing place," said Mars, "So much of who we were is contained in these vaults, it will give us back some of who we were as a people to have the catacombs studied."

"Especially the books," said Raski. "Once we can find someone to have them restored. It's an incredible treasure-trove that was just overlooked for centuries."

"Fortunately," added Mars.

"I'm surprised you left it intact," said Monct.

Draephus narrowed his eyes as his friends looked confused.

"Why would we not?" asked Raski, almost warily. "I mean… it's history. It's a huge and valuable piece of what we were fighting for."

"Well it's just that with all that wealth down there you could…"

Monct went silent. Draephus leaned forward, the wave of rage boiling up from the cold depths again.

"Could what?" he growled.

Monct looked frightened. Raski put a hand on Draephus' collarbone to restrain him as Mars sat up, possibly in preparation of having to dodge something large and angry in a long grey coat.

"I just meant," said Monct, choosing his words carefully, "that a historical treasure of that magnitude could have… funded…"

There was silence. Whatever Monct may have been trying to say was now lost. To Draephus, it just seemed proof that Astellis Monct was exactly what the rumours claimed he was – a daghuwai; a man willing to sell anything or anyone to the highest bidder in order to keep his own ass in comfort, regardless of who it hurt. Draephus felt Raski pushing him back, but Draephus would not be contained. There was a decorative glass bottle on the table, and he reached out to take it by the neck, breaking it on the coffee table there for stage dressing.

"Daghuwai BASTARD!" he screamed.

Khandid shrieked and ducked as Draephus launched himself over his four bandmates to land on Astellis Monct's desk, slipping on the glossy surface and sliding onto the floor as Monct dumped his chair and fled for his life. Draephus scrabbled to his feet and tore after the man, vaguely aware of Mars and Raski chasing after him.

****

Not terribly far away from where this was happening, Dahli and Diza sat on the floor, jaws hanging, blinking in unison as Dahli's favourite Gryphon made a serious effort to gut Astellis Monct with a chunk of broken glass. They watched as he charged after the hysterical talk show host, Mars and Raski in hot pursuit, trying to prevent their friend from doing something law enforcement probably would not approve of. This left Khandi and Yuri alone on the set. They looked at each other, then the audience. Then, as Monct screamed in the background for help, accompanied by the sound of breaking glass, overturning objects, and Mars and Raski shouting at Draephus to put the man *down*, already, Khandid scooted around Monct's desk, righting his chair and sitting in it. He rifled the top drawer of the desk, then pulled out a stack of blue cards.

"Well look who we have next, noted author of children's books, Melari Khanin! Come out Melari, mind you don't slip in the blood and broken glass and… whatever pieces Draephus is leaving."

The author scurried out, if for no other reason than to get away from the riot. The trio sat on the stage and looked at each other.

"Heia," said Khandid. The three flinched as something large was knocked over.

"Heia," said Melari. "Uh… loved your last album."

"Thanks," said Khandid. "Actually I did it all by myself, I just let the others have some credit."

There was the boom of a large hand-held weapon being fired, and all three flinched again.

"Should we do something?" asked Melari.

"We are," said Khandid, leaning back in his chair and putting his feet on the desk. "We are staying out of the way of Draephus CZimcocious and a daghuwai. That very much counts as something.

So! Tell us all about your new book! Raski just loves 'Renny Redhir and the Magic Leaf.' We read it to him all the time."

Melari tried to look perky, as if nothing at all strange was going on. "Oh, well then hopefully he will love 'Renny Redhir Finds a Stone'. Of course it's no ordinary stone…"

In the dark and quiet of Dahli's house, she and Diza just stared at the Visual as Khandid Stracona interviewed a writer of popular children's stories, while in the background Raski could be heard screaming at Draephus to not kill Astellis Monct.

"Well," said Dahli. "I'm willing to bet this is one of the most surreal things I will ever see in my life."

Chapter Three

The girls left the house, walking down the dim streets to the home of Dahli's grandfather. He had little to do with Dahli and Teirra, for reasons the pair never understood. All they knew was he would help them out if they happened to be in deep trouble, but apart from that seemed to want them to just stay away. Teirra thought it was because Dahli looked so much like their missing mother that the old man could not stand the sight of her. But whatever his reasons, he bore them no hate; that much he made clear. He just could not bear the sight of them.

The old man was apparently asleep; the lights were all off and the house was silent. They glanced about for his feralyke, but the mighty beast was nowhere to be seen. As Dahli and Diza made their way over to the garage, they hoped that the bellowing monster did not come flying out of the night to rip them apart seconds before realising who they were.

"Boo?" called Dahli softly. "Boo, come here fellah. Boo!"

"Why `Boo'?" asked Diza.

"Because he likes to leap out at people from behind corners," said Dahli. "Boo!"

They heard panting, and from around a corner stepped a huge shadow, his massive shoulders rising into a hump, great triangular head hanging from a neck as wide as the base of the cinder-block skull. Nocturnal eyes gleamed at them from the shadows.

"Hi Boo," said Dahli, getting down on her knees to greet the animal. The beast lumbered over to her, the dual rows of teeth protruding from a mouth that took up almost all of the head. He snorted in his joy at seeing them, and rubbed his hairless head against Dahli, thumping his tailless hindquarters into her lap. She rubbed his head, making his tiny ears flap comically.

"Who's a nice ugly feralyke, huh? Who's a nice ugly ferry-werry?"

Boo snorted and panted, then, as large pets were wont to do, sneezed all over her shirt.

"YUCK! Thanks, Boo."

Boo sneezed again, then hoisted a leg to scratch his ears,

displaying massive, hairless testicles. Dahli looked at Diza.

"It's a good thing I like him or I could be seriously grimmed-out here right now."

Diza giggled, and patted Boo's head. "He can't help it if he has no dignity."

They patted the creature for a few minutes, then, after giving him a hug around his thick neck, Dahli and Diza left Boo to his own devices and entered the garage. There inside, sat the old grey conni. It rested in lumbering, solemn style in the garage, a relic from ages past, stodgy and of ill humour. It was not capable of great speed, but it made up for it in grandiose dignity. A queen in full array was scarcely more pompous than the old grey conni.

Dahli unlocked the door with the spare set of keys she had fished out of Teirra's underwear drawer. Then, with Diza working the brakes and steering, Dahli pushed the vehicle down the driveway and onto the road, all under Boo's careful supervision. The conni cruised along slowly at the prodding and heaving of the two girls, who had to push it some distance before they could start the great engine. It rumbled into life without a hitch, and, with its underage drivers at its helm, the girls and the noble old conni set off in search of adventure. Diza reached out and snapped on the radio, screeching and giggling as she heard the Gryphons.

"Gonna be a good night! Oh! I wanted to ask you if you would come with me to the hospital this weekend."

Dahli snapped her gaze to her best friend. "HOSPITAL?!"

"Oh nothing seeeeer-i-ous," drawled Diza with her lazy accent. She reached into her jacket pocket and pulled out a piece of paper. "Remember when we had to go get checked out, see if we were fertile? Got my results. I'm fertile and disease-free. So, I'm donating half my eggs, and the rest I get to keep for me, do whatever I want with them. Even make an omelette. Did you get your results? Maybe we could donate together, then spend the day being waited on hand and foot by all the pretty men."

Dahli loved Diza, but, for a brief moment, she wanted to choke her. Instead she tightened her hands on the wheel. Finally she spoke.

"I'm not fertile. Even if I were, I can't have children, I carry two of the viruses the Grey Boys set loose in the water. The doctors took one look at my blood and took out my ovaries before they had a chance to turn into big rotting tumours. In fact one of them had started to do just that."

Silence fell in the car for a little while. "I'm sorry," said Diza quietly. She fidgeted uncomfortably, playing with the piece of paper she held. "But you said you didn't want children, so, it should be okay."

"There is a difference between choosing not to have children, and having the choice taken from you," said Dahli. "Who knows, I might have changed my mind."

She glanced at Diza, and could tell her friend was genuinely sorry for her, and relented. "Look just forget it, it's not your problem. I'll take you to the hospital, sit with you while you make like a chicken, then eat your bad hospital food and help you fend off the boys."

Diza smiled. "Thanks."

"But I ain't baby-sitting."

She laughed. "Well you won't be asked to baby-sit for a long time. I bet you'll be sitting for Czamki before me, way he's falling all over that new girl. That brings the female population in this area up to her, you, me, your sister…"

"Atania," said Dahli. Both sucked in a lungful of air and yelled; "EEEEEEYEEEEWWW!"

"…and two others we don't know," finished Diza.

They laughed, and Dahli said "Yeah it's a regular female population explosion. So what they do they do with the eggs?"

"Make baby Sferkkaans."

"Well DUH, but you need a Mommy Sferkkaan as well as a Daddy Sferkkaan, unless the articles I've read are seriously mistaken. With one woman to every eight hundred men, and not all the women able to bear, that means some poor woman's gonna be real busy."

"Well they're making use of some of the technology left behind by the Kryphisians. They have all sorts of stuff for making babies."

"Yeah," said Dahli. "Making babies, altering babies, programming babies to grow up and attack specified targets and fight for entertainment purposes…"

"The point is," said Diza, interrupting Dahli before she could work up to a full rant, "they can use the devices to raise normal babies, not Breeds. And," at this point Diza began to giggle, "I heard they have an artificial uterus for the guys."

"NO WAY!" said Dahli, and both screamed with laughter. "Can you imagine Yuri Stracona pregnant? That would be so sad. He'd look like a barrel impaled on a javelin. He'd spend eleven months trapped on his back and bleating."

"HE'D BE CUTE! He could do twins and a world tour."

"Diza, much as I admire your devotion to him, have you looked at him? He's a Breed. He was bred to be pretty: to sing pretty, look pretty, act pretty, play pretty... He's pretty. He's also easily as smart as a wet cardboard tube and probably as tough."

"Dahli Sandiniti, you're mean."

"Why thank you." Suddenly Dahli gasped, and abruptly slammed on the brakes. They jolted to a stop, Diza bouncing up in her seat and nearly hitting her head on the roof. "THERE HE IS!" yelled Dahli. "Lyrellyn CZim-Relyn. Oh sex on legs, gorgeous, baby I want him, grrrrrrrrrr..."

Diza giggled, and both watched with hungry eyes the beautiful young man stepping delicately across the road, his long crimson coat with its array of jungle fowl plumage flowing out behind him like the tail of an exotic bird. His complexion was silver-white, and he turned his head to look at the girls from behind an elaborate mask of red and black make up. He gazed back at them, smiling, moving across the street with slow grace. They watched him like predators.

"Baby baby baby I want that oh yes I do," said Dahli.

"Good luck," said Diza, "Czamki says he likes boys."

"What?" said Dahli, "you mean on purpose?" She rolled down her window and stuck her head out. "Come on, Lyrellyn, come to mama!"

He reached the curb and paused. He gazed back at them, smiling, then raised a black-gloved hand to his lips, putting his finger in his mouth and sliding it out suggestively. Then he turned and walked away. They watched him go.

"I don't care if he does like other boys," said Dahli, "one day I'm going to catch him behind the school and do naughty things to him." She began following him slowly in the vehicle as he strolled along, the long skirts of his coat swaying as he moved with an easy grace. His boots had heels on them five inches high, made out of glittering and deathly sharp blades. He cast a sidelong look at the girls, then put his head up, pretending not to see them as they followed in the huge grey conni.

"He is so pretty," said Dahli. "I heard his mama was a Grey Boy."

"In that case, she would have to be a Grey Girl," said Diza. "And don't let him hear you say that, his daddy is a Bird of Prey."

"What, for real?" said Dahli, surprised. Diza rolled her eyes.

"Dahli, you should try reading something other than music reviews. Look at him. The coat with the feathers, the red lines in his make-up, the bladed boots, not to mention the big fat capital CZ at the start of his last name. It's against the law to wear that unless you're a descendant of the old Imperial Houses. You're looking at a living, breathing piece of history."

"I hate history. It's so violent. *'Here we are, we're Sferkkaans, we play music and we make pretty things and oh clart we've just been invaded by a violent race of highly evolved clart-muffins and beakers.'* It's depressing." She stuck her head out the window. "Hey, pretty bird, can I give you a lift?"

Lyrellyn cast a glance at her, amused, then looked away. "My daddy doesn't like me taking rides from strange girls," he said airily.

"Oh come on, we're not strangers, we're in your math class."

"I said nothing about not knowing you. I said you were strange."

Dahli and Diza exchanged glances. Then she stuck her head out the window again. "I'll show you where the feralyke bit me."

"NOT interested."

"Diza's fertile, I'll let ya mate with her."

"DAHLI!"

"Ah, some other time," said Lyrellyn. "But I'll give you a kiss if you tell Czamkiar I like him."

"Done!" Dahli stopped the conni, and Lyrellyn stepped off the curb and over to the vehicle. He leaned in, and gave Dahli a lingering kiss full on the lips. His lipstick tasted of shooberries. Then he laughed, and stepped away, waving.

"Good night Dahli, night Diza."

"Night," they said, watching after him. Then they pulled away and continued on to their destination.

****

"I'm hungry," Draephus muttered as he staggered out of the studio, stopping to rest against a brick wall.

They had left by a back exit, and stood now in an alley, away from the crowds that Mars and Khandid seemed to love. Yuri would be with Khandid, silently wishing that he was someplace else. Raski and Draephus had decided to leave as quietly as possible after the incident with Astellis Monct. The talk-show host was currently locked in his dressing room, likely calling the LEOs and anyone else he could think of to protect him from Draephus. Raski had finally managed to get Draephus to leave off his quest to kill Astellis, but Draephus had not given the idea up; he just wanted to find out for certain if Monct really had been a daghuwai during the war.

Draephus closed his eyes and drew in cool spring air. He waited for the wave of dizziness to pass, for the darkness to leave his vision. He thought he might be ill. Raski sighed.

"Come on, old man," he said, taking Draephus' arm and draping it around his neck. "Uncle Raski will feed you and put you to bed. Then we'll find someone to clean that coat of yours."

"The coat's fine," bitched Draephus, allowing Raski to lead him along.

Raski was probably willing to debate that, but Draephus was volatile right then, and not open to any sort of criticism. He left the subject of the rancid coat alone. Instead, he opened the door for Draephus to get into his own vehicle, a sleek little black beast that looked as though it could think. After loading Draephus into the passenger seat, he went to the driver's side and got in. He started the conni, and they headed into the night. The little black conni slipped along the wet streets, its engine a quiet hum as it navigated the dark, damp lanes.

"I left Vesper's conni…" mumbled Draephus.

"We'll get it tomorrow. Any place you want to go?" Raski asked the slumped figure in the seat.

Draephus was virtually lost in his coat as he sat limp, slouched down. His glasses obscured the part of his face above his collar. The tip of his cigarette poked out, sending up a thin blue plume of smoke. His hat was resting on the dashboard, and Draephus picked it up and put it on his head, creating an illusion that the coat was empty and smoking.

"Wherever," monotoned the coat.

"Want to talk?"

"No." The coat fell silent for a moment, then added, "Later."

"Sure," said Raski. "Hey you like seafood, don't you? I know this place, serves really good food."

"Hate restaurants," droned the coat.

"Well this place is pretty quiet, you'll like it. Besides, I know you. I bet it's been days since you ate anything."

The coat said nothing further. They pulled into the parking lot of the small, waterside restaurant. Lights shone off of the placid seawater, and the building was perched beside a floating wharf, waves softly lapping at the edges. The building was styled like the house of a seafarer; in fact it had been just that in centuries past. Heavy construction of hardwood and stone had contributed to its longevity, and the old house looked peaceful and inviting.

Raski parked the conni, opening the door and stepping out of the leather-covered interior, then closing it. He walked around to Draephus' side and opened the door, watching as the slouched figure began to lean towards him. Draephus half fell out of the vehicle, catching himself and dragging himself to his feet to walk to the little restaurant. It was opened, which meant the latest transports from the South Continent had arrived, and the fishing boats in the north had managed to make a catch. Fish were one thing they had in plenty, but the little silvery delights had moved deeper and further out into the ocean, making them harder to catch.

Fish, it seemed, did not care for war any more than people did.

They went inside, Draephus following Raski as they entered, oblivious to the looks his attire received. The host led them, at Raski's request, to a table far inside, near the fireplace and a large window. Draephus seated himself and promptly ordered a noxious distillation called a Kryphisian Brain Surgeon. The host looked downright offended, but went to get the drink. Raski probably would rather Draephus didn't have it, but knew better than to talk him out of it.

"What do you want to eat?" Raski asked, leafing through the list of items served, most with a note next to them reading "if available". Draephus slouched in his seat and shrugged, shaking his head. He made no move to pick up the list.

"Hey, they serve shaumaus here. You like dead raw fish on vegetables, don't you?"

Draephus nodded. "Sure." He stared down into the contents of his glass, falling silent once more.

A server came back to take their order. Raski rattled off a list of items for their dinner, since it was likely many of them would not currently be in stock. Trade was still spotty at best; just because someone had money did not mean the desired item was available to buy. Raski seemed to ignore the occasional glances the server was casting at Draephus, who could well have been dead if one was going by appearances. The server took their order and went on his way. Draephus lit another cigarette, and Raski pulled out his own pack, noticing he was halfway through it.

"How many cigarettes does that make for you today?" Raski asked.

Draephus thought, then opened his pack and stared into it. "How many to a pack?"

"Thirty."

Draephus thought again, then, as he put the pack into his pocket, said, "This is my seventy-third."

Raski winced. "You should stop for the evening."

"Going to make me?"

Raski reached across the table and rummaged in the coat pockets, taking the pack. He put it in his own pocket, then took the cigarette from Draephus' hand and mutilated it. "For the moment, anyway."

`Here it comes,' thought Draephus as Raski moved his chair alongside his own.

"Are you okay?" he asked softly.

Draephus rubbed slowly at his aching shoulders. "I hurt."

"Are you going to need a doctor?"

"No," said Draephus, rubbing at his neck. "I should be all right. I'll just lie up for a few days, the conni was worse off than I was."

Raski nodded. "Just as long as you're all right."

"Fine," droned Draephus. He put one crusty-gloved hand over Raski's face and gently, but firmly, pushed him away. Raski withdrew to his own space to await the food.

****

"How much trinta do you have?" asked Dahli as they parked the mighty grey conni a short ways from the restaurant. Diza pulled her wallet out of her pocket and went through it.

"I've got eight."

"I've got ten," said Dahli. "So let's just order salads and pretend we're just not that hungry."

"Right," said Diza.

The two got out of the vehicle, and walked down the road to the wharf next to where the restaurant sat. They passed a beautiful black conni in the parking lot, pausing briefly to admire it. Then they made their way into the restaurant. Their boots made light thumping sounds on the floor of the solid structure, turning to a muffled pad when they stepped into the building and onto the rug-covered floor.

Their appearance generated immediate interest; the restaurant fell silent, and every pair of eyes was on them. The two smiled and waved, long used to the attention they received for merely being female. The host showed up in moments, and led the two girls to a table, presenting them with lists. He did not offer them wine, they noticed, and, when he left the table, he took the little basket with its small pots of assorted powdered intoxicants with him. The pair slowly perused their options.

"What does it mean when they leave the prices off of the food?" asked Diza.

"Means if you have to ask, you can't afford it," said Dahli. "Maybe we could just sneak off."

"Nah," said Diza, "it's not going to be more than eighteen trinta for two salads." She put her list down. "I hope." She watched as a server arrived with a tray of drinks and began placing them on the table. "We didn't order those!" she said.

The server indicated four young men at the bar, and smiled. The two girls stared back, blinking at him, the men, then the drinks.

"Of course it probably would have been just fine if we arrived without a single trinta between us," said Diza.

More drinks followed, along with desserts, costly dishes, and a platter of fiercely expensive shaumaus. The delicate and artfully prepared fish, which came from the clean waters of the furthest parts of the ocean, sat on a silvery plate, dabbed with spices and sitting prettily in a golden marinade. Nothing on the table was in their price range, but that was fine. They were not the ones paying for it.

They ate slowly, lingering over the fine foods, most of which arrived with names and telecom numbers. The plates began to stack up. Both took their time eating, not wanting to get full too fast. This was a very rare treat in their lives; a chance to actually stuff themselves and be completely sated in a time when often markets and restaurants, as well as pantries, were bare.

"What are we going to do if we can't finish all this?" asked Diza. "I never had that problem before! It was always 'oh it's all gone and I'm still so hungry!' Look at this fish – I bet it was still swimming just a few hours ago."

"It's okay, Diza, they let you take the bits you can't finish with you. Eat what you can and take the rest."

Diza and Dahli watched as a platter containing an entire roast loamwai lowered to the table. Loamwai were closely related to redhir, and easily as cute, but a loamwai weighed five times what its little cousins did.

"Okay," said Diza. "Never in a million years are we going to be able to eat this all."

Dahli looked up at the server, feeling a little scared and overwhelmed. "Are you really going to let us take all of this? You must realize that no matter how badly we want to, we can't eat all of this."

"We didn't mean to cause a problem," said Diza.

The man smiled and addressed them both. "I think people are just happy you are both here and well, donselles. Do not concern yourself. Little girls, these days, are too rare not to be spoiled."

Dahli would have liked to have argued the "little girl" part, but with everyone falling all over themselves to be kind, she decided to say nothing about it.

"Is the washroom functional?" she asked.

"Yes! Right down the hall, donselle," he answered. "Just next to the men's room."

****

Draephus picked at his meal. He'd managed to eat most of the delicately flavoured fish, but after days of drugs and distillations, his stomach was objecting to the light spices. Raski had eaten his own considerable meal, and was working on dessert, when Draephus got up and began heading for the washrooms. He was going to be sick.

He walked into the men's room, finding only one other person in there, some beaker who promptly turned up his nose at the scruffy figure he saw. In a happier mood Draephus would have tried to shove the man down the toilet, but at the moment his only concern was his roiling stomach. He walked into a stall and immediately threw up his fish.

The beaker was gone by the time Draephus staggered out of the stall. He wandered over to the sink, removing his shades and turning on the cold water. He rinsed the foul taste out of his mouth, then splashed some of the chill water onto his face. He drank a little, then decided to put something simpler into his stomach than the spiced fish. He dampened his hair, and stared at his bruised face in the mirror. He was acting like a lunatic, and Vesper was still alive, possibly with years to go. What happened when he died? There was still the South Continent, with its beauty, and drug runners, and nib-sized revolutions. He could go back and end his days frying his brains on the mushroom drug and running shipments up to Touskania…

Draephus sipped some more water. He'd been to the South Continent. He had stowed away on a shuttle when he was fifteen. The idea had not been to go to the South Continent, just to get as far away from where he had been as possible; away from the bombings, the disappearances, the fires, murders, and death squads. He had ended up further south than most people cared to go, straight into the eerie other-world that even the Kryphisians left alone, save for a few scattered patrols. He had been terrified for his own survival, until he took up with a group of boys around his own age. They taught him how to get by in the strange place he now found himself. From them he learned how to forage for food in the depths of the jungle, how to create the sympathetic magicks that he still used in his day to day life, and how to make the deadly pit traps. Draephus had dug a few of those pits when he became a little more serious about his `mushroom exports,' as he called the frequent, quick, and always tense runs into Touskania with a load of drugs derived from the spiny fungus.

It was also on the South Continent he had learned to play the drums, or at least to play them in a way he would not have in Second City. He had already been playing for around five years, and by the age of fifteen he was pretty good. When he wasn't tending to his mushrooms or his traps, he would travel the five hours out of the jungle to Touskania, and make his way into the city's underground. There he would find the mushroom dens, and the small packs of musicians who gathered there. Musical instruments were not easy to come by, and drums seemed to be the only ones readily available. He would stare at the drummers as their hands flew over the skins, creating twining rhythms that sent the people around them into a leaping, pulsing frenzy of dance. For hours he would watch, then he would slip off into the night, back to his own shack to practice the rhythms he had heard in the city. He had been good, but, left on his own to work and change the rhythms, he soon surpassed mere description.

    Draephus stayed on the South Continent for three years, living in seclusion with only his faelins for company. He called them his, but they did not truly belong to him. They were a tribe of about forty, living in the jungle. It had taken a long time to win their trust, but once he had, they became valuable allies in guarding both him and his mushrooms. He'd grown very fond of all of them, as were most of the drug runners he knew. There was a bond between the runners and faelins, an almost spiritual joining. The runners relied on them heavily for numerous things, and not just to know what the weather would be. That was an easy trick to learn. On days of impending cold, or violent rainfall, they were never to be seen, and only occasionally heard howling to one another across the expanse of trees. The howls would be reflected off the leaves of the amplifier plants that grew wild there; a plant that had learned to cope with the lightless days by absorbing certain sound waves and feeding off of them. But if the day promised to be hot, the faelins would be there in the yard, faces raised to where they instinctively knew the sun would be, even under the heavy Sferkkaan cloud cover. Then they would sway in the warmth, worshipping a star they could not see on that shadowless planet.

    The faelins also knew if anything was in the dense foliage that shouldn't be, and if there was a Night Stalker within miles, then the faelins would set up a noise that could be heard straight across the jungle. It gave everyone plenty of time to get underground, and cover their faces with heavy cloths to muffle their breathing, while the large, spider-shaped devices roamed silently through the trees. The unmanned Kryphisian machines, standing taller than most Sferkkaans, could hear a heartbeat, even a breath, and, like most spiders, could fit into virtually any hole. That was why it was important to have enough time to slow one's heart, so it wouldn't be heard racing amongst the other, calmer hearts of the jungle animals. Draephus still saw the Night Stalkers in his nightmares. He remembered too clearly lying in a small dirt hole like a frightened animal, a cloth over his face, his eyes squeezed shut as he concentrated on not alerting the deathly-silent animatronic spiders, poking carefully though the undergrowth. He would try to fall asleep, to be unconscious and unable to react to the scratching, digging, and relentless seeking…

At the age of eighteen he returned to Second City, which sat perched alone and aloof on its tiny island just off the mainland of the lower North Continent. He returned with almost two million trinta in drug money, an illegal shipment of drums, and a long scruffy coat, the first expensive item he had ever bought. He also arrived with his two favourite faelins, Bacca and Czanda, they not wanting to stay any longer in the uncertain world of the jungle. They had opted to remain with Draephus, and maintain the watch over him they had been keeping for three years.

Draephus moved himself, his faelins, and his drums into a demolished castle on the actual island part of the city, built centuries before the great floating platforms had been added, and the city enlarged. The castle was little more than ruins with a heritage, but he loved it. He and the faelins spent many damp, shivering nights in it, undetected by the Kryphisian patrols, careful to do nothing to alert the invaders to his presence.

Occasionally he would travel into the city, making his way into the Cylinder's lower depths in search of others like himself. The Cylinder had been built by the Kryphisians, the Sferkkaans at the time having no way of constructing a gigantic cylindrical tower of glass and metal. To them, the thing looked like some freakish bone poking out of the earth of the island on which their city perched. To the Kryphisians, it looked like a shining example of their superiority as a race, and they moved all their highest and most revered members of the invasion force into it, along with their families, servants, whores, and fighters.

It had been meant to intimidate the Sferkkaans into submission, but Sferkkaans were not easily intimidated. What they lacked in technology, they made up for in cold, cunning, craft. While the Kryphisians looked down from their lofty apartments through golden windows, their Sferkkaan pets were kept in the windowless darkness of the lowest levels. And while the Kryphisians threw lavish parties and plotted destruction, the Sferkkaans dug out underground dens, tunnelling to the street, stockpiling food, weapons, clothing, water, candles, medicine, and anything else they could think of. Then, one very dark and terrifying night, the partisans boiled up from the depths and started killing. Only the children were spared, smuggled to Kryphisian bases clutching toys and pets to sob to their own people about the night the walls came alive, and the blood ran in small rivers across the floor and down the halls. In the morning, the Kryphisians had looked out of their fortified bases and saw the Cylinder draped with banners showing the Imperial Gryphon, the sidewalk below covered with bodies.

After that, the Kryphisians never returned to the Cylinder. Officially, the reason was listed as "too impractical to maintain". Unofficially, the Kryphisians did not dare, knowing they would never be able to secure it. The Sferkkaans kept their prize, and the partisan groups moved in, using it as a base, and home. Music came to thrive in the deep cold underground, and the few bits and scraps of their own past were carefully hidden there. Treasures were locked away in secret vaults, protected from the invaders. South continent spiny mushrooms were imported, and in the darkness, Sferkkaan life grew. Musicians came to hide there, along with poets, artists, soldiers, farmers, miners, builders… the base of the Kryphisian-built Cylinder provided everything the Sferkkaans needed to dig in and lash out at their oppressors.

The Kryphisians responded to this by having the architect hanged.

In one of the infamous mushroom dens, Draephus found a handsome young dissident who played the best sepulchord he'd ever heard. Draephus and Raski liked each other from the first time they met, and soon Draephus had moved Raski in with his drums and faelins, where they would be safe from the cold and wet. They kept Raski's small flat as a back-up place to store weapons, food, and other things, and it was there Draephus had his chaotic first encounter with Vesper. At first, Draephus and Raski worked together better as musicians than revolutionaries. Raski was all for the New Empire, and fighting the oppressive forces that held reign over their planet. Draephus figured that since the Kryphisians had already been there for so long they should try to forget about them and live their own lives. This made him crashingly unpopular in the mushroom dens, especially with a slight, green-eyed poet named Mars David, and a six-foot, eight-inch Breed just back from the labs named Yuri Stracona. Instead of making them see his point of view, Draephus found himself agreeing with them, and he and his money joined the Revolution.

There were times of relative peace mixed in with the raids and sabotage, when, in the deepest levels of the Cylinder, Draephus and his friends would meet and play their music. Their music quickly became in high demand, but something always seemed to be not quite right, until one night Khandid Stratavarus stepped out of the crowd to play. Tiny, pretty Khandid was at the time earning a decent living infiltrating Kryphisian posts and selling the information he stole to the highest bidder, and selling his body to the Kryphisians. A night with Khandid could cost a man everything, including his life. More than one of Khandid's clients realized too late it was a very bad idea to bed a man with a single black line painted beneath his eyes, and bearing the last name of one of Sferkkaa's most famous generals. Khandid had been bred a warrior, from a very long line of warriors. Tiny, cute and cuddly on the outside, murder machine on the inside.

He also played a pretty good quinticord, and, with him in the group, all the band needed now was a name.

The Gryphons at that point in time were no music group. They were a band of Kryphisian pilots making use of an ancient Sferkkaan symbol. They had gryphons painted on the sides of their warplanes, and people seeing the symbol would often come running out of their houses to cheer what they thought were their own pilots, only to find their homes and families suddenly destroyed by a rain of laser fire. It was an easy way for the Grey Boys to find out who the rabble-rousers were, and it earned them the unending hate of those loyal to their emperor.

It was Khandid who came home with a map of the Kryphisian base, and it was Raski who decided to rig the planes with explosive devices. It seemed to always be Raski who thought of these things, and he was always the first one to volunteer to go out and bomb whatever needed blowing up, usually with Mars right behind him. Raski would have been content to simply rig the planes, but Mars had another idea. So as Raski silently and swiftly attached the detonators, Mars attached some sort of homing device to the bombs the planes carried. Then they scurried away in the night back to the Cylinder, and waited.

They had not known the Gryphons were scheduled to put on some sort of show for a visiting dignitary, but when they found out it just made things all the sweeter. Raski and Mars stood side by side, each holding a device that would send a signal to both planes and bombs respectively. As Draephus stood with Raski and Mars in an abandoned penthouse in the Cylinder, they watched as the Gryphons soared majestically by, banking, rolling, turning in perfect unity.

"They fly really well, don't they?" said Raski.

"Yes," said Mars. "So well I almost hate to do this."

Mars flicked the switch on his own remote first. The bombs on the fully-loaded warplanes broke free and went straight for the base, slamming into the buildings and destroying them. Raski activated his next, and the pair watched as the pilots were flung from their seats into the air high above the city. Moments later the planes began to explode, one after another, raining flaming debris down onto the Kryphisian dignitary.

"Well that is going to be a bit embarrassing to explain to the officials, isn't it?" said Mars, watching as the pilots slowly parachuted downward.

"Yes it is," said Raski. "They must just feel dreadfully silly; accidentally launching themselves out of their planes before blowing up the base."

"Absolutely. I should say that they're mortified gryphons now."

"Oooh we should call the band that," said Raski.

It was voted out four to one, but somehow it never went away, and when they finally crawled out of the underground after the war was over, they brought their name and their hordes of subversive followers with them. Six years had gone by since the day they blew up the planes, and they now had fans all over Sferkkaa, not just Second City any more. They had been rewarded for their work by the Emperor Stratavarus, though none of them wanted much. Draephus couldn't recall what the others had been given, but he had asked for the castle ruins. He'd always wanted a castle. The Emperor was a bit reluctant to give Draephus a ruined building, but if that was what he wanted, then he could take it and enjoy. With the money he already had, Draephus proceeded to rebuild it into a proud symbol of the

Sferkkaan past.

'Funny,' Draephus thought as he sipped some more of the cold water. 'Here I am, a hero, a noted musician with money to throw around, friends who love me, and I still feel like clart on the road.'

He washed his face carefully, trying not to irritate his stitches, and gently dried himself with a towel. He looked at himself for a time in the mirror, studying his swollen eyes. Then, putting his shades back on, he headed for the door.

He had almost reached the door when it suddenly flew open, the edge of it striking him square in the face. He staggered back, bringing his hands up over his eyes, and felt the warm stickiness of the blood that flowed from the torn stitches. He shook his head, stumbled, then collapsed onto the cold floor. A young girl with short red hair stood in the doorway and looked around.

"Oops," she said, "wrong door. Well, good thing nobody's in here." She was about to leave before her error was discovered, and stopped dead.

Draephus slowly struggled to his feet, dazed, bleeding, raising his head to look at his assailant. The girl brought her own hands up to her mouth in horror, and likely recognition as well. He struggled between the thought that this was only a stupid accident, and the notion of just killing her anyway. Then, as his temper cooled and she did not move, he reached for the door handle. Pulling the door open, he motioned for her to leave. She dropped her hands and shook her head.

"No that's okay," she said. "I'll just go drown myself in the toilet."

Her cheeks were burning red. He let the door go and reached into his pockets for his cigarettes, remembering Raski had them.

"Don't worry about it," he said.

He reached up to remove the shades, peering at the blood on them with a slight scowl on his face. The girl unfroze, and, grabbing up a towel, she dampened it in the sink. As Draephus moved over to the sink, she wrung out the towel and turned to press it against his bleeding wound. He jerked his head back, suspicious of the object coming abruptly for his face. Deciding she probably was not trying to kill him, he lowered his head to allow her to wipe the blood away.

"I'm really sorry," she said after a moment.

He shifted. "Don't worry about it."

"Well it's not really nice to go hitting people in the face with a door."

"I suppose," he said. He lowered his gaze to the front of her shirt and contemplated it. Across the front of her shirt in glaring yellow letters read `World Tour', and beneath this a monumental Gryphon wreaked havoc on a silhouetted city.

"You could offer me a cigarette," he said, still studying the shirt. "Raski took mine."

She set down the towel and reached into her pocket for her cigarettes and lighter. She gave him one, then lit the cigarette for him, and put the items into her pocket once more. She was acting coolly enough, but it seemed pretty obvious she was mortified to her very boots.

"So," he said after a time, "you hang out in the men's washroom of fancy restaurants a lot?"

"I feel so stupid," she muttered. She rinsed the towel out, seemingly unable to look at him. "You really whacked yourself," she said, dumping the towel into the laundry hamper.

"I did, huh?" he said dryly.

Her cheeks turned redder and she hid once more behind her hands.

"I'd like to die now."

"Did you see that concert?" he asked, indicating her shirt.

"What concert?" She lowered her hands to look at her shirt. "Oh! Yeah, I did. I stole the money off of my sister for tickets, then I had to sneak out of my bedroom window to go to the show. My best friend Diza and I managed to get backstage, but the road crew threw us back into the crowd. But at least that got us into the front row." She glanced up as he grinned at her.

"Was it worth it?"

She smiled back at him. "I thought so."

He turned to the sink and washed the blood from his hands, then from the glasses. He noticed there was a chip in one of the lenses. She seemed to notice this as well, and as he stared irritably at the glasses, she asked casually, "Are you going to throw those out?"

He gave her an amused sidelong glance, then passed her the glasses. "Here. And don't feel bad, I can't get any uglier any way."

"You're not ugly," she said, taking the glasses. She did not say anything about them, but he noticed the way she folded them into her hand, drawing them close to her chest. "You should eat something, though, you don't look well."

Draephus stared at her for a moment. "That's why I'm here," he said dryly.

She flushed red again. "Sorry. Bad habit I have."

"Uh-huh," he said. "Have a few of those myself."

She smiled again. "Thanks for the glasses," she said, almost shyly.

He reached into an inner pocket of his coat and pulled out a second pair of the glasses. "I always carry a spare," he said, "people keep stealing mine." He carefully set them on his injured face.

"Maybe if you haven't had food in a while you should try soup. Anything too heavy might make you sick."

He contemplated telling her to šukat off, then nodded. "Okay," he said, "I'll do that." He pulled open the door and stepped back. "After you," he said.

She was about to step out, but paused, looking up at him. "Can I ask a question? The CZ at the start of your name. Who…I mean, what royal house…?"

He shook his head. "No idea. That's a question lost to the ages." He laughed, a cold, mirthless sound. "It may not even belong to me. A few families tacked that onto their last names in the hopes it would save them. Fat bloody good it did any of them. What's your name? I mean since you clearly know mine."

"Dahli."

"Dahli," he repeated. "Nice to meet you."

She nodded, clearly feeling uncomfortable and a little intimidated. She offered him an Imperial salute, then stepped out ahead of him as he laughed quietly at the gesture. She went off to the women's washroom, still holding the glasses, and he returned to his seat. Raski glanced up as Draephus came over to the table.

"Are you all right?"

"Got sick," said Draephus, sitting down. "What's this?" He indicated the food before him, a bowl of clear soup and a small salad.

"I suggested to the server that you may not be feeling too well, and he thought soup would be better than the stuff you had been eating."

"What's with all these people trying to feed me soup?" bitched Draephus.

"What?"

"Oh, nothing," said Draephus, "just talking to some young Gryphon-watcher who proceeded to nag me on my eating habits."

"Marry him," said Raski.

"Her."

"HER?! Where?"

"She's about fifteen, Rask, we'd be doing her and ourselves a bigger favour by leaving her alone."

Draephus tried a little of the soup, thinking about the girl he had been talking to. He began to feel a little guilty about the way he had acted.

"I think I was a little nasty to her," he said.

"Tell her that you're sorry you're a clart."

"Yeah, I think I will." As he said this, he spotted a young boy with a basket over his arm, dressed in a manner popular with the fisher-folk centuries back. He was the adopted son of the owner, and a part of the atmosphere of the restaurant, supposedly a poor child selling flowers to earn a few trinta for food. Draephus motioned him over.

"Yes?" the boy inquired.

"Two bloodflowers, if you have them." said Draephus.

He did, producing two from his basket, passing the red-black flowers bound by lace to him. Draephus paid him for the flowers, the boy then wandering off to another table.

"Pretty," said Raski.

"Yeah," said Draephus. "Got anything I can write on?"

Raski hunted through his wallet. "Let's see. Parking ticket, speeding ticket, business card, parking ticket, dried flower, and half a song written on a piece of newspaper."

"Pass the speeding ticket."

Raski did. "What ya gonna write on it?"

"Nothing until you loan me a pen."

Raski handed him a pen. Draephus took it, staring down at the blank side of the ticket. Finally something came to mind, and the pen began to move across the paper. When he was finished, he returned the pen and folded the paper up, thrusting it into the lace binding the flowers. He called over a server.

"Yes?"

"There's a young girl, about fifteen, with red hair, wearing a

Mortified Gryphons tour shirt and a pair of dark glasses. Not sure where she's sitting. Would you give her this?" He passed the server the flowers.

"Certainly." The man took the flowers and left in search of Dahli, while Draephus tried to eat his soup.

****

The server found Dahli with little difficulty.

"Donselle?"

Dahli looked up, the over-sized shades obscuring most of her face. "Yeah?"

"A man in a long coat and wearing dark glasses asked me to give these to you."

Dahli took the flowers, looking about for the giver, not seeing him. "Thanks," she said softly.

"From him?" Diza asked. Dahli had told her the story, and she had been unable to believe it. She craned her neck around to see if she could catch a glimpse of him. "Was Yuri with him?"

"No, I think he was with Raski, he mentioned him." Dahli gingerly took the note from the flowers, not quite believing what she was seeing. She opened it, finding a cartoon on the back of a paper she recognised as a speeding ticket. It was of five small Gryphons on a branch, each one obviously a member of the band, each with his name written next to him in case there was any doubt. There was a tall, skinny Gryphon marked `Yuri', seated next to a tiny one with its mouth open, prattling on mindlessly. This one was marked `Khandi'. The next one, `Mars', stared out of the paper with large blank eyes, head screwed to a silly angle. `Raski' had his mouth opened to the point of obscuring his head, laughing crazily.

The fifth Gryphon sat a ways off by himself, tail around his feet, black circles around his swollen eyes. Above it was written, "I couldn't think of anything to say so I drew you this stupid cartoon." Draephus had signed his name beneath this.

"Let's see! Let's see!" Diza was practically bouncing up and down in her seat.

Dahli passed her the cartoon, Diza snapping it up and staring at it. "Oh isn't it cute!" she exclaimed.

"Yeah," said Dahli, gently caressing the flowers. Raising her eyes, she looked at Diza and said, "I am in shock."

"Why didn't you come and get me?" hissed Diza.

"What was I gonna do? 'Oh, sorry I whacked you with a door. Hold on a second, I gotta go get Diza'."

"Yeah, okay. Hey, maybe if we hurry, we'll see him in the parking lot."

They had their bounty of food packed up, then ran out of the restaurant just in time to see the black conveyance they had admired earlier start into life. The headlights came on, and the machine slowly pulled forward, gathering speed as it moved away, swiftly disappearing down the road.

"Was that them?" asked Diza.

"I don't know," said Dahli, "I think it was."

"Nice conni," said Diza. "Did you see Raski, too?"

"No, just Draephus." The realization of what had occurred suddenly sank in. Brandishing her bloodflowers, glasses on her face, she went running and leaping down the street towards their own conni, chanting, "I met Draephus! I met Draephus!"

"Big deal," said Diza, following her.

"I met Draephus!" Dahli sang, landing feet first in a puddle. "I met Draephus!"

"I'm sure he feels much the same," said Diza.

"You're just jealous," said Dahli. "I met Draephus!" She stomped in the puddle again.

"You're right, I am," said Diza.

"Sorry, but I did mention you to him."

"Very High Cylinder of you."

"I thought so," said Dahli. "Come on, let's go to my place and get this food put away. Teirra and Atterick won't believe their eyes! We'll divide it up when we get home."

"Dahli I can't take any of that home, my father will know I wasn't at your place all night!"

"Oh, right. Okay. Well we'll just store your half at my place."

"All right. Let me wear the glasses, you have to drive."

They drove the conni back to her grandfather's house, parking it carefully after having to push it back into its place. They said good night to Boo, then ran the last few blocks to Dahli's. They barged through the door, immediately barrelling upstairs to the bedroom.

"Where are you going to put your cartoon?" asked Diza.

Dahli glanced about her room, then walked over to a small book shelf, sitting down before it. She pulled a large book off of the shelf. Opening it, she carefully set the cartoon between its pages, then closed the book once more.

"I can't wait until Teirra sees this!"

"I'll put on some music," said Diza.

She walked over to a cluttered shelf, littered with small tubes. She picked one up, and shook out of it a thin, silver cylinder. Moving over to the small stereo deck on Dahli's dresser, she pushed the cylinder into a slot and then turned up the volume. Moments later The Mortified Gryphons came pouring out, the small amplifier plants on the table angling their leaves in order to absorb the maximum amount of vibration before reflecting it back as sound. The plants had gone an odd shade of indigo from a near-constant diet of Gryphons. Diza tossed the cylinder cover to Dahli. There was a picture of Draephus on it.

"You met him," said Diza.

Dahli snatched up the cover, pressing it to her face and screamed into it, "I did! I did! I did!" She lowered the cover and looked at Diza, her face flushed with excitement. "You know who I'm going to tell?"

"Who?"

"Atania Nightwing!" Sucking in great lungfulls of air, both girls bellowed; "EEEEEYYEEEEWWW!"

"But she doesn't like the Gryphons," said Diza. "She only listens to Vortex. And track bands."

Dahli made a face. "Atania listens to track bands? You mean that musical debris you take home and mix yourself, to make it sound like what you want? Eyew, now I hate her even more. But anyway, she'll be sick because I met somebody famous and she didn't."

"Don't let her touch your cartoon, it'll wither up and turn black."

"I won't, I'll just show it to her." Dahli opened the book once more and gazed down at her cartoon. "I'm not going to sleep tonight."

"So what, there's no school tomorrow."

They turned the cylinder up to a mind-numbing level so they could hear it when they ran downstairs to put away the food.

Chapter Four.

Raski's house would have been silent save for the soft whisper of a receiver in the darkness. The receiver was never off in his home, he couldn't stand the quiet. Raski turned on a light, then adjusted it to a low setting.

As Draephus seated himself on a long, low couch, he suddenly found himself thinking about how not long ago it had been dangerous to enter this house, to enter the domain of Heirrina. When Raski had met Heirrina, he did back flips to get her to notice him. She hated the music he played, and was not interested in having a sepulchord player as a husband. However, Raski had persisted in true Jervyas style. He wrote her ballads and sang them to her over the 'com when she wouldn't answer the door. He sent her flowers, jewellery, and once a fiercely expensive conveyance. Heirrina's friends all thought she was mad for ignoring him. He was attractive, they said. His hair is too long, she countered. He's famous, they said. No privacy, she said. He's rich, they said...

Heirrina did not have a response to that. While Second City had survived the long years of war relatively untouched and unscathed, the rest of Sferkkaa had not fared nearly so well. A nice house and food enough were little more than hopeless dreams to most of the population. Of course, the first fight Heirrina had with Raski was her violent objection to how much money the band was pumping into rebuilding their shattered homeland. Things did not improve when Raski flat-out refused to stop the funding, and when the other four Gryphons sided with him, she began doing everything in her power to cause a rift. Marrying him was a sure way to cause havoc, and she finally agreed to it. Mars took Draephus aside and asked him what he thought of this. Draephus said he thought it sucked clart, and Mars agreed.

The scatters started shortly after they were married, and the other four Gryphons knew that all was not happy and well when The Rask manifested one day with all of his beautiful thick black hair hacked off. Then Draephus, who had always been welcome in Raski's home, suddenly found that he was no longer. He would find himself being stared at coldly, disapprovingly by Heirrina. When he tried to talk to Raski he found his friend morose, if not snappy. Raski still tried over-hard to please Heirrina, but the fact remained that she hated his lifestyle, she hated his friends, and she never had a kind word for him, or even a tone of voice lower than a scream.

The scat hit the turbine the day Delaes Randerick showed up. Delaes, being a social creature who knew the Gryphons, took it upon himself to throw Mars a birthday party. Delaes' parties were indescribable acts of worship to the great god Indecency. Certainly nothing to be missed in any event, especially not when the guest of honour was a close friend. Heirrina did not want to go, but this time Raski would not take no for an answer, and said he was going with or without her. Heirrina bent and came along, and it was at the party she ran into a man much more to her liking than the horrible Raski. She came home after two days to find her things on the lawn, the lock on the door changed, and a sign on the door reading; 'Now you won't be bothered by my friends any more. And they won't be bothered by you.'

Raski had begun to feel better once his hair started to grow back.

Draephus stretched out on the expensive couch, Raski seating himself next to him and passing him a drink. He knew Raski had a fair idea of what was bothering him, but was probably more than a little afraid to ask. He also knew he'd find out when his friend was ready to tell him. Raski did not have long to wait.

"Vesper's sick," Draephus said quietly. "The virus has finally become active."

Raski shifted a little uncomfortably. "I'm sorry," he said softly.

"Yeah, me too," said Draephus. He stared into the dark, red-gold contents of his glass. "It's funny, you know, I always knew it would show up, but I thought he and I were used to the idea."

"How is Vesper?"

"He was pretty upset, understandably," said Draephus. "More so than I would have expected from him, he seemed so accustomed to the thought that he was going to die. But like I said, you probably never really get used to the idea."

"No," said Raski, "I suppose you don't." He slipped his long, dark hand into Draephus'. "How are you?"

"Me? I don't know. Tired, sick, depressed. I wrecked my vehicle, wrecked my face, beat up some fellow like it would make a difference. You and I have the opposite problem, Raski. You got something you thought you wanted, and couldn't wait to get rid of, and I got something I wasn't looking for, and don't know how I'll live without."

"Perhaps we should both try to get some sleep," Raski said, likely not knowing what else to say.

"Yeah, okay," said Draephus. He rose to his feet and crossed the floor to the winding stairs. Stopping partway up, he looked back at Raski.

"You coming?" he asked quietly.

Raski got up and followed after him, the two walking up the curving stair to the upper level, then following the long hall to Raski's bedroom. They stepped into the large chamber, which seemed silent at first, but then Draephus realized he could hear the vague sound of music coming from someplace. He was not surprised. The war had left them all with strange quirks. Raski couldn't tolerate silence.

Draephus stopped in the large room, glancing around at the centuries-old wooden panels. Like himself, Raski had a taste for the past, and the calm, dignified refinement of it. He turned to look at his friend, watching as he closed the great wood and gilt doors that boasted Imperial Gryphons. Once the doors had graced the summer palace of a deceased Emperor. Now they were the only thing left of a structure that had survived eight hundred years before its utter annihilation.

Raski stepped across the black marble floor, his movements uncertain, almost cautious, and the two stood close, sensing each other, circling one another like strange animals. Then Draephus gently caught Raski, pulling him close, slowly drawing him against his chest.

"We've never done this before," said Draephus softly.

Raski shook his head, his fine black hair framing his face, his dark skin making his blue-white eyes shine eerily. "Draephus this is so wrong…"

"I know," said Draephus. "I know. And believe me I don't want to hurt you or Vesper. I just…"

He gasped, and began to shake, fighting desperately to hold onto his emotions. He felt Raski take him into his arms.

"Draephus," said Raski softly, "it's okay to cry you know."

Draephus shook his head, swallowing back his tears, holding Raski tightly. Then he kissed him as though his survival depended on it, and Raski stopped questioning him. They fell into a pattern that had become so very familiar during the course of their time fighting. It was almost reflexive, and though they had never been with each other, they both knew the steps to this dance, and the reasons. During times of heightened fear, many of the fighters in their circle of friends and acquaintances would huddle together for comfort, often of a sexual nature. It was better to spend what may be one's last hours alive in an act of passion and comfort, than let one's nerve turn to raw sewage, rotted away by tension and fear.

Draephus kissed Raski, tasting him, holding him hard against his chest. For a time, Raski tolerated it, but then fought the tightness of the embrace, and Draephus eased his grip. Raski pulled back, gasping.

"Oh, we like to play rough, do we?" said Raski.

"I'm... not good at this."

Raski looked at him quizzically. Draephus reached out and carefully touched his friend's face. "Vesper... I dunno. I guess because he's small and sick, everything has to be a fight with him. To prove he's not as small and sick as he is. If I want to get on top I almost have to beat him into submission. And... I've never...had...anyone other than him."

Raski grinned, and kissed Draephus. "You don't have to beat me into submission," he said softly. "We have all night. Nothing exists outside of this room, or outside of this moment. Tomorrow will never come. We are safe here. And nothing we do has anything to do with the rest of our lives. Tonight is just you and me."

Draephus smiled slightly, without humour. He kissed Raski again, pulling him close, but carefully this time, as though he really was not sure what he was doing. "Okay."

Raski kissed him, taking Draephus' large, scarred hands between his own. His movements were soft, almost submissive, letting Draephus take control of the situation, allowing him to guide him over to the huge, ancient bed. They lay down on the soft, deep mattress, kissing, slowly exploring one another. Draephus opened Raski's shirt, gently removing it, stroking his hand over the dark, softly shining skin. He kissed his throat, grinning as Raski pressed close, making a soft purring sound of pleasure. Draephus pulled him closer, touching him, kissing him, relishing his gentleness. He wished that, just once, Vesper would relax and let their lovemaking be like this.

Raski just let Draephus take his time, lying back, eyes closed, languishing in the feel of the gentle caresses, the soft kisses, and his scarred hands moving across his skin.

"This is nice," he said quietly.

"Yeah," said Draephus. "It is."

He undressed Raski slowly, lingering over every part of him, kissing him, tasting him. He slid off his pants, then lowered his head to kiss his lower stomach, breathing in the scent of him. He moved his head, kissing slightly lower, then gave the penis before him an experimental swipe of his tongue. Raski purred with pleasure, and Draephus did it again, slower this time, then took the large member into his mouth.

Raski gasped, shifting beneath him, reaching down to stroke his dark hands over Draephus' hair. He made a quiet sound of pleasure, moving his hips. The music played faintly in the background, and Draephus couldn't help but grin when Raski turned it up.

He ran his hands over Raski's dark skin, stroking him, feeling the muscles, and the occasional scar. There was a huge one across his collarbone, from when a malfunctioning laser pistol had exploded, burning his flesh and breaking the bone. It never healed quite right, but it did not seem to trouble him. Draephus hardly noticed it, far more interested in exploring the beautiful body beneath him. Raski made a soft moan, his body gleaming in shades of black and silver in the subdued light. When had he become so damn beautiful?

They said nothing. There was no need. Raski gently pushed Draephus off, moving to lie across him, their naked bodies moving together fluidly, Draephus' pale skin showing in stark contrast. They kissed, touching each other, Raski's long hair falling loose and wild over his broad shoulders. He worked his way down Draephus' body, then gave him an impish grin before lowering his head to take Draephus' stiff shaft into his mouth. Draephus clutched the black silk bed covers, tilting his head back and swallowing hard.

Why oh why had they never done this before?

Draephus waited until he was nearly ready to explode before he stopped Raski, gently catching him and drawing him up. He did not want this to end too soon. He drew Raski up to lie beside him, kissing him, wanting just to touch him. His hands roamed over his body, feeling the lines of his muscles, kissing his flesh. It was almost spiritual, just to make love, to touch another body and not have to worry about when the battle would begin between dominance and submission, life and death. It was just the two of them: the rest of the world was gone, and they had all the time the universe could give them.

Draephus didn't know where the bottle of oil came from, he did not much care. He uncapped it, and poured some out, smelling the rich, musky aroma. He slowly rubbed it between his hands and sniffed, then looked at Raski, who simply tried to look innocent.

"All those times I told you I loved your cologne, it was this?"

Raski giggled, sounding like a demented hyena. Draephus shook his head and smiled, then began smearing the pale golden oil over his friend's body, stroking him, massaging him, just for the pleasure of feeling his living flesh. He started at his throat, working slowly down, caressing him, touching him, past the shattered clavicle, down over his broad chest, his flat stomach, then taking his hard penis in his large hands, stroking it slowly. Raski made a sound of pure want, and Draephus lowered his head to take it into his mouth once more.

He poured more of the oil into his hands, rubbing it between his palms to warm it, then sliding them underneath Raski, following the line of his hips, down to his buttocks, finally to the hot flesh between them. Still with Raski's cock in his mouth, he began slowly, teasingly, touching the opening he found, inserting the tip of one long finger into his anus, carefully working it deeper. He remembered vividly how damned much it hurt when Vesper did this; he wasn't about to do that to Raski. Raski knew four ways to snap a man's neck. No need to risk a reflexive response.

Raski uttered a small cry of pleasure, moving his hips, thrusting into the wet heat of Draephus' mouth. He cried out as he felt a second finger join the first, working its way in, then beginning to slowly slide back and forth inside of him.

"I thought you said you were bad at this!"

Draephus grinned, raising his head. "Just...feeling my way around."

"Ha ha."

Draephus didn't lower his head again to take Raski's wet penis back into his mouth, he was too fascinated watching his friend's response to the fingers inside of him. He was panting, head flung back, eyes closed, lips parted in pure pleasure. Draephus was sure he had never enjoyed it that much. He stared, almost hypnotized, continuing to pleasure his friend with one hand while he began coating his own stiff cock with the oil. Almost as an afterthought, he withdrew his hand and positioned himself between Raski's thighs. He placed his hands on his hips, and slowly pushed into him, closing his eyes and gasping as he felt the tight heat envelop him. It was almost too good to be real, and he had to shake himself back to some semblance of sense in order not to forget Raski.

    He lay over top of him, and began thrusting into him, feeling Raski's long legs move up to hold him, letting him penetrate deeper. They kissed, lips parting, tongues meeting, merging. Draephus thrust slowly, languishing over every incredible moment, basking in the peaceful gentleness of it. Outside he could hear the rain start to fall, and Draephus could hear himself speaking to Raski, but he had not the faintest idea what he was saying. It didn't matter anyway.

    His orgasm seemed to start somewhere in the pit of his gut, and shot out like an overwhelming explosion of pleasure. He heard himself scream, thrusting deep into Raski, the peace of their coupling broken as both hit their climax. Raski rolled violently, and they both fell off the bed, neither caring as they clutched one another and bit, faint touches of blood mingling with sweat and oil. Draephus thrust into Raski, feeling the other man's semen splash hot and wet onto his body. He cried out, emptying himself utterly into him, and, for one eternal moment, both were silent, shuddering as the feeling slowly, finally, passed. Eventually, they relaxed, and finally separated. Draephus withdrew himself, and collapsed to the floor like a dying animal, coughing.

    "You okay?" asked Raski, sitting up.

    Draephus hacked out a spray of blood. "Dandy."

    "Come on, old man, let's get you off the floor."

    They managed to crawl onto the bed and under the covers, moving into each other's arms. Draephus continued to cough, finally managing to get himself under control. He kissed Raski, stroking the damp and tangled black hair.

    "I didn't know it could be like that."

    Raski kissed him, then snuggled close. Draephus coughed explosively one last time, then reached for the drawer in the side table, opening it and rummaging around. Raski raised his head.

"And just *what* are you looking for?"

"Cigarettes."

Raski rolled his eyes. Draephus hauled out a fistful of pamphlets and looked at them. Raski promptly took them away from him before he got a good look, rolling over to stash them in the drawer in the table on his side of the bed.

"What are those?"

"Nothing that concerns you. Go smoke something."

Draephus lit a cigarette. "Rask you know I'll just read them the first chance I get."

"It's nothing to do with you. You're turning into Khandi, he's nosy too. DRAEPHUS!"

Draephus simply pinned Raski down to the bed with his weight, reaching for the drawer and pulling the pamphlets out to look at them, while Raski tried to shove his large friend off him. Finally he gave up and simply glared at him. Draephus drew the cigarette out of his mouth and exhaled a blue cloud.

"This is all about that experimental artificial embryo environment crap. Rask, why are you reading up on this clart, it's all Grey Boy technology. Who was thinking about getting this thing installed?"

Raski yanked away the pamphlets and tossed them back into the drawer. "Me. But you don't have to talk me out of it, I don't qualify."

"Raski I didn't know that. Hey what do you mean you don't qualify?"

"Get *off* you oaf, I can't breathe."

Draephus moved off Raski, and watched as he sat up, hair rumpled and skin gleaming. "I don't want to talk about it. Okay? The doctor took one look at my blood and threw me out of the clinic. Any child I fathered would be riddled with birth defects, so they're not going to let one slosh around in my guts in an artificial environment for eleven months. So I don't need to be interrogated about it, okay?"

Draephus was shocked and hurt at the defensive tone of Raski's voice. "Well, what makes you so sure I would have talked you out of it?"

Raski crossed his arms and fixed Draephus with a look, and Draephus conceded the point.

"Okay, I don't think anyone in this band has any business making babies, not with our history. But, this clearly meant a lot to you, and... I'm sorry we won't get a chance to make fun of you when you blow up into an off-balanced hormonal eating machine."

"Thank you."

"Who did you want to father it?"

"Who else? You."

"*ME*?! WHY IN THE NAME OF THE NEW EMPIRE *ME*?!"

Raski shrugged, and said quietly: "Because you're my friend."

Draephus stared back at Raski, jaw open, just gaping in shock. Then he put his arms around him and pulled him close, burying his face into the heavy mane of black hair. For a long time, the two just held each other, saying nothing. Then, after a while, Raski began to speak.

"You asked me once a long time ago why I hated the silence so much. Why I couldn't stand it."

"Yeah, I did," said Draephus quietly.

Raski drew back, looking at Draephus with luminous blue eyes, his long black hair hanging loose around his shoulders.

"When I was little, my parents moved to a small village and into an enormous house – the biggest house I ever saw. Since almost every male in the area had gone off to fight, I found myself the only little boy in a houseful of women. There was my mother, her sisters, my cousins, my sisters, neighbour women... there must have been twenty women living in that house, and me – their little prince." He managed a slight smile. "To say I was spoiled was an understatement. There was never silence in that house. Even in the middle of the night, somebody was up. There was endless music and laughter and movement. Then... one morning... I woke up to the most horrible, ghastly silence."

Draephus reached out to take his hand. Raski lowered his head, and when he spoke, there was a quaver to his voice.

"I walked around, looking in all the rooms. There were bodies in all the beds, under the covers, as if asleep. Every single one of them, all still, all locked in a type of sleep I did not understand. Even my Aunt's three month old baby daughter, perfectly asleep in her cradle, cold and still. I tried to wake some of them up, but when they did not respond, I left the house and went across the street to the house of this old man, named Daricus. I told him that my family was playing a very bad trick on me. He gave me an almaniki, and as I sat on the porch eating it, he went across the street to look in my house. He came back after a little while, and told me that they were not playing a trick. A bad fairy cast a spell on them, and they would sleep a very long time – until I was a grown man. I could stay with him for a while. He went back to the house, got everything from my room, got the food from the freezers, and nailed the doors and windows closed. That was the last time I was ever in that house again."

Raski drew a shivering breath, trying to steady himself. He squeezed Draephus' hand and began to speak once more.

"When we toured Trae Dae Mu a few months ago, I went back to that town and saw the house. It's still there. Still sealed. Still silent. There's a sign before it now, though. It says 'Respect, Please. The Jervyas Women are Sleeping'."

"That's when you came back after being gone for three days and did nothing but crawl into bed with me and cry," said Draephus.

"I'd never mourned them before," said Raski. "I spent my childhood believing they were just asleep. By the time I was old enough to understand, it really never sank in. It wasn't until I went back to the house that I realized… they were *all dead. All* of them. My childhood home where I was so happy was nothing more than a giant crypt. I made arrangements with the town to have the house and yard fenced off and to just leave it. After all these years… there is no point doing anything else. The jungle has claimed so much of it already. But after that horrible day when I awoke to the sounds of nothing… I could never stand the silence. Then I began to think that if I had children of my own, in a way I could bring them back. But I should have known better than to wish."

"Raski…"

Raski should his head. "Just shut up and hold me."

****

Raski and Draephus lay in a comfortable heap, tangled together. The soft light of morning came through the window, turning the wood panelling lining the walls into gold. Raski made a small sound of protest as Draephus gently pushed him onto his back to take him one more time.

"Draephus…" he muttered sleepily.

Draephus kissed him. "Ignore me, you're having a dream."

"More like a recurring nightmare." He remained limp and submissive as Draephus mounted him yet again, then lazily draped his arms across his broad shoulders. "Khandi will be here soon," said Raski softly against Draephus' neck.

"Šukat Khandi."

Raski grinned, his eyes closed, head on the pillow in a halo of black silk. He was so pretty Draephus found himself just staring at him; the sheen of sweat over his dark skin, the glint of white between his parted lips. How did Raski manage to have perfect teeth? Draephus himself was missing most of his back teeth on his lower right jaw; the result of a blow to the face with the butt end of a very large weapon.

Raski drew a breath and writhed beneath Draephus' body, moaning in pleasure, and Draephus kissed him, wanting to linger in this bed with him for as long as he was able. He was still a little overwhelmed by their conversation of the previous evening, touched by the idea that Raski would want a family with him. Secretly, however, Draephus was rather relieved that Raski had been declared unfit for breeding; it spared Draephus from having to tell his friend that no reputable doctor on Sferkkaa would let him father children. True, his blood was relatively free of diseases, but what Raski did not know, what no one other than Draephus knew, was that he suffered from a rare and aggressive form of arthritis; one caused by a virus that only manifested in people who had spent considerable periods of time in the deep jungles of the South Continent. Within ten years his joints would be virtually destroyed, and he would be completely crippled. Before he died he could look forward to the remaining bone in his body honeycombing and becoming like crumbling masonry. One day his ribs would simply be too weak to support his chest, and would collapse, killing him. Not even Vesper knew Draephus had the illness, and Draephus saw no reason to tell him. Vesper would be dead before the disease began to take a noticeable toll on him. Why worry the little guy? And Raski had enough to deal with. He wanted to think Draephus' relatively clean blood meant he was healthy.

The bedroom door opened, and Khandid poked his head in. "I've got coffee!" he trilled. He paused. "Oh. Well it's on the counter when you want it."

Draephus continued his slow love making, nibbling a tasty

spot on Raski's neck. Raski freed one hand from beneath the covers and waved. "Good morning, Khandid."

Khandid raised one eyebrow and smiled. "Certainly is for *you*," he said dryly, and left.

"Little twerp," muttered Draephus.

"Ignore him," said Raski softly.

They finished making love, and Draephus rose from the huge bed to pull on his old combat pants, then make his way downstairs to share Khandid's coffee. It was a rare and welcome treat, and he accepted a cup from Khandid with an even rarer smile. He closed his eyes and breathed in the fragrance.

"Where did you get this?"

"Fan mail," said Khandid. "Someone likes the noise we make enough to mail me two pounds of the stuff all the way from the South Continent. Won't it be lovely when we reach the point where we have highly evolved and astonishingly futuristic things like… oh I don't know… trade, and reliable mail?"

"We have trade, and mail. Things are getting better; it's just… sporadic, painfully slow and expensive. At least we have communication, and most countries are working together to rebuild." Draephus savoured a mouthful of the brew. "Oh that's good. Now all we need is some milk and… Khandid Stracona I take back every rotten thing I ever said about you, even the things that were true."

Khandid laughed as Draephus accepted the small container of milk. "My neighbour has a moo-moo cow."

"As opposed to a regular cow. I'm going to kiss you."

Khandid accepted the kiss, and laughed. "My, you are positively sweet today. You ought to come over here and play in Raski's bed more often."

"Yeah, about that…"

"Say no more. '*Nari nuisse*,' am I right?"

"Bang on."

Khandid nodded, and sipped his coffee. 'Nari nuisse' was an old expression, and though it was not easy to explain, every Sferkkaan knew its meaning. The literal translation was "it happened somewhere else." The implied meaning; 'it happened but there's no need to mention it to anyone else'. Khandid was familiar with the expression; he had more than a few 'nari nuisse' events in his past himself.

Draephus made his way over to Raski's large daybed,

stretching out on it with his head propped up so he could sip his coffee while watching the doings of the small creatures out in the tangle of wildflowers and weeds Raski liked to call a garden. Raski himself was slowly making his way down the stairs and over to Khandid, walking as if he were a century old and reaching a shaking hand for a cup of coffee. Khandid passed him a cup, and raised an eyebrow. A silent conversation took place that Draephus pretended not to notice. Raski showed Khandid a length of distance between his two hands, then held up four fingers. Khandid's eyes bugged and his jaw dropped. Raski laughed quietly.

"Honestly, I don't know how he manages to close his pants."

"Well I won't offer you a seat, then. FOUR times?"

"I couldn't keep him off me."

"No wonder he's in such a good mood."

Raski grinned. "I'm not feeling too badly myself."

Both began snorting and giggling. Draephus raised his head and looked at the pair, brow furrowed. "What are you two cackling about?"

"Nothing," they lilted innocently.

Draephus grumbled, but settled once more on the daybed, watching the little creatures in the soft misty rain. He smiled, very faintly.

"Nice to know I'm worth a bit of kitchen gossip," he said quietly to the tiny fat bird that was settled on the window sill. He watched the bird, keeping one ear cocked for his two friends, who were whispering and giggling.

"ENOUGH, already!" he grumped.

"Oh you are no fun," said Khandid.

Draephus grumbled. Khandid brought him more coffee as an appeasement, then looked at Raski.

"So what shall we do today, Raski Jervyas?"

"Why I don't know, Khandid Stracona. We could... pop into the Gryphon's Roost."

"A fabulous idea, Raski Jervyas, will you do the honours and turn on the computer?"

"I shall, Khandid Stracona."

Draephus turned his head and looked at the pair. "I don't believe you two! You'll go blind reading that stuff, you know."

"Oh come on, we can't help ourselves, it's like picking at a scab, you know you shouldn't but you just have to," said Raski.

"You're war veterans, have a little self-respect and decorum," Draephus grumbled.

Khandid and Raski looked at each other. "We'll have to quit the music industry, then," said Raski. "OH GOOD! Lady Nightfall is on, AUGH by all that is sacred to the Empire I loathe that alleged woman."

Khandid seated himself next to Raski. "You don't think Lady Nightfall is a woman?"

Raski's blue eyes gleamed eerily in the light of the screen. "If she is, then I'm Straif Mannechek. And my fingers just don't move that fast on the sepulchord. Oh look, pictures. This ought to be good."

Draephus heard the click of a mouse, and braced himself for the shrieks, grumbling and muttering to himself. Finally he could not resist asking.

"What's so funny?"

Raski was screaming with laughter, a sound not unlike demons being tortured. Khandid had tears in his eyes. "Stay over there, you don't want to know, believe me. Oh that is SO not Mars' body. And what is he doing with Draephus?"

Raski coughed and reached for his cigarettes. "I'm not even sure that's his hair. And what is with that bow?!"

"It's holding on that giant trouser snake."

"We have to show that one to Mars. Oh hey, there's been an update to the Draephus gallery! Let's go look!"

Draephus winced. Raski clicked the mouse.

"Oh, YES! It's by SkyBird, I love his stuff. Oh, nice shot of Yuri. I bet he took that down in Touskania. It's a good one of Mars, too. The boy has a good eye, I'll give him that."

"Come on, get to the fun stuff," said Khandid.

"The message board it is! I'll just sign in under my true identity; Fwuffy-Wuv…"

"You're a sick man, Jervyas."

"Oh and what's your screen name, Stracona?"

"I will have you know I am Puffy Bun-Tarts."

"PUFFY BUN-TARTS?! Oh I am so outing you on the official fan listing."

"Not if I out you first, Fwuffy. Oh look look look! There's Mars!"

"Where? Which name?"

"Right there, 'Blue Shade'. Let him know we are here."

Raski typed out a message. "Heia Blue Shade! Come up a half note and I'll meet you!"

The pair waited to see if Mars recognized the reference. Moments later he sent a response.

"You come down, I'm afraid of heights."

Raski laughed. "He knows it's us, great. Now let's see what Lady Nightfall has been up to. Oh look, apparently you and Mars are having an affair. Hey! There's an update on that badly written story in which Draephus rescues you from the prison camp."

"Oh good, I've been dying to find out if I live."

"Why am I always the whip-waving maniac? I wanna be the hero. Mars is always the hero."

Draephus sighed and rolled his eyes, leaving Raski and Khandid to their nonsense. Finishing his coffee, he settled onto his side to nap. In a couple hours he would have to make the long drive to Avalair to help out a friend, but for right now he could just rest.

****

Dahli wore the dark glasses Draephus had given her to school on Oneday. All the days of the Sferkkaan week were currently nameless, the populace harbouring a violent dislike to the names the Kryphisians had given them. Therefore, the nine days of the week had numbers, and so it would remain until somebody could dig up a historian who knew what the days had been named eight hundred years ago. Dahli had thought over bringing her cartoon, deciding Atania wouldn't believe her anyway, and there was no point in risking its disappearance. So it remained in the book at home.

She walked into the school, tromping down the hallway. She greeted the occasional person, and her favourite duone, which, in the adolescent mind, was not always the same thing as a person. She made her way to her locker and glanced about for Diza, but saw her nowhere. She hoped her friend was not home feigning some terrible illness; school was never any fun without her. Dahli took her books out of her locker and then made her way to the first class of the day.

Czamkiar was seated in his usual place at their table, and next to him was a girl Dahli had not yet met. She had to assume this was the new student Czamki had been trying to impress, and the girl perked up as she saw another female enter the room. She smiled widely, and Dahli smiled back, walking over to the table they occupied.

"I am so glad you're here, it's been so long since I saw another girl," she said, an obvious wheeze in her voice as she spoke. There were traces of ash still under her fingernails, and Dahli knew without asking that she would have come from the city of Avalair. The entire city was covered in ash. There was even a name for the dull shade of the stuff peculiar to the area; Avalair Grey.

"You must be one of the last people taken out of the city," said Dahli. "What's your name?"

The new girl looked mildly embarrassed. "Avalarian, after the goddess who supposedly built the city. My dads thought it was cool or something. Frankly I feel pretty dumb standing up in class and declaring myself to be the goddess of the sea. Anyway, there are lots of people who still need to come out of Avalair, but they won't. It's their home, regardless of the toxic ash and underground fires. When Big Dad said we were moving here so I could actually meet other girls my age I nearly did handstands. Little Dad really didn't want to move but when I started to lose the ability to breathe he caved pretty fast."

"So are you adopted or are you a Breed?" asked Dahli. Czamkiar pulled out a small bag of nuts, picked from the tree in his back yard, and they began helping themselves.

"Well technically I'm a breed," said Avalarian as she shelled a nut. "I don't have a mother, but I haven't had anything done to alter me. They took some genetic material from Big Dad and Little Dad, tinkered with it until they had a female embryo, then I spent nine of my eleven months as an unborn baby sloshing around in an artificial environment in Little Dad's guts."

Czamkiar flinched. "Now that is one thing I will NEVER do, EVER! You know I heard those can rip apart your abdominal muscles."

"Well there is a chance of that," said Avalarian. "I mean let's face it, girls are designed to have babies and guys aren't, but guys are all we have. And surveys have shown that babies who get to develop inside a living body are all healthier and more emotionally stable than the ones who grow in a purely artificial environment. Little Dad didn't seem to have any trouble. In fact he's thinking about doing it all over again."

"Let me guess," said Dahli, "Little Dad is really one of those massive guys from East Touskania who could carry eight babies in his guts and not notice."

Avalarian giggled and shook her head. "Not a chance. During the war he was a Whip, like Khandid Stracona. He's not as tall as I am, and his waist is smaller."

"A Whip?" said Dahli. "That must get interesting at times."

"Yeah," said Avalarian, "especially since our neighbour is a clart-blossom who won't stop wearing Little Dad's trigger-colours when he's outside. One of these days Little Dad's going to cut him to rags and it will be his own stupid fault. So what's the current female population of this area?"

"Seven," said Dahli. "Including you."

"Seven girls and about five thousand guys lining up for the pleasure of hearing one of them say '*Eyew, get lost you freak*,'" said Czamki.

Dahli laughed, but noticed that Avalarian seemed rather afraid of him. Dahli reached out to carefully clear away an errant blob of eyeliner from Czamkiar's face.

"How do you get your eyeliner and lip paint on so thick?" she asked, upper lip slightly curled as she surveyed the smears of black around the youth's eyes.

"I melt the cream. All the boys do it. Hey, did you manage to catch the Gryphons on the Visual the other night?"

"Of course," said Dahli, "and why were you watching them? I thought you said you now had no interest in the band."

"I wanted one last look at Khandid. You're sure he's a guy?"

"Yes, Czamki," Dahli said. "Oh – I am also to inform you that Lyrellyn CZim-Relyn says he likes you."

Czamkiar raised an eyebrow and seemed to think about that, then shrugged. "Well maybe I will give him a call. At least somebody likes me. Hey that ship full of people from Earth is gonna be landing in another day. It will be setting down right on that huge paved spot near the edge of the city that used to be where the Grey Boys kept their own space ships. Are you gonna go see it land?"

"I don't know," said Dahli. "It depends on when it comes down. It's pretty far to the landing pad, and if it's too late there's no way Teirra will let me go. But I am gonna go out and see it the first chance I get!"

"We should all go together," said Czamkiar.

"Supposedly they're studying our languages," said Dahli. "So we should be able to talk to them at least a little."

"Great!" said Czamkiar. "So any Earth girls can call me a freak in my own language."

Dahli hugged him. She was dying to tell him of the events that had transpired, but decided to wait until later. She took off her dark glasses and carefully placed them in her book bag, then glanced at Avalarian once more. Definitely scared. The girl was afraid of him. Czamkiar seemed oblivious as he glanced around the room.

"Heia where's Diza?"

"I don't know," said Dahli. "She spent the respite at my place, but she went home about eighteenhour last night....oh, there she is."

Diza walked into the room, strolling casually over to the table where her friends were sitting. She dropped her books onto it and sat down.

"I was at your place last night," she said to Dahli.

"Okay," said Dahli.

"So where were you while you were at Dahli's?" asked Czamkiar.

"Never mind," said Diza primly.

Czamkiar smiled. He was an attractive youth, one of the fair High Northern Sferkkaans. His hair was a pure shining platinum, and his skin soft white. His eyes were a deep blue, as opposed to the slate grey eyes of a Kryphisian, which was the only way to tell the two races apart; that and his delicate, almost bird-like bone structure. He was frequently the subject of discussion among the other kids in the class, but he was rather shy, preferring to spend his time with Dahli and Diza. This gave him the appearance of having the fabled Northern attitude, and more than a few people thought Czamkiar was cold and arrogant. Avalarian seemed to think he was just scary.

"Heia Czamki," said Dahli, "you wouldn't mind going into the hall and seeing if I dropped my biology book, would you?"

Czamkiar looked mildly surprised. "I don't see a millitron tied to your ass."

"Please?"

He rolled his eyes. "Fine. Make the white kid with the bad

eyeliner go get your book so you can talk about him while he's gone."

Dahli looked at Diza. "See? I told you High Northerners were smart."

Diza giggled. Czamkiar rolled his eyes and, with much drama befitting one going to his doom, left the room. Avalarian breathed a sigh of relief, and was quite clearly close to tears.

"Sorry," she said. "It's just the white skin and the white hair. I know his eyes are blue and not grey but... I've seen Kryphisians up close and..." She leaned close to Dahli and Diza. "They *do* things to women, you know, *disgusting* things. I overheard my dads one night talking about how they caught this one woman, tied her to a bed and... and forced her to have sex with them. I mean have you ever heard of such a thing?! They beat her and made her do disgusting things and they didn't stop until she was dead. It just... really stuck in my mind and ever since then... I just can't stand the sight of white."

Dahli and Diza exchanged glances, their eyes wide, astonished and disgusted to learn this. Diza suddenly shuddered, and looked at her male classmates.

"Seven of us, and five thousand of them," she said softly. "Makes you pretty šukating glad our guys don't do things like that."

Dahli felt sick to her stomach, and oddly vulnerable and frightened. She wished she had something to pull around herself. She'd never been afraid of boys before, but this information put a cold splinter of fear right into her heart.

"Yes, because what life for us would be like otherwise is just too horrible to contemplate," said Dahli.

The trio of girls sat in silence, the tension broken when Czamkiar returned, his makeup a good millimetre thicker than when he left. He smelled of shooberries and sat down in a swirl of white coat-skirts. Avalarian fell silent with his return.

"It just figures we'd have science first thing Oneday," crabbed Diza. "I hate science."

"I wonder when they're going to start making us cut stuff up?" muttered Dahli.

"Actually," said Czamkiar, "I heard that just before we have mid-year break, we're supposed to hack up something."

"Oh goody," said Diza, her voice dripping sarcasm.

"Like what?" asked Dahli, leafing through a book.

"A faelin," said Czamkiar.

Dahli looked up, horrified. "A faelin? You mean like, arf, arf, yip, faelin?"

"That's what I heard."

Dahli looked over at Diza, her expression unchanged. "That's sick. That's the sort of clart the Grey Boys would do. That's really šukating sick! We can't do that! They...they're people, aren't they?"

"The Emperor hasn't had a chance to evaluate that yet," said Diza, "and he's under a lot of pressure from the scientists to not ban them as test animals."

"I'm not hacking up any Faelin!" Dahli stated with a dismissing wave of her hand. Her tone was rising. "I don't need the Emperor to tell me they're human! THIS IS THE SORT OF CLART THE GREY BOYS PULLED ON US!"

"Shhhhh," said Diza.

"I could be wrong, you know," said Czamkiar. "Maybe."

"Where did you hear it?" Dahli demanded.

"From a couple of duones. They seemed to think it was a good idea."

Diza rolled her eyes as Dahli launched into a rant, then glanced at Avalarian, who was clearly astonished. Czamkiar played with his chewing gum and looked over his notes, too accustomed to her outbursts to pay any heed any more.

"GREY BOY SYMPATHIZERS, ALL OF THEM!" yelled Dahli. "I WON'T DO IT! WHAT DO YOU MEAN `THE EMPEROR HASN'T HAD A CHANCE TO EVALUATE THAT YET'? YOU MEAN THERE ARE BETTER THINGS TO WORRY ABOUT THAN A BUNCH OF FAELINS KEPT IN CAGES AND BEING SLOWLY CUT APART? IT'S A ŠUKATING ATROCITY! THEY'RE ALL A BUNCH OF GREY BOY SYMPATHIZERS, ALL OF THEM!"

"Well, it's good to know Dahli made it to class, anyway," said Duone Bathers as he walked into the room. The children he taught referred to him behind his back as 'Duone Blathers', due to his tendency to drone on and on, oblivious to whether or not anyone was actually listening. Dahli slouched down in her chair, staring ahead at the Duone as though he was a large and particularly unpleasant bug.

"Good morning," he said, depositing a large stack of paper onto his desk. "I hope you all had a good respite. So who's a sympathizer this week, Dahli, the cooking duone?"

"What's this about us cutting up a faelin for mid-year?" she demanded.

"Oh," said Duone Bathers, "yes, we'll be doing that, but most likely we'll be doing it before mid-year."

"I won't." said Dahli flatly.

"Now there's no need to be squeamish," said Bathers. "It will be dead when we get it. It's being donated by Second City Research Labs."

"Very High Cylinder of them."

"Now there's no need for that. We'll all..."

"It's sick and I won't do it!" Dahli shot back, eyes glowing an evil green. "They are intelligent beings!"

Duone Bathers rubbed his eyes. "It's too early to argue with you, Dahli," he said, his tone laden with the sort of weariness that can only come from finding oneself in yet another endless debate with a self-elected arch nemesis. "They are not intelligent, they are animals."

"Animals that are nearly genetically identical to us. And I'm not arguing, I'm stating a fact. I won't dissect a faelin."

"Well then what do you suggest?" said the Duone in a magnanimous tone as he leaned against the chalkboard.

"Something non-feeling. Maybe one of those big-ass scientists, they're pretty unfeeling."

It was at that moment another student elected to show up in class, arriving in a swirl of needlessly frilly and aggressively feminine bows and ribbons popular with some Earth girls. It was none other than Atania Nightwing, aka EEEEEEEYYYYYYYEEEEEWWWWW!

"I think it was very generous of Second City Labs to donate a subject to aid in our education," she said primly, seating herself. A few people in class groaned, one or two made gagging motions. Dahli fixed her eyes on the girl with the rolls of huge curls in her hair, bound up with lace-edged ribbons.

"You would," Dahli sneered. "I'll bet you think baby torture is a hoot."

"Maybe," chimed Atania flippantly, staring at Dahli's well-worn tour shirt. "But at least I have more than one shirt to wear."

"Oh good," said Dahli. "Fashion tips from a Vortex fan, the only band known to give its fans cavities."

"All right," said Duone Bathers, stepping in. "Dahli, if you object to this then I suggest you write a letter to the principal. Atania, if Dahli wants to wear that shirt until it dissolves, that's her business. I'm sure she has other Mortified Gryphon shirts at home."

"Dahli's just trying to meet a musician," put in one of the boys in mock defence.

`Dahli did,' thought Dahli, and smiled.

****

Draephus watched as Delaes Randerick paced in a circle, sighing. He seemed stressed and unhappy. He flung his head back and stared at the wide expanse of black glass, behind which the audio technician sat.

"Can we start it again?" Delaes asked in a weary, annoyed tone. Marachani lit a cigarette and looked bored. There was a click.

"Sure," said the technician.

"You're screwing up," said Marachani flatly.

Delaes glared at the man, then adjusted the tiny earpiece through which he could hear the music. It began, and he concentrated hard on the music, waiting for his cue. It had almost come up when he heard the music jerk to a halt.

Click. "Sorry," said the technician.

"Oh, fantastic. Best I've ever heard you," said Marachani.

Delaes glared at the man. Draephus would have liked to shoved Marachani's face through the glass, but that would leave Delaes without a quinticord player as well as a drummer. When Delaes snapped at the man, it was with the usual breathless run-on sentence.

"It's not me it's this studio for the love of the New Empire why do you insist on recording in Avalair I'm shocked this building is still standing."

Marachani was used to Delaes' nervous run-on sentences, and the way he seemed to rattle off whole paragraphs without pause or breath. "Because, in case you have not noticed, we are broke, thanks to you and dear little Rysta over there."

Delaes smiled thanks at his sepulchord player Rysta as he passed him a cigarette. Delaes and Rysta often quarrelled, but had no difficulty being civil, even friendly. And certainly neither was afraid to stick up for the other, and it was Rysta who now turned to face

Marachani.

"How is it our fault? And have you seen what's going on out there?" Rysta waved an arm to indicate the city beyond the studio walls. "Have you had a good look at this region? Do you know how difficult it is to stop an underground fire? We gave away the band's money to help put out the fires, on the assumption we would just earn it back. Well we haven't yet but we still might."

"There just should have been something else we could have done," Marachani muttered.

"Like what? I don't know about you, but during the war I sat in a little underground chamber and monitored enemy transmissions. That doesn't really qualify me as a firefighter. What did you do, Delaes?"

"I hid in storm culverts and shot things and you know I was really rather good at it but again no firefighting skills not that I would want to fight a fire really and anyway Marachani you spectacular stack of clart you do realize I assume that we all live here so the money really went to saving our own asses?"

The music blared, just for a second, and Delaes flinched. Draephus could tell he'd had enough of noise for one day. He wanted to go home, climb into a bath and listen to something calm, soothing, and not by Bad Influence.

Draephus had known Delaes a long time, and knew him very well indeed.

"Ready, Donsa Randerick?" asked the sound technician.

"Yes yes," said Delaes.

It had been a bad day. The equipment in this studio was all a hair away from death, and Marachani had decided to compound the situation as much as possible by behaving like the clart he was. The music began, the cue came up, and Delaes belted the first line of the song just as the memory board packed it in. He screamed, causing the towering studio amp-plants to abruptly turn his way, echoing his scream back at him, but everyone assumed it was in response to the board failure. Draephus however had a suspicion it was something else, and as Delaes stalked out of the studio and headed for the washroom, Draephus followed after him. Entering the washroom, Draephus close on his heels, he locked the door and leaned against it, permitting himself to slide down to the floor. He had a drag of his cigarette.

"I want to go home," he mumbled.

Draephus managed to ease himself down to the floor, lacking Delaes' easy grace. "You want me to take you?" he asked.

"I may as well I mean I have to leave now anyway my cycle has begun with a vengeance a day early and I am not prepared."

He drew on his cigarette slowly, lovingly. His breath began to hitch, and he squeezed his eyes shut, finally managing to control himself. When he spoke again, he was on the verge of tears.

"Yes home is a terrible long way away isn't it?"

Draephus drew Delaes into his arms and held him tight. Delaes had told him his story, long ago, about his home. It haunted his dreams at night; a warm jungle place with a brilliant yellow sun set in a clear blue sky, not shadowed as it was here. He could even recall the feel of the trees, smooth and warm, pleasant to stretch out upon in the afternoon heat, while the elders either dove for fish or swayed in the sun, worshipping its life-giving rays. Delaes could even recall his mother, though back home the word was 'nirith,' not mother, and it was written, not spoken. Faelins had the gift of literacy, but not one of them could say a word. He still saw his nirith lying near the watering hole in the blazing sun, long and slender, stretched out on the sand, eyeing him with loving, flame-green eyes. Nirith worried about him; he could see it in those eyes. Delaes wasn't the same as everyone else. He didn't move as well as they did, in fact by their standards he was downright clumsy. His hair and eyes were the right colour, but his skin was white, not rust. Sometimes his nirith would pace over to him on all fours and wrap her mouth about the back of his neck, as though telling him to stop being different right this instant, but that was far beyond his control. Sometimes he felt her thin, sharp incisors lightly scrape his flesh, but she never made a mark. She would never hurt him.

Delaes had been too young to recall what had become of her, or how he had come to Sferkkaa, but he knew that was when this horrible masquerade had begun. That was when he had been taught to dye his hair from red to black, taught to wear the dark brown contacts over his green eyes, and to hide who he was. `He' was how he was referred to, and he supposed it was appropriate, if not exactly accurate. He was male and female, as were all faelins, and despite having a Kryphisian father, Delaes considered himself faelin. He wasn't terribly fond of Sferkkaa, or its inhabitants, save for a few individuals. But even his best friends did not know about this, save for two very close ones, one being Draephus. Bad things happened to half-faelins. They disappeared. Delaes had known two. Both had become careless as to whom they revealed their secrets to. Both had vanished without a trace. There was no way Delaes was ever telling anyone other than the two who knew. But they had their own secrets – they would not be telling each other's.

There came a pounding at the door, and both Draephus and Delaes jumped, startled.

"Delaes, get out of there!" shouted Marachani.

"You can't tell me that you have to get in here so badly that you have to be rude."

"Well finish getting it off with Draephus."

Delaes and Draephus heard him stomp off.

"He's a real little bundle of love and joy, isn't he?" asked Draephus.

"Isn't he a delight?" said Delaes as he stubbed out his cigarette. "I'd shoot him if I could find another quinticord player of his ability but I have to get home the blood is flowing and I'm not prepared and I don't want to have an accident because trust me Marachani would report on his own mother I'm just thankful for black leather."

"We really do have to teach you to speak in sentences."

"Arf."

Draephus smiled and kissed his nose. "Come on, I'll take you home."

Draephus helped Delaes off the floor, and the pair left the bathroom running into the audio tech as they did so. He looked upset.

"I don't know what happened," he said, "I'll get it fixed in a moment."

"Don't worry about it I'll be back tomorrow I've got a screaming headache that should give you enough time to fix the board shouldn't it?" said Delaes.

Draephus was amazed the tech understood Delaes. But he had been with Bad Influence a long time now.

"Tomorrow would be wonderful, I can take the board apart tonight and find out what is causing all of these problems."

"Forty trinta says its ash all right I will see you tomorrow then PEOPLE and Marachani we are leaving I shall see you all tomorrow morning I am going home I have a headache."

Delaes left the studio, Draephus following, heading for his black conni; a fiercely expensive air-con. He got into it, pressing a switch to slide the roof back.

"It is too dark on Sferkkaa just far too dark and too cold and the reek of Avalair burning is making my nerves fray honestly fire is to be feared why do these lunatics insist upon holding their ground?"

"No place else to go," said Draephus quietly, getting in the passenger side.

"I'm was just glad I live in the area built on a massive plate of rock since fire usually has a very hard time burning through stone."

Delaes jumped as Marachani suddenly came up beside him to stare at the vehicle.

"Where'd you get this?" he asked, his tone slightly accusing.

"It was a gift," snapped Delaes.

"From whom?"

Delaes glared at him. "From a friend do you mind?"

"What did it cost?"

"More than I have."

"More than the whole band has, you mean."

Delaes started the engine, which was virtually silent, then looked at Marachani once more. "Are you implying I am stealing money from my own band?"

"You said it, not me."

"Yes but you thought of it so perhaps we would be better off wondering where your hands have been." Delaes pulled quickly out of the lot and headed off down the road.

"I could have him shot," said Draephus.

"Not unless you can find me another quint player."

"I could loan you Khandi after I shoot Marachani."

Delaes smiled. "Don't tempt me."

****

Delaes parked the air-con, in the parking lot of the large sprawling apartment complex. The Gryphons might all have private estates, but he was not a member of that group, as much as he would like to be. Bad Influence lived in much more humble quarters, though few who saw Delaes' place would call it humble. Once the apartment complex had been the home of high-ranking Kryphisian officers, and had been surrounded by lush grass and great trees. The trees still stood, but the lawns had been replaced by large communal gardens. Machines, the Sferkkaans had in quantity. Food was something altogether different, and everyone in the building was obligated to help out raising and tending the vegetable gardens, as well as the large flock of brilliantly coloured jungle chickens, carefully guarded in what had once been a general's walled garden.

Everyone, that is, save for Delaes' long-time and unseen companion, J'Vanni.

Information about him was sparse and spotty, and none of the public knew how accurate any of it was. The facts were limited to small handful; he lived with Delaes, and he was a most gifted musician, though his style in no way matched that of the man he lived with. He had fought in the war, as had almost everyone else, and apparently had developed a severe emotional disorder. He did not come out of the apartment, he did not answer the phone, he did not open the door. Rumours ran rampant that the hauntingly beautiful and almost disturbing music he made was actually Delaes, though the people who knew Delaes laughed at the notion. They did not know who was making the spectral melodies that fans snapped up eagerly, but it most certainly was not Delaes.

J'Vanni Dei Syncopius was a ghost.

Delaes entered the building, moving quickly in his fast, easy strides, keeping up a constant stream of conversation as he made his way down the hall of the apartment building towards the elevator. He had lived here for years, and knew most of his neighbours. He was the darling of the building, though a few tenants were distressed to learn that his image as a bubble-brained nervous wreck was not an image. Draephus struggled to keep up with the lanky half-faelin.

"Heia Donsa Keer how's your hip I heard about your accident terrible you shouldn't live alone Marist darling how are you give us a kiss I'll call you later Miski don't pick your nose Marist your child is picking his nose again Miski you keep that up I'll never let you into my house to play the millitron again who knows WHAT you'll get onto the keys and WHY is this lift taking so long?"

Finally the lift came into place, and Delaes stepped into it, Draephus managing to catch up at the last moment. The doors closed, and Delaes doubled over in pain, clutching his lower stomach and swearing softly. As the lift rose, Delaes began breathing deeply, forcing himself to calm down and relax. He ran one hand through his dark hair, then rested his face against the cool of the lift's wall. As the door of the lift opened, he stepped into his penthouse.

"J'Vanni are you home?" he asked, walking stiffly into the room. The question was a household joke; J'Vanni had not been out of that apartment in five years. He eased himself down into a chair and curled up on its softly upholstered seat.

J'Vanni stepped out of their home studio, his long, white hair brushed back from his pale, aristocratic face. He was tall, and very well proportioned, strong, though his height gave him the illusion of being slender. The long, blue-grey coats he wore made him look almost delicate, though Delaes had personally witnessed him pick up and move very large and heavy objects with little effort. He peered at Delaes from behind small, round-rimmed glasses for a moment, then turned and headed for the bedroom. When he spoke, his accent gave him a strange, mechanized sound.

"I'll get a blanket and the hot pad."
"And a pillow."
"Yes, love. Why don't you just crawl into bed?"
"I can't make you feel sorry for me if I'm in bed."
"He has a point," said Draephus.
"Behave and make me a drink and be grateful you don't menstruate and you better be nice to your faelins."
"I'm always nice to my faelins," said Draephus. "You know that. I was nice to them before I even met you."

J'Vanni emerged from the bedroom with the requested items. "So how do you like your conni?"

"I love it though of course now everyone thinks I'm embezzling money from the band whatever possessed you to buy me such an expensive toy?"

J'Vanni sat on the floor before Delaes' chair and draped the heavy quilt over him.

"Because it was your birthday," he said. He placed the hot pad over Delaes' stomach, and waited for Delaes to raise his head so he could put a pillow under it. Then he sat back and smiled at him. "And I love you," he said quietly, the fondness reflected in his slate grey eyes.

"Always knew you Grey Boys were a bunch of mushes," said

Draephus.

J'Vanni just ignored him, and kissed Delaes. Draephus just had a swallow of his drink and wondered at what point in his life he had become the guardian of defected Kryphisians and half-breed faelins.

Chapter Five

The school day wore on slowly, classes dragging by painfully. The fastest hour of the day was lunch. One class blurred into the next, and by the time the day was over, Dahli felt numb in the head. She dropped her homework into her woven bag and, bidding Diza and Czamkiar goodbye, headed for home.

She lugged her books upstairs to her room and immediately set to her homework. Not that Dahli was any great fan of homework, but she loathed knowing it was sitting in her room, waiting to leap at her seconds before bedtime. Best to get it done and out of the way, and there was not much to wade through anyway. The only thing that was really going to be a pain was a project she was doing for history class. She was supposed to be researching events in a city, and had drawn Second City as her area. The problem was, Dahli realized as she opened her notebook to stare down at the blank pages, that she knew nothing about the city she called home. How was that possible? She had lived here fifteen years; surely she must know something….

Nothing came to mind.

Dahli moaned and feigned weeping as she realized she would have to get books from the library. Or rather, from what was left of the library, it having fallen victim to their own pilots after some groutnoll mistakenly thought the Kryphisians were using it as secret base. She glanced up at the clock, and saw that she had little time to get to there. Pulling on the chipped glasses Draephus had given her, and a jacket to guard against the damp, cool spring air, she left the house and set out for the library. Most of the rubble had been cleared away, and Dahli giggled as she read the graffiti spray painted across the ruin; "Pilot to base – Whoops!" Next to that, someone else had written "The Imperial Sferkkaan Air Force – Defending You Against Subversive Literature."

The Air Force certainly knew who had blown the place up, but they weren't telling. Dahli could not help but wonder if it had been Raski.

The books that had survived the bombing were now in a small annex across the street. Dahli entered it, and groaned as she saw none other than Atania Nightwing behind the desk. The day just kept getting better and better.

"Well, well," said Atania. "If it isn't Dahli Sandiniti. Sorry, we don't have any books on used up ugly Ra musicians."

Dahli ground her teeth. "I'm looking for books on the history of the city."

"You're telling me you can read?"

"Just point me towards the books before I report your hair to the department of health for making me sick."

"No. Find them yourself." She flipped her hair, which was golden and bound up with frilly bows, then adjusted the front of her pink ruffled blouse to make sure the low neck went even lower. What exactly she was trying to show off, Dahli wasn't sure. She'd seen bigger bug bites. Did Earth girls really wear this stuff? It looked like a bad joke as far as Dahli was concerned.

Dahli glanced discreetly to the left. There were four boys from her class gathered close by, obviously more interested in Atania's low cut blouse and bug bites than any books. Of course getting a boy to pay attention on their world was hardly difficult. Dahli suddenly gasped loudly as if Atania had told her something shocking.

"You have viruses A-9 AND A-11?! That's HORRID! Poor you! What do you do about the violent uncontrollable gas and diarrhoea?? And the worms you picked up can't make things any easier; I mean parasites are just soooooo disgusting. You know if you wanted to lose a few pounds like the earth girls you could have just stopped gorging yourself on that hoarded pile of sweets your family has hidden away in a back room. You must be very clever to acquire such a large pile, what with luxuries like that still so very hard to find and most people in Second City having to rely on the victory gardens and fishing to get by."

Atania was horrified and outraged, and stared at Dahli as though frozen to the spot with hate and violence. The boys seemed to melt into the walls. Dahli just smiled and walked away, leaving her to sputter and choke on her loathing.

Dahli went through the few precious books available on the history of Second City, but, as she feared, there were none on recent history at all. However she did find a good one on the time when Second City was no more than a tiny but fertile island, ruled over by a series of Lords and Ladies, dwelling in a great castle. It seemed the castle still stood, restored to its ancient glory, on the far side of the island. It would be a long walk, but it could be worth it to see the ancient statuary and cemeteries, not to mention the castle itself, and she might find something interesting to mention in her paper.

She wondered briefly what sort of things they would learn when Draephus CZimcocious had the books in his catacombs restored. She'd really like a look at those!

She was not permitted to check the book out; books being too rare currently to risk their disappearance. So she took notes on what she wished to look for, and then set out, heading east towards the island proper. She was in no hurry; she roamed along the streets, leaving behind the city and its endless reconstruction, noting as the houses became larger, more decorative. Lawns became larger and larger, corralled by tall fences and hedges. Great leafy trees over hung the streets; huge shadowless monsters that protected the street from the rain. This was an area where many Kryphisian officers had lived, and it had survived the war almost untouched. These houses were now used as orphanages for children bred in Kryphisian labs; parentless male babies who had the good fortune to escape genetic programming to make them a tool of the invaders.

Sferkkaa would have a second generation. With luck, there would be another after that.

She made her way out of the residential areas, and was now walking past woods and dense bushes along the side of the road. She left the city entirely behind, seeing no houses at all now, and only the occasional vehicle passed her. She walked on, glancing up at the threatening sky. Though the rain was constant on Sferkkaa, it varied in intensity, everything from the finest of mists to downpours that could strip trees of their leaves with their violence. Currently it was just a light rain, and she hoped it did not turn into a deluge.

She was not thinking about anything in particular; her report, Atania, what Duone Bathers had said about the faelin. Dahli wondered if writing to the principal would do any good, then considered writing to the Emperor about the faelin situation. Clart, she'd write them both, why not? Maybe she'd get Diza and Czamkiar to write as well.

The cultivated trees ended, and the road became rougher. She continued on, gazing at the fields she now saw. She'd come quite a distance, she realized, she would have to take the transit back if she wanted to be home at any reasonable hour. In the meantime, it was just nice to walk.

Masonry began to appear in the fields; tall ghostly statues, centuries old, of proud men mounted on the strange, leggy destris, or on some mythical creature. Small monsters crouched in the mist, dark and sinister. There were swamps in this area, and, as the light began to fade from the sky, they emitted a strange glow, brought about by gasses and the weird, luminous plants that grew there. The endless rain had cleared to the faintest mist, and the rising moon was a vague, white glow behind the Sferkkaan haze. She heard no sound other than that of her own breath, and the tread of her shoes on the road. Ahead of her a small animal paused, looking at her with enormous white eyes before galloping clumsily away. Dahli could still make out the occasional statue; silhouettes in the mist erected to remember by-gone battles, but now they were beginning to look frightening, as if she were being watched by the dead.

She was relieved to finally find the castle. It was set quite far from the road, resting upon a gentle hill. Behind it was a wall of huge, pristine trees, a dark barrier of living growth in the failing light. She was surprised to notice some faint lights in a few of the windows, so vague Dahli had to assume they were from either candles or a fire.

"Does someone live here?" she asked herself softly, her breath misting in the cold. The book had said only the castle was restored, not inhabited.

She paused before a towering iron and stone gate and stared up at the castle. Above her head, mounted on their posts, two giant birds of prey glared down at her. Their wings were partly raised and spread, beaks open to tear flesh. She glanced nervously at them, telling herself they were just stone and nothing to fear.

She jumped when she heard the sudden thunder of distant drums, startled though the sound was not especially loud. She listened, eyes wide, watching the faint flicker of candle light, realizing she knew the song, recognizing the heavy, pounding rhythm. It was 'Rain Forest' by The Mortified Gryphons, and she grinned.

"Hey, someone's playing my favourite song," she said to the stone birds, and waited for the quinticord and sepulchord to make their cue. And waited. And waited. And then she realized this was not a recording; this was someone playing the drums.

The drumming stopped, then resumed, varying the beat, the pacing, alternating them, as if someone could not make up his mind if he liked the song the way it was or wanted to change it. Then the sound grew louder and stronger, and Dahli would have known that resonance anywhere.

"Draephus?" she whispered, uncertain, but there was no mistaking it, no one who lived on the planet could mistake that sound. No one played the drums the way he did, and no one had the variety of drums that he did. Then there was the sheer level of power he put into it, as if he was trying to kill them. She read somewhere that Draephus broke more drumsticks during a live performance than any other drummer alive, and if he ran out he just used his hands, cutting them to bleeding shreds.

Funny, Dahli thought, she had always known that the Gryphons resided in Second City, but she'd never thought to go look at the places where they actually lived. It certainly never occurred to her that the old castle out on Headquarters Road was *his* castle, which was absolutely ridiculous because every Gryphons fan alive knew he lived in one. She listened to the drumming; wondering what went on inside this structure. Was he alone? She wondered if he was sober; it seemed like he drank an awful lot, judging from the rumours she had heard. He seemed to smoke a lot, too. She thought about the man she'd spoken to briefly, the man whose face she had wiped blood from. He seemed miserable, angry, but then, what happy person would live way out here in this place?

The drumming stopped suddenly. Dahli kept her eyes fixed on the castle. She watched as a light, seemingly by itself, moved from window to window. It then went upstairs, where it finally stopped. It was a vague light, difficult to see, and then, abruptly, it was gone. Dahli continued to gaze at the castle until the lights of the approaching transit vehicle woke her from her trance, and she stepped into the road to hail it.

It was getting quite late when she arrived home. A hard rain had begun to fall, and her hair and jacket sparkled with tiny beads of water. As she entered the house and removed her jacket, she heard Teirra call her name.

"Yeah?" she responded.
"Where did you go out to?" Teirra asked.
"Out," said Dahli casually. She removed her wet boots, then wandered into the kitchen. She found Teirra at the table with her books spread out before her, having to do with some course she was taking. Dahli couldn't understand this, why wait all those years to get out of school, and then go back? But, she mused, it must be different when you *wanted* to be there, instead of *having* to be there.

"Out where?" Teirra asked.

"Well," said Dahli, thumping down into a chair and suddenly seizing an apple out of a basket on the table, pouncing on it as if it was about to vanish. "EARTH BERRIES! I love these things!"

"They're called apples," said Teirra dryly.

"I don't care if they're called clart-muffins, they're awesome! Where did we get them from?"

"The market. A man brought his harvest in. Now where were you?"

Dahli tore into the apple and chewed with obvious, almost obscene, delight. "I have to write this paper for history class about some of the things that happened in Second City a million years ago that no one cares about any more, so I went out to take a look at the castle on Headquarters Road."

"Oh?" said Teirra. "I wouldn't mind doing that myself one of these days. Those castles must have been miserable places to live."

"Yeah," said Dahli, thinking about Draephus and his castle with the eerie figures surrounding it. "I suppose they must have been okay at one time."

"One would assume."

"Is Atterick at rehearsal?"

"Yeah."

"Let's go into his drawers and tie his underwear all in knots."

"Let's not."

Dahli grinned, eating her apple. The room was quiet, and she let her mind roam at will, unconcerned with any one subject. Her thoughts wandered from Draephus, to Atterick and his own band Titan, and from there off to various other things. She snapped out of her reverie when Teirra spoke.

"Atterick fixed the kuvon, it's running again."

"Oh, that's good." said Dahli.

The kuvon had been in the garage for some time; a massive, two-wheeled machine beloved by Sferkkaan and Kryphisian soldiers alike for its ability to travel fast over poor terrain, and its virtually indestructible design. Atterick had dragged this one out of a pile of ruins that had once been a maintenance shed and brought it home, labouring over it every chance he got. The machine had been badly damaged, though not beyond hope. The biggest problem Atterick had was just finding parts; they had to be scrounged from other kuvons. The machines were no longer in production with the ending of the war, the factories in which they had once been assembled by the thousands now given over to manufacturing things necessary for agriculture. Sferkkaa did not need more kuvons; it needed crops. Dahli had thought the kuvon would never be fixed, and now it was finally running. She remained outwardly cool, but inside she was dancing. Grandpa's conni would not be the only vehicle to go for a late night cruise without its owner, and she wouldn't have to deal with Boo to get it.

Dahli was still thinking about this a couple hours later when she went to bed. She walked into her bedroom, and was promptly bitten on the leg by her homework, which was lying in ambush all over the floor. Dahli stared down at the offensive scattering of paper, and with a resigned sigh, sat down on the floor to finish it.

****

Draephus stopped practice early, his shoulders, elbows and wrists too sore to continue. He refused to think about what this meant, telling himself he had simply been pushing himself too hard. Unaware of the lone figure by the gate, watching the light of his candle, he walked to the upper level and into his bedroom, setting the candle on a small bedside table. Bacca and Czanda were both asleep on his bed, taking up as much of it as they could, which of course was the job of any good faelin.

Draephus seated himself on the edge of the bed, feeling his joints burn. He rummaged in the drawer of the small table, taking out a metal case and a length of tubing. Opening the case, he pulled out a hypodermic needle made of gold and glass, and a bottle of clear fluid. With practiced skill, he filled the needle to a specific level, then tied the tubing tightly around his arm. Locating a vein, he pushed the needle into his arm, emptying the contents into his bloodstream before deftly snapping off the rubber tubing. He withdrew the needle, and set it aside, then drew his arm up to stop the small hole left behind by the needle from bleeding. Within seconds the pain was gone, and with his last coherent thought, he blew out the candle and lay down on the bed, still dressed. The faelins growled at the stink of the mushroom drug that wafted from his body, but though they shifted positions, they did not leave him.

It was in the cold small hours of the morning that the telecom rang. Draephus made a quiet noise, leaden and disoriented from the drug in his system. He forced himself to roll to his back, still deep within the murky depths of the extremely powerful and illegal concoction's grasp. He was still dreaming, his eyes closed, and he whispered to one of the faelins.

"Bacca. Telecom."

The delicate, slender creature leapt off the bed, moving gracefully, lightly. Bacca could walk upright; he simply didn't care to. It was more fun to prowl, to move silently down the hall and slip with the grace of a jungle cat down the staircase. Then he leapt with the speed and elegance of his kind onto the telecom and grabbed up the receiver in his mouth. He had hands, and he could use them, but then again, this was more fun. He turned his green eyes to the upper landing rising almost twenty feet over his head, and, gathering himself like a spring, he leapt straight up, catching hold of the tapestry draped over the railing, and discovering belatedly that it wasn't secured to anything.

Bacca fell heavily, landing hard on the stone floor with the tapestry on top of him, and made a sound of pain and unhappiness. Taking the receiver out of his mouth, and rising to his feet, he walked with obvious chagrin up the staircase. He entered the bedchamber and handed Draephus the receiver, and climbed onto the bed next to Czanda. His companion said nothing, but Bacca sensed he was being laughed at. The two yipped quietly at each other, nipping, while Draephus slowly raised the telecom to his ear.

"Heia?"

"Heia handsome."

Draephus grinned. "Handsome? I'm sorry you have the wrong number."

Vesper laughed. "How are you?"

"Mph. Stoned."

Draephus could almost hear the eyeroll. "I don't like you taking that garbage."

"It stops the pain."

"No, it *masks* the pain, and the pain is trying to tell you something."

"It's telling me to stop playing the drums and I'm not listening."

"Have you asked Dr. Arang about it?"

"Yes, and he said stop playing the drums."

Vesper sighed. "Draephus I worry about you."

Draephus tried to sit up and couldn't. "Aw don't worry about me, Ves, please. It's just standard joint and muscle pain that comes with beating on drums day and night. A little mushroom resin and I'm good."

"You're sure."

"Would I lie to you?"

"Yes, absolutely, if you thought you had to."

'*Little creep knows me too well*,' thought Draephus. "I'm fine. I really am. I did some mushroom and I just had a nap. I'm good, really."

Vesper sighed heavily. "You're not good, there is something wrong with you. You always seem to be in pain."

Draephus made himself sit up. Now was not the best time for this conversation; he was still fogged from the drugs, and emotional from the last few days. He could hear the quaver in his voice as he spoke, hating it, unable to stop it.

"I'm fine, Vesper, I'm fine. It's not me we have to worry about, it's you. At worst it's a… a touch of arthritis but if it makes you happy I'll go see Dr. Arang." He swallowed, telling himself it wasn't a lie, not really.

"You promise."

"I promise," Draephus growled, teeth grinding. "I'm too high for this clart, can we fight about something else, please?"

Vesper laughed. "Okay, where were you the other night? I called, and all I got was barking."

Draephus sagged, guilt weighing him down and threatening to crush him like a bug. Scruffin' lovely, when he said he would like to fight about something else he did *not* mean that literally. Well there was no way he could lie about this; Vesper would find out.

"I… spent the night at Raski's."

There was a long pause on the other end of the line. Vesper was used to Draephus spending the occasional night at his friend's house, and having Raski over. But there was a hitch in Draephus' voice, telling him this time they did more than argue music and drink too much.

"You…?"

"Yeah."

"And may I ask what you did at Raski's?"

Draephus wanted to hang up, to flee, to just escape this conversation. He did not have an excuse or a justification, and he could not lie, would *not* lie to Vesper. He cleared his throat.

"Um… well…"

"How many times?"

"Four."

"FOUR?! How in the name of the New Empire did you perform FOUR times? You never did *me* four times in one night!"

Draephus shot back a response he regretted the second it was out of his mouth. "Yeah well maybe if you didn't make it a damn fight for superiority every time I *would* do you four times in one night!"

Vesper gasped. "You underhanded, back-stabbing, vicious…"

Oh this was shaping up to be a big one, Draephus thought, rolling his eyes. He loved Vesper, and he knew Vesper loved him. The problem was that together they were like oil and flame; dangerous and sure to explode.

"Yeah I am," Draephus snarled. "But why can't we *once* just be together without it being a fight? Why is it always a battle? Why do I feel like I have to pound you half to death just to have a chance to hold you? WHY IS IT ALWAYS A DAMNED FIGHT, VESPER?"

Vesper went silent briefly, surprised. "I… I didn't think it was an issue."

"It *is* an issue, and I hate it! I just…" Draephus felt the tears come to his eyes. He drew in a steadying breath, then snatched up the used needle, driving it into his leg, the tip puncturing flesh and scraping bone with a grinding, popping sensation. He gasped and convulsed in pain, but it stopped the tears. That was all it needed to do. He drew a breath to steady himself, and resumed speaking.

"I just want to be with you. I love you, you're my whole world. I don't know why you feel you need to fight me, I really don't, but I'm tired of fighting and you've proved your point, I know you're strong. I've always known you're strong. Now I just want to be with you."

Vesper was quiet for a little while. "Is that why you slept with Raski?"

"No, I slept with Raski because I'm a free-roaming disaster and I just really, really needed to hold a living body in my arms. I… I don't want to try and justify it. I don't have a justification. I know I shouldn't have done it."

Vesper was quiet again, as if processing. "Was he good?"

Draephus felt a headache begin to build up behind his eyes. "Vesper, why do you want to know that?"

"Morbid curiosity."

"Yeah, I would say he was good."

"Better than me?"

"Vesper nobody could ever be better than you."

Another pause. Vesper was definitely working something out in his mind. "Do… do you think maybe you and he could… have something?"

Draephus did not like the direction this conversation was taking. "What do you mean?"

"I mean do you think you and he could have a relationship? If I wasn't here?"

The full impact of the question hit Draephus like a fist in the gut. "I am NOT going to sit here and start planning my life around your death!"

"Well you are going to have to because I'm dying."

"Don't do this to me, Vesper."

"I just want to know you will have something to fall back on when I'm gone! This isn't fun for me either, sitting here worrying myself sick about you alone, shooting mushroom resin into your veins. I don't want you to die just because I did, I want you to live."

"Vesper, I can't DO this right now!"

"Promise me something."

"No."

"PROMISE ME!" Vesper screamed.

Draephus winced at the tone, grinding the needle in a little deeper. "Promise you what?"

"That you won't make me worry away my last days picturing you alone in that castle, slowly rotting away. I want you to set up an ancestor's shrine for me, so I can watch over you. And if you so much as *think* about doing anything stupid, I will claw my way out of the grave so I can come beat your skull in personally."

Draephus squeezed his eyes shut, his body shaking. He thought he was going to vomit. "Fine. I promise. I swear."

"Draephus?"

Draephus ground his teeth together, grinding them so hard he felt one chip with the force. He was trembling, almost vibrating, but he would not let the emotions out. He refused.

"Draephus," whispered the soft voice. Vesper awaited a response, but when he did not receive one, he spoke again. "It's okay… about you and Raski. I… always felt it was just a matter of time anyway. I'm not angry. I just… I just needed to know I'm important too."

Draephus forced himself to breathe, making himself calm down. "Vesper you are the most important thing in my life. I will love you forever. No one and nothing could ever replace you."

"Raski is important to you, too."

"Yeah he is, I'm not going to say he's not, but... he's not you. No one on this whole planet is you. And whether you are alive or not, no one will ever be you. I can't replace you and I won't try."

Vesper seemed satisfied. "Well, you can sleep with him if you like." Draephus rolled his eyes, a gesture Vesper seemed to hear. "Don't roll your eyes at me, CZimcocious," he chided quietly. "Make love to him if you want. Have babies with him. But you do it with somebody else and I will kill the both of you."

Draephus managed a small, dispirited smile, and again Vesper seemed to hear the gesture. He and Draephus knew each other very well.

"Do you want me to come home?" asked Vesper softly.

"Yes," whispered Draephus. "Of course I do."

"I meant right now."

"Yes. But don't. This trip means a lot to you, and I want you to enjoy it."

"Are you sure?"

Draephus nodded. "Yes. I'm sure. Enjoy it. Are you in pain?"

"On and off. It's not bad."

"Well if you are near Trae Dae Mu, I have a couple friends there I want you to look up."

"Draephus..."

"Don't argue with me you little creep, just do it."

"I'm *not* taking mushroom resin!"

"Fine. Be that way."

"Thank you, I will." Vesper laughed. "I love you, you know that."

"Yeah, I do. Don't be gone too long. The faelins miss you."

"Just the faelins?"

"Me too. I love you."

"Love you too. Get some sleep."

Draephus nodded, and sighed as he heard Vesper hang up. He set the telecom down and dragged himself to a seated position. He was depressed and angry and sick and he didn't care what Vesper said; he wasn't making love to Raski again until Vesper had quietly passed away and a suitable period of mourning had passed.

He yanked the needle out of his leg and stared at it, watching with fascination as the blood dripped off the point. He set it aside, then skimmed out of his pants to look at the deep, ripped hole oozing blood from his thigh.

"Somehow I don't think this is what Neil Young was referring to when he sang about the needle and the damage done," he muttered.

He removed his pants and tossed them aside, then reached into the drawer for a new needle, this one also gold and glass, and prepared another shot. He didn't want to think about anything, not Vesper, not Raski, not the way his bones were already warning him of their impending failure, not the ethics of starting a new relationship when the old husband still had a few good months left, possibly even a few good years.

He wondered if cuddling and kissing was okay...

He tightened the rubber tubing, holding one end in his teeth and shot the drug into his arm. Then he heard someone clearing his throat, loudly. He looked up guiltily, tubing in his teeth, needle in his arm, pants on the floor, and a bloody stab wound on his leg. It was Raski, and Draephus just *knew* that Vesper must have called him first and told him to get over here and find out what was wrong. Draephus suddenly thought he knew why Vesper was not entirely opposed to he and Raski being together; it meant they could gang up on him.

Vesper was small, and Vesper was sick. But by no stretch of the imagination was Vesper stupid. Draephus grinned in a hopefully-placating manner around the tubing in his teeth.

"I'm going to kill you when you come down, just so you know," said Raski.

Draephus dropped the needle in the drawer and snapped off the tubing. "Sleep beside me, Rask," he said quietly, lying down on the bed and drifting far, far away.

****

The next two days of school dragged on and on. Duone Bathers and Dahli had another confrontation about the faelin in Science Class, so, newly motivated on the subject, she used her study period that day to rattle off two heated letters, one to the principal, the other to the

Emperor, both smouldering with many creative descriptions and choice words. She dropped the letter to the principal off at his office at the start of her lunch hour. Then, as she was leaving school for the day, Dahli realised that she did not have the address for the Emperor.

    It never occurred to Dahli to do something as mundane as try to find the address. Within moments she was boarding the transit, heading for the half-collapsed but still magnificent building in the middle of the city, where the Emperor went about the business of trying to put his homeland back together.

    The building was a huge, grand affair, centuries old, spreading across its expansive lawn. Its turrets imperiously surveyed the area, flags blowing gently in the spring breeze. From their great height, stone animals glared down; huge mythical birds and mighty dragons. The vast windows were of stained glass, covered by iron bars wrought into the likeness of spears. At the peak of the arched entrance, carved into the stone frame high above the heads of the four uniformed guards that stood vigilant at the entrance, was a coat of arms. The figure cut into it was blurred and obscured by age and moss, difficult to make out. Then as she drew closer, she realized it was the symbol of the Emperor who reigned centuries ago, before Second City came under Kryphisian law. It was a Gryphon.

    Dahli strode up the wide, stone stairs, trying to look as if she had every right to be there, inwardly quaking. One of the blue-uniformed guards, a tall fellow with grey eyes and strange, bluish-grey hair, came down to meet her. His three comrades watched her with interest.

    "Heia," she said and smiled.

    One of the guards returned her greeting. He had dark hawk's eyes, set beneath heavy brows, and there was no denying the uniform gave him an air of intimidation. She blushed slightly, and shifted her position to put the other guard between them.

    "You scared her," remarked a third man.

    "I did not, I'm adorable."

    "Then it must be your breath."

    The guard standing before Dahli grinned at the interactions of his friends, then asked; "Do you have business here?"

    "I wanted to give this to the Emperor," she said, beginning to feel rather foolish. She passed him the envelope, and he took it in his gloved hand, opening it, checking for anything that did not look quite right. His eyebrow raised as he caught a few words of the note. Dahli felt her face become flush.

"So you wish to be a diplomat when you grow up?"

Dahli snatched her note back. "Look I realise that there are probably larger issues in the world than the one I wrote about, but could I please give it to him?"

The guard removed a small device from his belt and pressed two buttons on it, speaking to someone briefly. A few minutes later a tall man with dark red hair came out, moving at a quick walk. He made his way down to them, stopping as he reached the guard.

"Yes?"

"Tibor, this young girl has a note for the Emperor."

"I'm fifteen," put in Dahli defensively.

"This woman has a note for the Emperor," amended the guard.

Tibor smiled at Dahli. "I'll see that he gets it."

"Really?" said Dahli, unwilling to trust her letter to anyone. "You're not just patronizing me."

"I leave the patronizing to the foreign officials," he said.

Dahli shifted nervously. "It's just that this is on a topic I feel rather strongly about."

"And you're afraid that it will get lost in the shuffle. Well, would you feel better if you gave it to him yourself?"

Dahli stared at the man, her eyes becoming wide. She had a feeling that, had she not been female, the letter would have been taken and used to start a fire some place. But being a girl on Sferkkaa had definite advantages. She smiled.

"Yes. I would."

"All right, follow me." Tibor turned and walked back up the stairs, Dahli following along behind him, her stomach doing strange things, her eyes watching the sway of his long coats as he walked up the steps.

The inside of the building was cool and dim, voices and footsteps echoing in the cavernous halls. The floor was of decorative stone tile, icy cold, cut and coloured to form great mosaics. Tapestries hung on polished stone walls alongside carefully preserved paintings of the men and women who had inhabited the halls before the coming of the Kryphisians. The embassy was six hundred years older than Draephus' castle, built in the glory days when Sferkkaa had no modern technology of any kind, space travel was the dream of lunatics, and life was mostly peaceful. To hear the soft sounds within the embassy was to hear life as it had been in ages past. Dahli was almost afraid to breathe, lest she inhale a ghost.

Dahli was trembling slightly when they reached the mighty doors of solid timber, leafed in gold, carved with the gryphon insignia. She was about to decide if she should run or not, when Tibor flung open the doors.

There, directly across from her, sat the Emperor Stratavarus. He was a small man, slim, with a thick mane of red-gold hair. He was seated at an enormous desk of heavy, aged wood, and behind him the stained glass window let in multi-coloured rainbows of light. Tibor led Dahli into the room, and as she stood before the huge desk, she felt as though she had fallen into someone else's dream. Then he looked up, and she almost cried out as she saw his eyes were the same unreal shade of red-gold as his hair.

Stratavarus blinked at the small, terrified teenager across his desk, his golden red eyes lined in black. He was dressed in the red and black uniform of royalty, and wore the Imperial patterns on his face; the lines of black descending from his eyes to spread across his cheeks and become gold and red feathers, matching the ones in his red hair. It gave him an intense, other-worldly expression, and she felt herself begin to back up. Behind her, Tibor stood with an amused expression on his face. Tibor had been working with Stratavarus since he had come to power, and knew exactly what to expect from the man, which was anything and everything.

Dahli shivered under the pinning gaze of the man's red eyes, watching him as he lifted a cigarette from a crystal ashtray and placed it between his lips. He drew on it, and casually exhaled smoke. He set it once more in the ashtray, his movements slow and purposeful as he slowly rose and leaned across his desk to study her. He stared at her for what seemed to be forever, then suddenly yelled, "BOO!"

Dahli screamed, her letter flying out of her hand and cart-wheeling off across the room. It struck one silk-papered wall and tumbled to the floor. Dahli clamped her hands to her face and giggled nervously, shaking her head.

"We'll be fine now, Tibor," she heard him say. "If I need you for anything I'll throw the paperweight at your door. Sit down and tell me your name."

`*This is the man we have in charge of the planet?*' thought Dahli, not entirely certain if she wanted to come out from behind her hands. At last she did, finding that he had crossed the room to retrieve her letter.

"Well that's my name, so I'm assuming this is for me. Sit, sit. Tell me what's on your mind, that's what I'm here for, rather like an exalted psychiatrist."

"Thank you," said Dahli, a little weakly. She dared to take one chocolate from a box on his desk, then sat down in a sprawling, leather-covered chair. She bit carefully into it, savouring the taste. She'd never had chocolate before, so she slowly enjoyed it while he opened the letter and began to read. This only took a few moments, and then he glanced at her from over the top of the page with those transfixing eyes.

"I take it this is a subject you feel rather strongly about. Frankly I'm rather reluctant to name the entire staff of Second City Research Labs as a `bunch of Grey Boy sympathizers.' Would you care to expound on this theory, or are you just paranoid?" He waved the letter back and forth between two fingers.

Dahli drew in a breath, slowly exhaling. "I was rather upset when I wrote that, so I guess I was a little hard."

"No, not at all. Frankly, I believe very deeply that all science duones are `Kryphisian want-to-be's'."

"All right, I was very hard," she said, growing a little annoyed. "But this is wrong, and it's sick and I want to know what the šukat you're going to do about it."

Stratavarus sat back in his chair and blinked. "My dear donselle, precisely how small do you think this planet is? Sferkkaa is a very large place indeed, and no matter what the people think I am, I am still but one man, and I can't be everywhere at once. The very city I call home is still little more than ruins, and however willing the people are to help, there is ever so much to be done. Do you realise that some parts of this planet are still so isolated that they do not even know the occupation is over? I realise you may think this very cold of me, but I haven't had much of a chance to think about faelins."

"But surely you could find some time for them!" Dahli sat forward in her chair, green eyes meeting gold.

Stratavarus gazed calmly at the girl before him. "What is your name?"

"Dahli Sandiniti," she said, wondering if he was going to put her name on some secret file and list it under 'dissident'.

"Dahli," he said softly, the word becoming something wonderful when he said it. "I am not disagreeing with you. And I'm not dismissing your concerns. In fact, I like you, you're tough. Look, let's discuss this over lunch, shall we? Then at least if we come to blows we can throw food at one another, which is infinitely softer than furniture."

Before Dahli could reply one way or another, the man before her snatched up a lump of metal she assumed was the paperweight and heaved it across the room at a badly dented door. "Tibor!" he yelled.

Tibor opened the door and thrust his head into the room. "You banged?"

"Have somebody bring lunch. If you're going to work me like a feralyke the least you can do is feed me. And hand me back my paperweight."

"I am not the one who threw it," said Tibor as he bent to pick up the grey lump, shapeless from two years of hurling. He placed it on the desk.

"Yes, yes, but I'm Emperor and you're my secretary, so that means you have to get my paperweight."

Tibor left without comment to this, and Stratavarus sighed heavily. "We'll eat in the day room, shall we? So good to have someone drop in who doesn't want something."

"But I do, remember?"

Stratavarus thought for a moment, then said, "Oh yes, the faelins. Lunch first, politics later."

They left the office and strolled down the eerie, silent halls, Stratavarus keeping up a wandering line of talk as they walked. His thigh-high boots made virtually no sound on the stone floor, though his heavy velvet coats rustled softly. He was not significantly taller than she, which likely indicated he was from the area; the men of the coastal regions of the north continent having traditionally been small of frame. That was the subject of many jokes – the further north one went, the smaller the men became. Unlike Dahli, he seemed to know everything about the city he called home.

"This is a tapestry from the reign of Emperor Rivar. I have a guard named Rivar, I quite like the man. You would have seen him on your way in; dyes his hair blue. Dreadful. Says it's natural, well if it is I'm a seagull. That would make that particular piece of wall trash around two thousand years old, which is slightly younger than I feel on any given morning. I should not even have this post, you know, I'm not descended from the Emperor's line at all, I'm descended from his General's. Didn't even want the post, to tell you the truth. But I've a very faint trace of Imperial blood, so that makes me Emperor. They don't like it when I mention I used to be just another whore in the lower levels of the Cylinder. There's a portrait of my ancestor, General Stratavarus. Did you know Khandid Stracona and I are cousins? This is the General's favourite underling, Windsoar. He was always two steps behind the General, from what I hear. Great story about Windsoar; he was shot and left for dead in the South Continental jungles. The General had people out looking for him, but they couldn't find him, and after a while they just assumed the Night Stalkers got him. Nasty things, Night Stalkers. It was very hard on the General. They were, by all indications, lovers, but back then you just did not talk about such things. Then one night, five months after being used for target practice, who do you think crawls out of the swamps and bushes? Couldn't kill him, and many tried. The Kryphisians certainly hated him. Odd they never got him. They got the General, though. Apparently they had to put him in his coffin with a shovel."

  Dahli didn't know whether to be appalled or delighted. Granted, it was not the sort of thing one wanted to hear before lunch, but it would look good on her history paper.

  They reached the day room; a large, airy chamber with a window that spanned the entire width of the wall. It looked into a garden, alive with rare flowers, fruiting trees, and small, fuzzy animals. Dahli stepped forward to examine them, and realized they were…

  "Touskanian Cave Spiders," said Stratavarus. "Aren't they cute?"

  "Bleh!" said Dahli.

  "Oh come, don't be that way, they're cute."

  "BLEH! And there are… *dozens* of them!"

  "Well they don't like to be alone."

  "What do they eat? Each other?"

  "No, don't be absurd. Fruit, mostly, and the occasional rat or unwary spelunker."

  "Grim. Totally grim."

  "You can teach them to speak, too."

  "DOUBLE GRIM!"

  Stratavarus laughed. "Well I quite like them. Hello, babies!" he said as a few of the black and gold horrors leapt onto the glass and hung there, wandering across the surface of the window.

  "Erk," said Dahli. She watched as one wandered over to stare at her with multiple beady black eyes.

"Don't eat me," it said, quite clearly in a tiny, high-pitched cartoon voice.

"You have absolutely nothing to worry about!"

At either end of the great chamber was a huge fireplace, both currently lit, and in the dim light of what had become a very rainy day they sent out a warm orange glow across the room. Lunch was already being set up on a long table; various things steamed in a most appealing manner. Stratavarus motioned for Dahli to sit, and she selected a chair from which she could look around the highly elaborate room.

For a while, no one said a word. Dahli ate slowly, studying everything on her plate as though food had become a new and unusual thing. In fact everything looked a little odd, and she suddenly realised what it was she had eaten in Emperor's Stratavarus' office. Touskanian chocolates had been highly sought during the occupation; simple confections sweetened by the thorny South Continent mushroom. Dahli glanced up, noticing the wonderful way that the light from the fire smeared. Brightly coloured spots hung in the air. The pale curtains blew softly with no wind to help them.

"Is the air supposed to be that colour?" she asked, watching the spots.

Stratavarus glanced up at her. "Beg your pardon? Oh, yes, the chocolate. Sorry, I wasn't thinking. Oh well, you only had one, you'll be coherent, if distracted. How is the food?"

"It's very good," said Dahli, staring down at her plate. "But I really would like to talk about the faelins..."

"So would I. Interesting creatures, faelins. Perfectly designed for leaping from tree to tree. They are the closest a wingless creature has ever come to flight. Unfortunately they can also clear a thirty foot room in one leap to bite your nose off. They always go for the face."

"Well if someone had me in a small cage and was cutting me to bits, that would certainly be my choice." Dahli looked up as she heard loud voices shouting in the hallway, arguing heatedly. The noise finally moved away, and Dahli looked back towards the Emperor.

"Are you using me as an excuse to hide from someone?" she asked.

"In a word? Yes. Absolutely. Continue."

She rolled her eyes. "I just don't see how we, as an intelligent race, can justify it! They're people!"

Stratavarus fixed her with those disturbing reddish eyes. "They are not people, donselle. They can walk upright, yes, they have hands, yes, but they are not people, they are faelins."

"Well what about the rumours I have heard that Sferkkaans and Kryphisians have bred with them?"

"Utter nonsense. If it had happened, we would know about it."

"Well what if it was true?"

"If it was true, then I would be obligated to look into the matter, yes. And I intend to look into matters regarding faelins, but frankly I cannot spare them any time or thought right now. Donselle, have you had a good look at this city? Have you noticed how many homeless people we have? How we have more mouths than food, how we have people living in shacks without basic necessities, and so many Kryphisian-made orphans we had to set aside a neighbourhood for them? Do you have any idea what it feels like to sit up at night, staring at little charts, trying to decide how to divide up rations, knowing that no matter what you do, someone is going to go hungry? And we are the fortunate ones! We're an island, we have fish, we have desalinization plants for fresh drinking water, we have orchards. The death rate in Avalair due to starvation, toxic gasses released by the underground fires, not to mention the fires themselves, is staggering. And then there is the next city, and the city after that." He gazed at her, his expression sympathetic. "Child I am not unfeeling. I am buried."

Dahli felt her eyes begin to grow wet, and she lowered her head, feeling defeated. "I didn't think of things that way. I just felt so bad for that poor little guy." She made herself look up. "Isn't there something you can do?"

The shouting that had passed by earlier returned. Stratavarus pointed towards it.

"Do you hear that? That is a delegation from the east coast I was supposed to meet with four hours ago to discuss how we are going to clean up all the lovely oil and chemical spills the Kryphisians left for us to play with. If you feel truly strongly about this, then go forth and organize. Find like-minded people. Come up with a strategy. And when you have your committee in order and your goals set, I will be delighted to give you Imperial approval. But if you are waiting for me to do it, then you and the faelins will have to wait a very long time."

Dahli sniffed, and wiped at one eye with the back of her hand,

and smiled. "I think you're a great Emperor," she said softly.

The door opened, and Tibor appeared. "I'm sorry, I can't stall them any longer."

Stratavarus stood up. He gave her a smile. "It was lovely meeting you, I'll send in Rivar to walk you to the door." Then he was gone, departing in a swirl of red and black velvet. Dahli resumed eating and awaited the guard.

****

The day had been quite warm, though very wet, but the rain had slowed at last to a very fine mist, and the cloud cover was almost golden when Dahli arrived home. She walked up the stairs to her door and entered the house. She felt disillusioned and despondent, but not defeated. She just needed a plan. The trouble was she had no idea what that plan may be.

"Atterick? Teirra?" she called as she entered the small house. There was no answer, and she immediately headed for the kitchen, where the keys for the kuvon would be. She took them down from their peg and studied them. Surely it wouldn't hurt to take the kuvon for a short ride, just a treat to cheer herself up. Dahli made a quick inspection of the house to make sure Atterick and Teirra were truly gone, then headed for the garage.

The kuvon was a large one, silver and shining black. Atterick had painted it himself, crafting it carefully into a work of art. It was a big machine; a bit too big for Dahli, but she gamely mounted it anyway. Inserting the key into its slot, she started the machine up. Then she left the garage and made her way onto the road.

The wind whipped through her hair and clothes, causing her eyes to stream. The powerful kuvon tore down the road, moving with just a little too much aggression. She hadn't realised how strong the machine was, but that didn't stop her from riding it all over the neighbourhood, knuckles white with trepidation. She rode everywhere; to her school, past the houses of various enemies, including Atania Nightwing, and up and down different streets. She even travelled as far as the outskirts of the Cylinder, but one look at the dilapidated houses, the ruined connis, and a quick glimpse of what looked an awful lot like a burned body convinced her that she didn't want to be there. She turned around and began to head out of the man-made part of the city, back towards the actual island....and the castle.

The gate was open as she halted the kuvon near it and shut off the engine. Ahead in the dimming light she could see a black conni waiting in the driveway. She thought she recognised it from the restaurant, but couldn't be certain. It certainly hadn't been there the last time she had been here, sitting still and silent, its back end turned contemptuously towards her. From the castle she could hear nothing, but there were lights on. Or rather, candles lit. She wondered if he had any power in the place at all.

She toyed with the idea of going up to his door, but only briefly. It was one thing to sit at the bottom of his driveway and listen, but to walk boldly into his home was too much. He probably had more than his fair share of people taking liberties with his privacy. Why else would he be way out here? He was human; he had the right to hide in a castle if he wanted to. She found the concept of him being a real person strange. He'd always been a laser print on the wall, a heavy pounding rhythm on a music cylinder. But this was his home, his land, his space. She found herself wondering what he ate, what his bathroom looked like, where he slept. All these things she'd never considered before. Who did he sleep with...?

The kuvon slowly began to slide. She'd stopped it near a drainage ditch, far enough away, she had thought, to keep it safe. However she had forgotten to consider how heavy the machine was, and how soft the ground. The kuvon shoved away the earth, tilting far to one side. Dahli was forced to dismount, and she grabbed at the handle bars in a desperate attempt to right the machine, but it continued its slow, relentless slide into the ditch. She dug her heels into the earth for leverage, but it simply tore beneath her. Then, as she grappled with the thing, she heard the unnerving sound of a conni door closing, and the engine humming into life. She looked up, cold with horror, and saw the black conni briefly flash its lights. Dahli hauled all the more fiercely at the kuvon, her boots sliding out from beneath her as the machine dragged her into the ditch. She felt her backside strike cold, wet earth, felt the muck grinding into the fabric of her pants. She pulled, but the kuvon pulled harder, and as the conni crept down the driveway, she was anything but out of the ditch.

Dahli was almost in tears as the conni stopped at the end of the driveway. The kuvon by now lay on its side at the bottom of the ditch. Fortunately there was no water to damage the engine, but that was beside the point. She was mortified to her very core to be caught here, of all places. She sat in the mud at the midpoint of a wide, deep scrape in the earth, knees drawn up, arms around her shins, staring at the kuvon. Dahli heard the conni door open, then slam, and heard slow footsteps move towards her. She found herself hoping it was all a bad dream. She felt him sit next to her, smelled the warm scent of his body, and the reek of that awful coat. It was faint, but definitely there. A sickly-sweet smell, like…

Death.

She couldn't, or rather wouldn't, take her eyes off of the kuvon. Dahli heard Draephus open a pack of cigarettes, then light one. She continued to stare into the ditch.

"Nice kuvon," said Draephus in his low, roughish voice.

"My sister's husband's," said Dahli softly, wiping quickly at one eye.

"Clart like this happen to you a lot?" he asked, his voice gently teasing.

Dahli managed a small laugh, then sniffed. "Only when you're around, it seems."

"It was the birds."

"What?" asked Dahli, finally raising her head to look at him.

"Those birds," he said, pointing at the carved stone creatures on the gate posts. "A friend of mine claims they're haunted. He says they can cause bad things to happen."

Dahli studied the looming shapes. "They look evil enough," she said. "Do you think they can?"

Draephus shrugged, drawing on his cigarette. "Don't know. Frankly I think Khandid made that up because he keeps driving into the posts."

Dahli laughed, despite herself. She felt a little less silly now. Even dumping the machine into the ditch no longer seemed quite the tragedy it had moments ago.

"So why aren't you out with your boyfriend, instead of hanging around driveways?" he asked.

"I don't have a boyfriend. Never really felt the need to have one. Besides, most of the boys I know are either complete clart-blossoms always doing stupid stuff."

"I know. The problem is we grow up but we never stop doing stupid stuff."

Dahli looked over at Draephus and saw he was grinning. He looked terrible; his face was still bruised and his eyes were red-rimmed, but he seemed cheerful enough. She began to laugh, shaking her head.

"Oh, I feel so ridiculous."

"Don't," said Draephus. "You'll be laughing about this in, say, forty years."

"If I don't shoot myself first."

"Don't do that either. Here, I'll get your kuvon out of the ditch."

He stood up and flicked his cigarette away, then removed his famous coat before descending into the ditch. Dahli's jaw dropped and she stared, first at the coat, then at him, because she honestly had not realized the thing came off; she was reasonably certain no fan had ever seen him without it, and she was willing to bet the other Gryphons hadn't either. Not that she was complaining; he was wearing a ripped sleeveless military shirt that showed off his powerful arms, and a fair portion of chest. Then there were the clinging camouflage pants and the flat-soled boots, and that sexy silver armband around his upper left arm. Ooooohhh… yeah. Dahli wished she had brought a camera. She decided to forget about being embarrassed and just enjoy the show.

He made his way to the machine, grasping the handlebars and hauling it upright, lifting the front end off the ground to free the wheel of the mud. He threw one leg over the back of the kuvon, starting up its mighty engine. He probably knew there was no point in trying to take it up the side of the ditch; he'd never get it out that way. However, there was an area not far away where the ditch became very shallow, and he could ride it out. He started the kuvon forward, charging through the muck, down the ditch and, at last, out of it.

It must have been a long time since he had been on a kuvon, because as the front tire hit pavement, he couldn't seem to resist one high-speed run on the black and silver machine. He tore down the road, flying past Dahli, driving a short distance before slowing the machine and expertly spinning it around to head back in her direction. It was quite clear to her that he had not only driven a kuvon before, but that he had taken them over the rough, muddy terrain for which they were intended. He slowed the machine and pulled up beside her.

"Nice kuvon," he said, dismounting.

He held it for her as she got onto its leather back, then released the handlebars and stepped back a pace. He turned and walked over to the expensive black conni; a beautiful piece of machinery that probably cost as much as Teirra's whole house. He snatched up his coat before he opened the door, then paused and looked back over his shoulder at her. "That's an interesting name you have. Do you know what it means in Eastern?"

She shook her head. "No, what?"

"`Fearless'," he said. Then he got into the conni and pulled away, giving her a wave as he slipped off down the road.

Dahli drove carefully, following the tail lights of the conni ahead of her for most of the way, until he turned down another road. She kept on for home, and as she finally pulled into the garage, she vowed to never be caught anywhere near Draephus CZimcocious' castle ever again.

"`Fearless'," she muttered as she began cleaning mud from Atterick's kuvon. "There's lots of stuff I fear. Death, pain, humiliation, Atterick after he sees mud all over his machine..." But she was smiling as she filled a bucket with water to soap away the muck.

****

Draephus thought about Dahli in a wandering sort of way. He mused upon how both times he had met the girl she was in some sort of compromising position. First she hits him with a door, then he catches her trying to drag a kuvon out of a ditch before his house; certainly a kid with a nose for trouble.

He drove to the edge of the city, to where Raski had his large house. Draephus had been spending a lot of time there; too much in fact. They were getting a little too cozy with one another, and Draephus could see something ugly coming out of this if he didn't put the brakes on. Tonight, he was just going to return Raski's vehicle to him. He had been using it while his own was being repaired.

"Times have been worse, and times have been better," Draephus said out loud to himself, "but nothing is ever as bad as the present."

He pulled into Raski's driveway, before his large, beautiful stone and wood house. The huge windows were dark, save for the soft glow of candle and fire light. As Draephus stepped out of the vehicle, he was enveloped by the scent of night-blooming jungle lamps, the large flowers just opening, their luminous stamen and fragrant scent a lure to the large moths upon which they preyed. Faint music came from within the house, and Draephus sighed. Oh this was not going to be easy. He sighed again, and trudged up the path to the large door, taking hold of the handle and turning it. He felt sick inside, but made himself walk into Raski's house and close the door.

"Draephus?" said a voice from the room at the top of the stairs.
"Yeah, it's me."
"I wasn't expecting you tonight."
"Am I interrupting?"
"No, it's okay. I was just trying to meditate."

Draephus grinned and walked up the short flight of stairs into Raski's living room, and stopped, hearing himself gasp audibly as he saw his friend. He stared, as if he had never seen him before.

"Wow," he breathed.

Raski was from the South Continent; a land of deep jungles and beautiful people. Raski had the dark skin and blue-white eyes of the inhabitants, and in his rare moments of quiet, he practiced their traditions as well, partly from habit, and partly as a way to keep his tattered nerves from becoming worse. Clearly he had been meditating when Draephus intruded. He had lit a circle of candles, and a brazier of rare incense, which sent up plumes of rich perfume. He was clad as he would be if he still lived in his native village; his black silken hair long and loose around his shoulders, his neck draped with amulets of quartz crystal and amethyst, his chest bare. Slung low around his hips was the traditional long skirt the men wore, called a 'khatra', woven from the fibres of the khatrin plant and dyed vibrant colours. Draephus knew the patterns on each khatra were unique and very symbolic, but it wasn't a desperate attempt to understand the intricate pattern that caused his eyes to follow the lines of the garment all the way down to Raski's sandals. Both his throat and his pants were suddenly uncomfortably tight, and he coughed.

Raski raised a quizzical brow. "See anything you like?" he asked dryly.

"Wow," Draephus managed.
"Draephus you've seen me in this get-up a hundred times."
"I know, but… wow."

"You're drooling on my floor." Raski walked slowly over to his friend, and loosely draped his arms around his neck. "And you know as well as I that we have to stop this. It was supposed to be one night."

"I know, and that's what I came over to say to you, but… I think we crossed a line we can't uncross. Raski I am so in love with you. I mean I know, it's not a surprise, I think we've been in love with each other our whole lives, but…"

"I know," said Raski softly.

"This is all so damned complicated. We can't do this to Vesper, I mean we just can't."

"I know."

Draephus stared at his friend of so many years, bringing his hands up to rest them on his waist, thrilling at the feel of him in a way he never had before. Vesper had said it was okay, but Draephus had not told Raski. He did not want to make things even more complicated, and he certainly did not want his feelings for Raski to become entangled with Vesper's death. He stared into his friend's blue eyes, a thousand images going through his mind, all of them glorious, all of them impossible.

"I want you," he breathed, his voice husky with desire.

"We can't," said Raski, quietly, firmly.

"You're right, we can't." He gently drew him close and held him, closing his eyes, lowering his head to smell his dark skin, breathing in the fragrance of exotic oils from far away. "This is all my fault, I never… I never should have…"

"And I could have said no, but I didn't," said Raski. "We made this mess together."

"Yeah, I know." Draephus raised his head and looked into Raski's eyes, his own still blackened with bruises. Suddenly an idea came to mind. He did not know if it was a good idea, but the logical part of his brain was not currently engaged. "I'm going to suggest something."

"Does it have anything to do with that metal pole in your pants?"

"No." Draephus gently pushed Raski back, needing a bit of distance, needing to think if this was a good idea or not. He didn't know. He slowly removed his coat, dropping it to the floor. Around his upper left bicep was an armband of what looked to be silver, wrought into the likeness of two snakes entwined. He took it off, and held it in both hands, looking down at it, as if afraid to meet Raski's eyes.

"I… I found this, not too long ago, in one of the lower areas of my castle, an area I haven't had a chance to restore yet. Do you know what it is?"

Raski shook his head. "No. It's beautiful though."

"It's called a promise knot. Centuries ago, wealthy people gave them as a sign of commitment, of a promise that must be fulfilled. The promise could be anything; a promise to pay off a debt or to show up for an important event, or… a promise to continue something at a later date."

Raski swallowed nervously. "I… don't think I understand."

Draephus finally managed to raise his head and look at Raski, staring into his eerie, blue-white eyes.

"I love Vesper. I know you love him, too. That's why we can't do this to him, especially not now that he… that he's sick. He's going to need us, and we can't let him down." He held up the silver band and showed it to Raski. "This is my promise to you; that I will be a good and faithful husband to Vesper. And, when… he doesn't need me anymore, and if you want to, we can… pick this up where we left off. We can't do it now, and I don't want my feelings for you to get messed up with death and guilt. I love you. If our relationship is going to move from friendship to love then I want it to have a fair chance."

Raski looked as if some invisible force had struck him, and he rocked visibly, eyes growing large. Draephus watched as he put a hand out to steady himself, then began slowly sinking, his movements almost convulsive, his breathing coming in loud wheezes.

"Oh clart," said Draephus. He held onto him and slowly sank with him. "Raski? Raski, breathe, come on, Rask, you know how to do it. In, out, in, out, that's a good boy, breathe… no I said BREATHE not CRY! Awwww… šukat. Fine. Cry. See if I care."

Raski cried against Draephus' chest, and Draephus knew from long experience that Raski's crying jags could go on for a considerable period of time. However, he seemed to gather his composure rather quickly. He looked up at Draephus, eyes shining, and kissed him. It was a gentle kiss, though Draephus sensed he would have liked it to be much more impassioned.

"I accept your promise," he whispered. "Though I can't believe you'd want to try and start a relationship with me, with all our history."

Draephus grinned. "Well I like my men complicated."

Raski's eyes took on a playful glint. "You'd marry me?"

"Sure I'd marry you, why wouldn't I?"

"And we could have a family?"

"Sure," said Draephus, with all the enthusiasm of a man being asked if he would like a vomit sandwich.

"You don't want a family?"

"Rask we've been over this, we can't have babies."

"We could adopt."

"Or we could castrate ourselves with rusty implements."

"If you want me to take that promise knot then you have to promise me kids."

Draephus rolled his eyes, admitting defeat. Then he kissed Raski's brow. "Fine. I also promise you a family. How many of the rotten little ankle biters do you want?"

"Five."

"Wonderful. Fine. I promise you five children. But it's your job to keep them away from my drums."

"Fine." Raski stared at Draephus, the smile fading from his face. "This is morbid, you and I planning a life after Vesper's death."

Draephus nodded. "Yeah. But, I made another promise, this one to Vesper."

"And what was that?"

"He made me swear I wouldn't make his spirit worry by remaining alone the rest of my life, and that I would set up an ancestor's shrine for him in the castle, so he could always watch over me. I think he'd like a castle full of children." Draephus stroked Raski's long silken hair, looking down into his eyes. "I have to leave, or else I'm going to make love to you right here on the rug."

"First show me how to put this on."

Draephus did, gently locking the heavy silver device around Raski's arm. "There." He touched his face. "Makes it a little easier to walk out of here tonight."

"Yeah. Makes it easier to *let* you walk out." They gazed at each other, then Raski said dryly; "Wait, if you drove my conni here, then how are you getting home?"

"That's… a really good question. Rather blows my big romantic exit."

"Well I'll take you home in the morning. In the meantime you're sleeping in the guest room."

"But I usually sleep with you."

"Yes, but that was when I was pure and innocent and didn't know you have two feet of snake in your pants and could go all night like a pneumatic hammer."

"It's *not* two feet."

"It's still not getting into bed with me. We're supposed to be good boys now. If we are in the same bed someone's going to end up pregnant."

"You're right. We are going to be bastions of virtue," said Draephus, grinning.

"Uh huh. Now get your bastion away from my virtue before it rips out of your pants and attacks. And don't leave anything unspeakable on my sheets."

"Fine. Where would you like me to leave it?"

"You really are horrible, you know that."

"Yeah."

They held each other, looking into one another's eyes. Their resolve was weakening fast, and Raski was just about to say maybe once more would be all right, when his 'com rang. Reluctantly he pushed Draephus away in order to go answer it. Draephus lit a cigarette and tried to get himself under control, feeling a little shaken. He'd never felt like this for Vesper, and in a way that was a bigger betrayal than having actually taken Raski to bed. What he felt for Raski was incredibly powerful, and it had him spooked. Was this love? He'd always assumed that was what he felt for Vesper, and… he *did* love him. But suddenly he had to wonder, if something happened and he could only save one, which one he would rescue.

He glanced to the figure standing by the small carved table on which the 'com sat, his long black hair slipping over his strong shoulders and silver-black skin, the fabric of his khatra caressing his thighs…

Raski hung up the 'com and looked to Draephus. "Mars is at your place and your faelins are having fits."

"Having fits?" said Draephus quizzically. "They only do that when there's a…"

The thunder boomed so loudly that small objects on the shelves rattled, and both screamed like a couple of kids finding a monster in the closet.

"Storm," finished Draephus, feeling his heart pound in his chest.

"I do believe this qualifies," said Raski, coughing as he fought back another crying fit. Draephus walked over to him to hold him, intending to comfort him, but Raski shook his head, waving him back.

"No way, don't come over here. I want you so badly I can't

stand myself, but I can't live with the guilt after."

Draephus nodded, and back up a step. "Why is Mars at my place?"

"He went there to find us. The ship is landing tonight, and Khandi's cousin wants an informal meet-and-greet before the big formal production he knows we won't show up for. Speaking of meeting people, I have to change."

"You mean our beloved emperor," grinned Draephus, as Raski began heading for the stairs that led to his bedroom.

Raski shook his head. "Bizarre, isn't it? I still have a hard time thinking of him as something other than the little skinny white guy who used to run an apothecary out of a dead Kryphisian truck."

Raski vanished into his room, and Draephus put out the candles. After a few minutes, Raski came back downstairs, dressed for the stormy night, jeweled clips shining like white fire against his black hair. He paused at a mirror to apply some silver-blue eye shadow, a move that was not lost on Draephus.

"Blue eye shadow, huh. Are we expecting to see the unseen?"

Raski glanced at him. "We don't know them, and a little ohwendai magic can't hurt when dealing with strangers. Come on, let's go pick up Mars and then get to the ship."

****

Dahli was just coming out of the garage after washing the kuvon when she saw Diza coming up the walk. It was getting late by now, and Dahli had to wonder if she felt like company at the moment. She felt as if she had some kind of plague; a carrier of a virus that made her inflict embarrassment on herself. But at the same time it was good to have someone to share her adventure with. The two girls met and walked up the stairs to the house, entering without saying a word. Dahli went into the kitchen to make them a snack of sliced apples, while Diza set about making a fire in the fireplace. Finally Dahli came out of the kitchen, food in hand, and seated herself beside her friend.

"I met Draephus again tonight," she said, a wry smile crossing her face.

"You two are getting to be old friends," teased Diza. "What did you hit him with this time?"

"Nothing. He caught me hauling Atterick's kuvon out of the

ditch in front of his house."

"Oh no, Dahli!"

"I felt like such a groutnoll," said Dahli. "A complete, utter beaker. He probably thinks I'm some sort of deranged fan watching his every move."

"I'm sure he doesn't," said Diza.

"Are you kidding?" said Dahli. "Can you imagine what it's like being him, how weird it must be? All you have to do is pick up a newspaper and you can read about his every move. I've never even been in his house, but I know he likes to bake khasa-bread and eat it with fried fish. His whole life is on display, and he probably thinks I'm just one more tourist peering into his fishbowl."

"Well, what were you doing outside of his house?"

"I don't know," muttered Dahli. She sighed, then said, "Peering into his fishbowl, I guess. I was just...standing there...wondering who this person is. Then the kuvon went into the ditch and he came out of the castle."

"Did you talk to him at all?" asked Diza.

"No. Well, sort of. He asked me why I wasn't out with my boyfriend, and I said I didn't have one because all the boys my age are brainless clart-muffins."

"What did he say to that?"

"He laughed and said he knew because he used to be one." Dahli fell silent for a moment before she spoke again. "He seems scary. I mean, there's something kind of strange about him."

"You, of all people, saying Draephus CZimcocious is strange? Oh what I wouldn't give for a recording of that!"

Dahli grinned. "Yeah, okay, I know I'm always the first one to defend him, but....he seems like someone who could fly off the handle at any given moment. I felt it when I first ran into him, but I thought that it was just because I had hit him with the door. Then I felt it this time, too. There's all this tension surrounding him, like something is eating at him. There's a lot of anger in that man. I'd hate to be on the receiving end of it."

"Oh come now," said Diza. "The man has enough money to buy Second City. Clart, I'd like to have those kinds of problems. Was Yuri with him this time?"

"No Diza. I promise, if I ever meet Yuri Stracona, I'll call you. Are you staying over tonight?"

"Sure," said Diza, "that way I'll have someone to be late to school with. Hey, where are Atterick and Teirra?"

"Atterick's band is playing at a club and Teirra's with them, so we'll be alone for a while. They're down at Ayre's Music Hall."

"Wow," said Diza, "I'm impressed. Some real big names go down there to see the bands."

"Yeah I know. Maybe Atterick can bring home somebody else famous for me to embarrass myself in front of."

"Maybe," said Diza, "but if his band is playing Ayre's Music Hall, then they're pretty good." Diza poked at the fire. "Maybe `Titan' wasn't such a pretentious name after all."

"Let's face it," said Dahli, "`Mortified Gryphons' isn't such a hot name either."

"It stinks," said Diza. "I wonder how they arrived at that one?"

"No idea, and they haven't said in any of their interviews. I'll ask Draephus the next time I run into him." Dahli's tone was dry. She put her face into her hands. "Ugh! I feel so stupid."

"Oh I'm sure he thinks it's funny."

"I don't. Anyway, as long as we're talking about them we may as well play them." As Diza bounded up the stairs to get Dahli's collection of Gryphon cylinders, Dahli yelled, "Get `Nothing Wrong Here'."

"I'm sick of that one. I want to hear `Gryphons In Yer Basement'."

"May as well play them both."

"May as well play them all." Diza came back downstairs with a small box full of cylinders, forty-two in all, including singles, bootlegs and solo recordings. She dropped them onto the floor in a pile. "Let's start with the first one and work our way down the line."

Dahli searched for the first cylinder and pulled it out of its case, thrusting it into the stereo. The console glowed into life and seconds later the eerie notes of the Mortified Gryphons' first popular song, `I'd Rather Believe', drifted out. Then Mars and Raski joined together in their strange but transfixing harmonies. Dahli looked at the picture of Draephus on the side of the cylinder, then dropped it, sighing heavily.

"I don't want to go to school tomorrow, I'm too embarrassed."

"Oh sure, you just haven't done your history paper."

Dahli went cold. "Oh, clart."

"What?"

"I *haven't* done my history paper." Dahli flopped onto her back.

"Clart!"

"Oh we've got hours, we can make something up."

"Sure, Diza." Dahli sat up once again. "Even if I do something it will look like garbage because I won't have time to do a good copy."

"Well, it's going to take the Duone more than one class to get through all the papers. Start it tonight, tell him tomorrow that you forgot it at home, and then finish it tomorrow night."

"Yeah, all right. Except I'm not going to school tomorrow, I'm sick." She crossed her eyes and hung out her tongue.

"Oh poor Dahli," said Diza. "Well come on, I'll help. Oh! The ship from Earth lands tonight, do you want to go see it tomorrow?"

"Yes I would," said Dahli, "but isn't it way out at that old Kryphisian base?"

"No I heard they changed it, the emperor decided it would be nicer for the visitors to be closer to the downtown area. So they will be landing on that wide level paved spot near the city center where the Kryphisians were planning on putting up something or other. Once the space ship leaves they're gonna rip it up and convert it into more garden space, but for now it's a landing pad."

"Oh! I know the place. That's really close! Let's go now, maybe we can see it land!"

The two froze, listening as the usual soft patter of rain abruptly became a violent torrent.

"Tomorrow," they said in unison, as the thunder exploded like cannon fire.

The two girls worked, flipping through history books and using the stories Stratavarus had told Dahli. By the time they were ready for bed, they had accomplished a reasonable amount of work. Enough, at least that Dahli could turn in her paper if she had to. She climbed under the covers and fell into a heavy sleep, dreaming of blue eyes, bruised and red-rimmed.

Chapter Six

Gemma was sick to her stomach with nerves as the gigantic ship slowly lowered to the ground, settling delicately on a massive landing pad easily the size of several city blocks. The ship would serve as a hotel while the visitors were there; providing some sense of familiarity on a completely alien world. Gemma stood, looking out the window as the city street slowly rose up to meet them, and there was the faintest tremor as they landed. There was a brief silence, then the ship vibrated very slightly as panels drew back, revealing an entryway that led to the street one floor below, making the hotel illusion nearly perfect. They were now free to come and go as they pleased. Assuming they wanted to go outside. As the ship had come below the Sferkkaan cloud cover, there had been a tremendous explosion of thunder, almost as if some god was warning of their approach. As Gemma gazed outside, the rain began to fall more heavily.

Vidar walked over to Gemma, and she reached out to take his hand. She suddenly felt like she was far too small and young to be this far from home. Vidar squeezed her hand reassuringly.

"Is be okies, Gemma. Dey just wants to makes music! Nots eats us."

"We hope," said Gemma. "How do I look?"

"Likes little princess!" he said, indicating her green and white gown. Gemma rarely wore gowns, but she heard that there was a chance the Emperor himself could show up to greet them. She had no idea how to greet an Emperor, but she wasn't about to do it in jeans and a t-shirt.

"Wish it wasn't raining," said Gemma.

"Rain is alls dey be gettings here," said Vidar.

"I know," said Gemma. "I just miss sunlight. Oh God, Vidar, I am so nervous, what if I offend them?"

"So who cares if you offend a bunch of space aliens?" said a voice. Gemma rolled her eyes as Mickie appeared.

"Mickie I don't know if you realize this," said Gemma, "but this is *their* planet. *We* are the space aliens."

Mickie shrugged, and Gemma felt her patience wear thin.

"Mickie you better be nice; you're representing our home – we all are. We don't want them to think we're a bunch of jerks."

"Who cares what the fuck they think? I'm Mickie Pastors, who gives a shit about them?"

Gemma looked to Vidar. "He's going to get us all killed, isn't he?"

Vidar was staring coldly at the brat. He said something in Norwegian that sent shivers down Gemma's spine, and walked away. She resumed looking out the window, currently one storey above the street. It was dark, clearly well past sunset. The streets were wet, broken, and silent. Her first sight of Second City made her think of a zombie apocalypse; all it lacked was actual zombies. Then someone poked his finger into the crack of her ass, and she turned to see Mickie smirking at her.

"You try that again and I'll kill you!"

"Yeah, yeah, you loved it. Admit it."

Gemma wasn't really sure what to do about the assault. She wanted to beat his face into a bloody pulp then puncture his bladder while screaming "YOU LOVE IT, ADMIT IT!" but she lacked the physical strength.

"You're a hateful little bitch," she said, "I wish you'd been thrown out an airlock. Pig."

She stormed off, heading for the newly-revealed lower level, almost crashing into Mystique. Before the older woman could ask what was wrong, Gemma spoke up.

"Is anyone coming to meet us?"

"Well if they ain't, I changed my underwear for nothing," she said.

Gemma snorted with laughter. "TMI," she giggled. "But the streets out there are empty! You'd think they'd want to be… here…"

Gemma's voice slowed as from over Mystique's shoulder, through the gigantic observation window that rose three stories of their huge ship, she saw a vehicle pull up. It was small and black, gleaming like wet midnight, faint blue flames licking around the wheels and causing steam to rise. It did not seem to roll so much as hydroplane, and it was not until the little vehicle stopped that she realized it had been travelling slightly above the actual street.

"I want that," said Gemma.

Mystique turned to look at the vehicle. "Me too. Okay – I'll steal the car, you hold them off."

Gemma laughed, watching as a similar car pulled up, this one pale grey.

"Got to be the welcoming committee," said Gemma. She took Mystique's hand between her own. "Oh God I am so nervous I may pee."

K-Shot suddenly arrived. "I saw cars – *awesome* mutherfuckin' cars, one of which I *will* be bringing back home with me. Wonder who is in…? Ooooooohhhhh…. Shit."

Gemma, Mystique, and K-Shot watched as a familiar form got out of the car; it could only be Raski Jervyas. His skin was the colour of ink with a strange, almost silvery undertone to it, like hematite. Then he turned his head to look at the ship, and Gemma, K-Shot and Mystique all screeched briefly in unison at the way his blue eyes glowed, and in roughly the same key. They screamed again when he blinked and his lids flashed silver at them.

"That shit just freaks me the fuck out," said K-Shot. "Why do his eyes glow in the mutherfuckin' dark?"

K-Shot and Mystique looked to Gemma. She drew her trusty phone out of her bag, seeking information.

"Here we go, I found a National Geographic article," she said, and began to read aloud. *"I have since learned that the pale blue eyes are a logical adaptation to life in a jungle that is really quite dark. The human eye lens is smooth and… well… lens-like. The lens of the South Continent Sferkkaan is actually made up of tens of thousands of little reflective surfaces that catch the light, refract and re-reflect it, and enable them to see better in the dark. Pale blue reflects light, whereas dark lenses would absorb the light."*

"So what this all boils down to is stick Raski Jervyas in the dark and his eyes will glow, is that right?" said Mystique.

"Pretty much," said Gemma. "Like a kitty."

"Kitty my ass," grumbled K-Shot. "More like a vampire." He craned his neck to get a better look at the newcomers. "He's got some serious blue eye shadow happening there."

"Yeah," said Gemma. "Wonder what that means?"

As she tried to find the meaning behind Raski's make-up, a second man got out of the car – small, pretty, with a cascade of long fuchsia-tinted hair held more or less in place by an old slouch hat. He had three bottles in his arms… and four inch heels on his boots.

"I have *got* to find out where these boys buy their shoes," said Mystique.

A third figure emerged from the vehicle, hat in place, wraparound shades hiding his scarred face, flipping his long coat around himself.

"Oh yay," said Gemma. "It's Mr. Crazy-Pants. Did you see him try to gut that talk show host? Why is he here?"

They watched as Raski walked over to Draephus, nuzzling up to him, speaking softly. Draephus smiled faintly, and the pair nipped each other affectionately. Mystique raised one perfectly plucked and drawn eyebrow.

"I bet I know why he's here."

"May not be the reason you think," said Billy, coming to stand with the trio, watching Raski and Draephus nip and nuzzle. "I know what it looks like to *us*, but to them it may just be 'hi how are ya?' Much of their language is gesture-based."

"Yeah well if any of them try to nibble me, I'll show them a few gestures of my own," said K-Shot.

The second car opened its doors, and out stepped Khandid and Yuri. The Earthlings watched the Sferkkaans communicate; nipping, nudging, touching… Gemma glanced at Mystique, who was staring at Khandid Stracona as if he was a medium-rare steak covered in all her favourite toppings.

"That little Khandid, there… ooohh he makes me shiver."

K-Shot stared at her, affronted. "He WHAT?!"

"Well he's adorable!"

"He's so white he glows in the dark."

"And you're so black that when you sleep on a dark sheet I have to whack the bed with a pole to find out where you are. He's still cute. What's the matter? You think you can look at other ladies but I can't look at other men?"

"That ain't a man. I'm not sure what it is, but if it's male, I'm a sarcastic fringehead."

Mystique crossed her arms. "Uh-oh, everybody watch out, somebody's been watchin' animal shows again."

"The point is, *all* I do is look."

"You're so cute when you're jealous."

"It's okay, K-Shot," said Gemma. "She really only wants his shoes."

"Them too," said Mystique.

"You're gonna get a spanking in a minute," said K-Shot. "And what are those guys waiting for?"

"My guess would be whoever is driving that dragon," said Billy.

They watched as an enormous red and gold vehicle pulled up, moving almost like a serpent as it drew to the curb and settled on the pavement. Gemma became aware of more bodies gathering in what was now the foyer of their little intergalactic hotel. Brian Taylor spoke from somewhere over her head.

"Cripes they all look like a post-apocalyptic 80s hair band."

"Well I guess the post-apocalyptic part is right," said Billy. "Those bombed-out streets behind them ain't no movie set."

More people were arriving now, many Gemma had scarcely seen in the four months they had all been travelling through space together. They watched as the Sferkkaans began unloading what appeared to be crates, instruments, and bottles.

"Looks like the hosts are bringing the party," said K-Shot.

"From what I gather, they party hard, too," said Billy. He laughed. "Check out Khandid. Gotta get the war-paint just right."

Khandid Stracona was touching up his makeup in the side mirror of the vehicle when another car pulled up, similar to the first. The doors opened and out stepped a skinny, leggy man with long dark hair. He was dressed in tight black leather, and had an oddly foxy face. Exiting the other side of the vehicle was a skinny teen boy with long legs, high heels, and hair almost to his backside. He had a wide band of black with blurred edges painted across his eyes.

"Get Sigge!" cried Billy, and someone ran off to get him. Moments later the tall lean blonde appeared near Billy, trailed closely by Vidar.

"Ja what is you wantings?" he asked.

Billy pointed the boy out. "Straif Mannechek, Sferkkaa's fastest quinticord player."

Sigge perked up visibly. "Oh boy we is seeings tonight who is da fastest player on two planets!"

"Who is that with him?" asked Gemma.

"Do not know," said Billy.

"Delaes Randerick," said Brian. "Check out the makeup, grey and black bands blurred together. What's that?"

"Am I the only person here who studied?" Gemma demanded indignantly. Not getting an answer, she looked it up. "Black and grey bands blurred over the eyes. Sniper. Apparently, if he wants to, he can blow your brains out from three miles away."

"Did I miss anything?" asked a voice.

Gemma looked up as Missy Morgan came down the stairs in a hurry, cowboy hat firmly in place on her head. She, like Corey Hillman, was here to bring country music to Sferkkaa. Except in her case it was the fun kind of country that made a person want to learn how to line-dance. Gemma liked her; she was fun and rowdy and silly, and had once trapped Mickie in an air lock and threatened to shoot him into space. That had made her popular with pretty much everyone but Mickie. Missy hopped down the stairs as fast as she could and looked out the window.

"Wow," she said. "I do believe I see several men in sore need of a makeover. And what is up with the blue eyes that glow like kitty-lasers?"

"Those blue eyes mean he sees better in the dark than we do," said Brian. "Okay, we better be on our best behaviour, I'm pretty sure the guy in the really long car is the one in charge of the planet."

The man who exited the vehicle was small, with an amazing cascade of red-gold hair. He was wrapped in a large silvery-blue fur cloak, and as he stepped out of the vehicle, the seven men bowed. Or rather, six of them did, and one tried very hard. Before Draephus managed to hurt himself showing his respect, Mordrett Stratavarus hastened over to him and drew him up. They spoke briefly, and Draephus managed a chagrinned smile. The formalities over, they began pulling things out of their vehicles; mostly instrument cases and bottles. Then the back door of the imperial vehicle opened, and something stepped out in a flurry of black and red feathers. It rose to approximately seven feet in height, and came to stand behind Mordrett. Mystique looked to Gemma.

"What is *that*?" she asked. "And where does *he* shop for clothes?"

Gemma didn't even have to look up the answer to the question; she had been hoping to see one of these warriors desperately.

"Imperial Bird of Prey," she said, eyes shining. "Sacred warriors charged with protecting the emperor. The elaborate outfit traditionally served to tangle enemy weapons, making it harder to injure him in a fight. Check out the way his boot heels glint. He'll have blades mounted on his gloves and gauntlets as well. GOLD FEATHERS IN HIS HAIR! HOMIGOD he's a royal bird! That means he didn't earn the post in the war, it means he is a direct descendant of the warrior lineage!"

Gemma squealed, oblivious to the eye-rolls of her companions.

"Are you sure you want to be a singer-songwriter?" teased Missy. "You sound like a historian to me."

"Well I'm only fifteen, I can always change my mind," said Gemma. "But this stuff is all so cool. Look, see? Emperor first… hey why is Khandid Stracona walking with the emperor?"

"Maybe they're friends," suggested Missy as Gemma consulted her phone.

"Nope," said Gemma after a moment. "Cousins. If Mordrett dies, Khandi is in charge of the realm Oh this is good, Khandid's political slogan is 'If elected – will not serve'. That should make for a fun case of anarchy."

"Well here they come," said K-Shot.

"Hey!" said a voice, none other than Mickie. "Where are all the bitches?"

"Right there!" said Missy. "Can't you see them? They're everywhere! Callin' your name!"

"Where?" demanded Mickie.

"Can't see them," said Brian. "They're invisible ninja groupies. Sferkkaa's full of invisible ninja groupies."

"I'll answer the door," said Mystique. "Just so the first Earth person they meet on this ship isn't Mickie."

"Hey!"

"I'll let the others know," said Missy, and ran back up the stairs.

"Oh crap," said Brian. "Does anybody speak Sferkkaan?"

"We all just assumed Gemma did and left it at that," said K-Shot.

Gemma squeaked. Mystique held her hand out to her.

"Come stand by me, baby girl, someone needs to say hello."

"I'm not sure I know how to say hello! Oh God, they're gonna burn us all at the stake, I just know it."

"They're not gonna burn us at the stake," said Brian.

"Yeah," said K-Shot. "Where will they find dry firewood?"

Brian and K-Shot snorted and snickered. Mystique opened the door, and there before them stood Mordrett Stratavarus. Gemma thought he could not be much over five feet tall, although with the heels he was wearing it was hard to tell. Khandid Stracona was even smaller, dressed in a spectacular outfit of blue and white with a long flowing coat. He was in full makeup, complete with a black line beneath his eyes and a fine gold line beneath that, with a break in it just before it reached his hair. Gemma wished she knew what that meant, but now was not the time to go diving for her phone. She cleared her throat, and carefully went through a short greeting.

Gemma did not miss the way they and their companions nearly strangled holding back their amusement, nor the way Mordrett's eyes blinked, as if asking himself if he had heard her correctly. She felt her face begin to turn purple as he cleared his throat. When he spoke, it was with a heavy, throaty accent that made her want to swoon.

"Donselle, I do not believe you said what you intended. Your inflection was… rather off."

"What did I say?" asked Gemma warily.

"Well your hand gestures were… incorrect. What you said was 'Greet me, I have carrots in my panties'. Which is actually an improvement on what your ambassador said to me four months ago."

"I…don't have carrots in my panties," she mumbled.

"Well we shall be thankful for that, since I do and it would be highly improper for the Emperor to be wearing the same thing as a guest. Are you going to invite us in?"

Gemma thought her face was going to explode she was blushing so violently. "I'm so sorry, please come in, all of you. Do you all speak English?"

"Most of us," said Khandid. "We come bearing the universal gift of friendship – alcohol."

"Yeah, friendship, unexpected pregnancy, jail time, and my last album!" said Billy cheerfully.

Khandid passed him a bottle of something silvery-grey. "Drink that *veeerrryyy* slowly, my friend."

Billy laughed. In the light, Gemma could see Khandid's white hair had streaks of pale pink in it. It was very long, and thick, and made her think of unicorn manes. His eyes were almost pastel blue, and she had the impression he was wearing some sort of over-sized contact lens. His bones were fine and light, and she could not help but wonder if he was exceptionally tiny, or typical of Northern Sferkkaan males. He was so pretty, she felt oddly compelled to sit him on her lap and brush his hair.

Mickie suddenly barged in front of her and took Khandid's arm. "Don't waste your time talking to Billy, come talk to me, baby."

Khandid allowed Mickie to lead him away, but he did not look pleased. Nor did Yuri, who followed them up the steps to the main gathering area. Gemma moved out of the way, allowing the visitors to come inside and out of the rain. The next person inside was the Bird of Prey, and he was as scary up close as he was far away. He walked just behind Khandid and Mordrett, the feathers on his cloak rustling softly as he followed the pair up to the enormous common room of their ship-turned-hotel. The remaining visitors scooted in as the Sferkkaan rain began with a vengeance. Gemma felt herself turn cold as Draephus came in, closing the door behind himself. He smelled like death, and looked like someone had just dragged him out of his own grave. There was nothing pretty or delicate about this man – he was big boned and broad shouldered, and very tall. She noted he was wearing flat-soled boots. This was not a man who needed heels.

"Well we've brought you to our leader," said Mars, handing Mystique an unlabelled bottle of clear, pearl-grey liquid. "Allow us now to ply you with liquor."

"Are you trying to get me drunk and take advantage?" she teased.

Mars' large green eyes shifted nervously, as if trying to decide if she was joking. "Is that an option?"

"No it is not an option!" K-Shot took Mystique's hand and led her away. "Of all the women on the planet to hook up with, I have to find one with an alien fetish!"

"And such is the way of things," said Mars. "I'm adorable, why doesn't anyone love me?"

"You're short," said Raski.

"I am not. You're just mean."

"You're exactly the right height," said Gemma.

"There," said Mars. "The donselle agrees with me." He took Gemma's arm. "Let us go upstairs and find out what your companions are doing to our emperor. He's not much but he's the only emperor we have."

Gemma nodded, then watched Straif head up the stairs past them, wondering how he moved so easily in heels. She had always been under the impression that walking in heels was a female ability, and suddenly she was up to ears in men who moved as if they had been born in them. And then she was distracted from her train of thought by Delaes Randerick opening his mouth.

"Look at that rain I really hope we don't have to go out in it any time soon you know I really don't mind it if I'm home but I just hate driving in it!"

Those still in the foyer just stared, blinking. Delaes stared back.

"What is something the matter am I not speaking properly?"

"Do you… breathe?" asked Billy.

Delaes gave Billy an affronted look. "Yes of course I breathe I'm a living being don't be ridiculous if you can help it STRAIF what are you doing up there did I not tell you to stay close these people may be *very* weird."

They watched Delaes head up the stairs into the main gathering area. Billy looked to Raski.

"Um… does he breathe?"

"We're not certain," said Raski. "All we know is he is very highly strung, and has yet to discover the joys of punctuation. Oh – and he bites. Do not come up behind him; he really doesn't like it."

"Hard to believe he was a sniper, with all that energy," said Billy.

Raski shrugged. "Hard to believe only five years ago he was living in an underground bunker, and I was flying night missions over the jungle. But, anyway, *nari nuisse*, as they say. We will leave depressing things for another day."

"Or the day after that," said Mars. He turned his attention back to Gemma. "Let us go upstairs."

"Your heels are higher than mine!" she said as they went up the flight of steps.

"Because he's short," called Raski after them.

Gemma laughed. "It's just strange to see men in high heels like that."

"Yes we've been meaning to speak to your men about their complete lack of fashion sense," said Mars. "No lace, no makeup, no high heels, no corsets…."

"On my world, women wear those things," said Gemma.

"Ludicrous," said Mars dismissively. "How can you justifiably put a woman in a corset? Women are fluid, they gain and lose weight with their cycles, things shift with pregnancy… Absolute nonsense."

"Some women *like* corsets," Gemma said teasingly.

"Well I'm not going to stand on a street corner and tell people what to wear, but it just seems nonsense to me that such a restrictive item of clothing should be put on a woman."

Gemma liked him. He felt... safe. She did not know any other way to describe him. She just enjoyed his presence, and how he didn't seem to have any urge to be "masculine" or "manly". He simply was what he was. She stayed close as they went quickly up the stairs. She glanced back to see if Raski and Draephus were following, and saw they were standing together, alone, nuzzling and speaking softly. It was a little startling to see two men pressed so close, clearly intimate, all but kissing as they held one another. She said nothing about it, deciding it was none of her business. Instead she finished climbing the stairs with Mars, and smiled as she saw virtually every musician on the ship was there, including their families. And Mickie, of course, standing possessively close to Khandid.

"Is your friend okay?" asked Gemma. "Mickie is kind of a creep."

"Creep?" questioned Mars.

"A very unpleasant person."

"Ah. Well if Mickie does anything Khandid does not like, he will pay for it. Khandid is a trained assassin with dozens of kills to his name, and Yuri will defend him if he feels the need."

"I think Mickie will have a fit once he realizes Khandid is a male."

"Oh. One of those, is he? Must be frightening to have such a fragile hold on one's self-identity. We completely lost ours. Since we have nothing more to lose, we do not worry about petty things so much."

"I was reading about the war, and what it cost you," said Gemma. "I can't imagine losing so much."

"Be grateful for that," Mars said softly.

Gemma watched as Draephus and Raski walked by, close to each other's side. She had a feeling they were a couple, but it was hard to tell. Sferkkaans spoke many languages, and two of them simultaneously; combining spoken word with body language and a type of sign. The closeness may mean nothing at all...

Then Mars attracted her attention by nosing her, and that was the moment she realized she really was on another planet. Oh this was going to take some getting used to. She looked to him.

"What?" she asked.

He smiled. "Please don't stare at Raski and Draephus; they are trying so hard to keep their affair a secret."

"Then they're both really bad at keeping secrets."

He shrugged, then looked around. He sighed heavily. "We've lost Yuri."

Gemma looked around, and was stunned to find she could not see the Sferkkaan anywhere. "He's seven feet tall! How could you lose him?"

"It is one of his many talents – turning invisible."

Mars slipped away to find Yuri, leaving Gemma alone in the crowd. She didn't think she had seen this many people in the common room of the ship ever; in fact some of these people she had never even seen at all. It was as if whole families had materialized out of the woodwork. People were laughing and drinking, food was being brought out to share, there was music… didn't parties take planning? This had come out of nowhere. Back home her mother took a month to throw a party, and would obsess over every detail. This, however, seemed much less formal. Gemma smiled as she saw Missy corner Mars. The little Sferkkaan man had gone only a few feet and managed to end up with a drink in each hand. He watched Missy with wary curiosity as she sashayed up to him, standing several inches taller than he in her cowboy boots.

"Do you have horses here on your world?" asked Missy, batting her eyelashes.

Mars looked uncertain as to why she would ask. "No…?" he said slowly.

"That's too bad. Well how about we save one anyway, and you can ride me instead?"

Missy opened her shirt and showed him a very nice pair of full, firm breasts. Mars stared, clearly stunned for a moment. He then threw back one of the drinks, handed the empty glass to Raski, picked up a random bottle from the table, and grinned.

"*Ai sikate*," he said, and left with Missy. Raski looked to Draephus.

"Well we had to go to another planet, but we finally found someone who would have Mars."

"I'd have Mars!" said Mordrett. "But my husband would kick my head off."

"You take Mars, I'll take your husband," said Raski. "Hey where did Yuri get to? Khandi, you lost Yuri."

"Yuri is self-losing," said Khandid, looking around. "He can't have gone far. Check anything with a lampshade on it. How long have you and Draephus been having an affair?"

Raski had just been taking a drink when Khandid said that and choked, coughing whatever liquor he had been drinking out in a spray. Raski then stared at Khandid with heated indignity.

"You're a nasty little man."

"It was just a question!"

"We are not having an affair," growled Raski.

"Well it's not my fault you're not having an affair, no need to get nasty about it."

Draephus said something to Raski, apparently asking if Khandid had asked what he thought Khandid asked. Gemma braced for Draephus to have another violent outburst, but his reaction to what Khandid said was minimal. Maybe he wasn't a complete freak after all. She decided to chance a question.

"Raski? What's a daghuwai?"

Gemma had no idea how much English Draephus spoke, but he clearly caught at least a small part of that question. Most likely "daghuwai". Raski sighed.

"So you saw that broadcast."

"Yeah," said Gemma. "Actually… a lot of us did."

"Yes a lot of us did and wish to know why you didn't finish the hateful little snot off," said Delaes. He turned his head sharply to find Billy staring at him. "YES I BREATHE why would I not breathe you know I would really like to know what you have been reading about Sferkkaan biology I'm not a plant you know."

"Of course not," said Billy, still staring at Delaes in rapt fascination.

"Because plants breathe and we're not certain you do," added Khandid.

"You're all horrid I'm going to go drink something."

Draephus nudged Raski, who looked at his friend with obvious affection. Raski said something, and Draephus grinned like a corpse. Dear God in Heaven he was creepy. Raski turned his attention back to Gemma.

"A daghuwai is like a mercenary, but… worse. He fights for any side that will pay him, but lacks any loyalty to any side, regardless of pay. He will play as many sides as he can against each other, and when the players are dead he comes in and claims what is left. Food, ammunition, provisions of any sort, it does not matter to him. Often he will take even from surviving children and leave them to starve and freeze. Draephus and I have cleaned up after daghuwai; we have picked the corpses of frozen infants from the floor where they were left beside their dead parents, in one case even the baby was robbed of all clothing." The blue eyes became cold and eerily empty. "We don't like daghuwai."

"Is Astellis Monct one?" she asked in a small voice.

"He may be. There is no proof. If he was then someone will get him for it. Probably Draephus."

"Or me," said Mordrett. "We *do* have a war-crimes tribunal."

"What happens to them once they are convicted?" asked Brian. "Jail?"

"Oh, no, we don't incarcerate baby-killers," said Mordrett, filling his glass. "We shoot them, chop up the bodies and feed them to the scavengers. Wild things need to eat as much as we do, and it seems only right that those who scavenged are scavenged themselves."

"That's a little harsh, don't you think?" said Mystique.

Mordrett looked to her. "My dear donselle – I am not spending resources my government does not have feeding and housing child-killers when I could be feeding and housing children. Parasites, we do not need."

"Do you kill all your criminals? What about political prisoners?" challenged Brian.

"Depends on the politics involved," said Mordrett. "If he is advocating free room and board for baby-killers, we send him off to the eastern areas to build houses and schools. If he's just an asshole who doesn't know what he's talking about because he comes from a planet where he does not have to worry about where his next meal is coming from, or if his daughters, sisters, and female acquaintances of any kind are going to live to see the dawn, then I pour more wine and walk away."

Mordrett filled his glass and walked away, leaving Brian to stew. Gemma sucked back a smile. Then Corey Hillman's wife Mercy walked into the room, carrying their tiny daughter.

"Someone wants to say good night to Daddy," said Mercy. She blinked in surprise as Raski smoothly swooped in and took the baby. "I'm gonna want that back," she said.

"Have no fear, I won't run away with her. Hello tiny baby, what's your name?"

"This is Lisa," said Mercy.

"Hello Lisa, I'm Raski. Nice to meet you."

Lisa may not have been able to speak, but her facial expression said it all as she stared at Raski's pale blue eyes. Then she let out a blood-curdling shriek and began wiggling to escape. Raski returned the distressed infant to her mother.

"Sorry," he said. "It's the eyes. Lots of babies react that way."

"I react that way every time I see you," said Khandid.

"The feeling is mutual. Why is your hair pink?"

"I couldn't make it paisley." Khandid cocked his head, looking at Raski, as Mickie sulked beside him. "If you and I had a baby, what colour do you suppose it would be?"

"Pastel grey with pink highlights," said Raski. Mystique fought to stop herself from spraying her drink through her nose in amusement.

Gemma watched as Corey stood up to take his tiny daughter, muttering something that made her jaw drop. Raski may not have caught what Corey said, but Brian did. He stopped Corey a few feet away, and spoke to him in a low voice almost too quiet for Gemma to overhear.

"You better watch that kind of talk, because in case you haven't noticed we have both black people *and* gay people on this ship, and in the case of old Willis Joplin over there, some who are both. Now just because Raski has no idea what you called him does not mean I won't be happy to explain it to him."

Corey just glared and walked away, grumbling. Mercy hastened after him, and Gemma walked over to Brian.

"So how long until the Sferkkaans throw us off the planet?" asked Gemma.

"I have no idea," said Brian, shaking his head. "Bloody hell there really is one in every crowd, isn't there? I'm sure Raski heard him, if he asks what those words meant…"

There was a sudden flurry of blue and white, and Mickie screamed in pure terror. Gemma watched, eyes large, jaw hanging, as Khandid Stracona leapt straight up, kicking out with his boot-blades, aiming right at Mickie. People scattered as the tiny warrior twice more leapt up, a blur of silvery blue and white, striking and lashing so fast that he transformed into something looking very much like a white bird in flight. Gemma suddenly understood why the Sferkkaans dressed the way they did in a manner she never would have comprehended otherwise. The fighting style was like traditional Japanese martial arts, though with less restrained movements. This was about intimidation as well as defense, and in full flight with his coat and hair blowing, it was almost impossible to determine where to aim. There was no way to tell what was Khandid and what was whirling fabric, hair, and blades.

Within milliseconds it was over, and Khandid landed to stand over Mickie and scream at him in Sferkkaan. Then Khandid walked away, dropping onto the couch and wedging himself against Draephus. Mickie Pastors sat on the floor, sheet white, breathing hard, the front of his pants wet, clearly terrified. Both of his ears had long triangles cut out of them, and across his eyes and throat were cuts so very fine they were almost too small to bleed. Instead they leaked just the thinnest line of blood, then stopped. This had clearly been a warning; Gemma had no doubt that, had Khandid wanted to, Mickie would be down on all fours looking for his eyes while he bled through massive holes in his throat.

"Well the good news is Raski is probably no longer wondering what Corey called him," said Gemma, as Draephus cuddled Khandid protectively. Moments later Yuri materialized from whatever hiding-hole he had been lurking in to stalk menacingly toward Mickie. Raski gently caught him and turned him away from the cowering boy to where Khandid was seated instead. Gemma walked to Mickie and stood over him.

"You loved it. Admit it," she snarled.

Mickie got up weakly, shakily. He walked away quietly, shaking visibly, the arrogance all knocked out of him, at least for now. Khandid watched him go with a look in his eyes that implied he was sorry he hadn't killed him. K-Shot blinked at Khandid, trying to process what he had just seen.

"How the fuck did you do that?!"

"Years of practice," said Straif.

"Can you do that?" asked K-Shot.

"I can do a variation of it," said Straif.

"Can we see?" asked Gemma.

He brought a hand to his stomach. "No, sorry. I… had surgery recently. I'm a bit sore. Besides I'm really not small enough."

K-Shot raised an eyebrow. "Straif I don't know if you have looked in the mirror lately…"

He laughed. "No I mean North Continent small. Like Khandi. Khandi's northern, I'm eastern, Draephus is western, and Raski is southern."

"Yes the land of high humidity, high temperatures, and NO sun," said Raski.

"There's… no sun anywhere, as far as I can tell," said K-Shot.

"Yes well there is Second City lack of sun and then there is South Continent lack of sun," said Straif.

"It's like being on the bottom of the ocean, but wetter and darker," said Raski. He looked at Khandid. "Don't you think you've sucked up enough snuggles for now?"

"No," said Khandid, still pressed against Draephus while nibbling Yuri. He paused briefly to turn big blue eyes up to Draephus, then puckered for a kiss. Draephus responded by wrapping his mouth around Khandid's upper face. As Khandid screeched and wriggled, Raski looked to K-Shot.

"You have to forgive Draephus, we don't let him out much."

"I have to ask this," said Mystique, as Khandid managed to free himself from a slobbering and began immediately touching up his make-up, "and please forgive me if this is none of my business… but… what is with all the nibbling? I really want to know how I should react if someone does it to me. You guys all seem… pretty tactile."

"Well Yuri and I are married," said Khandid. "And the rest of us are close friends and we've known each other quite a while, even the brat over there." Khandid indicated Straif. "So we do tend to touch and kiss and cuddle."

"So… for close friends," said Mystique.

"As a general rule, yes," said Khandid. "But… you are not the first person from Earth to point out our tendency as a race to nibble. Not even the first visitor from another world to mention it. A Kryphisian general roughly eight hundred years ago commented on it, so we've been a nippy bunch for at least that long."

"We used to punch each other in the face, but we took a vote and decided the nibbling starts fewer fights," said Mordrett.

"We did," said Khandid, nodding.

Mystique just raised an eyebrow. She looked at Yuri, then at Khandid, her dark eyes shifting between the pair.

"He's a lot taller than you," she noted.

"That's why we keep the stepladder in the bedroom," said

Khandid.

Gemma was startled by an odd ringing noise. She looked to Draephus, who reached into the pocket of his coat and drew out something that resembled the old "clamshell" style cell phone. He opened it, then looked to Raski as a lot of furious barking came out of it. He sighed, closed the phone, then rose to his feet.

"Something wrong?" asked Brian.

"The pets woke up," said Raski.

"Your dog can use the phone?" inquired K-Shot.

"Faelins," said Raski. "They were asleep in the back of the car, I guess the rain woke them up."

"Pets?!" said Gemma excitedly.

"Noise makers," said Khandid. "But Draephus loves them."

Gemma waited in anticipation to see what these creatures would look like. She was unprepared for what she did see – something like the tailless offspring of a lemur and a greyhound, with deep red skin, long silky red hair on the head, a fox-like face and eyes that blazed like green fire. They tore into the gathering room like any over-excited dog, racing around and barking at random things. Then both headed straight for Delaes, knocking him flat onto his back in glee. As Delaes screeched and flailed, Draephus walked back to the couch to sit beside Raski. He watched his friend get gnawed, nibbled, slobbered, rolled on and barked at, then called a single word to them.

"*T'niski!*"

One of the creatures turned and, in a single leap, cleared twenty feet of space to land on Draephus. The second galumphed along noisily to bounce into his lap. They curled up against him, looking utterly content.

"What the fuck is that?" asked Brian.

"It's a faelin," said Raski.

"Yeah but what is it?" He tried to pet one, but stopped when it tried to eat the watch from his wrist.

"It's… red and it barks," said Raski. "That's about how far we got in the research. Delaes are you okay over there?"

Delaes picked himself from the floor. "NO I am not okay I am anything BUT okay and what have those things been eating it smells vile YECH I've been licked and YES I BREATHE!"

"Did I say anything?" asked Billy, eyes large and innocent.

Raski tossed him a bottle. "Here. That'll take care of it."

As the others interacted, Gemma continued to surreptitiously watch Draephus. He scared her, but she wasn't sure why. There was something very disturbing about him; the way he sat, ankle of his right leg resting on the knee of his left, cigarette between his lips, wrap-around sunglasses obscuring much of his face… he reminded her of a painting she had seen once of Baron Samedi, Haitian voodoo spirit of the dead. He was a man who had only come because his friends asked him to. Otherwise he would be home, in his castle, with its catacombs filled with the dead…

"Why do you wear sunglasses?" she asked, trying to get her mind off the idea that somehow she was at a party and Death was one of the guests. "I mean it rains all the time, why do you need them?"

"You will find out," said Raski. "The cloud cover sometimes becomes very high and thin. And believe me, there *is* a sun beyond the clouds. The light filtering through the clouds reflects off all the moisture in the air and creates a glare that can be quite painful."

"Of course Draephus wears them because he gets into fights and makes a mess of his face," said Khandid. He then repeated the statement in Sferkkaan. Draephus seemed to ignore him, stroking the soft hair of his faelins. Then he pointed at Khandi and said something. Instantly both creatures were on him, licking and barking.

As Khandid fended off the faelins, Sigge brought out his Fender Stratocaster, then looked to Straif. The youth dove for his own instrument, and the two promptly traded to check out what each other had. More drink was brought out as well as assorted instruments, and soon the musicians were doing what they did best – playing. There was so much more Gemma wanted to ask, but for now conversation was giving away to music. She would have to save her questions for later. Instead she went to stand beside Straif Mannechek and watch him play. He smiled at her, his face carefully made up, his long hair, flowing lace sleeves, frock coat, and thigh-high boots with the killer heels all just so.

Gemma had no doubt she would be able to find a boy to make friends with on Sferkkaa. She just hoped her ego could take him being prettier than she.

****

Dahli and Diza were dragged out of bed by Teirra the next morning, despite moans, groans and protests. The two ate breakfast, and finally were pushed out the door with the possibility of only being slightly late. But they could fix that. They meandered along slowly, going down alleys, stopping to gaze in shop windows, and following the progress of a large bug as it wandered over some rubble. The first class was science, and both were certain that, whatever they were going to be when they grew up, they weren't going to be scientists.

"Are you still seeing Randish?" asked Dahli as they tramped along.

"Yeah," said Diza, breaking into a grin. She looked over at her friend. "Would you like to meet him? I'm meeting him at the Contempo after school, why don't you come along?"

"Sounds like fun. Does your dad know about him yet?"

"My dad would clart in his pants," said Diza. "He'd lock me up for the rest of my life."

"So… that would be a no, I take it."

Their aimless wandering paid off; the two arrived halfway through class. If they had taken the route that led down to the old storm drains they could have missed it completely, but Diza was afraid of the gigantic plague rats that waddled up and down the pipes. Duone Bathers was less than impressed with their time.

"Well, well. So glad you two could make it."

"Good," said Dahli. "We're glad to be here."

She flashed Atania her worn and weary Gryphon shirt, then took her seat next to Czamkiar. He was wearing so much flavoured lip gloss that she could smell it, and he was casually painting his fingernails. His eyes peered out through circles of heavy black, cheeks painted into dramatic, skeletal angles. Dahli fought an urge to tell him his lips were on crooked. He was trying very hard to appear as though he did not notice the looks a couple of boys were throwing him. Sadly the one person he did want to notice, Avalarian, was paying no heed to him whatsoever. In fact she had even moved to a new table to be away from him. Then the door opened and in came Lyrellyn CZim-Relyn, limping along carefully. Duone Bathers sighed heavily.

"And what is your excuse for being late?" he asked.

"Fell off my heels," he said, and seated himself at his desk.

Bathers ground his teeth in annoyance, but did not reprimand him; he wasn't about to chastise a boy of Imperial lineage, no matter how distant. Then Lyrellyn cast a look at Czamkiar, and froze, eyes large. Czamkiar sighed, and Dahli fought back a giggle. Avalarian would not look at him because she was scared of his white skin. Lyrellyn was clearly in love.

"Great," Czamkiar grumbled. "I can just see how this conversation is going to go. 'Heia, Dad? I'm dating a Bird of Prey. If I marry him, your own son will be a Lord and you will be a peasant.' I bet he'll love that."

"There are worse fates," said Diza.

"Yeah," said Czamkiar. "I could be dating a Siriusian."

Diza clobbered him with her book bag. Bathers was about to say something, when another boy spoke up.

"So when is it arriving?" asked the boy. Apparently Dahli and Diza had arrived in middle of discussion.

"Next week," said Duone Bathers. "I decided that since it has to do with what we are currently working on in class that I would bring it in."

Dahli listened to this, unwilling at first to ask what was arriving, but the knot in her gut told her it was likely the faelin. She wrote her question down on a pad of paper and pushed it towards Czamkiar. He quickly scribbled a reply; the faelin was due to arrive just after the two-day respite and come Four or Fiveday, they would dissect it. Dahli passed the note on to Diza, then sat silent, eyes focused on Duone Bathers, just staring. She did not know what she was going to do about this, but she was not about to cut up the faelin.

Dahli hadn't run across an actual breathing faelin more than two or three times in her life. Apart from being used as lab animals, they were also kept as status pets by the wealthy. They made excellent pets, she'd heard, though unpredictable. There had been an incident a few months back where a man who had lived with only his faelin for a number of years had gotten married. When the fellow brought his new bride home, the faelin had been waiting. As the woman entered the room, the creature leapt, felling her like a prey animal, and went straight for her face. Close to two hundred stitches had closed the wounds, and several cosmetic operations restored most of her good looks. The man shot the faelin.

Faelins came from the steaming jungle planet of Faela, a young planet bursting with bright and unusual creatures. The faelins were a deep rust colour, their hair a dark red, their eyes a heated, luminous green. They were slender, long limbed beings, inquisitive for the most part, rather trusting and non-aggressive. The race had been discovered many years ago by a convoy of Kryphisian trade ships. The ships had pulled into orbit around the then-nameless planet, waiting to make contact with other freighters. It was during the wait that a few of the people aboard the ships decided to send down a shuttle to see if there was life.

There was not only life, there was soon a booming trade in faelins, and the creatures ended up everywhere. The more fortunate ones became pets of the Kryphisian generals, the not-so-lucky ended up in labs and other, less savoury places. The military used them to guard their buildings, preying on the faelin's easily-influenced nature. Nobody raised the question as to what exactly a faelin was, be it human or animal, until the much doted-on pet of some military figure presented him with twins. The babies were fair-skinned with white hair. Neither was a faelin characteristic, though the man insisted it was simply some quirk of the genes. Then the question was brought into being, and remained a topic of discussion and theory until modern times.

There were two main differences which scientists used to support the argument that faelins weren't human. First, they were hermaphrodites, both male and female united in the same long, red body. But more than this, faelin could not speak. They were by no means mute; they could make a whole array of sounds. They barked, yipped, howled, growled, snarled, trilled, and roared. The most common sounds were the barks, yips and trills, which seemed to pass as conversation. Barking was reserved for play and for friends. Howling was pure distress, and growls were fairly multi-purpose. As a former Duone of Dahli's had once put it, growls "could mean anything from 'I love you' to 'you're going to lose that hand in a moment'."

The only faelin Dahli had ever had any real contact with was Sikine. He had been the pet of her seventh-year Duone, and the man's constant companion. He didn't accompany him to school, but that was the only place he didn't go. Markets, parks, concerts and parties were everyday dealings to him, and Sikine never let 'his' Sferkkaan out of his sight. He had to wear the mandatory leash, but even this had been gotten around. More than once Dahli had seen Sikine up a tree or trailing along after the Duone with his leash either draped around his neck or tied loosely around his waist. This way, if anyone reminded his owner that he had to wear a leash, he could respond, "He is wearing a leash."

It was Sikine who coloured Dahli's whole image of Faelins. Once when Dahli had been travelling down a back road, she saw Duone Ryer's green conni bounce by. Duone Ryer, however had not been the one driving. Dahli could have sworn neither of them was sober. She had thought about them frequently since they had moved away last year, and missed both of them.

Dahli thought about her old Duone's companion. Surely that was what he had been, a companion, a friend. Nothing that could learn to drive was a pet. Certainly it was nothing to be stuck in a lab and dissected. Dahli stared at Duone Bathers, her green eyes focused on his face. She could see his lips move, but she could hardly hear a word he said. She was far away in her own mind, thinking...

****

School let out for the day, finally. Dahli was spared having to explain where her paper was as the Duone had put off collecting the assignments until tomorrow. Dahli, Diza and Czamkiar left the school and walked down to the Contempo, a popular hang-out for both teenagers and leftover revolutionaries, unsure as to what they should do with themselves now that the war was over. It was, in fact, the only place in Second City where one could get a cup of coffee; albeit watered down and ludicrously expensive. Trade with the South Continent was spotty at best, and coffee was a luxury, not a necessity of life. In fact the only reason the Contempo served coffee at all was because the same worn-out revolutionaries that haunted it made trips down to the South Continent to bring up the beans. As Dahli walked into the café, she had no idea at all she was in the same room with a man who mere days ago had given a small sack of coffee to Khandid Stracona.

Dahli spotted Randish the moment they entered the place. He was the only Siriusian present, and there was no mistaking him as anything other than someone who lived in the Lower Cylinder. His eyes were obscured by cords of long, shaggy hair that spilled down over the collar of his over-sized black jacket, and it was hard to tell where the hair ended and the coat began. The hands that rested on the table top were large and broad, the oversized knuckles giving them a spidery look. His features, what Dahli could see of them, were beautifully chiselled, the lips largish and sensual. His skin was dark, so when he smiled at Diza's approach his large, white teeth with their gigantic canines glared into view like a feralyke's smile. Then, as if recalling the all-too-useful looking devices, he forced his lips back down over them. He stood up to greet them, rising above their heads on long, leather clad legs. His tall boots were fastened with an array of straps and buckles. More buckles were attached to the wide belt that circled his hips. Silver chains hung in careful artistry from the black jacket and a studded leather collar rested around his throat. As Diza stepped forward to put her arms around the neck of the hairy, rangy being, Dahli could fully understand why her friend did not want her father to get a look at her boyfriend.

"Dahli, Czamkiar," said Diza, taking the creature by one long wrist, "this is Randish."

"Hi," said Czamkiar. Dahli found she was unable to say anything.

"Have you been here long?" Diza asked Randish as they sat down. She made an attempt to clear some of the heavy cords of hair out of Randish's face, and Dahli was startled to notice he actually had eyes – big brown ones.

"No," he said, his voice soft, and rough. "Just a few minutes." He held up a flat, rectangular object. "Server gave me a list. You read it to me."

"What do you mean, `you read it to me'?"

Randish thought about this for a moment. "You read it to me...please?"

"Can't you read?"

"No."

"Randish..." Diza gently chided, and he grinned that awful toothy grin, resting his head against Diza's shoulder. Dahli found it fascinating that he actually had to crouch to be able to look her in the eye.

They each ordered their food, Randish asking for shaumaus. He flinched when Dahli lit a cigarette, an animal reaction to the smoke. She recalled Diza saying he was from off the planet, and after only one or two puffs, she stubbed it out.

"He's sweet," Dahli commented later, when Randish had gone to the washroom.

"Isn't he just?" gushed Diza, all smiles.

"He's hairy," said Czamkiar. "Are you sure he's got an upper face?"

169

"Clart," said Diza.

"How'd he get to Sferkkaa?" asked Dahli.

"Same way they all did," said Diza. "He was caught by the alien poachers and brought back as a lab animal. Except shortly after he arrived the Emperor declared that there were no more experiments to be made on Siriusians, and the ones that wished to remain on Sferkkaa had to be provided for. After the ones who wanted to go home were brought back, all expeditions to the planet were banned."

"So how come the Emperor didn't ban experiments on faelins as well?"

"Siriusians don't bark," said Czamkiar.

Dahli picked at the food before her thoughtfully. "I wish I knew of a way to stop Duone Bathers from bringing in that dead body."

"Not much we can do," said Diza. "You did everything you could, you even went and saw the Emperor about it."

"I guess," said Dahli, "but it makes me ill. Oh well. Maybe I can't stop him, but I don't have to participate in this, either. Hey when are we going to go see the space ship? It landed last night."

"Tonight," said Diza. "I can't go now, I promised Dad I'd help him start the back yard garden."

"Yeah we have to start ours too," said Dahli. "No planting veggies now, no eating veggies later. Why can't we grow candy trees?"

"Well we all have to do it whether we like it or not," said Czamkiar. "Lyrellyn gave me a box of goldenspear seeds. I'm too scared to plant them."

"Goldenspear?!" said Dahli. "You mean those succulent delectable little pieces of yellow deliciousness most people would kill to have??"

Czamkiar was blushing furiously from under his makeup. "They're hard to grow and I don't want to waste them! He gave me eight seeds! If his dad catches him giving them away he'll skin him."

"Grow them inside in a closet," said Diza. "Anyplace hot, damp, and dark will do it."

"Boy he really likes you, doesn't he?" said Dahli.

"Yeah, he does. I asked him not to give me such fancy presents in the future, especially since I really like Avalarian. It's not right getting gifts from someone I'm not sure I like. I'd like him a lot better if he wasn't a boy." Czamkiar sighed. "Thank you Kryphis for making a very awkward time in my life ever so much more so."

"You could always ask out Atania," said Dahli. The name was greeted with the standard "EEEEEYYYEEEEEEEEWWWW!"

"Actually *she* asked *me* out," said Czamkiar. "Right after she saw Lyrellyn give me the seeds, and a kiss. Suddenly I was the most fascinating boy in the school. She doesn't want me. She just wants me because Lyrellyn does, so I must be valuable, right? Well even if Avalarian doesn't like me I'll never go out with Atania. I'd go out with Lyrellyn first because at least I know he really likes me."

"Wow," said Dahli. "Czamki that's really awful."

He shrugged. "Yeah, well, nothing I can do about how ugly she is on the inside. I'll just make sure I take really good care of my goldenspear so Lyrellyn doesn't get into trouble for giving it away."

"You know, Czamki," said Dahli, "Going out with Lyrellyn a couple times might be a good idea. It will give you a chance to get to know him better. Maybe you and he could get to be good friends."

Czamkiar seemed to consider this. "Yeah. I guess there's no reason to not make friends with him, right? I mean he's pretty nice." He gave Diza a puzzled look. "How do you know how to grow goldenspear?"

She shrugged. "Wishful thinking I guess. We don't get anything fancy for our allotments but I can still look through the books at all the things I would like to have in my garden. Wish I could do what Draephus CZimcocious is doing."

"What's that?" asked Dahli.

"Hiring about twenty people to restore the old fruit and nut orchards behind his castle, the big beaker," said Diza, annoyed. "He doesn't lift a finger but he manages to abide the laws stating vacant land must be used for farming while not changing his castle grounds an inch. Meanwhile me and Dad have to dig out the dead barrelwood tree ourselves to plant kaisa because that's all that will grow in our area. Bleh!"

"Grow puppy-noses," said an old man at the table beside theirs.

The four looked to him. He was old and mangy and had clearly fought in many battles. He was also drunk.

"Grow puppy-noses," he repeated.

"Puppy-noses?!" said Dahli. "You mean those big floppy blue flowers with the black center?"

He nodded. "You plant several rows. Half of them you harvest the flowers for fresh salads, the other half you let go to seed to have for the winter. You can get eight or nine harvests of puppy-noses and still have fresh vegetables in summer and stores for the winter." He smiled at them blearily. Diza laughed.

"Thank you! I had no idea they were edible!"

"You can also grow snow-buttons," said a younger man at another table. "You dry them and they make great seasoning for all sorts of different dishes."

Diza looked stunned. "You mean those grow in mushy boggy soil?!"

"They love mushy boggy soil," said the younger man. "In some parts of the island they even grow wild."

Diza began making notes. Dahli had no idea if Diza would have any luck growing either puppy-noses or snow-buttons, but anything was better than a garden full of kaisa.

****

The group of friends finished up their meal and parted ways, Dahli and Czamkiar watching Diza walk off with her enormous, shaggy boyfriend. He made her look like a child, his huge hand engulfing hers.

"We should follow after them," said Czamkiar, "so we can pick up the pieces in case he trips and falls on her."

Dahli narrowed her eyes and grinned wickedly. "Yeah, well, if he falls on her I don't think she will let him up, and she doesn't need us for that." She linked her arm through Czamkiar's. "Come on, I'll walk you home."

Czamkiar did not seem to hear her. He was looking across the street to a leggy, skinny boy in high heels with red and black feathers on his coat. After a moment, he looked to Dahli.

"I'm gonna go talk to Lyrellyn. See you at the ship later tonight?"

She smiled. "All right. Later."

They parted ways, and Dahli continued on her own way home. She greeted Teirra and Atterick as she came in, heading upstairs to her room to finish her history paper. This did not take as long as she had feared it would, and supper was almost ready by the time she came back down again. Dahli decided that it must have been Teirra's evening to cook; she didn't smell smoke. Atterick was seated in a chair near the fireplace when Dahli came downstairs. His eyes were closed, chin resting on his chest. Dahli brought her face mere centimetres from his and asked loudly, "Are you awake?"

"No."

"Oh." She sat down on the floor, ignoring the fact that there was a roomful of perfectly good chairs. "How long is your band playing at the music hall?"

Atterick yawned, stretching. "Well, we were only supposed to play until Sevenday, but it looks like we'll be asked to stay another two nights."

Dahli grinned. "Atterick, the great new Ra musician of the year."

He laughed. "Not yet, but maybe someday."

"Do you suppose I could sneak in to see you play?"

"Not likely, but if I meet anyone famous I'll be sure to tell you."

Dahli grinned. She briefly considered showing him her cartoon, but decided against it. She wasn't sure why, but there were reasons she wanted to keep it to herself other than the obvious ones. It was hers, and she didn't want to share it.

She ate her supper and finished her homework, then went to meet Diza and Czamkiar down by the spaceship.

****

"I am a horrible person," was the first thing Czamkiar said as he approached Dahli and Diza on the sidewalk opposite the gargantuan bulk of the interstellar ship.

"Why?" asked Dahli.

"Lyrellyn asked me over for dinner on Eightday evening. I said yes. Now I'm stealing his seeds and eating his food!"

"Czamki it's not theft if he gives them to you," said Dahli. "And you don't have to accept them. Say no if you are not comfortable accepting things from him!"

"Well I thought I may as well say yes since you were the one who said I should give him a chance," he said ruefully.

"Oh so now this is all my fault. Scruffin' lovely," said Dahli.

"Everything is your fault," said Diza. "We took a poll and the emperor agreed."

"Charming," said Dahli. "Well we're being charged by an alien teenager, I suppose that's my fault too."

"Yes," said Diza and Czamkiar in unison.

173

They watched the girl run to them, clutching some sort of rectangular device to her chest. Her eyes were brown and large, and her long brown hair was held back with pink clips with sparkling bows on them. Certainly nothing Dahli would wear, but then this girl was from rather far away. She spoke with a ponderous accent, and her hand gestures were so clumsy as to be nearly incomprehensible.

"I am so happy to feralyke birds with age!"

Dahli, Diza and Czamkiar were unaware that they were currently giving the girl the exact same look their emperor had quite recently. She rolled her eyes and consulted the device she had. Then repeated herself.

"It's so nice to see someone my own age, it's been months! I just had to come say hi!"

"Heia," said Dahli. She and Diza snapped their attention to Czamkiar as he began speaking a language they did not know. The newcomer was clearly so excited that he could speak her language she nearly hugged him.

"Exactly when and where did you learn to speak 'Earth'?" demanded Dahli.

Czamkiar smiled. "Where there are girls, there is a way," he said.

"You got thrown out of languages class and the duone called it a mercy killing," said Diza.

The girl looked nervous, clearly not understanding what was going on. Since Czamkiar was not likely to tell her, Dahli borrowed the translator the girl held and explained, while Czamkiar grinned and looked wholly unrepentant. The girl laughed.

"That is like me and math. My name is Gemma."

"I'm Dahli," said Dahli. "This is Diza, and this is Czamkiar."

"Please come in, it would be so nice to have someone to shaumaus with!"

"All right," said Dahli. "I haven't had a nice shaumaus with someone in ages."

Diza elbowed her. Together the four crossed the street to the ship, entering the wide door and slowly walking up the stairs to the main gathering area. There were instruments set out, plugged in and ready to play, as well as tables with bottles and glasses arranged neatly on their surfaces.

"We had a party here last night," said Gemma, using her

translator. "It was the informal greeting of the arrival on your planet."

Czamkiar picked up a random red feather from the floor. "I see Lyrellyn's dad was here," he said.

"Bird of Prey," said Gemma, her eyes sparkling. They laughed. Czamkiar fell into the role of translator, just to make it easier to speak without having to use the device.

"Well you learned that phrase pretty well," said Dahli. She seated herself on one of the large couches, and noticed a puff of some sort of fluffy matter come out. She picked it up.

"One of the guests had faelins," said Gemma.

Dahli looked up. "Draephus CZimcocious was here?!"

"Yes, last night, with his faelins. One of them chewed the couch. How did you know it was him?"

"I *looooove* Draephus," said Dahli. "He's my favourite of all the Gryphons, and probably the only person who owns faelins who would have been here last night. I can't believe you got to meet him and his faelins!"

"I didn't like him," said Gemma.

Dahli's head snapped in the direction of the other girl, her eyes large. "What?! *Why?!*"

"He is cold," she said softly. "I hated having him in the room. He smells like death. He feels like death. He frightens me."

"Well he's been through a lot," said Diza. "To be honest we all have, though some had it worse."

"A bath wouldn't kill him," said Gemma.

Diza put herself between Dahli and Gemma, trying to avert a fight. "Look I'm sure he bathes, and believe me he's not my favourite either. But he's been through things we can't even imagine, and the smell may not be his fault. It could be anything."

"I think it's that coat," said Gemma. "Does he take it off or has it grown onto him?"

"It. Comes. Off," growled Dahli.

Gemma was holding her ground. "Well it smells and I'm sure he could get another. I can't imagine how his friends put up with it."

A thin little form walked into the middle of the conversation, wearing only his pants and nothing else. Dahli felt her breath catch in her chest as she recognized the man, even without his trademark slouch hat, and saw what he looked like beneath his clothing. Mars David was nothing but sinew and bone and scars, with an odd lump near his spine that looked like a badly-healed break. He had clearly been in the shower recently, as his long hair was wet, and he smelled of moisture and soap. Dahli watched him walk over to a table, pick up a bottle, and pour himself a drink. Then he turned to Gemma, speaking very softly, and very coldly. Dahli had no idea what he was saying. She was too busy staring at the marks all over his body; feralyke bites that were badly healed, the marks of Kryphisian torture devices, and a long slash across his chest, possibly caused by a knife. His long hair hid some of it, but not enough. It frightened Dahli to think what this man, who always seemed so bright and happy and playful, had survived.

By the time Mars finished speaking, Gemma looked as if she would like to burst into tears. He had a long drink from his glass, refilled it, then returned to whatever it was he was doing on the ship. Dahli and Diza remained quiet as Czamkiar said a few things to Gemma, who shook her head and rose to her feet.

"I'll be right back," she said, and left hastily. As soon as she was gone, Dahli and Diza turned to Czamkiar.

"What did Mars say?" asked Diza quietly.

Czamkiar looked shaken. "He was angry. I mean… *angry*. He said if Draephus smells like death it's because he's had to crawl through it on his stomach. And if Draephus smells like death then they all smell like death, because they were all crawling through it together. And snippy little children, who are fortunate enough to have no idea what sorts of things they did to stay alive in the depths of the Cylinder, should just keep their judgmental little declarations to themselves."

"Wow," said Dahli. "That's… harsh."

"Well it's no secret all the Gryphons are close," said Diza.

Dahli leaned close to Diza and whispered; "Yeah but that coat does smell."

"Yeah but there is a difference between knowing it smells and knowing exactly *why* it smells. Mars knows why. I think that's the part we're missing here," said Czamkiar.

The three sat in silence for a moment, then Dahli said; "Mars David just walked by wearing nothing but his pants and we did nothing about it. What is wrong with us?!"

"I'll save the Mars-molesting for when he's not breathing fire," said Diza. "Hey do you suppose Yuri was here?! I would love to meet Yuri."

Dahli would normally take the opportunity to make cracks about

Yuri Stracona, but she was reluctant to do so with Mars David in close proximity and ill humour. And speaking of Mars…

He returned to the room, dressed now, picking up cushions as if looking for something. There was a woman with him, with long red hair and fair skin. She was quite a bit taller than he, and both were speaking quietly, with a great deal of intensity. If Mars was aware of the three teenagers sitting on the enormous couch, he gave no indication. He found what he was looking for; some small object Dahli could not identify, then turned to the tall woman with the red hair. They spoke intensely, and rather angrily. Then Mars drew out the object, which Dahli saw was his telecom. As the woman continued to try to talk to him, he called a number, then began speaking to someone.

"Draephus? Heia. Can you come get me? Well I *sound* upset because I *am* upset, can you please come get me? At the space ship. All right."

Mars snapped the 'com shut, put his hat on over his wet hair, and abruptly moved past the red-haired woman. She crossed her arms and looked defiant. Dahli listened to the sound of his boots clicking down the stairs, and then the sound of him pushing the doors open angrily. Through the windows, Dahli, Diza and Czamkiar saw him cross the street, heading for a corner that had a street lamp. They watched him stop beneath it, clearly upset. When they looked up, they saw the woman with the red hair was gone.

"What did they say?" whispered Dahli to Czamkiar.

"He said; I told you because I like you. She said; you should have told me before you came to bed with me. He said; if I thought it was anything that could affect you then I would have. After that it was just sort of more of the same, then he called Draephus and told the woman not to worry about it, he'd take his diseases and go."

"Wonder what class of virus he has?" said Diza.

"Can't be anything too bad or he wouldn't be out walking around," said Czamkiar. "These people from Earth don't understand – we're *all* infected with something or other. I guess it scares them."

They watched Mars David stand across the street, looking tiny, smoking a cigarette in a pool of light beneath a street lamp. He was shivering.

"I'd go out there and hug him if I thought he'd let me," said Diza.

"I think he needs some alone time," said Dahli. "Besides, there's

Draephus. Wow. He must have been close."

Raski's black conni pulled up before Mars. Draephus got out of one side, Raski the other, and moments later Mars was being cuddled and hugged by his friends. Raski wrapped a long cloak around Mars, and the three got into the vehicle and drove away.

"Poor baby," said Dahli. "Wonder what he has?"

"Heia," said a slightly raspy voice. The three turned to see Gemma standing there, looking a little deflated and sad.

"Sorry," she said. "I didn't know his smelly coat was a source of planetary pride."

"It's not," said Czamkiar. "We're all just… rather protective of him. And I think Mars wasn't really upset with you. I think you just happened to get in the way of an already bad mood."

Gemma sat down on the couch with them. "Yeah Missy was really upset with him earlier. Screaming she didn't want whatever diseases he had. Does he have a disease?"

"Gemma," said Czamkiar quietly, "everyone you sit beside, or talk to, or pass on the street, has a disease here. Every single one of us. The ones who are contagious are in hospitals. The rest of us who are not contagious are out wandering the streets living our lives. I have R-8. That means I'm prone to issues with my major organs. Dahli has C-969, which means she has bio-toxins living in her liver. Diza has X-11. That means she's ugly and she smells bad."

Diza walloped him with a pillow. Gemma laughed.

"I didn't know that. I kinda wish they had told us. That's why Missy had a fit – we have some pretty bad viruses on Earth, too. Ones that make you bleed out your eyes before they kill you."

"Yeah they should have told you," agreed Dahli. "But you can tell Missy that Mars does not have anything she can catch. And I'm sure he didn't mean to be nasty to you. It's just that he and Draephus are really good friends."

"Draephus is pretty good friends with Raski, too," Gemma said. She leaned in to gossip, clearly glad to be away from any arguing. "Last night when the party had been going on for a few hours, and everyone was pretty drunk, I was going to my room when I found them together in the hall. And they were kissing. Not like… kissing. But like… really… I mean bodies rubbing together and everything!"

"Please tell me you took pictures," said Dahli, as Diza mimed wiping drool from Dahli's chin.

Gemma reached for her phone. Sferkkaans certainly had cellular phones, but Dahli had never seen one like this. Gemma tapped the screen, seeking something.

"I think I want one of these," said Czamkiar.

"You'd just break it," said Diza.

Gemma finally found what she was seeking, and showed Dahli the photo. Dahli stared, eyes wide, jaw hanging. It was Raski Jervyas, his back against the wall, eyes closed, lips parted, his arms draped around the neck of the taller man holding him. Draephus' large, scarred hands were resting on Raski's ribs, having pushed Raski's shirt up to expose the gleaming black skin, and they were kissing as if there was absolutely no one else in the world.

"If you ask me," said Gemma dryly, "they like each other."

"Who do I have to kill for a copy of that photo?" asked Dahli. "I'm shameless. I'll stoop to anything."

Gemma smiled. "Well if we haven't got off to too bad a start with me saying Draephus is scary, then I'll trade it to you to show me around the city tomorrow."

"Done," said Dahli and Czamkiar at the same time for completely different reasons. Diza just rolled her eyes.

"We have school tomorrow," said Diza, "but after school will be fine."

"Great!" said Gemma. "I have school too. Come by when you're done. It'll be fun! Now I just have… one question." Gemma turned her head and looked into Czamkiar's blue eyes, smiling as he gazed at her.

"And that is?" he asked.

Gemma fluttered her eyelashes. "Where do you boys buy your shoes?"

He grinned. "I'll show you."

"Oooh I bet you will. Dahli? Where do I send the photo?"

"Good question," said Dahli. "Here's another good question – is your fancy phone compatible with our technology?"

Gemma shrugged. "Must be. Khandi used my phone to send a copy of this picture to some place called The Gryphon's Roost."

****

Draephus wasn't sure why, but there was something about being in Raski's black conni that made himself, Mars and Raski act like fools.

They tore down the unlit road at an insane speed; sailing over every slight bump as they roared through the night like a black comet, trying to stay alive long enough to reach the music hall.

"Turn on the receiver," said Raski, not seeming to notice when Mars cornered on two wheels. Draephus reached over from the back seat to turn on the receiver, and the three were confronted with the dubious honour of hearing themselves.

"Turn it off," said Mars.

Raski lunged forward to prevent his friend from doing so. "No, no, wait, I want to hear this. Listen."

They did, Mars sighing.

"Did you hear that?" Raski yelled. "That progression stinks, it always stank. It sounds like somebody's messed with the speed."

"If you hate the quinticord line, you should have complained to Khandid while we were recording it," said Mars.

"Ah you can't tell Khandi anything," said Raski with a dismissive wave of his hand. He sank back into the passenger's seat.

"I don't know about that," said Draephus, "I've heard you tell Khandid lots of things."

"Yeah," said Mars. "I've heard you tell him he's an unartistic pink nightmare, and that he doesn't know a quint line from a brain haemorrhage."

"Hard to understand why he doesn't pay any attention to you when you offer such constructive criticism," said Draephus.

"Yeah and you hang out with little girls in restaurant bathrooms, so what does that make you?"

"Šukat you, man!" yelled Draephus in mock rage, pouncing over the seat at Raski. He accidentally crashed into Mars, who lost control of the vehicle, and suddenly they were hydroplaning in circles on the wet black road. Draephus was thrown back into the rear seat, while Mars fought madly with the wheel. He felt the conni begin to tip, but miraculously, it did not flip over. Instead it wound to a stop, dead in the centre of the road. The three in the vehicle were silent. There was no sound, save for the disembodied voice of the announcer coming out of the small speaker.

"That was the Mortified Gryphons with another great song, `Flying to the After-Life,' with a wonderful and unusual quinticord arrangement by Khandid Stracona, one of the greatest musicians of our day..."

Mars weakly turned off the receiver. He rested his face against the steering wheel, breathing deeply.

"I think I just gave birth," he said in a strained voice.

Raski's head popped up from beneath the dash. "Hey man, you're not birthing anything in this conni, these seats are leather."

Mars swatted weakly at Raski as Draephus climbed into the front seat.

"I'll drive," he said. Mars nodded and climbed over him to get onto the back of the vehicle. Raski sat up, and, as Draephus started the conni forward, continued his tirade.

"`Great musician'? Khandid? I'm gonna call him up just to tell him he's a clart. Pass me the 'com."

Mars handed Raski his personal telecom, which he accepted, and dialled Khandid's number.

"Hello Raski."

"Khandi you're a clart."

"You're just annoyed because I wrote `Flying to the After-Life' and you didn't. And because the man on the receiver justifiably called me a great musician."

"You heard that?"

"I called in and requested it."

Raski stared at the 'com in his hand for a moment. "WHY WOULD YOU CALL UP AND ASK TO HEAR A SONG YOU WROTE!?"

"Because I know you hate that song, and I also know you go crackers when you can't hear the receiver. So I told the man who I was and asked him to play that song and say how great I am. So now you're annoyed and I got what I wanted. Good night, Raski."

"Clart," said Raski, then hung up, shaking his head. He thumped back into his seat. "He realises now I am going to have to retaliate."

They finally reached Ayre's Music Hall, parking before the grand structure. The Music Hall had been built long ago, painstakingly crafted into a beautiful and acoustically perfect music room. It was one of the most popular places to go for an evening, frequented mostly by professional musicians and those who worked with them. It was the best place to hear new bands and new styles of music, and playing there was considered a necessary milestone along the path to fame.

Mars, Raski and Draephus stepped out of the conni, pausing to watch the small, orange satellites blaze by, trailing light that reflected on the wet street. They crossed the pavement, jogging up the steps that led to the aged structure, darting inside to get out of the rain. They walked into the great ballroom, stopping to look around.

"See anybody famous?" Raski asked as Mars shook out his long, damp hair.

"I don't even see a table," said Mars. "Wonderful. We get to stand in the middle of the floor all night and look stupid."

"Why not?" said Draephus. "We get paid to stand on stage and look stupid."

"Lies, all of it," said Raski. "We're too good-looking to look stupid. Hey there's a table."

They made their way over to the table. It was in a bad location, too close to the towering amp-plants for comfort. The jagged leaves had gone strange shades from too many different types of music, and were vibrating gently from the crowd noise, occasionally twisting to follow a passer-by. However the table did present a good view of the stage. They would have no trouble seeing the band when it came on.

A server materialised by their table, a tall, leggy young man with a lot of shaggy black hair. "Heia. Can I get you anything?"

"A tall, good-looking man, hold the ice," said Raski.

"We don't serve those," the man said. "We only serve guys who look like you." He turned to Mars. "What would you like?"

"Just wine," said Mars.

"Hey," continued Raski to the server, undaunted by his earlier remark, "what are you doing tonight?"

"Burning your solo album."

Draephus burst into laughter, a horrible rasping sound that was more like coughing than laughing. Raski tried and failed to look offended. Mars grinned quietly. The server took Draephus' order and dodged off into the crowd.

"Oh, poor Raski," said Mars fondly. "If you weren't so obnoxious people wouldn't say these things to you."

"Yeah, I guess," said Raski, pouting slightly. Then he brightened. "Okay, plan for the evening. I'm going to pick up the band."

"Why?" asked Mars.

"Role reversal." said Raski. "What about you?"

"Oh I don't know," said Mars. "I just want to have a few drinks and hear the music."

"Draephus?"

Draephus shifted in his seat. "Probably just end up picking a fight."

"Okay," said Raski, "it's a race. Let's see who gets drunk, naked, or killed first."

Mars sighed, shaking his head. Then, catching sight of someone he knew, he rose from his seat and darted off into the crowd. Once he was out of view, Raski leaned forward to give Draephus a soft kiss.

"You're not really going to pick anyone up, are you?" Draephus asked quietly, resting his brow against Raski's.

"No," said Raski. "Everything I want is sitting right here at this table, and is definitely worth waiting for. I just wish we didn't have to hide."

"Well Vesper said we didn't have to, but…"

Raski nodded. "No, I am in full agreement with you. Vesper's your lover and he's my friend, and I think we should definitely wait." He grinned, his eyes glittering. "But I reserve the right to watch you walk and fantasize."

"Watch me walk? Raski you and I both know I don't walk. Stagger, stumble, lope, and fall, yes. Walk, no."

"You stumble and fall all you like. I'll catch you."

Draephus stared into the pale blue eyes. "You shouldn't have to catch me."

"I don't have to catch you. I do it because I want to."

They gazed at each other, staring into each other's eyes, understanding each other on a level no one else could. Then the server came by with their drinks and they sat back in their chairs. Moments later Mars appeared, dropping into his own seat. Then the lights dimmed, and they waited for the band to make their appearance. It was a group called Titan, and while this was the first time Raski, Draephus and Mars were seeing them live, they were not exactly unheard of. Raski in particular made it his business to know who and what feralykes were nipping at the heels of the Gryphons, how much of a real threat they were, and he knew each and every member of Titan by name.

This detail would have scared the clart out of Atterick had he known it.

Raski watched the potential competition with the same sort of coldness he used to regard the enemy aircraft he had rigged to detonate. The five came onto the stage amidst some applause and cheering. First was the drummer, Atterick, who slipped behind his set. Then the striped quinticord player, who called himself by the Earth name of Anthony, stepped across the stage on long skinny legs to a place over by the keybarr. The other three members of the band emerged as well; Taischa the lead singer, Amber the keybarrist from some other indeterminate place, and finally Luka the sepulchord player.

Anthony picked up his quinticord, the warmth of his hand causing it to glow into life. Fine laser lines appeared, running down its length, and the device quietly informed him that it was in tune. He snapped a switch that would allow him to record his performance, and the tiny memory chip in the instrument also glowed into life. Taischa stepped to the front of the stage, hanging himself off of an antiquated stand-up microphone of which he was fond. Then Amber started a low haunting melody, the soft, eerie sound filtering up beneath the applause of the crowd. As the audience fell silent Anthony and Luka could be heard as they came up under the keybarr, quinticord and sepulchord weaving together into a low, undulating harmony. Atterick awaited his cue as Taischa began to sing in his sultry tones, sinewy body swaying to the music.

"They're good," Raski called above the music.

Draephus nodded. "Better than we were when we first started out."

Mars was squinting at one of the people on stage. "What is the quinticord player?"

"Striped," said Raski.

"Oh, no clart, beaker. But what is he? I've never seen a striped alien before."

"Probably a Breed," said Raski.

"Probably painted," said Draephus. "Five trinta says he'll start to run halfway through the set."

The set wore on, and the stripes remained solid. This led to other theories as to what he may be, and finally Mars announced that he was going to go ask the man after the set.

"Oh sure," said Raski. "'Excuse me, but what are you?'"

"I'm sure I can come up with something more tactful than that," said Mars.

"Yeah well you talk to the stripy guy, I want to talk to the little thing they have playing sepulchord."

Mars stared at Raski for a long moment. "You aren't going to do anything to mortify me, are you?"

"I don't know, I haven't done anything to seriously embarrass you in a long time."

"Don't," said Mars.

"Need I remind you that you are a *mortified* gryphon?" said Raski.

"Please, once in a day is enough," said Mars.

The trio ceased their conversation when the quinticord player began to sing. He had a way of moving his body that didn't look quite believable, or perhaps it was the long coat with its high ruff of coarse, bestial hair that caused the illusion. His own mane of long dark hair hung over his fair-skinned features in a veil as his crooning voice rose up into an agonizing scream, trailing off as though into a void. The Gryphons exchanged glances.

"They're good," said Mars.

"Too good," said Raski. "In another year it will be `The Mortified Who?'"

"Not likely," said Draephus.

"Hey," said Raski, "look at what happened to `Nevermind.'"

"They blew themselves into oblivion," said Draephus. "And besides that the lead singer killed himself so it's no wonder they're not around anymore. Even when we do retire, we'll still be The Gryphons. Nothing can take that from us."

"Unless they start calling us has-beens."

"Lighten up, it'll never happen. You always get so morbid when you see young groups with lots of talent and potential. Before we got famous you used to get morbid when you saw established groups."

"It's just that..." Raski began.

"Raski," said Mars, preening his still-damp- hair, "don't worry about it. We're supposed to be enjoying ourselves, not contemplating suicide. Some of us have had a rotten enough time already."

Raski fell silent for a brief time, then said; "I just don't want to be watching a `Where Are They Now?' show and see us on it."

"Well you could always go to school and learn a trade," said Draephus. "I mean if this clarty band we're in doesn't break the billion-trinta mark soon we may as well call it quits."

Raski glared at his friend. "You're such a sarcastic clart, Draephus."

****

The set came to its conclusion, and the band stepped down to enthusiastic applause and cheering, unaware as to exactly who was watching them. Atterick joined a red-haired woman at a table, his four band-mates following in a loose group. All save for Taischa, who went to a back room behind the bar.

"Were we all right?" he asked.

She laughed. "Yeah, fair to mediocre."

Atterick kissed her face, then leaned back in his seat. Draephus glanced at Raski, smiling faintly at the predatory light in his eyes as he stared at the younger performer. He nudged him gently.

"Raski, they're kids, not fresh meat."

Raski gave him a sidelong glance. "Every new band is the enemy. They are better than we were starting out. We need to make sure they don't get better than we are now."

"You are so hot when you're evil."

Mars looked at them. "Are you two having an affair?"

"No," said Draephus and Raski in unison.

"Really? Because I've never heard you call Raski 'hot' before."

"Get me another drink and I'll even call you 'hot'," said Draephus.

Raski picked up his drink and rose from his chair. "Okay, people, I am going in to enemy territory."

"Take this," said Mars, handing Raski a pen. "In case you have to dig your way out of a prison camp."

"What, no rib?"

Raski began walking to the table, watched by Draephus and Mars. He approached Luka, who blinked and stared back, eyes wide, clearly recognizing the man approaching. Luka opened his mouth to say something, but nothing came out. No one else even noticed the intruder until he walked up to the table and spoke.

"Good set," said Raski, "you were great."

Luka stared back at the man whose style he had been trying hard on stage to emulate. "Thanks," he said, his voice a little weak.

Atterick made himself stand up and extend a hand to Raski. "Hi, I'm Atterick. This is my wife Teirra, this is Anthony, and Amber, and this is Luka. Have a seat."

Raski accepted the hand. "Hi, you're the drummer. My friend over there was watching you, he was pretty impressed. I could tell because he blinked once."

"Your… friend?" asked Atterick.

"Yeah, Draephus," said Raski happily, sitting down. "He's sitting over there." Raski indicated the general direction from whence he had come. He turned his blue-white eyes towards Luka. "Been playing long?"

"Twelve years," came the soft reply. The expression on Luka's face was one of wary disbelief. That expression did not change when Mars decided to make himself known as well. He walked up to stand behind Raski's chair, resting his hands on the tall back. He looked down at him fondly, long, fuchsia-dyed hair spilling from under his hat and trailing down to lie across Raski's shoulders.

"Are you bothering these people?"

"No, but I am sure you will."

"I doubt that," said Atterick. "Have a seat." As Mars seated himself, Atterick asked, "What brings you down here?"

Mars shrugged. "Just thought we'd come in and hear the band. Draephus said he heard you were good. He was right."

"That's pretty high praise, coming from you," said Atterick.

Mars just smiled. Next to him, Raski once more turned his attention to Luka, who still had the same I-don't-believe-I'm-talking-to-you look on his face.

"Nice old sepulchord you have," Raski said.

"Really?" said Luka. "It's a bit old, it acts up sometimes."

"It's a Legri, though, isn't it? Get it fixed and hang on to it. You can't beat them. I had one, but I sold it. Dumbest thing I ever did."

Mars lit up a cigarette, exhaling smoke. "I doubt that. I happen to know you have done stupider things just today."

"Find a planet," said Raski.

Mars and Raski grinned at each other, then they both turned their attention to Anthony simultaneously.

"Listen," began Mars, "I realise this is rude but we just have to ask..."

"They're real," said Anthony.

A chair being pulled violently from the table announced the return of Taischa. He thumped down into it, not seeming to notice those about him. He sat motionless, eyes fixed ahead, a dull smoking anger enshrouding him.

"Did you talk to him?" asked Teirra gently.

Taischa said nothing for a moment. "Yeah I did." His tone was quiet. He stared into his glass as he spoke, indicating he did not much wish to discuss things. "He asked me to come over and see him when we finished playing." He set down his glass, then suddenly noticed Raski and Mars. Taischa stared, and shook his head once, blinking, as if trying to convince himself that the two strangers at the table really were Raski Jervyas and Mars David, not an illusion.

"Heia," he said.

"Heia," said Raski. "We just came by to tell you we thought your band is great."

Taischa seemed to brighten a little at this. "Really? Thanks."

The server came over to the table. He paused when he saw Raski, a wary look on his face.

"Baby!" exclaimed Raski.

"I thought you'd left. I mean, what would you like?"

"Are you available?"

"Absolutely not."

"Then I'll have another Brain Surgeon."

The server took their orders and went his way, Raski watching him leave. He sighed.

"Looks and money, and still no one to love me."

Mars kissed his nose. "That's because you're an obnoxious clart."

"And you're short."

It came time for the second set. Mars watched Anthony as he rose and began walking over to the stage, one eyebrow raised, green eyes fixed on his lean frame. As if sensing the look, Anthony stopped and looked over his shoulder at Mars, then, after a pause, returned to the table.

"I'm singing this set; think you… might want to join me? First song is 'Watching It All' by…"

Before Anthony could finish asking, Mars bounced out of his seat. "Try and stop me, that is my favourite song. I'll do the high parts."

Teirra and Raski watched Mars leave with Anthony, then Raski sighed. "Abandoned again."

"I think Mars likes Anthony," said Teirra.

"Yeah well there's a whole lot to like," said Raski. "Be nice to see Mars hook up with someone who can put up with his nervous disorders and fondness for explosives."

Teirra looked at Raski. "He's not seeing anyone?"

Raski gave her a crooked smile. "Nope. He's sweet and pretty and intelligent, and an absolute šukating mess emotionally. Spent a few months in a Grey Boy prison. He met a very nice girl last night, shared some of his personal information he thought she should know, and she threw him out. Everyone wants the pretty lead singer, but no one wants his issues. And I love Mars to pieces but he's… a mess."

Teirra swallowed, turning slightly green. "I heard that part about the prison. I wasn't sure it was true."

"It's true. Makes him a little… nervy, I guess the word is. Most people want to be with Mars David, the famous singer. What they get is Mars David, the guy who had to dig his way out of a torture chamber with his dead friend's rib. They're *not* the same person."

Raski smiled as he watched Mars hop onto the stage between Taischa and Anthony, both of whom were considerably taller than he. Mars looked from one to the other, then darted off to return moments later with a drum case. He placed it before the microphone and stood on it.

"He's awfully cute, though," said Teirra.

"Yeah, he is, and he knows it, and so does Khandid. The pair of them make my teeth hurt. That's why we have Draephus, to cut down on the sugar content. Speaking of Draephus, I should go get him." He paused as he noticed Teirra break into a large smile.

"My younger sister would be bouncing off of the walls right now," she said.

"Is she a Gryphons fan?"

"She's a Draephus fan. Completely and hopelessly in love with him. She even took up the drums a while ago."

"Tell her he snores and leaves his clothes strewn all over the place."

"She won't care. She'll probably pull my head off because I got to meet him."

Raski turned in his seat and motioned Draephus to come over, and grinned when he saw his friend's head fall back and his eyes roll. At last he relented and stood up, walking towards the table.

"So you guys really did fight in the war," said Teirra. "That's not just hype."

"No, we all fought," said Raski. "I was the only one actually in the military, though. I was a fighter pilot, at least until I was shot down and died and a very determined doctor brought me back. Draephus rigged doors and windows to do funny things upon closing. Didn't you?" Raski said as Draephus sat down.

"Among other things." Draephus thumped himself down into the seat next to Raski, his blackened eyes hidden behind his shades.

"Her sister is in love with you," said Raski.

"Poor child," said Draephus.

Raski smiled, running his hand through Draephus' sandy hair. He turned his attention back to Teirra. "So what about you? What did you do in the war?"

"Dressed like a man and kept my mouth shut, mostly, me and my sister both. Hid in the catacombs under the old city with some refugees and a couple of defected Grey Boys who wouldn't let us drink the water."

Raski's eyes lit up. "Jai and Shalsairas, right?"

"That's them! Do you know them?"

"Yeah, I knew Jai and Shal, we all did. Loved those guys. Just sickening what happened."

Teirra blinked. "What happened? What do you mean?"

Raski looked at Teirra, then glanced to Draephus, who said quietly; "They were murdered a few months back. Someone tracked them to their hiding place and butchered the both of them."

Teirra's jaw dropped, and her eyes filled with tears. "No. No tell me that's not true! I loved those two, if it hadn't been for them I'd be dead, and so would about one hundred and fifty other people! They were heroes!"

"Yeah, well, sadly, to someone they were just another couple of Grey Boys," said Draephus quietly. "And if I ever find out who, I'm gonna return the favour."

****

The band played their three sets for the night and left the stage. Mars seated himself next to Anthony, a move not lost on the others seated at the table. The server came around to take orders for the last drink of the evening. Raski didn't order anything, and Draephus was face down on the damp, sticky surface. The hall was going to close soon, but the newly-minted band of friends were not quite ready to part ways yet. It was Anthony who came up with a way to encourage them to stay around a little longer.

"We were going to have a sort of a gathering after the show," he said to Mars. "Like to come along?"

"Sure," he said.

"Yeah, over at our place," said Atterick. "Nothing much."

"Sounds good to us," said Mars. "Be nice to mingle with some normal people for once."

Raski grasped Draephus' head and raised it from the table. "Draephus?"

"Mph?"

"We're taking you someplace else to pass out. Is that okay?"

"Mph."

"Good boy."

They left the music hall, Anthony getting into the conni with Mars and his friends, and followed after Teirra's old conni.

****

Dahli awoke, and she lay listening to the sounds below her in the living room. Dahli had returned home after visiting a couple hours with Gemma, and had been asleep, but the noises she heard were strange enough to wake her. It wasn't like Teirra and Atterick to have people over, and this alone was cause for curiosity. She got out of bed and dressed, then brushed out her long red hair. Satisfied with her appearance, she headed downstairs in her bare feet. The sounds were ones she was familiar with; musicians amusing themselves. She heard a short burst of disjointed harmony, then someone said; "That was awful."

Then there was that laugh. High, a little crazed, a sound that would make a person's skin crawl on dark stormy nights. It brought Dahli up short. She had heard that sound before, it was one she would know anywhere. It sounded for all the world like Raski Jervyas. She stood on the stairs, frozen in her tracks, listening. She heard a quick riff on a sepulchord.

"Hey Mars, remember this?"

There was a lilting, silly spat of music. "Yes!" said a voice. "Oh don't remind me."

`It's them,' she thought. `Here, in my house. It can't be them. Could it?'

She continued down the stairs, pausing for a moment at the base of the steps, composing herself. Then she turned the corner.

Raski was holding Luka's old sepulchord, working sounds out of the aging instrument that Luka could never coax from it. Mars was seated next to Teirra, talking animatedly with her about something, seemingly enjoying himself. Dahli blinked and shook her head, trying to determine if she was dreaming. She decided she wasn't, and very nearly fled back up the stairs. Conquering this urge, however, she headed casually across the floor to the kitchen, needing a moment to hide and gather her wits.

Draephus turned around when he heard someone come into the room, and he stopped as he saw who it was. Dahli stared back at him. The two studied one another for a moment.

"Heia," he said.

"What are you doing in my kitchen?" came out of Dahli's mouth before she had a chance to stop it.

"Getting a glass of water. That okay with you?"

"Yeah, sure."

She smiled at him, and he returned it. For the first time in her life she saw him under an unflattering light, and she had to admit that there were better looking men in the world. His eyes still had bruises around them, and the partially grown-in eyebrow showed a ragged scar. His coloration was grey at best, and the coat was too hideous to mention. He dumped the water left in his glass into the sink, and walked over to Dahli. He grinned maliciously, showing a chipped canine tooth.

"You're gonna rat me out to my sister, aren't you?" she said.

"Absolutely."

He hung an arm around her shoulders, and the two walked into the living room. Teirra saw the two come out of the kitchen and sat bolt upright. She opened her mouth to say something when Draephus pointed to Dahli with his free hand and said to Raski; "This is the culprit who whacked me with a door."

"Congratulations," said Raski. "You have done what many have attempted, and never survived."

"You two know each other?" said Teirra.

Draephus looked down at Dahli. "Yeah, to an extent." he said.

"Dahli..." began Teirra.

"We don't actually know each other," said Draephus, "we just… run into one another on occasion."

"You whacked him with a door?" questioned Atterick.

"Yeah," said Draephus. "I was in the men's washroom of this fancy restaurant, and just as I'm about to leave she comes breezing in and nails me with the door."

"I said I was sorry," said Dahli.

"It's okay," said Draephus, "I think I needed it." He studied her for a moment. "Isn't that the same shirt you were wearing the last time I saw you?"

"No, this is a different one. Teirra finally talked me into washing the other one, and now it has holes in it."

Mars nudged Teirra. "Talk him into washing his coat."

"No," said Draephus. "The dirt is the only thing holding it together."

"Yeah," said Raski. "Dirt, blood, booze, puke..."

"Not to mention the colonies of insects that have made their home there," said Mars.

"I don't have to take this from you guys," said Draephus. He seated himself on the couch, wrapping his coat about himself. Dahli seated herself in a chair not far from him.

"Oh come on," said Raski, "who better to abuse you than the people who love you?"

Draephus lit a cigarette and ignored the comment. Dahli thought he seemed edgy, and tense, as if he really didn't want to be there. She hoped he didn't leave too soon. Her heart sank as he suddenly asked; "Is there a distillation shop around here?"

"I believe so," said Teirra. "I think it's just a short ways from here."

"Two streets to the left and straight down, I think," said Atterick.

"Wait, wait," said Teirra, exhaling a cloud of smoke from a pipe Anthony had passed her. "Two streets to the left, then straight down to the...oh what's that thing, that building that looks like a wart in bondage? You turn right at the wart..."

"How about if I show him?" Dahli suddenly piped up.

"How do you know where the distillation shop is?" demanded Teirra, grinning.

"The route Diza and I take to school takes us right by it," she said. "Besides, you couldn't give directions to your left ear right now."

"Could too, if I had to," Teirra smiled.

Dahli looked at Draephus. "Do you want me to show you?" All

the while she kept thinking `please say yes, please say yes, please say yes...'

"Sure," said Draephus. "Otherwise I would end up wasting my time looking for a giant wart."

They left the house, walking down the flight of stone steps, across the yard and onto the street where Raski's black machine waited for them. Draephus flung open the door and sat down on the midnight-coloured upholstery. Dahli got in the other side, feeling a little intimidated at how nice the vehicle was.

"Identify yourself, please," said the conni.

"Draephus."

"Good evening, Draephus." The conni started into life. There was a soft hiss as the steel shield slid back, revealing a computerized console, green lights flitting back and forth as the vehicle thought out its next move, then quietly raised itself up onto its axels. The headlights opened, sending forth beams of white light.

"Ready for takeoff," said the conni.

"Yeah, well we won't be going that fast, okay? Gear down a little."

There was a pause. "We won't?"

"No."

There came another pause. "Well, you do realise that I am a high performance vehicle. Asking me to behave like a transit is highly insulting to me."

Draephus glanced over at Dahli, who was laughing. He sighed. "I don't believe this, I'm arguing with a machine. Just drive, will you?"

The black conni lunged forward, hurtling down the road. Dahli was flung back in her seat, laughter stopping dead.

"What is our destination?" inquired the conni.

"Mars' house," said Draephus. "I want to get a vehicle that doesn't argue back."

"Oh," said the vehicle. Then; "Well, fine."

Dahli laughed again. "Whose is this thing?"

"Raski's," said Draephus. "It was given to him by Khandid. And Khandid won't say where he got it. Hey conni, where'd you come from?"

"I'm not speaking to you, you're rude."

Dahli screamed with laughter, rolling in the seat with hilarity. "Could Raski have programmed its computer to act like this?" she asked when she could.

"He could have, but he didn't. This thing was given to him with the attitude pre-programmed. Khandi couldn't have done it; he's smart, but altering complex computer programmes is not his area of expertise. He must have had someone build it for him."

Dahli wiped her eyes, then reached out to touch the soft leather covering the computer board. "What a perfectly wonderful vehicle."

"Don't encourage it." He growled as he heard the song playing on the receiver. "Oh CLART I wish they would give that šukating song a rest! Šukat!"

"Rain Forest!" exclaimed Dahli happily.

"I'M SORRY I WROTE IT!"

"Why? It's brilliant! It's so beautiful! I listen to it in the dark all the time."

"Sick to death of it. Besides it's wrong. No matter how hard I tried I couldn't make it sound like the jungles. It's just wrong. Wrong and bloody awful and Satellite Base Four plays it a hundred šukating times a day."

"Because it's beautiful!"

Draephus made a rude noise, and Dahli laughed.

"Well if you didn't like it then why did you record it?"

"Because Raski and Khandi took my coat and wouldn't let me have it back until I said I would!"

Dahli howled with laughter, and Draephus grinned.

"Yeah you can laugh; you don't have to deal with them on a daily basis."

"Ah you love them, I can tell."

"I do. I adore them. And if you tell them I said that then I'll put you in the trunk." He grinned at her. "C'mon, I'll show you Mars' flowers."

They reached the elaborate estate Mars called home. The great mansion sat dark and silent on its hill, the only light of any sort coming from the luminous flowers that grew around the wide, sweeping alcove jutting from the building's front. Behind the house was the channel that separated their little island from the mainland. The black water lapped gently, smooth waves broken by the light drops of rain that fell. Plants blinked on and off, startled into darkness each time a rain drop touched them. In the distance, the tiny specks of light that were the city of Avalair looked like surreal spots floating in a void. The Sferkkaan night was perfect, the horizon gone for the hours of darkness. Even the quiet hiss of traffic was not to be heard.

Dahli walked over to one of the flowers and crouched before it, sheltering it from the rain with her hands. It remained dark for a little while, then softly it glowed into life, raising its delicate purple head. She stared at it for a time, then moved her hands away. At the first touch of the rain its light went out, petals folding closed, head nodding as though in sleep.

****

Draephus leaned against the front of his own trusty vehicle, watching the young girl. He knew it wasn't her fault, but she was depressing the clart out of him. He watched her play with the flower, making its soft light shine. He'd been half-hoping she'd do something to make him hate her, like climbing all over him in the conni or having a hysterical fit at the sight of Mars' house. But no, he took her up to the place, and all she was interested in was the flowers. It made her endearing. It also made him deeply sad at the thought of how much of his own childhood had been lost. When he had been her age he had been growing illegal mushrooms, surviving in a fallen-down shack that the animals didn't want, and grieving the loss of two sisters and both parents. The eldest had simply disappeared one day. The youngest had been around the same age Dahli was now when she was caught by a Kryphisian patrol and brutalized until she died. His only thought then had been money, and how to get it, and how to keep it so the Grey Boys didn't get it. He'd lost so much in his life that he didn't know if the hole would ever be filled. He knew he had a brother somewhere, but there was no way to find him in the chaos. It was only in the last few months the hospitals had been able to start keeping track of births and deaths; there was certainly no way to track down one man who may well not even be alive. The hole had seemed a little less deep with Vesper in his life, but even he would be gone soon, and Draephus was having to face the crushing guilt of no longer knowing exactly what he felt for him.

Draephus walked over to Raski's vehicle, opening the door and sitting down on the leather seat, closing the door before reaching for the 'com. He picked the small device up, then fished a scrap of paper out of his coat pocket. Reading it, he slowly punched in a very long number. Eventually, he heard ringing, then someone answered.

"Heia?"

"Heia," said Draephus. "I'd like to speak to Vesper, please."

"And who is calling?"

Draephus felt himself becoming annoyed. "It's his husband, Draephus. Who the šukat are you?"

"I'm his new husband. You don't call here anymore; he came down here to get away from you, to die in peace. He's sick of you."

Draephus blinked in shock. "What? Look I have no idea who you really are but I want you to put Vesper on right now."

"No. He's with me now. You go away and leave him alone. He doesn't need you anymore."

Draephus suddenly was blindingly angry, rage flashing up inside of him like the violent burst of fire from a bomb. "You get Vesper and you put him on NOW!"

The line went dead, and Draephus flew into a frenzy. Up by the front of the house, her attention fixed on the Jungle Lamp, Dahli would be unaware of the savage rage enveloping Draephus. She could not even hear him; the conni too well insulated for his screams of hate and agony to reach her. He raved and pounded the dashboard, splitting the flesh of his hands, spraying blood. He had made one mistake, ONE, with Raski, and he had felt lower than dirt. Now he finds out that Vesper had fled to the South Continent never to return, to marry some other man? It couldn't be true, it just could NOT be TRUE!

He dialled the number again, and got the same male voice.

"I WANT TO TALK TO VESPER!" he screamed, and the man hung up.

Draephus lost his mind, and began tearing apart the vehicle from the inside. What had he done to deserve this, what had he ever done? He had the sudden horrible feeling that the only thing wrong with the world was him, and that if he was dead then everything would be fine. A weight sank into his chest, making it difficult to breathe. He thought he was going to be ill. He lit a cigarette and drew on it deeply, and regretted it when the inside of the car began to spin.

Vesper… Vesper had left him? Gone to the South Continent… forever? It couldn't be true. It just could NOT be true! Vesper wouldn't do that to him! Once more he dialled the number. This time the man answered just long enough to hang up. Draephus shattered the phone against the dashboard and screamed, feeling himself splinter within. It was too much. It was far too much. He struggled to remain coherent. He had to go, he had to get out of there, he had to leave, had to numb the hurt. He wanted to get to the distillation shop now.

He stepped out of Raski's destroyed vehicle and walked to his own, feeling as if he was standing above himself. He unlocked the door of his conni, an older vehicle with opaque windows, the body of which was painted a dark stormy grey. A Celestial Hunter, it was called, though Draephus couldn't imagine taking anything as big as this thing hunting. He started the engine, the bright headlights illuminating the drive. Dahli left the flower to itself and walked over to the conni, getting into it. She sank into the soft leather seat.

"Nice," she commented.

"You like nice vehicles?" he asked.

It was an insinuation of sorts, though Dahli wasn't exactly sure what he was implying. She glanced over at Draephus, and had the weird feeling that this was not the same man she had arrived with.

"Yeah I like nice connis," she said. "Probably everybody does."

"Uh huh," he said. "This is an old fellow. I hate new connis."

"It's beautiful," she said, a little uncertain now of what to say to him. She touched the polished wood on the door.

Draephus tore out of the driveway, the conni throwing back white gravel before its tires caught, sending them forward. Dahli seemed frightened by the ferocity with which he took off. She watched his face as he drove, studying the strange expression she saw. Draephus was aware of the way she was looking at him, he just could not seem to be able to do anything about it. He felt as if he had splintered into a thousand fragments, and only a few of them were functioning.

Was he dying? He might be dying. Where was he, anyway? Was the war still on…?

****

Dahli could tell something was very wrong with the man beside her. This was definitely not the person she had arrived with. This was somebody else, not the shaggy, jaded, but basically gentle Draephus CZimcocious. She didn't know who this madman was, but he seemed to be in agony. Something had happened, literally while her back was turned. She took hold of the door handle and held on, then noticed the hands on the wheel were split and dripping blood.

"You're bleeding!"

He shook his head slightly, as if uncertain how to react. Dahli wondered if he even knew where he was. Had he taken some sort of drug? Was he stoned?

"Are we going to the distillation shop now?" she asked, for want of anything useful to say.

The look in the blue eyes implied Draephus CZimcocious had left and now this groutnoll was in charge. "Why? Aren't you happy just to tag along, we gotta have a destination too?"

Dahli looked away, hurt. "No, I guess not."

"Anything I want to do is fine by you, right?"

She didn't like his tone. The sneering sarcasm stung like wind-blown sand. She stared down at her lap, saying nothing. She could feel her hurt turning to anger. Draephus breathed in and out a few times, as if trying to calm down. Dahli watched him try to take command of himself.

"It's got a good stereo," Draephus said, sounding as if he was fighting to be the person he was a few minutes ago. "Try it."

She reached out and turned the device on. A cylinder positioned itself in the play slot, and a moment later she heard the soft sound of jungle pipes playing.

"I didn't know you liked pipe music," she said. It seemed the only thing to say.

"Oh sometimes," he said. "What about you?"

"I like some of it," said Dahli, "I haven't heard that much."

"Guess you just listen to what everyone else does," he said flatly.

Dahli shrugged. "I guess."

"How very individual of you."

They found a nearby distillation shop. Draephus pulled over in front of the small store and got out of the vehicle. Dahli watched him head into the building, puzzled and hurt. She wondered what was going on, what had gone wrong. She wasn't used to being attacked for everything she said, and his coldness was more than merely upsetting, from him it was devastating. She watched the rain fall outside. It was becoming heavier now; it looked as though it may turn into a downpour. She turned her head and looked at the steering wheel, which was covered in blood. There was something on the seat, and when she picked it up she saw that it was a piece of the black telecom she had seen in Raski's car.

She felt cold, setting it down as if afraid he would notice it had been moved. Something had happened, something bad. He wasn't just being a creep for the sake of being a creep; something had broken inside of him. She considered getting out of the vehicle and heading for home on foot, even though she was not familiar with this area, but then Draephus came out, walking through the rain as though it did not exist. He got back into the conni, thrusting a bottle down between the leather seats before lighting another cigarette. He glanced at her.

"So what are you so miserable about?"

Dahli stared at him, her eyes narrowing with anger. Broken or not, she wasn't about to take abuse lying down. "You're not exactly being nice."

"Oh. Am I supposed to feel sorry for that? Am I not living up to your expectations?"

"I wasn't expecting you to put on some big show," she snapped, "I was just happy to meet you."

"Yeah well you've met me. And guess what. I'm a clart."

She stared back at him, eyes narrowed. "No," she said evenly. "You're not."

"Oh, well you'd know better than I would what I'm like."

Dahli thumped back into her seat, arms crossed over her stomach. "Look, just take me home, all right?"

"Why should I?"

"So don't!" she yelled. She threw the door open. She tried to get out of the conni, but suddenly his hand snapped around her wrist. She looked over her shoulder, frightened, seeing him staring back at her. His grip upon her arm loosened, and for a moment she saw the other Draephus emerge; the one she liked.

"Come on," he said in a softened tone. "I'll take you home."

She considered leaving anyway, but after a moment she said; "All right."

She sat back in the seat and shut the door, and watched him as he held the wheel, staring straight ahead. He was shaking visibly, coming apart before her very eyes.

"Are you okay?" she asked quietly.

"I'm good," he said, starting to shiver so hard it was approaching convulsions. "I just… ah… can't quite remember how to make the conni go."

Dahli nodded slowly. She didn't know what was wrong with

him, but clearly he needed more help than she was able to give. She touched his shoulder gently. "Okay, well, how about you just sit here, and I'll go to ask someone."

He nodded. "Yeah, okay."

Dahli slipped out of the vehicle and looked around. The shop Draephus had just come out of was closing, but across the street was a small after-hours club. She doubted they would let her in, but she could ask the bouncer to call an ambulance for her. The club was set between two decaying warehouses, one gutted by fire and falling down. The street was littered by debris, and as she stepped across the road towards the club, Dahli could see figures lurking in the shadows. She was afraid, but she boldly walked towards it as if she had every right to be there. It wasn't until she reached the establishment that she noticed Draephus had followed her.

"Quite a dump, isn't it?" he said. She noticed he had brought his bottle with him, and wondered how long he'd get away with that.

The club was smoky, dimly lit. The floor consisted of worn, bare planks. A band played badly on the filthy floor. A few feeble light bulbs glowed different colours from the industrial-looking ceiling above the band. A vague, acidic smell filled the air, and it took Dahli a time to realize it was old vomit.

"Lovely," she commented.

"Lead singer has all of his clothes on this time," Draephus remarked. "He has a beautiful body. Can't sing worth clart."

He couldn't, and Dahli cringed as his voice hit a flat note. He was, however, pleasant to look at. She decided that was why he qualified as lead singer.

"Heia," said a voice, and the pair turned to see a large man coming towards them. He indicated Draephus' bottle. "Sorry, but you can't bring that in here."

"What if I just drank it and tossed the bottle?" asked Draephus.

"Well, hurry up."

Dahli knew he hadn't had so much as a sip out of it when he raised the bottle, tipping his head back and swallowing. She and the large man watched as Draephus allowed the fluid to drain down his throat, a fine clear line of liquid trailing down from the corner of his mouth. The he lowered his head and offered the man a bleary smile, turning the bottle upside down to show it was empty. The man nodded, then as he turned to walk away Draephus wound up and threw the bottle at him, bouncing it off of his head. Dahli was shocked, rooted to the floor with horror. Draephus just stood there with a huge grin on his face.

"Come on, groutnoll."

The man charged him, Draephus snatching up chair and swinging it with little accuracy. He missed the man completely, succeeding only in knocking himself off balance. The man leapt onto Draephus, punching him so hard that they both fell onto the floor.

A second man came towards the fray, the first one landing knee first on Draephus' stomach and punching him again. Dahli suddenly unfroze herself and grabbed the discarded chair. Wielding it over her head, she meant to bring it down on Draephus' assailant when the second man caught her about her waist from behind. Chair and all, he dragged her kicking and swearing to the door and, with a mighty heave, threw her into the street. She hit hard, cracking her hip and elbow as she landed. Draephus came flying out after her, landing like a sack on the wet pavement. The rain poured icily down upon both of them.

Dahli picked herself gingerly off of the ground, rubbing her sore elbow. Draephus was also trying to lift himself off of the pavement, but he was shaky and unable to stand. He had only managed to get to all fours when Dahli walked up and kicked him as hard as she could in the ribs. He dropped without a whimper. Bending down, Dahli grabbed him by the collar and began hauling him across the street, moving inches at a time through the heavy rain towards the grey conni. She made it to the conni and opened the door, trying to haul him into the passenger's seat.

"Come on, get in!" she yelled at him, tears lost in the rain. He made no attempt to do so at first, then managed to get up on all fours and crawl into the passenger's seat. Dahli got in behind the steering wheel. She fumbled through his pockets for the keys, his blood dripping onto the pale grey of her jacket. She found the keys and started the conni, then tore away from the club, tires spinning before gripping the road as they drove off.

Dahli had some trouble finding her way out of that area of the city, and by the time she drove up to the front of the castle she could tell that the sky was beginning to lighten. She reached across Draephus and unlocked the door.

"I hope I never see your face again!" she screamed at him.

Draephus tried to say something, but Dahli turned in her seat and, with both feet kicked, him out of the conni and into the mud near the moat. He hit the ground bonelessly, lying in a heap as she spun muck out of the driveway.

Dahli was so furious she almost couldn't see. Ahead of her loomed the two stone pillars upon which rested the huge, demonic birds. With a sudden wrench of the wheel she drove the conni against one, hearing a scream of metal as she scraped against it. There was a jolt as the rear bumper caught and tore partially off. Dragging along behind, it continued to scrape against the ground as she drove away.

****

Dahli had parked Draephus conni a short way from her house, not wanting her sister to see what she had done to it, and walked the remaining distance home. She could hear her sister as she entered the yard and began walking up the stairs, listening, slowing to stand on the steps and watch what was happening inside her house.

"Well where could they have gone to?" Teirra asked, a concerned edge to her voice. She turned to look at Raski, Mars and Anthony. All three were soaked, as if they had been roaming the streets and arrived home not long before she did. "Did you see them?"

"No we didn't," said Anthony, playing nervously with the keys to his conni.

Raski ran one long dark hand through his black hair. "Look, Teirra, I know you're worried, but trust me, Draephus wouldn't hurt Dahli."

Dahli narrowed her eyes as she studied his expression. She could see that he was telling the truth, or at least what he believed to be true.

"I've known Draephus a long time," Raski continued as he seated himself on the couch. "He's irritable but generally harmless."

Generally harmless, huh? Nice. Wonderful. Well Donsa Jervyas was about to get an ugly little reality check about his dear friend. She stomped up the stairs and opened the door, then slamming it behind herself to make sure everybody knew she was home. Her long hair was lank and dripping wet. Her eyes were red from crying, her clothes were torn from when she had been thrown out of the club, and there was a huge smear of blood on the sleeve of her grey jacket. She sniffed and wiped her nose with one bloodied hand, gazing back at the five shocked people.

"Dahli what happened?" Teirra asked, her voice somewhere

between horror and anger. "Are you all right? What happened?"

"I don't know what happened!" Dahli yelled. "One minute he was fine and the next he was completely insane. He had some sort of seizure, and started being really abusive, and then he picked a fight with this guy and got us thrown out of a club. He was too drunk to get off of the road so after I kicked him in the ribs I dragged him into the conni and drove him home. I don't know where the conni is, I dumped it after I threw him into the mud in front of his castle. Somebody should probably go rescue him before he drowns in his moat." Dahli paused for breath and to wipe her nose on her sleeve again. She was yelling to keep from crying. "I should have kicked him in the face but he was lying on it!"

"But he didn't hurt you?" Teirra asked.

"No he never laid a hand on me." She stepped around Teirra and faced Raski. "What's wrong with him, anyway?"

Raski had been fixed to the chair ever since Dahli had come in, both he and Mars rooted to the spot with horror at the sight of the young girl covered in mud and blood. He stared back at Dahli, slowly shaking his head.

"Dahli I'm sorry. I don't know what happened. He doesn't usually act like that."

"Oh so I'm privileged I guess," she bellowed.

"I'm really sorry," he said quietly, "this isn't like him. I don't know what happened. Something must have set him off, he… he's been under a lot of stress…" Raski's voice trailed off, realizing how lame the excuses sounded. "He… had a seizure?"

"Some kind of fit," said Dahli. "He forgot how to work the vehicle and he was shaking so hard I thought for a moment he might be dying. Then he went completely insane. Excuse me - I gotta go redecorate my room."

Dahli turned and ran up the stairs to her room and began ripping down the posters and throwing them into a huge pile on the floor. She then returned downstairs, heading for the kitchen. She opened the storage closet door and pulled out two large boxes, then once more to her room, brushing past Raski as she went back upstairs. She began ripping the sheets off her bed.

"We could always go to the castle and push him into the moat," she heard Raski say to someone.

"SOUNDS GOOD TO ME!" Dahli yelled, shoving things into

boxes.

"We should at least go to the castle," said Mars quietly.

Dahli heard them leave, and her sister Teirra come up the stairs and into her room. The posters were a shredded pile in one corner of the room. The Gryphon bed sheets she and Diza had made were in one box, along with her tour shirts, head bands, pins, jacket, concert booklets, banners, taped interviews, framed photos, and finally, one chipped pair of opaque glasses.

Dahli said nothing to Teirra as she grabbed up the pile of posters. They made a huge armload, paper blooming out on all sides. She moved past Teirra, hauling them downstairs and stuffing them into the fireplace. Taking a lighter out of her pocket, she then set fire to the stack, tending it as the posters burned in strange blues and greens. When the paper was gone she returned to her room, closing the boxes full of stuff and dragging both up to the attic. Depositing them in a corner, she once more went to her room and began to undress.

"Dahli..." began Teirra.

"I'm all right," said Dahli quietly. "I'm just unbelievably angry."

"You'd tell me if he had done anything to you, wouldn't you?"

Dahli dropped her bloody jacket onto the floor, gazing at her sister. "Of course I would. You know I would."

"It's just that we don't talk so much anymore."

"Well that's hardly surprising," said Dahli. "You're married and taking classes at the university, and I'm off getting messed up with maniacs." She removed her shirt and dropped it to the floor. "I need a bath. Do I have to go to school today?"

"Under the circumstances, I'd say no."

Dahli smiled. "That's why you're my favourite sister."

"I'm your only sister."

Dahli smiled sadly. "Be nice to know where our only brother is. And our mother."

Teirra nodded. "Yes. It would. Do you miss mom?"

"No," said Dahli. "Mom… Mom is happy. She's okay. But I miss Tanzikar."

"I miss him too. He'll turn up one day."

Dahli nodded. She picked up her jacket and frowned at it. "Groutnoll ruined my jacket."

"Dahli that's an awful lot of blood. Are you sure he was okay? I don't like to think he's hurt."

"It was only a little cut. It bled really badly, but just for a short time. He was more drunk than anything."

Her anger became tainted by guilt. He'd been sick; there had been something really wrong with him. He had not just been mean and hurtful for the sake of it; he'd been in an incredible amount of pain. But Dahli was fifteen, and like most teens she preferred to hold what felt like the moral high ground than consider the fact that Draephus may have suffered some sort of violent seizure. Besides, if he was just being nasty, then he was okay…

"Pass the jacket," Teirra said. "The blood should come out if we wash it before it dries."

****

Draephus had made it onto the bridge when he heard the conni pull up. He was half afraid that it was Dahli returning to kill him, but then he heard a familiar voice.

"DRAEPHUS! CLART, MAN, GIVE ME ONE GOOD REASON I SHOULD LET YOU LIVE!"

Draephus didn't much want to live at this point, so he saw no reason he should reply to the comment. He couldn't move, he was soaked to the bone and sick. His ribs had been re-broken, either when he had been thrown out of the bar or when Dahli had kicked him. He lay on the bridge and hoped he would die before Raski reached him.

He didn't.

Raski crouched down next to the miserable heap, touching the wet sandy hair. Draephus was shaking like a feralyke with the foaming rage, his face covered in blood. He smelled like everything his coat had ever been exposed to. Raski sighed loudly.

"Mars, open the door, will you? I'll try to drag cheese-head up the stairs. You're only the drummer, you know, we can replace you."

Draephus managed to stagger to his feet with Raski and Anthony helping him, and he stumbled blindly along as they led him into the huge ancient structure. They walked up the wide flight of stone steps, past a pair of sentinel birds and into the dramatic expanse of the main room. Daylight was just beginning to show through the stained glass window, and the room was a kaleidoscope of colours as Raski dumped Draephus onto an aged gilt couch. He stared down at his friend for a moment, then turned his blue eyes to Anthony, a wisp of black hair in his handsome face.

"Well?" he said, his voice tight with hysteria. "How do you like us so far?"

Chapter Seven

Draephus opened his eyes, feeling pain envelop him like a tight steel band around his chest. He shifted, trying to get comfortable, but was unable to find a position that was any better. In fact a couple of them were decidedly worse. He reached for the bedside table in which he kept his needle and drugs, but gave himself only a very small amount, just enough to take the edge off the ache in his bones. He had to call Vesper. He needed to talk to him, and he couldn't do that if he was too high to talk.

"Bacca. Telecom."

The faelin made a rude noise and shook his pretty head. Draephus sighed.

"Bacca, please don't make me argue with you."

Bacca made a series of low 'rrrrrrr-rrrrrrrrrr-rrrr' noises.

"Well who's got the 'com, then?"

"Hhhrrrrpht."

"Well go tell Raski to bring it here when he's done."

Bacca hopped off the bed to do as he was asked, returning in just a few minutes with Raski. The faelin hopped onto his usual perch on the bed and settled down, while Raski sat carefully on the edge of the bed, looking into Draephus' eyes.

"What happened?" Raski asked. "Do you realize you went mental on a little girl?"

"Don't yell at me, Rask, please."

Raski's eyes were blue ice. "You're lucky you're drawing air. Now would you care to share with me what came over you last night?"

Draephus squeezed his eyes shut. "Vesper's not coming home. I called last night and some guy answered and said that Vesper was with him now, and he's not coming back. And I kept trying to call, and... I went nuts. I came apart, I... I remember sitting in my vehicle and Dahli saying she would get someone and... that's about it. What do you mean I went mental on a little girl? I didn't hurt her, did I?"

"No, according to her you didn't lay a hand on her. But you scared the life out of her. What were you doing to break your hands?"

"I... I think I picked a fight with your conni. Raski..."

Raski swore quietly, grinding his teeth. He picked the telecom up and dialled a number, listening to a distant ring. Draephus was able to hear the entire conversation.

"Heia?"

"Heia Vesper? Raski. Just wanted to thank you for the brilliant job of emotionally destroying Draephus. Really good. Very thorough. He may even have had a nervous breakdown, we'll still sorting that one out."

"What are you talking about?"

"I'm talking about having the guy you're shacked up with tell Draephus that you're not coming back. Really classy. I guess that makes up for the one time he slept with me."

Vesper sounded horrified. "What guy? What are you talking about? Who…?"

Raski hung up, and passed the 'com to Draephus. "Here. You two fight, I'm going to go into the kitchen and scream before I make you lunch and possibly dump poison in it."

Draephus watched him go, and sighed heavily. "Šukat," he muttered quietly, answering the 'com as it rang. Vesper was already screaming.

"I never said I wasn't coming back!"

"Vesper…"

"What is going on? WHO said I wasn't coming back? When did you call?"

"Last night, really late. It would have been late morning where you are. A man answered and said he was your new husband and you were not coming back and I should just leave you alone."

Vesper put the 'com down. Draephus could hear him yelling at someone, and the person shouting back.

"Mirlai! Mirlai you šukating waste of meat did you tell Draephus you were my husband and I wasn't coming back?"

"Maybe. Why? He hurt you, didn't he? Let him… VESPER!"

Draephus heard the loud explosion of a large hand gun discharging, and the frantic sound of someone fleeing the room. Then the 'com was picked up.

"That was my cousin, Mirlai. And if I was a better shot his alleged brains would be all over my wall."

"It's not true?" Draephus asked, his throat tight, eyes burning with tears.

"No, it's not true. Draephus do you honestly think for one

moment if I was going to leave you I would do it in such a vile manner?"

"I dunno," he muttered. "Sorta thought I deserved it after what I did."

Vesper laughed quietly. "Draephus if I was ever going to leave you, I would have done it by now. And I would tell you I was going. Sleeping with Raski doesn't quite qualify. Yes, I was angry about it, yes we had a huge fight, but… I know what he means to you. Truth to tell I have been counting on it, because I love you. I want you to live. Don't you understand that? All I want is to see the light come back to your eyes."

"But then why did your cousin..?"

Vesper sighed. "He probably thought he was doing me a favour, giving you a taste of your own medicine, who knows. It's none of his business what goes on in our family. Draephus I am so sorry, are you okay?"

"No," he pouted. "I had a fit and now everyone hates me."

"Oh no one hates you." Pause. "What did you do?"

"Broke my hands beating apart Raski's dashboard, killed a phone, and apparently started a fight in a club that resulted in me getting my vehicle stolen after I was kicked into my own moat."

Vesper turned to mush. "Awww… so you do care about me, you big brute."

"I love you. I just want you here with me. I guess now you can't come home, the last shuttle north would have left yesterday, and there won't be another one until the rainy season is about to start."

"You're right," said Vesper softly. "But it will be okay. I'm doing really well. That's where I was when you called – at the doctor's office. I've got a few tremors and some shortness of breath, but the doctor says for my age and considering how advanced the illness is, I could likely have another five years."

Draephus sat up, forgetting the aches in his body. "Five years?! Vesper that's fantastic! They were talking months when you saw the doctors up here!"

"Well they have different ways of treating the illness here, and the warm air helps, too, makes it a lot easier to breathe."

"Maybe we should look into moving down there, then."

Vesper laughed. "Um, no. I am not enamoured of all the things they have down here with multiple legs, many of which are truly huge. I woke up this morning thinking there was a stray cat on my bed and it was a bloody cave spider."

"Yeah they do get big down there," Draephus grinned. "Okay, in that case I'll look into making the castle warmer. Oh baby I am so glad you're okay. And that you love me."

"Of course I love you."

Draephus lay back down, wincing in pain. "At the risk of starting another fight, if you're going to be okay then why are you still nudging me in Raski's direction?"

"Purely selfish reasons. He was talking about getting an artificial uterus. So you're going to get him pregnant so I can play with the kids before handing them all tired and pukey with full diapers back to their mother."

Draephus rolled his eyes. "Vesper, I'm barely housebroken; do you honestly think I can be trusted with a baby?"

"No," Vesper laughed.

"Well Raski and I talked and… we're waiting. We both love you. We're not getting together until… it's… appropriate. I'm not sure what the word is."

"Until I've cacked."

"Vesper can you please not...?"

"Just a sec." There was the explosive discharge of a firearm. "Šukating spiders."

"Vesper, stop shooting things."

"Yup. Just let me get this last one."

Draephus winced as the gun went off again. "Baby stop shooting the spiders." He smiled. "I love you."

"I love you too. I'm sorry my cousin put you through that, I don't know what he's using for brains. Week-old shaumaus, I think. You rest. Get better, and fix Raski's conni. Tomorrow I'm heading for Trac Dae Mu, I'll be out of communication for a couple weeks, but I'll call you next chance I get."

"Okay babe. Love you."

"Love you, too."

Vesper hung up, and Draephus shut off the 'com and set it aside. He looked up as Raski came into the room.

"So how are things?" he asked.

"Good," said Draephus. "Vesper still loves me, and the new treatments the doctors have him on down there are really helping."

"So all is well."

"Yup. Better than I could have hoped for."

"Good. Now if you don't mind my asking, WHY THE ŠUKAT DID YOU KILL MY VEHICLE?"

Draephus grabbed Raski and tossed him onto the bed, stroking his hands over his body, kissing him passionately. When it ended they were both breathless and aroused, staring at each other with want.

"I thought we were waiting," said Raski.

"Yeah but Vesper could live another five years. I have to remind you of what you're waiting for." Draephus kissed him. "Vesper was hoping we'd breed."

"Oh suddenly you want a baby. Well forget it; no one's giving me a baby. I've got C-3 and C-4 both, they don't let you carry a baby with those viruses zipping through your bloodstream. I'm lucky I can walk upright." The pale blue eyes glinted. "We could probably get away with putting one in you, though."

Draephus stared down at Raski, wanting nothing more than to give him everything his heart desired. He was going to have to tell him that he too was afflicted with an ailment that would ultimately prove fatal, but... not right now. Not now. They both needed a break from the pain and angst. Draephus kissed him softly.

"Yeah, maybe. We'll hash it all out later. In the meantime I have to heal up, then..." He trailed a finger over Raski's fine features, "I have to find your conni a new dashboard and telecom."

"Yeah, you do, groutnoll." Raski kissed him. "But I love you anyway."

They gazed at each other, Draephus feeling himself growing hard, want warring with pain and what was right.

"Gonna be a tough five years," he said.

Raski brought one long leg up, moving his hips beneath Draephus. "Very tough. Long and hard, one might say."

"Raski..."

"You started it."

"Sadly I have to end it, too." He kissed his throat. "But it's not because you aren't turning me on so badly that I think I'll never be able to walk again."

"Then kiss me, and we'll eat. Then to make sure we behave, I'll go home."

Draephus did, then carefully moved off of Raski, watching his friend leave the room to continue making lunch. He settled himself against the pillows and closed his eyes, and that was when Khandid showed up.

"What happened to *you* last night, get your ass-hairs ripped out?"

"Heia Khandi," said Draephus wearily.

"Don't 'Heia Khandi' *me* you malcontent, what was up with that little fit you threw in that old club?"

"What fight? What club?"

"Were we drunk?"

"Nooo…" said Draephus. "We were smashed. Stop shouting. Raski already came in and screamed at me. Mars will be up next I think."

"No Mars is on the 'com having a heated disagreement with Missy. She wants to know if he gave her anything."

Draephus sighed loudly. "He doesn't have a disease! I mean… he does. But he's not contagious. What is this girl's issue? Mars is little and adorable and sweet. There is nothing not to love."

"Except his lovers all seem to leave him very quickly," said Khandid.

"Yeah I've noticed that," said Draephus softly. "I've always wondered about that, too."

"We may have to face the idea that something is very wrong with him and he is not telling us," said Khandid.

Draephus shook his head. "Look whatever is wrong with him, it's not contagious and not our business. If he was dying he would have told us."

"I suppose you're right." Khandid lay down beside Draephus on the bed. Draephus opened one eye to stare blearily at Khandid.

"And what exactly are you up to?"

"We love you, you know," said Khandid. "Even when you're a šukating moron."

"Thanks Khandi."

"Stop being a šukating moron."

"Later."

Draephus suddenly grabbed him and began kissing him, as Khandid wriggled and screeched, trying to free himself. Draephus grinned as Khandid managed to squiggle free, only to end up in a large knot of blankets.

"I'm stuck!" he complained.

Draephus untangled him. "There you go. Khandi I am sorry about what I did…"

Khandid sat up, flinging back his long white hair. Draephus just smiled at the pretty little thing. What was it Gemma and Mystique had called him? A unicorn? Yeah Khandi was pretty enough to be a mythical creature.

"Draephus I am not the person you need to apologize to," said Khandid, arranging his long white hair.

"Yeah, I know. Man I can't believe I would act that way with a kid…"

"You have to at least try," said Khandid.

"I know. You're right. I will."

"Good."

They relaxed on the bed until Raski came upstairs with lunch for Draephus. He grinned at Khandid.

"So what shall we do this afternoon, Khandid Stracona?"

Khandid sat up and stretched. "Nothing, sadly, I really do have to go, but I'll call later to see how Donsa Booze-Brain is doing. Bye!"

Raski and Draephus watched Khandid scoot out of the room rather hurriedly, then exchanged glances.

"What did he do?" asked Draephus.

Raski sighed and gave Draephus his tray. "I don't know but I have a funny feeling we'll find it on that awful fan site."

"You go look," said Draephus. "I'm too sore."

Raski did. Draephus carefully picked at his breakfast, too sore and tired to be able to think about his actions the night before. Not that he wanted to; it made him sick to think he could let his anger take over so completely…

Raski returned after a few minutes, walking over to the bed where Draephus now ate.

"How drunk were you and I the night we had the party with the aliens?"

"I don't know about you," said Draephus, "but I'm pretty sure I managed to replace all my blood with booze. Why?"

"Apparently I let you push me against the wall and engage in some vertical naughtiness. Publicly."

Draephus stared at him. "You're kidding."

"I kid you not. I've got my back to the wall and you've got

your hand up my shirt and there is no one else in the world. And someone took a photo and our own darling little Puffy Bun-Tarts posted it to the Gryphon's Roost."

"I have a headache," said Draephus. He sighed heavily. "Well you're the band manager, what are you going to do?"

"I have no idea. I mean we can't deny it's us, and no one is going to believe you're just trying to keep me from falling down."

Draephus grinned. "That good, huh?"

"Let's just say the fans seem to like it, though a couple confused individuals are certain for some reason I'm with Mars and are calling you all sorts of names for breaking us up. Although some seem to think you were with him."

Draephus sighed loudly. "Where did that rumour come from? I never was with Mars. I've been with Vesper, and you, and that is the list of people I have had sex with. Have you ever been with him?"

"Not me. But he and Khandid were a couple briefly, before Yuri."

Draephus raised an eyebrow. "Khandi and Mars, huh? There's a photo I'd like to see."

"Don't get yourself excited. Anyway I'm pretty sure the source of all band rumours is tiny, white, wears stilettos with razors in the heel, and has a fondness for pink highlights. We should make up a few about him."

"You assume he'd care," said Draephus. Both he and Raski stared at the 'com on the bed as it began to ring.

"Your 'com," lilted Raski sweetly.

Draephus answered it. "Heia?"

"Heia Donsa CZimcocious, this is Sarellis Estea at Satellite Base Four, how are you today?"

Draephus glared sourly at the 'com. "How did you groutnolls get this number?"

Raski began to giggle, coming to sit on the bed to listen in as Draephus reached for his cigarettes.

"Well we were just checking the Gryphon's Roost…"
"Oh yeah."
"And we came across this photo…"
"Uh huh…"
"And… it's a pretty amazing photo."
"Yeah."

"Have you seen it?"

"No Raski told me about it when I woke up."

"I'm sorry, when you…?"

"When I woke up."

"So he spent the night."

"I have no idea." Draephus looked at Raski. "Did you spend the night?"

"No I showed up at about five in the morning and dragged you out of the moat," said Raski.

"What were you doing in the moat?" asked Sarellis, clearly delighting in the conversation, as were his listeners.

"Probably drowning," said Draephus. "Hey Raski, where's my coat?"

"I shot it," said Raski. "It became sentient and tried to eat Mars."

One of Sarellis' co-workers could be heard laughing in the background. Sarellis himself was giggling. "So about this photo…?"

"Look, Sarellis," said Draephus. "I am not the only guy in the world who got drunk off his ass and pinned his best friend against a wall, so…"

Draephus abruptly tossed the 'com to Raski and went to the bathroom to get sick. His bones burned like death and fire, and he was suddenly in so much pain he thought he would pass out. Fortunately Raski had not seen him stumble or most of Second City would be hearing him lose his mind over Draephus' condition. He could hear Raski from the bathroom.

"I'm sorry, Donsa CZimcocious had to take another call in a different room, could I take a message? My opinion about the photo? Well I was pretty drunk at the time but that thing digging into my leg was at least the size of a… What's that? Uh, no, hate to disappoint you but that was just drunken stupidity, we are not a couple and have no plans to get together at the moment. In the future? Oh it's possible, but honestly Sarellis, if everybody who got drunk and made out with a friend in a hallway married them, then everyone in the city would be married three times over. And he *is* my best friend so if we had a relationship and then broke up, who would I cry to?"

Draephus grinned through his pain and nausea. "You could always cry on me, Raski," he whispered. "Because I'll never be the cause of your tears if I can help it."

He closed the bathroom door to be sick in peace. Let Raski handle the interviews and fluff about naughty photos. He was good at it, and he liked it. Draephus cleaned himself up and staggered back to bed, collapsing onto it. The call had ended, and Raski reached out one hand to stroke Draephus' hair.

"I know I said I would go, but I think I'll stay and keep an eye on you. At least for a while. Tell me why I love you, you big mess."

"I don't know why," said Draephus quietly, wishing he had taken a larger dose of the mushroom. "But I'll never stop being grateful you do."

****

Dahli awoke sometime around the hour she would have usually been coming home from school. She fell out of bed and dragged her tired body to the bathroom, her thoughts wrapped up in having a long, hot bath. She filled the tub and more or less fell into it, being a bit too soul-weary to worry much about grace. There were times when one needed to flop; this was definitely one of them.

She submerged herself, coming up a moment later, sputtering. She pushed her hand through her wet hair, then reached for the soap. It was at that moment she recalled what she had done with Draephus' conni. Her eyes grew wide, and she paused as she realised that, yes, she had the man's vehicle. She had stashed it in an abandoned garage, next to a burned-out house. It was only a few blocks from where she lived, sitting in patient grandeur with its key still in the ignition. A slow nasty smile crossed Dahli's face. She knew what she was doing that evening.

****

It was past dark when Dahli ran up the stairs to Diza's house, knocking at the door. She heard the slow, heavy pace of Diza's father coming down the hallway. Then he opened the door.

"Well heia," he said as he saw her there. "How are you?"

"Oh fine. Can Diza come out to play?" Dahli grinned at the childish expression, the old man smiling back at her.

"Sure," he said in his slow manner, which always made him sound as though he was uncertain. His eyes moved to the sleeve of Dahli's jacket. "That's quite a stain."

The blood had not completely come out. There were still traces of it on the sleeve and shoulder; faded, but still visible.

"I know," said Dahli, "a friend of mine borrowed it and got something on it."

The man nodded, then turned and wandered further into the house. "Diza, Dahli is here."

Diza came downstairs, grabbing her coat as Dahli made a motion for her to go outside. Diza called goodnight to her father as she walked out the door.

"So what are we up to tonight?" she asked as they walked down the steps.

Dahli was grinning. "We're going for a ride."

"Ride? You got your grandfather's conni?"

"Better. Come on."

"I thought we were going to see Gemma…?"

"We will."

The two ran down the street, Dahli leading Diza as they turned the corner to where the grey conni sat. From the front there was no sign of the damage, and it was obviously an expensive machine. Diza prepared to walk past it when Dahli grabbed her sleeve.

"Where are you going? This is it."

Diza stared at the grey conni. "Dahli," she said, reaching out to touch the hood, "where did you get this?"

"Stole it. Come on."

"Stole it! Did you?"

"Yeah. Come on." Dahli got into the conni, shutting the door and starting the engine. It came into life with a soft rumble as Diza got in.

"Where did you get this?" she asked. "Whose is it?"

"I told you, I stole it." The conni pulled away from the curb with frictionless ease, prowling down the road. "Rides better than my grandfather's, doesn't it?"

"Yeah, it's great. What's this stain all over my seat?"

"Blood."

"Are you seeeee-rious?" Diza's voice went up in pitch and volume.

"Yeah, take a look at it."

"WHAT HAVE YOU BEEN DOING?"

"Look, nobody died, okay? I haven't killed anybody. The seat just happens to be stained and it just happens to be blood."

Diza sighed, shaking her head. "One of these days, Dahli Sandiniti, you are going to get into big trouble."

"Maybe," said Dahli, grinning. "Let's drive by Lyrellyn CZim-Relyn's house before we go pick up Czamki and Gemma."

****

The prospect of getting into trouble didn't make Dahli give back the conni, and as the days went by and no one came for it, she grew confident that there was no trouble coming. She and her friends took the conni down back roads, ploughing through brambles and swamps, and over small streams. They burned rubber on the paved sections of the decrepit old roads, tires screaming as they churned up clouds of blue smoke. They bounced it through bushes, over knolls in the road, and scraped it past trees. Diza tried questioning Dahli about how she had acquired the conni, but got no more information other than it was stolen.

They kept the conni hidden a few blocks from Dahli's home, housing it in the old garage. They drove it to school, parking it always out of sight. They took friends joy-riding in it, and, on a suggestion by Czamkiar, they spray-painted the hood with Bad Influence's stylized logo. They covered the body with surrealistic feralykes, leering figures, and a board fence for background. They dubbed the conni the `Creeping Malaise', after a song by afore-mentioned Bad Influence. Dahli wondered frequently as she and her buddies redecorated the conni exactly when Draephus was going to try to reclaim it. Perhaps he had given it up as lost, or maybe he was hoping she would give it back. There was no way she was bringing it back *now*. Once or twice, as she flung open the doors of the old garage and saw the still-noble vehicle, desecrated as it was, she felt small pangs of guilt and worry, but she quickly shrugged them off. After all, he could afford it.

****

The Creeping Malaise was about to find a less playful, more sinister, use, though the warm Sevenday Dahli drove it to school she was unaware of this. It was simply an average day, with the promise of a hot respite as she parked in the usual place. She and Diza planned to drive into the woods, dragging Randish, Gemma and Czamkiar along for good measure, and spend some time out there, maybe build a fire and catch some fish to toast. As she jogged up the stairs to the school, feeling the warmth of the day on her back, the last thing on her mind was dead faelins.

The day had progressed normally enough, until science class. There had been the usual run-ins with other students she didn't like, work to be done and assignments to be passed in. It would have been a wholly forgettable day if she had not walked into the science room after lunch to see the half-grown, reddish body lying cold and motionless on its board.

She stopped, staring at the dead faelin. It had an odd, dehydrated look to it, even the eyes, which she could see under partially open lids, looked dried. The bright, livid green had faded to some nondescript, dead colour. The dark red hair even looked dead, dry and cold. She stepped closer to the body, oblivious to the other students who stood there. As she drew near she saw the tattoo on the right forearm, an identifying number which sat beneath a row of symbols indicating the creature's age, owner, and grade. This one was stamped a lab animal. Others, more finely built with superior parentage were stamped as pet, show or breeding stock. A faelin's whole life was dictated by a series of marks burned into its skin. Evidence of experiments took the shape of half-closed scars on the abdomen, some long and thin, other more like punctures. The body had an underdeveloped, weak look, as though it had little opportunity for exercise during its brief life.

Dahli turned in horror from the body on the board, feeling a sickness in her stomach. She sensed the unusual silence of her classmates as they also spotted the body, gathering around and staring at the dead, cold form. Somehow she knew that they hadn't expected it to look as much like them as it did.

Duone Bathers entered the classroom, dropping his books and papers on the table as he always did, not paying much heed to his students. Dahli stared at him as he sorted through the papers, and realized she had never truly felt hate before this moment. Duone Bathers glanced up and caught her gaze, and was actually startled by the look she gave him. The disgust, the hate, the hot loathing she felt shone through her green eyes like a beacon, and he dropped his eyes back to the stack of paper. Dahli suddenly walked forward, marching straight up to the desk. Her anger had taken over to the point where any respect she may have had for the man had gone out the window.

"That," she said, pointing to the faelin, "is the most disgustingly sick thing I have ever seen."

Duone Bathers let out an irritated sigh. "Dahli, that was a laboratory animal, their purpose is to be used in experiments to aid research."

"Their purpose," said Dahli, her voice rising, "is to be on another planet, leaping from tree to tree, scratching, hunting, barking, having babies and carrying on as they have for thousands of years!"

"There are plenty of them left on Faela." said Duone Bathers. "There's no reason why we can't use a few, they're not an endangered species."

"I'm sure the ones in the labs don't feel that way."

"Dahli," the man straightened and looked at her. "Go to your seat. On Oneday we'll dissect it. If you have problems with that, I suggest you talk to the principal."

"Šukat the principal!" Dahli yelled, startling even herself. "Šukat the principal and most of all, ŠUKAT YOU!"

The entire class was absolutely silent. Duone Bathers just stared stupidly at her, unable to believe his ears. Dahli herself was a little overwhelmed by what she had just done, uttering one of the choicest of foul words to her Duone. For a long moment, nothing breathed within the class Then Duone Bathers broke the silence.

"Look, I can see you're upset," he said quietly. "Why don't you just take the rest of the day off, start your respite early."

"I'll do that," said Dahli.

She turned and strode from the classroom. She left the school and headed for the spray-painted conni. Reaching it, she got in and sat behind the wheel, hands shaking. She reached for the glove compartment, opening it and taking out a pack of cigarettes. She lit one, tossing the pack back and slamming the compartment closed. Dahli puffed at the cigarette, staring out the window but seeing only the body of the young faelin. She saw in detail the scars, the tattoo, and the dried, hopeless eyes. She sat and smoked a while longer, feeling her resolution harden. As she started the conni and drove away, she still wasn't certain exactly what she would do, but she knew she was going to do something.

****

Draephus stood directly across the street from Dahli's house. He had a cold, frightened knot in his stomach; a sensation all too familiar to him these days. He rocked back on the heels of his boots, hands in the pockets of his coat. There were traces of mud still visible on it, though most of the muck had fallen off.

He hadn't been there long, but he was already considering getting back into Raski's conni and slinking off. He hadn't wanted to face Dahli ever again after the way he'd acted, but guilt and Raski had both nagged him into some attempt at an apology. Šukat, she could keep the conni if she wanted, so long as he got a chance to say he was sorry. He doubted she'd accept, but it was worth the try.

He saw her come walking down the street, wearing the same grey jacket he had last seen her in. As he watched her go by, unaware of his presence, he noticed that the she was not wearing the ever-present Gryphon shirt. She looked preoccupied, lost in some thought as she headed up the stairs of her house, pausing to unlock the door. As she entered, he took a deep breath and forced himself to cross the street. Bad scene number three million and two coming up…

****

Dahli had just hung up her jacket when she heard the knock at the door. The sound puzzled her, she couldn't think of who it could be. She walked down the hall to the door and opened it. The two stared at each other for what seemed to be forever.

"YOU'RE THE LAST SON OF A FERALYKE I WANT TO SEE!" Dahli yelled.

"Dahli..." he began, taking a step towards her. She swung the door shut so hard that when it hit Draephus saw stars and his knees went weak. Shaking his head and asking himself if this was worth it, he pushed his way in as far as he could with her holding the door closed on him.

"Look," he said, "I want to apologise..."

"For your existence? Gonna take you a long time going door-to-door, now get lost!"

"Dahli..." Draephus began again.

"Shut up! I don't want to hear it!" She turned and walked away, Draephus following after her.

"Look, I behaved really badly..." he tried again.

"NO ŠUKATING CLART!" Dahli screamed at him. "COME TO THINK OF IT, I MAY HAVE NOTICED! NOW GET OUT OF MY HOUSE!"

"Dahli..."

"OUT! OUT! OUT!"

"Can I explain myself?"

"You were raised by child-beaters, right? You hurt me, clarthead. I'm not a sounding board. I'm not a vent for your head problems." She took an ineffective swing at him.

"I realise that! That's why I'm here!"

"I DON'T WANT YOU HERE!" Dahli screamed so loudly that the cords stood out on her neck and her face was virtually purple. "And I don't want your apologies or your excuses! And if you want your conni back, then here's your keys!"

She flung them at him, forcing Draephus to dodge the small, fast moving objects. He probably hadn't expected this abuse. He reached out and caught her, gripping her by her upper arms, and Dahli, with neat accuracy, spat in his face.

The two just stood there, facing each other, neither moving. Then Draephus slowly released her, stepping back to wipe off his face. In one brief span of time he had gone from angry to confused and quiet.

"I'm sorry," he mumbled, then turned and headed for the door, departing quietly.

Dahli went to the window and watched him go, a tall figure in a long flapping coat. He walked quickly over to the sleek black conni, getting into it and driving off. She watched until she could no longer see the conni, then turned abruptly from the window. Šukat him, she thought, though not quite with the finality she would have liked. She found herself feeling just the smallest bit sorry for him, though she wasn't exactly sure why. Nor would she have admitted it. Certainly nobody with his fame and wealth needed any pity from her.

She went to the kitchen and began making tea, not really needing a cup, but wanting something to do with her hands. On impulse, she walked back into the living room, getting down onto her hands and knees and peering under a chair. She found the heavy golden object with its array of keys, and sat back on her heels, gazing down at it. The object was shaped like a bird's skeletal foot, a strange, finely detailed device. She turned it over in her fingers, then rose to her feet, putting the keychain into her pocket before returning to the kitchen.

Teirra came home not long after this whole ordeal. She found Dahli at the kitchen table, elbows resting on it, chin in her right hand. In her other hand she held a smouldering cigarette, and before her sat a cup of tea. Teirra halted in the doorway, staring at her. Dahli stared back.

"You're smoking," said Teirra.

"I am," said Dahli. "You would be too if you walked into science class and found a dead faelin on a slab."

"So, they brought it in, did they?"

"Yeah, they did." Dahli tapped her ashes into a tray. "It's not right, they're not animals. Why can't anyone see that?"

"Faelins are big business," said Teirra. "They're expensive. I wouldn't chance a guess at what a show quality one would bring."

"The faelins pay more than the people who buy them." said Dahli morosely. She crushed out her cigarette with a violent motion. "I'm going to stop them from dissecting that body. I don't know how, but I am."

"Dahli," said Teirra, "I hope you're not planning anything crazy."

"No, I'm not." she said, even though she was.

****

She met up with her friends later that day at the Contempo, finding them seated at a small table away from the poets and people born too late to be part of the Revolution. As Dahli sat at the table, she leaned forward and said; "Anybody want to break into the school?"

Diza and Czamkiar stared at her, while Randish kept eating. He seemed undisturbed by the question.

"Are you seeeeee-rious?" asked Diza.

"Yes, I am," said Dahli. "I want to steal the faelin."

Randish kept eating. Diza and Czamkiar fell silent as they contemplated Dahli's statement.

"I don't know," said Diza. "We could get into a lot of trouble. And they're going to know who did it."

"Then I'll do it myself," said Dahli, hailing a server.

"I'll help," said Randish suddenly, his mouth full. "They can't catch me, I live in the Cylinder. Technically, I don't exist."

"Good," said Dahli. "Now, what about you guys?"

Diza and Czamkiar looked at each other. "When do you want to do this?" Diza asked.

"Tonight," said Dahli, a weird gleam in her eyes.

"How do we get in?" asked Czamkiar.

Dahli leaned back in her seat. "Beats the clart out of me. Let's go to the concert in the park, we were going to take Gemma and do that anyway. We have to wait until it's late before we do anything."

"We can't take Gemma with us to do this," said Diza.

"I know. We'll go to the concert, show her around the city a little more, then take her home. By then it should be late enough…"

****

The air was cool as the four made their way from the spray-painted conni towards the darkness of the school. The vague glow of a few emergency lights was the only illumination around the silent structure, casting long, skinny shadows behind the intruders. They approached the building cautiously, and peered in through a low window at the eerie pale blue glow of the handful of night-time lights left burning.

"Well?" said Diza. "How do we get in?"

Dahli looked around. She knew there were no houses close at hand, but she wondered if perhaps there were people in the darkness, watching. She pulled out the keys to the Creeping Malaise and passed them to Diza.

"Diza you're the getaway driver. Get the conni and park it right about here."

Diza turned and ran for the conni, glad to get out of going into the school without having to bow out of the operation. Dahli felt the weight of the prybar she had brought from home, steeling herself. Finally she raised the bar, thrusting one end under the sill of the window. She pried at the heavily constructed window, hauling down with all of her weight, and at one point raising her feet off the ground and dangling, cursing and swearing. Finally she gave up, putting her feet down on the concrete and stepping away from the bar.

"Randish, you try."

The large alien stepped forward, and, grasping the bar, threw his entire weight down on it. The window shattered, wooden sill splitting apart and allowing the iron bar to drive into the glass. There was an enormous noise of breaking wood and exploding glass, and Dahli and Czamkiar covered their heads and shrieked. Randish cleared the glass away with one gloved hand, then hoisted himself into the building, Dahli and Czamkiar following him inside. They found themselves in a classroom. Crossing the floor to a door, they opened it cautiously and peered into the hallway. They saw no one.

"This way," said Dahli, stepping forward and motioning the other two to follow. They ran down the corridor, shoes making too much noise in the empty building, squeaking and thumping loudly on the polished floors. They reached the stairs and ran up to the second level, abandoning caution as they charged to the science room. They reached it, Dahli grasping the door handle and discovering it was locked.

She swore, kicking the door, then took the prybar from Randish. She had come too far to be stopped now. Dahli wrenched and pulled, working the prybar back and forth, hearing the door begin to splinter. She pushed the bar in further, heaving and pulling. She pushed it in further still until she heard a great cracking noise and the door broke open, drifting back to bump into the wall. They barged into the room, Dahli running over to the window to look for Diza and the conni. Spotting them, she turned her attention back to the others, who now stood by the dead faelin.

It had been placed into a sort of cold storage box for the respite, to prevent it from decaying. Dahli had to wonder why it had simply been on the table when she had come into class, and if Duone Bathers, for whatever reason, had wanted everyone to get a good look at it.

`Don't let this happen to you,' thought Dahli as Czamkiar lifted the lid of the box.

"We'll need something to put it in," he said. "We can't take it by itself, and it will weigh too much in the box."

"There's a tarp in the art room," said Dahli, and the three tore off to get it. More broken doors, she thought as they broke first into the class, and then into the storage closet. They were moving fast now, becoming concerned about how much time they were taking. They removed the body from the box and placed it in the tarp, wrapping it up. Then Randish picked up the body, and they quickly left the school.

"What took you so long?" Diza demanded as they ran up to

the con. Czamkiar took the keys from her hand and opened the trunk. He helped Randish load the body into the space, then slammed the lid closed.

"Let's get out of here," he said, the group scurrying into the conni. Czamkiar tossed Diza the keys, and they tore out of the schoolyard in a way that would have made Raski Jervyas proud.

"Now what?" Diza asked. They were all terrified, shaken by what they had done, with the exception of Randish. He didn't seem worried.

"We go home," said Dahli.

"What?"

"We were only supposed to go out to the concert, maybe have something to eat afterwards. If we're gone too long it won't look good. So we park the Creep and go our separate ways like nothing happened. Tomorrow night we bury the body."

The group parted ways at the abandoned garage; Czamkiar and Randish heading off on their own. Diza and Dahli walked together until Diza reached her own door. The two bid each other good night, then Dahli kept on through the dark and silent streets to her own house. She slipped into her home as quietly as she was able, spying Atterick asleep in his chair. She crept past him, up the stairs to her room, finally slipping into her personal sanctuary and quietly closing the door. Dahli breathed a sigh of relief. She shed her clothes and turned off the light, climbing into bed, and lay staring at the ceiling for a very long time.

****

News of the break-in was on the receiver the next morning when Dahli made her way into the kitchen, pretending not to hear it as she set about making breakfast. She could feel the coldness in her body, the sick nervousness as Teirra's eyes burned into her back. Dahli thought she was going to vomit when she heard her sister speak her name.

"Yeah?" Dahli said, as calmly as she could.

"Someone broke into the school last night."

Dahli looked over her shoulder at Teirra, an incredulous sneer on her face. "Who would break *into* a school?"

"I was hoping you could tell me. The only things missing were a tarp and the body of a faelin."

Dahli was so scared she honestly thought her bowels were going to let go. She tried her hardest no to show it.

"WHY WOULD I TAKE IT?"

"I know how you felt about it."

"Oh, yeah, right. So I just bust into the school and take it. One, how would I get it out of there, and two, where would I put it? And three, why would I want to go handle a dead body? I wanted to keep them from cutting it up, not take it and make a keepsake out of it."

Teirra wasn't buying her story and Dahli could see it in her eyes. Teirra didn't know how her sister had removed the thing from the school, or where she had put it, but she was convinced that Dahli had indeed done so.

"Dahli..." she began.

"Teirra, I don't have the body, and I didn't take it. But I'd like to shake the hand of whoever did."

"You could be in a lot of trouble, Dahli. Damaging school property, theft..."

"I don't have it!" Dahli yelled. "I don't know who does. I hope they gave it a decent burial."

"Okay," said Teirra softly.

Both fell silent, Dahli turning back to making her breakfast. The quiet continued for another few minutes.

"Atterick and I were going to go down to the beach today and spend some time there. Do you want to come along?" asked Teirra, her voice light.

It was a challenge, Dahli knew, a dare to break routine and turn down a trip to the soft white beaches of the east side of the island. It would also give Teirra a chance to keep an eye on her, to watch for clues that would incriminate her. Dahli shrugged.

"I don't know, are you sure you can trust me not to break into anything?"

Teirra sighed. "I think so."

Dahli found herself wanting to throw something and start screaming, but she couldn't very well try to get rid of the body in broad daylight, anyway.

"Sure," she said, "okay."

****

The day was hot for late spring, unseasonably so. Dahli stretched out on the warm sand, gazing up at the protective haze. She felt calmer now than she had earlier. She closed her eyes, feeling the sand between her fingers as she thought about where they would bury the faelin. It would have to be someplace secluded, where no one was likely to come across it. She wondered how long it would take her, Diza, Czamkiar, and Randish to dig a grave. They would need a pick and a shovel. Dahli considered buying flower seeds to sprinkle over the grave, musing about how long it would take the foliage to grow back over the hole. Grass and brambles grew quickly, and they could toss some leaves and branches over the area. With any luck, caution and planning, no one would ever find the spot.

But where to put the body? Dahli mulled over several possibilities. There were swamps along the back roads, where the ground was soft and easy to dig, but they were popular places for people to drive off-road vehicles. They may not have enough time to bury the faelin before somebody came along. Maybe they could bury it off the side of the road, in the deep bush. Sure, who would find it out there? Dahli dozed in the hot sun, content that the adventure would soon be over.

She called Czamkiar when she got home later that afternoon, asking him to get Diza and meet her down at the Contempo. She then changed her clothes and left the house, convinced that Teirra had given up the notion that she had the body. Dahli walked down the street to the old garage, keys jingling in her pocket. It was a fine day, and she was feeling pretty good. Or at least she was until she reached the garage.

The smell seeped out as soon as she opened the garage door. It was not very strong, but it was there, the sickening-sweet smell of spoiled flesh. Dahli felt her mouth water as though she was going to vomit, and her stomach rolled. She turned her head aside, hearing the sound of the flies buzzing as they sought the source of the stench. She took a moment to recover, then inhaled a breath of clean air before walking into the garage.

The smell was worse once she got into the conni, where the body was confined. Gagging on the reek, she rolled down her window as fast as she could and drove out of the garage. As she paused for a traffic light, she opened the other window to air the vehicle out, and it worked to some extent. Dahli drove as fast as she dared to the Contempo, feeling a knot in her stomach as she continued to smell rot. She glanced out the window, glad to see the day was ending and it was becoming dark. When she reached the Contempo, she left the conni running and ran inside the building to get her friends, finding Randish among them. Dahli walked hurriedly up to the table.

"I'm parked outside," she said in a quick, quiet tone. "Can you please hurry? The conni stinks like you would not believe."

The three stared back at her. "Stinks?" inquired Diza. She had a horrified look on her face. Dahli nodded.

"Yeah. Look I'm going to drive around a bit before someone gets a good sniff. You people hurry." Then she left the restaurant, getting into the conni and heading off to circle the block.

She had driven around the block five times before she saw her friends in front of the Contempo. She stopped the vehicle and threw the door open for them to get in. She couldn't help but notice that her hands were white on the steering wheel.

"Smell isn't *that* bad," said Czamkiar from the back seat.

"Isn't that *great*," said Randish. His voice implied that his nose was wrinkled in disgust, but no one could see through the hair.

"It was worse when I first got the conni." said Dahli. "Sitting in the garage it was so bad I thought I was going to be ill." She turned a corner, guiding the conni out of the city. "So does anybody know where we can get a shovel?"

There was silence.

"Anybody?" said Dahli, a little helplessly. Diza and Czamkiar were quiet. Randish stared down at his long, strong hands.

"Come on, Randish," said Dahli, "Siriusians live in caves."

"We don't dig them ourselves."

The group drove on, heading further out of the city. All was silent within save for the soft sound of the receiver and the hum of the engine.

"I have an idea," Czamkiar suddenly said. "If we took it into the woods we could use branches and stuff to dig the grave. The ground would be soft enough."

"That would be all right for a shallow grave," said Randish. "We want something deeper and more permanent."

"Randish is right," said Dahli. "We're going to need something to dig with. I wish I knew where to get something. HEY! My Grampa gardens, he'll have a shovel." Dahli turned the conni around sharply, heading back towards the city.

They parked the conni a safe distance away from the old man's house. Dahli got out and slipped quietly into the yard, and as she did so a familiar large figure bounded off of the porch to greet her. She bent to pat Boo's head, rubbing the furless monster's ears. She gave him a final slap before heading towards the gardening shed, Boo tagging along, his small rump trying to keep up with his huge weight-lifter's shoulders. He sat down by the garden shed door, dual rows of teeth and huge nocturnal eyes giving him the look of a demented cartoon. Boo watched as Dahli tried the door and found it locked.

"Clart," Dahli muttered, pulling once more on the door.

She walked around to the small side window, managing to get her fingers under the sill. She pulled and the window came open, but the space was narrow. She thrust her head into the opening, finding she could fit that part in easily enough. Putting her arms in next, she pulled herself clumsily head-first into the shed. She slowly squiggled inside, almost falling and landing on her skull. She managed not to kill herself as she lowered herself to the ground, then stood up and dusted herself off. Dahli reached for the light, finding the string and tugging it, illumination suddenly filling the small, cramped space. There were stacks of pots on shelves, seedlings were lined in neat rows on a little rack, and in one corner there was an array of gardening implements. She examined these, finding hoes, rakes, and a couple of spades, but nothing that looked as though it could do the job she had in mind.

Grampa probably didn't bury many bodies.

Dahli continued to look around, though by now she had decided she probably was not going to find a large shovel. She decided to take the spades; they were sharp and better than nothing. She reached out to take the smooth shafts in her hand when she suddenly heard Boo race off at a great rate, roaring nightmarishly. She heard the screech of two surprised youths, young boys who made a practice of cutting through the yard. Dahli quickly turned off the light, crouching down in the small shed as she heard the feralyke continue to bellow. She saw the yellow porch light come on through the window, and a moment later heard the front door creak open.

"Boo! What are you making all that noise about? Come on, get inside!"

Dahli listened to her heart pound as she heard the feralyke tear up the stairs and into the house. The door shut, and she breathed a sigh of relief. She waited in silence until the light went off, then, taking the spades, tossed them out the window and climbed out after them. She then pushed the window closed, and, spades in hand, ran across the lawn, climbing over the low fence and heading towards the conni.

"What took you?" said Diza, her hand over her nose. With the conni stationary the smell had once more filtered through.

"I almost got caught," said Dahli, thrusting the spades into the back seat of the conni with Randish and Czamkiar. She then got into the driver's seat and started the vehicle forward, pulling neatly away from the curb.

"Do you think these will do it?" asked Czamkiar, examining the spades.

"I don't know," said Dahli. "I guess they'll have to, but who knows how long it will take us to dig the grave."

"It's getting late," said Diza, "we had better find a place soon or else we won't have time. And that thing smells bad enough already."

"Kinda smells like home," said Randish musingly.

"Great," said Dahli, "that really makes me want to keep your planet in mind if I ever move off of this one. I think I'd rather move to Faela."

"Great conversationalists, those faelins," said Czamkiar. He and Randish both began barking and howling loudly.

"Okay!" Dahli yelled above the noise. "I get the point. And I'd fry in the sun anyway; their planet isn't protected like ours. And speaking of faelins, there's a back road. Maybe there will be a place to dig a grave."

They turned down the road, driving slowly over the pot holes. Trees lined the way, old and bent, their trunks rough and grey, standing like grizzled spirit guardians. Grass grew long and wild on road's unpaved surface, and at times it seemed the old thoroughfare had been swallowed completely by the encroaching wilderness. The bush was thick and high, a virtually impenetrable barrier.

"This is going nowhere," said Dahli after a while. "There's no way we'll get through this stuff. Let's go back."

They went back to the main road, driving about until they

found what appeared to be a suitable spot. Upon closer inspection, however, it proved to be a swamp, and they spent a tense few minutes trying to get Randish out of the muck. They finally hauled the big Siriusian out of the bog, but it had been a scary turn of events. They went back to the conni and were on their way again, continuing in their quest for the Great Faelin Burial Site.

"This is clart," said Czamkiar, exasperated. He was in the front seat with Dahli now, while in the back seat Diza was wiping muck off Randish with a towel which had been left back there. "It's almost the middle of the night and we still haven't found a spot. I don't even want to think about what the body looks like after baking in the heat all day."

Dahli didn't answer. She suddenly pulled over to the side of the road, stopping the conni. Off to the right she looked out across a misty field, the eerie shapes of statues in the vague light of the headlights.

"Okay folks," said Dahli, "we have found our spot." She opened the door and got out. She walked around the conni and down the ditch towards the field.

"Dahli!" yelled Diza as she and the other two followed her. "This field belongs to someone!"

"Uh-huh," said Dahli, knowing exactly to whom it belonged. "Come on, let's pick a spot."

The four scaled the simple wooden fence, thumping down into long, tangled grass. As they walked they could feel the softness of the earth beneath their feet. They passed statues, some tilted at odd angles, slowly sinking into the ground. The unnerving cold sentinels were everywhere, and loomed periodically out of the fog to watch the four pass by, and in one place great birds and men on destris stood guard near a group of ethereal goddesses, down on their knees as they wept into their stone hands.

"Someone was busy for a few hundred years," whispered Czamkiar as they passed a multi-faced monster with impossibly large teeth.

"Yeah," said Dahli. "I wonder who made these, and why they all face in the same direction?" She shivered as she realized the monuments all stared towards Draephus' castle, like a silent army of the damned, daring him to come forth.

"Who knows?" said Diza. "Hey look! We can bury the body

there!"

The place Diza indicated was a tiny grotto created beneath the limbs of several enormous, bent trees, hung with mosses and lichens. Within their shrouding embrace was a miniature natural pool, little more than a puddle, a run-off from the thin stream that wormed apologetically past. A tiny winged being bent her face to the pool, her young features a mask of surprise. One small hand hovered just above the surface of the water. Behind her and the pool, shadowed far under the mighty trees, was enough space to bury the faelin.

"Right," said Dahli. "I'll get the spades."

"No it's too late now." said Diza. "We'll have to do it tomorrow."

"But then we'll have to leave the body another day!" said Dahli. "It's going to smell even worse. Let's at least start the grave, since we're out here."

She ran back to the conni, bounding over grass and brambles, returning shortly with the spades. Dropping one to the ground, she took the other and shoved it into the earth, removing a chunk of the rich, dark soil. The digging was easy, and Dahli cut the edges of the grave. She removed the top layer of grass with care, so it could be replaced later. She set the pieces aside in careful array, rather like a jigsaw puzzle. Then, once this was done, she set about digging with a vengeance. The soil heaped up as she went, driving the spade again and again into the ground, tearing out more earth.

She didn't ask Czamkiar to take over; he simply did when it became obvious that she was too tired. Rising from his seat on the ground, he took the spade and continued work on the hole. Dahli sat down on the ground, winded and sweating. The air was cool, and she could feel the sweat quickly drying on her body, leaving a chill. She watched Czamkiar dig for a while, then, when he grew tired, Randish took over. The hours came and went silently, slipping by unheeded. After three hours of digging, Dahli and Diza went to get the Faelin.

The stench that wafted out of the conni's trunk was revolting, and Dahli had to resist the urge to vomit. She could feel it rising in her stomach, and she fought it down as she reached in to grab one end of the rolled tarp. Diza reached in to take the other and they lifted it out of the trunk, carrying it back to the grave site. The hole Randish was standing in was thigh-deep on him, making it waist-deep on Dahli and Diza. Dahli stared at the hole critically, then shook her head.

"It still isn't deep enough. Look why don't you guys just go home, it's getting pretty late. I'll finish this myself. No sense all of us getting caught for being out too late."

"No," said Diza wearily, and sighed. "Look my dad won't be home in the morning, he goes to work early. I told him I was spending the night at your place because I had a feeling we would be out too late. We can go to my place and wash our clothes so you won't have to go home all muddy. I mean it still doesn't solve the problem of Teirra wanting to know where we were, but we may as well finish."

Randish was still digging. Dahli watched him for a short time, then said; "All right."

They dug down further, and when they finally could dig no more, the pit was chest-deep on Dahli. All were sore and tired. Blisters had formed on their hands and broken open, leaving painful, oozing sores. They placed the faelin in the hole, then sat on the grass to catch their breath. They had no idea what the time may be. Above them the sky showed no sign of brightening, but all were anxious to finish the job and be on their way. It was Dahli who first went to the heap of dirt and began doggedly throwing it back into the hole. This took decidedly less time than the digging had, and soon the hole was full. They replaced the grass, pressing it down by walking on it, the four of them milling about on the one small area; heedless of how comedic they looked doing so. Then, in silence, they took the spades and left the solitary grave beneath the trees.

Diza's father had left by the time they arrived; four dirty, tired figures. They beat most of the clotted muck off outside, then threw their clothes into the washer. They sat about the kitchen table, quiet and bleary, drinking tea in their underwear. Dahli lit a cigarette with aching fingers, noticing Randish was too tired to care. She stared at the tattoo on his forearm, one very similar to the Faelin's. She was almost startled to notice it, but then recalled that was why he was on Sferkkaa; he too had been brought down to experiment on.

Dahli studied the Siriusian. He looked ordinary enough, save for that ridge of hair down his back that descended from somewhere beneath the tangled mane on his head. His hair was stringy enough after the work that she could see his eyes, which were a soft warm brown. Inside his great chest was a pair of enlarged lungs, and a huge heart to make better use of the thin, hot atmosphere of his world. The biggest problem Siriusians had living on Sferkkaa was the fact that this world was not as warm as their own, and those big, heat-absorbing lungs easily caught bronchial diseases. Dahli then recalled that he would have an inner lid to help protect his eyes from the flying sand. One good yawn also reminded her of something else, and she stared at the ragged carnivore's teeth with the awe of the exhausted. Diza came to sit next to him, pushing her hand through his dark, heavy hair. A little dried mud fell out, and she smiled.

"You need a bath."

"Are you going to make me take one?"

"Won't be the first time I've wrestled you into doing something."

Czamkiar was too tired to notice the interaction. He stared ahead, his blue eyes surrounded by red, a streak of mud on his left cheek. His eye make-up was halfway down his face.

"Well," he said, "here it is, another typical morning at Diza's, with everybody at the table drinking tea in their underwear."

"We don't wear underwear on Sirius," remarked Randish. He stared into his mug. "We don't drink tea, either."

Czamkiar look at Dahli. "So now what?" he asked.

Dahli exhaled smoke, stubbing out her cigarette. "From now on, it's my mess alone."

Gryphons – Book II
'Take the Long Way Home'.

Chapter Eight

Draephus searched under the debris of the previous night's party for the telecom, completely unaware he was running a cemetery for faelins. He could hear it, ringing persistently beneath the mess of glasses, clothing, bottles, ashtrays, drug paraphernalia, and other bits of crap. He found the telecom under Raski, who was curled protectively around it behind the couch Delaes Randerick was presently passed out on. Draephus thought this was probably the last party he would ever throw in his home as he pried the 'com away from Raski and managed to get it to his ear.

"Heia?" he croaked blearily. His stomach threatened to evict last night's merriment.

"May I speak to Draephus CZimcocious, please."

Draephus didn't much like the officious tone of voice. It sounded too much like a LEO. Beneath him, Raski squirmed. Draephus kissed his face.

"Yeah, talking."

"Donsa CZimcocious, this is Officer Astor of the Second City Legal Enforcement Department..."

Draephus went cold. He'd had enough problems with the LEOs to be wary of any contact with them, and the fact that there was enough highly illegal drugs currently lying all over his house to get him put away for life didn't make him any happier. Not that the LEOs had time to waste on the occasional user, but if they showed up and found this pile… well... there *was* such a thing as pushing one's luck. Fifteen pounds of mushroom powder and resin was a bit much to claim as being for personal use only.

"Officer..." drawled Draephus. "How's it going?" Both Delaes and Raski sat up, Delaes weaving appreciably.

"Donsa CZimcocious, do you own a psychedelic Celestial Hunter?"

"Psychedelic? No mine's grey."

Across town, the officer looked out his window at the smouldering wreckage that had once been a beautiful vintage conveyance. "Well it's been vandalized, Donsa CZimcocious. The original colour may have been grey."

Draephus groaned, trying to think of any distinguishing features that would be visible through several coats of graffiti. He finally recalled the time Khandid had accidentally broken a bottle of ink in the back seat.

"Is there a hand print in black ink on the back seat?"

"Yes, there is."

"Should be mine, then."

"Well, we have it, we were wondering if you would like to come claim it."

Draephus sighed. "Sure. I'll be right down." He passed Raski the telecom, staring fondly at him, gently touching his face. "Come on, Rask, let's to down to the LEO department and get my conni."

Having determined somewhere in his still-inebriated brain that they were in no danger, Delaes Randerick flopped over once more with a small, childish noise. Draephus walked over to him, picking him up and carrying him upstairs to a guest room.

"You're cute when you're asleep," he told the skinny, leggy man. Delaes made a small noise, but that was the only response he gave. Draephus carried him into a room and placed him on the bed, watching as his faelins hopped up to join Delaes, snuggling with him.

"You guys sure like Delaes," Draephus remarked. He watched them as they yipped and nipped each other, as if fighting over who got to sleep beside the unconscious man. Czanda finally let Bacca have the privilege, Draephus raising an eyebrow. "Look, every time Delaes comes to visit, you two start acting like clartheads. Now if you can't play nice then you're both going in the Bad Faelin Box, *without* cookies."

Bacca shook his head and made a rude noise.

"Just behave."

"Pfft."

"I don't have to take that from you. Me Master. You… alternate life form. Respect me. Or I'll discipline you. And I mean it this time. Really."

Bacca made a rumbling noise, then put his head down, closing his eyes. Draephus sighed and left the room, making his way downstairs in time to see Raski stand up and look around at the spread of chaos. It had taken the Gryphons, Bad Influence, and about two hundred of their best friends to make the mess. Now as the day broke on Twoday morning, Draephus wondered how large a transport they'd need to haul the debris away. A transport, and paid workers. Once the mushroom resin wore off, Draephus would be in far too much pain to move.

"I've seen explosions that didn't look this bad," said Raski.

"That's because this wasn't an explosion, it was a riot." Draephus began sorting through the wreckage, finding a body rolled up into a ball inside one of the two enormous fireplaces. Draephus slowly uncovered the face, and grinned.

"Well well, lookit this, someone tossed away a perfectly good quinticord player. Wanna see what the world's fastest quintist looks like asleep?"

Raski blinked. "Straif Mannechek is passed out in your fireplace?"

"The one and the same. Little darling must have showed up with Delaes, he's been trying to talk him into leaving Vortex and joining Bad Influence."

"Well what do we do with him? We can't leave him in the fireplace; the man's a god of the music world!"

"So genuflect and I'll carry him upstairs and stick him beside Delaes."

Raski did. Draephus rolled his eyes, and picked up the tiny youth. No sooner had Draephus hoisted him, however, when one eye opened. It looked from Draephus, to Raski, and back again.

"Why do I smell like a barbecue pit and how did I get here?"

"You were in the fireplace, and we have no idea."

Straif Mannechek, sixteen years old and not known for his brains, stared at Draephus nervously. "Are you gonna hurt me?"

"Would you like me to?"

"No."

"Then I won't. C'mon, you're a baby, you're not supposed to be found passed out in the fireplaces of people you don't know."

"I didn't have anywhere else to pass out."

Draephus took Straif up to Delaes' room, placing him down beside him and covering him over.

"Want a bedtime story?" he asked.

Straif gave him a sour look. He was small even by East Continent standards, and he was not about to lip off to a man he knew to have killed over two hundred people in the war.

"I'm fine," he said.

"Glass of milk? Cookies?"

Delaes sat up. "Draephus will you kindly stop teasing the child I would really rather not have to get out of this bed and find something to hit you with not with my head and stomach feeling the way they do at the moment and I am going to be sick where's the bathroom?"

Draephus pointed, and Delaes got out of the bed, fleeing in the direction indicated. Draephus looked back down at Straif, feeling an odd urge to just cuddle the youngster protectively, knowing the boy was far too young to realize just how very exceptionally talented he was, and how, despite what he was being told, Vortex would come apart without him. Straif was a pawn in other people's games, and Draephus hoped he had the bravery to leave Vortex and join up with a band that would protect and appreciate him.

"Okay I'll stop teasing. And you don't have to be scared of me."

"Don't have to be scared of you? You once killed a man with a kaisa!"

Draephus sighed and rolled his eyes as once again he was confronted with his own myth. "It was *not* a kaisa. I don't quite remember what it *was*, but it was definitely *not* a kaisa. And Straif, there was a war on, and he was trying to use my lower intestine to hang me with. I don't kill people just for fun. In fact I would much prefer to not have to kill anyone ever again. I certainly have no reason to hurt you, so don't be scared. Just lie down until you feel better, help yourself to whatever I have in the kitchen, and if I catch you drinking again before you're twenty, I'll spank your ass. *Shi-dah?*"

"What?"

"Understand?"

"Everything but that last word."

Draephus groaned inwardly. "Lie down, get some rest, we'll sort out how bright you're not later."

Straif did. Draephus left the room, trailed by Raski.

"I have to check on something in the woods before I go," said Draephus.

"Ohwendai?" asked Raski.

"Yeah, I wanna see if it's working this time."

"I'll come with you," he said.

Draephus nodded, heading carefully down the stairs. Man he

was starting to hurt. After he went to see the LEOs he was going to make his friends positively ecstatic and do what they had been telling him to do – go to bed and let himself heal. The war was over, he could do that now.

Draephus was about to ask Raski if he had any wards of protection before he went to a place of magic, but then remembered Raski was never without wards of some sort. The bright flashing jewelled clips he liked to wear in his hair and the sparkling bracelets were not simple decoration that looked beautiful against his black skin – they were made of a type of white crystal that could only be found in caves on the South Continent. Cut and polished, they flashed like the scales on a fish, and had been valued for centuries as a means of reflecting bad magicks back at their caster. Draephus went to get his knife, bag, and staff, and the pair headed down the path that led to the pond, followed as always by Bacca and Czanda. Reaching it, he paused.

"Mind yourselves, my family!"

Something slowly prowled off through the grass. Raski took Draephus' arm, a little unnerved.

"Very impressive. You've been keeping up with your spell-work I see. Is that a daeha?"

"I think it might be," said Draephus, watching the grass bend with the passing of the creature. "It came when I began casting magic in this area. Seems happy enough, and if it is a daeha, I'm not going to do anything to scare it off. I can use all the guardians I can get."

Draephus and Raski followed the path that led behind the pond, and down into the clearing, both murmuring the simple tunes to keep the carn-crows away. Then as they reached the clearing, Draephus paused and held up one hand.

"Yes, yes, yes, I see you, Brother Bird. What news have you for me today?"

The bird may have been the same one he had caught weeks ago when he last tried this spell. In fact it may even have been the same beetle. Both gave the impression of staring at him in annoyance.

The new twig was even more dead than the last one had been.

"I don't get it!" said Draephus. It's not working. It is absolutely not working. Bird – you're not trying!"

He released the bird and beetle as Raski went to inspect the twig.

"Wow," he said. "Draephus I am truly impressed. This is a twig from a Nightwood tree."

"I know."

"They're unkillable! I cleared three out of my yard, threw the bits into a pile to dry for firewood, and the *bits* grew! I now have fourteen!"

"I *know*, Rask."

Raski stepped back and shook his head. "I have to say I am absolutely in awe of your abilities. You killed an unkillable tree using sympathetic healing magic."

"Yeah scruffin' lovely, Rask, now why is it not working?"

Raski just slowly shook his head. "I have no idea. All I can say is the illness you are trying to heal is stronger than this simple spell. Have you called Shaktra Mannis? She'd know a spell that was stronger."

"Called her a few times, I didn't get an answer. But considering she's on the South Continent, and the seasonal floods are underway, she could very well be out rebuilding her house."

"Yeah," said Raski. "Well we could always go call Harli, he's an ohwendai man."

Draephus nodded. "Yeah. And his magic is stronger than mine, he'll know something."

"And Draephus," said Raski softly, "when Vesper left, he had months to live. Now he has years. Don't despair – the magic *is* working."

Draephus nodded, and managed a smile, looking to Raski. He wanted to go to him, hold him and kiss him, but to demonstrate open love for another in this place of healing would likely have some powerful consequences. Then his attention was caught by the sight of the carn-crow landing on the earth before him. It was a powerful, ugly, beast, and it gazed at Draephus with red eyes, beak open, making soft sounds as if it was trying to speak. He slowly backed up a step as the monstrous creature creaked and cackled, gazing straight at him. Then it walked over to the dead twig and pulled it from the ground, letting it fall before walking away.

Draephus and Raski cautiously followed it, watching as it walked over to a very small sapling that had been uprooted by some curious animal. It picked the tiny tree up and turned to walk back to Draephus, who knelt and accepted it. He then gave the crow his entire bag of red beans, which seemed to please it endlessly.

"Thank you, Brother Crow," said Draephus.

It took the bag and departed, leaving Draephus holding the tree. Raski walked over to him to look at the tiny plant.

"What does this mean?" asked Raski.

"I don't know," said Draephus. "Carn-crows are random magic, neither good nor bad, but dangerous and to be respected. So if one tries to speak to me and then gives me a tree, you can bet I'm going to plant it. Come on, let's get this little fellow into the ground, then go get my conni."

Draephus planted the tree, then he, Raski and the faelins departed. As they left the clearing, Draephus noticed the grass rippling, and watched to see what, if anything, this meant. That was when he noticed that someone had dug up a portion of the ground near the little winged statue, then very carefully replaced the top layer of plants and earth.

As if someone was hoping no one would notice they had been digging.

****

Raski cleaned himself up before they left; Draephus didn't bother. They drove to the large, functional and painfully ugly building downtown, and the two walked into the structure, listening to their feet make hollow, echoing sounds on the cold stone floor. The two walked up to the main desk, reigned over by a large man in uniform. He glanced up at the two with mild interest, as though smelly, beat up, and hungover celebrities were an everyday occurrence.

"Can I help you?" he asked.

Draephus paused, his attention focused for the moment on his stomach. It calmed down, and he relaxed. He had no desire to toss here, of all places.

"Name is Draephus CZimcocious," he said. "I'm here to identify my conni."

"Officer Astor has been waiting for you. You'll find his office just down the hall."

The two found the officer, and Astor led them out to the compound where the vehicle was being kept, crossing a short grassy expanse to the fenced-in area. Feralykes ran up to investigate them briefly, then went about their business of guarding the compound. Officer Astor made a motion for Draephus and Raski to follow him.

"It's over here," he said.

When Draephus saw his conni, he began moving faster, jogging up to the vehicle, stopping before its broad nose. He stared, horror-struck, at the wild colours, the weird lurking figures, and the Bad Influence logo. The windshield was cracked, and as he moved around to the side he saw the enormous crease along the side where Dahli had driven it into the stone pillar. He yanked the door open and winced as it screamed in protest. He thrust his head inside, pulling it out quickly as the stench of rot hit him. He gagged, resting a hand on the roof of the once-noble conni to steady himself.

"Is this your vehicle?" asked Astor.

Draephus composed himself, slowly turning to face the man. "Yeah. Where did you find it?"

"In the possession of a fifteen-year-old girl named Dahli Sandiniti. She's in custody now. Would you like to press charges?"

Draephus looked at the ruined upholstery, the debris strewn about the interior. Oh she'd been mad, all right. Furious. Draephus could barely recall anything past the conversation with Vesper's cousin, but apparently he had made an impact, and Dahli had returned the favour in spades. They were even. There was no need to continue the situation.

"No," he said softly, "that's all right, she didn't hurt it."

Officer Astor nodded, then gazed in puzzlement at the Bad Influence logo on the hood. "I thought you fellows called your band the Mortified Gryphons…?"

"We're really big Bad Influence fans," said Raski.

The officer looked sidelong at Raski, who was grinning like an idiot. "Just as well you don't press charges," he said. "Donselle Sandiniti is in quite enough trouble already."

"What kind of trouble?" asked Draephus.

"I can't specify, but bad trouble. Anyway, just sign the form stating this is your conni and you can take it."

Draephus signed his name, taking his keys from the man. At least he still had his bird-claw keychain, he mused. Vesper had given it to him, and he would have hated to have lost it.

"So what do we do with it?" asked Raski, staring at the vehicle. "Burn it?"

"Have it repaired, I guess."

Raski nodded, and watched as a tire suddenly began deflating loudly, complete with sounds effects that would have had any eight-year-old rolling in hilarity. He put an arm around Draephus.

"My lover, that child was some kind of pissed at you."

****

Dahli awoke to the harsh sound of the morning bell, and rolled out of bed automatically, before her brain had time to fully register that she was awake. She sat on the edge of the cot, a bad taste in her mouth. Her hair was scruffed up at odd angles, and her back and shoulders ached. She had learned to get up without thinking about it, just sit up at the sound of the bell. It made life easier. Since she had four-and-a-half months left of a six month sentence, anything she could do to make life easier was worth it.

Diza had come to visit her a few times, bringing letters from some of the people at school. Many of these were from people she did not even know; it seemed she had become something of a local hero, which struck her as odd. She hadn't taken the faelin to gain the approval of a lot of kids who, for the most part, had never cared she existed.

Teirra had come to see her, too. After the initial outbursts of rage and tears when Dahli admitted the entire story to the news media, Teirra hadn't said much about the incident at all, resigning herself to the idea that Dahli was determined to make her point. The school had offered to drop the charges if she gave the body back, but she'd refused to do so. She also refused to name her accomplices, and insisted she had acted on her own. Nobody believed that, of course; the LEOs had pictures of the tracks up and down the school hallways, including a spectacularly large set that could only have come from an adult male Siriusian. However there was nothing anyone could do to get her to implicate her friends.

Dahli was as loyal as she was hard-headed. That meant she got to enjoy her prison sentence alone.

Dahli ran her hand over her face, musing upon that warm Oneday when she had marched cheerfully into the office of Second City News Services and announced the whole story. Somehow she honestly hadn't expected it would come to this. Summer would be long gone by the time she got out. At least with the educational programme within the institution, she wouldn't be behind in her school work.

"What a plus," she muttered sarcastically as she rose from her cot and wandered out of her cell, making note of the fact that it was the first day of the week. "I don't like Oneday," she grumbled quietly.

She picked listlessly at the crumbling paint on the walls as she walked down the hall. Prisons were expensive, and there were more pressing things to spend the money on. It was cheaper to simply send prisoners to Second City than it was to build more penitentiaries and detention centers, and there would be no more built until sewer systems, running water, and electricity were available everywhere in Second City, as opposed to only a few areas, and the underground fires were finally put out in Avalair. In the meantime, law-breakers were kept in rather nasty cells, and the bare handful of female inmates was segregated to a few rooms of prisons meant for male inmates. Those who complained received the same form letter from The Emperor;

"If you can't find something better to do with your time than break the law and bitch about the prison that YOU put yourself into, then go šukat yourself."

Behind Dahli trailed the two girls with whom she shared the cell, Crystal and Ember. Fine, upstanding girls, both of them. One was a thief, and the other had beaten up an old man. Both were from far away; Dahli wasn't certain where exactly. Dahli was the first person they had met who had stolen a dead body. They had all exchanged stories one night as Dahli shared out the cigarettes Diza had smuggled in to her. Dahli liked them well enough, they were okay. At least they were somebody to eat breakfast with.

They filled their trays and took their places at a long table. The food wasn't bad, usually, just bland and very basic, as though the stuff had been cooked by people with no imagination. The Emperor's stance on the food in prison was much the same as it was on the décor – if you don't like it, don't do anything to come back here. Dahli took a bite of something that may have been toast and chewed thoughtfully.

"Well?" asked Crystal. "How's it taste today?"

"Liiiike..." Dahli took another taste. "Old paper soaked in ditchwater."

"Always one of my favourites," said Ember. She took a bite of a brownish square. "Yeah, that about sums it up."

One of the inmates was making her way around the small room that served as the women's mess hall; there were only six females in the detention center altogether. She was handing out the day's mail, and dropped four letters in front of Dahli before wandering on her way. Dahli picked the letters up and looked at them, Crystal and Ember eyeing her a little enviously. Probably no one in the whole place got as much mail as Dahli did. There was a letter from Atterick and Teirra, one from Czamkiar, and another from Diza. The fourth letter had no return address, and she didn't recognise the handwriting. The letters were blocky, printed rather than written, with a slight quaver to them. She assumed it was from one of the many teenaged fans she now had, and she opened this one first. There was no date, no perfunctory greeting, it simply began with a line;

Heia donselle. Quite the number you pulled on my conni.

Dahli blinked and re-read the line, then continued down the letter;

Got it re-painted, but they're still working on the upholstery. And I can't get the smell out of the trunk. I didn't figure out what it was until I read the story in the newspaper. Raski keeps calling it the `Reek-mobile'. I haven't told him what the smell is. I'll wait until it's been fixed and he's in it. Then I'll tell him.

Why am I writing you. Good question. I don't even know if you'll read this far. I didn't put my name on the envelope so you wouldn't see it and toss this letter away without at least opening it. After all, I'm the last son of a feralyke you want to see, right? You're pretty tough, takes a lot of nerve to do what you did. Sorry you ended up in there. No place to spend the summer.

It's fourhour in the morning, I haven't slept for days so I don't know if I can be held responsible for writing this. Raski walks up to me today and says; `What do you call a guy who hangs around musicians?' I said `What?' and he says; `A drummer.' I was so tired that by the time I figured it out, he was gone and I couldn't thump him for it. I think I'll telecom him in a moment or two and ask him what a five-letter word for clarthead is.

Anyway, take care. I'm gonna call The Rask and then maybe go to bed. Or maybe I'll take a wander out to this little pond in my field I sometimes go to. It's a good place, good quiet place. Has trees all around it, and a little statue. I like to sit there sometimes and watch the world go by.

Here's my address, you can write if you want.
- Draephus.

Dahli read the letter twice, astonished at what she was holding in her hand. He'd written her. She had no idea why he had, but here was the letter, in his own handwriting. Why would he even bother trying to communicate after what she had done? And the remark about the pond; had he found the body? He must have, why else would he mention the pond specifically? That was probably the reason for the letter. He wanted to let her know he was aware of the faelin, and that it was all right with him that she had buried it in his field.

Maybe he wasn't such a clart after all.

She read her other letters, taking her time with them as she ate her breakfast. Then she replaced them in their envelopes just in time to be chased out of the mess hall. It was time for classes now, which were a wholly different experience than they had been in the `Real World', as Dahli had come to refer to life outside the detention centre. There was no šukating around, not if she wanted to eat or spend any time outside of her cramped, musty cell. Sitting by herself in the room was no fun, she had learned from experience. Better just to be a good little drone and follow orders.

Their instructor was a man named Donsa Sappil. Dahli assumed he was a man, but truly she wasn't even certain if he was from their planet. Donsa Sappil was the only person in the whole place Dahli truly liked. He had time for all of his `little delinquents', and if one wished to learn, he would teach. If one wished a fight, he'd go for that, too. He had a face like a rock with a headache, but he was a fair teacher, and he alone of all the instructors seemed to have the affection of his students rather than their grudging respect. Dahli gave him a smile as she walked into class. He smiled back and passed her a note on pink paper; a reminder that she had a counselling session later that day.

"Awwww… I don't wanna go…" she whined.

"Now, Dahli," said Donsa Sappil, gently chastising, "what did I say about the councillors?"

"Just humour the idiots so I can get on with my life?"

"Smart girl. Take your seat."

Everyone had to go to a councillor once a week, it was mandatory. And it seemed there was no one who did not despise the two councillors. The first of the two, Donsa Newark, had decided sometime in early childhood that there was no one on the planet he could not bully into seeing things his way. He was what Crystal called a `friendly monster'. When one first met him, he seemed an attractive, helpful and sympathetic person. According to the stories Dahli had heard, he was anything but. He could be belligerent, insulting and abusive.

Dahli had the second of the two, Donsa Ris. She wasn't sure who was worse, and several times she found herself wondering if it would be less of a pain to have Newark insult her than it was to be frustrated to madness by Ris. She honestly couldn't decide who was the more loathsome of the pair. However, of the two, Ris somehow seemed less dangerous than Newark, who appeared to delight in abuse. He had, indeed, elevated it to an art form. Dahli thought about the drunken and snide Councillor Dowan back at school, and wondered if all councillors were such a mess, and if that was how they came to be in the profession in the first place; they were patients who had been promoted. As far as she was concerned, `Greasy Ris' served only one purpose. She saw him once a week, and this would be the seventh time she had seen him. She was now seven weeks into her sentence. At least he helped her keep track of time.

She got through her three hours of class, and began heading for the laundry room. It was only tenhour by this point, and she had two hours of dirty laundry to look forward to before lunch. Then, after lunch, she got to clean floors. Yay! If she survived she vowed never to leave Teirra with all the laundry ever again. And dishes, she'd *never* stack up dishes either. She'd done piles of them, and it was like a nightmare, scraping plates and washing them in water so hot it turned her skin red. Then there was always bed-making, that was fun, but not as much fun as cleaning toilets. Dahli swore some people sat up all night just thinking of new ways to clart on the seat. She couldn't understand *why,* because chores were rotational and everybody had to do the same ones. But then maybe it was funny when somebody else had to do the cleaning.

She walked into the laundry room's steaming heat. Upon

spotting her, one of the two girls dropped the load she was holding and slogged wearily out of the room. Dahli picked up the clothes and stuffed them into the ancient washing machine. No one ever seemed to have anything to say, they just put clothes in, took them out, folded and sweated. It was hot work, and hard. Dahli was always glad when it was over.

By the time lunch rolled around, Dahli was in a haze. Nothing made sense; the heat had cooked her brain. When the bell rang announcing the end of her time there, it seemed too good to be true. She dropped the load of dirty laundry she held and stumped towards the door. As she left the heat of the room and felt the cooler air against her damp, sweaty flesh, she mused upon how she was going to deal with Ris in this state.

She located Ember and Crystal in the mess hall, and slumped down beside them with her tray. "I hate laundry," she grumbled. "I'd rather go naked than wash anything else." She stared down at the dubious-looking bowl of soup. "What is this clart?"

"We don't know," said Ember. "How's it taste?"

Dahli took a sample. "Liiiike...decaying meat, boiled. The noodles have a distinct, snot-like texture. No idea what the brown things are."

"That's disgusting," said Crystal morosely, allowing some of the clearish broth to dribble off of her spoon.

"I want some real food," said Dahli, dropping her spoon into her soup with a small splash. "And some real clothes, and cigarettes. Who's gonna break out and get us some real food?"

"I will," said Ember. "What do you want?"

"Everything. Absolutely everything. Whose idea was it to come here, anyway? I'm going to be mad by the time I get out of here."

"You'll survive," said Crystal with a little sympathy.

"I wanna play my cylinders," pouted Dahli. "I want to go for a stroll at night, watch the Visual, and sleep until thirteenhour."

Ember laughed. "Look at it this way. Every hour that goes by is an hour closer to all those things."

"Yeah," said Dahli, "but every hour with Ris is like an extra two days on my sentence. I'd rather do anything than see him. He frustrates the clart out of me. I'm sick of him trying to get me to confess to having some sort of fascination for dead bodies."

"Ah, just admit it," said Ember, "I admit to everything he suggests. That way he thinks you're learning to be honest with yourself."

"But I DON'T like dead bodies!" said Dahli. "And I'm not going to say I do just to make him happy."

"Oh sure you do," said Ember, "Come on, just admit it. You think about that cold, smelly flesh..."

"I'm trying to eat," said Dahli.

"Okay," said Ember, "You eat *that* clart, and you won't own up to liking dead bodies. You have problems."

Dahli grinned. "I like little boyyysss…" she leered.

"Well at least now you're being honest with yourself."

"Yeah," said Dahli. "Now do you think they'll let me out if I ask real nice?"

"Doubtful," said Ember. "Very doubtful."

Lunch passed all too quickly, and Dahli was not even allowed the privilege of lagging on her way to Ris' office. If she was late he would submit a report and have a few of her meagre privileges lifted. Dahli had an hour in the yard coming up that day, and she wasn't about to lose it.

It was exactly thirteenhour when she arrived at his office, knocking once before entering. She stepped into the small, over-warm room. His office always had a stuffy, rancid smell to it, as though he never left it. Dahli wondered idly if his house smelled the same as he did. As far as she could tell he never bathed. His hair was always slicked back with its own oil, and his skin had a shiny, greasy look to it. His shoulders were always liberally covered in dandruff, and he wore dark colours to ensure that it was noticeable. Dahli didn't know if she was glad she had eaten before she had seen him. Certainly she could not have afterwards.

He stared at her as she sat down, piggy eyes watching as though her smallest action could relay information to him. He continued to stare for a long moment, then said, "How are you today?"

"Fine," said Dahli, "and yourself?" She didn't really care. But he was attempting to teach her how to hold a conversation these days. As if she had ever had any difficulty. But he seemed convinced that she had difficulty communicating. Draephus could have assured him that she could get her point across just fine; loudly and clearly and painfully.

"Good," he said, though it was an appraisal of her new-found conversational abilities, not a comment on his health. Dahli could already feel the irritation rise as she watched him scribble in his notebook. "Now," he said, "is there anything you'd like to discuss?"

"Yeah," said Dahli. "The food here stinks. The stuff we had today tasted like somebody died in it."

"I'm sure nobody did," Ris soothed consolingly.

"Well, I hope not," said Dahli, just so he wouldn't begin to formulate some thought that she like to eat dead bodies. She wondered if *he* was the one with the body fixation; he seemed to think about them an awful lot.

"Now let's talk about the faelin," he said, his voice cutting into her thoughts. Dahli couldn't wait to hear what new and wonderful ideas he had come up with today. "Tell me again why you took it."

"I thought it deserved better than to be cut up by a science class."

"You felt you should protect it?"

"I suppose you could say that."

He nodded thoughtfully. "Why did you feel this way?"

"I think any normal person would feel the same way. I like to think I live in a place where dismemberment of a person is distasteful if not illegal."

"Of a person?" said Ris. "You consider faelins people."

"Yes," said Dahli. "They're more closely related to us then Siriusians. A Siriusian and a Sferkkaan can't reproduce. A Sferkkaan and a faelin can."

"I see," said Ris. "But there are no documented cases of this happening."

"Yes there are," said Dahli. "What about General Medarine, two hundred years ago? I studied him in History. His faelin gave birth to white-haired children who could speak."

"Legend," said Ris with a dismissing wave of his hand. "Or more likely slander. Just like the one of the First Emperor of Sferkkaa being born of a red deer."

"Might be true," said Dahli. "A red deer? When you look at the legend they may even be talking about a faelin."

"How would it have got here?" countered Ris. "We had no interplanetary travel that long ago."

"It is well known that the Kryphisians travelled to many planets, including Faela and Sferkkaa, long before they became hostile towards us. It was from them we acquired our knowledge of space travel."

"Yes, yes, yes, but that is fact, not fiction. Kryphis *does* exist, they are real. The rest of it is just legend."

"All legends have a basis in truth," said Dahli.

"Well, perhaps at one time these too held some grain of truth," said Ris, "however, what we are discussing is pure myth, a child's bedstory. I understand you live with your sister. Where is your mother?"

"Where do you think?" she snapped, surprised at the amount of rage the question aroused in her. "She left the house one day and never returned. That's when Teirra had to look after me. I was nine, Teirra was fourteen."

"Do you miss your mother?"

Dahli shrugged. "I don't know. I think the strain of looking after me under the circumstances made her crazy."

"You feel qualified to make a statement on your mother's mental state?"

"I don't need to go to a fancy school to learn what crazy looks like."

"I see." He nodded, looking thoughtful. After a moment he reached out and picked up his pen, scribbling into his notebook. "So," he said as he wrote, "perhaps what you were actually doing when you broke into the locked school and took the Faelin, burying it in what you concluded was a safe place, was rescuing your childhood self and hiding it where it would be safe."

Dahli wanted to scream at him. Then she recalled what Donsa Sappil had said. "Maybe. You could be right, I guess."

Ris smiled, evidently pleased with the progress Dahli was making. "So what you did in effect was make a belated move to defend yourself."

"Does that mean what I did was normal?" Dahli decided to shift from argumentative to enthralled. Sure, she'd play up to him if it made him happy. He was easier to get along with that way.

"Normal, yes, but it was not right to steal the body. You understand that."

"Yeah, I guess," Dahli stared down at her shoes, the chastised child.

"Will you tell me where the body is?"

"No."

"You don't wish to return what is not yours?"

"Not anyone else's, either. It's against the law to own another person."

Ris ran his hand down over his face in agitation. "Look, we've discussed this before. A faelin is not a person."

"Sure it is. They walk on two legs, stand upright, feel emotion, have two arms, two eyes, hair, teeth, noses, skin...only difference is they bark and we talk. A lot of people lack speaking ability. That doesn't mean they're not people."

"But a faelin is not human."

"I see," said Dahli, mimicking his voice. "And are you an anthropologist? Are you qualified to make that statement?"

Ris slowly leaned over his desk. His face was red, his jowls quivering dangerously. "I DON'T NEED A DEGREE TO TELL ME THAT ANYTHING THAT BARKS AND SPENDS THE BETTER PART OF ITS LIFE UP A TREE EATING BIRDS IS NOT HUMAN!"

"I didn't say they weren't a little strange. We probably acted much the same a few thousand years ago."

Ris was on the verge of exploding. His entire body may come across the desk top at any moment to throttle her. Then he turned his pig-eyes up to the clock on the wall.

"You hour is up," he said, seeming relieved. "You may leave. I expect you to be back here at the same time next week."

"Sure," said Dahli. "I'll see you then." She stood and walked to the door, being certain to say good-bye so he wouldn't think she was lapsing in her conversational abilities. Then she left, heading deeper into the building. Washing floors was going to be a joy after that.

It was after supper when she finally got her hour outside, and she thought it was probably the most depressing hour of her life. The sun was low in the sky, a warm orange glow behind the purplish-grey of the cloud cover. The birds chirped lazily in the trees across the street from the large concrete lot in which she stood. Other inmates roamed the bleak yard, or else stood in small groups and talked. A few of the boys were kicking a ball around, but Dahli was alone in her section; there were only a few other girls in the whole facility, three of them from a place so far off they did not even speak the local tongue. None of them currently had outside-time.

The detention centre was divided into two parts, one for female inmates, and one for male, though the section for female inmates was, understandably, much smaller. When out in the yard, Dahli could see the youths in their section. Usually they were hanging from the chain link dividers like apes, trying to get the attention of the girls. They, like Dahli and most of the girls she sometimes shared the yard with, had committed non-violent crimes. One boy, a scruffy youth named Shae, was in for stealing feralykes and selling them. Dahli liked him, and would speak to him whenever she saw him.

She searched the grounds for Shae, but didn't see him. She did however see one kid hanging upside-down on the fence like some impossible frog, trying to impress her. Well she was definitely impressed. She hoped he didn't fall and splash his brains all over the concrete.

Somehow Dahli suspected it would be a *small* splash.

Dahli wandered over to the high mesh fence that separated her from the street and the fields across it, listening to the hum of power surging through it as she stared at the distant skyline of the city. Dahli could hear the distant sound of the traffic, and found herself wondering how far she'd get if she did manage to climb the fence. Then a guard strolled by, and her thoughts turned to how much her sentence would be extended if she tried. She didn't want to stay here any longer than was necessary.

Dahli thought about Czamkiar, Diza and Randish. They'd be down at the Contempo right now, or maybe over at Czamki's, and suddenly the time she had to spend in this hole seemed like forever. What if she never got out? What if she died in here, or did something stupid and got more time? She was developing a fixation with that thought; it plagued her dreams at night. She saw Ris coming towards her, saying she would have to stay another year, or sometimes twenty. When she had these dreams she would wake up in a cold sweat, and it would be a long time before she could calm down.

Dahli watched the day end, the softly-coloured Sferkkaan haze darkening. Three tiny satellites shot by, round balls of rapidly moving orange light. They flew towards the city, where they would reflect off of the silvery glass of the tall buildings. Dahli tried to recall what their purpose was, and couldn't. Another trio of the little satellites shot by, and she yelled after them; "Hey! Take me!"

A couple of people standing close by laughed. Dahli watched after the lights until she could no longer see them, feeling depressed. She'd sent herself to this place; somehow she hadn't expected that at all. She thought there would have been some sort of a reaction to what she had done, but six months in a detention center was not what she had envisioned. She thought she would have brought enlightenment to the masses about the plight of the faelin. A few people had contacted the media, declaring she had been right to take the faelin, but it seemed the outcry had been fairly short-lived. In the end, she was in jail, the faelins were still in their cages, and everything seemed to have been for nothing.

****

'Lights Out' came, and Dahli and her roommates stayed under the covers just until the guard roamed past to make certain they were asleep. Then they all converged on Ember's bed, where they would make use of the dim light of an outside lamp to read their letters to each other. This practise had become an almost nightly ritual, one for preserving sanity. It was a form of excursion, a trip outside of the centre. Ember read her letter first, since it was her bed. The first of her two letters was from her mother. Letters from Donselle Analia were always full of weeping and wailing, promises of an early death, and very long sentences. Listening to them, Dahli could understand why Ember would do anything, even break the law, to get away from her. On paper she was funny; in real life she would be a nightmare.

The second letter was from her morose brother. His letters were never terribly entertaining, save for rare moments when he would be so blackly depressed he was funny whether he meant to be or not. Then Crystal read her one letter from her painfully dumb boyfriend. Dahli found it difficult to believe anybody could actually be that brainless, and often wondered if it was an act. As Crystal finished reading, Dahli shook her head.

"Somebody had better take good care of that boy. Doesn't sound like he could do it himself."

"He's not very bright," said Crystal fondly. She replaced her letter in its envelope. "Now you read yours."

Dahli read the one from Czamkiar first, as she always did

when he wrote. Ember and Crystal had seen him briefly when he had come to visit Dahli, and now both were in love with him. The infatuation had not worn off despite the fact that he did not write terribly exciting letters. They invariably began with; "Hi, I'm writing to you in Math class..." or, "I'm in Science right now..." Not that Czamki was so smart he could afford to miss a class.

Diza's letter was next, filled with loads of information about who was doing what to whom, and who knew about it, and why they'd done it, and where and why. In short there wasn't much happening at school that Dahli wasn't kept current on. Duone Bathers apparently had not tried to get a second faelin, and many parents and guardians were not pleased there had been one in the class to start with. At least that was one small victory.

Next came Teirra and Atterick's letter, filled with a dual portion of 'we-miss-you' and smug notations about places they had gone. Teirra apparently wasn't so old that teasing her younger sister didn't still hold some appeal.

"Well," said Dahli, putting the letters away, "that's it."

"You got four letters," said Ember. "You're holding out on us."

"Oh you don't want to hear that one. It's just some guy I know. It's boring."

"From your boyfriend?" asked Crystal.

"I don't have a boyfriend," said Dahli.

"Then who is he?"

She squirmed, dreading the inevitable hysteria that would ensue should they turn out to be Mortified Gryphons fans. "Just… someone I sort of know."

The two studied her. "Come on, Dahli," said Ember. "You know we're not going to take 'no' for an answer."

"I just don't know what you're going to think when I read it. It's not as though I actually know him or anything." Dahli briefly went to her own bed, pulling the remaining letter out from under her mattress, returning to Ember's bed and sitting on it. Drawing a deep breath, she took the letter from its envelope and read it.

"There," she said when she had finished.

Crystal and Ember stared at her. "You *know* him?" said Crystal, her voice filled with awe.

"Not really. I hit him with a door, then I stole his conni. I guess we're sorta pet enemies. I'm surprised he didn't say something like `*ha ha serves you right'* because I'm in here."

"Write and ask him to lean on some people for you!" said Ember. "He'll have you out of here in no time!"

"No," said Dahli quietly. "I mean, first of all, I don't think he would after what I did to his conni. Second, I don't know him well enough. The times I have been with him total a few hours. And the last time I saw him… I sorta spit on him."

"You SPIT on him!?" Ember yelled. She was abruptly shushed by the other two girls. They listened for the guard, but when they did not hear him coming, they kept talking.

"You *spit* on him?" Ember repeated quietly.

"He was making me angry," said Dahli, making a mental note to not mention she had also kicked him in the ribs. "Anyway, he left after that. And now he knows what I did to his conni, so I doubt he would do anything to get me out of jail."

Dahli's two cellmates just stared at her. "Dahli," Ember finally broke the silence. "You are just not real. How could anyone spit on Draephus?"

"I was getting back at him for starting a fight in this club he and I had gone to."

The two girls were silent, exchanging glances. "Aren't you going to write him back?" asked Ember.

Dahli looked down at the letter she held, turning it over in her hands. "I don't know," she said softly. "I'll have to think about it."

Ember put her hand to her breast and did a perfect imitation of her mother. "She gets a letter from a Gryphon and he includes his address and she doesn't know if she will write the Gryphon back."

"Where did we go wrong with the child?" asked Crystal.

They went to bed shortly after this, falling asleep in the all-too-sterile room. Crystal and Ember dreamt nothing. Dahli dreamed of running through the halls of the centre, trying to find an exit.

****

The days all seemed to blur into one, and after a time Dahli realised she was having difficulty recalling what happened when. It seemed she had only seen Ris yesterday when she had to see him again. The end of the week reprise was no different than the weekdays; schoolwork and chores happened all the same. Every morning they rose at sixhour, and they were in bed by twentyhour. Twice weekly they were permitted into the yard for exercise. As though they never got any, Dahli mused as she scrubbed the floors one day. When she did not have studies or chores, she sat in her cell and stared at the walls. They weren't in there to have fun, she realised. As she had heard Raski Jervyas say in an interview once; *jail is to let you know you've done something stupid.* She doubted she'd ever do anything to ever warrant more of this deathly boredom.

She was in her cell doing a little wall-staring one day when the guard walked in. Dahli pried her gaze from the flat surface to look at the man.

"That wall has almost eight hundred bricks in it," she announced.

"Wonderful," said the man. "I'll put that in my book of useful things."

Dahli grinned. "Come back next week and I'll tell you how many bricks are in the whole structure."

"I can hardly wait. Well, can your counting wait awhile? You have a visitor."

"Really? You mean like somebody I know from the Outside, like a real person?" Dahli was fairly leaping up and down, the guard watching her warily.

"Yeah, now calm down and I'll take you out to the visitors' area."

Dahli followed the guard out of her cell and down the long, dim corridor to the visitors' area. The guard stepped forward and opened the door, Dahli walking in to find the tiny room full. Teirra bounded forward to greet her, Atterick, Diza and Czamkiar not far behind. Dahli let out a screech and grabbed her sister around the neck, hugging her tightly.

"Everybody's here!" she exclaimed, looking about at her friends and family.

"You look like clart," said Atterick.

"Oh, thanks, groutnoll. Let's see what you look like after spending all your life indoors." She threw her arms around him. "Oh, Atterick, in a weak moment sometimes I even miss you. How's the band?"

"Not bad. However Anthony has been spending so much time with Mars that I worry the Gryphons may give him a better offer."

Dahli grinned, then behind him spied an array of brightly-wrapped packages on the small bench near one wall. "Have you been shopping?" she asked. "What are the packages for?"

"Right, Dahli," said Diza.

"No, really, what's up?"

Diza stared at Dahli as though she had lost her mind. "It's your birthday, groutnoll."

Dahli had known she had a birthday coming up, but in the sealed-off world of the centre, she had no idea when this day would come. There were no timekeepers other than the relentless clocks in the building. Dahli stared at Diza with a stupefied expression.

"My birthday?"

"Yes!" said Diza. "Didn't you know?"

"No," said Dahli. "I guess I lost track of time. I didn't think it would be my birthday for a while yet."

Her voice had become quiet, and the increasingly familiar feeling of depression crept up on her. It was her birthday, and she was spending it here. Had it really only been eight weeks?

"Well," said Teirra. "Since we wasted our money on you, hardened criminal that you are, would you like to open your presents?"

"Oh, sure," Dahli said in her familiar rant. "You break into *one* building and steal a lousy body and suddenly everyone thinks you're a criminal." She was trying very hard not to let circumstances ruin the day. She picked up a small, slim package from Teirra, then shot a sly look at the bored guard.

"Gee!" she said loudly. "My very own metal file!"

The guard yawned and ignored her. Dahli unwrapped the box and opened it, finding a slender chain made of the fiercely expensive, smoky-grey metal czilbein. She drew it out slowly, gazing at it with wonder. Even in the bad light of the small visiting room, it shone with the surreal glow that made it so valued.

"Teirra, it's beautiful!" Dahli turned it over in her fingers. "Thank you."

"I thought you'd like it," said Teirra. "And if you have your own czilbein necklace, it will stop you from borrowing mine all the time."

"No it won't," said Dahli. "Of course, it will be awhile before I'm borrowing jewellery from you." Dahli picked up the next box, this one from Czamkiar. The package was rather large; Dahli tore the paper from it, opened the box and peered in.

"A bird cage, Czamki? It's nice, but why a birdcage?"

Diza picked up a small box and passed it carefully to Dahli. "In case someone gets you a bird."

Dahli took the box and gently opened it. She reached in and took out one of the two, blue-white birds. She placed it inside the cage, then put its companion in with it. They flitted from perch to perch, cocking their heads as they studied the people around them.

"Do you like them?" asked Diza.

"Yeah, I do," said Dahli. "They're so tiny!"

"They sing nice," said Diza, "and they're smart. You can teach them to come when you call."

"What are they for?" asked Dahli. "I mean other than the fact that they are adorable."

"Pest control in the garden," said Czamkiar. "You let them loose in the morning and they spend the day clearing bugs off the plants. Then they return in the evening to when it's safe and warm. I remembered last year when the bugs ate all your plants."

"What are you going to name them?" asked Teirra.

"No idea," said Dahli, studying the tiny white creatures, which had yet to utter a sound. Then she grinned. "I'll call this one Delaes..."

"Dahli Sandiniti, if you name that dear innocent bird `Delaes', I'm taking it back right now!"

Dahli laughed. "All right. I won't call it Delaes. Maybe I'll call him Draephus."

"Now there's a name I never expected to hear you utter ever again," said Teirra.

"Yeah, well," said Dahli, "I don't know if I hate him as much as I thought I did. He wrote to me. He apologized for the way he acted and said I could write to him if I wanted."

"Will you?" Teirra asked.

"I don't know. I'll have to think about it. I'm still pretty angry at him." Dahli laughed a little. "Remember when I would have shed blood and switched sides to have gotten a letter from him? Now he's just some person I'm annoyed with. I think I liked him better as an unreachable demigod."

"He say anything about Yuri?" asked Diza casually.

"No, Diza. If I ever get a letter from Yuri Stracona, I'll be sure to let you know."

    Diza smiled at her friend, reaching out and squeezing her hand. "Just don't hit him with a door."

    "Or kick him in the ribs," said Czamkiar.

    "Or steal his conni," said Teirra.

    "Yeah funny how *he* is not the one who seems to be mad at *you*," said Atterick.

    "He'd never dare," said Dahli. "I'd beat him up."

    All too soon it was time for everyone to leave. Dahli felt a sick, leaden sensation in the pit of her stomach as she watched Teirra gather up her presents to bring back to her bedroom, which seemed so far away and unreal. She could feel tears starting to sting her eyes, but she fought them back.

    "Hey, Teirra..." she suddenly said.

    Her sister glanced back at her. "What?"

    "Is all of my Gryphon stuff still in the attic?"

    "Sure it is. I wouldn't throw out that."

    "Maybe someday if you and Diza are feeling ambitious, you could… put it back in my room for me?"

    Teirra smiled. "Sure."

    She stepped forward to give her a hug, and Dahli was hard pressed to stop the tears. She managed to keep them back, watching as Teirra, Atterick, and her friends left. It was only after they had gone that she permitted the tears to flow.

Chapter Nine.

Draephus sat on Ysith Beach, a stretch of glittering white sand on the far side of the island. The island had two good beaches, but Ysith Beach was rarely used; hellish battles had been fought here, and there were still dead soldiers lost somewhere in the surf and deep sand, as well as unexploded bombs and flares and other devices of war. The only people who came to the mile-long stretch of sugar-white sand, flowering beach shrubs, and small trees were people like Draephus, who had fought here, and lost friends and pieces of their physical and emotional selves, wandering down to the tide-line to drink at night with the dead. Draephus was sitting mere meters from where but a few years ago he had crouched with a long-muzzled Night Stalker gun, firing at creatures that were once Sferkkaans, turned into mindless killers by Kryphisian technology.

He'd earned his lines of make-up, and medals; he just didn't like to look at them.

The early summer breeze that blew was cold, and he shivered a little. His glazed, faded blue eyes watched the softly rolling waves in the darkness of the night. He had spent a lot of time here when he had been younger. He and Raski would come down with some friends and swim in the ocean. But that had been a long time ago, and it gave him an eerie feeling to be here now, alone. He briefly detached from reality as he wondered where his old friends had gone, forgetting for the moment that they were somewhere under the sand upon which he sat. He then shook his head when he thought he heard someone call his name.

He tried to light a cigarette, but couldn't make it connect with the fire. He tried closing one eye and that seemed to help. He closed the lighter and replaced it in his pocket, then dropped his free hand down to the soft white sand, reaching for the bottle he had brought with him. His arm ached slightly as he lifted it. He thought about Raski as he drank some of the burning liquid from the bottle, thought about all the times they would sit together on this beach. They would lean on each other drunkenly, talking and philosophising. Draephus wondered how many songs had come into being on this beach, and then shook his head. Life had changed so much in the past few years, mostly for the better. The war was over, Vesper had a few more years added to his life, and Raski had said he would wait for him. So what was he so miserable about? Apart from the fact his bones were slowly turning into powder, and his joints into tormenting balls of fire, and his days as a musician were rapidly coming to an end because no one who had to shoot mushroom resin six times a day in order to be able to move could have the speed and reflexes needed to play the drums, his life was great. Mushrooms eased the pain, but they did not improve one's comprehension or co-ordination. Draephus would not long remain a drummer, and that meant either replacement or dissolution of the band. Great. Nothing like going down in flames and taking your friends along for the ride. He had to tell them, but… not yet. Not now. Things were good. Let them stay good a little longer.

He heard his name again. Some šukating seabird, he thought for no rational reason. Then he heard footsteps approaching.

"I don't believe it," said a voice. "Draephus CZimcocious. I cannot believe that there are people on this planet who will actually pay to see you, when there were so many times I would have paid to get away from you."

Draephus looked up slowly and stared for a long moment at a face he knew he should know. Finally he recalled the name. A drugged smile spread over his face.

"Namerea. What are you doing here?"

Namerea sat down next to Draephus. "Just out for an evening walk. It's been a long time since I've seen your ugly face. How are you?"

Draephus wavered, then without meaning to, slowly fell over backwards. "Fine," he said, his voice distant.

Namerea laughed. "So I see. What are you doing out here in this state?"

"I'm a hero. I can get into my altitudes wherever I like. Hey, Namerea, you think I should move Raski into my house?"

"That's up to you."

"Actually, it's up to Raski, and whether he wants to child-mind me constantly, or just continue to do it on an occasional basis. Poor Raski. He'd be so happy if I wasn't always making life hard for him."

"I'm sure he doesn't mind. Speaking of life, how much longer do you think Vesper will survive?"

"I don't know," said Draephus. He took a swallow from his bottle. He wanted to just lie there forever. The sand had become soft and warm. He took another drink, not bothering to question how Namerea knew about Vesper. "I spoke to him tonight. He's in Trae Dae Mu with some buddies of mine. He sounded all right. It could be years before he gets sick enough to die."

Namerea nodded. It did not matter that Draephus had his eyes closed; he saw the gesture. His mind began to drift to other things, the main topic being the quality of the drugs he had injected, his joints still sore despite the narcotics.

"Lousy resin," he bitched. "You can't get good resin in Second City, but I was out of the South Continent stuff. I wouldn't share this garbage with people I *didn't* like, never mind my friends."

"Just as well," said Namerea. "You're alone."

The last two words rang through Draephus' mind almost leeringly. He *was* alone, wasn't he? He opened his eyes and studied Namerea calmly. He smiled back at him, a warm affectionate smile. A tiny black crab fell out of his mouth. Draephus thought nothing of it.

"Well," said Namerea, "perhaps if you have any left I could try it and tell you if it's as bad as you think."

The statement held implications. Mushroom resin lowered morals and inhibitions to the state of virtual non-existence in some people. That was the main reason that the Kryphisians had been so opposed to the stuff. Can't have people having fun.

"No," said Draephus. "I'll keep it. I may need it."

The beach was becoming longer. Draephus could feel it stretching and changing beneath him. Above him, the sky began to gently lower, the cloud cover softly approaching. Soon he was hidden in warm fog. However the sand was getting cold. As the beach continued to stretch, the sand layer grew thinner. White objects, thin and twisted, began to rise out of the thinning surface.

"What are these?" Draephus asked quietly as the bones grew all around like demented plants.

"Things you've buried," said Namerea. He pulled a bone out of the sand and held it out to Draephus. He stared at the offered object, then shook his head.

"I won't take back what I have disposed of."

"But you want it back, don't you? Don't you want things to be the way they were before life stopped being fun? You could stay with me on the beach."

"No," said Draephus. "I admit I have been thinking about how good it would be to come hide on this beach again, in the past, hanging out with old friends, but I can't. They're dead, you're dead, the past is dead. Only place to go is forward. And I'm gonna do it, even if I have to crawl."

Namerea's features were beginning to slide into odd positions. The skin on one cheek was beginning to develop what appeared to be worm holes. "Are you sure you won't stay?"

Draephus slowly forced himself to a seated position, reaching for his bottle. "No," he said, and sighed. "Sorry. I can't."

He slowly pushed himself to his feet, then looked down briefly at the seated corpse. The sand was once more thick and soft, hiding the skeletons. He turned and began trudging away, heading down to the water's edge. The walking was easier here, and the dark water lapped over the toes of his boots to form tiny whitecaps. He was staggering, his movements stiff and wooden. He stumbled along, like a feralyke with the foaming rage. He could feel Namerea's eyes on him, watching him go, hating him because he could.

"Heia Draephus!" called the specter. "Before you go… maybe ask Vesper about Jai and Shal."

Ask *Vesper*? Ask Vesper *what*? He never even met the two…

Draephus paused in his tracks and looked out over the water. The waves were small and gentle, edged in silver, soft, and inviting. He loved the water, loved to swim in it, to dive as deep as he could into the ocean, and watch the doings of small incomprehensible creatures until his lungs screamed for air. He wondered how cold the water was as he began walking into the ocean. It felt warm enough. He waded in up to this waist, feeling how peaceful everything was. Perfect for a late evening swim to wash away his own dark thoughts and misery.

He tried to leap forward, but the weight of the wet coat permitted him only a clumsy flop into the darkness. The water closed over him, and suddenly he realised it wasn't warm at all. It was colder than a tomb.

****

Khandid Stracona lay under a warm blanket on his bed, gazing out the open balcony doors as he watched the sky lighten. In the background, he heard the complex sounds of Yuri playing his quinticord, picking out impossible musical combinations. Musically, Yuri was something like a secret weapon; a six-fingered, self-taught quinticord player was bound to attract some attention. More than one musician had called demanding to know what in the Emperor's name they had done on this or that song.

The music stopped, and Khandid heard Yuri set the quinticord in its stand. A moment later he walked onto the room where Khandid lay. He strolled over to the stone railing surrounding the balcony and stared down into the garden, watching the luminous flowers glow softly. Khandid studied Yuri's long back and smiled.

"What are you thinking about?" Khandid's tone was amused.

Yuri pushed his long black hair out of his face, a heavy curling mane that went down to his thighs.

"I was just thinking about that girl...what's her name...the one who hit Draephus."

Khandid thought for a moment, then said; "Oh you mean Dahli Sandiniti."

"Yes, her."

"Whatever for?" Khandid rolled luxuriantly onto his stomach, blinking sleepily at the new day.

"Well, you knew she is in jail?"

"No, but that's not surprising, what with hitting people with doors and stealing their conveyances. Only so much of that society will tolerate, you know."

Yuri glanced over his shoulder at Khandid and smiled. "That isn't what they locked her up for. Don't you ever pay attention to the news?"

"I don't have to, love, I hear it from you."

"She stole a dead body."

"Oh Yuri it's too early in the morning for necrophilia."

Yuri rolled his eyes. "Think, Khandid, back to the days when you used to have intelligence."

"I'm a professional musician now, love, I don't have to think."

"She was protesting the dissection of a faelin. Claims they're human."

"She and Draephus would have lots to talk about. He's always on the same tangent. He used to keep faelins when he lived on the South Continent. Apparently all the drug runners had them. Practically worshipped them. That's where he got the pair he has now. "

"I don't think they should have jailed her," said Yuri, watching the rain.

Khandid glanced up. Yuri was a black silhouette against the brightening sky. "What do you suggest?"

"Make her repair the damage she did, obviously. If she isn't any good with tools, at least make her pay for the work that has to be done. But I don't think they should have put her in jail. I think perhaps somebody should have begun looking into the situation. The Grey Boys did so many things to us I'm surprised we have the audacity to experiment on anything alive."

"Well I'm not surprised that you feel this way. After what they did to you."

Yuri looked at Khandid. "You mean like putting inserts into my bones to make me taller?"

Khandid flinched. "Yes, that. And other things."

"Like the fact that I owe my very existence to Kryphisian scientists, who decided to mix the chromosomes and DNA of several different creatures and came up with me? I don't even know what I am, and trust me, it weighs on my nerves heavily at times. I've no parents, no siblings, and no place of origin." Yuri shook his head. "We have no business as a race experimenting on the faelins. Someone should let that girl out of jail. I'm going to talk to Raski about it. He knows everything."

Khandid sighed. "Let it lay, Yuri. Our revolution is over. Let Dahli fight her own. The time has come for us to just do what we are good at and let others fight the wars. I for one have had a belly full of causes."

"But we can help."

"But it's not our battle anymore. If we keep leaping onto every cause that comes along people are going to start to think that we're another one of those bands who can't deal with the fact that the war is finally over."

"I suppose," said Yuri. "Of course, if we don't stay politically active to some extent, then all of our fans will abandon us, and Vortex will become the most popular band on Sferkkaa."

Khandid roared with laughter. "VORTEX? REPLACE *US*? Oh, there's a thought. How did that *last* wondrous ditty they came up with go? `I'm so glad to see you, dribbling with goo, icky icky poo, woo woo woo.'* Something to that effect. *`I think of you all the time, even when I have no brain, I think of you when I pick my nose, and when I go down the drain`*."

Yuri smiled. "That's not *quite* how it went."

"Basic concept though. Do you know why they called themselves `Vortex'? In honour of the space between the lead singer's ears, no doubt. Replace us in the charts. I never heard of such nonsense. You've been awake too long."

"Perhaps. I'm hungry. Let's have a bite to eat and then I'll go to bed."

"I like that idea. Turn on Base Four, we can hear what's going on in the world."

They walked into the huge kitchen. Khandid began to dig through the cold box while Yuri turned on the base receiver.

"...was found washed up on the shore of Ysith Beach early this morning. He was brought to Second City Hospital, unconscious, with a large quantity of drugs in his system. Hospital staff are saying little at this point, though one doctor did comment that his situation is grim..."

"Sounds like something Draephus would do," said Khandid, head within the cold box.

The telecom sent up its soft electronic beeping. "I'll get that," said Yuri, when Khandid made no move to do so. He walked into the next room and lifted the receiver.

"Heia?"

It was Delaes Randerick, the fastest mouth in Ra Khan Roll.

"...always was a lunatic you know but by the New Empire this is beyond anything I ever thought he would do I just had my receiver on for a moment because a friend of mine thinks I should listen to the news more so I only turned it on what was he doing do you think it was a suicide attempt but that really doesn't sound like Draephus he'd never kill himself because he wouldn't be able to beat people up does Raski know?"

Yuri gave his head a shake. "Delaes, what are you on about? Better yet, what are you on?"

"I only had some mushroom and a few rams of some other stuff you're not telling me that you haven't heard you people are all so disgustingly tight with one another..."

"Heard *what*, Delaes?"

"They found Draephus on Ysith Beach just an hour ago Yuri I'm sorry I thought you would know I was just calling up to ask how he is he hasn't any family but you know that you don't have any family either do you well I'll go now I'm sure you have people you have to call I'll talk to you later."

There was a click. The telecom fell silent in Yuri's hand. He set the device down and walked into the kitchen slowly, feeling as though reality had just left the premises. He paused in the doorway to watch Khandid stuffing his face.

"Khandi..?"

"Whaf?" he said, his mouth full. He poked about inside the cold box for anything interesting.

"That *was* Draephus they found on the beach. Delaes just called to ask how he is."

Khandid abruptly straightened up and looked at Yuri, simply staring at him for a long moment, blue eyes huge with disbelief.

"Call Raski," he said finally, "he'll want to know."

Yuri went back to the com and called Raski's number. He heard the com beep once, then Raski snatched up the receiver.

"Heia?"

"Raski? It's Yuri. They…"

"I know, I'm on my way to the hospital now."

He dropped the 'com, not managing to get it onto its hook. Yuri heard Raski cross his room at a run and bound down the flight of stairs, banging the door behind him.

Yuri sighed and hung up the 'com. "He knows."

****

Raski's black air con settled down onto the hard surface of the hospital parking lot with a quiet sigh. The door slid open, and he leapt out of the dark interior, running into the huge, impersonal grey structure that served as the temporary hospital until the new one could be built. He barely managed to avoid a stretcher being pushed by an orderly, and went at a dead run for the doors of the critical ward, where he knew Draephus would be. He almost made it, but at the last moment two large men dressed in hospital uniform caught him. Raski struggled and kicked in protest.

"Let go of me, my best friend is in there!"

"Donsa, you can't go in there," one of the men informed him, trying to keep his patience with the wriggling Jervyas.

"But I'm all the family he has!" Raski struggled, then, deciding this was going nowhere, tried to climb over the man like a very large cat.

"Donsa if you do not calm down we will be forced to sedate you!"

The orderly grabbed Raski, wrenching one arm behind his back, using his free hand to get him by the scruff of the neck. The grip was extremely painful, and most people would have gone down to their knees. But most people hadn't been trained to behave counter to what pain told them. Raski flung himself backwards at the wall, stunning the orderly. The grip released as the man slumped to the floor, just in time for the second man to pounce on Raski.

"Release me you clart!" Raski snarled at him. "What kind of hospital hires people to beat up concerned relatives?"

"Donsa Jervyas, if you and Donsa CZimcocious are related, then I am the Emperor."

"Pleased to meet you." Raski grabbed the orderly's arm and, using his own body weight as leverage, threw the man over his shoulder.

"Raski!"

Raski looked over his shoulder, and was relieved to see Dr. Arang walking towards him.

"How is he?" Raski asked.

Dr. Arang was a very tall man, quite imposing, with dark hair turning grey at the temples. During the war he had led troops in battle, and now found he preferred putting people back together as opposed to blowing them apart. He had known Draephus and Raski for a number of years, and dreaded saying anything to Raski about Draephus' condition because he knew how badly he would react.

"It does not look very good. We are doing what we can, but he arrived in very bad shape. To be truthful, I'm afraid for him."

Raski swallowed. "I want to see him."

"Later, we can't let you in right now."

Raski suddenly had a horrible feeling; one borne of his own experiences in a hospital during the war. His blue-white eyes became large.

"What did you do with him?"

"We haven't done anything with him," Dr. Arang tried to assure him.

"Then why won't you let me see him?"

"Because we are still working on him!"

"You mean you're warehousing him for body parts, don't you? Using bits and pieces of him to save other people with a better chance."

"Raski, that does not happen in civilian hospitals, and the only time it happens in military ones is in times of extreme crisis, and only with patients who have…"

The knife was enormous; Raski kept it in a spring-loaded device that attached to his arm, hiding under his sleeve. With a flick of a switch it would appear in his hand. It could even be simply aimed and fired like a gun, though the spring was not powerful enough to send the blade very far. Raski clicked the switch and the huge blade shot into his hand. He pointed it at Dr. Arang, eyes crazed.

"You're going to take me to Draephus and you're going to do it *now*!"

"No," said Dr. Arang, calmly, firmly. "You're going to put the knife down before I call security and have you shot."

Raski was outraged. "You can't shoot me, I'm a war hero!"

"And so am I, and I out-rank you. So sit down and shut up."

The egos came out to play, one diplodocus as large as the other. "I'll have you know I have an Order of the Empire *and* an Imperial Gryphon, awarded posthumously, I might add!" Raski snarled.

Dr. Arang looked puzzled. "Posthumously?"

"Long story."

"I'll bet. But the truth is a drunken monkey could get an Imperial Gryphon! I was on the ground, down with the troops. I'm a *real* war hero, not some sissy fighter pilot!"

Raski stared at the man in astonishment, blinking, asking himself if he had really just heard what he thought he had. Then he let out a blood-curdling shriek of pure rage and hate. He lunged for the doctor, who realized belatedly he had just intentionally pissed off a man with a knife. He tossed his clipboard to an orderly and ran for all he was worth; Second City's greatest doctor being chased by its most beloved sepulchord player. Dr. Arang fled into a storage closet, slamming the door shut and barring it just seconds before Raski hit the thing, running full speed and leaping to throw his entire body weight against the door. It shuddered and cracked, but for the moment, it held. Raski staggered back, stunned and panting, and suddenly felt something poke him in the shoulder muscle. He spun around to find himself face-to-face with another doctor, who waggled an empty hypodermic needle at him.

"Nighty night, Donsa Jervyas."

"I'm putting your name in my book of people to be rude to," said Raski. Then he dropped gracelessly to the floor.

****

It was dark when Raski opened his eyes. He was sweaty and uncomfortable. For a long moment, he was unable to think of a way to amend the problem, but then he thought maybe he should kick off the blanket. He did, then, with a movement much like a dead fish on a line, sat up. The world was a little confusing, and he had to think about where he was. Then a figure on a bed next to the stretcher he occupied moved, and Raski recalled where he was.

Raski hopped off of the stretcher, a little afraid to get too close to this person before he verified exactly who it was. Dr. Arang had been dealing with Draephus, and consequently Raski, for years, and he wasn't above putting Raski's drugged form in the psychiatric wing.

Dr. Arang was not as fond of Raski as Draephus was.

Raski drew close to the still form on the bed, reaching out one dark hand to rest on the soft green covers, breathing a sigh of relief as he recognized Draephus. The room was dim, and it was difficult to see clearly, but Draephus didn't look good. Of course, the dermal patches on his temples that monitored his heart, breathing, and brain didn't help, nor did the eerie glow of the small machines that pulsed and blipped to themselves. Raski put his hand over Draephus' and squeezed gently, then glanced about the room nervously. The silent hospital frightened him, and despite the sleepy feeling that still gripped him, Raski felt the hair on the back of his neck rise. He recalled the feeling from days when he and Draephus would start to get jumpy down in the Cylinder, waiting for something to happen. He hated it, and he hated this hospital.

He glanced about for a receiver, not seeing one. For a moment panic gripped him, then Raski breathed deeply, trying to calm himself. He had not slept in a silent room since he was a child. Silence scared him. During the war, and his time as a pilot, silence meant the Grey Boys had severed communication and were coming to get you. And hospitals were usually where they brought you to finish you... slowly. He looked down at Draephus once more, unconscious and helpless. Maybe the Kryphisians were all gone, but why take any chances? Raski climbed onto the bed, putting himself between Draephus and the door, determined to hold vigil all night.

The hours of darkness slowly dragged by. Raski stared into the night and thought about what his life had been like just a few short years ago. Things were definitely easier now that he was simply a musician, and he didn't have to hide in the fouled and psychotic depths of the Cylinder. But after a lifetime of fear there was no place to leave the strange little paranoias that had become an essential part of his survival. He never turned the receiver off in his home, and he didn't own a Visual because of the fear of monitoring beams being projected through it. He'd heard things about the Grey Boys being able to transmit subliminal hypnotic messages through the telecom, and only had one because there were times when they were needed. He had dozens of little traps all over his house; floors would be covered in a fine layer of dust, delicate threads were strung across doors and windows, clothes arranged just so in drawers and closets and covered with a thin layer of scented beads...all set up so there would be no getting into the house undiscovered. Not that Sferkkaa was so lacking in technology that there was no electronic surveillance equipment. Raski had some of the best, but he was familiar with such things. He knew that sensitive equipment could be rewired, but that there was no way to get around a hall full of powder without disturbing it.

Surveillance equipment could fail, but dust never sleeps.

A nurse came in at daybreak, gently shooing Raski off of the bed before examining Draephus, leaving after only a few moments. Despite having been told not to, Raski once more settled himself onto the bed, waiting for daylight.

Dr. Arang was the next person Raski saw, and he was a little more firm about not being on the bed. He sent Raski into the hallway while he looked over Draephus, and Raski stood by the door, shifting anxiously from one foot to the next, looking like an overly large child. After a short time, Dr. Arang walked quickly out of the room and almost managed to dodge Raski, but he planted himself squarely before him. Dr. Arang stopped and sighed heavily.

"Doesn't he ever get sick of you?" Dr. Arang snapped.

"Oh, *there's* a question, like I'm the one that breaks into *his* house at fourhour just to see what he's got in the cold box. How is he?"

Dr. Arang was opening his mouth to answer, when Raski heard someone call his name. Dr. Arang looked in the direction of the call and sighed loudly, rolling his eyes as he saw the three remaining clowns, Khandid, Yuri and Mars, accompanied by their other little pal, Delaes.

"He's not good," he said, answering Raski quickly in order to escape the group.

"He's not going to die, is he?" asked Raski.

"I doubt it, but it's a possibility that can't be ignored at this point. He was doing well for a while but the monitors are starting to indicate a build-up of fluid in his lungs, and there are indications of other problems. Now if you will excuse me..." He brushed past Raski and was gone.

"How is he?" Khandid asked as he walked up to Raski.

Raski stood quietly, shaking and upset. He pushed his hand through his hair tensely. "Sick," he said quietly. "Really sick."

He turned and walked into the room, followed by his friends. Raski seated himself on the edge of the bed, the others positioning themselves about the room, all eyes on the motionless form.

"Someone should call Vesper," said Mars.

"I would if I knew where he was," said Raski. "But we can't very well get on the telecom and place a call to Vesper when he's somewhere in the South Continent in the Hiscoth Mountain Range."

"Anyone else we can call?" asked Khandid.

"As far as family goes, we're it," said Raski. He looked at Delaes. "What brings you here?"

"Well I heard on the receiver that he was sick so I called Khandid and Yuri and I thought that since they were coming down to see him that I should perhaps tag along as well even though personally I'd rather not be in a hospital they really rather make me uncomfortable did you know..."

Raski put a hand up, stopping Delaes' endless sentence. "I meant, what brings you to Second City? I thought you were in Avalair, recording."

"Oh yes I *was* but the session was brought to rather a rude close you know the clart we've had playing quinticord for the last two years finally up and quit right in the middle of a track so I'm without a quint player not that I miss him not that *anyone* misses him but it would have been nice to have had some warning now I'm not so sure I have a band and honestly someone ought to take the lot of us out into a yard somewhere and shoot us."

"I'll do it," whispered voice, and Raski's attention snapped down to the figure on the bed.

His eyes were still closed, but there had been no mistaking the voice. Draephus lay still for a moment later, then he drew in a laboured breath and spoke. "Course, if my life was half as confusing as yours I would have shot myself by now." He opened his eyes and looked around. "Everyone's here. Am I going to die?"

"No, groutnoll, we just wanted to yell at you for trying to drown yourself," said Raski.

Draephus smiled. "That's what I keep you around for."

Raski smiled at his friend. Then, moments later, Dr. Arang came into the room with several other people and some ominous-looking devices.

"You'll have to leave now," he said quietly. He looked pointedly at Raski. "That includes you."

"You can't make me leave."

"Donsa Jervyas," he said, holding up a syringe. "Either you leave, or I stick this in you and your friends carry you out."

Raski stared sourly at the needle, then leaned closer to Draephus. "They're kicking us out in order to perform some horrible experiment on you, but I'll be back later."

Draephus smiled, then reached a hand up to touch Raski's face. "I'll be here. Feed my faelins. And don't give Bacca any fish, he'll barf it all over the rug."

Raski grinned. "I should give him a whole *bucket* of it to pay you back for worrying me. We'll be back later."

"Kiss me."

Raski kissed Draephus softly, and then he and the others left.

****

Later that evening, Dr. Arang walked into the hospital room, and looked around at the four weary figures seated around the bed. He sighed and shook his head, understanding their concern and indeed paranoia about leaving Draephus alone in a hospital, but was still irked by their constant presence. It was like having to wade through a chamber full of guard animals to check his patient.

"Well," he said, drawing their attention. "Since you are here, I am obligated to ask if you have all had your blood work done. Can't have you spreading nasty diseases."

They nodded. Khandid sat back and yawned. "We all had that done ages ago."

"Do any of you have anything that might affect Draephus' recovery?"

"No," they droned, like bored school children.

"Nothing in the 'A' category?"

"No," said Khandid. "I have F-17 and K-4, but that's it."

"I have A1-2," said Mars quietly.

Raski, Yuri and Khandid all snapped their attention to Mars, staring at him in shock.

"Mars…" began Khandid.

"I'm just a carrier of the dormant virus," said Mars quietly. "I could potentially give it to any children I fathered, but it's not doing anything to me, and I'm not contagious. I just can't have kids, and if at any time I start to spew blood from my nose and mouth then I know it's become active and some nice soldiers will have to come shoot me and burn my body before I start an epidemic."

"I had no idea," said Raski. "Mars I'm so sorry…"

Mars just waved him off. "I'm fine. But now you can stop wondering why I can never get anyone to stay with me more than a day. Hard to have a romance when people are wondering when you'll accidentally murder them. Hard to keep friends, too."

"You were in Avalair at one point during the war, weren't you?" said Dr. Arang.

"We all were," said Mars, as Khandid seated himself beside him and wrapped his arms around Mars' neck. He began crying on his shoulder.

"I thought so, that's the only place I know of where you can pick up an 'A' level virus. Have you been checked recently?"

"I go in every week, like they tell me."

Dr. Arang nodded. "I'm still going to schedule someone to look at you."

Mars nodded. "Yeah, that's fine."

Dr. Arang gazed at him for a while, clearly feeling a profound sympathy for Mars, wishing he could help. But as of yet, they had no means of fighting the 'A' strain viruses. Finally he turned to Yuri and Raski. "What about you two?"

Yuri yawned. "Q-233."

Dr. Arang nodded, then looked at Raski. "And you?"

"C-3, and C-4."

Dr. Arang looked surprised. "Really? C-3 *and* C-4?"

Raski nodded. "That's what they told me."

Dr. Arang walked over to him, taking his head gently between his hands and looking into his eyes, his expression sceptical as he examined Raski.

"You play sepulchord, don't you?"

"Yeah."

"That takes a lot of dexterity. Ever have any trouble speaking?"

"No."

"Ever suddenly drop things you are holding, or have your knees give out from underneath you?"

"No."

"Ever soil yourself?"

"Not since I was three."

Dr. Arang smiled. Mars sat forward in his chair, his expression one of curiosity.

"Is something the matter?" he asked.

"Well," said Dr. Arang, "neither C-3 nor 4 is especially problematic on its own. However in combination they work to destroy the brain's ability to tell the nerves and muscles what to do. People with C-3 and 4 develop tremors, they have trouble walking, speaking, holding onto objects, things of that nature. In more extreme cases the bowels will cease to function, the eyes begin to vibrate, and the heart and lungs will either cease to function, or will behave so erratically as to cause death." He picked up Raski's hands and examined them. "I don't see anything here to make me think Raski has C-3 and C-4. Where did you have your blood work done?"

"Second City Health."

Dr. Arang nodded. "They're good, but they're also very busy, and 'Jervyas' is a relatively common surname. 'Raski' is not uncommon either. It's possible they mixed your test results up with the results of another 'Raski Jervyas'. I think it's best we test you again."

"I hate needles," Raski muttered. "And if I find out I have AA-1 then I won't be amused."

"Well if you have AA-1 then your friends will have to start looking for a different sepulchord player, because I will be legally obligated to quarantine you immediately and permanently. Not that I haven't often wanted to. But I don't think you have AA-1. If you did, I suspect you and the rest of the band would be dead by now, or at the very least be bleeding out of their eyes."

"Eyew," muttered Khandid against Mars' neck.

"Hate when that happens," said Yuri. Mars snorted with laughter.

Dr. Arang held out his hand to Raski. "Come along, woolly lamb. Let's take you down to paediatrics and get your blood work done. If you're good I'll give you a sweet."

"Groutnoll," grumbled Raski, but followed Dr. Arang out of the room.

Chapter Ten

Gemma watched Diza and Czamkiar sit on her bed, watching the TV in her room, checking the news for any word on Draephus CZimcocious' condition. They had been coming over more now that Dahli was in jail. They seemed rather shaken by her arrest, and Gemma found it flattering they immediately gravitated toward her. However she could have lived without Diza's boyfriend Randish, who looked like the bastard offspring of a heavy metal guitar player and a werewolf. She really did not care for the length of his teeth.

"Any word?" she asked. Not that she actually cared, and she could not think why Diza and Czamkiar would. But it seemed the polite thing to say.

"Not yet," said Czamkiar. "I wish I knew if he was alive. Oh look, there's Mars!"

Mars David emerged from the hospital looking pale and exhausted. Gemma watched him speak briefly, then moved past the reporters. Someone stopped him, and asked him something. Mars answered, and the person ran off. Mars just shrugged and waited. The Sferkkaans laughed.

"What did I miss?" asked Gemma, truly regretting now she had not spent as much time learning their language as she should. She meant to do something about that.

"Well Mars came out and said Draephus was really sick, but chances were he was going to get better. Then that guy in the blue shirt asked him if he needed anything, and Mars said yeah, supper, so the guy went to get it for him."

"Only on Sferkkaa," said Gemma.

"Well even for famous musicians, supper is hard to come by," said Czamkiar.

Gemma looked at him, curious. "Wait – the Gryphons don't get extras?"

"*What* extras?" said Czamkiar. "There *are* no extras. You have food or you don't, it's as simple as that. Everyone who lives on Second City Island has to contribute."

"But you have all this cool technology, I mean… you have cars that fly over water and radio stations on satellites and…"

"Toys we have," said Czamkiar. "Our next meal is a little harder to come by. My last meal was yesterday morning. Doesn't matter how much money you have, if it is not there, it is not there, and money won't buy that which does not exist. Even the Gryphons have to contribute."

Gemma watched as the man on the TV hurried back with a basket for Mars, who hugged him and thanked him before retreating into the hospital. Gemma shook her head in confusion.

"Wait… I don't understand… does the hospital not have a cafeteria?"

Czamkiar stared at her. "Stocked with what?" he asked.

"Well I don't know, there must be something! You have restaurants, don't you?"

"A few."

"So you must have food. So why didn't you go there to eat?"

"I went. It was closed. The transport from Trae Dae Mu sank. So the restaurant is closed and the market is empty, and the man on the steps before the hospital clearly knew this, so he brought his favourite rock star something that he probably grew in his own garden."

"I just find it hard to believe that the Gryphons at least could not afford extra food!"

"As I said – you cannot buy what does not exist," said Czamkiar. "And even if they could, they would not."

Gemma did not understand that at all. *She* certainly wouldn't starve if she could afford to eat. It made no sense to her, any more than this attitude of "we're all in it together". Would anyone really know or care if the Gryphons stockpiled food? It seemed silly to her.

There was a tap on her bedroom door, and then it opened, revealing Brian. He looked to Czamkiar, Diza and Randish, and smiled.

"Heard your tanker sank."

"Yeah," said Czamkiar. "Some dumb fish is eating my lunch for me."

"Well me and Billy and Missy just made shaumaus for the first time, you want to join us?"

Czamkiar translated, and Diza and Randish nodded readily in agreement.

"Wait," said Gemma as they followed Brian to the kitchen.

"Doesn't 'shaumaus' mean 'converse'?"

"No," said Czamkiar. "'Shaumwisse' means 'converse'. Shaumaus is marinated raw fish served on almaniki leaves."

"Oh thanks a lot, you know you could have told me!"

"Why? It was much more fun hearing you tell us you had no one to food group with in a long time."

"Czamkiar you're evil."

"That's what the makeup says!"

"Does it?"

"No."

Brian scrutinized Czamkiar's makeup. "I believe it says you are learning to be a Whip, and your father was in the military, am I right?"

"Yeah," said Czamkiar. "I haven't don't much with my life yet."

"Well you're only fifteen. That little Straif Mannechek had some interesting paint, though."

"Yeah, when he was ten his parents died, and he spent the last year of the war smuggling messages for the partisans from place to place in Avalair, as well as doing a few assassinations when he had to. He's got a medal from the emperor on his wall and an A-class virus in his lungs that will kill him before he's twenty-two."

"Fuck me," said Brian softly. "He's just a baby!"

"Yeah," said Czamkiar. "He's sixteen, but as we all learned, babies can die too. Most of the famous musicians came from the Cylinder, and Avalair. We will lose most of them in the next fifteen years. That is partly why we are so protective of them. You should get Randish to take you to the Cylinder; you are a musician, you would fit right in. Especially since you play Metal. It is becoming very popular there."

"I'd need a translator," said Brian.

"I can translate. But we will have to do your make-up or they won't let you in. People there don't like blank faces."

They seated themselves at the large table in the kitchen, joined by Missy and Mystique. Gemma noticed that the Sferkkaans ate quickly, but carefully, not wanting to waste anything or act like a pack of starving animals. Gemma had to admire their restraint – if it had been twenty four hours since her last meal, she would not be as gracious.

"So tell me something," she said. "Do women here just not wear make-up, or are they not allowed to?"

"Some do," said Czamkiar, "especially the ones who fought. We *do* wear make-up purely for vanity, but most of it tells people who we are. Or were."

"The Gryphons don't," said Brian. "Or rather most of them don't."

"They do when something important is going on. But with Raski, his stripes do not all fit on his face. And Yuri Stracona has no stripes. And Draephus… they do not make stripes for what he did."

"What did he do?" asked Brian.

"Smuggled drugs. He brought mushrooms up from the South Continent. I'm not sure but I think he also fought on Ysith Beach in one of the last battles. But mostly he smuggled drugs."

Brian laughed. "What did he bring them up for?"

"Pain relief," said Czamkiar. "And for the soldiers too badly hurt to help, to sedate into death. Better than screaming one's life away."

Brian shook his head. "Good god that is horrible."

"It went on for eight hundred years," said Czamkiar. "We had to face it. People died. It did not matter if they were good, or talented, or babies. They died. And they did not choose how they died. The mushrooms Draephus brought up saved many people from a death in agony. We still use it for many things, both legal and not."

"And not?" said Brian.

"Oh I am far too young and innocent to know about that," said Czamkiar, smiling.

Brian laughed. "Oh I am sure. So do I have to dress like a Sferkkaan as well as get painted up like one?"

"Would you like to? I can teach you to walk in heels and a corset."

"Well how can I turn down an offer like that? Okay, dinner, then shopping?"

"Yes!" Czamkiar turned to Gemma. "Would you like to come?"

"Sure!" she said. "But are people going to look at me funny if I want to wear high heels and corsets too?"

"Gemma you are a girl," said Czamkiar. "You could dress up like a farm animal and no one would mind. But they might think you are a lesbian."

"I have a question," said Missy. "How do you treat lesbians here?"

"I don't know. I never thought of it. It is hard enough to find a female lover on this planet with only one woman to every eight hundred men. I can't imagine being that one woman. She must be very lonely."

He looked to Diza and spoke. She smiled slightly, then nodded. Czamkiar looked to Brian. "Diza is coming too."

"And me!" said Mystique. "I am not going back to Earth in a year with no Sferkkaan shoes. And you are going to teach me how to wear my make up."

"Oh what's this, a gay-boy party?" said Mickie, walking into the room.

Czamkiar looked at Mickie, raising an eyebrow. "Is that supposed to upset and offend me?"

"Well you're a little faggot, aren't you?"

"If you are asking me if I am homosexual, then no. I am not. If you are asking me if I have given very serious consideration to dating other boys because there simply is no one else, then yes. And if you are implying that I should somehow be ashamed of that, then you're an idiot."

Mickie appeared to be on the verge of coming at Czamkiar, when the Sferkkaan youth showed one tall boot heel.

"Mickie I have boot-blades too."

Mickie left immediately. Czamkiar turned back to his meal.

"I can't *use* them, yet, but I have them," said Czamkiar, and grinned.

"Boot blades?" said Gemma. "Don't you have to be a warrior to have those?"

"Lyrellyn asked me to wear them," said Czamkiar.

Gemma felt a wave of annoyance and jealousy. "Lyrellyn. The boy whose father is the Bird of Prey. The one who wants you so bad he gets a nosebleed every time he looks at you."

"Yes," said Czamkiar. "He wants to teach me to use them."

"Oh I just bet he does," said Gemma.

"Jealous, hon?" asked Missy.

"I don't care what he does with his stupid boots," grumbled Gemma.

"Oh that's good," said Czamkiar. "I was worried you were jealous."

"I'm not jealous!" said Gemma heatedly.

"We know, sweetie," said Mystique.

"I really am not! I don't care what Czamkiar is off doing in some room with some other boy. It's none of my business."

"Actually it's usually in the garden behind his house near the fountains," said Czamkiar, smiling.

"I'M NOT JEALOUS!!! I hate all of you, you're totally ruining my life. I'm going to go get changed."

Gemma departed, heading for her room to dress in something a little better suited to the endless Sferkkaan rain. She had only been on the planet a brief time, but she was already beginning to think of the rain in the same terms the Sferkkaans did –

Not raining = high cloud cover, fine misting rain.
Damp = slightly denser cloud cover, light rain, some fog.
A bit wet = medium rain, no fog.
Raining = Black skies, rain hammering down, occasional mud slides.
Storming a little = You round up the animals, I'll start building the ark.
We should probably stay in = was that ocean there when we went to bed?

Currently it was "damp", and Gemma wanted to make sure she stayed dry. First she sent a note off to Facebook.

Going shopping on an alien planet. This should be interesting.

She met up with Czamkiar, Diza, Randish, Brian, Missy and Mystique by the front doors, and together the group went outside into the wet Sferkkaan night. Gemma looked nervously around at the bombed-out buildings.

"That is so creepy and scary. It gives me nightmares. I hate thinking what might be living in them."

"Could be anything," said Czamkiar lightly.

Gemma scowled at him as he got into the car. The rest followed, with Brian getting in behind the wheel. Like K-Shot, one of the very first things he had done was buy himself a Sferkkaan car. Like K-Shot, he was having a hard time figuring out the dashboard.

"Do you want me to drive?" asked Czamkiar as Brian glowered at the dash.

"Yeah I think you better."

They switched places, Czamkiar removing his high heels in order to drive, then turning on the radio. Gemma groaned loudly.

"I hate the radio station they have here!"

"What, Satellite Base Four?" said Czamkiar. "What's wrong with them?"

"The only Earth music they play is by dead guys no one cares about!"

"On behalf of Sferkkaans everywhere we apologize for liking what is good and not what is popular, which do not always go hand in hand. Personally if it is a choice between 'Set the Controls for the Heart of the Sun' by Pink Floyd and any of that clart by Mickie Pastors, then Floyd wins."

"What Earth bands do you like?" asked Brian, grinning. It was clear to Gemma that Brian liked Czamkiar too. Great. Soooo nice that her would-be boyfriend was more popular than she was.

"Lots," said Czamkiar. "Mostly art rock and progressive rock, like Yes, Emerson Lake and Palmer, Pink Floyd, Queen, the Moody Blues…"

"Dead guys no one cares about," said Gemma. "I wish they would play that Sferkkaan band… what is their name? Straif Mannechek plays for them, I think they're great!"

"I like the Rolling Stones, too," said Czamkiar. "And Led Zeppelin."

"More dead guys no one cares about," said Gemma.

"The Rolling Stones are not dead," said Czamkiar. "They've merely reached an age where it's no longer safe to move them, and a sneeze could prove catastrophic."

Gemma just watched out the window as they pulled into a narrow street that was clearly one of the oldest parts of the city. The buildings were stone and timber, carefully repaired, restored to their antique glory.

"So this is what Second City used to look like," said Brian.

"This is the original heart of the city from centuries ago," said Czamkiar. "We are on the island itself here. Out by your ship we are on the extensions that float on the water. Here we are on ground."

"It's beautiful," said Missy. She was quiet for a few minutes, then said "Hey, Czamkiar? Do you know Mars David?"

"He lives in Second City. All the Gryphons do. I've seen him once or twice playing in the… I do not know what the Earth-word for it is…*grassekaarmoet* in the park on hot days, but I don't know him."

Brian slowly sounded out the word, then said "Do you mean that shallow pond in the park?"

"I think that is what you call it, but a *grassekaarmoet* is a specific kind of pond. But yes it is a pond."

"He can't afford a swimming pool?" asked Gemma.

"He could but I think he's lonely," said Czamkiar. "He seems to like to be where there are other people."

"You understood that argument he and I had a few weeks back," Missy said.

"Yes."

"What disease does he have?"

"I should think you would know that better than I," said Czamkiar.

"I didn't really give him a chance to explain."

"Whatever it is," said Czamkiar, "It cannot be contagious or he would by law be in a hospital and either quarantined or sedated into death."

"Jesus H. Christ on a cracker," said Brian. "You guys don't fuck around, do you?"

"Some of the A Class viruses are brutally painful," said Czamkiar. "Who wants to live endlessly screaming? Even the most powerful of pain killers don't work. We cannot help them. All we can do is stop their suffering."

"What if they are not in pain?" asked Brian. "What then?"

"They live in the hospital with the other patients and do what work they can. So they can contribute and have as full a life as is possible." He glanced at Brain. "We do what we can. Sometimes it is not enough. But when you have a man whose breath spreads carcinogens that can kill children, animals and anything else he comes into contact with, what do you do with him?"

"So Mars can't… give me what he has," said Missy.

"As far as I know," said Czamkiar, "the only thing Mars David can give to anyone is bloody good vocals and an excellent šukat."

Mystique looked to Missy. "And was he excellent?"

"Let's just say that, for a man who doesn't get much practice with women, he was better than a lot of the ones who do."

Czamkiar stopped the conni on the empty street before a small shop, and the group exited the vehicle. The street was silent, and dark, giving Gemma a creepy feeling that the Sferkkaans did not seem to notice. They hurried across the wet sidewalk, and into the shop, which was much warmer and more inviting. Gemma closed the door behind them, and looked around the inside of the little store. She supposed it would be called a boutique at home. The walls were the same stone and timber they had been on the outside, and the floor was made of thick wooden planks. Rows upon rows of racks and shelves carried everything from boots to jackets to eyewear to shirts and underwear and pretty much anything else she could think of. A display case made of glass and wood carried bags, bowls, and boxes of powdered items, most of a narcotic quality, including several dried spined mushrooms.

Gemma crept closer to look at the mushrooms. They were silvery-grey, with an undeniably phallic shape to them. The spines were long and thin, eerily bone-like, and the fungus looked more like a medieval torture device than a natural mushroom. She carefully reached out one finger to touch it. Then something enormous and black with glowing blue eyes that she had not noticed before stirred behind the counter.

Gemma shrieked and turned to flee, crashing face-first into Missy, and both fell into a shelf full of shirts. Moments later, Czamkiar was helping her to her feet.

"What is wrong with you?" he asked wearily.

"There was a monster back there!" said Gemma.

"Yes and his name is Askari, he owns the shop and makes the clothes. Honestly, Gemma, do they let you roam free on your world?"

Something huge and hairless with a gigantic head and round bulging eyes bounced out of the back room to see what all the noise was about. Gemma screamed again and fled for the car, and this time nothing was blocking her way. She left the shop and dove into the vehicle, closing the doors and locking them. Within the brightly lit shop, she could see Czamkiar, Diza, Brian, Missy and Mystique helping to right things, and cuddling the furless monster with the protruding teeth. It seemed happy and friendly, and no one appeared interested in following her out to the car. Well fine, then. She didn't care.

Gemma sat in the car and sulked while her friends shopped. After a while she drew out her phone to update her Facebook status.

Sferkkaa sucks, and the guy in the shop is a freak. This place is totally ruining my life.

****

Dahli awoke suddenly, and lay perfectly still, listening to the sounds around her. An alarm was ringing off in the distance, somewhere in D Section. Across the room Crystal and Ember stirred and sat up, also awakened by the alarm. All had heard this sound before, during drills, but the detention centre didn't do drills in the middle of the night. The girls were quiet, making no move. Dahli wondered if her roommates were as frightened as she was.

A guard ran by, followed by two more. The alarm continued to ring, on and on without abating. That was unnerving in itself, but there were other sounds, too. There were yells and screams, and once she thought she heard the strange, throaty hum of a laser pistol. Dahli huddled under the covers, eyes squeezed shut, pillow over her head in an effort to escape the sounds she heard. The alarm rang on, and now Dahli could hear other inmates prowling about like restless animals, nervous and uneasy.

Another group of guards ran by, five this time. Dahli sat up. "What's happening?" she asked.

"Sounds like something down in D Section," said Ember. "I wonder how bad it is?"

"Bad," said Crystal. "Real bad, listen to it." The three were silent. The noise was louder now, shouts and commotion reaching a higher pitch.

"That's more than a couple people trying to break each other's necks," said Crystal. "Sounds like a riot."

The noise wore on, neither growing nor fading. It seemed the fray was still contained within D Section. Then a second alarm went off, of a different sound than the first. This one seemed closer.

"Can't be a riot," said Ember. "If it was a riot they would have the old siren on, the one that makes that sharp beep."

"Well it's something," said Crystal. "I think it's getting closer."

"Have they broken into this section?" asked Dahli nervously.

"I don't think so," said Ember. "I'm not even sure what that is."

The alarm rose and fell, howling away into the darkness. No lights had been activated; the only illumination came from small emergency lanterns. A series of laser pistol shots exploded, these frighteningly close, and seconds later two youths ran by, clad in detention centre uniforms.

"It's broken out," said Dahli, her heart pounding.

"It's not a riot," insisted Crystal. Then she sniffed the air, catching a whiff of something.

"What's that smell?" Ember asked. Down the hall someone began to scream, answering their question for them.

"Fire! The whole place is burning!"

The alarm wailed as several more people ran by. Then the fire was upon them, sweeping down the hallway like a wave, fast and violent. Mercifully it was a short blast, as if it was the warning shot of a dragon. Trapped in their cell, the trio screamed as something in the room exploded into flames, igniting one of the beds. Dahli leapt out of bed while Ember grabbed her flaming mattress and turned it over. It hissed and crackled, sending up billows of black, oily smoke as Crystal used a cup to throw water on it. Dahli grabbed her own mattress and threw it on top of Ember's to smother the flames. Smoke filled the room and rolled out into the hallway, covering everything in soot, plunging the room into reeking darkness. They could hear other inmates screaming, adding to the calamity. Another siren went off, virtually unnoticed amidst the chaos, while guards began herding hysterical inmates towards the exits.

Dahli searched around the room for anything that could be used as a weapon. She had a feeling that she may need one. She examined the metal frame of her bed. It was one solid piece, welded together.

'Obviously', she thought wryly, 'so no one can take it apart and use a portion of it for a weapon. Duh.'

She looked about for anything else that may have possibilities, but there was nothing. Should the electronically controlled doors fling open, there was nothing she could use with which to defend herself. Outside the cell, bodies clashed and fought behind a thickening veil of smoke, rats struggling to see who would die last. The noise all around was like that of a battle. The flood of bodies had stopped flowing by and was now clogging the corridor. Dahli could no longer see Crystal and Ember in the room. She felt only a growing terror as the air became a toxic cloud, and her throat and eyes burned. She heard herself screaming as she began throwing herself against the cell door, trying to escape certain death.

Something exploded, and with the mad confusion of animals stampeding, the wall of bodies began to move on. Some ran back the way they'd come, most moved forward. Then all was plunged into total blackness as even the small emergency lights went out, and there was only the non-light of the fire in the distance. The electronic door slid open, and without a second thought, Dahli was through it. She paused in the hallway, disoriented, then, choosing the least obstructed route, ran down the hallway.

It occurred to her to head for the yard, and wait there for the nightmare and chaos to end, but she had no idea where that was in all the smoke. It was as if the detention center had become an alien landscape. She dodged down unfamiliar halls, strange and frightening in the dark. At one turn she saw a body lying across her path, and like a wild animal she chose the next opening she saw rather than cross the corpse. There was no sense to the route she had chosen; all she wanted was to get out of the building. Here and there she encountered small spot fires and the smoke was not so thick, but she could still hear the screaming in the distance, and try as she might, she could not seem to escape it.

She turned a corner and accidentally plunged headlong into a small knot of fighting people, blundering straight into the midst of about ten combatants taking advantage of the situation to settle old scores. Two of them turned on her as she crashed into them, and she felt one of them seize her arm. She turned and struck out at him, but was thrown to the floor before managing to make contact. She rolled quickly, not waiting for her attackers to pin her. A hand seized the collar of her shirt, two more grasping her ankles, and she was thrown onto her back. She could see one of her attackers now, a rangy, dark-eyed youth with a pock-marked face. Dahli struck out wildly in terror, and it was an act of divine intervention that guided her hand to his nose, striking the soft cartilage and breaking it. Blood spurted, and he retreated, howling in pain.

With her assailant suddenly on the defensive, Dahli felt a rush of rage well up inside of her. As he sat with his hands over his bleeding nose, she snatched up a length of pipe someone had discarded and brought it down across his ribs. There was a loud crunch, and he screamed in pain. Wielding the pipe once more, she broke his knee for good measure. Her second assailant fled. Dahli let out a crazed war cry and charged after him, scattering people as she went.

She pursued the youth for some distance, but eventually lost both him and herself. Tired and winded, she seated herself upon the cold grey floor, looking around. This area of the building was unknown to her. It was badly damaged; doors hung open and askew, blankets, clothing and mattresses lay scattered, shredded and burned. The metal frames of beds were leaning against walls or thrown haphazardly into the hall. There seemed to be no one else about, at least not close at hand. In the background, the ominous sound of fighting rumbled on, but it was far off and of no immediate danger. However the stench of smoke still hung in the air, and the thought of the building burning down with her in it was very much on her mind. She rose to her feet and began searching for an exit, still hearing the alarm ring.

Dahli made her way down the hall, moving slowly and carefully as she searched the area. She roamed the dark halls, finding nothing, not even a flight of steps that led downstairs. She would have to go back the way she had come; assuming could find her way back. She hadn't realized the detention centre was so large. Every corner she turned revealed only more cell doors, more debris on the floor. She knew that in her flight from the fire and subsequent rioting that she had gone up a set of stairs, but where?

She found a mattress, one which was not as badly burned as the others, and sat upon it. The alarm still rang on, but when she strained to hear any other sounds, she could not detect any. Had the riot stopped? If so, then why was the alarm still on? She wrapped her arms about herself, feeling the cold of the building take hold. On the wall beside her sat her silhouette, formed by the soft glow of an outside light coming in through the barred window.

The alarm stopped abruptly. Dahli had become so accustomed to the noise that she had almost ceased to hear it. Now the quiet was louder and more worrisome than the clanging. Still and silent, Dahli awaited the small night lights to come on, to send out their soft, sterile glow and announce all was well. The lights did no come on, and as time passed, the dark and stillness began to nibble at her like a deranged mouse. She stared nervously around, wishing so strongly she was home in her own bed that her stomach began to feel ill.

She closed her eyes and visualised her room; the large spreading dresser with its huge mirror, the soft blue-grey carpeting with the little bald patch near the closet door where a mouse had chewed it. She could see her reading lamp, and her bed with its Mortified Gryphons bed sheets. She and Diza had painstakingly made these themselves. There were dark blue, with soft grey and light blue constellations painted over the background. An open patch hung in the sky without any reason for being, a rope ladder dangling from it. A man hung onto the ladder, looking down at an immense gryphon, which stared back with a malicious cartoon smile. It was the cover from one of the older recordings; `Nice Knowing You'.

Draephus came to mind then, and the letter he had sent; the apology she would not accept in person. She didn't know if she accepted it now, but it would have been wonderful to have his imposing frame seated next to her. Perhaps she would write him, if the letter still existed and she still had his address. She wondered if he would make any further attempt to contact her. She couldn't imagine why he would, other than to possibly seek compensation for what she had done to his vehicle.

There was an unexpected scream of feedback from an intercom coming to life. Dahli's attention snapped towards the source of the sound, a small startled gasp escaping her. She waited anxiously for the voice to come on and announce all was under control. What did come out was not comforting.

"We've taken over!" a voice raved fanatically. In the background Dahli could hear banging and pounding, loud authoritative voices demanding the door be opened. The voice in control of the microphone laughed crazily. "No way! This place is ours!"

The voice droned on, screaming with all the zealous insanity of a new dictator. She listened as he broke into song, howling the words to a Bad Influence song in a voice that quavered and cracked, or lay as flat as a dead man's pulse. He sang the wrong words, sometimes intentionally, sometimes not. Alone in the dark of the emptied section, Dahli found it the most frightening thing she'd ever heard.

"*...I'm gonna take off all my clothes,*
And shout and run around,
I'm gonna jump right off a cliff
And land right on the ground..."

Dahli knew the song, had it at home in fact. When Delaes Randerick sang it, it was merely another bizarre and pointless Bad

Influence song. When this guy sang it...well...he sounded like he would do it, but not without taking someone with him.

A voice suddenly cried out in the dark; a yell, then running feet. Dahli leapt back into the security of a darkened cell. Crouched down behind the destroyed remnants of a bed, she watched as a youth ran by, pursued by two others. She listened as their footsteps faded; remaining huddled down behind the bed. The voice on the intercom continued on. It seemed the whole place had gone mad.

She remained hidden for hours, listening to the insane voice. The light of an exterior lamp slowly gave way to day. Outside the window she could hear birds chirp and trill, oblivious to her plight. Her stomach began to growl, and her mouth had begun to feel like the stuff that filled the mattresses. Still she would not move from her hiding place. She had already had a sample of what would happen to her should she be found by the wrong people; and she wasn't too fond of the idea of being raped or beaten, or both.

Did Sferkkaan men commit rape? Or was that just something Kryphisians did? Oh man, she hoped it was just something Kryphisians did! She huddled in her hiding spot, terrified. Surely the chaos couldn't go on much longer, surely someone would have been called in to help deal with the mess. The voice on the intercom droned on. A brief scuffle broke out, uncomfortably close. Dahli squeezed her eyes shut and pulled the remains of a blanket over herself, hoping to pass as debris.

The voice suddenly changed from fanatic to frantic. "HEY...HEY! LET GO YOU CLART! YOU ŠUKAT YOUR MOTHER, GROUTNOLL!" There was the thud of an object striking flesh. "LET ME GO YOU GREY-BOY SYMPATHISER! YOU USED TO WORK FOR THEM, DIDN'T YOU?"

The screaming voice faded away, and a second calmer, more authoritative one took over.

"This is Warden Shayer. The fire is out, the riot is over, and we are resuming command of this centre. Those of you who have barricaded yourselves in D Section arc commanded to release your hostages immediately and surrender, and no further time will be added to your sentences."

Dahli gasped in horror as laughter broke out not far away, and something smashed against a wall.

"Listen to him, will you? `Release your hostages.' EAT CLART!"

The voice echoed from a point down the hall. Suddenly she began to wonder just what section she was holed up in. She heard no more from the voice down the hall, but she didn't have to. She only had to think about the words it had uttered to know where she was.

She decided to stay where she was, hiding in the debris, waiting for the people down the hall to fall asleep and then try to find her way out. Whether this was a good idea or not, she didn't know, but the thought of being trapped on the wrong side of a barricade with a group of hostage-holding lunatics didn't much appeal to her.

*****

The hours dragged on. She had become stiff and uncomfortable; her legs had gone to sleep from being in the same position for too long. She shifted as slowly and quietly as she could, and stretched her legs to let the blood move. She heard nothing from the voice down the hall, and she wondered how many people were down there.

Dahli turned her head to look out the cell window. It was small and square, horizontal bars crossed by diagonal ones. From outside she heard the sleepy titter of birds starting to awaken. The sky was heavy and dark, the clouds thick, obscuring the soft haze that was the sky.

Dahli dozed off for a brief time, sleeping in starts and stops. Once she was awakened by the intercom starting up with its usual scream, and the voice of Warden Shayer again demanding that D Section be opened up. This was met with yells and obscenities, the strident voice of one individual rising above all to state that the hostages would be killed if their demands were not met.

"What do you want?" Shayer asked. "What are your demands?"

"We'll get back to you on that, now get out of our ears."

Dahli swore that, come nightfall, she would try to find her way out of D Section. With any luck she would be able to avoid the crazies down the hall. They seemed to be keeping to the one cell for the most part; presumably that was where the hostages were being kept as well. She wondered what sort of weapons they had. Laser pistols were a possibility, if they had managed to capture one or two of the guards. Clubs were more likely than the pistols, or knives. She couldn't think of what else they may have. She knew from conversations with former soldiers that people could make weapons out of anything. Dahli shifted herself into a more comfortable position and listened hard for any nearby movement.

It was going to be a long day.

Chapter Eleven

`It's strange to be here,' Draephus thought, `very strange. It's funny how things take on a different perspective when you know you aren't supposed to be alive.'

He had died in his sleep. Dr. Arang had told him he had simply given up and stopped breathing. Draephus drew in a laboured breath and wondered why he had taken that midnight swim anyway. He hadn't thought he was trying to kill himself, but what other reason was there for what he had done? The fact that he had very nearly succeeded scared him, and the knowledge that the mucous that now tried to plug his lungs still may get him was even scarier.

'Welcome to wanting to live, clart-head. Welcome to being hooked up to a half-a-dozen machines and having to deal with the thought that death may come and get you without your consent.'

What had he been thinking when he had jumped into the water? Was he out of his mind? When he had opened his eyes after his brush with death Dr. Arang had been there, sitting on the edge of his bed.

"Congratulations," he drawled. "You've got the worst case of pneumonia we've ever seen. We think it may even be a new strain. You're famous."

Draephus couldn't speak, but he did manage an obscene gesture, which seemed to please Dr. Arang to no end. He gave him a pat on the shoulder before leaving him in peace. This lasted roughly ten minutes, then Delaes and Raski blew in, armed with a huge collection of wildflowers. Flowers would have been Raski's idea, picking them on their own would have been Donsa Hyperactive's. Delaes was the single most tense and nervous person Draephus knew. He never sat down for long, went for days without sleeping, and started every morning with a run, going for miles at a pace that left most in the dust. Draephus had once jokingly asked Delaes what he was running from, and Delaes had screamed with hysterical laughter for a long, uncontrolled time before collapsing in tears. Draephus never asked him again. They all had their pursuing monsters. As Raski approached the bed to talk to Draephus, Delaes vibrated quietly in a corner.

"Delaes and I brought you some flowers," he understated. The huge, crazed collections of flora exploded from their glass containers, filling the air with the scent of the summer Draephus was missing. He smiled slightly.

"Hey," said Raski, "Dr. Arang says you're going to get better as soon as they remove the extra teeth you use for biting people's heads off. You'd better get out of here soon; I'm really getting rather tired of babysitting your faelins and people calling me at all hours to ask how you are. You won't believe who called this morning. J'Vanni Dei Syncopius, the crazed composer. The first time anyone has heard his voice and he breaks solitude to ask about you of all people. Someone should tell him the war is over and it's all right to make music now."

Delaes spoke up. "He makes music he just doesn't sing you know I really wonder if he exists or if he's some sort of fictional character I mean has anyone ever seen this man?"

'I'm willing to bet you did, and very recently, too,' thought Draephus. But J'Vanni had more reason to hide than Delaes did; one look at those soft, expressive, slate-grey eyes would be enough for most people to know what he was.

"He has to be real, he called me," said Raski. "And I can understand why he doesn't sing, he's got the strangest accent I ever heard. Like a seductive computer, some kind of machine experiencing feelings it shouldn't. Put the hair up on the back of my neck to hear it. Hey is our presence a bit too much for you right now? We can leave if you're tired."

Draephus smiled and shook his head. Delaes had turned on the small Visual and had begun to listen to the news. From its place on the wall opposite from where Draephus lay, it began to broadcast the day's events quietly.

Raski took Draephus' hand, then said; "Hey Delaes, turn that off."

Delaes made a move to do so, but Draephus shook his head, indicating that he wanted the device left on. The Visual spat out sounds and images of what had occurred over the day. Another revolution was happening on the Southern Continent. That happened so often that it was a wonder anyone bothered to report it. Then on to the cute stuff. The Emperor was remodelling his bathroom, obviously a story of political importance. Draephus wondered if anybody had noticed that he had reconstructed an entire castle. No one had done a news report on that. Then story came on about a fire and riot at Second City Youth Detention Centre. It seemed six people had taken hostages and barricaded themselves into one of the sections. As of yet no one had asked for anything.

"Well they may not have *asked* for anything," said Raski, "but I suspect they'll *get* something, all right. And it will probably leave bruises."

The news reporter prattled on. "...also believed to be amongst the hostage-holders is Dahli Sandiniti, the young girl who caused something of a fire in the scholastic system when she stole a dead faelin from her school on what she called `political grounds.' It is not known if the two incidents, the theft and the riot, are linked in any way, but the possibility is being examined."

Silence fell in the hospital room as jaws dropped. Delaes uttered a short, shocked laugh.

"What is she doing?" asked Raski.

Draephus suddenly began coughing loudly. He gasped and struggled to breathe as though his lungs had just collapsed. A delicate beeping came from the many monitors, and an attendant ran into the room. Seconds later Delaes and Raski were evicted from the room, ingloriously shoved into the hall.

****

They remained there for a short time, until Dr. Arang came to say that Draephus was all right, but he was going to be asleep for a while and they would have to come back later. Then the pair wandered off. Raski and Delaes left the hospital, getting into Raski's black vehicle and driving away. Delaes turned on the receiver, and out came the latest syrupy tunc from Vortex.

> "...It's so nice to see you,
> smiling like you do,
> you know I love you,
> I hope you love me too.
> I think about you all the time,
> even when you're not there.
> I think of you when I brush my teeth,
> and when I comb my hair..."

Delaes shrieked and turned off the receiver. "That group is really atrocious I cannot believe the Emperor declared them a government-protected band they really ought to have that status revoked but then that is probably the only thing keeping people from killing the whole group be a shame about the quinticord player he's the only one with any talent how come they have Straif Mannechek who is extremely talented and cute and I have Marachani who is mediocre and ugly like a feralyke's back end but oh yes he quit didn't he?"

Raski let Delaes rattle on as he drove easily down the quiet streets towards his home.

`Like a little bird,'* thought Raski, *`one of those little ones that get up at fourhour in the morning and trill outside of your window non-stop until you want to pull its cute fluffy head off.'

He tried to think of what else made a continual racket, and almost instantly Draephus' faelins came to mind. Bacca and Czanda would perch thirty feet off the ground in the great wooden beams of Draephus' castle and trill non-stop, calling and cackling to each other and scarcely draw a breath. Draephus loved it, and often incorporated the sounds his faelins made into his music. There was definitely something very compelling about their cries and calls. Many of their vocalizations were truly unearthly and beautiful… much like the singing style of a certain lead vocalist Raski knew.

Raski glanced at Delaes as he rattled on. Nah. Couldn't be. Could he?

"Hey Delaes, you know that song 'Avalair Grey'?"

"I should hope so I did write it."

"That cry you let out towards the end, is that you, or is that synthesized or a millitron or what?"

"How dare you of course it's me you know very well I don't synthesize my vocals I'm very proud of my voice."

"Well you do have a beautiful voice but… come on. One musician to another. It's synthesized."

"Oh you are SO asking for a slap it is my voice and it has not been altered in any way!"

"Well then let's hear it."

Delaes gave him an annoyed look, miffed his talent should be held suspect. Then he let forth a haunting, mournful cry that rose and fell, lingering for an impossibly long time, hanging in the air like the wafting perfume of despair. It brought tears to Raski's eyes just hearing it, sending a shiver down his spine. That cry had made Delaes and his band famous. It also sent Draephus' faelins into a complete frenzy, and they would return the call, matching it note for note, then repeat it for hours, almost as if it held some significance for them. Raski glanced at Delaes again, studying the small face, the long delicate limbs, large eyes, and slender build. He'd seen it before, but not on another Sferkkaan.

Dahli and Draephus both claimed faelins were intelligent beings, and not merely humanoid animals.

Maybe Dahli and Draephus were right.

Maybe faelins and Sferkkaans could cross breed after all.

They arrived at Raski's house. It had begun to rain by now; a heavy ocean storm that turned the sky black and obscured the view from his windows. Raski hurried up the walk to get out of it, but Delaes stopped to stomp in the mud puddles. Raski paused on the porch to watch him; a leggy, skinny figure blurred by the falling water, dancing with a surreal grace, a black smear in the darkness of the storm, laughing.

"Delaes!" Raski cried. "Get in here, or else I won't let you sit on the furniture!"

Delaes came running, metal-tipped boots scraping droplets of water off of the flagstone walk as he continued to dance, bouncing past Raski and into the wide entrance of the house. Silver beads of water were flung from his hair and scattered about the room, striking the large windows and melding with the raindrops that slid down them. Raski grinned at him.

"Want some music to go with that performance, Delaes?"

Delaes whirled to stop, eyes bright. "Do you have `Birdseed Tea'?"

"I'll look in the kitchen."

"NOOO...that's not what it is groutnoll it's a J'Vanni Dei Syncopius song."

"In that case, no, I don't."

"What do you have?"

Raski checked his music collection. "`Bragging to Fire' and `Pensive Moments in the Fifth Hour'. Then we have the classic `My Songs All Have Really Long Titles, Therefore My Album Should Have One Too'."

"I don't really like those ones oh here I have one in my pocket." Delaes fished the thin silver cylinder out of his pocket and threw it to

Raski. "It's his latest."

Raski caught the object and turned it over in his fingers to read the name on it. He felt a mild chill go through him, as though he had been overheard in a private conversation. The cylinder was titled; `Don't You Wish you Knew What I Looked Like?'

Raski stared at it for a long moment, and thought about the accent he had heard when speaking with J'Vanni – an accent he kept thinking he *should* be able to place. He then tossed the cylinder back to Delaes, who bounced over to the stereo. The broad, shiny leaves of the amp plants twisted like primitive radar, following him in anticipation. Raski walked into his kitchen and picked up the telecom, punching in the number Donsa Syncopius had given him earlier that day. He heard the device ring at the other end, then heard it being lifted.

"Hello?" spoke the strangely accented voice.

"J'Vanni? This is Raski."

"How is Draephus?"

"Fine, he's fine. He sends his regards. Hey, I was just listening to your latest recording. It's very good. Love the title."

There was silence from the other end of the line. Raski waited a moment, then said; "So what *do* you look like?"

The pause continued, then the voice came back, speaking quickly.

"I am glad to hear Draephus is doing fine. Send him my love. Good day, Jervyas-Kaif."

The line went dead. Raski stared at the device for a long moment, startled by the man's abruptness. Slowly, he hung up, still trying to place the accent.

"`Kaif'?" he repeated softly. Like the accent, he knew that he should recognize the word, but it too eluded him. "What is a `kaif'?" He then called to Delaes; "What is a kaif?"

"It's a hole in a mountain!" Delaes yelled as he bounced into the room. He had removed his coat and was dressed in a tight black leather outfit that was just a little tighter than it ought to be. Raski studied him critically.

"Are you getting fat?"

Delaes paused, blinking. "Fat? Me? I think NOT what is to eat I'm ravenous which is really strange because I was positively ill this morning."

There was a bowl of reddish-orange settins on the table and

Delaes picked one up. Holding the fruit with both hands he tore into it voraciously, hardly bothering to chew, a clear thin line of juice making its way down between his fingers. He ate the soft fruit, seeds and all, then walked past Raski and to the coldbox, opening the door. He leaned inside, Raski watching him.

Oh there was something very odd going on here. Something very odd indeed.

"Do you have any almaniki juice because I am positively dying for some oh yes you do here it is."

Delaes stepped back, holding a carton. Raski watched Delaes up-end the carton of juice and drain the entire contents down his throat.

"Delaes, you hate almanikies, you said the smell of them alone was enough to make you gag."

"I know which is why I can't figure out why I want them so badly now."

"Delaes, are you quite all right?"

Delaes blinked innocent brown eyes at him. "Never better just hungry."

"Well help yourself to the coldbox. But those pants don't fit you right as it is."

Delaes shrugged. "I'll get new pants."

Raski continued to scrutinize Delaes, his mind working. There was something definitely up. Delaes hated almanikies. The small blue fruit were an acquired taste, and people who did not like them tended to continue not liking them throughout their lives. They didn't wake up one day and start gobbling them down. Then a light went on over Raski's head.

Pregnant. Delaes was pregnant. He had an artificial uterus put in and... no he couldn't be pregnant. Candidates for the artificial uterus were screened carefully, and they were not given to just anyone, not even wealthy and famous musicians. Delaes would have had his health checked, his friends would have been interviewed, and he would have to be able to prove he had a calm and stable home life as well as a partner to help him raise future children. Delaes was a bundle of nerves, and so far as Raski knew he didn't have a husband. The fact that he lived in Avalair, albeit on the outskirts, was in itself enough to get him refused. And even if Delaes didn't say anything about having such a device implanted, news of these things tended to leak. People would know.

Of course, if he was half-faelin he might not need an artificial womb. He might already have his own…

****

It was early evening when Raski drove up to Draephus' castle, Delaes in the seat beside him. He could hear the yapping and howling of Draephus' two faelins before he even opened the vehicle door.

"They must be frantic," said Raski. "Draephus has never been away this long."

"Certainly do make a noise what does he do with them when you're on tour?"

Raski rolled his eyes. "Brings them."

"Oh that must make getting a hotel reservation interesting."

"Tell me about it."

They left the con parked by the bridge, walking across the wooden planks over the moat to the great door. All around was encroaching darkness, lit only by small luminous insects, and the glowing eyes of the frogs at the edge of the pond. Soon the perfect night would have settled, and they would be locked away in another time; before electricity, before conveyances, and before wars. Raski paused on the bridge and looked around, wondering what it would be like when he too called the castle home. Finally he resumed walking to the door. As he reached for the handle, he heard a body hit the door with a resounding thud, then fall to the floor.

"You have to wait until I get it open, groutnoll!" said Raski.

Czanda made an unhappy noise. Raski unlocked the door, and was immediately pounced upon by two desperately worried and distressed faelins. Bacca leapt into his arms and bit down on the collar of his shirt, chewing it; a sure sign the creature was very upset.

"Well I guess I'm sleeping here tonight," said Raski. "Can't leave them alone. C'mon, critters. Let's get you fed then I'll run a bath and let you two soak the castle down."

"Sleep *here* you honestly can't be serious I could never sleep here well yes I did once but that was different I certainly could not sleep here *alone*!"

"So stay with me."

"As much as I would love to spend the night in a haunted house trying to keep you off of me I can't I have to get back to Avalair and rescue Rysta his building collapsed and he's been staying in a shelter."

Raski gave Delaes a quizzical look as he walked through the door and up the steep flight of stairs that led to Draephus' main sitting room.

"His building collapsed? I thought that housing complex was new."

"It was but the underground fires found a vein of something combustible and just followed it all the way down munch-munch-munch until it hit foundation."

"Is Rysta all right?"

"Oh he's fine he's just not looking forward to staying with me for a few days you know it's funny he and I drive each other nuts but we're always the first to stand up for each other."

"Rysta's a good guy," said Raski. "He's just a little… screwed in the head."

"Well I daresay I would be as well if I went to bed one night having a wife and two daughters and woke up to three corpses to this day he won't drink water no matter what's been done to purify it."

"Yeah, I know how he feels," said Raski.

Raski walked into the kitchen, carrying Bacca over to the table and setting him on the polished wood inlayed with mother-of-pearl to form patterns of flowers. He then walked over to the cold-box, opening it, and sighed.

"You have got to be joking, what is this clart?" Raski pulled out a package and read something in Draephus' handwriting. "Bacca, Threeday evening snack." He pulled out another. "Czanda, Twoday breakfast. What is this? The man is *insane*. We're on *limited* rations, and they don't give us celebrities any little extras. So what does he do? Blows his ration cards on the faelins and starves." Raski shook his head. "No wonder he's nothing but bone and sinew. And why do you two arfers each get your own package, anyway?"

"Arf!" declared Bacca.

"That's not an excuse."

"Arf arf arf! RARF!"

"Really. Well, I was just asked to feed you, not comprehend you. And it's a damned good thing because I can't."

"Rar-arf!"

Raski smiled, and looked down at the packages he held. "Why do you two get different dinners?"

"They're different varieties," said Delaes.

"They're what?"

"They are two entirely different types of faelin surely you can tell that."

Raski looked at Bacca, then Czanda. They sat on the table, blinking at him with luminous green eyes. Both were red, roughly the same height, with a lot of long silky hair.

"Sure," he finally said.

Delaes rolled his eyes and took one of the packages, walking over to the wood stove to light a fire and heat it.

"Bacca is taller with longer bones and a deeper chest and a more flexible spine because he is an arboreal which means he lives in the tree-tops."

"Uh-huh. And Czanda?"

"Better suited to life on the ground but he can and will head for the tree-tops if he feels threatened."

Raski stared at the faelins. The faelins stared back.

"Well if you say so. All I know is if I could have chicken and fish three nights a week I'd sit up in a tree and bark too."

"Arf!"

"Yeah rub it in, ya skinny red arfer."

Raski glanced over at Delaes, eyes flicking up and down his body. He leaned back against the counter, watching Delaes light the woodstove. He drew a breath, and kept his voice casual.

"You know there's a chance I don't have C-3 and C-4."

"Raski that's wonderful of course it's not if it turns out you have something worse but I hope you don't."

"Yeah me too. If I'm relatively clean, they'll let me have kids."

Raski thought he saw a nervous flinch, but couldn't be sure.

"Well who would you have them with?" asked Delaes

"Draephus."

Delaes screamed with hilarity, dropping down to the floor in convulsions of helpless laughter. Raski rolled his eyes.

"He's my best friend, what's wrong with getting him to father my children?"

"YOU HAVE TO ASK!?"

"He loves me. I love him."

Delaes was still giggling. "I have no doubt you both love each other but honestly Raski do you have eyes the man is a shambling disaster I mean I love him too but do I want him putting a baby in me absolutely not!"

"So who *did* put a baby in you?"

That stopped the laughter cold, as if Raski had struck him across the face. Delaes stared at him, dark eyes full of fear as he slowly rose from the floor, unwittingly finding himself standing near the table on which the faelins perched, side by side with Bacca. He reached out one hand to place on the creature's shoulder.

Oh yeah. Definite family resemblance.

"Delaes, it's okay. I'm your friend."

Delaes shook his head. "It's not okay it is absolutely not okay you have no idea how very UN-okay this entire situation is."

Raski walked over to him, taking him by the shoulders. "Then explain to me," he said quietly.

Delaes shook his head. "No."

"Delaes…"

"Someone or something will hear it doesn't matter where we have this conversation someone will find out I already told you more than I should I should never have come but Draephus was so sick I didn't want him to die without saying goodbye…"

Raski gently drew his friend close, holding him, stroking his hand over the long hair. "It's okay. I won't tell anyone. Look, Delaes, no one has to know, okay? Here's what we can do. We can take you down to the South Continent. You can have it there, and we can say you adopted the kid."

Delaes was shaking. "And what if it has white hair and grey eyes?" he asked softly.

Raski felt his stomach drop. "Grey eyes? You mean the father is…"

"Kryphisian."

Raski closed his eyes and breathed in and out slowly several times. "Man, Delaes, when you screw up, you screw up *allllll* the way, don't you? Where did you find a Grey Boy?"

"In my apartment he lives with me I'm in love with him we get along great I'm a freak and he's a monster but I love him."

"Look, not all Grey Boys are monsters, even I know that."

"It doesn't matter to most people does it?"

"I guess not." Raski gently pulled Delaes closer, stroking his hair. "Do I know him?"

Delaes smiled. "J'Vanni Dei Syncopius."

Raski grinned. "Oh so THAT'S why we never see him! The little shit hides in your apartment pretending to be a High Northerner with severe emotional disturbances!"

"Well the emotional disorders are quite real he's been through some awful things I mean one day you are a private music teacher for children of wealthy parents and then they come drag you away and put a gun in your hand and tell you to kill these people who have never done anything to you…"

"A lot of us had that happen, Delaes. I mean I'm sorry for him, but…"

"You don't understand you don't understand the way they raised him you…"

Raski grabbed Delaes by the forearms, giving him a gentle shake to get his attention. "Delaes, breathe. Okay? Speak in sentences. I can't help if I can't understand you." He reached up to stroke his face. "Calm down. Breathe. That's a good boy. Now. What don't I understand?"

Delaes breathed, trying to control his non-stop nervous babble. "There is a caste system in place on their home planet that is very strict." He forced himself to breathe. "'Dei' means 'teacher' you do not choose to be a teacher you are raised a teacher and because you are working with innocent children you are expected to be innocent yourself that's…"

"Breathe, Delaes."

Delaes did, fighting to speak in a concise manner, fighting to express himself. "They raised him to be a music teacher. They raised him in an isolated community. Away from war, away from rape, away from murder, crime, violence. They raised him in a little controlled paradise. Then, because they were running out of soldiers, they gave him a gun, and sent him to war. And until that moment… he had no idea people killed each other."

Raski tried to comprehend what that must have been like for J'Vanni, and couldn't. He could not imagine being raised to have no knowledge of the violence people were capable of, only to be one day expected to kill like a trained soldier. There simply was not an emotion he could reach for he thought would even come close to the overwhelming horror and fear and revulsion this gentle man must have experienced.

"What did he do?"

"What do you think he did he went insane that's what he did and when his unit pulled out they left him behind because he was useless and that was when Draephus found him."

"Draephus…?"

"Found him took him in took care of him hid him and introduced us once he got a bit better and Draephus set him up in an underground communications center so he could help our side without having to kill." Delaes stopped, suddenly looking thoughtful. "I guess we didn't fight for *our* side we fought for *your* side because I don't see anybody worrying about half-breed faelins and emotionally destroyed music teachers other than Draephus and that weird kid who stole one I mean a faelin not a music teacher."

"Delaes, I…"

"I have to go I can't stand here chatting I have to get Rysta and I have to get home and I have to plan out a way to save my own neck."

Raski caught hold of him. "Delaes, nobody knows you're pregnant other than you and me, and possibly the father. So calm down."

"I really do have to get Rysta."

"Okay, go pick up Rysta. But if you need help with anything, Delaes, you can come to me, okay? That includes finding you transportation to the South Continent."

Delaes nodded, and smiled. "Thanks."

Raski stroked his hair, then kissed him gently, watching him depart. He sighed, and looked at Bacca.

"Aren't you glad you don't have to worry about this crap?"

He shook his head, long red-gold hair flying. "Pfffffthrp. Arf!"

Raski smiled. "I'm starting to understand what Draephus sees in you guys."

Chapter Twelve

Dahli waited until darkness had settled in completely before she made her move. She crept slowly out of the cell, looking down the hall to where she knew the crazies to be. There was a vague illumination coming from one of the cells, but she heard nothing, saw no movement. Slowly she began making her way down the hall, away from the light, her bare feet made no sound on the cold concrete floor as she crept along, uncertain if she was going in the right direction.

The air around her was cool, and she could smell the aftermath of the fire. Her heart banged painfully in her chest, and there was a nervous tightness in her stomach. Every fear she had ever felt before had been rendered infantile at that moment, a baby's apprehension of shadows to be warded off by a warm hand. She knew at this moment she was experiencing actual terror. She was barricaded inside a portion of a youth detention centre with a group of dangerous people, anyone of whom could see her and either take her hostage or kill her.

She walked quietly, keeping to the middle of the hall, hoping this would give her small advantage. If she was seen, she wanted a chance to react, and fight. She wasn't going to be picked off like the head of a flower, stupidly awaiting disaster. She negotiated the hallways carefully; avoiding any debris that would make a noise should she step on it. She tried to calm herself, distracting herself with thoughts about the first thing she would do when she got out. She'd call Czamkiar, and have him go get Diza. They'd go down to the Contempo and have some real food, not the stuff they served here. They could stay for a poetry reading, or head down to the city park for one of the evening concerts. She would forget all this clart, and just go back to being herself. It would be absolutely glorious.

She tripped, suddenly and loudly, over a jumble of unidentifiable metal, landing on her face. Dahli was terrified; she did not even feel pain as she awaited the sound of running feet, telling her she had been heard. She wondered how she had missed the tangle right before her; perhaps thinking about being down at the Contempo instead of where her feet were going was not the best idea.

She slowly, quietly, began disentangling herself. Freed of the debris, Dahli continued down the hallway, feeling a little more confident that she was alone. If someone had been stalking her, then they would have had the perfect opportunity to attack when she had tripped.

She heard the sudden sound of a summer downpour, and she paused, startled by the sound. She wondered if she would hear thunder; this was the season for it, and the electrical storms. Time to be out by the beach with a fire going, watching the ghostly flashes of lightening flit about the sky. She wondered if the dead faelin cared about what she had tried to do. No, probably not. By the time she had taken it, the thing was well on its way to the next plane of life, probably already up a tree, chasing birds and barking arf arf arf at all his dead buddies from the lab. Did they have thunder storms on Faela? What a noise that must be, clouds booming and the whole pack howling and arfing.

Dahli turned a corner and stopped. Before her rose a grey wall of cinder block and mortar. There were no stairs. She had gone the wrong way, and now would have to go back and take her chances passing the cell. Well clart, why didn't she just stay back here until this mess was cleared up? Sure, how long could that be? She could go hungry for a while, and if she needed water, there where sinks in the cells. Or if worst came to worst, she could drink out of the toilet. And if *that* happened, then Dahli was determined not share that particular piece of information with anyone. No way was anyone in her class getting a chance to read about *that* in the papers.

Sighing heavily, she began searching for a secure place to sleep. Unable to find anything suitable, Dahli made a place out of things she had come across. Once finished, her hiding spot looked like a heap of trash thrown aside. Dahli hoped anyone who may happen across it would not question it. She slipped beneath the heap of matter and onto a pile of blanket remnants. She sat with her back to the wall and closed her eyes, trying to relax.

'Morning,' she thought. 'By then everything will be fine. The guards will have moved in and taken command.'

The night passed slowly, Dahli dozing off and on. She was afraid to fall asleep, but too tired to stay awake. She would lurch out of sleep every now and then to listen to the silence, to determine if anyone was close at hand. Morning found her more tired than she had been the previous evening, and no indication that anything had changed. On top of everything else, she really had to go to the bathroom. She crawled out of her pile and crept down the hall to another cell. Glancing about, she went into the cell and, not giving herself a chance to think, she hauled down her pants and sat on the toilet.

`Great,' she thought, `wonderful place to get caught. Hello, Donsa Maniac, can you let me wipe my backside before you kill me?'

Dahli managed to finish without seeing any maniacs coming towards her. She made her way back to her hiding spot, pausing to glance out a window. Nothing spectacular came to view, just the prison yard, and beyond that, the main highway that ran into Second City. She wished she was on the other side of the road and far away from all this lunacy. Come nightfall, she decided, she would creep back down the hall and see how things looked.

The day wore on. Fear had given away to boredom and hunger. Dahli lay inside her shelter, dozing for lack of anything better to do. She did not want to risk doing any spying during the day, and reading material was non-existent. Well, there was that piece of a letter she had found under the sink. Even this wasn't particularly fascinating. There was little to it other than idiotic ramblings about some party that the writer had attended. Discarding the letter in favour of a nap, she drowsed away the day, until once more night slipped into the building.

When she awoke again, she was surprised to find it was not only night, but quite late. When she left her jumbled bed to peer outside the barred window she could feel the silence of the sleeping city. It had to be somewhere in the dead zone between when the last clubs closed down, and the first of the early morning workers awakened. A perfect time for doing some investigating. Once more Dahli ventured into the hall. Silently she walked along, this time carefully avoiding the pile of trash she had previously tripped over.

Turning a corner, she was confronted with the cell she would have to pass. No sound came from it, which was hopeful. Perhaps they were all asleep. Dead would have been good, too. Much safer than asleep, but she would have to take what she could get. Slowly, carefully, Dahli moved forward, trying to be as silent as possible. Blood pounding in her ears, she stealthily came up to the cell door and listened very, very hard. No sound came to her. There were no stirrings to alert her, no words exchanged that she could hear. Then, with a burst of bravado, she thrust her head around the corner.

The cell was full of sleeping bodies, some on the bed, some on the floor. It was easy to tell who the prisoners were, all five of them. In one corner three boys were bound together in an uncomfortable heap, asleep despite the knots. Next to them was an older man with his back towards her, so she couldn't see his face. Beside him was one of the guards. He was awake, and as she looked at him, he stared straight back at her. His eyes were green, she noticed, quite nice. She glanced back at the four figures on the bed, the captors. They were all snoring peacefully, which was fine with her. She turned her attention back to the guard, and then, frightened half out of her mind, stepped silently over to him. He was close to the door, so she did not have to venture far into the cell to reach him. The ropes binding him were tight, and she had to force herself to be calm and not make matters worse by simply tugging wildly at them. Finally she managed to remove them, and, dropping the bonds aside, she motioned for the man to follow her.

He rose to his feet carefully. He steadied himself for a moment against the wall, waiting for the circulation to return to his feet, then walked out of the cell. She was relieved that he didn't seem to want to take on the four armed youths by himself.

"How did you get back here?" he asked her when they were a distance from the cell.

"I was already back here," said Dahli. "I got lost looking for an exit when it looked like the whole building was going to burn down. I was at the back of the section, hiding and hoping somebody would clear up this mess, and with a little luck, survive it."

He nodded. Dahli was glad of his presence, he at least knew his way out of D Section. Just getting away from this area was going to be like a day off school. Now that they were past the cell, she felt much more relaxed and confident. They would get out of this, she was sure now. In just a few minutes, they would have left this area and its madness behind.

They walked, her bare feet silent, his boots making quiet sounds. Dahli's main thoughts now were on her stomach, she was hungry. But bed would be nice too. Yeah, bed then breakfast. She'd just saved the guard, maybe they'd let her sleep in. They'd better, or she'd start a riot of her own. She thought about asking if she could go home now, but thought that would be pushing things. Oh well, a chance to sleep in once would be nice, she could ask for that.

"Are we almost out of here?" she asked softly.

"Just a short ways further," he said.

Suddenly, with the finality of a dropped brick, he fell. He simply landed flat on his face. Dahli stopped and stared at him in surprise. What did this clart think he was doing? It didn't occur to her that anything was wrong. He was a guard; he was one of the people in charge of this place. Nothing bad could happen to him. She was reluctant to touch him at first, but when he still did not move, she grasped his shoulder and turned him over.

The knife had gone into his heart. She had not seen or heard the silent object as it had flown through the dark to strike him down. Now, as he lay there with the blood running dark and thick across his shirt, she still couldn't quite believe it. However, when realization did take hold, she immediately turned to flee. She spun around and bolted straight into the chest of the boy standing right behind her.

"Boy he's deader than clart on the road. Too bad. I guess you have to come with me."

She ran, dodging the boy and heading back the way she had come, moving at a rate she didn't know she could. Why hadn't she thought that there would be people watching the hall? Why hadn't she just stayed down at her own end? Then she could have at least starved to death in peace.

Dahli didn't get far before she was tackled from behind and thrown to the floor, caught in a tight grasp.

"Come on, don't be like that," said her captor. "Just think, you'll be able to write all your friends and tell them you got to be a hostage. Fun, huh?"

`Scruffing lovely,' thought Dahli.

He led her back to the cell. She was pushed down into the guard's spot, and bound tightly, feeling frightened and angry and helpless. She glanced down at the older man who lay next to her, and realised it was Ris. Dahli stared in horror at his greasy face, his dandruff-covered shoulders. Then completely without thought, said; "Hey I don't want to sit next to him, he smells."

The youth stared back at her, an amused look on his face. Then he shrugged and kicked Ris in the backside. The man jolted awake with a cry.

"I'm sorry, Donsa Ris, but we'll have to put you in the hall," he said calmly, a little apologetically. "The other prisoners are starting to complain about the smell." He bent and grasped Ris' feet, dragging him out into the hall, leaving him there.

Those within the cell began to stir. One of the three boys tied up in the corner shifted and looked around to see what was happening. The four on the bed were tossing and complaining about the noise, but none of them bothered to take a look at what was occurring for a few minutes. Finally one of them did sit up. He blinked sleepily at Dahli's captor.

"Hey Tesh, what are you doing?"

Tesh stared back at the boy on the bed for a long moment, then slapped him across the top of the head.

"Well I could be setting all of our prisoners loose, but you wouldn't know, would you? While you were lying here dreaming about the sex life you don't have," He pointed at Dahli, "she managed to set the guard loose and almost got away with him. And where were you? You were asleep. I could have sat on your head and you wouldn't have known it. Maybe you and her should trade places, at least she uses her head for something besides holding up the top of her head." Tesh shook his head, a sneer of disbelief on his face. "You're useless, Cui."

Cui stared back at Tesh. "Not," he mumbled petulantly. Tesh slapped him idly, then turned his attention to Dahli. "What's your name?"

"Dahli."

He nodded, then narrowed his eyes at her. "What's your last name?"

She sighed. She had a feeling she knew where this was going. "Sandiniti."

"Dahli Sandiniti? Hey I know you, you're the one they put away for stealing dead bodies. What were you doing with them? Hey we'd make a great team, I could kill them and you could take them and hide them. I like you. Just relax, nothing dead in here for you to take off with. We'll let you know if we need you."

Dahli watched him leave the cell, then closed her eyes and leaned her head back against the rough brick wall. As those around her settled once more, her mind turned to Draephus. Maybe she should have asked him to get her out of here, what would it have hurt? Never mind that she would be paying him back for the rest of her life for what she did to his conni. Most likely he would have told her to go take a course in reality, anyway. Why should he help her? She sighed heavily. He would be home in that ancient castle of his, sound asleep without a care in the world.

`Must be nice.' she thought as her backside began to hurt on the cold, hard, floor.

****

Delaes walked out of the lift and stepped into the large, softly-illuminated apartment. The warm room welcomed him, and he felt himself relax as he stepped across the deep carpet. He threw himself down into a leather covered chair and closed his eyes, feeling a dull throbbing in his head. He rubbed his eyes with his long fingers, then dropped his hand into his lap, sighing as he looked out over the crumbled remains of Avalair from the huge picture window.

"Gia?" he called. "Are you home?"

There was the sound of footsteps coming down the hall. A moment later a tall, elegant figure entered the room. He paused, gazing fondly at Delaes, his long white hair held back in a ponytail, his blue-tinted glasses shielding his tell-tale grey eyes.

"You look tired."

Delaes stared back at the Kryphisian. "I feel like I should be dead."

J'Vanni walked into the kitchen, returning a short time later with a delicate cup full of scented tea. He sat next to Delaes, surprisingly graceful for such a large man. He passed the cup to him, smiling affectionately. Delaes accepted the cup, then leaned his head against J'Vanni.

"I am so tired I could cry," he said as he felt the large hand gently rub the back of his neck.

"How is Draephus?"

"Good he's recovering slowly he's quite ill but I think he will all right I'm more worried about you and I frankly."

"Why worry about us? We're fine."

Somewhere in the back of the apartment, something with a horrid, almost demonic, voice shrieked "YUCK!" at the top of its lungs. J'Vanni sighed.

"Piska, come here."

There was a rush of wings, and a huge golden bird flew

towards him, landing on the floor before him. The creature stared up at him with golden eyes, the hooked beak and curved talons leaving little question this was a bird of prey.

"What's yuck?" J'Vanni asked the bird.

The creature skipped off, returning shortly with a dead mouse. "That's not 'yuck', that's dinner."

The bird picked the mouse up and, with a deft movement of its head, threw it away.

"Piska…"

"YUCK!"

J'Vanni narrowed his eyes. "I had best not discover you have been after the chickens again."

Piska hopped onto his ornate perch and began preening. J'Vanni sighed, then turned his gaze to Delaes once more, grey eyes soft and affectionate. Delaes gazed back at J'Vanni. Things weren't fine. They were far from it. Their whole carefully built little hidden world was about to be torn apart, and by him. Delaes felt sick. There was no way to say it gently. He felt his stomach clench, and he breathed a little harder.

"I'm pregnant."

J'Vanni blinked, then slid off the chair and onto the floor, almost as though he was pushed. Delaes sat forward, concerned for him.

"Gia?"

"Oh," J'Vanni said softly. He took off his glasses and ran his hand over his face. "Oh," he said again.

"That's your great comment on this?" said Delaes.

J'Vanni looked up at Delaes. He shook his head. "I don't know what else to say."

Delaes stared down into his cup. "I'm sorry."

"Sorry? Whyever for? It's not your fault. It's not either of our faults, we took precautions, it's not our fault they didn't work. Frankly given the fact that you're half Faelin and I'm Kryphisian I'm really rather astonished we *can* breed."

"Well we can and we did and what are we going to do?"

The door opened, and in stepped Rysta, dragging his bags with him. Piska immediately flew over to him, landing on the arm of his leather jacket.

"Hey Picky-bird. You being a good boy? Give me a kiss."

Piska gave him a gentle peck on the lips, ruffling his feathers and making soft sounds. Sensing he was invading a personal moment, Rysta walked towards the guest room he had used in the past, Piska balanced on his fist. Delaes and J'Vanni watched him go, then J'Vanni leaned forward, taking Delaes into his arms. He could feel a cold tingling all through himself, his arms could hardly do what he wanted. Delaes was shivering as well.

"We've got a lot to think about," said J'Vanni quietly.

Delaes was incapable of saying anything, he was crying quietly. J'Vanni held him tighter, trying to be supportive as his body tried to collapse. They were dead, it was that simple. They could hide for a while, but how long before someone began to question whatever story they came up with? And then there was the baby. Which one of its accursed parents would it resemble? How would they account for its appearance? J'Vanni spoke soft Kryphisian nonsense to Delaes, his own eyes becoming wet. He kissed his face, then set up a soft rumbling purr in an attempt to calm Delaes, but could only keep it up a short time. He was not in the mood for it.

Delaes Randerick was one of very few people on Sferkkaa who knew Kryphisians purred.

"I'm a disaster."

"No you're not." J'Vanni pulled back a little so he could look into Delaes' eyes. "You're the one who showed me how to have a good time, remember? You're the one who taught me not to take myself so seriously."

But Delaes had ceased to hear J'Vanni. "Gia what am I going to do I know nothing about children or childbearing I don't even know anything about being pregnant except how to get pregnant, and I've done that Gia what am I going to do?"

J'Vanni gently kissed Delaes. "You're going to calm down. Just sit here, I'll get you a blanket, some more tea..."

"A bowl of kiska nuts?" Delaes asked hopefully.

J'Vanni rolled his eyes. "A bowl of kiska nuts, then we'll light the fire and relax. Nothing has to be decided this instant. We need to calm down and think."

"Oh good I love procrastination." said Delaes.

J'Vanni kissed him, then rose and left the room, walking down the long hallway to their bedroom to get Delaes a blanket. He stepped into the chamber and promptly collapsed, quivering uncontrollably.

He honestly thought he was going to die, that the huge surge of emotions would kill him. He put his hands over his head and whimpered quietly, trying to get a hold on himself. He managed to finally get off of the floor, but the room looked surreal, strange. He was shaking hard. Despite all his efforts, his knees buckled once more as his vision suddenly blackened.

"Delaes!" he yelled in panic, and heard him come running down the hall. Delaes ran into the room and knelt down at his side.

"Gia?" he said nervously, and felt J'Vanni's hand on his arm. They sat together in silence for a long time, the room slowly growing dark as J'Vanni wrestled with his fear.

"I'll be all right," J'Vanni whispered. He was still shaking hard, but seemed to be calmer. "Could you help me to the bed?"

Delaes helped J'Vanni up, carefully leading him over to the large bed. Together they climbed under the thick covers and held each other. Both were exhausted, and before long they fell asleep.

*****

Delaes awoke sometime before daybreak, knowing J'Vanni was already awake. He rolled to his side and looked at his face, reaching out to touch him.

"What are you thinking?"

"Here's what we'll do," said J'Vanni. "We will go down to the South Continent, hang out, relax, enjoy the tropics. While we're down there we decide to adopt a war orphan. Draephus knows people who can forge the papers. No, that won't work. Too easy to figure out phoney papers. Too easy to trace. You and some woman have a baby. She didn't want it, the result of a one-night type thing, and we stay on until the baby is born. Conditions down there aren't good, she dies in childbirth. The way things are right now, no one will ever find out. We'll be safe; we can keep the baby, and our necks."

J'Vanni looked over at Delaes and grinned. Delaes smiled and drew close.

"That's why I married you you're smart."

Delaes reached up to touch J'Vanni's face, parting his lips as he bent to kiss him. Then J'Vanni moved down Delaes' long body, resting his head on his lower stomach, listening.

"I can hear it," said J'Vanni softly.

"That's the kaisa I had for dinner last night."

"It is not," J'Vanni grinned, then said; "It's a heartbeat."

"Stop talking to the baby and get up here and talk to me."

J'Vanni did, his body covering Delaes' as they embraced, bodies merging as they settled together. Outside the window the sky began to slowly brighten, and the two figures on the bed were mercifully unaware of the electronic beam aimed through their closed window, listening now to their lovemaking just as it had been listening to everything for the past twenty-four hours.

****

"My life is totally ruined!" Gemma informed Czamkiar.

The Sferkkaan boy stared back at her steadily, blinking large blue eyes at her. "Really."

She showed him a blue shirt liberally festooned with pink flowers and sequins, pointing out a stain so small that a person would have to be invasively close to see it.

"My favourite shirt is totally destroyed."

"Really," he said again.

"I can't replace this! I'm on another planet!"

"Dreadful," said Czamkiar.

"Are you being sarcastic?"

"Me? Goodness. No. I was just pondering how best to inform the Emperor of this tragedy. He does take bad news so very hard."

"Well what do you do when you get a stain on your clothes, Donsa I'm-Still-Stuck-in-the-Eighties?"

"I get my scissors and thread and scrap fabric and fix it."

Gemma stared at him. "You can sew?"

"Can't you?"

"No. I can't do any of that. I don't have to." She looked at her shirt, then made a noise of frustration. "GOD this makes me so ANGRY!"

"Yes, it is a tragedy that rivals the first invasion."

She made a face at him. He held out one gloved hand.

"Pass it here, donselle, I shall see to this great crime."

Gemma managed to find him some sewing supplies, then seated herself in a chair and watched him work. It was early in the day, and was as dry and sunny a day on Sferkkaa as she could hope for. She had decided to make use of it by calling up Czamkiar and asking him to go shopping with her, wanting to see the city in what light there was.

"I didn't think boys could sew."

Czamkiar glanced at her. "The only thing a girl can do that a boy cannot is have a baby, providing the boy hasn't had an artificial uterus implanted. Your planet is so bizarre. Everyone is screaming about what everyone else can and cannot do. Are you so lacking in personal accomplishments that you must forever make up ridiculous rules?"

She shrugged. "I don't know. I never thought about it. But come on, you guys aren't perfect either."

"No," said Czamkiar. "We just do what works best for us. If we were perfect, Dahli would not be locked up in a detention center that just had a riot. I wish I knew if she was all right."

"I'm sure she's fine," said Gemma, not knowing what else to say. "She's smart, isn't she? She'll be okay."

Czamkiar shook his head, his long white hair moving softly. "I hope so. She is smart, but she also acts without thought at times. And I am lonely without her, and Diza."

"Yeah where *is* Diza? It's been a few days since I saw her."

"She's not allowed to speak to us anymore," he said, putting tiny delicate stitches in the shirt. "For some reason her father does not approve of her spending time with kids who steal corpses."

"Gee I can't imagine why."

She watched him work, feeling that sense of annoyance and dissatisfaction with him. He was just so damn.... *girly*. He sewed, he wore make-up and high heels, dressed like a fairy... She'd been hoping to meet something big and manly and macho on Sferkkaa, preferably something that would impress her friends back home. Instead she got something that looked like the little prince that the hero had to rescue in a bad gay romance.

"Wanna play dress-up?" she asked brightly.

He paused in his sewing and gave her a side-long look. "Are you planning on putting me in a baggy shirt, pants that look like I am smuggling thirty used diapers, and one of those stupid hats? *Nai-nan*. I still have to be seen in public after you leave the planet."

"Oh come on, it will be fun."

"For the Emperor and no one else."

"Just for my interview?"

"What interview?"

"The producer of an entertainment show sent me a list of questions, they want to talk to me. I mentioned you, and they want to see you too."

"And what am I?"

"Well I told them you were this boy I've been seeing."

"And you want me to look more like someone your Earth friends will approve of."

Gemma sighed heavily. "Czamki…I really like you a lot. Honestly, I do. I just want…"

The blue eyes became cold. "You want your friends to approve. Well you may tell them that I am Czamkiar of Second City. My mother was a fighter pilot. My father built bridges where the enemy swore no bridge could be built. My grandparents died defending a bunker in which many children were hidden. And when night fell it was my job to sneak into the fields and steal what I could from the Kryphisian game yards because I was the smallest and fastest. And I do not give a šukat what your little friends think of me."

Gemma felt her face flush red, and her eyes became damp. "Czamkiar I'm not trying to insult you. I'm not! I really like you! I just… I mean I have to go home and live with these people."

"Gemma, a few moments ago your life was ruined because your favourite shirt had a spot. Now it is ruined because the boy you like wears make up. Then it will be ruined because your friends will not approve of the make-up wearing boy."

"Stop making fun of me, this is important to me!"

"I am not making fun of you. I am simply wondering how long you are going to let shallow little brats ruin your life by the hour. You don't hear *me* complaining that you insist on dressing like a boy."

"I DO NOT!"

"Do," he said flatly. "High heels, make-up, pink sparkly clothes… and I have to be seen in public with you."

"Well that's not fair! This is how girls dress where I live!"

He smiled at her and blinked long lashes.

"I really do hate you," she said.

"Did I ruin your life?"

"YES!" She watched him sew, thinking about what he had

said. "Well how do girls dress here? Dahli and Diza are always dressed so…"

"Drably?"

"I was going to say 'practical' but yeah 'drab' works too."

"Dahli and Diza *do* tend towards more basic outfits. If you want something more flamboyant you have to show your accomplishments."

She wrinkled her nose. "I'm not sure I've accomplished anything. Does travelling to another planet count?"

"Only if you built the ship yourself."

"I was the Chubby Bunny champion at summer camp."

"Stuffing food into your mouth and trying to talk is *not* an accomplishment," he said dryly.

"I write my own songs, does that count?"

"Yes. On this planet, it very much counts."

"Oh good! Now what do I have to do to get my gold eye shadow back?"

"Prove Imperial lineage."

He clipped the thread, then tossed the shirt to Gemma. She caught it and held it up, examining it.

"How did you do that?!"

"I just added a couple of tiny pleats on either side, one to hide the spot and the other to…"

"OHMIGOD this is like SUPER CUTE!"

"You're welcome. Is your life no longer ruined?"

"You are just never going to let that go, are you? Can we go clothes shopping now?"

"I suppose." He watched as Gemma grabbed a camera and aimed it at him. She took his picture, and eyed the photo critically. Well he was pretty, no denying that. She sent the picture to her Facebook page with the comment *"Oh well, not much I can do about the way guys look here."*

"Done?" he asked.

"Yup! Let's go!"

They left the ship, heading into the bright day. Gemma pulled on her sunglasses the moment she got outside. The Sferkkaans were right; the brightness caused by the high cloud cover, sunlight, and moisture in the air caused a glare that was very painful.

"It's beautiful out here!" she said. "Well apart from the

burned-out buildings. But look how bright the flowers are! And look at the little birds over by that stack of cinder blocks! They're like little jewels! There's so much colour!"

She suddenly spied a boy about her own age, but it was hard to tell through all the finery. He was perched on five inch blades, and had streaks of crimson and black across his face. His long coat was scarlet, and sported black and red feathers around the collar. His hair showed red and black feathers also, as well as the single small gold feather with the black line showing servitude to the imperial line.

"Oh wow, look at that boy over there! Love his coat. That's a little baby Bird of Prey, isn't it?"

Czamkiar looked in the direction she indicated, and Gemma did not miss the way he started when he saw the other boy. She narrowed her eyes.

"Is that Lyrellyn CZim-Relyn?" she asked.

"Yeah," said Czamkiar.

"Well what's he doing here?"

"Probably just looking at the ship."

"Or stalking me," said Gemma.

"Gemma, Imperial Birds of Prey do not stalk."

"Says you! What's he gonna do, follow us down a dark alley and kill us?"

"I very much doubt he's going to do anything worse than try to steal me."

"That's bad enough! GOD my life is totally ruined."

"Well it's only the fourth time today. I'm sure things will get better."

Lyrellyn CZim-Relyn approached with a slow magnificence that came with being a royal warrior with a bloodline that flowed back centuries. If he had been another girl, she would have found his presence far more daunting, but he wasn't. Czamkiar preferred girls to boys, and that was something Mr High-Boots couldn't change. However she could not fault his sense of intimidation. The feathers, the blowing coat, the band of scarlet across his eyes, and the slow, purposeful 'clink!' of the golden blades on his boots striking the pavement… yeah he was definitely trying to get her to back off.

"Czamkiar, so nice to see you. This must be your little friend. Oh my, she's adorable, isn't she? And such charmingly masculine clothing! It really is just too precious."

"The cast of the Rocky Horror Picture Show called, Lyrellyn," said Gemma. "They want their clothes back."

He chuckled at her in a cruel, condescending way that would have made Dr. Frank N. Furter proud. "Too bad."

"All right," said Czamkiar. "That is enough. Gemma, Lyrellyn, you are both my friends, I would like you to please be nice."

"Of course," said Lyrellyn. "I shall treat the young man with the utmost respect."

"Hey it was the Sweet Transvestite who started it," said Gemma.

"And I'm ending it," said Czamkiar.

Lyrellyn bowed his head. "As you wish, Czamkiar. Permit me to escort you around the city. We can use my conveyance."

Czamkiar seemed a little uncertain, but was probably just not wanting to start a problem with a boy that he'd known a long time.

"All right," he said softly.

"Wonderful," Lyrellyn said.

He deftly inserted himself between Gemma and Czamkiar, body-checking her out of the way with a force she didn't expect. He took Czamkiar by the arm, and began leading him away. Gemma growled and took out her phone, taking several photos before sending them to her Facebook page.

"THIS is what I have to put up with. I not only have a boyfriend who looks like a girlfriend, but my competition looks like a cross between Dr. Frank N. Furter and a parrot. MY LIFE IS SO TOTALLY RUINED!"

Chapter Thirteen

Tesh was making Dahli nervous. No, he was scaring the clart out of her. He had worked himself into a frenzy during the night and attacked one of the hostages. It was during the attack that Dahli realized that the boy he was beating was Shae, the youth she sometimes spoke to in the yard. Tesh had beaten him senseless for no reason she could see, simply lashing out at him while Shae lay bound and helpless. He laid on the floor now, his handsome face bruised and swollen. He was unconscious, but still breathing. Dahli hoped Tesh would leave him alone before he killed him.

She had finally met the knife-thrower, the one who had killed the guard. It was the youth she had put the run to in the hallway, one of the pair who had tried to assault her. She recalled his pock-marked face, just as he remembered her. Even now she could feel his eyes upon her. So far Tesh had offered her protection, but she had seen how unpredictable he could be. Anything could set Tesh off; a sneeze, a yawn, and he would fly into a rage. Tesh seemed to have a special dislike for Shae, and he was not hesitant to express it. She felt a sympathy for him she dared not express openly.

Pock-Face tore a piece of bread apart and ate it, his eyes still on Dahli. She studied her feet and pretended not to notice him, acting distant, as though lost in her own thoughts. Most of the time she forced herself to think about the good things in her life. She recalled watching the Gryphons on the Visual with Diza, stuffing their faces and drinking in every tiny detail. She thought about the things she had done in school, and how far away all that was now. She had been stupid to steal the Faelin, she thought, unable to keep her mind from settling into darkness. Not wrong, but stupid. At the very least she should have kept the stunt to herself. Why had she not realized she would end up here? She had honestly thought she would solve everything, that all those people who dealt in the lives of faelins would roll over and say; "You're right, this is cruel." Then everybody would go home and life would be fine.

Dahli stared at her cold feet, feeling Pock-Face stare at her. This wasn't the way it was supposed to turn out. She thought perhaps she was feeling sorry for herself, and that bothered her a little. She wondered if Draephus was here how he would handle the situation. Why was she thinking about him, of all people? Well, he did make two attempts to apologise, even after she hit him again, stole his conni, hid a body in it, and spit on him. Maybe he wasn't such a clart after all.

She mused on him for a while, then her mind wandered to school, to home, to places she would like to be. She cluttered her mind with nonsense so she wouldn't have to think about where she was. She recalled the tiny white birds Diza had given her for her birthday and tried to think of names for them. Spot and Spit. No, Trinity and Eek. Or how about Convalescence and Incontinence? Why not? She sighed quietly.

Thinking up silly names would have been more fun if she had someone to share them with.

Shae stirred beside her and whimpered. Something had broken inside of him, Dahli just knew it. She was waiting for him to die, wondering why Tesh wanted to hurt him so badly. Just then Tesh came into the cell. He was worked up about something. He walked past her and looked down at Shae. Dahli held her breath, but then Tesh turned and walked away, beginning to pace about the cell. Suddenly he snapped his attention to Pock-Face.

"Hey Pimple, you're going down to the barricade. We're going to make some demands." Tesh was shifting his weight from foot to foot, looking nervous and crazy. "Food and blankets. And a Visual. And it has to be a big one."

"They're not going to give it to us," said Cui.

"It's worth a try," said Tesh, ignoring Cui. "Tell them we want out. And Cui, if you get any stupider I will personally scruff you up the ass with the business end of Pimple's knife." He turned his eyes back to Pimple. "Now go."

"Aren't you coming?"

"No, cranium-clart, I'm not," Tesh stared at him crazily. "Go."

Pimple left, and Tesh sat down on the bed he had proclaimed as his own. Some of the wild look was gone from his eyes. He lit a cigarette, exhaling blue smoke. He looked at Dahli and held one out to her.

"Like a smoke?"

"Hands are tied," she said calmly.

"Oh," he said. "Yeah, I guess you can't smoke like that. So

what are you in for, Dahli?"

He seemed to like saying her name, he said it a lot. He also liked to get her to repeat the faelin story. Endlessly.

"I stole a dead body," she said.

"Yeah? Why did you do that... Dahli?"

She shrugged. "Just crazy, I guess."

"Just crazy. What did you dooo with it... Dahli?"

"Buried it. I wanted to bury it so it wouldn't get dissected by my science teacher."

He nodded thoughtfully, looking less crazy now. "Hey I wonder where Pimple is with the food, I'm hungry."

He rose to his feet and wandered into the hall again. He began to pace, making Dahli fearful once more for Shae's safety. Tesh however seemed to have forgotten about Shae for the time. He left him to lie in peace, or at least without further torment.

Tesh was beginning to show signs of violence by the time Pimple finally returned with the food and blankets. He explained to Tesh that the other demands would take a little longer, and this settled him somewhat. However he was still volatile, just looking for something to set him off. All around him were quiet, hoping he would find something else to occupy his mind. Finally Tesh lay himself down on his bed, curling himself into a knot and pulling a blanket around himself. Dahli relaxed as his breathing slowed and deepened. She closed her eyes, leaning her head back, exhausted from constant fear and tension, her body beginning to weaken from hunger.

Her head jerked as she almost fell asleep. She found sleeping difficult, unable to get comfortable in a seated position with her hands behind her back. She was so tired she could have cried, feeling strained, frustrated and miserable. She half-dreamed, half-fantasised that the guards would break through and rescue them from these mad people. Next to her, Shae slept on in his misery. Dahli wondered how badly off he was, and if he would die.

Tesh himself seemed deeply sleep, curled up comfortably and looking almost harmless. All around her were sleeping bodies, captors and captives alike. Except for Pimple, she noticed, he alone was awake and watching her. The look made her nervous, a prey animal noticing a predator on the prowl. Tesh continued to sleep like the dead. Dahli closed her eyes and pretended to drift off. She relaxed her breathing and tried hard to move into pleasant forgetfulness.

A type of sleep encased her, and she began to dream, seeing herself talking to her friends from school. The images that flashed in her mind were broken and disjointed, making no sense. They were simply pieces of what her past had been, something that seemed so far away. She couldn't believe she had hated school so much, she would give almost anything now to go back and to carry on the way she had before. It would even be good to see ol' Atania Nightwing, she of prissy manners and simpering ways. And those two beakers who used to always sit at the back of the room, what had their names been...?

Eventually Dahli fell asleep.

****

Morning came. Dahli stayed where she was. She was so hungry now that she was beginning to feel dizzy. She reached up to scratch her nose, and realized someone had untied her. She heard the sound of eating going on around her, and this alone made her look up. There on the floor was the bag of food that Pimple had brought the night before, laying open. Nobody made any moves against her when she reached in and pulled out a few items for herself. For the most part, the cell was quiet. Dahli could tell Tesh was getting bored with the situation, as were his little buddies. She was not certain what they thought they would get out of this ordeal; she recalled the request for the transport to the South Continent and wondered if they honestly expected to be given it.

She finished her own meal, and then pulled a few things out of the sack for Shae. As she set the food beside him she kept an eye on Tesh, waiting fearfully for him to explode. He looked at her and she froze, feeling a cold sensation run through her. Tesh stared back at her for a moment, then decided to ignore what was happening. Deciding it was safe, Dahli helped Shae into a seated position.

He was from the more southern reaches; he had the beautiful dark skin, the straight black hair, high cheekbones and clear blue-white eyes of people from the South Continent, but he was not as dark as Raski Jervyas. He was in fact a beautiful silvery-grey colour, implying one of his parents was Northern. People of his race had long been immortalised in fables for their great intelligence and cunning, a myth that had continued so long through the years that people had come to accept it as fact. Dahli didn't know if this was true or not. She tore a package of dried food open for him, and held it as he reached in one shaky hand to take some of it. She watched him eat and tried not to think about the bloodied mess that was now his face, or the horrific images of the night before.

"How do you feel?" she asked mechanically. She stared at the packet of food as she spoke, not making eye contact. Shae glanced quickly at Tesh, who was not paying any heed to them.

"Like clart," he replied quietly. "How about you?"

Dahli smiled slightly, humourlessly. "Like clart."

Shae ate slowly, his body too sore to allow much movement. By the time he finished, Dahli could tell he was exhausted. Carefully, he eased himself down onto the floor, resting so his head was near Dahli. Then he began speaking softly.

"I know this fellow; he's a friend of mine. He has a sign over his fireplace that reads `Clart Happens'. Well, one night I'm at his place with a few people, and we're drinking and carrying on. Now he has this exercise equipment in his living room, and he decided to work out. So he puts some weight on this thing, gets onto the little bench and hoists the weights. Problem: the weights are too heavy. We're all down the hall having fun and drinking, and he's in the next room stuck on his back with these weights on his chest. Matter of fact, they're so heavy that as he's struggling to get them off, he makes a mess in his pants."

Dahli sat unmoving, listening to all of this and wondering to what great end it was going.

"Anyway, a couple of us finally go look for him, and we find him on his back with the weights on his chest and clart in his pants. So we get the thing off of him and put it on the rack, and while he's in the bathroom getting cleaned up, we change the sign over the fireplace to `Clarts happen'."

Dahli waited to find out what this had to do with anything. When no explanation came, she asked; "So what is the point to this?"

"There isn't one. It's a story about a guy I know who messed his pants."

Dahli was quiet for a moment, then turned her head to stare at Shae. "That was the most useless tale I think I ever heard."

"Thank you."

She stared at him for a time longer, then laughed quietly, shaking her head. She reached out and took his hand, smiling as he squeezed it.

The days wore on. In other parts of the Centre life was back to normal. In here clart just rolled on and on, like a forsaken giant faecal lump down a hill. Tesh was King-Clart, Dahli supposed, and then there were all the little corporal clarts, and finally the prisoner clarts. Ris, who had been silent and terrified through all, was just clart. Certainly as the only adult Dahli figured he should have done something other than sit and look terrified. The clart rolled on, and the clart was mind-numbing. Fear had given away to boredom and frustration. Dahli was weary of the whole ordeal; it was time for it to end.

****

Tesh had left the cell, leaving Pimple in charge, which was much like leaving the ceramic feralyke in charge. Currently he seemed asleep; his head was down and he was breathing deeply. Dahli slowly stood up and stretched, keeping an eye on him. She had learned it was Tesh who had untied her for some reason; maybe it was his own lame attempt at consolation, she didn't know. She did know Tesh would let her wander around, whereas Pimple wouldn't, and if he woke up to find her gone he would have a fit. Dahli supposed Tesh knew there was no way for her to escape; if she retreated to her old corner she could starve, and if she tried to go over the barricade then she would be killed. Pimple just liked to bully her, but she needed to stretch her legs. Dahli glanced down at Shae. He was asleep as well, and when she glanced out the window she was surprised to notice it was dark. One more day gone. May as well go for a walk.

She wandered to the doorway of the cell and stopped, blinking. The three uniformed men at the end of the hall didn't seem real, and she stared at them, puzzled, as they made their way quietly along. They spied her a second later, their faces masks of apprehension, fearing that she would sound the alarm. Dahli looked back at them, then began to casually stroll away from the cell, making her way out of the line of fighting. She put her hands up to show she wanted no part of this. Once more, the men began to advance.

She was almost into the other cell when suddenly Cui bore down from out of nowhere, screaming. He had a laser pistol he was waving around, and he threw himself at her, throwing both of them into the cell Dahli had been walking towards. She stumbled and fell into the room, hearing Cui throw the barred door shut and fire randomly through it. The blue light of the laser pistol glowed momentarily, a silent indication it had gone off. He screamed something out into the hall and then laughed crazily, enjoying the whole disaster. Someone shot back, and once more the silent laser glowed its deadly illumination. He turned to face Dahli.

"Why didn't you tell me they were coming?"

"Tell you?" she screamed back, still sitting on the floor. "Because I was glad to see them! Unlike you I don't want to get old in here!"

He stared at her for a second, as though that wasn't something that had ever occurred to him, then spun around to fire his pistol once more. He hit one of the three men, and he stumbled back, screaming, his arm a smouldering stump.

"Leave me alone or I kill the prisoner!" he yelled wildly. Dahli wondered if he noticed that Tesh hadn't come back, and that his fellow hostage-holders had already given up. She decided he hadn't as he continued to rail on. "Do you hear me? I got a laser, and I'll use it!" He fired some random shots.

Dahli glanced about the room for something, anything, that she could use for a weapon. She overlooked the broken piece of shelving the first time she saw it, her mind not taking it in. She had to look at it two or three more times to realise she had found what she was looking for. She glanced over at Cui, but he was too busy yelling and shooting to pay any attention to her. She picked up the piece of shelving and advanced carefully. Raising it above her head, she brought it down on him with all the force she could manage.

Cui yelled in pain and surprise, the pistol flying out of his hand as he grabbed hold of his bloodied, mangled ear, the board having not quite struck where Dahli had intended. She saw the pistol land on the floor, and without hesitation she pounced on it, picking it up in shaking hands. The soft green glow of the computer cross-hairs told her calmly where to aim. She raised it and pointed it at Cui.

Pulling the trigger was an accident, a reflex squeezing of the finger. The blue light glowed silently forth, and his upper chest exploded. Suddenly the world was entirely without sound, and Cui's shattered form collapsed to the floor. She stared at the body, the pistol slipping unheeded form her fingers. The very world was frozen in time, stopped in its relentless spin as she stared in horror at what she had done. Slowly she sat down. Her hands found a charred, foul-smelling blanket, and she pulled it about herself, eyes never leaving the body on the floor.

A guard peered cautiously into the cell. She looked up at him, eyes huge and frightened as he slowly approached, his pistol pointed straight at her. He paused just before her, and when she made no sudden moves, asked; "Are you all right?"

Dahli swallowed, her whole body vibrating with cold and sickness. She wanted to cry, but she couldn't seem to do it.

"Can I go home now?" she asked in a quavering, dry whisper.

The guard put his pistol away and reached out a hand to help her up, leading her out of the cell. She was passed to another guard, this one a woman, and led out of the section, the blanket still clutched tightly around her.

The two of them walked along slowly, Dahli quiet and paying little heed to the world about her, the only thing running through her mind was the vision of Cui's body slumping to the floor. She was walked past the remains of the barricade, not noticing Tesh's dead body lying slumped next to it. She was led out of the nightmare of D Section and down to the showers. She scrubbed the dirt and oil from her body and hair, spending much longer under the running water than she would have normally. When she finally emerged, she was given clean clothes, then was brought to the Centre's doctor to be examined. She was declared fit and healthy, and then was led back to the point of origin; her cell. Crystal and Ember were both asleep. Dahli's own cot awaited her. She stumbled over to it and climbed in, flopping down heavily. Dahli heard the guard lock the door, and seconds later, she was asleep.

****

She never heard the morning bell; she slept through it as if she was made of stone. When she did awake it was early afternoon and she was alone. A quick glance at the clock in the hall told her lunch would have just ended. She wasn't hungry anyway, she was just tired. She drifted back to sleep for a time, awaking later to the sound of someone calling her name. It was the Center's doctor, back to give her a more thorough examination. She slept through this, scarcely noticing it, her limbs managing to react in the required way. Then the doctor left, and Dahli once more slid into pleasant nothingness.

She didn't rejoin the waking world until late morning of the following day. She didn't exactly feel lively, but she felt better than she had. A guard came in with some food, and as she ate, she was also told she was expected to be up with everyone else the next morning. She was also told that after the evening meal tomorrow night that she was to report to the Wardhead's office. Dahli had little comment about all of this; she simply handed the guard her empty plate and flopped down onto her bed again.

An hour passed before Dahli recalled her letter from Draephus. She thought perhaps it would have been destroyed in the fire, but she searched for it anyway. She peered under the mattress, knowing that it was useless, then she moved to the small trunk at the end of her bed. Here she found her letters. They were scorched and sodden, the ink smeared and unreadable in place. She returned to her bed with them and sat down, turning first to one of Diza's letters. She quickly put it down, feeling a little ill. The happy, nothing-wrong-here conversation that exploded out of it was too much, like turning on a light after having lain in darkness. Czamkiar was much the same, though not quite as bad. She decided her first thought had been right, it was the letter from Draephus she wanted right then. She sorted through the letters until she found the envelope with its largish, blocky letters. She carefully pulled the letter out and read it, then fetched a pen and paper from her trunk and began to write;

Heia Draephus.

*I was going to write Diza, she's a friend of mine, but I just read a letter from her and it hurt my brain. You for some reason seem a little closer. You can write me if you want to apologise some more, it gets lonely in here. I can't say boring, or rather I **won't** say boring. I was bored just a little while ago and I got all the excitement I'll want for the rest of my life. Anyway, you probably heard all about that on your mile-high Visual screen.*

So after I write this letter I will hand it over to the Detention Centre Office, so they can mail it after they read it. Then it will bounce gaily along to your address where it will get buried under a stack of other letters and assorted keys to the rooms of lusting fans.

What's it like being you? I can't even remember that it was like being me. I have a hard time imagining what sorts of things plague you, but you must have problems or you wouldn't be human. People mailing you their unwashed underwear must be a curse unto itself.

I'm rambling. Tomorrow I have to go see the Wardhead about all the stuff that happened in D Section. I did some stuff that will probably get me into trouble. Nothing I want to talk about. I'm scared they'll give me more time. I already have nightmares about never getting out of here. I guess they'll question everyone to find out who is responsible for what. All I wanted was a place to hide because I thought the building was going to burn down.

*I have to end this now, or I won't have time to mail it. Maybe I'll talk to you again. And the next time Raski is picking on you tell him I said to leave you alone, or I'll mess up **his** conni.*

Take care.

- Dahli

She read the letter over two or three times, then deciding she was satisfied with it, folded it up and left her cell, heading for the Office. She stopped before its wire-mesh window and reached up to tap on its frame. She heard stirrings, and then the dry, disapproving face of the man who held reign there appeared behind the mesh, like that of some bizarre zoo creature.

"I'd like to mail this," said Dahli. She caught a glimpse of herself in a small mirror just inside of the screened window. Her face was bruised, swollen. Her eyes were red and puffy, her skin an off-grey sort of colour. She quickly averted her eyes back to the face in the window, passing him the letter.

"What is the address?" asked the man in a voice as dry and disinterested as his face.

Dahli read the address off of the bottom of Draephus' letter, the man writing it down on an envelope. He stuffed the letter into it and sealed it under the scrutiny of Dahli's eyes.

"When will it go out?" she asked.

The man glanced up at the clock on the wall. "In about two hours."

"Thanks," said Dahli quietly, and turned to wander back to her cell.

****

She welcomed the clang of the morning bell with more enthusiasm than she would have expected. As she dressed and shuffled out with everyone else to get in line for breakfast she welcomed the return to routine, the chance to get away from the new and ugly images that turned in her head. She hadn't thought about Cui since the night she had come back to her cell, and that worried her a little. She could think of the incident, but she could raise no feelings about it. It was as though a switch had shut off in her brain. She tried to recall what she had felt when she had shot him, but her mind refused to remember this. She was away from the feelings and images, left once more in the dingy interior of the waiting hall.

She got her tray full of slop and ate it. Then she went to the study hall and did her schoolwork. On and on the day went. She got a letter from Diza, which she read while down in the sweltering heat of the laundry room. When the bell announced supper, she once more got in line for food. Then as she choked the last morsels down, a guard came to take her to the Wardhead.

She was led down a hall to the huge office where the Wardhead held command. She was brought into the sprawling room and led to a leather chair set before the huge, darkly polished wood desk. Behind it sat Wardhead Shayer, himself large and sprawling. His ancestry traced back to the beautiful High Northern Sferkkaans, and he would have also possessed that haunting beauty had he not at some point in time decided he would much rather look as though he had been passed through a mill. He clearly drank too much, and the fair, delicate skin was a network of thin purple lines. But whatever his indulgences were, he did not waste time or words.

"Well, Dahli, tell me your side of the story. I have already taken statements from the other people involved in this incident, and I would like to hear your side before I make any decisions."

Dahli did, starting with awakening in her cell to hear the alarm bells ringing to the last horrific moments in the cell with Cui. It was as she was describing these events that she began to understand what she had done, and her voice faded off as she thought about this. Her mind drifted, and she felt cold. She thrust her hands between her thighs nervously, hunkering down in silence. She was oblivious to the notes Shayer was making. For a long time the office was silent, then he spoke.

"What were you doing in D Section?"

Dahli blinked as though awakened. It took her a moment to understand the question he had asked.

"I told you," she said. "I got lost."

"D Section is pretty far away. Why did you head for it?"

"I didn't *head* for anywhere. I was scared and confused. If anything, I was just trying to get away from the riot."

"Any you just happened to get past these people and into the far end of the sector without them finding you."

"Yeah."

"Then you just happened to get caught by them when you were trying to release the guard."

"I thought I said all of this."

"Dahli as I have said I have also taken statements from the others involved, and according to them they were all under the impression that you had gone down to D Section to meet with their leader, Tesh Varian."

Dahli stared at Shayer. "What?"

"They all claim that he told them you had come down to meet him, and that when you all escaped, you were going with him to the South Continent."

"What?"

"Donselle Sandiniti, I'm afraid I have to come to a decision that you may not like."

Dahli sat on the edge of her chair, feeling ill. A clock ticked softly on the wall. She was so tense that the muscles on her neck and shoulders ached, causing her head to throb. She hadn't done anything, wasn't that obvious?

"And what is that?" she asked softly, trying not to sound frightened.

"That according to the evidence I have, you were no mere victim. I have reason to believe that you were involved with Tesh Varian and his group. In fact, he died asking for you."

Dahli was finally beginning to understand what this man was saying. "Tesh Varian was a lunatic."

Wardhead Shayer watched her though blue eyes, gauging her reactions. She stared back at him, frightened. She had thought herself incapable of any bursts of emotion after all that occurred, but she suddenly found herself living in a nightmare, and she had to do something.

"He was crazy!" she yelled. "He was crazy and you know it! How could I have arranged anything with that madman? How could I have even contacted him? Why would I have even wanted to, since I didn't even know him? Where's Shae? He was in there, he'll back me up. Get Shae Wharren in here and ask him about that whole incident, or didn't you talk to any of the hostages for fear that you may find out the truth?"

"I'm afraid we haven't been able to talk to Donsa Wharren, he had something of a breakdown after he was rescued. We had to send him to the hospital. He's not here anymore."

Dahli stared at Shayer, then suddenly had something of a breakdown herself. There was a heavy paperweight on the desk, and she snatched it up, throwing it through a window and shattering the glass.

"I'm gonna lose my mind in this hole! If I die in here I'm going to come back and haunt you, you groutnoll!"

She didn't recognise the stressed, screaming person shouting insults at the Wardhead. She was seized and restrained, and as the guard held onto her the Wardhead read his sentence; she was to be kept imprisoned for an additional six months for participating in and inciting the riot, and pending the investigation into Cui's death. As for the hurled paperweight, that was good for seven days' confinement. Then she was dragged away, still demanding to speak to Shae.

Dahli was dumped unceremoniously into her cell and locked into it. She stood staring at the guard as he locked the door, but did and said nothing. She was not dealing with the time she was just given; it was too much for her mind to cope with. Rather she concentrated on the seven days ahead of being locked into her cell. Seven days without having to scrub, wash, sweat, cook, or chip moss out of the masonry. With punishment like that she should have bounced the paperweight off of his head.

She turned to her bed and sat on it, staring at the floor and shaking her head. What had happened? Had Tesh really said all of those things? She supposed he could have, he had been insane. But how could this happen? Something was wrong, she knew with all of her being that something was wrong. She glanced fearfully about the room, as though the answers were on the wall. She wondered if he could do this, then decided he probably could. How hard would it be? "I, Wardhead Clart-Breath, have reason and evidence to believe Dahli Sandiniti, she of the dead body fixation, incited a riot in order to escape. Blah, blah, on-and-on-and-on."

Maybe he could do this to her.

She climbed under the covers of her bed, wrapping them about herself. Maybe she would get lucky and die, she thought as she suddenly fell asleep, leaving behind a situation she found impossible to deal with.

****

Draephus was awake and alert when Raski came in bearing a fistful of letters. Draephus was breathing loudly, but at least he was doing it on his own, and Dr. Arang was pleased with his progress. The mean look was back in his eyes, and he was bored and nasty. Even Raski was only met with a minimum of warmth; Draephus wanted nothing more than his own home and his own bed.

"Well, you are your usual charming gentle self," said Raski. "Glad to see you awake and bronchial."

The blue eyes gleamed coldly. "Did you come in here to force me to get up and strangle you?"

"No," said Raski, "To bring your mail." He tossed each envelope onto the bed as he read off the name of the sender. "The Systole Drum Company sends you their kind regards, never miss a beat, do they? Hah! I'm so witty. Why do they write you? Surely they must know that all of your drums are handmade."

"They want to buy the design."

"Well that will never happen. This letter is from some woman named Kassina, never heard of her, but the letter smells really good, and one from somebody named Dahli Sandiniti in the Second City Detention Centre. How come none of my fans write to me from jail?"

"Yours are all in the madhouse." Draephus started to reach for the letter from Dahli, but he paused when he saw that the perfumed letter was opened.

"Raski..."

"Yeah, I know, I couldn't resist. Don't know how she got your home address, but she's really demented."

Draephus drew the letter from its envelope and glanced

through it. "Yeah, I agree. This is burning my fingertips." He crumpled the note up and tossed it into a wastepaper basket, reaching for Dahli's letter.

"From the deranged to the depressed. Girl isn't happy."

"Let me see," said Raski.

"It's private, you clart. I'm surprised you didn't open it anyway."

"Hey, would I open your mail?"

Draephus reached down into the basket to pull out the one Raski had opened.

"One letter!" said Raski.

"I hear about my letters before I get them, Rask. You go through my closets, my cupboard, my drawers..."

"No, man..."

"I caught you at it. You missed your calling in life. You should have been Legal Enforcement. Or a pervert."

"Not your drawers."

"Yeah, my drawers."

"No, that's not me. I go through your mail and your closets, but Khandi is the one who goes through your drawers."

Draephus stared at Raski for a long moment, who looked back at him with large, innocent eyes. He sighed.

"People wonder why I am violent. Did Khandi leave the pink panties in my suitcase before we went through border check, crossing into Telescheck?"

"Yeah, well, he didn't want them found in *his* suitcase."

Draephus was becoming annoyed. "Oh, wonderful. So there we are, going through border check into one of the most dangerous and unstable territories on the planet, people all over the place as we're being searched to make certain we're not carrying anything we aren't supposed to have, and out of my bag they yank these little pink underpants. Now how do you think I felt?"

"I stood up for you," said Raski.

"Yes, I recall. What was that you said? Something like; `Hey, those aren't yours, who did you steal them from?'"

"It was an honest question."

Draephus said nothing further, reading the letter. Dahli had accepted his apology. If things had been reversed, he wasn't sure he would have been so generous. There was nothing about him being in the hospital, probably she didn't know. Detention Centres didn't let information in. Part of the punishment, he supposed. Let the little clarts develop strange new fears, like maybe the world had disappeared.

"Raski, what have you got to write on?"

Raski reached into his wallet. "Uh, speeding ticket, parking ticket, signed order from my neighbours telling me to cut the noise..."

"That'll do. Got a pen?"

"Sure. Want me to go away?"

"No, I need you to mail it."

Raski sat in a chair, the room becoming quiet save for the distant sound of traffic, and of pen on paper. There was also the distinct sound of Draephus' breathing, a heavy, congested sound. He was still far from well.

"When are they going to let you out?" Raski asked.

"Soon. Probably sooner than they would like to. If I have to stay here much longer I am going to start killing people, you included. Let me write."

The room became quiet again, for about two minutes. "Hey, Draephus..."

There was a growl. "What?"

"Nothing."

Draephus looked up at Raski, who stared back innocently.

"I'm not going to talk to you if you're going to be nasty."

"I'm always nasty. What do you want to ask me?"

"Why did you jump into the water?"

Draephus turned his eyes from Raski to the paper before him. "I think," he said quietly, "that I was trying to die."

His pen slipped across the page, leaving a black trail as he drew. There was silence, Draephus keeping his eyes fixed on the small comical drawing he was creating. He heard Raski stand up and pace about the room. Boots wandered up and down the shiny floor, finally stopping.

"Why?" he finally asked.

"I don't really know," said Draephus, unable to look at his friend. "I just felt so tired. My family is dead or lost, Vesper is going to die, and there is almost no hope of ever finding my brother on the planet, if he's *on* the planet. Which I doubt. I think with the fame we have, he should have found me by now at least."

"Oh, quit beating up on yourself." Raski sat down on the edge of the bed. "You have no reason to assume that he doesn't want to talk to you. How old was he when he last saw you? What reason could he possibly have for hiding from you?"

Draephus was quiet. He didn't have a reason, just a lot of miserable emotions. He looked up into Raski's blue eyes.

"Why do you put up with me?"

"You're my friend. You put up with me."

"In other words, we're both too rotten to make friends with other people, so we had best stick together."

"Something like that."

Draephus smiled, reaching out to place his pale hand on the dark skin of Raski's neck. "You know, I should probably make some other friends so I'm not always dropping my emotional garbage on you."

"Wouldn't you need a different personality first?" said Raski.

"Wanna die?"

"Not especially."

"I love you."

"I love you too. Want me to shut up and let you write?"

"If that is physically possible for you."

"I can be quiet." Raski pouted.

"Oh, stop it."

A comfortable quiet fell on the room, Raski returning to his chair to gaze out the window as Draephus finished his letter.

Chapter Fourteen

Dahli received the letter from Draephus on the third day of her confinement, and it was like the most wonderful thing in the world. She was bored and depressed, and supper was a long way off. She had nothing to do, and the letter gave her something to fill her day with. She sat on her bed with it as though it was a great prize and tore it open, savouring the feel of the paper. She stared at the list of names in puzzlement for a moment, then turned the paper over to find the letter.

Heia Fearless.
I'm in bed, in the hospital. I drank too much and jumped into the ocean, so now I'm sick...in the body as well as the head.
Raski is here, he's been here pretty much since I was brought in. He won't shut up. He never shuts up. He even talks in his sleep. Raski Jervyas will have been dead almost fifteen years before he actually shuts up. I guess I had better strangle him now. Here is a picture of me strangling Raski.
I'd like to know why I put up with these people. Raski reads my mail and Khandid hides all the stuff he's too embarrassed to get caught with in my luggage. I'm going to write a song about those two and call it "If the People you Hate Don't Get You, Your Friends Will."
Sorry your attempt at taking over the Centre failed. Oh I know you didn't do anything, I know you aren't capable of something like that. Anyway, I wouldn't worry if I were you. Then again, this letter won't get to you for a day or two, and by then whatever is going to happen will have. Let me know the outcome, I'm interested. People seem to have a fascination with you these days; I guess you caused more of a ripple than you know. It may amuse you to learn that Khandid and Yuri are having rather heated debates about what you did, and how the situation should have been handled, and whether or not you should have gone to jail. Me, Mars and Yuri think they ought to let you go, and Raski wants to yell at you for beating me up. Good old Rask, I guess I won't strangle him. He's staring out the window, watching the people. Did you know he has a scar on his lower stomach that goes all the way down to his...oh never mind, here is probably a good place to end this letter. Let me know how things

work out.
    -Draephus

    -Oh yes, people do send me keys and underclothes. They also send me naked photos, bad portraits and for a very long time after Mars wrote that song "Things to do with a Kaisa", people sent us various kaisa recipes. That was a weird song, I hated it. Reading a cookbook at fourhour in the morning into a mic while high is NOT music. Don't know why it was so popular, don't know why anything we do is so popular, we're a group of weird people. Why do you listen to us? I assume you do, every time I see you you're wearing that tour shirt. Why am I still writing. Why am I here. Why does Raski Jervyas buy ugly shirts. Write soon. I'll send you a kaisa recipe. I've got lots.
    -Draephus.

    She read the letter twice, slowly, then took a glance at the list of names on the other side. He was sick, sick enough to be in the hospital, but was apparently on the mend. She re-read the remark about the scar on Raski's stomach. She hadn't known about that, and she wondered how Draephus did.
    "Send me a kaisa recipe," she mumbled, "I hate kaisa. I didn't know anybody liked that stuff."
    She smiled at the cartoon, then set the letter down. She found a pen and paper in her trunk and began a letter. She'd let him know what happened all right. They wouldn't let her see Shae, would not even let her send him a note. Dahli desperately wanted to talk to him; he alone seemed to believe her, that she had not been a willing participant in what had happened in D section. All of her thoughts and concerns came out onto the paper in a nervous flow. She wondered vaguely why she could tell him this stuff, but she felt that Draephus would be able to more fully grasp her emotions. She finished the lengthy letter, then read it over, shaking her head.
    `Fearless,' she thought, recalling her long-ago conversation with Draephus. `There's a whole lot of stuff I fear.' She put the letter into an envelope, writing the address onto it in her own fine hand. Then she sealed it and called a guard to mail it for her.

****

The days crawled by, but eventually her term of confinement to her room ended. Once more work resumed for her. Dahli found readjusting to the sixhour bell difficult, but she found it less painful than sitting in her cell with nowhere to go and nothing to do. She felt like she had once again become one of the living.

On her first day back at her chores, she was informed she would now be going to Donsa Newark for counselling, something she had pretty much expected. She doubted Donsa Ris would be doing anything for a while. She also found she would have some time outside after supper, and that made the day just a whole lot brighter. She had not been outside in over fourteen days, and her excitement at the chance to do so was almost amusing.

Supper took light years to arrive, and when it finally did Dahli ate so fast she nearly choked herself. Then she had to wait for the guard to come for her, and by the time she arrived Dahli was very nearly hanging from the ceiling with excitement. Finally she was led into the yard, left to herself on the wide concrete expanse. She stared upwards at the still-bright sky. Summer was in full glory, the air was warm and fragrant. Birds flew overhead singing, and a conni slipped by on the road beyond the fence, receiver playing loudly. Off in the distance loomed the city, more enticing than it had ever been.

`My nightmares were right,' thought Dahli, `I'm never going to get out of here. I'm going to die here.' She cast searching eyes at the youths in the boys' enclosure, looking for Shae. She didn't see him. Where was he? He must be back from the hospital by now.

She walked over to the fence, having no trouble at all getting the attention of several of the guys. As they approached, she said; "Have any of you seen Shae Wharren?"

"Nope," came the response from a tall blonde kid. "Last I heard he was in the hospital."

"I heard they sent him home," said another boy.

"Home?" said Dahli.

"Yeah, he was pretty messed up."

"Do any of you know his address?" she asked hopefully.

The boys looked at each other, then shook their heads. "Not us, but we can ask around."

"Thanks," she said quietly.

****

Dahli's first visit with Donsa Newark was right after the midday meal of the following day. Once more she found herself jogging down the hallway to keep an appointment with someone she much rather just not deal with. She wished she could just suddenly and mysteriously disappear. Anything would be better than going to see Newark. She had heard too many stories about the man. Already Dahli could tell this was not going to be fun.

She reached his door and tapped on it before entering. Newark was seated at a large desk across the room. The floor was covered in soft carpeting that looked new, and, unlike Ris' office, didn't have that musty, unwashed smell. Newark himself was a presentable-looking old man. He was clean, and the suit he wore, like the carpet, was new. His skin was darkish, his hair nearly white. As she stepped into the room, he looked up at her and smiled. She eyed him warily.

"Hello there, and you are...?"

"Dahli."

He consulted a book before him. "Yes, Dahli. Come sit down."

She crossed the room to the chair before his great desk and sat on it. She still watched him carefully, but she wasn't certain if it was because of the stories she had heard about him or if she was just becoming suspicious. She often caught herself eyeing people these days, when before she had just accepted them at face value. She had begun paying attention to voices, movements, and statements in a way she never had, dissecting people until she was sure she had them figured out. This was obviously not lost on Newark.

"My, you are a suspicious one, aren't you?"

Dahli stared at him a long moment. "Yeah," she finally said.

Newark contemplated her a moment, then consulted his notes. "I see you and Donsa Ris were discussing faelins. I used to own a faelin when I was young, his name was Buff."

"What happened to him?"

"Oh, he eventually died of old age. He was an odd sort, though. He seemed to think very highly of my mother, but he hated my father. Attacked him one day and tore a piece of his face off."

"Good for Buff." said Dahli.

Newark stared at Dahli for a long, questioning moment, looking into her distant, unfriendly eyes.

"'Good for Buff?' What is your reason for saying that?"

Dahli shifted in her seat. "Well considering what some faelins end up being used for, Buff was probably justified in biting your father. No telling what your dad was doing with him when no one was home."

She watched Newark's eyes narrow. "Are you suggesting that my father was having sex with animals?"

"They aren't animals, that is so obvious that it frightens me no one seems to think so. And they aren't known for attacking people unprovoked. Isn't that one of traits that makes them good pets? Also they are fiercely protective of those they care for. How did your father treat your mother?"

"My family is not up for discussion here," Newark said tersely. "Now what were you and Donsa Ris discussing during your visits?"

"Mostly he was questioning where I got my bizarre ideas about faelins. I think Donsa Ris was sadly lacking in his abilities as a councillor. Oh, we were also discussing my logistics for taking a dead one from the school and how my childhood influenced me to do this. You see he had it figured that subconsciously I was protecting my childhood self. I said `yeah sure' just to make him happy, but in all reality I was just so repulsed by the idea of dissecting a person that I didn't see how I had any alternative. Then of course I confessed the entire thing to the news media, so I think my motives were entirely political. Either that or I really needed the attention."

Newark concealed a smile behind his hand. "I see. And did you need the attention?"

"No. I just had some idea that I could make a difference. Maybe it was a useless move, maybe I just went about it the wrong way. I just object to the way that faelins are treated. This is the same stuff the Grey Boys used to pull on us."

"But Dahli, faelins..."

"Climb trees, eat birds, chew rugs, bark, bite, and if they get the chance, will present you with a dead smelly thing in front of house guests just to show they like you. No they don't make a very good case for themselves, but they have a great capacity for learning. People who have worked with them have reported there is virtually nothing that we can do that a faelin cannot do, save speak."

Newark nodded. "All right, you seem to have given this a lot of attention. But having owned one, I can tell you that they are very strange creatures."

"Not on their own planet." Dahli had already decided that Newark was not going to be as much fun to fight with as Ris.

"I suppose not," said Newark, rising from his desk to look out the window. "Well, unlike your previous councillor, I don't think your reasons for believing faelins are human are completely off the planet. But let us leave the subject behind for a time, if we may."

There was a small, open box of cigarettes on the desk. Next to this was a large and solid looking ornamental lighter. Dahli took a cigarette and lit it.

"Sure," she said.

Newark glanced at Dahli when he heard the lighter click.

"Rather defiant, aren't you? How are you dealing with life here?"

"I seem to get along okay," said Dahli. "I don't have any problems with my cell mates, and I mind my own business, which probably saves me a lot of grief."

"Good, good." He turned to face her, seating himself on the window ledge. For some reason, Dahli had the feeling he was working up to something. "Anything occur down in D Section you'd like to discuss?"

Dahli exhaled smoke, slumped low in the chair, feet out before her. "Apart from the fact that I have been wrongly convicted of being in on the riot?"

"You weren't?"

"What possible motivation could I have? I was almost halfway through my term here, and trust me, I'm not enjoying myself enough to want to stay."

"I believe the demand was for a transport to the South Continent."

"Oh sure," snorted Dahli. "I really want to go down there and join some mushroom revolution and risk getting my head shot off while a group of political know-nothings play `Whose In Charge Now?' And to think the Wardhead would let us go was just so far beyond rational thinking it was stupefying. Tesh was dreaming in colour."

Newark nodded, then said; "I see. Well perhaps I could help straighten this matter out with the Wardhead. Would you like that?"

She had dropped her gaze to the carpet by now, and she heard rather than saw him rise to his feet and cross the room towards her. She felt him rest a congenial hand on her shoulder for a brief moment.

"I could do a lot for you," he said. He was trying to keep his voice light and friendly, but there was no way to disguise the insinuation. Dahli turned her head and looked at him, a sneer of disgust and disbelief on her face.

"Now *you're* dreaming in colour. I'm out of here."

She left his office feeling depressed and exhausted. She resented being approached by the old man, and she was glad to wash away his slime during her evening shower. Maybe he *could* do a lot for her, she thought as the water streamed down over her face. She decided she'd let him know if she ever had an unbearable urge to be degraded.

****

The days came and went, and letters from friends and family were beginning to lose their appeal. They were full of trips and outings and happenings, of people met and things done. Dahli read the letters but felt only distance. She was no longer a part of what made up their daily lives. She was in the background, gone and out of sight, occasionally thought of. Their sympathy and outrage over the additional time she had gotten just seemed like lip service. She supposed she was being hard on them, but she couldn't help feeling bitter.

She thought about her letter to Draephus and wondered why she hadn't heard back from him. She thought about their tentative friendship and how it had begun. Something strange would come of the whole thing, that or it would just fade away, she becoming a distant memory and he just a drum beat once more. Dahli told herself this didn't bother her much, she couldn't really expect someone like him to take an interest in her for very long. Perhaps he had already given up on her, and that was why she had not heard back from him. Still, she did hope they'd continue to know each other for a little while longer. It was kind of fun to admit she knew him.

Dahli and a few other girls were elected to do yard work one fine day. Some were to clean windows, others were to sweep out the concrete expanse. Dahli and her co-workers found themselves on their knees scraping small plants out of the cracks in the concrete so that it could be repaired. It was hard work, but it was outdoor work, and just being able to feel the warm breeze was worth it. She scraped at the plants, digging them up and dropping them into a bucket. She already had a few feet of crack cleaned behind her. Scritch, scritch, scritch in the dirt, her gardening knife making strange, teeth-grinding noises. Working as she was, her concentration fixed on her task, she did not at first notice the presence of the man standing near her. Then as she shifted her position, she saw the pair of shoes confronting her. She looked up and saw Newark smiling down at her.

"Having fun?"

Dahli stared at him for a moment, then returned to her work. "That doesn't warrant a response."

"I just came to remind you that we have an appointment tomorrow."

"Yeah, I know," said Dahli, "after lunch."

"Yes, that's right." He fell silent, hovering near her. "Well, see you then." he added after a moment, then wandered away. Dahli chipped at the weeds and gave no indication of her thoughts.

She walked into his office the next day, seating herself in the chair opposite his desk. She stared straight at him, appraising his every move. He organised the things on his desk, pushing papers about, reading things, finally sitting down and looking at her.

"Let's be honest with each other," he said.

"Sure," said Dahli, smoking one of his cigarettes.

Newark leaned forward, his manner becoming serious, perhaps even malicious. A gleam came to his eyes as a thin smile touched his lips. "I can make things very easy for you Dahli. Or I can make things very hard. It depends on how you want it to be."

Dahli stared back at him, her eyes narrowing. She hadn't much liked him the last time she met him, he made her absolutely sick now. "Are you giving me an ultimatum here?"

"Well, that's a harsh word. I'd call it an arrangement."

"What if I told the Wardhead about this ultimatum?"

"You wouldn't want to do that, Dahli. You see, if your delusions get too far out of control, you will have to be transferred to the psychiatric ward. You may even have to be drugged to contain your outbursts."

She stared at him with narrowed eyes. "Yeah, huh? Now you're threatening me."

"No, no, you've got it all wrong." Newark smiled at her. "I'd like us to be friends, Dahli. Wouldn't you like to have a friend right now?"

She exhaled a cloud of smoke. "Got friends."

He sighed and leaned back in his seat, leather creaking. "Yes, you do, don't you? Well, as I see it, you don't have much choice."

"I'm not going for it. You can go play your games with someone else."

He was still smiling. "Oh, come on, Dahli, be reasonable. Think of what I can do for you. I could even arrange to have you let out for a few hours every week. You could go see your friends. You'd like that, wouldn't you?"

He'd never do it, Dahli knew. She's go straight to whomever she thought could do the most damage to him. People like him depended on secrecy. Dahli had no interest in making life easy for him. In fact, she could think of several people off-hand she would write to. Given half a chance, she'd go for his throat.

She exhaled smoke once more. "They publicly shoot child molesters, you know."

That rocked him visibly; he looked as though she had slapped him. Then he became angry. "I suggest," he said in a tense, heated voice, "that you take the time until next meeting to think things over. You'll see I am being reasonable. I could be very helpful to you."

She rose to her feet and left the office, shaken, angry and scared. She made her way to the laundry room, stepping into the hot, sweaty air and over to a machine. A bag of laundry sat before it, and she began stuffing clothes into the huge device. Time to write a few letters, she thought, time to stop this little game before it got too dangerous.

She wrote them that night. The guard saw her up, industriously scribbling away, and was going to make her go to bed until Dahli said she was working on an education-by-mail programme, and this was the only time she could find to do the work. The guard relented, and said if Dahli ever needed any help she could ask him, then once more went on his way, leaving Dahli to wonder how some people could be so wonderful, and some could make a person want to give up on the world.

Dahli wrote everyone she could think of, and at the end of the night, she had eight letters together, most of them to people she didn't know, the Emperor included. Damned if she'd let this clart get away with this. She wondered how long he had been doing this sort of thing. The sky was beginning to brighten as she addressed the envelopes and put the letters into the hole in her mattress before laying down to get a few hours' sleep. She would mail the letters during her lunch break.

Days passed, slipping by unhurriedly, with calm persistence. As the next meeting with Newark drew closer, she began to grow concerned as she still heard nothing. She had mailed the letters herself, surely at least Teirra would respond. No one was answering her, not even to say they did not know what to do. Finally the day of their meeting arrived, and still Dahli had heard from no one. She felt ill inside, hoping that some sort of miracle would happen to save her.

The mid-day meal passed, and Dahli walked down the hall to Newark's office. Nothing had happened, no one had showed up to save her. As she stepped into the office and saw him, she felt a clutch in her bowels, her stomach was an acid knot. She walked over to the chair and sat down, gazing at him warily. He had something before him on his desk which he was reading. He did not seem to notice her yet. He drew on his cigarette and exhaled, finally looking up at her. He studied Dahli for a long moment, then reached down and picked up the collection of papers he had been reading.

They were her letters.

****

The local media were everywhere. They were the first thing Draephus saw as he came out of the hospital, leaning on Raski's arm. He stopped short on the steps and stared at them with unfriendly eyes.

"Who called these people?" he growled, coughing a little.

"No idea," said Raski, and Draephus knew he had. That was just his style.

"No, huh?" Draephus coughed again. He was finally well enough to go home. He could think of about three nurses who wouldn't miss him. He sighed heavily and let Raski lead him down the steps. He could have happily picked a fight with the entire world.

One of the media people actually got up the courage to approach Draephus. He hadn't ever hit a reporter, but he was very good at making them think he would. He and Raski moved past the groups of people, Draephus not interested in speaking to any of them. Then he heard someone ask if he had any comments.

"Yeah," he said. "Stay out of the water, that clart will kill you."

"That's not nice," said Raski.

"Who are you, my mother?"

"I thought I was your wife."

"Šukat you and the entire universe."

"He's fine!" someone yelled in the background. "Let's go!"

Draephus ignored the remark and followed Raski over to his black vehicle. Sand leaked out of the coat at a steady rate, and there were small bits of sea weed clinging, dried, to the fabric.

"Where are we going?" asked Draephus. He got into the conni and slumped into the seat, ocean-scented coat wrapped about him.

"Home," said Raski. "Where do you think I am going to take you? Dancing? You just got out of the hospital."

"I don't want to go home."

Raski expertly handled the high-performance vehicle, taking it onto the road and speeding away from the hospital. "You're in no shape to go anywhere else."

"Oh, come on Raski, stop treating me like you're my mother."

"Gladly, when you stop acting like it."

"Delaes is throwing a party at his home in Avalair." Draephus searched for cigarettes, but found Raski had taken them. "Let's go there."

Raski found was becoming annoyed quickly. "No. You just got out of the hospital."

"Oh, I know that, let it go, will you?"

The conni pulled to a violent halt. Both were jolted in their seats and the door on Draephus' side flew open as Raski slammed his hand onto the automatic switch.

"Oh, that's just great!" he yelled into Draephus' shocked face. "*You* telling *me* to let it go. You're a fine one for letting things go, aren't you? Donsa Drunk-for-four-days. Picking fights, ruining your conni, drowning yourself in the ocean. Don't hand *me* your unused advice, *not* to the guy who ends up cleaning your emotional messes. Telecom calls at fourhour in the morning. `*Raski I'm drunk, I'm sick, I got beat up.*' I'm tired of watching you die by degrees, so either shut up and let me take you home or you can get out and *walk* to Avalair."

Draephus stared at Raski, astounded. He was unable to utter a sound. Raski had always given in to him before, he certainly had never turned around and yelled at him. This was an entirely new experience. The two faced each other, Raski trembling slightly.

'He means it,' thought Draephus, *'he'll throw me onto the street if I try to get him to go to that party.'* He stared at his friend a moment longer, then backed down.

"Maybe I'll just connect the telecom to the Visual and call him from home," said Draephus.

"We can do that," said Raski.

He closed the conni door, and they continued on their way. Draephus was too tired and defeated by the idea that he had finally pushed Raski to the point of threatening him to try to raise the idea of going to the party once more.

"Have you seen any letters from Dahli lately?" Draephus asked quietly.

"No," said Raski in an equally quiet tone.

"She should have written back by now. Maybe she doesn't want to talk to me anymore."

"Well, I doubt that," said Raski. He glanced over at Draephus, then rolled his eyes and sighed. "I'm sorry I yelled at you. Okay?"

"No. I'm sorry I made you yell. I just can't seem to get myself under control anymore."

Raski managed a weary smile. "Come on, old man, let's get home and call Delaes. Maybe there will be a letter there from your little friend. Here's a thought, if you're really that concerned, we can drive out to the detention centre one day and see her."

"Yeah, all right," said Draephus, then smiled faintly. "Pull over for a sec."

Raski shrugged and did so, turning to face Draephus. "Okay. What?"

Draephus gently took his head between his hands and kissed him softly, loving the way Raski seemed to melt beneath him. He stroked the silky black hair, drawing him close, feeling every nerve in his body come alive. He wanted him so badly…

The kiss ended, and Raski drew back, eyes lidded, panting softly. "What was that for?"

Draephus smiled. "Absolutely no reason at all."

****

They pulled up before the great castle, Draephus slowly getting out of the polished black vehicle. He grinned as he heard an inquisitive yip from within the castle. He cleared his throat several times before he could draw in enough breath to call out.

"*T'niski!*"

Raski listened as the faelins in the castle went mad, screaming and calling, running back and forth. He sighed.

"Did you have to whip them into a frenzy?"

"Doesn't take much to whip a faelin into a frenzy, Rask."

Draephus began walking towards the castle, moving slowly, breathing loudly. Raski hurried to his side and put his arm around him, kissing his face.

"They're going to knock you onto your butt, you know that."

Draephus grinned. "Yeah." He looked at Raski. "Stay the night?"

"I don't know, we said we'd wait," grinned Raski, teasing him.

Draephus coughed. "Come on, what am I going to do? I just got out of the hospital."

"Okay. But please don't put me in a situation where I have to say 'no'. I really don't know if I have the strength right now."

Draephus kissed his temple. "I wouldn't do that to you, Rask." He nuzzled him softly. "I love you too much."

They reached the door and braced themselves, wincing in anticipation, Draephus standing behind Raski on the little bridge that spanned the moat. Then Raski yanked the door open and a pair of red blurs shot by them. They tore past their beloved Master, over to the conni and landed on it, then looked around, puzzled. Draephus laughed.

"Over here, ya morons."

The faelins tore straight for him. Bacca leapt into his arms and bit onto his coat collar and chewed, making worried sounds. Czanda barked explosively, leaping straight up and down, hair flying, clearing at least seven feet with each vertical bounce.

"What's it like with an entire tribe of these things?" asked Raski.

"Insanity," said Draephus. "I'd love to have more. I'd have to import them, though. Don't like the faelins they have up here. They act too much like pets. I like these guys. Jungle-raised. They still have their brains."

Raski watched as Czanda accidentally bounced himself off the bridge and into the moat. "Yeah real geniuses. Won't these two have offspring? They are hermaphrodites; you'd think one of them would have had a baby by now."

Draephus shook his head. "They won't breed because their fertility cycle is controlled by external forces. Faelins take a year to make a baby. They mate when the temperature gets above a certain point, usually mid-spring. That way the babies will be born in mid-spring and there will be plenty of food available in the coming months. Trouble is we are rather far North. And South Continent spring is much warmer and wetter than any weather we get here. We need heat and we need humidity to make a baby faelin."

"Oh, the same thing we need to help you get better."

Draephus paused, and turned to look at Raski, still holding Bacca. "Raski have you ever seen faelins mate? Better question – have you ever *heard* faelins mate?"

"No."

Draephus giggled. It was a creepy sound. The only time Draephus giggled was when something unpleasant was about to occur.

"We'll see if we can get them to do it in the recording studio."

"Why do I have the feeling this will be one the next album?"

"I dunno, because you're psychic? C'mon Czanda you goof!"

Czanda managed to get out of the moat and onto the edge of the grass, wet and mucky. He then proceeded to roll around on the grass to get clean before leaping back into the moat to chase the ducks. Raski gave Draephus a sidelong look.

"I have to ask. What do you keep these things for?"

"Are you kidding? These are good jungle-raised faelins! They're security."

"Lover I hate to break this to you, but I have crept into your house plenty of times, and they watched. In one instance they even helped."

"But they know you, and they know you're welcome."

"Draephus those faelins couldn't protect you from anything more dangerous than a fish sandwich."

Draephus grinned. "You think so." He looked around, spying a small deer grazing near the moat. "How far away would say that deer is?"

Raski shrugged. "Twenty-five, maybe thirty feet. Why?"

Draephus turned Bacca so he could see the deer, then said quietly into his ear; "Fetch."

Bacca leapt, uncoiling like a spring and clearing the distance between himself and the deer, landing on the creature before it had a chance to react, killing it with the impact of his body. He then picked the deer up and paraded proudly back to his master with it. Draephus accepted the prize and looked at Raski.

"Like a bullet to the head," said Draephus, showing him the broken deer. "They go for the face, catch you by the jaw or the throat, and throw you backwards, snapping your neck or spine. At the very least they will peel your face right off your skull." He grinned. "Like I said, good jungle-raised faelins." He looked down at Bacca. "Now let's go clean this and give you your share."

The telecom was blinking softly when Draephus walked into the main room of his castle, indicating messages had been recorded onto the silver cylinder inserted into the receiver. Draephus set Bacca down to take the cylinder out and carried it over to the Visual, plugging it into a slot behind the sheet of glass while Raski took the deer into the kitchen to gut.

"What do I give him?" Raski called.

"The heart and the liver," said Draephus as he waited to see who had called.

The first message was from Delaes, calling to ask if he was still in the hospital, then deciding Draephus was since he had not answered the com. Khandid called, and then an old friend, Shaktra Mannis. She left her 'com number, Draephus writing it down. Shaktra talked on for a while, letting Draephus know what she and her husband had been up to, then bowed out, saying someone else wanted to talk to him. Then, onto the screen of the Visual walked Vesper. Draephus sat up with a jolt, staring at the small man who seated himself before the Visual to record his message.

"Hi there. Just called to see how you are, but I think you're still in the hospital. I found out you were sick from Delaes. I called him when I could not reach you. He said..." Vesper paused to draw in a lungful of air. "'Vesper darling so good to hear from you terribly sorry about Draephus oh but you haven't heard he is in the hospital but he should be fine so don't worry you know he jumped into the ocean coat and all probably the closest to a wash that thing has ever had.'"

Vesper grinned fondly at the face of the man he could not see, indigo eyes warm and affectionate from behind the black-rimmed glasses. "Hope you're feeling better. I'm in Anth right now, as you probably guessed because I'm at Shaktra's house. Tomorrow I'll be heading into the deep jungle for the mountains, me, my pack beast and four of the locals. I'll call you when I reach Trelf, which is a village just a few days hike from here. Take care. I love you."

The screen went black. Draephus erased the cylinder, replacing it in the 'com. "Delaes couldn't keep his mouth shut if it was sewn," he mumbled. He inserted a thin plug at the back of the 'com into the Visual, then dialled Delaes' number. A moment later a torrent of noise blared out of the screen. Draephus turned down the party.

"Draephus!" screamed Delaes in delight. "So good to see you oh look you're home how long have you been out so glad to see you feeling better wish you were here Mars is he was dancing on the table a moment ago he's still there but he seems to have misplaced his clothes oh well that happens I suppose."

'It certainly does at the parties you throw,' thought Draephus. "Hi Delaes! Raski wouldn't let me come, so I thought I'd call and watch. Who's there?"

"Everyone but you Anazampini is here all five of them you know those are the five meanest women I have ever encountered Rhaksault showed too but that's all right Vortex even came but I don't think they're having a good time everyone is avoiding them but you know for all that horrible sugar-coated music they write you think they'd try to make up for it by at least being interesting people and I called Harli but he couldn't make it you know the biggest problem I had throwing this party was finding a band to play." Delaes howled with laughter.

Draephus grinned, relaxing in his chair, watching the party. Raski was right, he decided. He was better off home.

Raski had checked the mail while Draephus had been talking to Delaes, but had found no letters from Dahli. There was a lot of other stuff jammed into the small mail box, but not one letter from the Detention Centre. Raski carried the letters and bills into the main room, along with the tea he had made, setting these onto a table next to Draephus' chair.

"She didn't write," said Raski.

Draephus sorted through the letters, then dropped them once more, sighing. "That really bothers me," he said. "I'm not sure why, but it does. What have you got to write on?"

Raski grinned, reaching into a pocket and pulling out some heavy, cream-coloured paper and matching envelopes, as well as a pen.

"Writing paper!" He passed these to Draephus, then turned his eyes to the screen. "Is that our own dear Mars running about unclad?"

"It is. I always knew he was too polite and quiet to be believable. I'm recording the party, so we can lift out the good bits and play them on his birthday."

Draephus began to write, thinking about Dahli and wondering why it bothered him so much that he had not heard from her. Perhaps too many years of fear had made him overly suspicious, he didn't know what was nagging at him. He glanced over at Raski, watching him for a moment. After Raski was in bed and asleep, Draephus would call some friends, some of his acquaintances from his days in the Cylinder. Perhaps there was nothing to worry about, but there was no use in taking any chances, and there was no one like an old South Continent drug-runner for getting things done. Draephus did not know if he would need Tricale or not, but his instincts told him something strange was happening. Best to be prepared.

The telecom rang, and Draephus signalled to Delaes to wait a moment. He turned down the Visual, then switched to another line.

"Heia," he said.

There was a pause, then a vaguely familiar female voice said; "Heia, Draephus?"

"Yeah?"

"This is Teirra Sandiniti."

"Heia. I thought I knew your voice. How's Dahli?"

Raski paused as he heard the conversation, listening from his perch on the couch.

"Well, that was what I was calling to ask you. I know she was writing you, so I thought perhaps you may have heard from her."

Draephus glanced significantly at Raski. "No, she hasn't written me for a while, not since shortly after the riot. But then I didn't think that much of it," he lied. "She doesn't really know me."

"Well that is really strange. Her friends Diza and Czamkiar have not heard from her either. I wonder if something is wrong."

"I wouldn't worry about it," said Draephus with a casualness he did not feel. "She may have just not gotten around to it. Have you been up to see her?"

"I went once since the riot, but they said that she was with her counsellor and I would have to come back. I'm going again in the morning."

"I'm sure she's fine," said Draephus. "The Centre would have called if anything was wrong."

"I suppose," said Teirra dubiously. "Well, thanks for letting me bother you. Hope you're feeling better." Then she was gone. Raski and Draephus looked at each other.

"Well," said Raski, "my interest is up."

Draephus nodded, turning Delaes' party up once more. Time to call Tricale. Raski studied Draephus' face, then sighed.

"What are you up to? I know that look, that is the same look you had on your face the time you decided to creep into the Grey Boys' main headquarters and blow it back to where it came from."

"I'm not going to blow up the Detention Centre," said Draephus.

"What are you going to blow up?" yelled Delaes.

"Nothing! Just get that thought right out of your head!" said Draephus. He looked thoughtful for a time. "Teirra is going down tomorrow to see Dahli. I'm going to go too. And if something stinks, I'm going to start calling a few people from the Cylinder." He smiled. "And I will get *them* to blow up the Centre."

Draephus called Teirra back. The 'com was answered almost immediately. "Heia?"

"Me again," said Draephus. "I just thought, if you didn't object, that I would come down with you to the Centre."

"So you think something is strange, too."

"I don't know what I think," said Draephus. "But if we go down as a group, then they may be a little more willing to be cooperative, and if they aren't, then I want to be there to put my fist through someone's head."

"Not before I get to. Atterick and I will meet you there at elevenhour, all right? They won't let us in before then."

"Fine. I'll see you there." Draephus hung up, slouching comfortably into his chair.

"Well?" said Raski.

"Teirra wants to blow up the Centre too."

"You're not blowing up anything without me!" yelled Delaes.

Draephus grinned. "I'll call you if anything needs exploding," he said, "I promise." Then he called a number Raski did not know. Raski shivered as he heard him start to giggle.

Chapter Fifteen

Time passed slowly for Dahli, the days dragged by like a slug over stones. She had made one more attempt to write Draephus, saying nothing at all this time about Newark. Again he appropriated the letter, confronting her with it, questioning her reasons for writing the man. He tormented her with the fact that he had read all her letters. There had been some very personal things in the letter to Diza, but at least she had never mentioned the faelin for fear someone may find the letters. Dahli wasn't certain exactly what he wanted from her, other than to terrorize her. With women being is such incredibly short supply she suspected his grand scheme was to break her emotionally so she would become his loyal little puppet and then go from there. However there was just one small flaw in his little plan. He didn't know her nearly as well as he liked to think he did.

She was in the laundry room again, washing more clothes. It was her turn to be there, and Dahli found for some reason she had taken a liking to this particular chore. Perhaps because in its own way, despite the loud machines, it was peaceful. It was too loud to talk, so nobody did. She was left to her own thoughts and devices, and she was always sorry to have the shift end.

She spotted the girl who had come to replace her, and Dahli dropped her load of clothes, leaving the laundry room still wearing the heavy rubber gloves meant to protect her hands from the harsh soap. The gloves sat next to her plate at lunch, oversized and ugly, a dull grey colour. Dahli said nothing as she ate, and her cell mates who were seated with her did not press for conversation. She had become morose and angry as of late, and they left her alone. Most people these days let Dahli be. She was an explosion waiting to happen.

Dahli brought the gloves with her out into the yard later, along with her bucket and weeding knife. She set down the pail and pulled them on.

`Good.' she thought. `Now I won't scrape my fingers up.'

Once more lifting the heavy pail, she walked over to the wire fence. `Lots of weeds here,' she thought, then paused to look up at the sky. Dark clouds had moved over the haze, and the normally shadowless daytime had become gloomy and threatening. It would rain, possibly there would even be lightning. Electrical storms were brutal in their part of the world, and all of Second City had been built to take them into consideration. The storms had never bothered her, but she could think of several friends who feared and loathed them. Faelins were known for throwing themselves into fits of terror when the lightening began, and the great bolts of blinding blue-white power stabbed down from the sky.

Dahli set her bucket down and tugged at the wrists of her gloves to make certain they were on tight. She glanced down at her shoes; ugly, blocky things, but tough. Then she leapt, catching hold of the fence and going up. All was quiet behind her. She kept on, her mind surprisingly cool.

She was almost at the top when there was a shout for her to stop. Dahli climbed faster. Once more the guard shouted, and by now she reached the top of the fence. She swung one leg over, but as she moved to the other side, she slipped, touching the wire with exposed skin. She was thrown by the jolt to the grass beneath. She was winded and her ribs hurt from the fall, as did her burned arm, but adrenaline picked her up. She rolled to her feet and headed across the field, those still in the yard screaming their approval.

****

Teirra and Atterick waited outside of the Centre, keeping an eye out for Draephus. Finally, at a couple minutes past the hour, they saw his grey conveyance glide into the parking lot. It had been restored to full glory, and the paint glowed softly in the muted light. It pulled up next to them and Draephus got out. Teirra was shocked to see how bad he looked, reminding herself that he had only been released from the hospital the day before, and probably should not have been out of bed. His breathing was laboured, and she cringed as she heard him cough.

"Are you all right?" she asked.

He shook his head and coughed again, wiping his mouth with the back of his hand, leaving faint smears of blood. From behind him two more figures emerged from the conni, and as Teirra saw them, her eyes became large and worried. The two men were both huge, looming behind Draephus like evil giants. One man was dark-skinned, his hair shaved off. Across the left side of his strong face were painted three stripes, and about his huge neck was a heavy leather collar. His clothing was a bizarre array of straps and buckles and chains, and very little else. On the inside of his right arm he wore a cage-like device, housing a heavy silver rod. Teirra didn't know what it was for and didn't want to. The second man was also quite dark, with his thick black hair combed forward into a fan over his heavy brow. He was dressed a little more conservatively, but not much. In the pit of his throat was a small tattoo, a bleeding flower. Like the device on the other man's arm, Teirra didn't want to know what this was.

"Do you get the feeling that maybe we leave Dahli alone too much?" said Teirra as the trio walked towards her. Atterick's eyes were huge. He said nothing.

Diza had been in Teirra's conni, and as she saw Draephus she opened the door and stepped out. Her facial expression changed drastically as she laid eyes on the two imposing-looking men. Draephus walked up to Teirra and Atterick, stopping before them, coughing miserably. He was much taller than Atterick, and considerably less healthy.

"Those two aren't friends of Dahli's, are they?" asked Atterick, indicating the two men with Draephus. He shook his head.

"No, they're friends of mine. Why? Do you have reason to believe your sister hangs out with South Continent drug-runners?"

"Well before all this, I would have said no," said Teirra.

Draephus coughed again, grinning. "Let's go inside before Raski shows up and drags me off to the hospital again."

The group walked into the Detention Centre. The inside of the building had a strange, dry, sterile smell. It always struck Teirra the moment she walked into the place, and it made her nervous. There was something hopeless about it, something decayed. She hated the Centre, she would be glad when Dahli was out of it. They walked into an office, a small wood-panelled box that scarcely held the crowd. From behind a desk a thin man looked up at them, then turned slightly pale.

"May I help you?"

Teirra pushed her way past Draephus and his two unnamed monsters. "We're here to see Dahli Sandiniti," said Teirra. The small man looked relieved that it was nothing more than a visit.

"I'll send someone for her right now." He pushed a square on the desk.

There was a thin whine, then a voice said; "Yeah?"

"Historius, can you bring Dahli here, please? She has some..." the man looked at Draephus and his buddies, "friends here to see her."

The intercom switched off, and the small man indicated a door for the six to go through. "We'll bring her in just a moment."

They walked into the visiting room, positioning themselves in various seats. Draephus coughed, then said something to the man next to him. Teirra jumped at the sound of the strange language, listening as the man answered him. They were speaking quietly, in an eerie-sounding tongue, which Teirra had never heard. She assumed it was South Continental, she recalled Dahli saying he had spent some time down there. She wished they would stop it, the language scared her. They did not keep it up for long, however, they only exchanged a few words. Then Draephus turned his eyes to Dahli's young friend.

"You must be Diza."

Diza didn't know if she was thrilled or alarmed that this man knew her name. "Yeah, I am."

"Dahli mentioned you to me."

"Oh good," said Diza, rolling her eyes. "She's probably told you all the things I'd rather not admit to."

Draephus grinned. In fact, Dahli had said very little about Diza, but she had told him one good story.

"She only told me about the time you went into the science duone's desk and left that..."

Diza gasped, eyes becoming large. "SHE DIDN'T! I DON'T BELIEVE SHE TOLD YOU THAT STORY!"

"I thought it was funny. How did you rig up that water pistol to fire urine upon the drawer being opened?"

Teirra and Atterick were staring at Diza, who hunched down into her seat. "Dahli Sandiniti is one dead beaker," she mumbled, and Draephus laughed. The sound was not healthy, but it was human, and the tension in the room dispelled a little.

The door opened and a well-dressed older man stepped into the room, smiling. "Heia," he said. He glanced at Teirra. "You must be Dahli's sister. I am her councillor, Dr. Newark. Is there something I can help you with?"

"Where's Dahli?" asked Teirra.

"Well, I'm afraid Dahli hasn't been feeling too well as of late, she asked me to..." Newark paused as everyone in the room stood up and looked at him. His manners faltered a little.

"The last time I was here I was told I couldn't see her," said Teirra. "I have had no letters from her, and I want to talk to her."

"As her councillor," said Newark, "I advise against it. She has been through a lot and I do not believe it conducive to her health to have visitors right now."

Draephus walked over to the man, standing before him. "Donsa Newark, do you know who I am?"

"No, I cannot say I have met you before."

"I'm Draephus CZimcocious."

Newark blanched. "Donsa CZimcocious. I'm sorry, I didn't recognise you."

"You don't have to know my face, just my name. Now that you know who I am, listen up. Either you bring Dahli Sandiniti here, right now, or my two friends are going to break every bone in your body. And while they are doing that I will 'com the Emperor to let him know that he should send some people down here to turn this place inside out, because a girl seems to have gone missing for no apparent reason."

Newark stared at Draephus, obviously frightened. "You can't do that."

"Can't I?" Draephus' voice was soft and calm. "Why, of course I can. Or don't you know I am a very powerful figure in this country? Isn't that what power is all about? Abuse? You're a powerful person yourself, you hold the line on a lot of young lives. Must get tempting to take advantage of that once in a while. Just sign a document, write a letter to the right people, and you can do whatever you want. But of course, you would never do that, would you? Nor would I have any interest in where you work and live in the future. These are simple times now. The war is over; I am only a musician now. I have no need for underground warfare. I don't even think I recall how to make a bomb, and I don't care how you live your life. Now, why don't you be a good man and bring Dahli here?"

Teirra, Diza and Atterick were staring at the scenario unfolding before them. Draephus was smiling slightly, his tone congenial. He had not raised his voice once, and never had his voice been threatening. He didn't need to be loud and angry; he was content to simply be dangerous. Newark began to shake, becoming an even whiter shade of pale.

"I'll bring her directly," he said. "But you realise, I have warned you. She is not at all well."

"We'll take our chances," said Draephus, and Newark left the room.

He was gone a very long time.

Teirra walked over to Draephus and said; "He's been gone too long, I don't think he's coming back."

"I'd tend to agree with you," said Draephus. He walked across the small, dingy room, taking the handle of the door and opening it. Two uniformed guards ran by. The man they had spoken to in the office was standing in the hall, looking worried.

"What happened?" Draephus asked.

"One of the inmates has just gone over the fence. I don't understand, no one has ever done that before. It's an electric fence, who would want to try to climb it?"

Draephus and Teirra both looked at each other significantly, both thinking the same name. It was one of the guards who made their concerns concrete. He came running down the hall and stopped before the thin man.

"Cusmar," he said, "call the Legal Enforcement downtown and tell them we have someone loose. Several people in the yard identified her as Dahli Sandiniti. Climbed the fence in front of half of the guards we have. She's heading south across the island, probably for the hydrotrans."

The group of people in the hall broke and ran, heading for the south side of the Detention Centre. They were immediately confronted with the extremely busy main transit route. Connis and freight vehicles roared past rapidly in an unbroken chain. Draephus and Teirra stared at the road in astonishment.

"Did he say south?" said Draephus. "He must have been wrong, how could she have gone across this?"

Teirra nodded. "He said south."

Draephus looked back across the Detention Centre, seeing an electrical fence surrounding the yard. This was the place she had been, it seemed. He looked back at the busy road. The guard had said south. Somehow Dahli had crossed that route; there was no other way to go from the yard. Draephus laughed quietly and shook his head.

"Fearless."

****

As Dahli Sandiniti was climbing an electrified fence, J'Vanni Dei Syncopius was starting his day. He was a late riser, and he had a routine. Run the bath, put the kettle on to boil, make the tea and leave it to steep while he had a bath. Today however Rysta had already made the tea. It was a small deviation in his routine, but upsetting and unnerving; he didn't deal well with change, ever since his breakdown he had a difficult time with any sort of little variation to his routine.

He felt Rysta come up behind him and rub his shoulders. "Sorry about the tea, I should know better by now."

J'Vanni shook his head. "It's all right. What are you supposed to do, sit on the floor like a lump until I decide to move?" He rubbed his eyes wearily, then shook his head again. "It's been years, it's time I stopped trying to control every tiny aspect of my world, it won't work and I know better, so why do I still try to do it?"

"Maybe because your own people raised you in this tiny little paradise and then tore it to shreds and destroyed you? You're entitled to your eccentricities."

"As are you. I can't believe you would even want to stand in the same room with me."

Rysta played with the long waterfall of white silk that was J'Vanni's hair. "Yeah, well, if I thought you had anything to do with the poisons they dumped into the water that killed my family I'd strangle you in your sleep. But you're just as much a victim as the rest of us." He kissed his head. "Besides, you let me play in your studio and sleep in your guest room. Where's Delaes?"

"Out attempting to find a ride down to the South Continent. We felt we could use a vacation."

Rysta snorted. "There's nothing going down there! It's the rainy season!"

"Well he wants to go. And who am I to argue with…"

"The mother of your child?"

J'Vanni spun sharply to look at him, grey eyes large with terror. Rysta watched him, then leaned forward and kissed his nose.

"Relax. There are many things in this world that send me into a frenzy, but baby Grey Boy-Faelins are not one of them."

"How did you find out?"

Rysta gently nudged J'Vanni aside so he could start breakfast. "J'Vanni, I've raised faelins, owned faelins, and bred faelins. I know a faelin when I see one. And even if I didn't recognise the large expressive eyes, small foxy face and long limbs, I knew the first time I heard him sing. Nothing has the range of vocalizations that faelins do, and that howl he lets out during 'Avalair Grey' is the warning call faelins let out to alert their little barking buddies a predator is around. I hate that song. Every time it played on the receiver my old faelin would go mental. Nothing sadder than a twenty-year-old faelin trying to rally the troops."

J'Vanni smiled. "But Rusty was so cute when he did it."

"Yeah it was scruffing adorable when he did it at threehour in the morning." Rysta looked at J'Vanni with dark-rimmed blue eyes, stubble on his handsome face, his long dark hair hanging loose around his shoulders. He placed his large hands on J'Vanni's upper arms. "The point is I love you, I love Delaes, and I'm not about to harm either of you. But I do have one very important question that I must ask before the two of you head south to have a baby."

"And that is?"

"Can I stay in your apartment?"

J'Vanni smiled, reaching up one long elegant hand to take hold of his friend's chin. "Now how can I say no to a face like that?"

"I heard Kryphisians have terrible eyesight."

"We don't. And there is nothing wrong with our sense of smell, either."

"Sorry. Everything I own smells like a house fire. I need to do laundry."

J'Vanni poured himself some tea, glancing up as his hawk flew in through the window, a large rat in his talons. He returned his gaze to Rysta.

"I know I probably needn't ask this, but…"

"I haven't told a soul, don't worry. But J'Vanni, you were awarded citizenship, there is no reason to not let people know you're Kryphisian."

"Rysta you and I both know that there are people who will kill me regardless of what I did during the war. They will kill me because of what they lost, and what I represent. And they will kill Delaes and our child for similar reasons. How dare two monstrosities begin a family when so many have lost their own? These are ugly times, Rysta, the wounds are still open and festering. It will be a few years ere we may speak of openness."

J'Vanni looked up as he heard the door to their large apartment open. He waited to hear Delaes' voice, and became puzzled when he did not. It was never good when Delaes was quiet.

"Are there no more transports heading south?" asked J'Vanni as he stepped into the living room. He paused, cocking his head at the man he saw before him; a man he knew, one he had not been expecting, but who was not unwelcome. He bowed formally and politely.

"Welcome to my home. Had I known you were…"

The words died on his lips as he saw two other men appear, one holding a Long-Muzzled Night Stalker gun. J'Vanni Dei Syncopius watched as the massive weapon was raised and aimed directly at his head. The muzzle seemed as large and damning as a black hole. The gentle composer stared, unable to move, having not the first idea how to react. There was a loud 'clack' of the weapon being cocked, and J'Vanni began to shake.

"Bye bye, Grey Boy," said the man with the gun.

Rysta came tearing out of the kitchen and leapt at the man, grabbing the gun. J'Vanni's first instinct was to flee, but there was nowhere to go. He darted back and forth like a bird in a cage, then spied Rysta's sepulchord. He snatched up the weighty device and brought it down full force on one of the attackers. Then there was a tremendous explosion. The world turned red, then black, and J'Vanni dropped to the floor.

****

Dahli did not know how she had managed to cross the transit route. But there had been no other way to go that she could see, so she had plunged headlong into the traffic, somehow managing to make it across all four lanes without being flattened. She didn't have a plan or a direction; her only thought was to go where the guards wouldn't likely follow. She headed straight across the uneven grass of the vacant field beyond the road to a low, artificial knoll in the earth. Housed in the side of the knoll was a narrow storm drain, and with no hesitation she bolted down it. She became momentarily trapped in the entrance, and for a wild moment, she had visions of being stuck there, helpless, waiting for her captors to come get her. Then she jammed through, falling down the short drop and banging her knees on the hard floor. She was bruised and scraped, but she would not feel it for a while. Right now all of her attention was focused on getting as far away from the Centre as she could.

She heard the rain begin with a mighty crash somewhere outside of the drain, but she did not think much of it. She had other problems, larger ones. The light had all but failed a few short feet into the tunnel, and she now found herself trying to run in darkness. She stumbled full force into walls, her feet slipping on the slimed floor. There was no way to tell where she was going, no forward or backward, or even up or down. She guided herself by trailing the tips of her fingers along the walls, following them as best she could. She kept on into the dark and silence, heading far away from the Centre and into the eerie void just beneath Second City.

The rain fell. Dahli was now walking slowly and carefully down the tunnels as the water began to rise. She was not afraid, not yet. But time wore on, and she was becoming painfully aware that the hours were slipping by, and there was no shaft of light to let her know of a place to allow her to escape the artificial night. The water was flowing at her ankles now. Dahli's legs felt so tired that she thought they were going to collapse. She had to stop wandering and sit for a time, even if it was in the water.

Dahli sat unceremoniously in the mire. Her hair hung lank and damp, wet from the murky water that dripped from a ceiling she could not see. Her clothes were soaked through, and her feet were beginning to feel strange and numb from being wet and cold too long. She sniffed and wiped at her nose, feeling the water gently push at her as it flowed on to other things, caring nothing for her plight. Dahli closed her eyes, trying to determine what she felt. Nothing. She wasn't frightened, she wasn't sad or depressed. She knew she could die down here; she had become all too aware of her mortality lately. Better to die in the drain, in the dark, than back in the Centre. Dahli thought about Shae Wharren and wondered where he was. She didn't think she wanted to know.

She swatted at the invisible water that dripped onto her head, then let her hand fall into the stuff that swirled around her. She began hearing voices speaking in her mind, saying different things, most unconnected with what was currently occurring. She heard Czamkiar complaining about his white hair, wanting to change the colour to purple or something equally abhorrent. Duone Bathers chastising her for not doing her work, her mother calling her in for supper when she was still very little.

`I'm going mad,' she thought. Then, clear as a bell, she heard Diza say; "Well it has to go somewhere!"

They had both been very little. They were playing with a hideously dangerous Kryphisian leg trap, buried into the concrete of a shattered building. They were dropping twigs into the device, watching the tiny razors lining the small hole disintegrate the sticks. Diza was wondering where the wood splinters were disappearing to, as there did not seem to be any left over when the blades stopped whirring. This question still had not been resolved when Teirra found them and made them get away from the thing, but Dahli could still hear Diza's young voice insisting, "Well it has to go somewhere!"

The phrase rolled around in her brain, not fading. She trailed her fingers in the water, which was rising higher still. Seated as she was, it now flowed around her hips, still running on to other places, as she had been. `Well it has to go someplace,' she thought again, then suddenly snapped out of her reverie. The water was most definitely running someplace, which was probably the ocean. This was rain water, not sewage; it would either go into the city reservoirs or, if the reservoirs were full, the ocean. Dahli stood up and began following the water.

She lost all track of time, all her thoughts wrapped up in following the water to its destination. She began to see light, little by little, seeping in from somewhere. Able to finally see where she was going, she began to run, plunging through the knee-deep water. She saw the vague outline of the drain opening ahead, and she charged for it. Suddenly however, the floor was no longer there as she fell into the channel cut into the floor, dropping into a massive cistern. She fought her way to the surface, gasping in a breath of air. She paddled like a rat in the fast-moving water, feeling herself being washed along against her will. Then suddenly she was spat into a great flood of water, falling with the rest of the excess into a second huge reservoir. She found herself briefly under water, but then she bobbed up, coughing and sneezing. She swam to the edge of the concrete tank, grabbing hold of the edge and pulling herself out. She tumbled three feet to grassy earth and lay there in the rain, coughing, waiting for her heart to stop banging.

"Well that escape plan sucked," she croaked, and slowly sat up to see where she was.

The lights of the city glittered off to her left, sparkling different colours in the encroaching night. Before her the waves of Shepherd's Strait washed gently against the shore, smooth and tranquil, separating Second City from the Mainland. Across the way, like a distant beacon, shone the bright lights of Avalair, calling across the water to her sister city.

Dahli looked down at her filthy, soaking-wet clothes. She would need a change. Even if she was not wet and muddy, what she had on was definitely not the sort of thing people wore of their own volition. She couldn't go home, there would be people waiting for her. She needed trinta for the hydrotrans, clean clothes, and shoes. There had to be...

Diza. She would go to Diza's house. Maybe they would not think of looking for her there. Dahli rose to her feet and set off for the dim lights of Second City.

****

The sky was just beginning to lighten as she reached Diza's house. She was exhausted, her legs and feet ached, and she was so cold she felt certain she was going to die, feeling her body weaken. She was thankful that Diza's bedroom was on the ground floor, and she didn't have to climb through anything. The house was dark and silent, and no one seemed to be lurking about. She made her way over to Diza's window and slid it open, crawling into the room. Diza sat up and blinked sleepily at the muddy, ragged thing in her room. Dahli sat on the floor, breathing heavily.

"Long walk from the Centre to here. Got a cigarette?"

"Dahli? What are you doing here? Half the city is looking for you. Are you all right?"

"I don't know. I'm so tired I could cry, and I'm filthy. I came to ask if I could borrow some clothes and money. I have to get out of the city."

"Yeah, sure." Diza got out of her bed and walked over to the large wardrobe in her room. She went through her drawers, finding

Dahli what she needed, including a good pair of boots she no longer wore. "Will these do?"

"Perfect," said Dahli. "Now, if I could just have a bath."

"Go for it," said Diza. "Dad has left for work, so there's just us. Have a bath, I'll make you something for breakfast."

"Don't turn any lights on," said Dahli. "I didn't see anyone watching the house, but that doesn't mean there isn't anyone out there. If they see lights going on all over the place after they know your dad is gone, they may start to wonder."

Diza nodded. She looked scared, Dahli noticed, and who could blame her. Dahli wasn't sure how well she herself could have dealt with an escaped friend climbing in through her window at this hour of the morning. She reached out and hugged Diza hard, then let her go, moving low under the windows towards the bathroom, starting a bath. A half hour later Dahli walked into the kitchen, clean and dressed. She sat at the table and proceeded to swallow her breakfast, Diza watching with fascination.

"Wow, is that ever disgusting."

"Whaf?" said Dahli, her mouth full.

"Your eating habits. Did you take a class in bad eating habits?"

"The whole place is a class in bad habits." said Dahli, and kept eating.

Diza picked at her own breakfast, clearly feeling nervous, as though she expected the entire Second City Legal Enforcement Department to come through the door at any moment. Dahli happened to glance up and catch the look.

"Wishing I hadn't shown up?"

Diza jumped, then turned her gaze to Dahli. "Yes and no. You know I'd do anything for you, but frankly, I'm a coward."

"What makes you think I'm not?" Dahli kept shovelling food into her mouth until the plate was cleared. "Besides, you're as brave as you need to be."

Diza smiled slightly. "I suppose. It was just a nasty thought, and I'm sorry. I want to help you any way I can."

"You've done all you can." said Dahli, standing up and putting her plate in the sink. She stared at it for a moment, then washed and dried it. "No use leaving signs all over the place," she said as she put the plate away. "Thanks for the clothes. I'll write to you when things have calmed down a little."

Diza stood up, concerned. "Am I ever going to see you again?"

"I honestly don't know." Dahli shook her head. "Yes, probably. I just have to get to a place where I can better think over how to deal with this."

"Dahli, what happened?"

Dahli shook her head. "Some other time. I have to go. I promise, as soon as I can, I'll give you all the details. I know you like a good horror story."

Diza narrowed her eyes. "I'm concerned. I don't want to know if you don't want to tell me."

Dahli sighed. "I know, I'm sorry. I'm just a little stressed right now." She looked out the window at the brightening day. "Great, how am I supposed to get anywhere in broad daylight?" Then she turned her eyes to Diza. "I need a pair of scissors, some hair paint, and make-up."

An hour later, Dahli crept out Diza's window, looking very different than she had when she crawled in. Her hair was now dark brown, and very short. Her fair skin had been painted dark, and, with careful artistry, she had changed her appearance drastically. She now appeared to be a woman from the South Continent, one a bit older than a mere sixteen. Teirra wouldn't have recognised her, and, secure in her disguise, Dahli began walking down the long winding street that would eventually take her to the hydrotrans. She felt better for her rest and breakfast, but her eyes kept wanting to close, and the bag of things Diza had given her felt heavy. But she kept on. She had a long way to go before nightfall.

****

Delaes was talking to Donselle Marist, she being the best person to pump for information regarding pregnancy. Fortunately it was a subject she was only too happy to discuss. His only other option would be to look up faelin breeders and he didn't think he could bring himself to do that. She already had a set of very young twins, as well as the infamous Miski, and was expecting another pair – a feat that had earned her free housing in an area of Avalair away from the toxic ash, as well a comfortable life paid for out of Imperial funds. No healthy woman who could produce lively and happy infants naturally was obligated to work to support them. Of course there was the matter of Marist being the only woman in Avalair able to have children.

She and Delaes had been friends almost from the moment they met, though they had very different lifestyles; she couldn't stand his music, and didn't have any of his cylinders. Her only complaint was her bedroom was directly beneath his recording studio. She didn't mind when his roommate/boyfriend/husband/whoever-he-was sat and composed half the night; she didn't hear him at all. But the best sound buffers in the world did not keep the famed Randerick vocals from penetrating her sleep. The sound proofing between his floor and her ceiling was extensive.

"Would you like more tea?" she asked, and immediately Delaes bounced up to make it for her.

"I'll get it," he said.

"Delaes," said Marist. "The idea was that I would get it for you."

"Well I realise that but I never get to do anything for you I really ought to come by more often or better yet why don't you come up and have dinner some night bring the family we don't have one and it would be good for Gia to be around children he misses them." He brought her a cup of tea, then bent and kissed her face. "Speaking of Gia I have to get home he'll be wondering about me."

"Tell him it was my fault, I forced you to stay here and drink tea. Oh! And tell him Miski will be late for his music lesson tomorrow, we're going to the doctor for a check-up."

In later years, Miski would be stunned to realize he had taken music lessons from J'Vanni Dei Syncopius. Right now, he knew him as Gia, the nice man with the blue-tinted glasses.

"All right I'll let him know and if you need anything come knock see you later."

Delaes stepped into the lift which would bring him up to his own flat, the device quickly bringing him to his own door. He opened it, stepped into the room, then stopped. Three men stared back at him, standing over two bloodied bodies. Delaes could not see the faces of the fallen, but the silver hair turned scarlet was enough to tell him who the body used to be.

He slammed the lift door shut and hit the button for the lobby, dropping to the floor with his arms over his head as the decorative glass and steel doors were shattered by the enormous power of the night stalker gun. When the lift finally stopped, Delaes bolted out of it, hearing the door of the second lift directly beside it open. A second blast narrowly missed him, searing the leather of his jacket. Suddenly Delaes' body recalled its faelin heritage. He fled at an incredible rate, tearing out of the building and down the street. He rounded a corner and came to a high fence. Without thought he tore straight for it, gathered himself together and leaped, catching the top of the eight-foot fence, swinging over the top and dropping to the ground in one motion. He hit the pavement running, knowing exactly where he was heading as he dove into a broken water pipe, one purposely exposed to help catch overflow from storm drains. His boots splashed in the shallow water as he ran, dodging and turning down a maze of pipes that would have confused a rat. The only light he had to go by was from small sewer grids above him. He continued to follow the pipes as they began to slope down, heading towards enormous underground cisterns. When he reached the first cistern he dove into it, heading down into the black water, the small amount of light left behind on the surface. He made his way to a pipe that led to the second cistern, following it into the second tank, then shooting to the surface, gasping, listening to the darkness, every muscle tense.

Nothing. At least not yet.

Delaes swam to the edge of the cistern and crawled out, running with water. Without thinking he rose up on all fours and shook like an animal, then got to his feet and kept running. He was on home ground now; deep in the heart of the underground water pipes that broke their way into ancient catacombs. Here he had lived and fought during the war, and he knew every square inch of this place. Even if he was followed, it was unlikely he would be caught

Ahead he saw the pipe branch off in two different directions. With no hesitation Delaes turned right, finding a doorway. He darted into it and slammed the door behind himself, barring it. He stood trembling, water running down his body, staring into the room he had occupied for so long before the Revolution had ended. Gradually, as he calmed, he looked around at the room. Once it had been almost cosy, decorated with quaint bits of stolen things, items donated by friends, and things he had made himself. Things that now all sat in a box in his apartment, which was unquestionably being ransacked. Delaes sat on the floor and looked at the ten by ten room. The walls were still painted cheery pink, the floor still soft grey. Everything else was gone.

Suddenly he heard something in the tunnel and he instinctively dropped to the floor, flattening himself, though he knew he could not be seen through the closed door no matter what position he was in. He covered his nose and mouth with his wet leather jacket so he would not be heard panting, and listened.

"I can't see a thing!" called a voice.

"Look he had to have come this way. He was a sniper during the war, he knows these tunnels as well as we do."

"Better," said a third voice, one Delaes knew instantly. His eyes became huge, and he felt a lump of bile churn in his stomach.

"You monster," he whispered. "How could you?"

"Well if he was a sniper then why are we hunting him? The Grey Boy, sure, but why go after one of our own?"

"He's not one of our own, he's a freak," said the third voice. "Things are bad enough for our people right now, we don't need Grey Boys and half-breed faelins breeding freakish half-animals and using up resources we can't spare. Come on, he must have gone this way."

Delaes huddled on the floor, listening as the trio departed for the other pipe. His eyes filled with tears, and he drew a shuddering breath as cold reality slowly gripped him, and the images of Rysta and own his beautiful, gentle husband lying on the floor in a pool of blood rose up to fill his mind. He drew a second shuddering gasp, and began to weep.

"You weaselling little monster I will kill you I swear by all that I have lost I will kill you."

Chapter Sixteen

Draephus stared hard at Tricale, who was seated across the room from him. Draephus was in bed, weak and tired from the previous day's excitement. He wasn't too terribly happy with Tricale at the moment, as Newark had been found dead during the night.

"I asked you to watch him."

Tricale shrugged. "This way I won't have to. You'll know what he's doing thirty-two hours a day."

"Did you have to make it so obvious?"

"It wasn't obvious. I thought it looked rather natural." Tricale smiled slightly.

"The man was found clutching a suicide note, hand written by somebody else, dead on the floor after having his head slammed repeatedly in the oven door."

"Poor man was obviously quite distraught."

"I would be too if someone was slamming my head with an oven door." Draephus closed his eyes, sinking deeper into the pillows. "No matter, I suppose. I can pay you to take a holiday down to Anth, they have some festival they throw every year going on right now. Take along your favourite person, if you have one."

"I do," said Tricale, rising to his feet. "One in very good health, may I add." Then he left the huge bedroom.

Draephus lay in bed, hating the man. He vowed never to contact him again, wondering why he had once spent so much time with him. Tricale had seemed such good company a long time ago. Either one of them had gotten crazier, or one of them had gone sane. Perhaps it was merely a case of one of them not noticing the war was over.

Draephus had been up much of the night, screaming at various individuals. Wardhead Shayer had been one of them, and he had virtually rolled over and urinated on himself in order to appease Draephus, something Teirra had greatly enjoyed watching. Obviously, people in the Centre worked on the assumption that most of the youths in there had no one to care for them. Certainly no one there seemed to have been braced for a dual attack by the girl's sister and some used-up revolutionary.

Draephus rolled onto his side in an attempt to get away from Dahli, but she did not leave his mind. He thought about her a lot lately. He kept recalling the girl watching the jungle lamps blink on and off in Mars' garden, and how innocent she was. He had seen too much that was innocent die, and the thought of something bad happening to her made him physically ill. Granted, he barely knew her, but at this point in time that hardly seemed to matter. He wasn't sure what did matter, except he had the weird feeling that at least some of this was his fault, and he wanted to make it right. In the course of a few hours, he had the rest of her sentence dropped, and, albeit rather inadvertently, Newark murdered. He had also stumbled across a boy named Shae Wharren, who was in the hospital and seemed to have a great deal to say on what had occurred during the hostage incident, and about what Dahli hadn't done. The media was tearing the Centre to bits, along with the High Courts. When the dust finally settled, it was quite likely some people would find themselves in cells very like the ones they had lorded over.

The bright light of the day shone through the multi-paned stained glass windows of Draephus' bedroom, but could not penetrate the heavy drapes about his bed, or his dark mood. Everything was going along so nicely, save for one problem. Nobody could find Dahli. He was having visions of her having headed off to the South Continent, never to be seen again. This was not a concern he had voiced to Teirra, who was already upset without him bringing up new thoughts to distress her.

The bed was deep and warm, and despite the emotional storm in his brain, Draephus found himself giving way to sleep. He had done all he could to make life right for Dahli, screaming at everyone he could to fix the situation. The letters she had written had been found in Newark's desk, like some sort of trophy. Draephus had them now, uncertain as to what he should do with them. They sat in his nightstand drawer, ready to be pulled out should they be needed. There was nothing left to do, save hope that Dahli turned up somewhere, someday.

Draephus rolled to his stomach and sighed, tired but unable to quiet his brain. The bed shifted, and he felt one of the faelins pacing on all fours on the bed, looking for a comfortable spot to sleep. It stepped on him twice, and this was enough to tell Draephus it was Czanda. He snorted loudly in his ear, then thumped down, body half-on Draephus, who wondered how long he would be able to put up with this. It certainly wasn't helping him get to sleep. Finally he threw back the covers, pushing Czanda off of his back, and staggered out of the room. He had a bottle of Doven's Smokey Mushroom in the hall closet, and if that stuff couldn't make his brain shut up, then nothing could. He found the bottle and was stumbling back to bed when he heard Raski come tearing up the stairs with a newspaper. Draephus was certain he was about to get yelled at for drinking, but Raski had something else on his mind.

"This is a bloody travesty! This is insane! How could something like this happen, how can we live in a world where things like this occur?"

Draephus made his way over to the bed, getting into it. "Raski, calm down, what..."

"Calm down, the man says! This is a bloody emergency!"

Draephus rubbed his eyes, then sighed. "I'm sure it won't escalate to that point. Raski, I'm sure we'll find Dahli before things get too bad."

"Dahli? This isn't about Dahli...don't you ever read the paper?"

"Rarely. Why, what happened?"

"WHAT HAPPENED?! VORTEX HAPPENED! THEIR NEW SONG IS CURRENTLY MORE POPULAR THAN OURS! THEY FINALLY LET STRAIF MANNECHEK WRITE A SONG, AND IT'S BEATING OURS TO DEATH! A LOVE SONG, NO LESS! I'M GONNA BE ILL! WE'VE BEEN HUMILIATED!"

Draephus stared at his friend. "Great Rask, just what I needed to cheer me up."

Raski looked chagrined, lowering the paper. "Sorry. It's stupid I know but… you know me."

He smiled. "Yeah. Come lie down, keep me and the faelins company."

Raski did, slipping into bed beside Draephus and resting his head on his chest, an arm across his waist. They had just made themselves comfortable when Raski's mobile 'com rang. He swore quietly and took it out of his pocket, opening it.

"Heia? Oh. Heia Dr. Arang." He rolled lazily onto his back, listening. "Oh you do? Well what's the result? Immediate quarantine?" Suddenly his eyes grew large and he sat up. "You're joking me." He listened, jaw hanging, and reached out one hand blindly, feeling for Draephus' arm and squeezing it. "I'm…? Th… thanks for calling. I… really appreciate it. Thank you."

Raski closed the 'com, his entire body beginning to shake. Draephus slowly sat up.

"Raski? Baby are you okay?" He swallowed, forcing down a feeling of dread. "What did Dr. Arang say?"

Raski closed his eyes and breathed deeply. "I… I'm clean. I'm the cleanest male on the island. I have X-82 and that's it. I can… I can stop worrying about if the next time I wake up I'm going to still have full use of my body. I can stop taking the preventative medications. They're going to wean me off the more potent ones and let my system adjust and if I want to then we can start talking…"

Raski began wheezing heavily. Draephus rolled his eyes, reaching out to draw him close.

"Dammit can you please just not do this to me every time you get good news? And now the tears, that's just scruffin' lovely." He was grinning as he said it, and pressed a soft kiss to his face, letting Raski cry. X-82. That was it. That meant any sons Raski had would be sterile, but his daughters would all be healthy and fully functional. And they were not currently lacking males.

"I'm happy for ya, Rask. I really am," Draephus said softly. "We'll put the pictures from your first sonogram on the next album cover."

****

She didn't know she had left the hydrotrans at the wrong exit.

A person familiar with the area could have told her, of course, but Dahli was currently avoiding people. Avalair had two ports. One was in the destroyed area of the city, and the craft would stop there briefly to pick up any refugees who had made their way to the dock. Further down the shore was a second dock, where passengers could get off in the safer, more habitable area. Had she debarked there, she would have quickly found the road leading out of the city to the rural areas. Soon she would have been amidst streams choked with ash, but already showing signs of recovery. Tiny brightly coloured fish called Speckle Fish would be burrowing in the mire, laying eggs, feeding on the algae, gradually wearing away the sludge so larger plants and aquatic creatures could move in. New trees and plants would be coming up through the burned and bombed areas, and redweed, which was always the first plant to reappear after a fire, would be colouring the landscape with brilliant red and dark shining green.

Instead she stepped off the small ship and into a world of silent grey death.

She had heard the description 'Avalair Grey', and she could recite the lyrics to the song from memory. It was one of her favourites, though she admitted readily she didn't understand many of the references. But as she stood shin deep in the distinctive blue-grey ash, that song came slamming home to her, and she understood it in a way she never had before.

She began walking slowly, mentally picturing how the snipers would lay down in the ash, rolling in it until they were the same colour, then sink down like strange monsters, peering through grey-streaked masks, waiting for hours or even days for the enemy to appear. Delaes Randerick would have been one of them, she knew. She had heard him mention it in interviews often enough, though she had a very hard time picturing him sitting still for so long. She'd seen him live on stage once; a skinny little figure clad in black running relentlessly back and forth while he sang, until Rysta stopped playing and told him to stand still because he was giving him motion sickness. It was odd to think she was walking where once he had fought.

A strange moaning wail started up, like the mournful cry of some enormous demon in its final death throes. It hung in the air and lingered like a snow-laden cloud, dark, low and ominous. Then it stopped. A few minutes later a second one began, further away, and from a different direction. She had heard these in the song as well; warning sirens, telling anyone in the area that the fires were shifting. The trick now was to avoid them. Well how hard could that be? Fire should show up no problem! Then from somewhere in the back of her mind, she heard Delaes' voice sing to her.

"Silently beneath our sleeping bodies the serpent comes for us,
And as we lie then so we die, and the demon-fire sates its lust…"

'UNDERGROUND fires, Sandiniti,' Dahli reminded herself. 'The fires are UNDER the ground.' She permitted herself a moment of smug satisfaction. And Duone Bathers swore no one ever learned anything lying around and listening to music. Pompous self-satisfied clart-sack.

"Okay," she said aloud. "Just... stay away from the sirens and... keep an eye out for anything you could fall into."

She gazed around at the sea of grey. Much easier said than done, it seemed, and already she could feel the ash settling into her nose and mouth. She set down her bag and dug through it, finding a light scarf she had grabbed, vaguely aware that she would be crossing Avalair and it would be covered in ash. She wrapped it around her nose and mouth, then took out a pair of goggles she had brought for the same reason, fitting them over her eyes. Then she closed up her bag and looked around for something to use to test the ground ahead of her. She kicked aside the ash, but that did no good. She had to get down on her knees and feel. She grimaced, hoping she didn't find a body. She did find something, however; it was... sorta soft and... kinda round...

A head shot up out of the ash. Dahli shrieked and fell back onto her butt, shaking in terror at the strange monster with a long nose and enormous baleful eyes. Then a hand came up and removed the mask, and Dahli exhaled a huge sigh of relief. The man she had awakened stared at her.

"Excuse me but do I come 'round and feel *your* bottom when you are asleep?"

"Sorry. I was looking for something to use as a walking stick."

"Oh." He felt around in the ash, then picked something up. "Here. It's the barrel off a night stalker gun. That should do."

"Thanks." She accepted the five foot length of metal. "Hey if I wanted to get out of the city, where would I go?"

"Dock's right there."

"I meant the other side of the city."

"Then I suggest you learn to fly. Avalair is cut in half by fire, you can't get there from here. Not unless you feel like trying the old army bridge they strung across some of the buildings in the center of the city. But I don't recommend it."

"I have to try," she said quietly.

"Then walk lightly."

She nodded, and smiled. "Thanks. Uh... sleep well."

He grinned at her, then pulled his mask back on, settling into the soft ash once more. Dahli rose to her feet and began slowly making her way into the heart of Avalair, using her gun barrel to gently prod the ground before her.

Dahli's first thought when she reached the center of the city was that ash-guy could have at least told her WHY he did not recommend coming this way. Then again he likely assumed she had half a brain and would know the place was an inferno.

The universe really did hate her, didn't it?

She stood on top of a building, gazing down fifteen stories at what she could only call lava. She had no idea how it got there; Avalair was not known for its volcanoes, but there it was nonetheless, following narrow trenches in the street, spitting, hissing and emitting a stench like some unholy monster's unclean bathroom. Delaes could have told her it was the result of some sort of thermal device the Kryphisians had created, which Sferkkaan freedom fighters had managed to detonate while it was still in the enemy's underground lair, but the information would hardly help her to cross it. She eyed the chain and cable bridge leading from one building to the next with trepidation, slowly approaching it, staring down at the metal planks. It seemed solid. But how to be sure?

She was tugging on the bridge to be certain it would hold her when she heard a noise behind her; a sort of slavering, snuffling noise. Dahli froze, listening to the sound of paws on the roof, slowly turning her head to see three very large and obviously starving feralykes. They normally ate fish, and reports of them attacking people on their own for the purposes of devouring them were few and far between. But these three looked like they would take what they could get. Their last meal was probably a distant memory.

Dahli stared at the feralykes. The feralykes stared back, growling, their ribs showing through their singed and dirty hides. Without warning, one lunged for her. Dahli scrambled to her feet and ran for her life, tearing across the swinging bridge, reaching the end and racing across the roof top to the second bridge. She could hear the animals tearing after her, paws scrabbling over the flat tar and gravel roof. She hit the second bridge and ran across it, still hearing paws tearing after her. Then she crossed the third and final bridge, and… the paws stopped. She skidded to a halt and looked back the way she had come, and was puzzled to notice the feralykes had not followed her across the third bridge. She stared at the starving animals.

"What's wrong with you guys?" she asked.

The animals stared at her, then one yipped and fled back

across the second bridge. Dahli sighed.

"That can't possibly be good," she mumbled.

Slowly she turned and gazed around the rooftop. She did not have difficulty spotting the thing that had terrified the feralykes. It was a dragonbird. She knew that without ever having seen one in real life ever before. Every Sferkkaan child had a storybook with a dragonbird in it. They were magnificent creatures that had spawned the image of the Imperial gryphons that adorned the old palaces and the Mortified Gryphons band logo. Legend had it that once, thousands of years ago, Sferkkaa had clear skies and a sun that shone down, and the dragonbirds brought the light to the planet. But an arrogant nobleman tried to capture the sun for his own purposes, and thus they were closed off from its warming rays, and the dragonbirds had been trapped on their world until such time as the sun chose to shine again.

The creature stared at Dahli with cold eyes the colour of gold, and the massive curved beak for rending flesh was less then a hand span from her face. Feathers the colour of fire formed a great crest on then enormous cranium, and Dahli could not help but notice the magnificent creature's head was roughly the same size as her entire torso. It was a male; she could tell by the red and blue tips on his crest feathers, and by how tall the crest was. Males and females shared nest duty, and he was firmly planted on a collection of debris roughly the size of Draephus' conni. Under him would be two cream coloured eggs, and somewhere above him would be their mother, scanning the area for food.

"I'm gonna die," said Dahli, watching as the huge crest slowly raised straight up.

The bird cocked his head, and made an inquisitive noise, then puffed up his feathers and shook. He didn't seem aggressive, but maybe he just hadn't decided whether or not he wanted to eat her. He stretched his neck out and picked at her bag. Curious, Dahli slowly opened it, and saw Diza had packed her a whole roast chicken. Brilliant. No wonder the feralykes had chased her. Diza's father would have a fit when he got home and found the thing gone. Slowly Dahli pulled it out.

"You want this?" she asked, offering him the chicken.

He accepted it graciously. She couldn't help but think the animal was at least semi-tame. He certainly was not afraid of her. Perhaps he had once been kept as a pet. She knew that several military outfits had kept a dragonbird or two as mascots; it seemed likely he had once been one. Either way Dahli did not much care, so long as he was not trying to eat her. Gingerly she bent down to pick up one of his fallen feathers, then reached out to touch the great golden beak. It was smooth and hard, but warm. She smiled.

"You'd need one big bird cage, and a whole lot of newspapers."

He made a quite noise of agreement, then looked up. Fortunately Dahli did the same thing, and thus was able to see the mother dragonbird bearing straight down at her. Dahli shrieked and fled, feeling the force of the wind of the enormous bird's passing. She ran for the far side of the roof, catching hold of a fire escape ladder and headed for the ground as quickly as she could, glancing up to see if the mother dragonbird was coming back for another pass. There was no sign of her. Apparently she was satisfied that the interloper was gone. Dahli paused on the ladder and looked down, all too aware that the ground beneath the ash could well be nothing more than partially-molten mire upon which the ash was resting.

She reached over her shoulder and took hold of her walking stick, pulling it forth and using it to prod the ground. She heard satisfying thuds. It felt solid. Slowly she climbed down off the ladder and began cautiously moving forward, testing the ground, but it was safe. She found only one more area of lava, but it was little more than a few listless threads, and no longer flowing. Soon they would be crusted over. Dahli managed to hop over them, feeling a few moments of utter terror as a couple of the places she hopped onto were not as solid as she would have liked. Still by the time she reached safety she had survived with only slightly melted boot soles, and a second pass by the mother dragonbird to make certain Dahli knew not to come around and flirt with her husband ever again. She had fire-walked the heart of Avalair, and come through unscathed, despite lava and feralykes and dragonbirds. Elated, she turned and kept on her way. She needed to find a safe place to sleep for a few hours, then she would continue on her journey.

****

Dahli reached the outskirts of Avalair by daybreak, and by mid-morning had left the destroyed city far behind. The landscape was a series of lumps and hummocks, churned up by war machines. The knolls had become covered in vegetation once more, and occasionally Dahli walked passed the carcasses of Kryphisian machines. They lay in the grass like strange, dead animals, light-eyes staring blackly ahead in death. Sometimes she would stop to look at them, touching their cold bodies. She would clear the grass away and watch confused insects flee, their homes disturbed. The bugs were almost as interesting as the carcasses they infested. Rising to her feet, Dahli continued on her way.

The sun was setting behind the cloud cover, and Dahli sat in the shadowless early twilight, eating some of the fruit she had brought from Diza's house. She was almost blind with exhaustion, and all she wanted was to find a place to curl up and go to sleep. She had grown so used to hearing no human voices that when she heard the man speak, it frightened her. She jumped, all senses becoming alert. She listened hard, but heard nothing that stirred fear in her heart.

"No, not over there, you stupid animal. Hey. Stupid. This way. No, not there, you can eat redweed any day, it ain't going nowhere. Oh, fine, have it. Just don't drop me this time."

Dahli watched as a man rode into view on a tall destri; a very badly behaved one. The leggy creature shook its thin, almost conical head, nocturnal eyes huge. It turned circles, paws scraping up the dust from the road, all attention on the redweed and none on its rider. Finally getting its way, the beast walked over to the low, blood-coloured shrub and began to chew. The aging South Continental man sat on its back, trying hard not to be amused at the creature. It chattered away as it ate, making small laughing noises in its high voice. The man patted the beast's long thin neck, smoothing down velvet-black fur.

"You're a stupid animal, yeah, you are. If I had any sense, I'd throw you into the ocean. Let the fish get you. Faelin meat, that's all you are."

The destri didn't seem too concerned with any of these threats. It chuckled and swished its tail, eating the redweed down to the ground.

"Okay, that's the end of it. Let's go home. You been stuffing your pointy face all day, now I want to stuff my pointy face. Now what, you dumb animal?"

The destri suddenly swung its thin head towards Dahli, large diamond-shaped ears perked, long whiskers moving forwards as it sniffed.

"What do you see?" The man looked, spying Dahli with pale blue eyes. "Oh, that ain't nothing to be afraid of, just a skinny girl. Hey, Skinny, what you doing way out here?"

Dahli swallowed, frightened but trying hard not to show it. "Just out for a walk."

"Some walk, Skinny. Avalair is a long way from here, and I know all the people who live in this area. You ain't one of them. Course, if you take walks like that often, could be why you're so skinny."

"I'm not skinny," said Dahli, fear becoming balanced by annoyance.

"Suit yourself, Skinny. You going to walk all the way back to Avalair, you better hurry, it's gonna rain on you."

On Sferkkaa, where the rain was constant, no one said it was going to rain unless it was going to storm in torrents. Dahli glanced up at the sky. "How can you tell?" she demanded.

"Cause I'm old and ugly, and that means I'm always right. Gonna rain all over your head."

"Is not."

"Suit yourself, Skinny. I'm going home for my evening meal. You wanna come? There's so little of you that one good blow and you'd fly back to Avalair."

"I'll be fine," she said.

"Okay. You like being wet and skinny, that's your business. You get sick of the rain, you come by my place. Just go straight down the road a little ways, I'm in the cabin on the left hand-side. Only cabin there."

Dahli watched the man turn the destri around and ride off. She followed him with her eyes until he was out of sight, then she lay down on the warm grass. Over her head, the sky gradually darkened. She would be just fine. The old man could wait up all night if he liked, she would be just fine where she was. A few moments later, Dahli fell asleep.

****

The sheer violence of the rain fall woke her a short time later, and she sat up with a cry. She was soaked right through her clothes, and she stared down at herself for a long moment, the rain streaming down on top of her.

"Why is this happening?" she asked aloud as the thunder crashed. She sighed heavily as she rose, picking up her bag. She wandered down the weed-grown road to the old man's cabin, whimpering and grumbling, her bag dragging along behind her.

It took her a little over an hour to find the small, ramshackle house. It sat by itself, surrounded by bushes and trees. The remains of a fence encircled it, covered in rot and moss. A group of feralykes, four in all, raised their heads and watched her from their vantage point on the dilapidated old porch. Ancient fruit trees, bent and gnarled, grew in a clump near what was the edge of the weedy yard. The stairs leading up to the shack were tilted and cracked. It was the most deserted-looking house Dahli had ever seen.

The feralykes made no unfriendly moves as she walked towards the house, but she kept a watchful eye on them anyway. She climbed the four small steps, walking past the feralykes to the door. As she reached it, she saw a light shining from behind the heavy shades, and she relaxed a little. She had not been looking forward to waking the man up to ask for shelter. She knocked at the door.

There came a stirring from within, then the sound of approaching footsteps. The feralykes rose to their feet at the sound, eyes bright and expectant. Then the door opened, and there stood the old man. He stared at Dahli for a long moment, then snorted in amusement.

"Only plants stand in the rain, Skinny. Come on in."

Dahli entered the shack, then paused. The room she now found herself in was a sea of chickens. The birds perched everywhere, sitting on the backs of chairs and eating out of dishes set on the floor. She slowly surveyed the room, eyes huge. One of the reddish birds hopped onto her bag and gawked at her.

"That's No-Toe," said the man. "See, she's missing one. I'm Harli. What do they call you?"

Dahli started as the man asked her name, and she stared at him for a terrified moment, at a loss as to what to say. He gazed back, then picked up her bag.

"I'll just put this away, and give you a moment to make one

up."

Dahli cursed herself under her breath, then walked into the small kitchen. Sitting down on a chair, she sighed heavily, then glanced about the room. Chickens were perched everywhere, and she rose slightly to examine the chair she was on. Not seeing anything other than wood, she sat back down.

Harli walked back into the room, heading over to the stove and peering into a pot. "So what's your name?"

"Atania Nightwing," Dahli said, smiling slightly.

"That's a good one, better than I could come up with in a short time. You hungry? Should be, you're skinny enough."

"I'm fine the way I am!"

"Okay, be skinny, I don't care."

Dahli smiled, shaking her head. "Boy, you sure are rude."

"I'm old, I'm allowed. See, if you can be skinny, I can be old and rude. The chickens don't care. You play an instrument?"

Dahli rolled her eyes. It was just her luck to be born on a planet where everybody had to play some sort of instrument to be considered normal.

"No," she admitted, scuffing one food on the chicken-speckled floor. "Well I play the drums a little."

The old man looked downright offended. "Well, what do you do with your time? Ever thought about learning?"

Dahli had the sinking feeling she was trapped in a cabin with a rude lunatic. "Yeah, from time to time. I'd kinda like to learn the drums."

"Good, be good for you to learn. And if you don't like the drums, try something else, maybe the quinticord. You know who taught me to play quinticord? Philo Rae. You ever heard of him?"

"No."

"Course not. When he died you were probably still trying to master sticking a spoonful of mush into your ear. Philo Rae was the greatest quinticord player ever lived. I used to follow him all over the country. Biggest, ugliest Siriusian I ever saw. Face like his, he'd have to sound good. And when he sang that sound just welled up and came pouring out like it was its own animal. Tell you one thing; you gotta smell a whole lot of clart in your life before you can sing like that."

Dahli glanced about the kitchen, then said quietly; "Well, I'm smelling a whole lot now."

Harli stared at her for a long moment, then suddenly howled with laughter. "I guess you are, I guess you are. I like you, even if you are skinny. You can sleep in the spare bedroom upstairs. Don't worry, I don't let the chickens upstairs."

The upstairs of Harli's house was in considerably better shape than the downstairs. The furnishings were new and clean, untouched by chickens. The bathroom was clean as well; Dahli had been terrified to think what it may look like. She set her bag down on the floor and began running water into the bathtub, peeling off her clothes. Her hands were gloved in the dark skin paint, and her face wore a mask of it. She had to scrub several times before it all came off. She was tired, and not thinking clearly. She had struck fair skin again before she realised what she had done, and stared at her hands in horror.

"Oh clart," she muttered wearily. She didn't have any more of the paint. What was Harli going to say when he saw she had gone up Southern and came down Mid-Northern? She sat back in the tub and stared at the wall ahead, too tired to care at this point. She giggled helplessly for a few minutes, firmly convinced she was going to lose her mind. She ceased giggling, then had a good cry, tired, stressed and frightened. She never wanted to emerge from the tub again, but decided Harli was probably going to eventually want access to his bathroom. She got out of the tub, dried, and put on her only change of clean clothes, tossing the dirty ones into the bag.

Harli tapped on the bathroom door. "It's late, Skinny. You can use the spare bedroom at the end of the hall. I'm going to bed."

"Good night Harli," Dahli said, rubbing at one eye. "Thanks."

"That's all right, Skinny. Get to sleep."

"I'm not skinny."

"Suit yourself, Skinny."

Dahli listened to his footsteps fade off down the hallway, then heard the sound of his bedroom door closing. She turned off the bathroom light and walked to her own room, closing the door behind her. It was a small, simply furnished room, with a bed, dresser, and nightstand. The chamber was illuminated by a Jungle Lamp on the dresser, and its warm, creamy fragrance wafted to her. Dahli dropped her bag, then walked over to the bed, sitting on its edge. The window was open, and she could hear the rain beat down onto the ground. Dahli sat on the bed for a long time, just staring out into the rainy night, a weary smile on her face. It wasn't home, but it was good.

****

Harli glanced up as Dahli entered the kitchen the next morning, and stared at her hard. Dahli stopped and looked back at him, blinking and trying hard to look innocent. It was a long time before anyone spoke.

"Are you going to change like that every time you take a bath? Cause if you are I don't know if I'm going to be able to get used to it."

Dahli smiled slightly. She figured Harli at the very least knew she had run away from somewhere, and without any more paint she could not continue to hide her colouration from him.

"That was a disguise. It washed off in the tub."

"And here I thought you was somebody respectable, and now I find out you're just one of them Mid-Northerners."

Dahli shrugged. "Worse. Part Eastern, too. Are you going to make me sleep with the chickens?"

"Don't make my chickens sleep with easterners," said Harli. "Now you sit down and pick up that spoon and eat. You're too skinny."

Dahli picked up the spoon and muttered; "I am not."

"Suit yourself. It's still coming down in rivers outside, you're not going out in that stuff, are you?"

Dahli glanced out the small window. The rain beat down hard, turning the yard into slick, deep mud. She sighed.

"Oh great. How can I get any travelling done in that?"

Harli stirred his tea, studying her from across the table. Then he shrugged. "No matter, Skinny. You can stay here another day."

Dahli smiled. "Thanks, Chicken Man."

"Chicken Man!"

"Yeah. See if I can be skinny, you can be a chicken man."

Harli chuckled. "Yeah I guess you're right." He pushed the tea pot over to Dahli. She poured herself a cup, and for awhile they just sat together in silence and watched the rain fall.

****

"Well good morning, Grey Boy," said Draephus softly.

J'Vanni made a small noise and slowly rolled onto his side, his face bandaged, swatting feebly at Draephus.

"Don' call me that."

Draephus seated himself on the edge of the hospital bed, taking hold of one long white hand.

"How are you feeling?"

"Bloody awful. Where is Delaes? Is he all right?"

"We don't know where Delaes is. He seems to have got away. I have people looking for him. Rysta's going to be fine, he's back at the apartment helping to clean up, and I took your hawk to a vet. He's pretty upset but he will be fine as well." He stroked J'Vanni's long hair. "So what happened?"

"I don't know. I don't really remember." He reached up to touch the bandages encasing his face. "What happened to me?"

"Well it looks a lot like you narrowly missed getting shot in the head by a long-muzzled night stalker gun. The projectile missed you, but those things emit so much in the way of heat and particles and crap that they can miss a person entirely and still cause a lot of damage. Personally I think whoever went after you wanted to make certain you didn't survive."

J'Vanni smiled coldly. "Well the only good Grey Boy is a dead Grey Boy."

Draephus lowered his head and kissed him. "Yeah well I promised I would look after you, and I plan on doing just that."

"You're just a sucker for lost causes, aren't you?"

"We lost causes have to stick together," said Draephus. "Do you remember who hurt you?"

"No. But… I have this strange feeling that I knew him. Did you say Piska is okay?"

"Your birdie is fine, and whoever hurt you has a very unique scar. They were picking flesh out of his talons. And it was not rat flesh." His telecom rang, and he drew it out of his pocket. "Heia?"

"Why are you never home? Are you avoiding me?" a voice gently chastised.

Draephus sat bolt upright. "Vesper? Vesper how are you? *Where* are you?"

"Fine, and on top of a cliff, being drooled on by a large herbivore. It's a beautiful early evening, I'm just settling down to camp for the night and I thought I would call you before it rains again."

"When are you coming home? I'm a disaster and the plants are all turning yellow."

"I'll be home in just a couple more weeks if I can't get down into the Kalihine Valley. But there are some caves in there I really want to see. They contain ancient paintings dating back thousands of years. But the wet season is coming up on us, and if we don't get at least three days of dry weather very soon we'll have to head back, or else sit on this wretched cliff until the dry season comes again. And I really don't want to. Blossom, stop chewing on my pack. How are things with you?"

"Fine," Draephus lied cheerfully. "Just visiting Delaes."

"Oh really? How is Delaes?"

Draephus did not like lying to Vesper, but there was absolutely no way he was admitting on the 'com that J'Vanni was badly hurt and Delaes was nowhere to be seen. Currently J'Vanni was in the Avalair hospital, while Raski and Mars crawled around his apartment like a pair of demented stoats routing out any listening devices before they brought J'Vanni back home. Personally Draephus would have liked to have moved him, but there really was no place to move to, and J'Vanni, sweet as he was, possessed the infamous Kryphisian stubbornness. He would not be moved.

"Oh Delaes is good."

"Put him on."

"Well he's in the bath right now. He has to enjoy the running water while they have it. It's Avalair; they only get a small amount allotted for bathing each day."

"Oh that's right. Well don't bother him, then."

They chatted for a little while, then Draephus ended the call and hung up, turning his attention back to J'Vanni. "I'm sorry about that."

"It's quite all right. Now if only Delaes would call. I'm very worried about him."

"Delaes is a smart guy, he probably went straight for the pipes. They won't find him down there."

"He's pregnant."

Draephus winced. "Did I not tell you two not to breed? I'm pretty sure I specifically told you not to do that."

"It was not planned, I can assure you. We were going to go down to the South Continent to have it, then return and claim the mother had passed away."

"You do realize there are even less women down there than up here?"

"I thought there were more."

"No. If you want to claim you found an actual breathing woman capable of having a child you have to go down to Charlendine."

"Charlendine? That's the other side of the world! You know I heard they get this frozen rain, it falls from the sky in a sort of white fluff. Is that true?"

"Yeah, it's called snow. It's very pretty. I've seen it."

"Well if Delaes comes back then we will go to Charlendine. Not that I will be able to see the snow, or anything anymore." He swallowed, clearly upset. "Draephus I am so afraid for him…"

"Don't worry, he'll come back. Delaes won't be able to stay in a huge hollow underground pipe with a baby, can you imagine the noise?"

J'Vanni smiled, although Draephus could tell he was on the verge of tears, even with most of his face bandaged. "I just want him home."

Draephus took J'Vanni's hand and gently squeezed it. "He will be home. We'll find him, I promise. You just rest. Do you have any idea who did this to you?"

"No. I mean… I'm sure I knew who it was but… everything is all confused now. I can't remember."

"Okay. It's okay, just rest. I'll stay here with you. Just rest Gia. We will find Delaes and you will get better and you will have a beautiful baby with long red hair who barks at parked connis."

"I hope you're right. I'm so worried."

"Just rest, Gia. It will be okay. I promise."

J'Vanni doubted Draephus would be able to keep that promise, but he was too tired and ill to do anything about the situation. Instead he quietly slipped into a heavy sleep, still holding his friend's hand.

****

Dahli came down the stairs, yawning. She paused about halfway down the steps to stretch. "Good morning, Harli."

"Morning? High on to afternoon. Why do you stay in bed so long? Counting the fibres in the quilt? HEY! CHICKEN! OFF THE TABLE!"

Dahli grinned as she sat down at the table. "So what are we up to today?" she asked as she took the cup of tea he offered her.

In the two weeks since Dahli had come to Harli's she had adjusted to his way of life. She helped with the care and feeding of the animals, and with some of the heavier chores that went along with them. She had learned how to brush the destri, whose name seemed to be 'Stupid,' and Harli had been teaching her how to ride Stupid as well as play the quinticord. Life had settled rather nicely, and Dahli wasn't sure she wanted to leave it for the trials of the outside world. She thought that if Harli asked her, she would stay on for a while.

"Gonna pluck all these stupid chickens alive, that's what. HEY! CHICKEN! OFF THE TABLE!"

Despite his words he picked the bird up gently when he moved it. He seated himself and began loading food onto his plate. Dahli smiled and also began to eat. There was silence at the table for a short time.

"You know," Harli suddenly said, "if I were a skinny girl named Dahli Sandiniti, and not Atania Nightwing, I'd listen to the receiver more often."

Dahli's fork halted its upward motion, and she looked across the table at Harli. "Really? Why is that?"

Harli chewed a mouthful of food, then swallowed. "'Cause I might find out that I've been hiding out with a crazy old chicken man for eighteen days when I didn't have to. I might find out that maybe due to a series of incidents at a Detention Centre, the rest of my sentence that I'm not around to enjoy has been dropped. And I might find out my friend Diza has since told a bunch of people I was headed for Touskania for some fool reason."

Dahli stared across the table at Harli for a long moment, blinking, trying to absorb what she had just heard. "What?" She slowly sat back in her chair, stunned. "They're not looking for me?"

"No they ain't looking for you, they're looking for Dahli Sandiniti, so they can tell her it's safe to come home."

"Do you mind if I use the telecom to call someone?"

"Is it local?"

"No."

"Go ahead."

Dahli picked up the telecom and carefully dialled her home number. She heard the distant sound of the device ringing, and then it was picked up.

"Hello?" said a familiar voice.

"Heia Teirra," said Dahli.

"Dahli is that you?" There was the sound of the 'com in the next room being picked up, and then she heard Atterick's voice as well. "Dahli?"

"Heia Atterick."

"Dahli where are you? We have been worried sick."

"I'm just outside of Avalair."

"Avalair!" yelled Teirra. "How in the New Empire did you get all the way past Avalair?"

"I walked. Well I took the Hydrotrans across the channel, otherwise I would have had to swim, but mostly I walked."

"How are you?"

Dahli pushed her hand through her hair. "I'm fine. I've been staying with a friend."

"You don't know anybody in Avalair."

"Do now. His name's Harli."

"Tell them I'm a cranky old man with a chicken fixation," said Harli as he mopped eggs off his plate with bread.

"I will not," said Dahli, then addressed Teirra once more. "He's a cranky old man with a chicken fixation. So tell me, is it true? Can I come home and stop bothering this man?"

"Yeah, it's true," said Atterick. "Dahli we have been so worried."

"I'm okay, don't worry any more. I'm fine."

"Where are you? Do you want us to come get you?"

Dahli thought about this for a moment, then said softly; "No, I'll make it on my own."

"Are you sure you can make it home on your own all right?" he asked. "You're sure you don't want us to come get you?"

"No, I'll be fine. I'll call you when I get to Second City, which should probably be in the next few days."

"Okay. Oh, you know that drummer you hit with a door and

beat up and robbed? The one whose name you once forbade us to mention? Well he wants you to call him. He's been helping us look for you."

Dahli was both shocked and delighted. "*Really*!?" she screeched, her voice hitting a pitch that sent the chickens fleeing.

"Yes, and he left a number. You want it?"

"*YES!*"

"Wait," said Teirra, "I don't think she deserves it after all she has put us through."

"You're right. Let's toss it out."

"NO!! No gimme please gimme I'll be good I won't beat up or rob another drummer ever again *or* steal anymore dead bodies."

Atterick sighed. "Well, in that case, all right." He gave her the number, Dahli using a bit of charred wood from the hearth to write it on the floor.

"Got it. Thank you! I'll be home soon I promise. I missed you guys so much."

"We missed you, too. Hurry home."

"All right. Bye."

Dahli sat back in her seat and looked at the code written down on the floor before her. She wondered if she should call him or not, then sighed. She happened to glance up and see Harli staring at her amusedly.

"You gonna call him?"

"I guess. Kinda… feels odd, though."

She picked up the telecom again and dialled. She heard the 'com ring at the other end of the line ring, and then heard a click, followed by a recorded message.

"Heia. I'm not home, I'm in Avalair. For those of you who know me and still want to talk to me anyway, just wait a moment and this call will be transferred."

There was a series of beeps, and then she heard another ring. The 'com was picked up.

"Heia?" said a soft, oddly mechanized-sounding male voice. Dahli almost dropped the 'com, briefly panicking, then recovered.

"Heia," she said, a little nervously. "I called Draephus, his 'com forwarded me to this number."

"Oh yes. I shall get him. Whom shall I say is calling?"

"Dahli."

"Just wait a moment please." He set the receiver down, then called down the hallway; "It's for you."

Dahli could hear their voices, slightly muffled but still audible.

"Who is it?" asked Draephus.

"A young woman who calls herself Dahli."

Draephus walked to the 'com, and she heard him grab it up. "Where are you?" he said bluntly.

"Nice to talk to you, too."

"Just cut the clart, we've been worried."

"I'm outside Avalair."

"Avalair? What are you doing in Avalair? How are you getting home? Is anyone coming to get you? Wait a moment." There was a pause, and for a brief time all Dahli could hear were muffled voices. Then Draephus came back on the line. "Uh, I'm kinda here keeping Gia company, he's a friend of mine, and he wants to know if it would inconvenience you a great deal to come over here for a bit. He'd like to meet you. I could come pick you up."

Dahli's mouth hung open for a moment, flapping uselessly. "Sure," she finally said.

She heard Draephus shift slightly, then exhale. "So where are you?"

Dahli looked at Harli. "Where am I?"

"Sitting in a chair in my kitchen."

Dahli rolled her eyes and sighed. "Where is your house?"

"Hold the 'com out."

Dahli shrugged and did so. Harli shouted; "She's here with *me* you dumb-ass!"

Draephus let out a rusty scream of pure delight. "HARLI!"

"You better believe it's Harli. Get your skinny ass over here. You know what to bring."

"Yeah, all right. I have an air-con, so I'll be there in about twenty minutes, longer if I get lost."

Dahli heard him hang up, and replaced the receiver. "Why am I suddenly worried?" she asked.

"I dunno. 'Cause you're smart? Who'll ride Stupid if you're gone?"

She smiled. "Who rode him before I was here?"

"I did, but he don't listen to my sorry ass." Harli snorted. "Maybe he ain't so stupid after all."

Dahli suddenly wondered if he was going to miss her. He seemed to have broken off from his usual continuous rant against the universe in general and chickens in particular.

"I'll miss you," she said softly.

"Oh don't start that, I ain't gonna miss you, skinny woman. I ought to send you off with a few of these chickens, wouldn't miss them either." He smiled as one of the birds hopped onto his shoe and sat there, looking blankly about. "You're a stupid bird, yes you are," he said to it.

He moved the bird and got up, leaving the room for a time. He returned a few minutes later with the old quinticord Dahli had been learning to play, and one of his hats that she had been wearing constantly. She liked it because it was floppy, and it sported long, brilliant feathers from the tail of his favourite rooster. Harli had three roosters in total, named Steve, Not Steve, and Also Not Steve. He dropped the hat onto her head, then passed her the old quinticord.

"I want you to keep these," he said. "That way I know you'll think of me once in a while. And you better learn to play that quinticord, because if I ever run into you again and you still can't play you're in a lot of trouble."

"Don't worry," said Dahli. "You're far too scary for me to think you're not going to come back and haunt me."

"You better believe it." He grinned at her, looking pleased with himself. He sat at the table again, and for a time both were silent.

"Yeah I'm gonna miss you, too," he said.

Chapter Seventeen

Delaes had not survived the war in the ashes of Avalair by being stupid. He wasn't. Flighty, nervous, and highly strung, most definitely, but not stupid. And he knew the best place for him to hide was in plain sight.

The hunters were still on his trail. They knew he was in the pipes, and the fact that two weeks later they were still popping up to torment him meant they could likely hear every move he made when he ventured into the higher pipes outside of his hiding spot. This was no place for a pregnant faelin. He needed warmth and fresh meat and trees, not cold dampness, expired rations, and a dark underground lair. And trees. Definitely trees – big ones. Delaes had often wondered what sort of a faelin he was; he apparently now had his answer. He was arboreal.

He had found a lower level where there had once been a small hidden base, and located a few things left behind; a mirror, a light, and various items used for disguise purposes. Delaes took out his dark brown contacts, revealing his own vibrant green eyes. He then dyed his hair back to its natural rusty red. A good roll in the iron-rich dirt was next, to stain his skin from white to red. Then he had to decide how much clothing to dispose of. It was true faelins as a rule didn't wear clothes, but it was not unusual for some owners to dress them up. Personally after a lifetime of clothing he wasn't sure he liked the idea of hanging about stark naked, and J'Vanni would have been mortified a thousand times over at the idea of his husband nude up a tree…

Poor beautiful J'Vanni. Delaes wondered if he dared hope that he was alive.

He finally decided to simply make his pants into shorts, leaving most of his clothing as well as his signature pieces of jewellery in his hiding hole. A little more rolling around gave him the scruffy look of the average pet faelin. He located a discarded faelin collar in the remains of the old encampment, then, wearing only ragged shorts and the collar, he prowled out of the tunnels looking greatly different from when he went in, and made his way to a park where people took their faelins to run.

There were two faelins in the park, along with a man who was clearly their owner. They were what Draephus would have called 'stupid house pets', faelins bred and raised to be quiet elegant pets that knew better than to crease a pillow or sleep on master's bed. They took immediate notice of Delaes, and bestirred their privileged and graceful selves to come sniff him. Delaes was in no mood to be sniffed. He was hungry and cold, and any faelin owner with half a brain would know he was pregnant. And a pregnant faelin was not a socially well-adjusted faelin. Delaes watched the pair approach, and narrowed his eyes.

"If you useless twats come one step closer there is going to be a very large vet bill in your master's future," he snarled.

The faelins stopped. They had heard their master speak often enough, but to hear words come out of one of their own was more than they were prepared for. They yipped and headed back for their master. Delaes found a huge and ancient Goldenwood tree, rising well over three hundred feet straight up, gigantic leaves making maximum use of the shrouded Sferkkaan sun. He climbed it with ease, heading up to the highest branches and settling comfortably on a wide bough two hundred and ninety feet off the ground; resting faelin-style on his right hip, body twisted so his upper body was supported on his elbows, arms crossed at the wrists. In the distance he could see his apartment building, a faint white tower flanked by rising trees. He lowered his head onto his arms and wondered if he would ever see the inside of his home again.

****

Draephus pulled up in a gleaming black air-con, the vehicle settling softly on the ground. He hopped out, grabbed up a couple bags from the passenger side seat, and ran up to Harli's door, barging in, not even bothering to knock. Dahli watched in astonishment as he pounced on Harli.

"Harli! How are ya? Still living with the chickens I see. FEARLESS!"

Dahli almost panicked as he grabbed her up and hugged her. She could hardly believe this was the same cold, dispassionate, and angry man she had met before, but he seemed desperately glad to see her.

"Heia," she said quietly. "Um… who are you and what have you done with Draephus?"

He smiled, and held her. "Yeah, sorry, when I get worried I get clingy."

"Awwww… you were worried about me?" she asked, smiling.

"No. I was worried about Harli having to live with you. Have you smacked him with a door yet, or are you saving that for a special occasion?"

"Groutnoll."

Draephus set her down, acting more like himself. He set the bags on the table and turned to Harli. "Just so you know, you owe Gia for an awful lot of booze."

"Hmph. Prissy Grey Boy. Surprised he *can* drink."

Dahli's eyes became huge as she looked at Draephus, jaw hanging. "You know a Grey Boy?"

"I do." Draephus cast Harli a quick glance. And the older man shook his head, implying he had not meant to leak that particular piece of information. They began hauling food and bottles out of the bags. "They're not all murdering bastards, despite what the propaganda says, and I happen to be pretty fond of this one. He's a good guy. I'll take ya to meet him. You spoke to him on the 'com. Harli, where do you keep your pans?"

"See the chicken with the blue tail on the counter? Under him."

"You're a sick man."

"I like chickens. What's wrong with liking chickens?"

"I'm worried about the extent to which you like them. C'mon, Steve, move the feathers."

"That's Not Steve," said Harli.

"What are you making?" asked Dahli. "Can I help?"

Draephus looked at Dahli, then looked at Harli. "Did you not explain what we are about to do here?"

"Nope. Don't explain things to skinny women who are gonna leave my ass all alone with the chickens."

Draephus looked at Dahli, and grinned. "Dahli, tonight, we make you a man."

"Oh goody," she said, a hint of worry in her expression.

****

It didn't hurt as much as she thought it would, though there was definitely some pain involved, mostly in the form of a plate of 'hrabaccaus'. It was a heavily spiced fish dish, served with sweet peppers that made her eyes water and assorted green veggies cooked in a fish sauce containing small oysters. It looked bizarre, it didn't smell especially appealing, but was so good she had two helpings.

"That was fantastic! So am I a man yet?" Dahli asked, smiling. The smile fell off her face as Draephus placed chilled glasses, two bottles of alcohol, and a small bag of ominous-looking round green candies on the table. She had a funny feeling that Teirra would not approve of whatever it is they were about to do.

"Not yet," said Draephus. "First we must teach you to drink like a warrior."

"But... I'm not a warrior."

"According to South Continent tradition, yes you are," said Harli. "You passed the three rites. Maybe you didn't *know* that was what you were doing, but that's what you did. You're a warrior. So you earned the right to a warrior's privileges; a plate of hrabaccaus and..." Harli picked up one of the green candies. "The Yri Babbi, the Tree Frog."

Dahli looked at the green candy. "Tree frog? Rites? I don't understand. What did I do?" She glanced up as she heard a conni pull up outside, but was distracted by Harli picking up one of the glasses.

"These glasses aren't cold enough, Draephus, you know better than that."

Draephus rolled his eyes and took the glass, going for a colder one. Harli turned to Dahli and continued speaking.

"In the South Continent, to be a warrior, a person has to complete three tasks. Now it used to be only boys could do this, but that's not true anymore. Lotta girls took this test, but we still razz them, tell them we're gonna make a man out of them. The first task is to complete a deed in silence, without being discovered, for a just cause. Well you did that when you took the faelin."

"But... I told everyone."

"Yeah, you did, but... you *chose* to reveal what you had done. You weren't caught doing it. So that was your first task. Your second task was to undertake a great journey in which you found knowledge. Everything you have been through right up until the moment you landed on my door step counts as a journey towards knowledge. I bet you're a lot wiser than you were."

"Definitely," muttered Dahli. "What's three?"

Harli grinned at her. "You fire-walked. Right through Avalair. Don't tell me you didn't. Not with those burns on your boots, and pant legs. And that feather in your pack, that's from a dragonbird, and they only nest near sources of heat. You completed the three tasks. That makes you a warrior. So, we are gonna throw you a warrior's party."

The door opened, and Dahli's jaw dropped as in walked Raski Jervyas and Straif Mannechek. She had seen Straif numerous times on the visual, but she hadn't realized how young he was. He planted himself beside her and picked up a glass.

"It's warm!" he complained.

"Shut up, brat," said Harli as Draephus planted a fresh glass in front of Dahli, one so cold she could almost hear it crackling. "We don't take clart from no under-aged smugglers in this house. Dahli this is Straif. He's just a fluffy little pretty boy now, but back when the war was on he used to smuggle messages from one base to the next in Avalair. Assassinated a few people too, probably by accident."

Dahli cleared her throat, thinking he had the biggest, greenest, most amazing eyes she had ever seen. "Heia."

"Heia," he said back, and grinned. "Let me guess. You know who I am and have none of my albums."

"Something like that," said Dahli.

He nodded. "I thought so."

"Because Vortex stinks," said Raski, seating himself at the table.

"They don't stink," said Dahli. "They cause cavities. It's like candy-covered vomit, there's no way of telling what part will rot your teeth faster." Then she looked at Straif. He was pretty and slender, with a long curling mane of thick dark brown hair, and sea-green eyes, masked in a soft line of black. He was so... damned... *lovely*. How could anything *that* beautiful be in Vortex?

"Sorry," she said.

"It's all right," he said. "I don't mind. We are pretty..."

"Vile."

"Yes."

"It's a šukating tragedy is what it is," said Raski, "The kid's a decorated veteran and he ends up with those snot-nosed groutnolls."

Draephus brought the remaining glasses to the table and seated himself beside Dahli. He picked up one of the round candies and showed it to her.

"Now pay very close attention, Fearless, because after two drinks none of us will be in any shape to explain it a third time."

"None for me," said Straif. "I'm pregnant."

Dahli turned abruptly to look at the pretty young male in his long frock coat and thigh-high boots, as did everyone else at the table. Even a few of the chickens looked.

"'Scuse me?" she said.

"Buhk?" said Also Not Steve.

"Yeah what the bird said," Raski said.

"I'm pregnant," repeated Straif. "Three weeks."

"You're *seventeen*!" said Draephus. "And you've only *been* seventeen for five weeks! Who gave you an implant?"

"Dr. Arang. Look, I *am* a veteran, young as I am, I don't need to remind you two that I was *ten* when I was running messages back and forth through the air vents beneath Kryphisian bases. I don't wear this black face paint for fashion; that's what it means, that I did covert work. I also have A2-78, which means if I want a family then I have to do it now, I won't be in any shape to do it when I'm older. If you want to scream at me for being too young to start a family then go call the Kryphisians, I'm sure they'll be very sympathetic."

"You're right," said Raski, "I'm sorry. But... clart, Straif..."

"I just can't believe Dr. Arang gave you an implant at your age," said Draephus.

"Well I went to him and said I wanted an implant." Straif picked up a candy and nibbled it. "He laughed and said no, absolutely not. So I said "Look, I *am* a veteran," and he laughed and said no again. Then I showed him my medical files and he scheduled me for surgery. I have maybe five years left to live. In three my body will be too broken down to have kids. I can't wait to meet a girl; there are not that many of them out there who would both want to be with me and be physically able to have children. If I want a family I have to do it now, I have to do it myself, and anybody who is horrified by my choices can go marry a feralyke."

"So who is the father?" asked Draephus.

"I'm not telling you, I know you, I'm not having you put him in the hospital."

"I won't hurt him, I promise," said Draephus. "Really. Honest. Okay I won't hurt him *badly*, just tell me it's not one of those pukes in your band."

"Oh, no, don't be ghastly."

"Then who?"

Straif looked extremely pleased with himself. "My'shlyin Achania."

Raski, Draephus and Harli sat back in their chairs, jaws hanging. There was a long, stunned silence, then Raski sat back in his chair and clapped.

"Bravo, kid!"

"Who is he?" asked Dahli.

"My'shlyin Achania is without a doubt one of the finest musicians in existence," said Raski. "The reason you never heard of him is he won't come out of the Cylinder's mushroom dens, he's not quite ready to believe the war is over. He's also one of the greatest fighter pilots I ever flew with *and* he is absolutely beautiful. Bravo, Straif, well done. Does he know?"

Straif shrugged. "I have no idea. I went up to him after a show and told him I was ovulating and he said fine. We went to his place and I spent the night, haven't seen him since."

Draephus shook his head and grinned, making that strange laugh that sounded more like a cough than anything. "Straif you are unbelievable."

"Well I wanted a baby not a boyfriend; I'm really not all that interested in men to tell you the truth, I just don't have very many options. I'll tell him next time I go see him play." He looked at Dahli with playful green eyes. "Would you like to come with me?"

"Go with you to a covert mushroom den in the base of the Cylinder?" she asked, not quite believing what she had just heard.

Straif nodded. "Yeah."

Dahli raised an eyebrow and thought about that. She had just been asked out by Straif Mannechek. It was almost more than her brain could take.

"Sure!" she said.

"Not without us you're not," said Draephus, and Dahli did not miss the way he seemed to exude both jealousy and protectiveness. She grinned at him.

"Awwww... you're so sweet."

"Šukat you," he muttered, but he was grinning. "Okay, now, on to business. We gotta get these frogs made before the glasses get too warm."

****

It was not until evening of the next day that they were in any shape to leave. Raski and Straif departed together, heading back to Second City. Dahli put her few things in Draephus' gleaming black vehicle, then she turned to sadly wave at Harli on the porch. They had been reluctantly saying farewell all day.

"Take care," she said quietly.

"Yeah you too. Call me, or I'll come looking for you."

Dahli laughed. "Yes I believe you would."

"You come visit."

Dahli did some mental calculations. "Tell the chickens I'll be back to see you and them in six weeks."

Harli nodded. "You better. Them chickens can get real ugly when people don't come by."

She ran onto the porch and hugged him fiercely, knowing she was going to miss Harli a great deal. She then returned to the air-con. She eyed the expensive vehicle, looking at it as though her mere presence could scratch the shining finish. She glanced up at Draephus.

"After what I did to your last vehicle I can't believe you came to get me in this. Actually I can't believe you came to get me."

He shrugged, looking uncomfortable, smiling slightly. "Yeah, well, I had a motive for driving this con."

"Which was?"

"If you get angry at me and trash it I don't have to care because it's not mine."

Dahli laughed, and the two got into the vehicle. She turned to Draephus, watching him as he started the con.

"On the subject of me getting angry at you..." Dahli said.

"You'd like an explanation for why I exploded that night."

"Yes. I think I am at least owed that," said Dahli.

Draephus pushed up on the throttle, and the con levitated. As they started to move, he said; "I'll tell you later, okay?"

Dahli nodded. "Okay." She smiled at him. "Thanks for coming

to get me."

"Yeah well it was the least I could do after ruining your life."

"Oh quit taking credit, I did it all by myself and you know it. Who is this Grey Boy friend of yours? Why does he want to meet me?"

"He's rather impressed with your stand on faelins. He would like to see things made better for them as well."

She shook her head. "If someone told me a year ago I'd be driving with you to visit a friend of yours who wanted to meet me, I would have fallen down laughing."

"Why? Doesn't anyone think I *have* friends?"

"That's not it and you know it."

Draephus laughed quietly, lighting a cigarette. Dahli waited for him to light it, then took it and put it in her own mouth. He sighed resignedly and lit another. He gave her a sidelong glance, looking amused.

"It's good to see you again, Fearless," he said.

****

Dahli stood nervously next to Draephus as he slid the electronic key into the door, opening it. She stayed close behind him as the door slid open, and she saw the blue apartment before her. There, poised within the room, was probably the single most beautiful individual she had ever seen. Despite the fact that there were black stitches visible beneath the white bandage across his upper face, she could tell he was beautiful. She thought perhaps it was the air of nobility he possessed, the regal demeanour with which he faced the door. He was very tall, well built, and he carried himself with quiet elegance. He looked more like an Emperor than Stratavarus ever could.

"Draephus?" he asked nervously.

"Hi Gia, it's me." Draephus motioned for Dahli to follow him into the room. She walked after him, closing the door behind herself. Draephus tossed his ratted long coat onto a delicate carved chair. "Gia, this is Dahli."

"Heia," said Dahli shyly.

Gia turned toward the sound of her voice and bowed slightly, his great mane of silver hair falling forward. "I am very pleased to make your acquaintance, won't you please have a seat? Donsa CZimcocious has gone into the kitchen to look for his lost manners, I believe."

"What?" yelled Draephus from the kitchen, obviously with his mouth full.

Dahli set her bag and quinticord down, sitting on a chair carefully, a little afraid it would break beneath her. Gia sat across from her, crossing his long legs. A huge golden hawk hopped from a perch near the window and onto the chair he sat on, making him even more impressive than he already was.

Dahli found herself staring at the blind man as though he was a large and very appealing piece of candy. She was pleasantly imagining what it would feel like to run her hand over the soft, gleaming fabric covering his stomach, when he spoke and ruined her daydream.

"I've been following your adventures on the receiver. You've been through quite a lot."

Dahli's eyes roamed up his long legs. "Yeah I guess I have. I haven't really had much of a chance to think about it yet. It will probably all sink in after I get home and things are quieter."

She thought about home, and forgot about how beautiful the man before her was. She didn't know if she wanted to go home. She didn't know if she wanted to talk about anything that had occurred to her with Teirra and Atterick. She wanted the entire time she had been in the Centre to fall into a large hole and vanish. Dahli abruptly felt very old, tired and sad, and she sighed heavily, shakily.

Gia cocked his head, listening. "Donselle?"

"Oh I was just thinking about the Centre. Sorry."

He smiled, very gently, and then he was pretty again. "Don't concern yourself. Let's see if we can't get Donsa CZimcocious to bring us the wine, na?"

The three sat and drank together for a few hours, talking with greater ease than Dahli would have thought possible. She was secretly pleased when Draephus thumped himself into the seat beside her, and she took advantage of his proximity to lean against him. He didn't seem to mind, and this also pleased her. She thought she could probably get used to this.

The topics ranged far and wide, starting with faelins, moving over to the Revolution, and getting stuck on what types of biscuits went well with tea before realising that was a pointless topic and going over to music. Dahli admitted that, although her heart belonged to the Mortified Gryphons, she was also quite fond of Anazampini and J'Vanni Dei Syncopius. The last admission seemed to amuse Gia to no end, and Dahli said, slightly defensively, that although a lot of people she knew seemed to regard him as downright strange, she thought he was wonderful. This seemed to amuse the pale man even more.

"What's your favourite composition?" he asked.

"Well I really like `Some People Who Haven't Deserve To,'" Dahli said, then paused, smiling, "but my absolute favourite is `Epitaph on a Small Insect That I Accidentally Stepped On.'"

He roared with laughter. "Oh you can't be serious."

"Why not?"

"It's awful, it's complete nonsense. Any resemblance between that and actual music is imaginary."

"Well I like it."

He laughed softly, shaking his head. "Oh that has to be the most amusing thing I have heard in days." He rose shakily to his feet. "Now I'm afraid I have to take a nap, this has all been rather much for me. Will you stay for dinner?"

Dahli was a little annoyed with him laughing at J'Vanni Dei Syncopius, but she still liked him.

"Sure," she said. "Thank you."

He nodded, then turned and headed off down the hallway to his room, still chuckling. Dahli watched him go, then looked up at Draephus.

"Well, glad he's amused. I like him. What happened to his face? That looks pretty recent."

"That's kind of a touchy subject. Basically what happened was some fringe group found out that he was Kryphisian and shot him. Fortunately they just grazed him, if that's the word. Night Stalkers do a lot of damage. He's lost his sight, and the doctors told him he would be permanently scarred, but I don't think he knows how bad it is. And I'm not gonna tell him."

Dahli pondered this, then looked to Draephus. "Harli wasn't supposed to let slip that Gia is Kryphisian, was he?"

"No, but he spends a lot of time alone, and the people who do come visit know about Gia, so I guess he thought since you know me, that you did too. Anyway… please don't mention it to anyone. He's already had one close brush with death. We'd like to keep him a little while longer."

"I won't," said Dahli softly. "I swear on my newly-gained status as a warrior and an adult that I won't."

"Thanks, Fearless."

Draephus sipped at his wine, falling silent, looking distant and tortured, as if he was holding something back. Dahli leaned forward, reaching a hand out to him.

"Are you all right?" she asked softly, touching his arm.

Draephus almost broke; Dahli could virtually see the crack opening up. He glanced away from her, shaking. He gained his composure, then said softly, "It's just that a lot has been going on, and as much as I'd like to tell you about it, I can't, I'm sorry. Let's just say I'm here to keep Gia company because he's going through a very hard time, and it affects me, too." Then he turned to look at Dahli and smiled, reaching out to put his large, scarred hand over hers. "But I'm really glad you're back."

There was an uncomfortable silence, and Dahli was suddenly very aware of how close Draephus was, and how blue his eyes were. She suddenly found him attractive, but not in the same way she had his pretty friend, nor in ways she had previously. He had suddenly become human, and a warm comfort replaced the tension. The man before her had just become her friend.

****

The evening cruised by slowly. Dahli ended up falling asleep on the couch for a few hours, and Draephus took advantage of the lull to entertain himself in J'Vanni's home studio. Many of the instruments in it were the inventions of either Delaes or J'Vanni, and Draephus wanted a chance to play with all of them before he had to leave. He was amusing himself by running a quinticord through the reverb on the millitron when he heard the door open and J'Vanni stood before him.

"Having fun?" he asked dryly.

Draephus grinned sheepishly, setting down the quinticord. "Yeah, actually, I was. You know, you really should perform live. Now that you... well, I mean the only way to tell you're Kryphisian is by your eye colour."

"And now that I don't have eyes I should tour, is that it?"

"That's not what I meant. You make incredible music, and all on these instruments that you made. It could be wonderful."

"Oh don't be ridiculous, Draephus, I'm no show man." J'Vanni walked forward cautiously, reaching the millitron and resting his hands on the gleaming black surface. He gently played a few notes.

"I'll bet you could be incredible," said Draephus. "Come on. Think about it. J'Vanni Dei Syncopius first live appearance at the Charlendine Year End Festival."

"Followed quickly by J'Vanni Dei Syncopius shot on stage at the Charlendine Year End Festival. Someone knows about me, Draephus. Knows about me, and my beloved scatter-brained husband. No." J'Vanni paused and fell silent. Draephus stopped next to him, watching the Kryphisian as his thoughts went out to his missing lover. "Do you think he's all right, Draephus?"

"He'll be fine," said Draephus, trying to reassure him.

J'Vanni shook his head, then sighed. "I love him, Draephus. I want him to come home. Well, take me to the living room, I shall keep the Donselle company while you make dinner."

"Have a fondness for burned kaisa, do you?"

"Not especially, no. Perhaps we will make other arrangements for dinner." J'Vanni extended his arm for Draephus to lead him.

****

Dahli was sitting on the edge of the couch with a bad taste in her mouth when the two walked into the living room. She gave Draephus a bleary smile.

"I guess I was tired," she said. "How long was I out?"

"A couple hours," he said.

Gia sat down on the couch next to her as Draephus sat on the floor and lit a cigarette. Gia's hawk landed next to his master, sidling closer to gently pluck at the long silver hair. Dahli cautiously touched the feathery, golden brown back. The bird turned to look at her, staring at her with the cold eyes of his kind, but he did not seem to object. Then he stepped regally over to her and put his head down for her to rub the back of his neck.

"Well you're friendly, aren't you?" she said, smiling. She

rubbed the back of the bird's head, wondering how much damage he could do with his huge, hooked beak and claws.

"He's very friendly," said Gia. "And very good company. I spent endless days teaching him to speak, but unfortunately the only word he learned was `yuck.' He uses it appropriately."

The huge bird stepped onto Dahli's arm, ruffling its feathers. "What's his name?"

"Piska, but we call him 'Picky'." Gia reached out to touch the large bird. "Now the interesting thing about Picky is he is the biggest problem with your theory about faelins."

Dahli's attention snapped to the man next to her, and Draephus, recognising the weird gleam in her green eyes, decided this was a good time to leave the room.

"Would you care to expound on that?" she said.

"Certainly. Now at the risk of having you hurt me, and I *have* heard about what you did to Donsa CZimcocious, I can assure you that faelins are not human."

Predictably, Dahli went off like a rocket. "THAT IS THE MOST RIDICULOUS THING I KEEP HEARING! OF COURSE THEY'RE HUMAN, IT WAS THE GREY BOYS WHO KEPT SAYING THEY AREN'T."

"Assuming for one moment the `Grey Boys' may have been right, and assuming you will stop shouting at me long enough to listen to me..."

Dahli closed her mouth and listened. Gia continued.

"Faelins are *not* human. They are faelins. They are a distinct race unto themselves, found nowhere else in all the discovered planets. Now let's look at Picky. Is he human?"

Dahli looked at the bird and smiled. "No."

"Would you hurt him?"

"No, of course not. He's a living creature, he has feelings."

"And that is where your feelings about faelins become confused. We should not be worrying about the faelins because they are like us. We should worry about them because they are alive."

Dahli glanced up at him, blinking. She stared at him for a long moment, then said; "I didn't think of it like that."

He reached out and put a hand on her arm. "We should not only concern ourselves with creatures that fit into our ideas about ourselves. The fact that a creature is alive is enough to give it respect.

Once the...`Grey Boys'... knew this too, but things change, sometimes for the worst. They are more to be pitied than despised. They will have to sit on their planet and wonder where their plans went wrong, and they will most likely never learn why, even though they once knew the answer." Gia shook his head, then sighed. "Anyway, enough said. What shall we eat?"

****

Dahli and Draephus departed after dinner, leaving J'Vanni to himself for a while. Rysta would be back within a couple hours, and J'Vanni assured Draephus he would survive for two hours. Draephus promised to return soon, then, as they entered the lift he mumbled, "He ought to just hire someone to look after him for a while."

"Why doesn't he?" asked Dahli.

"He's afraid to have anyone in his house he doesn't know, at least if he's by himself. Gia hasn't been out of that apartment for five years. If he wasn't friends with Delaes he would never even have made a recording..." Draephus stopped and went pale. Dahli leaned closer and peered at him, eyes narrowing.

"Oops," said Draephus, feeling her eyes on him. "Cold in here, isn't it? Wow this lift takes a long time to get to the lobby."

"A recording? That man has a cylinder out, and he hasn't been out of his home in five years? Gee let's see if I can figure this out. Could his full name be J'Vanni Dei Syncopius?"

Draephus gazed at her sidelong. "You're not going to hurt me, are you?"

"You let me make a complete fool of myself in there!" She whacked him on the arm. "No wonder he started laughing when I said I liked his music. At least I *liked* him, can you imagine if I thought his music stunk? Draephus how could you?" She whacked him again, then her eyes grew large. "Oh clart. I called J'Vanni Dei Syncopius a Grey Boy. TO HIS FACE! I'm gonna DIE...

"OW! Leave me alone, will you? He wanted to meet you and I thought you might be more willing to just talk if you didn't know who he was. And it's not the first time he's heard it."

"You should know better. I was perfectly willing to beat you up and I knew FULL WELL who YOU were." She whacked him again.

"Okay, that's it." Draephus grabbed her and slung her over his shoulder. "If you're going to act like a delinquent, I'll treat you like one."

Dahli just hung there for a moment, stunned. "Put me down or I'll brain you."

"Won't be the first time." The lift doors opened, and he stepped out, still with her over his shoulder.

Dahli thought about his words, then snorted. Instead of fighting with him, she dug through his pocket for his cigarettes, managing to light one in her inverted position.

Draephus carried her to the air-con and gently dumped her into the front seat, quinticord and all, then walked around to the driver's side. He got in and started the silent engine, the only indication of its presence being a soft vibration. He pulled back the throttle, and the vehicle lifted, turning silently before heading down the broken streets of Avalair. Occasionally as they drove they would see a figure dart off into the darkness of the city. Dahli didn't pay them any heed, but Draephus noticed them all, glancing at them in hopes of seeing one in particular.

They quickly left Avalair behind; soon the air-con had descended the boat launch near the Hydrotrans and was driving across the channel towards Second City. They moved quickly over the black water, suspended in the perfect Sferkkaan night between the two tiny points of light which were the cities as though they were in a tiny space ship, heading for regions unknown. Indeed the city they were now going to did indeed have an unfamiliar feel to it to Dahli, and she felt a little as though she could never face Atterick and Teirra ever again. She did not want to discuss the Centre, then or ever. She just wanted to forget about it.

She was brought out of her revelations by the slowing of the air-con, and she glanced at Draephus as he throttled down the vehicle, stopping it on the calm surface of the channel water. The phosphorous green light of the control panel gave him a strange, other-worldly appearance, and she stared at him questioningly as he turned to look at her. She half-wondered if he was going to toss her into the water.

"You asked me why I blew up that night," he said.

Dahli turned in her seat to look at him. "Yes, I did."

He reached out to turn off the receiver. Silence filled the near-dark air-con, and Dahli could feel the gentle rolling of the water beneath them. Draephus lit a cigarette, looking thoughtful. He reached out to idly pick at the metal frame of the receiver.

"I want to say that I didn't set out to target you. I would have gotten somebody that night; unfortunately you just happened to be the one."

There was more silence, and Dahli waited. Finally he spoke again.

"Every time something goes wrong in my life, I try to fix it by making as many people miserable as possible. I get drunk, and I get into fights. It's not that I think this is a particularly effective way of dealing with my problems; it just seems to be something I do. Days before I ran into you, the man I live with, Vesper, told me that the virus he has in his heart has become active, meaning, he's going to die. Anyway, he wanted to see the South Continent before he died. So I kissed him goodbye, smiled and waved as he got on an aircraft for the South Continent, and the moment he was out of sight I went right to the Cylinder. Started my evening by running my con into a pillar. Then I got drunk, got beat up, picked up, rolled, beat up again, found my way into some filth-pit of a bar where I ended up playing all night with cracked ribs for drinks. I crawled home a couple days later, just in time to make my appearance on the Astellis Monct Show, which I believe you saw."

Dahli's mind flashed back to the programme. "Yeah I did," she said softly. He smiled a little.

"I thought I had worked all the worst of it out of my system, but I guess I hadn't. Anyway, a few nights later, when you and I went out to get my con..." He fell silent, looking thoughtful. He drew on his cigarette, exhaling clouds of smoke, which turned eerie green in the light. He tapped the ashes onto the floor, then, remembering Gia's dire threats should he do just that, he began picking the ashes up. "…I tried to call him and got this guy who said he was Vesper's new husband and I should just get lost."

"Ouch," said Dahli.

"Turned out to be a misunderstanding, but…"

He fell silent again, and for a long time neither said anything. Finally Dahli spoke.

"I'm sorry about Vesper." she said quietly.

"Yeah well I'm sorry I unloaded on you."

"You… were not well," said Dahli.

"What do you mean?"

"You were... I don't know how to explain it. At one point you were just sitting in the con and shaking, and I knew there was something really wrong. It's... kinda the only reason I forgave you. Yeah you should not have taken things out on me. But... you were in pieces, and even I could see that. So... it's okay. I forgive you. And I am sorry I kicked you in the ribs and ruined your conni."

Draephus was quiet for a time longer, then shook himself as though coming out of a dream. He started the air-con up again. "Ready to go home?"

She nodded, and turned on the receiver. The Mortified Gryphons came blasting out. Draephus promptly turned off the device.

"Hey that's my favourite song!" Dahli protested.

"I'm not listening to myself going across the channel. Dahli!" he yelled as she turned it back on again. He grabbed for the receiver, and Dahli latched onto his arm.

"Come on, have a heart. I have forty-two Mortified Gryphon cylinders at home and I haven't heard any of them in over six months."

"Forty-two? Where did you *get* forty-two? Why would you *want* forty-two? Turn off that band now!"

"Make me, old man."

"That's it, you're in the channel now."

The air-con bobbed and rocked over the channel, the music stopping and starting, echoing off into the darkness and carrying for miles over the smooth water.

*****

They pulled up before Dahli's house at about mid-morning, soaked through. The seats of J'Vanni's con were wet as well, and there were puddles beneath their feet. They had both spent a fair amount of time in and out of the channel.

"Well, you're home." said Draephus, looking up at the little house.

"Yeah, I guess I am." said Dahli. She still felt some nervous tension within her stomach, but now she was at least ready to be there. She smiled at Draephus. "Thanks for the ride home."

He grinned at her, broken front tooth in full view. "Anytime," he said quietly.

The two sat together for a time in silence, then Dahli said; "Do you think I'll see you sometime?"

"Oh could be," he said casually. "Maybe you could give me a call sometime."

"Maybe," she said. She got out of the air-con, pausing to look back at him. "See you," she said softly.

He gave her a wave, and the door closed. Dahli stepped onto the sidewalk and watched the air-con lift, then fly down the street until it was out of sight.

Dahli walked slowly and quietly up the steps of her house, feeling almost as though she didn't belong there. Setting down the quinticord, she carefully opened the door and stepped inside. It was quiet in the little house. Music played softly within the kitchen, and she could hear Atterick and Teirra talking. Dahli placed her bag and quinticord down in the hall and advanced slowly down the hall.

She was a mere few feet from the kitchen door when she decided to change her approach and silently left the house once more, making her way down the steps. She stood at the bottom of them for a moment, then ran up them as hard as she could, bashing the door open and thundering across the floor to the kitchen. She leapt into the room, dirty and wet, with the rooster feathers on her hat askew.

"Heia people," she said, grinning.

Atterick and Teirra stared at her for a long moment, faces blank with amazement. Suddenly they both leapt on her with a vengeance, hugging her and demanding to know where she'd been and how she'd gotten home and how she was.

"I'm fine," she said, hugging Teirra. "I've been hiding with a crazy old man in a cabin full of chickens."

"Dahli we were so worried about you. We've been hearing so many horrible things about the place you were in..."

"Yeah well they're all true. I'm hungry."

"Dahli... did..."

"I don't want to talk about it. *Any* of it. I'm home, I want to stuff my face, call up some friends, and enjoy myself. I'd rather not think about anything right now." Dahli lit a cigarette and flopped down into a chair with a wet squelching noise. She giggled.

"Wow, home is so normal it's scary." She looked at Teirra and

Atterick, cigarette smouldering between her lips. "I really missed both of you. I can't tell you how often I have wanted to be back in this house, in this kitchen."

Teirra smiled. "We missed you too."

Atterick stood up. "You're hungry, huh? Well that sounds like you." He opened the coldbox. "What do you want to eat?"

"Anything, and lots of it." Then as an afterthought, Dahli said, "No chicken."

Chapter Eighteen

Draephus went home after dropping Dahli off, shedding wet clothes as he walked down the hall to his bedroom. He had called J'Vanni to make sure he was all right, and was relieved to learn Stratavarus had dug up someone to watch him. Pleased with this turn of events, Draephus poured himself a large belt of mushroom distillation and carried it up into his bedroom. Wearing nothing, holding the glass of liquor, he walked into his bedroom and dropped down onto his bed. Delaes still hadn't come home, but at least Dahli had, and Vesper seemed to be holding up well. Draephus felt some of the knots in his stomach melt away. He rolled onto his stomach luxuriously, like a large feline, and waved a hand in the general direction of the stereo ball. It glowed silently into life, and the towering amp-plants arced expectantly.

"Select Imperial Chant number 33," he said, and a moment later the soothing, rich music filled the room. Draephus closed his eyes and sighed contentedly. He smiled as he thought of Dahli. He liked her, genuinely liked her. Not very many people had been granted that honour. He suddenly reached for the telecom, and, without thinking about it, called her number. Dahli snatched up the 'com before it had finished ringing once.

"I'm home I'm home I'm home!" This statement was followed by rolls of demonic laughter. Draephus grinned.

"I know, I'm the one who brought you there."

"Oh heia!" said Dahli brightly. "Wasn't expecting to hear from you so soon."

"Yeah well I was just thinking of you."

"Yeah well there's coincidence, I was just thinking of you. Why did you let me go over the wall when you were only a few feet away, and had in fact come to get me?"

"*Let* you! I didn't *let* you do clart, Fearless. Why were you so inconsiderate as to wait for me to show up before you did it?"

"MAYBE I WAS GETTING YOU BACK FOR THE LITTLE JOKE WITH J'VANNI DEI SYNCOPIUS!"

Draephus laughed rustily. "Yeah all right, I'll accept that." He grinned fondly. "Welcome home."

****

Dahli talked on the com with Draephus for quite a while, finally hanging up after the mushroom he was drinking began to go to his head. Dahli came away from the telecom bouncing.

"I'm home I'm home I'm home!" she chanted. She bounced in circles around Atterick. "When does school start?"

"Last week," he said, watching her a little worriedly.

"So I can go tomorrow? My life can go back to normal?"

"Yes and yes. Who was on the telecom?"

"Draephus. He's my friend. He likes me. He thinks I'm fun. So does J'Vanni Dei Syncopius." Dahli was punctuating every statement with a bounce. Atterick was getting a headache watching her.

"Where did you meet J'Vanni Dei Syncopius?"

"At his house. Last night. We had supper there."

"STOP BOUNCING! You had supper with him? The man no one has ever seen?"

"I've seen him, he's beautiful. He's tall and very regal, and he has these *looonnng* legs that make you just want to... anyway, yes I met him."

Atterick stared at her sourly. "Great. *I'm* the musician, and *you* know Draephus and J'Vanni."

"Well what can I say, Atterick, maybe you just need to hang around more bathrooms."

****

Dahli awoke the next morning, flung back the covers and bounced out of bed. She was home, everything was fine, life was just the way it had been before. With the possible exception being that she was actually looking forward to going to school. She dressed and came downstairs, tail feathers on her hat waving. Teirra looked up in surprise as Dahli came prancing into the kitchen.

"I was just about ready to go wake you."

"No need," said Dahli. She thumped down at the table and poured herself a glass of almaniki juice. Teirra smiled at her fondly.

"I'm glad to see you back."

"I'm glad to *be* back, I can't *tell* you how glad I am to be back." Dahli drank her juice, then got up and walked over to Teirra, leaning over her shoulder. "What's for breakfast, assuming there is any?"

Dahli ate her breakfast, then left the house, heading down the road to where Diza lived. She reached Diza's house, heading up the steps to the front door. She knocked on it, and smiled as she heard the sound of Diza's father approaching. The door opened, and the man stood before her. Dahli opened her mouth to ask if Diza was coming to school, and he slammed the door in her face. As Dahli stared at the door in complete shock, she heard the man yelling through the house at Diza.

"I told you I don't want you hanging around with any of that group! That Sandiniti girl is back and I don't want her around, she's trouble."

Dahli stood on the steps for a time, then turned and walked away, heading once more towards the school, although with a lot of the bounce taken out of her. She walked down the sidewalk, feeling hurt and confused. She hadn't counted on this, but decided it was probably to be expected. She wondered who else had forsaken her.

Dahli turned the corner and stopped. Before her stood Randish and Czamkiar. The three stood and blinked at each other for a moment, then all three screamed in delight. Czamkiar's books went flying as he leapt on her, planting a gluey kiss on her face. He hadn't started wearing his make-up any thinner.

"Well good to see you two are still talking to me. I just got thrown out of Diza's place," said Dahli. She threw her arms around Randish's huge neck. She could have sworn he had grown a foot and gained one hundred pounds since she had seen him last.

"Oh none of us are allowed to talk to Diza anymore," said Czamkiar, picking up his books. He rose to his feet and stood carefully in his high heel boots, tossing back his white hair. He grinned at her broadly. "That's why we wait for her here in the mornings."

No sooner had he said this when they heard the sound of shoes racing up the pavement behind them. Diza charged around the corner.

"Is Dahli here? Oh Dahli!" Diza's books were the next ones to become air-borne, and she threw her arms around her neck. "I am so glad you're back! I'm sorry about my dad, he's decided that I can't talk to anybody fun anymore. When did you get back?"

"Yesterday. I wanted to surprise you."

"Well I'm surprised." Diza grabbed her around the neck once more.

The four walked down the sidewalk towards the school. Dahli smoked and talked, answering questions that her friends asked. They strolled along casually, but not so slowly they would be late. Diza couldn't chance her father finding out she was still hanging with the same crowd.

When they reached the school Diza gave Randish a kiss, and the huge Siriusian went off on business of his own. Then Diza went to class, while Czamkiar walked with Dahli to the school office to sign her back in. Dahli had tossed her cigarette away, but not before almost walking into the school with it. She decided she was a little too used to doing things her own way. It wouldn't do to come back to school behaving like a wild animal.

There was dead silence in the office as Dahli stepped into the room. Several pairs of eyes stared at her questioningly, but nobody moved to help her at first. Finally one person stood up and walked over. "Yes?"

"I want to come back to school," said Dahli. Then, a little more loudly, said; "Or don't you accept criminals?"

There was a sudden scurrying of activity about the room as everyone tried to look busy. Dahli and Czamkiar exchanged glances, shaking their heads.

A short time later Dahli was walking down the hall to class. She felt a little nervous, and she paused outside the door. She listened to the sounds within for a time, then stepped into the room, picking a seat. Unfortunately the only person in the room she knew was Atania Nightwing. But even Atania seemed a little reluctant to incite anything. Dahli leaned back in her seat and hoped the Duone wouldn't be too long.

The class door opened, and into the room stepped Duone Bathers. He walked cheerfully into the room, dropping his papers onto the desk. He greeted the class and began droning on about nothing in particular. That was one of Duone Bather's more outstanding traits. He would talk for hours about nothing. Dahli was silent, just watching. Atania glanced from Dahli, to Bathers, and back. Dahli sat back in her seat and said not a word.

Approximately half of the class had gone by before he turned around and squinted at the girl in the third row with the feathered hat on, and when he saw who it was, he froze. For a time all he could do was open and close his mouth.

"You're back!" he finally said.

"You say that like you're surprised."

"Well..." he sputtered, "Well, delighted, actually." He grinned at her jovially.

'Yeah right,' thought Dahli, noticing the sweat breaking out on his face. What was *wrong* with everyone? She decided she would ask Diza later if there was anything she should know.

Lunch time arrived, and Dahli met Diza and Czamkiar on the front steps of the school. She sat down between them.

"Half this school is terrified of me," said Dahli. "What is with these people?"

Diza and Czamkiar exchanged glances. "Well they're probably worried about the stuff they've heard on the Visual about you." said Czamkiar.

"WHAT stuff?"

"Haven't you seen the papers?" said Diza.

"No," said Dahli. "I've been too busy hiding with crazy chicken men. What's in the papers?"

"Well the riot for one thing," said Diza. "You did shoot that boy, didn't you? Then there was that councillor found dead in his apartment. Some idiot bashed his brains in with an oven door, then wrote a suicide note to leave on the table."

"Well I didn't do *that*!" said Dahli in surprise. She fell silent, becoming thoughtful. "I wonder who did?"

Diza shrugged. "A lot of people seem to think *you* did. They're saying some strange things about you, Dahli. They're saying that the Emperor had the rest of your sentence forgiven because you have links to bands of ex-revolutionaries."

Dahli uttered a noise of exasperation. "The only `band' I have any links to is the Gryphons."

Diza nodded. "And what were the Gryphons before the Revolution ended?"

"Oh and I'm supposed to believe that Draephus knocked off my councillor. That's just too silly. I get into some trouble and now everyone has lost their mind. What have you got for lunch? Teirra gave me sliced ocrish and I hate the stuff."

Dahli and Diza traded sandwiches and ate them on the steps, enjoying the warm, late summer day.

****

Draephus pulled up in his grey conni and stopped before the front gates of Gryphon Studios. He waited for them to open, then drove through and parked near the huge building. He turned off the engine and sat in the conni, lighting a cigarette. He tossed the lighter onto the dashboard, getting out of the conni and shutting the door behind himself. The air was becoming cool, and he pulled his trademark long battered coat about himself. Lowering his head, he walked towards the studio.

He entered the large, brightly lit building, making his way to the studio to find the other four members of the band sitting around waiting for him. Draephus broke into a grin when he saw them.

"Heia people."

"Where have you been?" said Raski. "Clart, man."

"Shut up, Raski," chirped Khandid. Yuri hung back behind him, trying to look inconspicuous and failing miserably.

"Can we all act like adults?" said Mars tiredly. He glanced about at the group, then consulted a piece of paper. "Now before we get to work..."

"Mars, Khandid poked me," said Raski as he and Khandid pushed each other back and forth.

"...I would just like to say that we should try very hard to remember we are friends. No matter how bad we think each other's ideas are, we should try to be diplomatic. Draephus, this means you. If you *do* get angry, and must throw something, please make certain it's not too expensive. Last year you tossed a several thousand trinta laser keybarr through the studio window in an attempt to brain Khandid. We'll have no more of that."

"Yeah!" said Khandid.

"Khandid," said Mars, "you are under no circumstances to reprogram Raski's sepulchord so that it only makes barnyard noises. Let's try to be professional, shall we? Raski, you are not allowed to pick on the technicians, the last five we had quit. The ones we have now used to work for Bad Influence, so we seem tame in comparison, but there is still no need to traumatize them."

There was an uncomfortable silence, with no one asking why Bad Influence were not using the technicians. Mars cleared his throat, pushing a wisp of hair behind one ear.

"My question right now is do we release this album before or after the Year End Festival?"

"I vote for after," said Raski. "We'll have new music to play at the festival and we won't have to rush."

"I agree with Raski," said Draephus.

"Oh you would, Donsa Not-Having-An-Affair," said Khandid.

"We are not having an affair," said Draephus and Raski in unison.

"Well then what *are* you having?" asked Khandid.

"A lot of unfulfilled sexual fantasies based on a solid foundation of knowing how badly we want each other but neither of us is willing to go behind Vesper's back," said Raski.

"Oh," said Khandid. Then – "An affair would be a lot more fun."

"Yes it would," said Draephus. He reached up to touch Raski's black hair. "But in the meantime we have vowed to be good boys."

"Aw that's so *swee*t!" gushed Mars.

"Oh I'm going to be sick in a corner," said Khandid.

"Just go stand over there and pretend to be a quinticord player," said Raski.

****

They took a break several hours later, and Draephus took advantage of the lull to wander down the hall and call Dahli. He punched the code into the telecom, then waited. A moment later Dahli answered.

"Heia?"

"Heia."

"Draephus!" she said, and Draephus smiled at the way her voice warmed. "Where are you?"

"Playing with the kids," he said. "We just stopped for a minute to grab a bite, then we're going back to work."

"How is it going?"

"Oh not bad. No fights yet."

"You people fight? You all seem so close."

"We are. We're family, we love each other. It's just that after being jammed in a studio for hours on end we happen to think that each other are no-talent clartblossoms who couldn't write lyrics to save the Empire." In the background there was a terrific crash. "Oop," said Draephus. "Sounds like someone is annoyed. This wouldn't be so bad if we didn't insist on doing things to each other. Once Khandid stashed feralyke dung on a plate in the coldbox just to see what would happen."

"And?"

"Let's just say I don't think Mars ever fully recovered. Anyway, what are you doing now?"

"Not a lot, why?"

"Want to come down and watch? I mean, it won't be real terribly exciting..." There was another crash.

"Or maybe it will be," she said "I'll see you in a bit."

"All right," he said, and hung up. Pleased with himself, he turned and headed towards the commissary.

****

Dahli arrived on Atterick's kuvon, parking it next to Draephus' grey conni. She took a few moments to look at the other connis before going into the huge and not terribly attractive building. A sense of nervousness and being someplace she shouldn't came over her as the uniformed security man let her in, and she walked past the enormous statue of a gryphon in the lobby. She was in unfamiliar territory, Draephus' home turf. She wondered about what the other Gryphons would think of her being there, and almost turned and left. If it hadn't been for the security man next to her lending some moral support, she would have.

He led her into the green room, where she could grab herself something to drink before going into the studio, then left her there. She poured herself a glass of hot tea and took a sip. It burned all the way down, then hit her stomach and ignited. Dahli shook her head, deciding not to take such a large swallow next time. Then she walked over to the coldbox and began going through it.

Raski stopped in the doorway and considered the back end he saw in the cold box. He was fairly sure it was not a familiar back end, and it appeared to be female. Therefore, he assumed, the front end that was now stuffing itself probably was as well. He entered the room, curious, and peered over the girl's shoulder. She was grazing her way through various munchies and delicacies, apparently unaware anyone was there. Raski watched for a time, then reached past her to get something for himself.

Dahli watched the hand come into the coldbox. It was a dark-skinned hand, long and beautifully formed. There was a ring on it, as well as a delicate chain about the wrist. Both looked very expensive. The hand grabbed a plate of smoked fish and brought it out. Dahli followed the hand with her eyes, turning to see its owner standing beside her. His black hair flopped over his eerie blue eyes as he stared back at her.

"The fish is good," he said.

"Heia Raski. I hadn't worked my way over to it yet," said Dahli. "Draephus asked me to come watch him play."

"Watch *him* play? No no no no… he is the drummer. He does not play. He is the guy who hangs around musicians." He cocked his head and looked at her. "You know I would have sworn you were older."

"Yeah?" said Dahli, picking up her drink. "I guess I will be eventually. Sooner or later I'll even be as old as you." Then she left. Raski had to think about the statement for a moment before he realized he'd been insulted. Then he followed after her, doing what he did best – being a nuisance. He waggled his eyebrows at her.

"So what are you doing tonight?"

"I have to be in bed early, I have school in the morning."

"Ah. Well, that puts me in my place. How about tomorrow night?"

"Go away," said Dahli.

He followed her to the studio, staying right behind her as she entered the room. Draephus looked up from a tape he was listening to and motioned her over.

"Heia," he said. Pointing at Raski, he asked, "Is he bothering you?"

"Yes."

"Oh good, I was worried he might have learned to behave in my absence."

Raski feigned hurt and walked away. Dahli sat down on a

stool next to Draephus where she could observe without being in the way.

"He caught me with my face in the coldbox," said Dahli, watching Raski go. "He's pretty, isn't he?"

"Oh yeah," said Draephus, glancing after his friend. "Yeah, he's *very* pretty."

Draephus grinned, ejecting a thin cylinder from the almost featureless black board. Then he yelled over at an unseen figure, "This one's not bad, we may even be able to pass ourselves off as musicians. If you listen real hard you can even hear the words to the song." He set the cylinder down and stood up. "Well nothing to be done about it. We'll just have to get the engineers to fix it and start all over again. Great day I picked to have you show up and watch."

"Problems?" she asked.

"Oh, well, yeah." said Draephus. "The engineers should have it cleared up before too long. Technical break down of the sort you'd have to ask them about. In the meantime all the music we had stored in the memory board sounds like a group of guys who can't play stuck in a sandstorm. Want me to show you around?"

"You don't sound too angry," said Dahli as they left the room.

"I was an hour ago." said Draephus. "I would have gladly eaten someone's brains for lunch. Here, let's go down this way... oh there's Khandi. Khandi!"

He turned to look at Draephus, blue eyes shaded by pink glasses. "Did my solo survive?"

"Well the technician says it can be restored, so… yes."

Khandi sagged with relief. "Thank whatever gods that used to watch us before the Kryphisians shot them." He turned to Dahli. "Heia! I'm Khandid. What are you doing hanging around this aging clart? You know rumour has it he's a dirty old man. I should know, I made it up myself."

"Khandid," said Draephus. "Don't you have something to do?"

"I did, but I'm finished now." Khandid turned his attention back to Dahli. "So where do you go to school?"

Draephus straightened, his eyes narrowing. For a moment he simply glared at the smaller man, then spoke very softly. "Khandid, go find something to do."

Khandid was miffed but hardly daunted. He turned his attention back to Dahli. "Nice meeting you. Come by sometime without the big ugly one." Then he left.

"Insufferable pink nuisance," said Draephus. "He gets on my nerves sometimes. Which of course is exactly what he is trying to do."

Dahli smiled. "He's pretty bold, isn't he? You wouldn't lose him in a crowd."

"We try," said Draephus. "Come on, I'll show you the control room. Oh and there's Mars, well well well."

"I'm being checked out, aren't I?" Dahli said. "It's not really surprising, girls are kinda rare animals."

"Yeah, I guess you are," said Draephus. "But Mars is at least too polite to be obvious about it."

"So can I assume the next person after Mars will be Yuri?"

Draephus grinned. "I doubt it. Yuri doesn't meet people if he can help it. I have no idea what he is doing in a band, other than he's brilliant and he's half the reason we're as popular as we are. But the man does *not* like to meet people. Oh, there he is. Watch... see? Looks around, spies me… spies *you*… note the body language. Do I stay and make nice, or do I try to creep away?" He grinned. "Poor Yuri. Heia Yuri, come say heia. This is Dahli."

Yuri clearly would have rather been anywhere else other than meeting Dahli. He towered above her, balanced delicately on long legs and five inch heels. He extended his hand towards her, a slow, formal gesture. She took his hand in hers. It was well formed, and very long. It wrapped about hers, gently engulfing and hiding it. It was his left hand, and she found his sixth finger almost as unnerving as his distant, muddy green eyes and slow, cautious movements.

"Pleased to meet you," he said, then he withdrew his hand and backed up a pace. He looked extremely uncomfortable, not knowing how to extract himself from this situation. Draephus was the one who saved him.

"If you're looking for Khandid, he's with the technicians."

"Oh, thank you, I was just looking for him." He nodded at Dahli. "Nice meeting you." Then he stepped carefully around the both of them, disappearing down the hall. He had just stepped out of sight when at the opposite end of the hall they herd Raski yell.

"Hey old man, are you here to play or to stand in the hall and look good?"

"I thought the board was bust."

"We unbusted it."

Draephus offered his arm to Dahli, and she took it. Together the two followed Raski into the main recording chamber. She spotted a familiar slender little form with long brown hair and the most amazing big green eyes, and felt her knees turn to goo.

"Heia!" she said.

Straif looked up and smiled as he spied her, fingers still slipping over the neck of his quinticord. "Heia! I didn't know you were here!"

"Draephus invited me down," said Dahli. "He didn't mention you."

"Oh he didn't, huh," said Straif.

Draephus made a show of looking around, as if realizing he was in the wrong room, then left. Straif just shook his head.

"I think he's hoping we'll get to be friends," said Straif.

"Friends with a boy? Gee I don't know…"

He smiled. "Want to go to the Cylinder tonight?"

"Sure." She leaned back against a carefully soundproofed wall, watching him play. "How are you feeling?"

He shrugged. "Okay I guess. I'm only a little over three weeks, so apart from throwing up every morning and having mad cravings for kaisa…."

"Eeeeeeeyewwww…."

"I fully agree but they're all I want to eat anymore. Anyway I'm hoping I'm not too pregnant to play the Festival. Are you going?"

"No. That would require trinta, *and* a sister who is willing to let me out of her sight after some of the stuff I've pulled recently."

Straif gave her that grin that made her want to melt. "Well it's another eight months. Plenty of time to talk her into letting you go."

"Straif, in eight months you will be nine months pregnant."

"Still leaves me another two months to go. I'll be fine."

"You will be enormous." She watched his fingers fly over the neck of the quinticord. "How… do you do that?"

"I don't know, if I think about it I can't do it."

There was a click, and a loud voice intoned; "Fearless…"

Dahli shrieked as she was startled, and sat down hard, hand over her heart. "WHAT?" she demanded, panting.

"The sooner you two stop talking, the faster we can get out of here."

Dahli picked herself up off the floor, smiling weakly. "I have to go now, anonymous voices from above say so."

"I'll be done soon," Straif said. "Then we can go."

There came another click. "Not without the Anonymous Voice from Above you're not."

Dahli left the room and went into the recording booth to sit beside Draephus. "You really are just a big stinky brat, you know."

"Well someone has to be," he said, and grinned.

****

Dahli called Teirra to let her know she would be late, then she and Straif got into Draephus' grey conni with him and Raski both. Before they left, she had gone into the bathroom and carefully painted the single blue line beneath her eyes; the line she had earned fighting for a belief. It wasn't much, but it was hers, and she was proud of it.

"You ever been to the Cylinder?" asked Straif as the conni started forward.

"No I like to stay away from places where dead burned bodies are lying around the parking lot."

"Ah that rarely happens," said Draephus dismissively, grinning.

"Very comforting," said Dahli.

The Cylinder was not far from the studio, but it may as well have been on another planet. The houses near where Dahli lived were still badly damaged and lacking pieces, but they had been cleaned and made habitable until such time as the neighbourhood could be rebuilt. But the area around the Cylinder was as it had been the moment the war ended. Broken vehicles scattered about, most burned, some still containing the rotting remains of their Kryphisian drivers and passengers. Carrion creatures still skittered about, remembering when this was a land for feasting, still hoping to find a crumb of flesh or drop of blood. Wild brambles grew over some of the carnage, and the streets were strange broken landscapes that had to be carefully negotiated. Across the broken remains of one wall, someone had scrawled a line from a Mortified Gryphons song;

> *"You stood upon a thin layer of death and called yourselves gods. Until the dried blood cracked, and what emerged, you had no words for…"*

"Always liked that line," said Raski softly.

"Yeah Yuri comes out with some good ones, for a guy who almost never opens his mouth," said Draephus.

"What's funny is I was nowhere near the Cylinder the night that happened," said Straif, "but to this day I have nightmares about it."

"The whole incident was a nightmare," said Draephus. "Sometimes I feel bad for those Kryphisian children, though. Can't imagine what they thought we were when we started coming out of the walls, floors, and closets."

They approached the formidable tower, jutting out of the cracked and broken pavement, rising from a graveyard of shattered black buildings. They slipped down a ramp to an underground parking lot, and Raski glanced at the pair of teens in the back seat.

"You two stay close."

"You have nothing to worry about," Dahli said, her eyes enormous as something huge with a humped back, long dangling arms, and the face of a feralyke loped past, giving her just enough time to see it and question her sanity.

They parked near a door, and Draephus got out of the vehicle, looking around carefully. Dahli watched him as the years dropped away, and she saw the man who had called this place home. His movements were dramatic and purposeful, knowing things were watching in the darkness. He drew out a laser pistol and loaded it, eyes scanning the gloom. He put the pistol into his coat pocket, then drew out a truly enormous knife from his boot, wiping the gleaming blade on his thigh before replacing it. Dahli watched as a few of the shadows skulked away, the message clear – these people were armed, and they knew what lay beyond the light. Draephus opened the door for Dahli.

"What were those?" she asked softly.

"*Varadasai*," said Draephus. "The Homeless Nightmares. They used to be Sferkkaans, but a few years in a lab cured that. They were roaming killers during the war, but now they have no masters and no homes. So they stay here, cleaning up scraps and keeping the rat population down."

"That's so sad…" said Dahli quietly.

"Yeah right up until the moment they try to eat you," said

Raski. "Come on."

Dahli stayed close as the four entered what could only be called a tunnel. The few small lights dotting the walls seemed to do almost nothing to illuminate it, and Dahli would swear they almost made the place darker. She crashed into Draephus' back as he stopped before a door and knocked.

"OW! Your coat's lumpy!"

"The coat's fine," muttered Draephus.

"Not if you walk into it with your face. Is this thing armour plated?"

Dahli poked at the coat experimentally as they waited for someone to answer the door. Straif began poking at the coat as well, the pair trying to figure out what the hard parts were. Draephus released a long-suffering sigh.

"What's your theory?" Dahli asked Straif.

"He's hoarding kaisa," said Straif. "No… wait… this thing over here is not a kaisa. This… kinda feels like an iron dildo…"

"Don't make me come back there," growled Draephus.

"Iron dildo?" said Dahli. "Exactly how practical is an iron dildo? It'll rust."

"It's not a dildo," said Raski. "He keeps the dildo on the left side."

"I'm feeling violated, here," said Draephus. "Okay – everybody stop poking. I'm sore and I'm grouchy."

"And in other redundant news," said Straif. "It rained today, feralykes eat fish, and faelins bark!"

Draephus sighed heavily once more and looked to Raski. "And you want five."

Raski took his arm, smiling. "Maybe more."

"I want a destri," said Dahli.

"If Dahli can have a destri then I want one too," said Straif.

"Are we there yet?" asked Dahli.

"Draephus, Dahli's touching me…"

The door opened, and they slipped into the room beyond it. The first thing Dahli noticed was the smell; not unpleasant, but heavy, as if the walls would never be free of it regardless of what was done to clean them. It was like flowers and wood smoke, with something mixed in. The next thing she noticed was the lack of chairs. The small, low tables that were scattered through the room were surrounded by large, firm cushions, covered with scrap fabric and leather. There was a pair of very large feralykes splayed on two of the cushions, snoring loudly, their naked skin pitted and scarred from past battles. At the far side of the room was a small stage, and lining the wooden walls were laser prints of various people and things.

A tall South Continental man had let them in, and he hugged Raski and then Draephus, before fussing over Straif like someone's concerned grandfather. Straif didn't seem to much care for this, and squiggled as the man spoke to him in a tongue Dahli did not know. However she could guess the words easily enough just from the man's gestures and tones. "You are too skinny, when did you eat last? Who put on your make-up, why can't you dress more like your cousin?"

Straif complained back in the same language as the older man took his face in one hand and re-drew Straif's make-up, widening the edges of the black band before blurring them properly. Dahli put Draephus between herself and the stranger before she found herself being subjected to the same treatment. The movement just drew attention to herself. When the man spoke, it was with a very heavy accent.

"You come out! You are next! Draephus who is that?"

"This is Fearless."

"Oh the troublemaker who climbed the fence and made you chase her! Let me see her!"

Draephus stepped aside. Moments later Dahli had her face clamped in what felt like a warm dry vice and was having her own make-up redrawn.

"Who teaches you children to draw your lines? How can anyone know who you are with such marks? Draephus, do you teach these children nothing?"

"They are not mine to teach!" said Draephus.

The older man gave Draephus a look that actually made Draephus back up. He did not relinquish his hold on Dahli's face, but he did point at Draephus with the other hand, the one liberally coated in pigment.

"You are ohwendai man. It is the business of every ohwendai man and ohwendai woman to teach the children! It does not matter who the child is, YOUR duty, Draephus CZimcocious of the Lost Royal House, is to teach the child! Where do they learn from if not their elders?! And if they do not wish to learn or to see, you MAKE them!"

The older man returned to the business of fixing Dahli's line, muttering and mumbling in a tongue she did not understand. Finally he was done, and stepped back to look at his work.

"There! Now you are right, and everyone will see who you are. You are Fearless. I am Bonnikkaar of the South. You and the Little Mother sit there. I will return."

Dahli watched him leave, then looked to Straif. "Well I'm suitably intimidated."

"Yeah let's sit down before he comes back."

"So am I now officially Fearless of the Mushroom Dens?"

Raski, Dahli and Straif seated themselves at the table Bonnikkaar had indicated, while Draephus followed after the man. Moments later a server came to set a beautiful blown glass object down on the table; a sort of strange pipe with long serpentine bits attached. With the pipe came a small basket of various items. Raski thanked him and began setting up the pipe.

"Well Fearless *is* your name in the dialect he speaks. It's not a bad name."

"No it's a great name," said Dahli. "I just don't feel it's always true. There have been plenty of times I was scared."

Raski shook his head, the clips with their white jewels flashing and glittering as his hair moved. "Fearless does not mean absolutely without fear. It means doing what needs to be done in spite of it. You've done that. It's why you are here. You're a special little girl. Wait! Sorry – you had your coming of age ceremony, you're a special woman. Anyway it's not easy to stand up when your knees are shaking. Much easier to sit down, especially when so many other people are telling you to do it. Everyone here understands that."

"Why did Bonnikkaar say Draephus was of a Lost Royal House?" asked Dahli. "Is he?"

Raski shrugged. "The capital CZ at the start of his name says there is some connection to the Imperial line. There's just no way to say how closely he may be related. That's why he won't wear gold. Khandid wears a broken line of gold because we *know* he has Imperial blood, but it was not from the family that actually ruled. His mother was a cousin. If he was a little closer we'd have put him on the throne instead of Mordrett. And then had to tape him to the seat because if there is one thing our little Khandi does not want, it's to try and decide who gets to eat."

"Yeah I don't think I'd like that responsibility either," said Dahli. She looked to Straif, and snorted with amusement. "Little Mother. That's cute."

"Yeah, adorable," said Straif. "I've got another ten months of it coming."

"Oh no," said Raski. "We are going to make sure that name sticks for a *looooong* time."

"Thank thee a bunch."

The server came back with bottles and glasses, and a pot of tea for Straif. Then he presented them with a bowl of what looked to be large, brightly coloured stones, and a small hammer.

"For Little Mother," said the server.

Straif growled. Dahli giggled.

"Do we get to share?" asked Raski.

The server gave him a swat. "No!"

The server left as Dahli and Straif snorted and giggled. Dahli picked up one of the stones, examining it.

"What are these things?"

Straif picked up one, and gave it a few strikes with the hammer. The outer casing fell away, leaving in his hand a round white morsel of soft flesh.

"They're called calurchi," said Straif. "They're some sort of little sea creature that builds a really hard house around itself. Because they are delicious and everything knows it!"

"I'd try one but I don't want to get a swat," said Dahli.

Straif hastily hid two in her coat. "Eat them when you get home. If I am caught giving them away then I'll have insulted Bonnikkaar and the others here in the worst way possible. Calurchi are very hard to collect, and in some places giving them to anyone other than an expectant mother will get you a beating."

Dahli examined the one she held, then hastily returned it to the bowl when the shell cracked open and a pair of accusing eye-stalks peered out at her. The server returned with three smaller bowls of calurchi for Dahli, Raski, and presumably Draephus when he returned. He gave Raski a swat, then walked away. Raski sighed and picked up one of the little things in the bowl.

"Oh I see how it is. Dahli and I get the calurchi that the expectant mothers didn't want."

Dahli returned the pair Straif had given her. "Let's just not risk insulting anyone."

He smiled, and inclined his head to touch noses with her. Oh she could get very used to this indeed...

"Want me to tell you about all the laser prints on the wall while we wait for Draephus?" he asked.

"Sure!"

Eventually Draephus returned, looking not particularly happy about something, but said nothing. He did, however, smile when Raski nuzzled up to him.

"What did Bonnikkaar say?" Raski asked softly.

Draephus touched noses with his friend, their lips nearly meeting. "Later. Let's just... enjoy ourselves."

They ate their calurchi, Raski setting up the pipe. More people arrived, some coming to say hello, some just sitting at tables. The feralykes refused to move and nobody made them. Then, just as Bonnikkaar came out with more tea for Straif, a man came and sat on the stage and began to play. Moments later he was joined by another man, who began to sing in a strange, haunting manner, and in a language Dahli did not know. She set down her calurchi and hammer to listen, not wanting to be rude.

Musicians came and went. Raski and Draephus sat close together, sharing the pipe, Draephus with his arm around Raski. Dahli finished her calurchi between songs, fascinated by the different types of music she was hearing, most for the very first time. She wished the area was less dangerous; she would love to come back.

It was getting late when the last musician of the night came on. Dahli heard herself gasp at the sight of him. He was about the same age as herself and Straif, or perhaps a little older. His long straight hair was held back with a jewelled clip, and his eyes were the pale, burning blue of the South Continent. But what truly enchanted her was the colour of his skin. He was black, yet not, and somehow golden...yet not really that either. She'd never seen anything like it, and she looked to Straif as she felt him nudge her.

"If Raski and Draephus had a baby, that's what it would look like."

Dahli glanced to Draephus and Raski. They were seated close, Raski resting against Draephus, blinking sleepily. She then looked back to the man on stage.

"He's not only pretty, he's talented," she said.

"That's who got me pregnant," said Straif.

"Does he know?"

"I don't know. I mean it's not exactly a secret, but I would like to tell him myself."

Dahli watched My'shlyin Achania play his quinticord, very nearly as fast as Straif, but with more complexity to his style. Of course My'shlyin Achania was older; as Straif grew older he would likely refine his style more as well.

By the time he died he would be nearly perfect.

Dahli suddenly began busily picking up the broken bits of calurchi shell on the table, being quiet, but forcing herself not to think of the fact that Straif was dying. For some reason it had just... suddenly struck her so hard...

She looked at the beautiful glass pipe on the table, then glanced at Raski and Draephus. There would be mushroom resin in the pipe, she realized. That's what this place was – a mushroom den. People would come to smoke, hear music, argue the politics of the day, plan attacks... they were a hidden world of dissidents and partisans that the average person didn't see. And she was in one...

She picked up one of the pipe stems and had a small puff of the fragrant smoke. It was an odd flavour, a bit like honey and dark earth.

"Go easy on that," said Raski. "Remember we use that stuff to kill pain and sedate the senses. We can't bring you back to your sister completely..."

"I can't feel my lower lip," said Dahli.

"You should probably put the stem down," said Raski.

"I thought I was an adult now!"

"Yeah and part of being an adult means knowing your limits," said Draephus.

Dahli watched as Raski nearly had a fit over what had just come out of Draephus' mouth. If even a quarter of the things Dahli had heard about Draephus were true, then he was not the one to be talking to her about limits.

She had one more puff of resin then put away the stem.

My'shlyin finished playing, Dahli and watched as Straif rose from the table to approach him. My'shlyin smiled as he saw Straif. They met, kissed, then left together to talk.

"What do you suppose My'shlyin will say when Straif tells

him?" asked Dahli.

Draephus shook his head, then looked to Raski, who was clearly almost asleep. "I don't know. But My'shlyin needs to know. Assuming he has not already heard. How about you? For a moment there I thought you were going to cry."

"I almost did," she said. "Just… suddenly realizing Straif is going to die. I mean… he has five years left to live. I don't know how he manages."

Draephus shook his head. "I don't either."

"What will happen to his baby?"

"Assuming he hasn't found someone to take on the role of co-parent, Raski gets it."

Dahli looked to the sleepy man. "Raski Jervyas… and a five year old."

"Yeah the idea scares me too," said Draephus. He smiled at Raski, stroking the silky black hair. Dahli leaned close and whispered into Draephus' ear.

"You are so stupidly in love with him that I'm surprised you don't glow."

He laughed quietly. "Yeah. I am. But my relationships are not up for discussion."

"Meanie. Heia, Draephus? Can we come back some time?"

He smiled. "Sure."

The three waited for Straif. Raski Jervyas was clearly ready to fall asleep at any moment. Dahli couldn't tell if Draephus was sleepy or not, but Dahli was certainly ready to find her bed. It was almost an hour before Straif returned, looking like he'd had more enjoyable conversations. His make-up was streaked and even some of his hair was damp. Dahli did not miss the cold angry look that came into Draephus' eyes.

"What did My'shlyin say?" asked Draephus.

Straif sniffed and began preparing to leave. "He was not pleased. He apparently didn't realize that when I said I was ovulating that I meant *'literally'* and *'right now'*. So he was pretty angry. Then he wanted to know how I knew it was his. Well I haven't been with anyone else."

"Give him a few days to calm down, he'll apologize," said Draephus. "This is a lot to spring on someone."

"Yes it is, and I should have told him what I was up to, but I was following a list of things that needed to happen this month and getting pregnant was on it. I should have added *'Ask My'shlyin if he wants to be a father first'* to the list, but I'm pretty, not brilliant. Anyway, let's be off. I'm exhausted, I want to soak in the bath and listen to J'Vanni Dei Syncopius. Maybe throw up at some point too. That or cry for no good reason while eating kaisa, which is a reason to cry unto itself. Maybe I'll just have a nice case of cramps coupled with a bit of spotting just to top the evening off. ŠUKAT they should really warn you about the hormones."

Draephus just smiled. "Come on, Little Mother, let's get you home to bed."

"Can I sleep at your place? I'd really rather not be alone."

"Only if you don't cry all over the faelins."

"I promise *nothing*."

They left the Cylinder, heading to Dahli's house and pulling up in the driveway. It was very late, the night was damp and a deep heavy mist lay over the ground. Dahli turned to look at Straif, reaching out to take his hand.

"I had a lot of fun. Thanks for asking me out."

"We could do it again sometime if you like. If you don't mind being seen with a hormonal teen boy who can't get his make-up on right."

"I'll have to introduce you to my friend Czamkiar."

"Is he pregnant too?"

"No but he likes to cry while eating kaisa the same as you." She then turned in the seat to lean forward and hug Draephus. "Night night."

She looked to Raski, and saw that he was asleep. Funny. She would have sworn that never happened. Then she looked to Straif, smiling. "Good night."

She climbed out of the conni, closing the door and watching as it silently vanished into the deep mist. Then she turned to walk up the stairs to her house, reaching the front door and stepping inside. She closed the door, then went to the kitchen to get some tea before she went to sleep. Teirra was awake, seated at the kitchen table.

"Have fun?"

"Yes. Lots. I heard a lot of new music and ate calurchi and drank tea and got to sit next to the most beautiful boy on the planet."

"Well I hope you were not the one smoking the mushroom

resin. You stink like a whole den of it."

Dahli sniffed her coat. "Oh. Yeah. That… was the people next to us."

"Are you making tea?"

"I was planning on it. Why?"

Teirra pointed to the clock, and Dahli's jaw dropped. She had exactly four hours to sleep before she had to get up and go to school. She sighed heavily, and just went to bed.

Chapter Nineteen

The next morning was dark and rainy when she awoke and Dahli lay in her warm bed staring at it. The telecom next to her bed rang, and she rolled over to pick it up.

"Heia?" she said groggily.

"I'm in my warm, soft bed," said a soft, teasing voice. "I have a nice fire going, and when I crawl out of it in, oh, say, two or three hours, I'm going to have a bath and a large, unhurried breakfast." Then Straif taunted, "And you have to go to school."

"May your quinticord be stolen by South Continent rebels, and may your baby be born with an extra foot, randomly placed."

Straif laughed, and Dahli heard him hang up. She hung up the telecom as well and kicked off the covers, sitting up on her bed.

She went through her full morning routine, dressing and eating breakfast before rushing out the door in order to catch up with Diza and Czamkiar. Randish was not there; they rarely saw him on days that were too cold and wet. He was for the most part confined indoors on colder days. His entire system had been designed to breathe the furnace-hot air of his planet, and the damp cool air of Sferkkaa settled in his lungs and caused bronchial problems. Diza frequently went over to visit him, but he would rarely be on the corner now that fall was settling in.

They walked to school, then parted ways for their separate classes. Dahli had language studies that day, which meant several hours with Duone Alsayers, a tall man fond of surveying students from his superior height and intellect. Dahli had never much cared for him as a person, but always regarded him as good at his job. He did, however, have days when he could make life hard for chosen students. Dahli knew the moment she walked into the class room that today was her day.

"We're going to do something simple today," Alsayers said as the class assembled, and somehow Dahli knew that it was going to be something she did not want to deal with. "Since the summer respite had not been over long, I want you to demonstrate your budding vocabularies by writing about what you did."

Mumbles arose from the class. Dahli put up her hand.

"Yes Dahli?"

"Can we use newspaper clippings?"

"Only for reference. I know the news people can write, I want to see if you can."

"I can't write," said Dahli, "I broke both my hands."

"Oh? And when was this?"

"As soon as I can find a big rock."

Duone Alsayers smiled patiently. "Good to see your time in the Detention Centre hasn't dampened your sense of humour any. The assignment is due in three days, we'll read them in class and critique them."

`Fun,' thought Dahli, and opened her book. Picking up a pen, she began to write.

WHAT I DID THIS SUMMER, BY DAHLI SANDINITI.

This summer I stole a dead body. It was neat. It smelled real bad and I had to carry it out of the school and bury it all by myself. Then I told everyone and I got sent to this camp for kids who do stuff like that. However some of the other kids there didn't like the place, even though it had lots of fun activities, like scraping moss off of the walls and washing floors. So they tried to take the place apart from the inside. I ran into them while looking for an exit. I asked if I could go and they said no and I said I had to because I left the water on in my room and they said sit down and shut up. So we did this for a few days and then some men showed up to tell us that it was time to go back to our rooms or else they would put large holes in us. After that the place became such a pain that I left, even though they did not want me to. I lived in the woods for a while, then a spaceship came down and took me to another planet so I would not have to write this stupid assignment. Duone Alsayers is a Kryphisian Militant and should not be allowed to teach. I think he houses small groups of revolutionaries in his basement and bleaches his hair.

THE END.

Dahli crumpled the paper up and stuffed it into her jacket pocket. She didn't want to write about the summer, she wanted to bury it. It wasn't something she wanted made the topic of conversation, any more than it already was. Then an idea came to mind, and she began writing furiously.

She had written quite a lot by lunchtime. When she heard the bell announcing that class was over she snatched up her books and left the room in a black mood. She dropped her books off at her locker, then set off in search of Diza and Czamki.

The day had dried up and become warm, and she found her friends sitting on the school steps. She sat down next to them with a thump and opened her lunch. Reaching in, she pulled out an enormous sandwich. Saying nothing, she took a huge bite, cramming her mouth full to the point where she could hardly chew.

"Hungry?" said Diza.

Dahli shook her head. "Angry," she said, when she was able to.

"Why?"

Dahli swallowed the rest of her mouthful, turning her green eyes to Diza. "Duone Alsayers wants us to write about our summer respite."

"Oh wonderful," said Diza. "And will you?"

"Sure," said Dahli. "He didn't say what summer it had to be, or even if it had to be the truth." She stuffed her mouth with food once more.

A tall figure came from behind them and stood on the steps before the small group. Duone Bathers watched Dahli eat, an amused smile on his face. Dahli noticed him and stared back with predatory intent.

"What?" she finally said.

"I just thought I'd congratulate you on your return to school."

"Uh-huh."

"So did you learn anything in jail?" he asked, the amused smile still on his face.

"Yeah," said Dahli. "That if you wear rubber gloves you can climb an electric fence, and that not all slime falls off a gastropod's hind end, some of it counsels the young and teaches science."

Duone Bathers studied Dahli, she ignoring him and seeming unconcerned with what he may be thinking. By this time a few of the students had gathered near her, some curious, some sneering. All backed up when she stood up abruptly and stalked off, her two friends following after her.

The rest of the day went quietly enough. Dahli was just putting her books away before heading home when she felt a presence behind her. Turning, she was mildly shocked to see Randish standing looming over her.

"Hi there," she said. "And what are you doing skulking about these halls?"

"Diza sent me in here to find you and drag you forcibly to the Contempo."

"She did, huh." Dahli closed her locker. "Well maybe I'll just drag you out, big guy." She reached up and caught hold of the alien's coarse ridge of hair on the back of his heavy neck, and pulled him along after her. Randish followed compliantly.

"Oh sure," said Diza as she saw the pair come out of the school. "I send him in there to beat you up and you drag him out by his fur."

"Give it up, Diza," said Dahli. "You couldn't set him on a deranged killer."

"That's for sure," said Randish.

"You made his hair all sweaty," said Diza, smoothing it down. "Are you up to coming with us? You didn't look like you were having a good day earlier, but I didn't want to just go without asking."

"Yeah I'll come," said Dahli. "That's about the best offer I've had all day."

The air was cool and fragrant as they walked down the sidewalk away from the school. They crossed the street and continued on their way at a leisurely speed. Randish ambled along next to Diza, a mountain of muscle and hair. Dahli could hear a faint wheeze in his breathing, and it worried her a little. He should have been at home, where it was warm, not out wandering the streets. But there he was, a veritable giant being led along by a girl half his size. He seemed content with life, if mountains can be content.

They reached the Contempo, walking into it and over to their favourite table. There were a lot of other people their own age, as well as the usual small collection of ex-revolutionaries. Randish sat next to Diza and rested his great head on her shoulder, black corded hair hanging over his face. As a server poured them each a mug of tea, Czamkiar sat next to Dahli and picked up the food list.

"What will we have to eat?" he asked.

"I have the biggest craving for shaumaus," said Diza. She

looked at Randish. "What do you want?"

He passed her a laminated sheet of paper, and Diza cast him a sidelong glance. "I ought to teach you to read."

"I'd about kill for some spicy hrabaccaus," said Dahli.

The server pouring the tea raised an eyebrow. "Not many people up here even know how to say that, let alone ask for it."

"Can I get some? I know it's only served at certain events, and I already had my coming of age party…"

"I can make some. And what would Donselle like to go with her hrabaccaus?"

"Tree Frog. I definitely want a Tree Frog."

The man paused, as if he was not certain he had heard her correctly. "I beg your pardon?"

"Tree Frog. Yri Babbi."

The man smiled in a pleasantly condescending manner. "Perhaps Donselle would like to choose something a little more…?"

Dahli rolled her eyes. Draephus and Raski had taught her how to deal with this situation. "Look don't šukat with me, groutnoll, I want a Tree Frog. Make sure the Silver comes from the Western coast of J'Halta, *not* the Eastern, and make sure it's cold enough to snap when it's going in. Layer it with the Green, don't stir it, and that frog better be dead when I hit bottom."

The man was clearly impressed. "Right away, Donselle."

The man left, returning shortly with a chilled glass, two bottles of liquor and a round green candy. He dropped the candy into the glass then poured in a layer of something that looked like mercury, swirled with clouds of grey. The moment it touched the small green ball it broke open, sending up wafting tendrils of something that smelled like flowers. As it hit the glass a faint crackling sound could be heard, and tiny fingers of what looked to be frost appeared. Next he poured in liquor the colour of darkest jade, then more silver, then more green. He next pulled out a lime and prepared to cut it, but Dahli waved it off. The man bowed and took a step back, waiting anxiously for Dahli to sample the concoction. She seemed oblivious to the fact that she now had the full attention of virtually every ex-revolutionary in the place. She picked up the drink and downed it the way Draephus had taught her; slow, in a continuous draught, catching the remains of the candy in her teeth to crunch.

Diza, Randish and Czamkiar looked around nervously as the

place erupted in applause. Dahli set the glass down and laughed.

"And was it to Donselle's taste?" asked the server.

"Wonderful, the best I have had yet."

"Then let me make you another."

"Please do."

Diza leaned forward. "Dahli where did you learn to drink like that?"

"The guys taught me."

"The guys?!" said Diza. "Since when are the Mortified Gryphons "the guys"?"

"Diza they're just people."

Diza drew a breath, putting her hand over her heart. "Blasphemy!"

Dahli snorted and giggled. "Draephus taught me. He said after what I have been through I had earned the right to drink them, and he taught me how to order one. Oh, and the lime is very important. You only need to bite the lime if the Silver is the cheap stuff to cut the bitterness. Very insulting to ask for a wedge of lime after you have already asked for the Western Silver, because it implies the bartender is cheating you."

She looked around at the decorations on the wall, seeing them with new eyes, smiling as she recognized the insignias, and understood now their meaning. Straif had taught her a great deal.

"Look, see the dragonfly with the burning wings? That is the emblem of the 'Arastins'. They were a fire fighting unit sent in to stop the jungle fires caused by Kryphisian bombers to drive ground troops into the open. And that there, that bleeding flower? That is the emblem of the 'Nocturnos', stealth troops, assassins mostly, they would infiltrate enemy compounds and go in and kill their fighters."

"Since when do you care about stuff like that?" asked Diza, a look of disbelief on her face.

"It's fascinating!" said Dahli, accepting her drink. "You have no idea how incredibly amazing it is to learn all this stuff! I spent days with people who fought in these battles and wanted to share with me what they did. Then last night I was in a Mushroom Den. I wished I'd had something to record it with, I could have written a book. It's like someone has opened my eyes and poured new colours into them."

"Mushroom den?!" exclaimed Diza. "You mean in the Cylinder?!"

"Yeah, I was there last night to hear some music. Next time I go you should come with me! It was the most amazing experience!"

"Mushroom distillate makes everything amazing, I hear," said Czamkiar, warily watching her down her second drink.

Dahli caught the candy and cracked it, savouring the sweetness of it. She set her glass down, and looked at her friends, blinking as she saw the way they were eyeing at her. As if they didn't know her.

"Come on guys, it's... it's our history. We walk daily through ruins of a war that only ended five... no six years ago, live among people who gave everything they had of themselves to make a future for us, and... what? That's the thanks they get? People who can't be bothered to find out what they did?"

"That's not what we're saying at all," said Diza. "It's just... you've kinda changed."

"Oh chicken clart, I have not. I'm still failing math. *And* science. Mostly because Duone Bathers hates me."

Diza smiled, but seemed uncertain, even a little intimidated. "I guess." She picked up Dahli's glass, meaning to taste the small amount left behind, but the server deftly plucked it from her hand.

"This is for warriors. Not children. I will bring you tea."

Diza stared, affronted and speechless as the man left. Randish leaned forward to face Dahli.

"So what did you do to qualify as a warrior, according to Draephus?"

She shrugged. "I met the three traditional challenges. I completed a task in stealth and was not caught, at least not until I blabbed it all over the place but apparently it doesn't count as being caught if you blab. I undertook a great journey in which I found knowledge, that would have been Harli, and I fire-walked. Of course I would have left that one out if I had known how to get *around* Avalair instead of heading through it."

A man at a nearby table stood up and walked over to her. He moved with a pronounced limp, and part of his face was hidden behind a leather mask. He spoke with a soft Eastern accent.

"Excuse me, Donselle. Did you say you fire-walked through Avalair?"

Dahli nodded, recognizing the crossed night-stalker guns on his old uniform jacket. This man would have been a warrior in

Avalair.

"What is your name?" he asked.

"Dahli Sandiniti."

He laughed. "Fearless!"

"Yeah I've heard that name before. It's not strictly accurate," said Dahli.

"I beg to differ; if you walked through Avalair I say it is not nearly accurate enough!" He turned to call something to the server, and the entire place seemed to erupt in noise. Diza's eyes darted nervously.

"What are they doing?"

Dahli looked around. "They seem to be throwing me the traditional warrior's drunken bash."

"And what does that entail?" asked Diza.

"Mostly it entails the four of us being fed food and booze."

"I can handle that," said Diza, pulling out her mobile 'com. "I better tell Dad where I am."

It was not long before the drinking had turned to dancing, singing and music playing. Dahli ended up being taught the words to a song in a language she did not speak. There was the exchanging of tales, and at one point Dahli was required to have some sort of flaming pale grey liquid poured down her throat as she knelt on a South Continent prayer rug. She didn't know how, but she managed to neither spill a drop nor be burned by the softly flickering flames, which seemed miraculously to stay just far enough away to avoid reaching her. As she finished she was raised to her feet, and a very large man with a heavy accent and slapped her heartily on the back.

"There! Now you are a man!"

She laughed, then peered down her shirt. "Then I think I had better do it again, I don't think it quite worked!"

"Give it time," said a soft, rough voice.

"Draephus!" Dahli screeched, and fell on him, hugging him tightly. She looked up at him, clearly intoxicated. "How did you get here?"

"Well a couple of friends called me and said you were having your victory party. I had to be here. Look who I brought."

Dahli peered around Draephus, and screeched again. "Straif! C'mere you adorable little hunk of man-meat."

He laughed and hugged her back. "You, my friend, are

baked."

"Only a little," she said, and hugged him again. Oh she could get used to hugging Straif. She liked hugging Draephus, too, but hugging Straif just brought up sooooo many more thoughts and ideas…

Draephus gently pried Dahli off Straif. "Hey show me how well you learned what I taught you."

"Absolutely!" She gestured to the server, who began making her another Tree Frog. It was then Dahli noticed Diza, Randish and Czamkiar were preparing to leave. "Hey guys, where are you going?"

Diza snorted. "Duh. We're going home."

Dahli sensed anger and resentment in her friend's voice. She walked over to her, and was astounded when Diza turned and walked away. Hurt and confused, Dahli followed her outside.

"Diza? Diza what's the matter?"

"You are!" said Diza, clearly angry. "I don't know who you are anymore! You're acting like you're one of them!"

Dahli blinked. "But… this is just fun! We're just having fun! Why are you so angry?"

"Because I don't know who you are anymore!"

"I'm me!"

Diza began turning away, but Dahli caught her by her arm and turned her towards her once more.

"Diza I'm just me! I'm still Dahli! I'm still the same person you listen to music with and do your homework with. I mean… we're still on for tomorrow, aren't we?"

Diza shook her head. "Look I don't think we should see each other anymore."

Dahli's jaw dropped, and her green eyes became huge, filling with tears. "But… Diza…"

"Forget it, Dahli. All this talk about change and revolution and faelins. And look at who you're hanging out with! Most of these people arc twice your age! If I keep hanging out with you then eventually I'll end up in the Detention Centre and I don't want to." Diza motioned to Czamkiar and Randish. "C'mon guys. Some of us have school tomorrow. We can't be out all night getting drunk with ex-revolutionaries. After all we're just children, not warriors."

Dahli stared as she watched Diza, Randish and Czamkiar walk away, feeling her eyes well with tears. She gazed after them, feeling people walk up behind her. Draephus came to stand at her left side, Straif at her right. She felt her heart break as her friends disappeared from view without so much as a backwards glance.

"Diza," she whimpered as Draephus put an arm around her.

"Let them go," said Draephus softly.

She shook her head. "I don't understand! She's my best friend!"

"She's angry," said Draephus.

"But why?! I wanted her with me! I wanted her to see what I see, I wanted to share with her every detail!" She began to shiver. "She says I'm not me anymore. Who am I?"

"You are who you always were," said Draephus. "You simply moved down your path more quickly than she."

"But I thought she was coming with me."

It was Straif who answered her, speaking softly. She turned to look at him, this boy who was not much older than she, but who had already done so much.

"Dahli, in life you are either the leaf or the wind. If you are a leaf then you go where the wind takes you, unthinking, affecting little, just blowing through the lives of others. If you are the wind, then you determine the destiny for others. You can affect where they end up in life, and to many people that is frightening. You both live on the same planet but in completely different worlds. Diza wants to be a leaf. You have chosen to be the wind. You have chosen to create changes. She fears where you may carry her."

"But... but I love her! And Czamki, and Randish. I thought..."

"You would be together forever?"

She nodded. Draephus gave her a gentle squeeze, lowering his head to kiss her hair.

"I'm sorry."

Dahli swallowed. "I just lost my best friend."

Draephus sighed quietly, and nodded. "If it is any consolation, I know just how you feel. Come on, let's get back to your party. You earned it. You deserve it."

"Will she ever come back?"

"I don't know. But the choice is hers. She could have rejoiced in what you accomplished, but she has chosen to remain a child instead. Likely a jealous one."

Dahli sniffed and looked up at Draephus. "Jealous? Of what?"

"She helped you to steal the faelin, did she not? Perhaps now she regrets not stepping forward with you, and resents missing out on what she sees as glamour and fame. Because she did not travel the road with you, she has no understanding of what you went through to earn it."

Dahli took his hand. "It doesn't feel like I gained anything. It just feels like loss on top of loss."

He squeezed her small hand gently. "I know. It feels that way right now."

"Perhaps not a total loss," said Straif.

Dahli looked up just in time to be pounced on by a white form wearing too much make-up. She embraced Czamkiar tightly.

"Czamki I'm so glad you came back…"

"Yeah, well, I don't know what climbed up Diza's butt and died, but… you've always been my friend and I couldn't just walk away."

"I'm glad." She kissed his face. "Come on. Let's have fun. Maybe Diza will calm down and we can talk to her tomorrow. Oh! Czamkiar, this is Draephus, and this is Straif."

"Heia!" said Czamkiar happily."

Straif just stared at him. "Wow. Do you know what your make-up says?"

"No, I had a guy at school put it on, I haven't seen it."

Straif took his hand. "Into the bathroom with me, young one, I can't be seen with a prostitute."

"WHAT?! I'll kill him!"

Together, the four friends went into the café.

Chapter Twenty

Draephus cleared his throat. "Heia, Teirra?"

Teirra sighed heavily. "I'm not going to be pleased, am I?"

Draephus cast a glance at Dahli, face down in the middle of the floor of his castle, Bacca and Czanda sniffing her suspiciously, occasionally barking at her inert form.

"Well... she's fine, she's *safe*, she's..."

Raski plucked the 'com from Draephus' hand. "She's passed out face down on the floor."

"WHAT?!"

Draephus took the 'com back from Raski, glaring at him. "We... threw her a traditional warrior's celebration and... she got a little... um..."

"*How* little?"

Draephus and Raski exchanged glances. Finally Draephus sighed.

"She's... well... pretty wrecked."

"But she's safe? She's okay? By the Empire the girl is turning my hair grey! Tell me she's safe."

"She's fine," said Draephus, "she's with us. We'll let the faelins chew on her a little bit then send her home when she can function."

Teirra made a noise of exasperation. "You can understand how I'm not exactly jumping for joy over having my sixteen year old sister passed out at the house of some man twice her age that I hardly know."

"Well I'm only physically twice her age. Mentally I'm like... twelve... thirteen tops."

"I'm not reassured," she said dryly.

"We'll bring her home when she can find 'up'."

"Thank you."

Draephus hung up, then turned towards Raski, gently drawing him into his arms, kissing him softly. Raski grinned up at Draephus.

"You didn't tell Teirra that we awarded Dahli the traditional virgin sacrifice as well."

"No reason to. Straif's not a virgin. Besides tradition says you don't have to tell the older sister that you gave the younger sister a virgin if all she did with him was talk." Draephus gently kissed Raski again, and groaned. "Gonna be a very long five years."

Raski nodded, then said; "Would you like me to spend the night?"

Draephus nodded. "Yeah. But… we have to behave ourselves. We promised we would. And I don't care what Vesper says about wanting us to have a baby, we're not doing it. I've already betrayed him once; I'm not doing it again."

Raski nodded. "I understand. Come on, let's get Dahli in bed and then get some rest. We've got a busy day tomorrow."

"Can you put her to bed? I… want to check on something."

Raski gave him one last soft kiss. "Okay."

Reluctantly they released each other, Draephus leaving the castle and heading to the clearing behind the pond; walking stick, knife and bag all in place. He mumbled the little chanting song that would keep him safe, and walked up to the cage on the stump, looking into it.

The beetle was hanging from the roof of the cage by its feet. The bird was asleep. Draephus sighed heavily.

"Bird, you are not trying."

The bird made a tiny noise. Draephus then went to check on the sapling the carn-crow had given him. It was not dying, but it was not growing, either.

"I do not understand any of this," he muttered.

He returned to the cage, opening the door and taking out the bird. He patted its tiny head, speaking softly to it before setting it within the depths of a climbing ivy on a tree limb to sleep the rest of the night away. Then he returned to the castle, leaving the offerings of seeds and beans as he went, trying to think what all this meant. The tree was not growing, the bird was not splitting the beetle… ah he would have to get some answers out of Harli and Shaktra. He wanted to see if they agreed with Bonnikkaar; that the magic was not working because there was nothing more it could do.

He entered the castle, putting away his stick, bag and knife before climbing the stairs to his room. There he found Raski, already asleep, face down in the pillows. The firelight shone across the dark skin of his back, and his long hair spilled across the pillow like a waterfall of black silk. Circling one wrist was a bracelet of white gems, sparkling and flashing with the motion of the flames.

Draephus walked over to the bed, seating himself on it and reaching out to remove the bracelet, which was shaped like some sort of millipede. Distastefully, Draephus set it on a night stand, then rose to his feet to undress. He winced as his bones let him know it had been far too long since his last shot.

He stripped his clothes off, then reached for the needle in the night stand.

****

Dahli woke up rather abruptly, keenly aware that she was not in her own bed. The problem was she had no immediate idea exactly where she was. Outside the day was warm, bright, and almost dry, and the light that filtered in through the windows was oddly multi-coloured. The sheets beneath her hand were thick and so very soft, and smooth. The cover over her was the same sort of fabric, stuffed with something that crushed in her hands, yet slowly expanded once more. Puzzled, Dahli sat up, and looked around.

She definitely was not home.

Someone had taken off her shoes and her jacket, but left her otherwise fully dressed before tucking her into the massive bed. It had great posts that rose from each corner, carved of a wood that seemed black at first, but was actually an extremely dark red. The headboard was made of the same wood, carved with images of deer in a flowering marsh. The cover had the same images, carefully embroidered in thread of green and gold, beaded with tiny gemstones. The bed was resting in the middle of the bedroom floor, where the light from the gigantic arched window with its stained glass depiction of an Imperial Gryphon cavorting in a field of golden flowers could cast its light directly upon her. The furniture was made of the same dark wood, including an elaborate cradle across the room, carved whimsically to look like a chariot being pulled by yet another Imperial Gryphon. She couldn't help but smile at it; she would have loved a bed like that as a small child.

Actually she would have loved a bed like that now as a quasi-adult.

As she was gazing around at the paintings, the windows, rugs, and the gigantic fireplace carved to look like two enormous dragons engaged in battle, something nibbled her hand in a 'pay-attention-to-me!' sort of way. She squeaked in surprise, then looked to the nibbler. It gazed back at her with eyes so green they seemed backlit by fire. She smiled at the creature.

"I know you," she said fondly. "You're Bacca, aren't you?"

"RARF!"

"Well I guess now I know I wasn't carried away by fairies to their palace on the sun. Wonder why Draephus took me…?" She rolled her eyes as the answer to her own question came to mind. "So my sister wouldn't beat the clart out of him when she saw me drunk. Clever boy. I've been a very bad girl this whole summer, it seems. Nothing but trouble and worry for the people I love."

She carefully stroked the faelin's silky hair, smiling as he nibbled and mouthed her hand. Then the second one hopped onto the bed, coming to investigate her. She'd never been so close to live, breathing faelins before. They were warm and silly and friendly, and she felt as if she could hug and cuddle them forever. She wondered how Draephus managed to keep them in such excellent condition; she knew he didn't get any extra rations. But then again, he was pretty skinny. Was he giving his food to the faelins? They certainly didn't seem to want for anything…

"All right, you two. I have to get up and find a bathroom or I'm gonna do to this sheet what I did to Draephus' conni."

She got up, followed by bounding red forms. They seemed to be four-legged for the most part, but that didn't stop them from getting up on their back legs and working the oil lamps that adorned the walls with paws very much like hands. That was more than the average feralyke could do.

She left the bedroom, and found herself on a wide walkway of wood and stone. To her left was the castle wall, to her right was a low rail and an open space that allowed her to look down into the main room of the castle. The walkway ran along one wall, eventually reaching a set of stairs. Beyond the stairs was a hall leading to other rooms on the upper floor. Below was a fantastic room with two massive fireplaces, each larger than her kitchen at home, one on either side of the enormous room. The rugs and furnishings were clearly centuries old, ornate and elaborate, the great upholstered chairs carefully carved to look like dragons and gryphons. One entire wall of the castle was a stained glass window; a mosaic of coloured glass cut and assembled in a framework of lead and gold to form the image of one of the nameless old gods, riding a black destri with flames leaking from its jaws and mouth. The god was nude save for a sort of long winding scarf of living flowers and vines, and in one fist he clutched a golden sword. He was followed by strange creatures, and women that were half bird, their breasts bare, their arms turned into wings. And, in the background, Dahli realized with a start was the field of stone creatures and statues where she had buried the faelin, immortalized as it had appeared in ages past.

She gasped quietly, staring at the field where she buried the faelin as it had looked over eight centuries ago. And in the distance was another castle, all traces of it gone now from the real world, and only its image set into the window left.

"I want to live here," she whispered as she gazed at the window. "I want to live in this castle and study the tombs and learn all the buried secrets. Then I want to find that second castle."

It was a long time before Dahli could tear her eyes from the window, and only because if she did not move she was going to wet herself. She found the bathroom, unaware that centuries ago this had been the private bath of the lady of the house. Once business was attended to, Dahli looked around the chamber. It too had huge windows. Here the scene was birds gracefully floating in a pond. Beside the window was a carved screen made to look like twining branches and leaves with little gems dotting it to resemble rain drops. There were even tiny bugs hidden amongst the twigs.

The toilet was clearly modern, but the sink was the ancient stone one that was clearly part of the castle. The bath, however, was a piece of absolute art. It was a deep, semi-circular basin with a mosaic of fish and flowering water plants in the bottom. Rising far above it, rearing high, wrought of some black metal, were huge destris, their immense paws hanging over the basin. Dahli noticed a note taped to the paw of one animal, and she went to look.

Heia Fearless, I had to go to the studio and deal with a few things. I got the water hot so all you have to do is pour it. Later. Oh, yeah – your sister hates me.

- Draephus

She read the note, then looked at the great metal animals. "Pour it? How do I pour it? I don't see a tap…"

Bacca solved the problem for her by pulling on the reins of one of the destris as Czanda put the plug in the bath. Moments later, rivers of hot water were pouring from the jaws of the destris and onto the faelins. Dahli looked at them. They gazed steadily back at her.

"You're not going to get out of there, are you?"

They stared at her. The answer appeared to be "No."

"Fine," said Dahli.

She was heartily sorry she gave in and let the faelins stay – they made a mess the likes of which she had never seen, dashing in and out of the water, biting at it, and barking like fools. Faelins, she learned, would bark at anything. At one point Bacca shoved his head underwater and proceeded to bark at the decorative fish, then leapt out of the basin to dash around the bathroom, spewing water everywhere. Fortunately somebody had thought to install a drain in the floor, or else she had no idea how long it would take to dry.

She finally got out of the bath and located a dry towel. It was going to be awfully dull taking a bath at home after this. She dressed and left the room, continuing her exploration of the castle. Escorted by the faelins, she examined the paintings and tapestries, and peeked into rooms. She found the bedroom where Draephus slept; the huge bed was unmade, and there was a faint sickly-sweet smell she associated with him. What was that smell, anyway? She'd never smelled it before in her life, and she didn't like it. Gemma had been right when she said it smelled like death.

Something glittered on a night stand, and she picked it up, examining the item. It was a jewelled insect, some sort of slinky, multi-legged horror from the South Continent, made of glittering stones and gold. She had seen Raski Jervyas wearing it last night, and knew it must be his. Draephus never wore jewelry.

"You know, for two guys who say they're not having a sexual relationship, you really act like you are," she said.

She set the bracelet down and left the room, heading to the end of the hall and opening a door. She found herself standing in a large room full of recording equipment, musical instruments, and… the drums. Not just any drums – THE drums, the set that held reign when the Gryphons played live, with the Imperial Gryphon on the bass drum. Quietly, as if afraid she was being watched, she walked over to them, examining them closely but not touching them. These were drums that saw a lot of use; stained and chipped and worn, some of the skins clearly newer than others, all obviously handmade and irreplaceable.

She walked around the imposing set and seated herself on the stool behind them. It was true Dahli had taken lessons, but she could not name half of these drums on a bet. Many she had simply never seen before, and a few shy and experimental taps revealed differing tones that were only ever heard on a Mortified Gryphon track. Save for one drum, which made an odd, dead thud when struck. A quick investigation revealed it wasn't a drum at all, it was some sort of container made to look like a drum. Upon opening, Dahli found tins of mushroom spines, cigarettes, and a half-full bottle of what she recognized to be mushroom distillate. And... that smell. That sweet deathly smell. Dahli very carefully picked up a spine, holding it gingerly. The spine itself felt like a shard of bone. At the base was a sort of sac, soft to the touch, ready to force its deadly contents into anything unwary enough to stand on it. A cursory sniff revealed it was indeed the source of the smell.

She put the spine back and closed the drum, moving hastily away from the huge kit, disturbed by the find. She knew about the spined mushrooms, though it was only a very basic sort of knowledge. They had been imported to use as a painkiller during the war. A tiny amount soothed battered bodies and painful muscles. A larger dose sedated burn victims and eased the pain. An overdose provided a soldier too damaged to survive with a peaceful death. They were still used for a number of reasons, mostly processed into pain medication. But the raw, whole mushrooms were illegal because it was so very easy to accidentally kill oneself with them.

What would Draephus need whole mushrooms for? And in such quantity that he actually stunk of it? Dahli was sure the other Gryphons knew he used them, or at least that seemed to be the implication Mars gave when he told off Gemma for commenting on the stink. And Dahli had by this time known Draephus long enough to realize that it wasn't that coat that smelled; it was Draephus.

She wandered over to one of the studio walls, and gazed at the photos hung there. The first she saw was a very young Draephus, not much older than she was now, shirtless and using a machete to clear branches from a pole. This was clearly the South Continent, judging by the jungle and the faelins. Even at that young age there was something cold in his expression; something lost that could never be replaced. There were a total of five photos taken in the jungle; Draephus clearing vegetation, Draephus smoking in front of his tiny shack, and three pictures of faelins. One showed a very proud looking faelin mother lounging beside…her? His? Her, Dahli supposed, her babies. Someone had written on the photo, assigning names to the creatures. Mama faelin was apparently Nemari, and the baby on the right was Scatter, and the baby on the left…

"Bacca, that's you!" she said to the faelin. "That's a little baby Bacca!"

"RARF RARARARAF!"

"Where's Czanda? Oh there's Czanda, look how little and cute you are! And there you both are, sitting on the roof of the shack. So cute."

"Arf!"

Dahli moved to the next set of photos, and felt her jaw drop. She stifled an involuntary laugh with one hand as she found herself looking at the Gryphons in the days before the war ended. One showed Raski and Mars making bombs while Khandid cleaned a laser pistol. Another photo showed Draephus with a grin on his face holding up a Kryphisian uniform with a lot of medals on the front and a big hole in the back. There was a picture of Khandid and Yuri curled together on some sort of mattress on the floor, both asleep, surrounded by bottles and glasses. Then there was one of the five of them together, looking shaggy and ragged and tired, holding some sort of very large gun with a Kryphisian insignia on it. Next to it was a photo of Raski, clearly not long after he was awarded his posthumous medal…

Dahli flinched and turned away from the photos. She left the room, disturbed by what secrets it held. She was hungry, and her attention was caught by the smell of something cooking. Was Draephus home? She hurried down the long staircase and followed the smell into the kitchen, and found herself wishing she'd knocked first.

Yuri Stracona was in the kitchen, alone, and her sudden appearance caused him to spook like a wild destri. She backed away from him, trying not to upset him any further. She didn't know what was the matter with him, but she did not like the feeling that she was stuck in a room with a frightened wild animal.

"It's okay," she said softly, edging away from the kitchen door in case he wanted to flee. "I'm Dahli, remember?"

She didn't think he did, and it was clear from the way he was behaving that she could not back away far enough or fast enough for his liking. She slowly retreated, keeping her eyes on him. He was a Breed, and Dahli had heard the term often enough, knowing that it applied to Sferkkaans who had been genetically manipulated to certain specifications. But face to face with Yuri Stracona in an enclosed place was giving her a whole new insight into what that term really meant. For the first time she was seeing him without his carefully planned wardrobe and makeup, and it was clear he was not Sferkkaan. Not anymore. For one thing, dressed in just his pants and a light shirt, she could see how very, very, delicate he was. His bones were so thin she wondered how he could support himself, and the left side of his face faintly showed a dapple-and-stripe pattern commonly seen on wild destris. The pattern followed the lines of his face and receded into his hair, where Dahli was surprised to notice small, soft feathers along his temple.

No wonder Yuri didn't like to meet people; one close look at him was all it would take to tell anyone what he was. When he knew he was going to be in public, he could hide his differences with clothing and makeup. Here stuck in Draephus' kitchen with some crazy girl he didn't remember, however, was very different, and the animals he had been infused with were controlling his reactions.

"Look I won't hurt you," she said gently, and took a step towards him.

It was a bad move. He kicked out like a wild thing and completely destroyed a chair. Dahli screamed as wood went in all directions and she found herself stuck in a room with a wild animal. Then something tiny and white arrived, and stood, watching as Dahli tried to get away from a highly agitated Breed.

"Yuri," said Khandid, "we've discussed attacking random strangers before, don't make me break out the sock puppets."

Yuri was making noises like a very unhappy destri. Khandid slowly approached him.

"Yuri... it's fine. It's just Dahli. You've met her before. She's not going to eat you. Come on, it's all right. Just breathe, okay? Come on, let's get you upstairs where you can calm down. It's all right..."

Dahli watched Khandid lead Yuri away, then slumped gracelessly to the floor once they were gone.

"I was nearly killed by Yuri Stracona. Thank you. Kryphis, for making my life needlessly exciting in random ways. 'Oh what did you do today, Dahli?' 'I was nearly kicked to death by a seven foot quinticord player who is also part destri! Yay!' I think I like the Gryphons better on a poster."

She was just getting off the floor when Khandid returned.

"Are you all right?" he asked.

"Yeah," she said. "Is he?"

"Yuri's a little spooked," said Khandid. "I'm sorry. If we had known you were here we could have prepared him for it, but… well I'm sorry. Part of the many joys of living with a Breed. I love him dearly, but between the two of us, we've killed more hall mirrors than you can imagine."

"Must be hard," she said quietly, helping to pick up the scraps of chair. "I keep asking myself why the Kryphisians hated us so much. I can't think of any answers."

"They didn't hate us," said Khandid, his voice equally soft. "To love or hate anyone requires a certain amount of emotion. They didn't care about us at all. They just needed what we had. And somehow that's much worse than hating us. At least if they hated us, I could say "Well they scrambled Yuri's brains and DNA to hurt everyone who cared about him," but they didn't. They did it because one of their generals really wanted a sexy anthropomorph to play with when he didn't have anything else to do. They rewired parts of my brain to kill anything of a certain colour because they were bored. Our pain and fear and sickness and loss didn't mean anything to them."

Dahli set pieces of the broken chair on the counter, wondering idly if it could be repaired.

"Sometimes…" she said quietly, "I feel guilty I didn't fight."

"Dahli you were ten when the war ended, how could you fight?"

"Straif fought."

"Noooo… Straif was a scruffy little urchin who mooched cigarettes and food off anyone he could and then sometimes ran messages. There were three instances where he had to kill someone to save himself, though he insists that just saving his own life does not count as bravery. It wasn't exactly safe, but we would have never let him fight. We all just wanted him to be a kid but there was no way to let it happen."

"I bet he was adorable."

"When you could subdue him long enough to hose the mud off, he was. Draephus and I once forcibly shoved him into a tub of soapy water like a bad feralyke and scrubbed him clothes and all. Then the war ends and the next thing you know the little monster discovers personal hygiene. Not a moment too soon if you ask me." Khandid looked at a smashed bit of chair he held in his hand. "Draephus is going to kill me, this is the second chair Yuri broke. Well we've figured out two of the animals running around his bloodstream – destri and a piptik bird. So he not only kicks and bites, he has an irrational fear of anything that eats birds. Now we just have to figure out what makes him want to eat snakes."

"Maybe he's hungry," said Dahli. "I've eaten a few when I can catch them."

"Permit me to expound upon that statement. Now we just have to figure out what makes him want to eat live, raw snakes."

"EYEW!"

"Yes, my thoughts exactly. He says they're crunchy."

"BLEH!"

Khandid finished piling the bits of chair on the kitchen island, and stared at it morosely. "I'll just have to find someone to repair it. Not that we are flush with artisans these days."

"Let me give it a try," said Dahli. "They have a really well stocked carpentry shop at school. I broke his conni, may as well fix his chair."

"Yes what was that little temper tantrum about? Why did Draephus lose his mind that night you wrecked his conni?" asked Khandid as he and Dahli began bundling up the chair pieces.

"Well he was stressed about Vesper being ill, then he called Vesper and got some man claiming to be Vesper's new husband," said Dahli. "And then the volcano blew."

"Has he apologised?"

"In his own shambling Draephussy way," she smiled. "Can't really figure out why he cares what trouble I get up to, though."

"He had two sisters, one older, one younger. The youngest was two years younger than you when she… well let's just say she ran into a pack of Kryphisians who had some very sick ideas about fun. She didn't survive. His older sister vanished. We have no idea if she is alive or dead. His brother is simply gone. So… I would say having a sixteen year old girl in his life who is not afraid to call him on his clart makes him feel a little less alone in the world."

"He never told me that," said Dahli, gazing at Khandid.

"Dahli he doesn't tell anybody anything, that's why he has me. I am the official dispenser of band gossip, rumours, incriminating photos, and breakfast."

"Well speaking as a fan, we gratefully appreciate your efforts with the gossip, rumours, and photos, but why the breakfast?"

"Years of habit. Every morning in the Cylinder, one of us would make breakfast. Being paranoid from all the death around us, we began to associate certain people with certain events. If Raski made breakfast, someone ended up wounded or sick. If Mars did, the mission never went well. If Draephus did, the mission not only didn't go well, there was usually an inadvertent explosion. When I did, things went smoothly. So it got to be a habit. Every morning I made breakfast. Now the war has been over for five years, and I still show up either here or at Mars' home or Raski's place and make breakfast. I have a rotating schedule. I'm the šukating breakfast fairy." He smiled at her, picking up a spatula and brandishing it like a wand. "So how do you like your šukating eggs?"

****

Khandid and Yuri left not long after breakfast, leaving her alone with the faelins. She spent an uneventful few hours cautiously creeping a few short feet into the catacombs and scaring herself silly until Bacca and Czanda decided they'd had enough of this. Then the 'com rang and she had a brief conversation with Vesper before taking a nap on one great leather couch in the middle of the gigantic living room. She stayed there until she heard Draephus drive up in his conni. He parked it, shut off the engine, and then she heard the door slam.

"T'niski!"

The faelins went mad, tearing down from the upper levels like red streaks. Dahli winced as she heard the inevitable impact with the closed door.

"Idiots," she mumbled fondly.

The door opened and Draephus came in, walking up the stairs

followed by his faelins. He grinned at her.

"Heia Fearless! How's the head?"

"Not bad," she said as someone came running up the stairs and into the room. It was Raski.

"Heia Fearless," he said. "I see you are back from the land of the inebriated."

She smiled a little self-consciously. "Just barely."

He grinned. Damn but he was gorgeous! Posters and photos just did not capture it. It was a shame; he was utterly lovely. Then his attention was directed away from her as Draephus walked over to give him a kiss. Dahli raised an eyebrow. Bet the fan listings didn't mention *that* little bit of trivia. She enjoyed the view while it lasted.

"Heia Draephus, you got a call while you were out."

"Oh yeah?" said Draephus. "From who?"

"A guy named Vesper. Claims to know you," she teased.

Draephus groaned, as if disappointed he missed the call. "What did he say?"

"Not much, really. Heia, how's Draephus, how are the barkers, is Raski pregnant, THAT one got my attention, I'm gonna post that one on the Gryphon's Roost."

Raski snorted. Draephus just looked puzzled.

"He... didn't ask who you were?"

"No. In fact he knew my name and everything."

Raski and Draephus exchanged glances, then Draephus moved towards Dahli, his expression puzzled. "He knew your name?"

Dahli nodded. "Well I assumed you mentioned me to him."

"No, I haven't. He's down on the South Continent. We haven't talked much."

"South Continent? No he's in Avalair."

"Avalair?!" said Draephus, looking surprised.

Dahli nodded. "Yeah, Avalair! I heard the warning sirens."

Draephus shook his head. "No you have to be mistaken."

Dahli snorted. "No way. Believe me, I walked through Avalair. I won't ever forget the sound of those sirens, no matter how long I live. Or how much I would like to."

Once more Draephus and Raski gave each other a puzzled look, then Draephus walked over to his telecom to check if it had in fact recorded the conversation. It had. He activated the cylinder, and listened to the phone call. Dahli's voice was first, cheeky and light hearted.

"Mortified Gryphons Fan Club."

Draephus and Raski gave her a weary look. She blushed. Vesper's voice was next, laughing.

"Really? Well I'm not sure I have my dues paid up, can I speak to Draephus anyway?"

"Only if you can play Rain Forest on your school desk with two pencils and the tin lid on your ink bottle."

Draephus gave her a look of disbelief. "Can you really?"

Dahli nodded happily. On the 'com, Vesper laughed again.

"Sorry, all I have are two almanikies and a watering can."

"Well he's not actually here right now, can I take a message?"

"I suppose. I was really rather hoping to speak to him. Are you Dahli?"

"Yeah."

"Heia I'm Vesper. How is Draephus, have his lungs cleared up?"

"Yeah he sounds fine. I'm not really the one to ask about his lungs, though, I haven't really been here for the worst of it."

"Is Raski pregnant yet?"

"Well not by me!"

Vesper's voice became excited. "But he's pregnant?"

"I really can't answer that, I have no idea, and they don't put information like that on the fan listings."

"No I suppose not. I was rather hop…"

"Here!" Dahli interrupted, pointing at the machine. "Listen!"

Draephus and Raski froze as they heard a sound that they, like Dahli, would never forget; the low, dirge-like moan of the sirens, warning all who heard that the area was unsafe. It was faint, obviously very far away, but there was no mistaking the distinct tone.

"See?" said Dahli, triumphant. "You tell me that's not Avalair."

"That *is* Avalair," said Dracphus quietly. "Why would Vesper be in Avalair of all places? And why would he have not told me he was there? There is no reason for him to be there, in fact with his health the air alone could kill him."

"Could it be they have the same sirens in the South Continent?" asked Raski.

"Where would he hear a siren in the jungle? They don't have

them in the jungle, they don't need them…" Draephus turned his head to gaze at Raski, blue eyes reflecting an indescribable look. "I've got to get to Avalair."

"Fine. Go. Just… don't breathe the air."

"I won't. I won't be near the inner city."

Raski and Dahli watched Draephus leave, getting into his grey conni and driving off. Dahli looked to Raski, confused.

"What's going on?"

Raski looked positively ill. "I'm not sure, but I really hope it's not what I think." He sighed. "C'mon, Fearless, let's get you home before your sister comes hunting us."

Gryphons – Book III
'Celebration Day'.

Chapter Twenty-One

Draephus drove to Avalair. He had to use the ferry, since he no longer had the air-con, then once he was across the channel he began making his way to an old outpost, one where Mars was once stationed that the Kryphisians never found. One that was only just within hearing range of the sirens.

It was early evening when Draephus pulled up before the dilapidated old house. Once it had been a beautiful little home, but decades of neglect and war had left it a blackened little shack with a snarling façade, its expression as dark and miserable as the events it had seen. It seemed gloomy and uninhabited, but that was what had made it serve so well as a hideout; it was laid out in such a manner that the main rooms were sectioned off from the others, forming a sort of house within the house. A person could watch the place for months and see no sign of life.

Draephus got out of the conni and went for the side entrance of the little house, opening the door and stepping inside. He closed the door, then followed the passage to the inner chambers, opening the door and striding in, overwhelmed by the familiar scent of the light oil used for cleaning the guns. There was only one figure in the room, and he was small and thin, his eyes just a little too intense from behind his heavy rimmed glasses. He jumped and whirled to face Draephus as he heard the door slam. The wide eyes became even wider.

"Draephus!"

"It was you, wasn't it?" said Draephus.

"What are you talking about? What are you doing here?"

"No I believe I am the one who should be asking that question."

Vesper stared at Draephus, blinking, jaw working. Draephus fought down the illness in his guts.

"It was all a lie, wasn't it Vesper?"

"I don't know what…"

"Don't lie to me, Vesper! Now tell me why you're here!"

The smaller man swallowed nervously. "My name's not Vesper," he said quietly. "It's Khalinyrs. There is no Vesper. He never existed."

Draephus had no words for what he felt, at least not at that moment. Later he would be able to get the feelings and emotions sorted; loss, rage, betrayal, pain, and terribly, terribly violated. For now he was just cold, his emotions shutting down.

"What are you saying?"

"I'm saying I had a job to do, and being with you made it easier," said Vesper. "I had to make you love me. I had to find out what moved you, attracted you, and mould myself into something you would care for. It was not easy. It would have been simpler to insert myself into Raski's bed, but Raski is too nervous. He would have been harder to fool for so long. No, it had to be you."

Draephus watched as the man he had loved turned to resume cleaning the guns, as if he didn't matter. As if he had never mattered. Draephus suddenly realized he hadn't. He lunged for Vesper, grabbing him by the arm and turning him to face him.

"You bastard! You owe me an explanation."

"I don't owe you a damned thing, frankly. Thanks to you finding me out my entire schedule is off. It was nearly blown when that groutnoll down on the South Continent told you I was leaving you for him." Vesper yanked his arm away from Draephus.

"So what did you need me for? Someone to look after you when your virus became active?"

"I don't have a virus," said Vesper quietly. "That was part of the persona. We knew of your tendency to take in and look after those in need. I had to make myself more attractive to you. So I..." He mimed a cough, "developed a virus."

Draephus stared at him in horror. "You were never sick? Never? Vesper I... I stole medication for you, I broke into Kryphisian labs, I risked my LIFE! I might have stolen medication from someone who really needed it! People may have died because of what I did for you! What did you do with the drugs?"

"Sold them. Used them to fund the movement. You know as well as I that ammunition is not cheap."

Draephus' breath was coming in gasps, and he felt the vomit rise into his throat. "You... you're leaving me for that guy on the 'com? What...? What is going on?"

"He is my next target. I told him I was leaving my abusive lover for him. You would have received a note and a box of small personal effects from the South Continent saying I had died down there. All I needed to do is complete my mission up here and I would be on my way."

Draephus had gone numb. Part of him had simply shut down, unable to take in what he was hearing as he watched the stranger that had been his lover turn away and once more resume cleaning the weapons.

"So… why… why did you want me to have a baby with Raski so badly?"

"I thought you would be less likely to want answers to questions if you had something new to focus on. A new relationship and a baby would serve as a suitable distraction. So I played the concerned dying lover who did not want the man he adored to end his days in loneliness." Vesper finished cleaning and loading the laser pistol. "Now if you don't mind, you've caused enough trouble."

Draephus suddenly thought of something. "Shaktra Mannis… you called me from…"

"I did go to the South Continent briefly, and I saw her. I pretended to call your number and get your machine, and we left that precious little message for you on a recording for later use. Then I came back. Of course I could not leave her alive to accidentally inform you as to my whereabouts…"

Draephus could feel his brain struggling to grasp what was occurring. "Wh… what did you need me for? What… what use was I?"

"You were of very *little* use, sadly," said Vesper. "You're closed-mouthed and paranoid and you don't share secrets with anyone. It took me years to find where you had stashed that Grey Boy and his little barking freak. Now that I'm finally close you're protecting one and the other has gone into the Avalair Underground, and now you show up at the old hideout. You've been nothing but a pain in my ass since we met. Having to play up to your nerves and neurosis and your sick sense of honour. I was hoping I could have driven you to suicide by now but you're tougher than you think." Vesper turned and pointed the pistol at him. "And now I have to think of what to say when Raski lets me know of your demise."

It surprised Draephus how well he recalled his survival skills. He dove sideways, feeling the silent blast of the pistol just miss him. He pounced on a long-muzzled night stalker gun, rolled to his feet, racked it, and fired.

The sound was like a shockwave; felt as much as heard. The recoil nearly broke his collarbone, throwing him into a wall. Then there was silence, and smoke, and the quiet rain of meat as well as debris jarred loose from the ceiling. He sank to the floor, shaking, willing himself to breathe. Then he grabbed a small waste basket and threw up into it before collapsing to the floor.

A lie. It was all a lie. Vesper never loved him. Vesper never existed. He was just a target, a means to an end. There was no Vesper. The man he loved, had killed for, stolen for, grieved, raged and wept for, was not real. Draephus curled into a foetal position and began shaking so hard he was nearly convulsing. It wasn't real. None of it. It was all just… a dream turned nightmare. He felt someone put a pair of arms around him, and he turned his head to see Mars crouching beside him.

"Mars? How did you get here?"

"Raski called, he said there was something odd happening in Avalair. From his description I decided to come here. Looks like my instincts were right." Mars glanced up and gasped at the bloody mess across the room. "By the New Empire, Draephus."

Draephus stared in horror at the broken remains of Vesper. No, not Vesper. A stranger. A man he didn't know.

"I… I don't understand," Draephus babbled, close to hysteria. "I don't understand any of this…"

"Just sit, I'll look around."

Draephus sat in a daze on the floor, eyes closed, trying and failing to comprehend what had happened while Mars looked around. Draephus had rarely come to Avalair during the war; he had only been to this place a handful of times. Mars had spent months at a time here, hence the lethal virus that now lay dormant in his blood. Draephus listened to him flit from one secret room to another, finally returning to where he sat.

"Come, we are sitting in a viper's lair. We don't want to get caught here."

Draephus opened his eyes, noticing the collection of file folders Mars was holding.

"What's that?"

"I'll show you later."

Draephus slowly staggered to his feet, shaking all over, hardly able to keep himself on his feet. He grabbed up the night stalker gun, and followed Mars out of the house to his vehicle, climbing into the passenger side and sitting down.

"It was all a lie," he said softly. "All of it."

Mars put the folders in the conni, then pulled out a couple low-impact incendiary devices. They would burn with the intensity of the sun, but there would be no explosion to draw anyone's attention. It would simply look as if the underground fires had claimed another area. Mars threw one into the ground floor window, then threw a second into an upper storey window. He watched as the flames suddenly flared up with a hissing whoosh.

"Ah how I miss doing that. Let's go."

They drove to J'Vanni's apartment, and Draephus sat on the same couch where not more than a few nights ago Dahli had sat and ogled J'Vanni. His eyes were glazed, and he stared forward at nothing, one hand idly rubbing the neck of J'Vanni's great hawk.

"What were they doing?" he asked quietly.

Mars turned over a paper, his long hair spilling around his shoulders as he bent over the folders laid out on a low table. "Well Khalinyrs, known to some as Vesper, was part of an extremist organization dedicated to killing the Kryphisians that had defected to our side, claiming that the only reason they would do so is to have a foothold for a return invasion. Our little Vesper was one cold-blooded monster, most of these execution orders are in his hand. He's the one who killed Jai and Shalsairas, and he's the one who had J'Vanni and Delaes attacked. Apparently Delaes is… half-faelin?" He turned his green eyes to Draephus. "Is that true? I mean… can that happen?"

Draephus nodded slowly. "Yeah," he said, his voice quiet and hoarse.

"And Khalinyrs hooked up with you because through you he could learn the location of these people."

"I never told him. I never even mentioned Jai and Shalsairas. I didn't keep anything about them, I destroyed all documentation of their existence and I never mentioned them."

"Thus explaining why it took so many years for him to find them. The story about the virus in his heart was so he would have an out after the mission was over. Looks like it became 'active' a week before killing Jai and Shalsairas."

"I… I can't believe I didn't know." Draephus laughed, a sick, humourless sound. "I actually apologized for betraying him. Can you believe it? I have *one night* with my best friend, and I actually said I was sorry. He was prepared to kill my friends and destroy my life and *I* was the one who said he was sorry! I wish I'd beaten him to death with my own fists!"

Draephus looked down at the scrap of silk he always wore around his ankle, because Vesper had given it to him, and tore it off. He then gave it to the hawk, who was delighted with the new toy and proceeded to rip it to small bits.

"You wouldn't have had much luck using your fists," said Mars. "From what I can see, Khalinyrs was a Whip as well as an assassin, like Khandi. He'd have slashed you to pieces."

"A Whip? But… he didn't have any triggers."

"He did, a *ton* of them. But he wore tinted contacts to prevent his being affected by them, same as Khandi does. That's what gave him that intense expression."

"What's a Whip?" asked a quiet voice.

Mars' head snapped up in the direction of the voice, then he rose to his feet, walking to the tall man with the bandaged eyes.

"We thought you were asleep," said Mars.

"I was," said J'Vanni. "But I heard voices. I was hoping Delaes had come home."

"No, not yet," said Mars quietly. "Come on, sit down."

He led J'Vanni to where Draephus was seated, waiting for him to sit down before taking a seat himself and proceeding to explain.

"A Whip is a type of fighter, perfected to kill," said Mars. "The… Grey Boys made them into something else. They took a form of combat perfected by Northern warrior-clans called Shi-Kha and turned it to their own purposes. Warriors trained in this method must be small, because it calls for speed and dexterity rather than brute force. Because many warriors trained in this combat were reluctant to fight each other, the Grey Boys programmed them to kill anything of a certain colour. They would then dress the warriors in their opponent's trigger-colours and leave them to slash each other to bleeding rags. Fights between Whips are fast, bloody, and usually a draw."

"And… Khandi is one of these?" J'Vanni seemed puzzled. "What's his trigger colour?"

"A specific shade of pale green. He's killed a few mixing

boards in the past."

"He also once went crazy on my stereo," said Draephus. He smiled faintly. "The contacts were a gift from the band, but they give him headaches if he wears them too long, so some days we end up having to blindfold him."

"And he has no control over this?"

Draephus shook his head. "Nope. None. If it's the right colour, he'll kill it. Doesn't matter what it is, all it has to be is green."

J'Vanni slowly shook his head. "How horrible."

"Yeah," said Draephus quietly. "Horrible."

Mars gazed at him, clearly worried. "Draephus?"

Draephus just shook his head. "I apologized. I actually *apologized*. I slept with Raski, and I told Vesper I was sorry." He laughed; an ugly hysterical sound. "I should apologize to Raski for sleeping with Vesper." He turned his head to look at Mars, gazing into clear green eyes. "I'm fine. I... I'm fine. Turn on the Visual, I want to find out if anyone noticed that shack was burned."

Mars did, then went into the kitchen to make tea. Draephus reached out and took J'Vanni's hand, squeezing it.

"How are you holding up?"

"Well much as I would like to put on a brave face I have to say I'm a complete wreck. I just want Delaes found and home and well and safe."

"We all do. C'mon. Snuggle up. Take a nap."

J'Vanni lay down, his head in Draephus' lap, closing his eyes. Draephus placed a hand on his slender shoulder, watching the news, forcing himself not to think about Vesper. He did not want to deal with it yet. He would wait until he got home, then he could hold Raski close and cry out the whole tale to him, and beg forgiveness for making him wait for a lie. No more pissing around. No more waiting. No more second guessing, He should have been with Raski all along. He would go home, marry the man he loved and who clearly loved him and give him as many damned babies as he wanted, and spend the rest of his life making up for what a piece of dirt he was. Meanwhile on the Visual, the news cut to an outdoor scene, and a group of people standing around a huge tree.

"Hey that's the old Goldenwood tree in the park," said Draephus.

"Oh I hope they're not cutting it down," said J'Vanni sleepily.

"There was talk they may have to after the last big storm we had."

Draephus used the remote to turn up the sound, and grinned as he saw the female reporter. "Hey Mars, there's a woman on the visual."

"Nonsense, they don't exist. They're a myth, like the sun." He stepped out of the kitchen. "By the Empire you're right. I think it's a female. With breasts and everything. We used to need those for something, didn't we?"

"What, breasts?"

"No, women."

"Yeah we made babies with them."

Mars raised an eyebrow. "A man and a woman? Making babies? Disgraceful. We all know that's something that can only be done with two men, extensive physical alterations, and a lot of alien technology, as nature intended."

They watched as the woman walked over to the Goldenwood tree. Draephus turned the sound up a little higher, and at last they could hear her more clearly.

"We're at Goldenwood Park, standing near the tree that gives the place its name. But it's not the tree that is drawing the attention today, it's what has been discovered up in the canopy nearly three hundred feet off the ground."

Draephus just stared at the screen, having the oddest feeling he knew what he was about to see. Then the camera shifted to show a slender form dozing on a branch. He slapped a hand over his face. The woman continued to speak.

"It's a rare arboreal faelin. Virtually all faelins in the province that includes Avalair are ground-dwelling, as the arboreal ones have a tendency to do just what this one has; head up the largest tree they can find. It makes them difficult for pet owners to control, and only one pet arboreal is known to live anywhere in this region. That would be Bacca, who belongs to drummer Draephus CZimcocious of the Mortified Gryphons. So Donsa CZimcocious, if you are watching this, you may want to check where your faelin is."

Draephus sighed heavily. "I think we just found Delaes."

J'Vanni sat up. "Can we go get him?"

"You stay here with Mars. I'll go get Delaes. I'll have him home in an hour." Draephus stood up, then paused, looking once more towards J'Vanni. "Does he have a leash?"

Mars was horrified. "Draephus! No of course he doesn't have a leash, he's the man's husband, not his…"

"There's one in the bedroom in the second drawer of the green dresser. Don't use the one with the red collar, he doesn't like that one, it chaffs. Use the blue one with the matching collar, he likes that one."

Draephus went to get the leash, leaving Mars to stare open-mouthed at J'Vanni, who sat demurely, long legs crossed, hands on his knees.

"Delaes Randerick and J'Vanni Dei Syncopius, playing with bondage gear."

"We *are* consenting adults, Mars."

"Yeah but…. NOBODY who can write songs like 'Pensive Moments in the Fifth Hour' should be getting tied up and spanked."

"Actually I usually do the tying and spanking while wearing my old teacher's uniform." He smiled a small, wicked smile. "He's such a naughty pupil."

Mars just stared in astonishment for a long moment, blinking. "Oh there is not enough brain bleach in the world for the mental images I am getting."

"Then it's a good thing I sent Draephus for the leash and not you because you probably don't want to know about the chain harness and the pants made out of…"

Mars shoved his fingers into his ears and began walking back to the kitchen shouting "LALALALALALALALALALALA….!"

J'Vanni sat, smiling faintly, waiting for Mars to fall silent.

"Eel skin," he finished. Mars shrieked.

Draephus came out of the bedroom with the leash. He bent and kissed J'Vanni's face, then walked out of the apartment.

He reached the park roughly twenty minutes later, stepping out of the grey conni and walking towards the Goldenwood tree. Draephus had never leashed either of his faelins a day in their lives, though he always carried one when out with them. He would shake it, and the small brass bells on the collar would ring, summoning them. Delaes' leash didn't have bells and small carved wards dangling from it, but he doubted Delaes would come to the jingling of bells anyway.

He walked up to the Goldenwood tree and stared straight up, cigarette smouldering in the corner of his mouth, paying no attention to the small gathering of people and the female reporter, his eyes fixed on the tiny form resting oh so casually on a branch far above their heads. Wow. He backed up a few steps, took the cigarette out of his mouth, and called.

"*T'nisk!*"

Delaes' head shot up.

"Bacca! C'mon, we can come play another day. Let's get home. It's going to be dark soon, it's almost night."

A man to Draephus' left made a sound of exasperation. "It's not going to come to you. They don't listen."

Draephus slowly turned his head to look at the man. "That's probably because you hit them when they do come."

The man's eyes grew huge, and he went white, then red. He said nothing more, and Draephus returned his attention to the form up the tree. He watched as Delaes rose up to all fours and stretched, then turned and began casually descending, moving head first on all fours like a jungle cat. He climbed down the tree, landed on the ground, then bounded over to Draephus, throwing his arms around him. Draephus picked him up and carried him to the waiting conni, loading Delaes into it, then getting in himself. He slammed the door shut, and started the engine.

"I have never been so glad to see you in my life," said Delaes.

"Don't speak yet," said Draephus quietly, "wait until we are out of here."

Delaes waited until they were out of the park, then reached out and took Draephus' arm. "How is J'Vanni?"

"Blind. But well."

"And Rysta?"

"He's good, too. He's still weak but he's going to be just fine. He says he's never rooming with you again, though."

Delaes smiled. "You know I really do adore that man when I don't hate him." He gave Draephus a sidelong look, but then lowered his eyes, saying nothing. Draephus swallowed the knot of bile in his stomach.

"I know who attacked you. Let's... let's just not talk about it. I... really haven't dealt with this yet. But... you're safe. This won't happen again."

Delaes nodded, falling silent. Draephus took him home, but did not stay to watch the joyful reunion. He didn't think he could stomach it. Instead he immediately set out for home, needing to be someplace safe and familiar and just as far away from the crap as possible. As he pulled into the driveway of his castle after being gone for thirteen hours, he saw a worried form on the moat bridge, wrapped in a long cloak, looking like something out of ages past. Draephus parked his conni and got out of the vehicle, hurrying to the figure on the bridge. He threw his arms around Raski and held him tight, and that was where everything came out. There was no more space for the pain inside to remain, and it all came out; the years he had spent protecting J'Vanni and Delaes, the overwhelming horror and pain of Vesper's betrayal, even the news about the viral arthritis eating his bones and ending his career. It all came out in one grotesque waterfall of hate and grief and fear.

By the time Draephus was done talking, it was daylight, and they were both cold and wet. Raski led Draephus upstairs, and this time when Draephus reached for the needle of gold and glass, Raski just watched. It all made sense to him now.

"I wish you'd told me," said Raski. He looked ragged and tired, and his black hair hung in lank wet clumps.

"I should have," said Draephus, preparing the shot. He carefully pushed the needle into the sac at the base of a mushroom spine and began drawing out the pure resin. "But I have this... habit of not liking to say bad things out loud. When you say them out loud, they become true. That's one reason I hesitated about having children. With the virus, I don't know if..."

"So you worry me half to death, thinking you're an addict. Well we will find out about whether we can have children with you having the arthritis. Will that be enough?" Raski asked quietly as Draephus took just a small amount of resin to inject.

"I don't want to take too much," Draephus said quietly. "I have something I want to do before I fall asleep."

"What's that?"

Draephus finished injecting himself, then set the needle aside to await cleaning. Then he reached for Raski, drawing him close and kissing him.

"Apologize for making you wait."

****

It was strange, Draephus thought. Strange to be lying here in this bed with Raski, watching the fire gently flicker in the massive stone fireplace, and the faelins curled up on the foot of the bed. It was strange, yet… very familiar and comfortable. He had an odd feeling of finally being home after far too long away, and he knew this is where he was supposed to be all along. He turned his head to see luminous blue eyes gazing at him.

"I was just thinking," said Raski.

"About what?" asked Draephus.

Raski slowly sat up, stretching, the light of the fire turning his black skin to fire-ember gold. "Is it all right with you if we wait a while before announcing our relationship?"

"Well I'm pretty sure Mars, Yuri and Khandi are already onto us, but yeah. Why?"

"I want to be able to do it when the time comes."

Raski smiled. It was the same sort of smile he used to get while sitting in their run-down flat and making bombs.

"Am I going to be horribly embarrassed?" asked Draephus.

"If everything goes right, yes."

"Oh good, I was worried there for a moment." He sat up to look into Raski's eyes. "Whatever makes you happy."

Raski kissed him. "The Year End Music Festival is being held in Charlendine this year, isn't it?"

"Yeah, it is," said Draephus.

"They were almost untouched by the poisoning," said Raski quietly. "Lots of beautiful, strong, women down there."

"And you're worried one of us will be tempted?"

"One of us," Raski admitted softly, gazing at Draephus.

"I wouldn't worry about it, Rask."

"Well it is an issue. You and I are not naturally inclined towards other men, we just…. Kinda gave up hoping we'd meet a woman."

"Yeah well in our case it was extra hard because she would also have to be willing to tolerate our various issues," said Draephus.

"But what if we go there and…?"

"Raski," said Draephus softly, "I won't meet anyone down there because I don't want to. Because I really do think that even if the Kryphisians had not poisoned half of our population, we'd be together anyway. What we have isn't about gender or preferences or any of that. I love you. I don't want anyone else, and anatomy has nothing to do with it. What we have is based on a very long road travelled together. I'm not looking for anyone else, and I really hope you're not either."

"I'm not. I'm just afraid. I waited a very long time to be with you. I didn't really realize that until the night we had sex, then… I understood what I was feeling."

"Then why do you want to wait to tell everyone?" asked Draephus.

Raski just grinned crazily. Draephus sighed. "Well I can't say I didn't know what I was getting myself into…"

"And you did promise me a family."

"And I did promise you a family," said Draephus wearily. "Assuming it's possible with me having this disease. But not right now. C'mon, lie down. I'm tired."

"All right. But I think you should know that tomorrow I am going to go to a doctor and ask about your condition."

"I don't want anyone to know," grumbled Draephus.

"They won't. I'll make sure they don't. But if you think you are making me wait this long to be with you, and then falling to dust, then you have another thought coming, Donsa CZimcocious."

Draephus smiled. "Well who am I to argue with the most beautiful man on the planet?"

****

As Raski and Draephus were finally falling asleep after a very long night, Dahli sat and daydreamed, alone on the steps of her school, staring off into the distance and thinking. Something had changed, and it was her. She sighed and shook her head, then looked around hopefully for Czamkiar. She had not seen him all day, and knew he was home with the flu, but could not help but hope he would appear anyway. He seemed to be the only friend she had left at school.

She stood up, toying with the idea of just skipping the afternoon, when Diza came around the corner and almost ran into her. Dahli stared at her in surprise, feeling both joy and sadness, just wanting her friend back. Diza stared as well, blinking, and for a long moment, neither spoke.

"I met Yuri," said Dahli lamely. "You... always told me if I met him you wanted to know, so... I met him. Um... yeah. That's... it."

"Well I'm sure he was thrilled to meet a big bad warrior like you."

Dahli sighed. "Look what are you so mad about? Because so far all you've done is act like Atania and you haven't given me one reason why you're so mad. We used to be the best of friends; don't you think you at least owe me an explanation?"

"Well why don't you just use your warrior powers to read my mind?"

Dahli gave her a look of pure irritation. "Look, tell ya what. Why don't you go down into the shop class, borrow a pair of pliers, go into the bathroom and remove that razor-edged aluminium tampon, then come back when you're feeling better. I'll wait."

Diza's eyes bulged, and her jaw dropped. "DAHLI!"

"What?"

"THAT'S HORRID! I'M GOING TO BE WALKING FUNNY FOR A WEEK!"

Dahli though about what she had just said. "Yeah that... was a little harsh."

"A *little*?!"

"Well," she said, her tone slightly defensive, "at least it made you briefly forget you hate me!"

Diza sighed, rolling her eyes. They stood together in silence for a little while, then finally Diza spoke.

"I don't hate you. I hate me. Because I'm a coward. I could have come forward and admitted that I helped but I was too scared. I didn't want to go to the detention center! I could have done a lot of things but I didn't because I was too scared. I've been eaten alive by guilt for the whole time and I can't seem to forgive myself, and the fact that you weren't upset with me in the least only made it worse." She began to tear up, her breath hitching. "And then Randish came and told me he has to go back to Sirius because the air is too wet and cold for him and I really liked him and I was just so mad..."

Diza's voice degenerated into hiccups and squeaks. Dahli moved closer to hug her tight.

"Diza, I'm so sorry, I know how much you like him. And why would I be upset with you? You're not a coward! You helped me when I came to you that night. How many other people do you think would have helped?"

Diza sniffled. "That's not brave, of course I'm gonna help you, you're my friend."

"It *is* brave," said Dahli. "You helped me every time I asked you to. That's very brave. Especially considering what I asked you to do. Which… in retrospect was sort of a lot to ask."

"Well you know the old expression," said Diza. "A friend will help you move, a real friend will help you move a body."

"Yeah," said Dahli. "So stop picking on yourself. I miss you."

"Yeah I miss you too. Besides, I would have had to make nice eventually. You have all my Gryphons albums."

"Good because I wasn't gonna give them back until you did."

Diza giggled, as did Dahli, feeling a tremendous weight lift from her shoulders. They moved apart, looking at each other as Diza wiped at her eyes.

"I'm sorry Dahli."

"It's okay. I'm sorry Randish had to leave. Was he getting sick?"

Diza nodded. "Yeah. It was just one lung infection after another and finally the doctors said he could go home or die. So this morning he boarded a transport ship back to Sirius."

"I'm really sorry, Diza."

"I know." She wiped at her eyes with one hand. "But… if you're a warrior, then I should be a warrior too."

"Well okay," said Dahli. "You already completed one of the tasks, which was to do something in secrecy with no one finding out."

"I did?"

"Yeah, when you helped me! That was a task done in secrecy!"

They began walking away from the school, their differences forgotten.

"What are the other two?" asked Diza.

"A journey to find knowledge, and a fire walk."

"I guess a trip to the library doesn't count as a journey to knowledge," said Diza.

"No, said Dahli. "But I think you completed that task too. I bet you learned a lot helping me with the faelin."

"Yeah that's for sure," said Diza. "So all I have to do now is fire walk!"

****

It was about twentyhour in the evening when Teirra, Atterick, and Draephus arrived at the LEO station. Dahli and Diza stared at them with sorrowful faces as the trio of adults came to stand before them, Teirra and Atterick looked angry and frustrated. Draephus looked battered and exasperated.

"Why are you here?" Dahli asked him.

"Because your sister didn't believe this wasn't my fault."

"This isn't his fault," said Dahli, as Diza nodded in agreement. Both girls were charred and covered in ash. Their minor burns had already been seen to, but nothing short of a bath and a hairdresser would fix the rest.

"What were you doing?" asked Teirra irritably.

"Well Diza wanted to be a warrior too, so we were… trying to firewalk."

"Firewalk?" inquired Atterick.

"Yeah," said Dahli. "But we didn't want to go all the way to Avalair and we didn't have a way to get there anyway, so…"

"So we went down to Ysith Beach, found some driftwood and set it on fire," said Diza.

"Ysith Beach?!" exclaimed Draephus. "What were you doing there?! The whole place is covered in old ammo and forgotten incendiaries and bombs and stuff you can't even imagine!"

"Yeah," said Dahli. "Well, we didn't know that at the time. And Diza was… kinda halfway across the coals when there was this "poof!" noise, and there was a spray of red and blue fire, and..."

"And shortly after that Legal Enforcement showed up," said Diza.

"We were arrested for setting off an incendiary device in city limits," said Dahli. "We told them we didn't, it was an accident. So they checked the fire and found a forgotten box of flares that had been there since the last battle."

"They dropped the charges," said Diza. Then added ruefully; "after they stopped laughing."

Teirra and Atterick just stared at her. Draephus slapped both hands over his face and walked away a few feet, shaking his head and saying something in a language she didn't understand.

"Look, can we just go home?" asked Dahli. "I'm really tired, and so's Diza."

"And so am I!" said Teirra heatedly. She pointed at Draephus, still addressing her younger sister. "Ever since you met that over-size juvenile delinquent, it's been one issue after the other!"

Draephus snapped his attention to Teirra, looking very much as if he would like to say something to her that would result in criminal prosecution.

"Teirra you can't blame Draephus for any of this. I would have taken the faelin anyway, I would have gone to the center anyway, I would have escaped anyway. We may not have firewalked, but that is all you can blame him for. That and… one really spectacular drunken bender…"

Diza looked to Draephus. "Does it count as firewalking if I blow up a set of flares by accident and scorch my own butt?"

"Ah I'll help set you up a proper firewalk," said Draephus.

"YOU WILL NOT!"

"Oh thanks!" said Diza. "Oh – tell Yuri I love him."

"It will just terrify him, but all right," said Draephus.

"ARE ANY OF YOU HEARING ME?!" demanded Teirra.

Dahli stood up, coughing, leaving little trails of dust behind her. "Yes I hear you, you would be much happier if I would stop doing the same dumb stuff that you did at my age, Donselle Caught-Stealing-Kaisa."

"Stealing kaisa?" said Draephus. "Why would anybody *steal* kaisa?"

"It seemed like a good idea at the time," growled Teirra.

"WHO IN THEIR RIGHT MIND STEALS A KAISA?!" demanded Draephus. "Have you ever eaten one?!"

"Yes," said Teirra through gritted teeth. "Plenty of times."

"Then why would you steal one?!"

"She found a large patch of dream-buttons and ate five of them," said Dahli dryly.

"Five?!" said Draephus. "Wow, you must have been circling the outer atmosphere…"

"This is not about what I did or did not do as a teenager!" said Teirra.

"Like running off with some weedy musician you met lurking

around the outer edges of the Cylinder and not coming home for five days and leaving your nine year old sister to fend for herself," said Dahli.

"Weedy?!" exclaimed Atterick, indignant.

"Five days?!" said Draephus. "You left a little kid alone for five days?! Gee no wonder you hate me. I'm a better parent."

"You got her drunk off her butt!" said Teirra.

"Yeah but I didn't leave her alone for five days chasing some guy's backside! Maybe you're not fit to look after her. Dahli, wanna come home with me?"

"SURE! Can I bring Diza?"

"Just get in the scruffing conni before I hurt you," growled Teirra.

They did, Dahli, Draephus and Diza fitting into the back seat, with Teirra driving and Atterick in the passenger seat being very quiet. The vehicle started off down the long dark road. After a few moments, Diza gave Draephus a slight push.

"You're practically sitting on me!"

"It's not my fault you have a huge butt."

"It's not my butt, it's your smelly coat!"

"My smelly coat is not taking up more space than your smelly butt."

"Is too."

"Is not!"

"Heia!" said Dahli. "Look the Icy Berry stand is open! I WANT AN ICY BERRY!"

"ME TOO!" called Diza.

"I want a destri!" said Draephus.

"No way, if you get a destri then I get a…"

The vehicle skidded to an abrupt halt in the middle of the road. Teirra turned in the driver's seat to stare at them. Her right eye was twitching visibly, and her teeth were grinding with near-audible force. She spoke with a terrifying level of quiet.

"Don't. Make. Me. Come. Back. There."

"'Kay…" said the three miscreants. There was silence for all of three minutes.

"I need a job," said Dahli.

"Yeah because none of us have enough to do between school, homework, and working the gardens," said Diza. "Why?"

"I want to go to the Year End Festival."

"That's not happening," snarled Teirra.

"I have to go! Straif invited me! Sort of."

"Straif?" queried Atterick. "As in Mannechek?"

"Yeah."

He sighed heavily. Diza looked at Dahli.

"So are you now dating a rock star as well as getting drunk with them?"

"Not really dating him. Besides I'm not sure he has anything on his mind other than the festival and getting his home ready for the…"

"I could probably find you something to do around the studio," said Draephus.

"That would be great." Dahli had a funny feeling that Draephus did not want her mentioning the baby. Fair enough. Straif would likely make the announcement when it was time. Meanwhile, she had to find a way to convince Teirra to let her go to the festival.

Chapter Twenty-Two

The school day crawled by like a dying snail. Then, after making plans to meet up with Diza and Czamkiar later that week, she made her way to Gryphon Studios. She stood before the huge gate and stared at the building. The parking lot was full of connis, all different, all expensive. Then she spied one she knew, an old grey one, carefully repaired and shining wetly in the muted light.

A uniformed man walked up to her as she stared at the vehicles. "Yes?" he said.

"I'm Dahli Sandiniti."

The man nodded, and opened the gate, allowing her in. She crossed the lot and entered the building. The halls had been quiet the last time she had been there, but now they were alive with sound. Some of the weight lifted from her chest, and she brightened as she saw a familiar shaggy figure step out before her. Her heart warmed even more as he showed obvious pleasure at seeing her.

"Heia!" said Draephus, looking a little surprised. "What are you doing here?"

"I just came to find out if you were serious about the job. Is that all right?"

"Yeah, fine, but I don't know what you'll think about the people wandering around this place."

"What's happening?" asked Dahli as they walked down the hall together. "It was so quiet the last time I was here."

"Yeah, I know," said Draephus. "Well what happened is things got slower and quieter until all we were doing was staring at each other. Finally we had to admit we weren't very happy with the way things were going. So while we were just sitting there, in cruises Straif Mannechek. Well he brought a friend, namely the sepulchord player from Anazampini, Contessa Rae. She's the granddaughter of Philo Rae, I'm sure Harli must have mentioned him to you. So we start to play, and Straif says; 'Hey, Slow Ferril is in town.' So we call him up and he comes over. I thought he was dead, myself. They don't call him 'Slow' for nothing. The man must be at least three million and two. Then Khandi got drunk and called Laude Ioko on the South Continent. He didn't come over, he told us to šukat off, sober up and go away. Anyway, people have been coming and going ever since, and we haven't stopped. The memory boards are still rolling, which is more than I can say for half the technicians. We sent out for food and cots. We've been pretty much living in the studio. When somebody falls over we throw him in bed and just keep on. I'm a little afraid to find out what we recorded sounds like. I recall thinking it was pretty hot at the time, so maybe it's all right. Oh, watch out for Khandid, I think his brain has melted. Or it least it should have by now, with all the stuff we have been collectively dumping into our systems."

"You seem fine," said Dahli.

He laughed, a harsh, ugly sound that she recognized all too well. She stopped in her tracks, and he turned to face her.

"What?"

"I know that *laugh*, I know what it *means*, and if you get ugly on me I'm gonna take that coat and do to it what I did to your conni!"

He seemed to sag, lowering his head. For a long time he was silent, then he said quietly; "I'm sorry. I… uh…" He suddenly began to shake, his knees collapsing. Dahli tried to catch him but it was like holding up a concrete tower. She somehow managed to get him into a lounge, half-carrying him over to a couch and lowering him onto it.

"Draephus what's the matter? Tell me, please. Talk to me. You can't…"

"I can't talk about it. I can't. I… can't talk about it. And trust me… you don't want me to."

"But if you…"

He turned his head and looked at her. "You don't want me to," he said quietly. "Just…"

"Draephus," she said quietly, "if you don't let some of this stuff out it's going to kill you."

"Yeah, probably," he said quietly. He picked at the edge of his coat. "Tell ya what. I'll…. uh… I'll tell you about it when I've had a little time to deal with it, okay? I've… got a lot to sort on this one and I'm not even sure what emotions I'm supposed to be feeling. The only thing I am sure that I am feeling is betrayal. Lots and lots and lots of betrayal tangled up with guilt and a lot of other crap. Let's just say… Vesper was not who I thought he was. The rest… I can't talk about yet."

"I'm sorry," she said quietly.

"Yeah me too. I'm going to miss him every day of my life,

but... well the after-math of the war is still being felt and there are still casualties stacking up. Probably going to be at least another ten years before it's really over, and even then... who knows."

Dahli reached out to stroke his hair. Funny, when she first met him, he flinched from her touch. Now he seemed calmed by it. He stuck a cigarette in his mouth and lit it, then let his head fall to her shoulder.

"I used to think if I was you then I wouldn't have any problems," said Dahli. "Because you were so rich and so many people loved you."

He seemed to think about that, then turned his head to look at her. "Let's go do stupid stuff with music and record it."

"Sounds good to me."

They left the small lounge and walked into the control room. Dahli stood behind the technician, looking down on the room below. Mars was on the floor, curled into a knot. Both hands were around the slender, silver rod of a microphone. He was singing in a clear, powerful voice that belied the position he was in. Behind him Dahli could faintly make out the towering amp-plants, vibrating gently with the sounds, and the vague shapes of people scattered throughout the room. It was dark, save for an occasional flash of light across the body of an instrument. There was a tiny explosion of flame as someone lit a cigarette, and then it disappeared.

"And people pay you trinta to do this," she said.

Draephus actually giggled, like a bad boy getting caught at something naughty. "They pay us a *load* of trinta to do this. We ought to be ashamed but we're not."

Suddenly Khandid lurched up against Draephus, grabbing hold of the larger man's arm to steady himself.

"I'm going to be sick!" he cheerfully announced, gazing up at Draephus. Then he turned his liquid eyes to Dahli. "Heia!" he chirped.

"Hi Khandi."

"Heia! So which one of you is going to marry groutnoll, here? You or Raski?"

"Raski can marry him," said Dahli. "My job is merely to threaten."

"Oh good. He needs that. He doesn't take the rest of us seriously anymore."

Khandid left. Dahli looked up at Draephus.

"So what's my job? Following you around with a big stick?"
"C'mon. We'll start you on something small."

****

Dahli for the most part that day found herself running around like a mad thing, trying to comprehend what everyone was doing. There did not seem to be any organisation to the madness, only a shifting stream of music that altered as some of the musicians stopped for a break and others took their place. Dahli's job seemed to mostly consist of bringing food, drink, cables, small pieces of equipment, and removing items no longer required. It wasn't especially hard, but with so many people there was no time to sit down.

Straif had shown up, much to Dahli's delight, and he and Khandid were obviously having a lot of fun playing off of one another's talents, occasionally upstaging one another. Raski was a shadow at the far end of the room, but she could hear his sepulchord in the background, an anchoring rhythm to the wild havoc Ferril was wreaking with his own instrument. Mars somehow managed to be heard above everyone else, his strong voice having no trouble competing with the other sounds around him. Meanwhile the great memory boards flickered and responded to the technician, taking all of it in.

"Is this usual?" she asked. "Do they always record like this?"

The technician nodded. "Yeah, from what I hear it's pretty normal. They have a five or six day jam session with friends, get out their ideas, and take it from there."

Mars suddenly reeled into the room, darting out of the studio and crashing into Dahli as she stood near the board. Supporting himself by hanging onto her arm, he said to the technician, "Are we good? I think we're bloody wonderful."

The technician smiled in acknowledgment, and Mars turned his attention to Dahli. "Hold this for me, will you?" he said. He passed her his drink and staggered out of the room. Dahli watched him go, wondering if everyone else was in the same shape. She turned her eyes back to the studio just in time to see Ferril fall over backwards, playing his quinticord from a prone position. Idly, she sipped Mars' drink.

"Ferril just turned seventy," remarked the technician.

"Do you think he broke anything in the fall?" Dahli asked.

"No the equipment should have withstood it."

Dahli thought about that, then sipped the drink once more. It was already affecting her, but the thought never occurred to her that there may be anything in it other than the obvious. She took another sip and watched Draephus from behind the glass.

She had seen him live in concert, and numerous times on the visual, but to watch him from so close was an altogether different experience. He was oblivious to all around him, eyes only on what he was doing. He crashed and hammered away at the drums, coat off for one of the few times in his life, the muscles in his neck and arms working as he played. He was a power drummer, and rarely sat down. The drum set was not the set he played in concert, but was still enormous; a huge sprawling array of everything from little hand-sized ones to colossal brightly painted ones that could only have come from the South Continent. He pounded and hammered like a madman, sinews and cords standing out. He was much more lean and thin than he looked beneath the imposing bulk of his coat; almost starved, and his shoulders were covered with bruises and scrapes.

"He's been fighting again," she remarked softly to herself.

Something was beginning to happen, something strange. Perhaps it was the loud colour of the liquid she drank, luminescent almost, and green. A liquor created from the distillation of a hibiscus plant from the South Continent. Some of the plant's fluorescent properties remained in the bottle of liquor. This particular drink was mixed with a tonic called silver...because it was. And there was something else... She took another swallow in attempt to identify the flavour, then continued to examine the fluid suspended in a tall clear glass. She smelled it, slowly, then touched it with her index finger. Metallic green dripped from the finger as she withdrew it. Interesting. A large drop formed on the tip, suspended. She licked it free, then held the drink aloft and swallowed, long and slow, until the glass was empty. Satisfied after a long voyage inside the depths of the glass that there was nothing more inside it, she glanced through the window which separated her from the band. She wavered, was she wavering? She saw the window come towards her.

'It's going to hit me,' she thought, and it did. The window gave her a bleeding nose.

She stepped back, feeling the technician's hand on her

shoulder. She looked down at it as blood dripped unhindered onto the white shirt she wore.

"Hey," he said.

Dahli followed the arm up to the source of the voice, and watched a napkin come towards her face. She looked at the technician, confused, as he held the napkin to her bloodied nose.

"It's not generally wise to try and walk through sound-proof glass."

"I didn't," she protested mildly. "It hit me."

"I see," said the technician quietly, a little amusedly. His face filled her vision, huge and surreal. Mars then reeled back into the room and came to rest against her. He hung an arm around her neck, his face even larger and more bizarre than that of the technician. Dahli watched it come towards her, shifting and altering. Tiny coloured specks filled the air. Then Mars dropped from view, temporarily disappearing, then, with a lurch in time, he was suddenly there again. He was talking, and she couldn't understand a word he said. Then time lurched again, and suddenly she and Mars were entering the commissary and he was wiping blood off of her face.

"Got to be careful how you drink that stuff," he was saying, but the words came out surprisingly slow for how fast he was moving. He didn't seem to move at all, but he was one place, then another, and then he was gone entirely. Dahli was left alone in a commissary full of bottles and bags and cups.

The bags she began to check out. One contained capsules, green ones. She took one, reasoning that since it was green it would counteract the effects of the drink. Then she poured herself a glass of some sort of thick, clear liquid and took a sip. It didn't taste like much, but her mouth and tongue filled with a tingly warmth. Then as she was heading out of the commissary she noticed a stack of lined paper and a pen. The sight of these reminded her of the report she had to write, and she took some of the paper and wandered off to find a place to write.

She had only just sat on the speaker and been writing for what felt like seconds, when she looked up and found Draephus beside her. All the paper she had taken was covered in her handwriting. She let him read what she had, and he seemed to like it. That was good enough for her.

"Does it make sense?" she drawled, her mouth feeling numb

and slack.

"Yeah I understand it perfectly," he said, watching something invisible fly across the room. As it left his range of vision, he once more turned his attention to Dahli. He took her glass and had a sip, then made a face and shook his head.

"You're drinking this straight?"

"Yeah. What is it?" she asked.

She wasn't too gooned to notice the look of absolute astonishment he gave her.

"It's šukating mushroom distillate, ya bean! Your sister is going to have me flayed alive! Stop eating and drinking out of unlabelled bottles and bags, you're going to get me either killed or arrested, possibly both."

She shrugged in slow motion, weaving slightly. He sighed, helping her down from her perch. "Come on, let's get some food into you."

They went into the commissary, and while he went through the coldbox, Dahli took the opportunity to check out another bag and pour herself some more Hibiscus liquor and Silver, mixing it with the mushroom distillate she already had. The bag she now investigated was full of tiny spined mushrooms. They were a sickly greenish white, with the occasional shade of grey on them. Dahli ate one, the spines proving to be soft. They tasted the way Draephus' coat smelled. She ate another one.

An arm reached around her, an electric blue arm with a ruff of white lace about the wrist. She sipped her drink and followed the arm up to a handsome but rather young-looking face, with an untidy mop of wild brown hair. She watched him eat a mushroom with drugged interest.

"Heia Straif," she said.

"Heia," he said, looking amused. "I'd be careful about how many of those I ate."

"Dahli what are you into now?" Draephus came up behind her and peered into the bag she had been eating out of. "How many of those have you had?"

"Two," said Dahli swaying. "Straif what are you doing here? I heard Vortex are in the studio, are you still with them?"

Raski drifted into the room and began going through the coldbox. Straif smiled slightly at Dahli.

"I am at the moment, though I don't think that will go on much longer, now that Marachani Kai from Bad Influence has joined."

Raski pulled his head out of the coldbox and looked up. Still chewing, he yelled, "WHAT?"

"I'm not supposed to know this," said Straif, turning large green eyes to Raski. "But apparently Bad Influence is dissolving. So my band has grabbed up Marachani Kai because he's a more low-key type quinticord player than I am, and I suspect I'll be kicked out of the band shortly. That's part of why I'm down here. I'm looking for a band. Too bad about Bad Influence, though. That was the one I wanted to get into."

"Bad Influence are breaking up?" said Raski. He looked upset and disbelieving.

Straif shrugged. "That's what Marachani says."

"Yes, well, the only comment you should ever believe coming from Marachani Kai is 'I've got a knife and I'll use it'," said Draephus. He looked down at Dahli, putting a protective arm around her. "You, my friend, are toasted."

Dahli's mind was once more at work, but only partly. Her etiquette centre had gone to another planet.

"Well I'm glad you're getting out of Vortex. They're awful. The only reason anyone buys their stuff is to laugh at the lyrics. How did that one song go? `I think of you when I pick my nose...' Oh, no that was the version Khandid released. Never mind." She waved her hand as though to clear the air of the comment. She began to slide down, and Draephus had to hang onto her. He grinned apologetically at Straif, who narrowed his eyes.

"Oh this is wonderful. I have to find out from your fans that the biggest band on Sferkkaa has been releasing comedic variations of our music? You couldn't pick on someone your own size?"

Raski staggered over to Straif. "My dear lovely young Straif, with the emphasis on lovely, there *is* no one our size."

Straif stared levelly back at Raski, then sighed. "Groutnoll." He tossed back his hair and stalked from the room.

"Blew that one, Rask!" yelled Dahli happily.

"You stay out of this. You're a nasty child. You ought to be given a good swat."

"And you're arguing with me so what does that make you?"

Draephus tried not to smile as he held onto Dahli, who looked

501

up at Draephus with liquid eyes.

"You don't think we hurt his feelings, do you? Because I really like him and I think he likes me, but that may be because I'm one of the only girls around here and his options are sorely limited."

Draephus just stared at her. "Wow. I am impressed. A full sentence in your condition."

"Did we hurt his feelings?"

"No," said Draephus. "And I don't want to see you grazing on anything that isn't food. You're supposed to be here to work."

"I'm on break!" Dahli watched the room start to distort, time was beginning to move in jerks once more. She nodded.

The next time she was aware of her surroundings, she was watching the band play. She was vaguely aware that a lot of time had passed since she had come into the studio, but she couldn't think how much. She didn't know any of the people in the room, and there was a different technician. She hadn't seen Draephus for quite some time, and she felt thick and heavy. She was tired and she knew it. She asked the tech where she could lay down, and he gave her directions to a room down the hall. It was furnished simply with cots and blankets, and there were bodies on several of these. As Dahli staggered into the sparsely furnished room she heard someone shift, then sit up.

"Dahli?" said Straif.

"Yeah, me," she said, and swayed.

"Figured you'd run out of energy sooner or later. How do you feel?"

"Mmmph," she muttered, and flopped down beside him on the bed. "Sick. I'm too heavy. I'm gonna go right through this cot and hit the floor and I'll just... split, y'know? Like ancient ruins."

"Better not go through the cot, then," he said.

"Guess not," said Dahli, and closed her eyes. "I'm sorry I teased you about your band."

"It's fine. I'm just annoyed over being replaced by a man I can out-play in my sleep."

"Yeah, that would bug me, too. But you're the best, you can find a real band."

"Yeah," he said quietly. "Well, I'll think on it. I have to decide what I want to do before the baby is born. Maybe studio work."

"Yeah," said Dahli quietly.

She settled closed to him, and exhaled quietly. She was asleep when Straif dropped the blanket over her, leaving his arm to rest across her back.

****

  Dahli awoke, uncertain as to how long she had been sleeping, but long enough that Straif had somehow transformed into Draephus. He was a lump next to her, and she rolled onto her side to look at him. He looked different when he slept. Not older or younger, just different. Perhaps it was that she could really see his face for the first time. When he was awake she seldom saw more than his eyes. He had a strong face, the cheekbones prominent and angular, the jaw rather heavy. The eyes were set deep within their sockets, which were dark-rimmed from lack of sleep. The nose was long and narrow, with a slight warp in it from previous altercations. She could even see the thin, ragged scar over the warp. The skin had a roughish, slightly grey look to it, and the stubble on the jaw was getting long. A large, silly smile spread over Dahli's face as she looked at him.
  "You're beautiful," she said quietly.
  "Beautiful!" came a voice from another cot. "I've seen baby-prints of that man, he was never beautiful. People sent his mother sympathy cards when he was born, and the doctor slapped his father."
  Draephus rolled onto his stomach and propped himself up on his elbows, facing the other cot. "Shut up, Khandi. And don't contradict Dahli, I think she has very good taste." He put his arm around Dahli, resting his head on her back.
  "Yeah," said Dahli, her voice muffled by a pillow. The weight of his head on her back and the closeness of his body were far from unpleasant. His breath, however, would have cracked masonry. Dahli chose to ignore his breath, but she couldn't ignore the nagging thought which had just crept into her mind.
  "What time is it?"
  From a third cot came another voice, this one a little irritable.
  "Twentythreehour in the evening, I believe."
  "Mars!" sang out Khandi. "You're cranky!"
  Mars rolled under his covers violently, but said nothing.
  "Oh," said Dahli, closing her eyes.
  "I'm hungry," said Khandi, leaping from his cot to Mars'. "HEY MARS!" he bellowed. "YA HUNGRY?"

Mars sighed heavily. "Death comes to us all in time, Khandi, why must you court it?"

Dahli felt Draephus get up, and her body missed his presence as he left the bed. She pulled the blankets up higher, not quite ready to get up herself yet. Neither was Mars, it seemed, and he snuggled down into the warm covers, closing his eyes as Khandid and Draephus left. The room was quiet, dark, and cool, and though she could not seem to get back to sleep, it was nice just to lie there.

Dahli was just beginning to doze off when she heard Mars roll over abruptly, flinging the covers aside. Disturbed from her near-sleep, she raised her head and looked at him. He was several feet away on his own cot, mostly dressed, breathing hard. His arm was hanging off the edge of the bed, and, as she watched, she saw his eyes open. He looked around, then closed them again. Puzzled, she sat up, and realized he was dreaming. Or perhaps not dreaming so much as having a nightmare. She wondered if there was anything she should do, but she was very reluctant to get too near him as he writhed, then began to thrash. She had no idea what was going though his mind, and the last thing she wanted was for him to mistake her for part of the nightmare and break her neck. He was breathing harder now, and she thought she heard him whisper something, but it was too faint to catch. Then he whispered it again, a little more clearly this time.

"Sint nu vai."

Dahli looked around, wondering if she should go get someone, or just let him be. He was starting to fight with something in his sleep, and he was repeating the phrase over and over.

"Sint nu vai. Sint nu vai. Sint nu vai..."

Suddenly he flung himself aggressively off the bed, and began screaming so loudly she was sure the flesh inside his throat must have torn, his whole body shaking with the force. She flung back the covers and was on her feet to get to the door when Khandi came racing into the room, clearing furniture as if he could fly, white hair blowing out behind him. He landed on the floor before Mars, catching and blocking at least three strikes from Mars that came so fast Dahli never really did know if she had actually seen them.

"Dahli hand me a blanket," said Khandid.

She did, watching as Khandid wrapped it around Mars and held him tightly as other people began to fill the room. Mars kept screaming until he suddenly went silent, his head snapping back, his small body trembling cruelly, eyes wide and staring at nothing. Slowly the convulsion, and the trembling, eased. Khandid was speaking to him, saying soft nonsense to calm him. It seemed as if it took forever, but finally Mars was blinking and looking at his friends in confusion, clearly uncertain as to what was going on.

"I had a nightmare, didn't I?" he said.

"Just a little one," said Khandid. "Are you okay?"

Mars slowly looked around, uncertain where he was as Draephus came to sit beside him on the floor as well.

"No?" said Mars in a small voice, his body wavering unsteadily.

"Well 'no' is a valid option," said Khandid. "I'll take you home for a while, let you get your bearings. Come on. I think you and Yuri both could use a little stability and quiet."

Draephus carefully picked Mars up, and, with Khandid close at his heels, left the room as Dahli followed. She went to the commissary, where she found Raski picking at his meal.

"Mars have a nightmare?" he asked.

Dahli nodded. "Yeah, looked pretty bad to me. Khandid is taking him home, he looked…"

"Confused? Scared? Lost?"

"Yeah, all of them," said Dahli. "Hey Raski? What does "*sint nu vai*" mean?"

"Is that what he was screaming?"

"Yeah. What's it mean?"

"Eastern dialect for "make it stop"."

Dahli felt her stomach become sick, and she found herself refusing almost violently to think about what that could mean. Draephus came into the room after a few minutes and walked over to Raski, kissing him softly, touching his face. She didn't miss the way Raski responded to him, and found herself feeling oddly jealous, the same way she felt when Diza first began seeing Randish. Then Straif came to stand beside her. She turned her head to look at him.

"Why does it bug me that Draephus has Raski and my best girlfriend Diza had a boyfriend?"

"Because having to share your friends stinks?" he said. "You know if you wanted me to I could help you make them a little jealous."

"I don't know," said Dahli, uncertainly. "I mean you've fought in the war and you're the fastest quinticord player in existence and famous and… my only accomplishment was not throwing up on the floor last night."

He shrugged a little. "I think you're cute."

"Uh huh. Do you *really* think I'm cute or am I just the only girl you've ever seen?"

"I think you're cute."

"I think you're hot sex on toast."

He grinned. She giggled and took hold of his hand, a little overwhelmed by the situation but by no means unhappy with it. Even if Straif had not been a famous musician, he was absolutely beautiful.

"Are you getting cavities?" asked Raski. "Because I'm getting cavities."

"Yeah I think my teeth are falling out," said Draephus.

"Groutnolls," said Dahli. "Hey… about Mars…"

"He's fine," said Draephus softly.

"Does he get nightmares like that often?"

"Not… so often anymore," said Raski quietly.

Dahli suddenly had the feeling she was prying. They clearly did not wish to discuss the matter.

"Sorry," she said. "I was just kinda worried…"

"He doesn't like to talk about them," said Draephus, "and we try to respect that. He rarely has the nightmares anymore, usually only when he's asleep in a place he doesn't usually sleep. Khandi will take him home, let him wobble around for a while until he remembers how to walk in his heels again, and then he'll be good."

"Very cute when Mars wobbles," said Raski.

"That's kinda mean," said Dahli, trying not to smile.

"Yeah but I'm his friend so I can say it."

They plundered the coldbox in the commissary, then sat at the table, eating cold leftovers and nodding over their tea. Dahli felt leaden and thick, as though her head was full of some spongy material. Across the table Raski was shaking like an old man, and even with his dark skin Dahli could tell he was grey beneath it. The only one who didn't look any different from the usual was Draephus. He had a thoughtful look on his face, and he turned to look at Raski.

"Hey Raski," said Draephus, "do you have any idea what time we went to bed? I'm not sure Mars is right about the time. We were all into the green stuff pretty heavy, and you can't keep track of time on it."

"Well I wasn't," said Straif. "Not in my condition. But I did have a couple mushrooms."

Dahli's eyes were huge. "Straif! You can't be doing that! You're pregnant!"

"It's all right," said Straif. "The baby spined mushrooms in moderation are okay, I already looked into it. I can have them, I just can't have more than two a day."

"And what if you have more?"

"My implant thinks I need to get pregnant again. And considering the model I have stores genetic material… it *could* happen. Which is why I have been limiting my mushroom intake to three every other week. But they don't have any effect on the baby."

Draephus made a face. "I'd just stop eating them 'til I was done being pregnant."

Dahli, Straif, and Raski stared at Draephus.

"What?" he asked warily.

"Nothing," said Straif, "we're just all sharing our mutual horror at the idea of you being pregnant."

"I'll ask the tech what time it is," said Raski. He left the room for a short time, then came back and sat down again.

"He says it's nine-and-a-half hour on a beautiful Fourday morning."

Dahli almost dropped her cup. Her eyes grew large, and the fuzzy muddledness left her head as her stomach convulsed into a knot. "Fourday morning? For real? It was Oneday afternoon when I got here!"

Raski shrugged. "You were as fried as the rest of us, Donselle. We were taking bets on whether or not you would even land this week."

Dahli was in a cold panic. "Teirra will want me dead. Where's the 'com?" She lunged out of her chair and ran for the telecom, picking it up and dialling her code. The 'com was answered by the first ring.

"Heia?" The voice was Teirra's, weary and concerned.

"Teirra it's Dahli."

"WHERE ARE YOU?" Teirra's voice tore out of the 'com so loudly that from across the room Raski jumped. "ARE YOU ALL RIGHT?"

"Yes, Teirra. I'm sorry, I lost track of the time."

"For three days? Are you with that groutnoll?"

Dahli closed her eyes and waited until she had regained her self-control. "Teirra," she said softly, "I was wrong to worry you like that, and I am very, very, sorry I did it. But you may not call my friends names."

There was a pause on the line. When Teirra resumed speaking it was with a quieter tone of voice. "All right I'm sorry, it's just I'm beginning to think Draephus is a *very* bad influence. Where are you now?"

"Gryphon Studios."

"Do you mind telling me what you were doing that was so fascinating that you didn't remember to go home for three days and nights?"

"I don't have an answer to that." Dahli pushed her hand through her hair. "Look, I'm going to go to school, and we'll discuss this when I get home, all right?"

Teirra made a noise of exasperation. "Just as long as you're fine. But I reserve the right to kill you."

Dahli smiled. "Sure. Talk to you later." She hung up the com and looked across the room at Draephus, Raski and Straif.

"Okay, how big a fool did I make of myself?"

The three glanced at each other, then looked back at her. "Well *we* didn't notice," said Raski, still shivering.

"That's not encouraging. I must look like garbage. I've got to get out of here." She snatched up her jacket from a chair, noticing a roll of paper in the pocket. She recalled the report she had written and was glad at least she had her assignment done. A brief flash out the window caught her attention, and she made a small sound of distress as she saw the skies were black, and the rain a pounding torrent. A storm was in full fury, and her light jacket was not suitable for such weather. To top things off, she noticed she had spilled something green and sticky all over her shirt, as well as some blood. As she stared down at it, wondering whether she should have a fit or not, she heard Draephus' voice cut into her thoughts.

"Well I can offer you a semi-clean shirt. Sorry I can't offer you a ride but… I'm in no shape to get behind the wheel."

She looked up into his faded blue eyes. They were puffy and red-rimmed. A smile crossed his stubble-covered face, and in one hand he offered her his own abused but relatively clean shirt. Dahli smiled back at him and took it.

"Thanks," she said softly. "And it's okay, I don't need a ride, the school's not far. What I need is a coat that can stand up to the weather."

"I'd loan you mine if I had brought it," said Straif.

She smiled. "Thanks. It's sweet but not real helpful."

Raski looked at Draephus, then gently nudged him. Draephus sighed, then hoisted the imposing might of his infamous coat and held it out to her.

"Here, it's made for the South Continent, so it will stand up to this."

Dahli stared at it. "You'd... let me wear the coat. *That* coat. The coat that no one on the planet will possibly mistake for *any* coat other than *that* coat."

"Well if you want to leave soggy footprints behind you all day…"

Raski got up and went for Draephus' shades and hat as well. "May as well make the picture complete."

Dahli took the coat and slid into it, astonished at the sheer weight of it. Then Raski came to put the hat and shades on her before stepping back to survey his work.

"Awwwww….. that's so cute! It's an itty-bitty Draephus!"

Dahli held up the sleeves and made them flap. "I can't find my hands."

"Perfectly fine," said Raski. "They're overrated, anyway."

Ten minutes later, a short form in an over-large coat, wearing a grey t-shirt, flat-soled boots with a piece of rag tied around the ankle, a hat and shades was seen leaving Gryphon Studios, walking quickly. Technically the rag around the ankle was no longer a piece of the complete Draephus CZimcocious "look", but Raski felt it needed to be there. It took only a few minutes to get to the school since she was hurrying and taking a direct route, but now that she was moving it was as if the ghost of everything she had been drinking in the days prior were rising to trouble her. By the time she reached school she was definitely feeling… *something*. It wasn't unpleasant but she doubted anyone would approve.

Despite the fact that she was late, Dahli stopped off at the washroom and had a look at herself in the mirror. Her eyes were puffy and red, at least where they weren't circled in black from lack of sleep. Her face was greyish and sallow-looking, and her lips had virtually no colour to them. Her hair was at all angles, but at least this she could fix. She wet it down in the sink, wondering what her breath must smell like. She rinsed her mouth out with water several times, then, in a fit of drug-addled brilliance, stuck her head under the soap dispenser and squirted some of the noxious substance into her mouth. Then she took in some more water and worked the whole mess into a healthy mass of bubbles before spitting it out. Finger-combing her damp hair, she put on the hat and shades, and, looking like a miniature version of Draephus, left the washroom and went down the hall to her locker to find out what class she was supposed to be in.

"Teirra is never going to let me go to the festival now," she muttered to herself. "She's going to hang me. Why can't I keep my fat dumb bum out of trouble?"

She froze as she felt an ominous twinge of pain in her abdomen. Oooohhhh.... no.

"Don't you dare, don't you even THINK about it, you stupid uterus! No! Bad reproductive organ! That doesn't work *anyway*, I should add. Useless troublemaker."

Normally Dahli would have taken further measures to address the issue of an impending menstrual cycle, but currently her common sense was floating somewhere in a used glass at Gryphon Studios. She walked into Languages as quietly and unobtrusively as possible, but there was just no missing her. Atania Nightwing was mortified when she got a look at what Dahli was wearing.

"She's finally snapped."

Duone Alsayers was somewhat amused, but not much. "So good to see you Donsa CZimcocious. Care to share with us where you've been?"

Dahli twitched involuntarily, then shook her head to clear it. "At my new job?" she said in a small voice. "With friends?"

"Did you get your report done?"

Dahli reached into her pocket and pulled out a mighty document, dropping it loudly onto the desk top from arm's length. There were a few subdued giggles.

"You *have* friends?" said the boy next to her.

Dahli turned her head to stare at him blearily. "I have to warn you, that at this moment my saliva is caustic, and you are not that far from me."

"Dahli you are not going to spit on anyone," said Duone Alsayers. "Now since it is no secret you had the most interesting summer, you read yours first."

Dahli sighed and stared down at her report. To her horror, the page was covered by scrawled little figures, some human, some bestial, all nonsensical.

"We're waiting," said Duone Alsayers.

"Yeah well you may have to wait quite a while," Dahli muttered as she sorted through her paper. Much to her relief she discovered it was not all written in the little characters. Relief, then further horror. It was all gibberish. She chanced a furtive glance around the room. Everyone was staring at her.

"Just read what you have," said Duone Alsayers.

"Okay," she said, knowing she was facing down the most embarrassing day of her life. She took a deep breath then began to read.

"Dark dark dark spinning light swooping across planked floor lurch. New day, all right, never know I'm gone. Lurch again still same day stuck out back in this joint how did I get in and how do I get out assuming I do at all then he walks into view and asks me what I want for lunch and I follow into commissary eat go back to speaker sit. So hard to think garbage loads of garbage should put a period in here somewhere someone offers me a drink don't know who thanks cool down here I'm so quiet that they just let me sit here asks me if I'm okay yeah fine gotta write this stupid report yeah okay gonna go sleep. Sleep? What time is it anyway get another drink some mushrooms ought to go find breakfast comes Draephus want to go eat sure do this later no wait I'll bring it."

Then the little figures resumed, and the next two pages were unreadable. As Dahli sorted through them, she heard Alsayers ask; "How long does it go on in this manner?"

"Uh," said Dahli, "I'm not sure. Some of it I can't read."
Why not?"

"Well it's in another language. Oh wait, here's a part... 'in the men's washroom somebody sure tossed in here the smell's so bad makes me want to add to the mess. Write on door can't read it. No good go back to kitchen more silver and green and wait for it to take effect oh wow Touskanian chocolate see you later where do you go when you die or do you just go what do you mean the memory board went down seven minute improvised drum solo and the board goes down someone's gonna be angry. Cui's dead, Faelin's dead I'll be dead too someday I guess."

"Duone Alsayers," piped up Atania Nightwing, "I think it is obvious that Dahli wrote this report under the influence of some hallucinogenic substance."

"Hey don't stop now," said the boy next to Dahli. "I was just beginning to understand it."

Dahli swung her head to look at Atania. Images smeared temporarily. "Yes, I was stoned. Nasty, nasty me. If you'd get that knot out of your back end maybe people would share their drugs with you, too."

There was a shocked silence. Somebody giggled. Atania stared open mouthed at Dahli, then looked towards Duone Alsayers.

"Dahli," said Alsayers, "are you quite all right? You seem a little spontaneous."

"Duone Al..." began Atania, then was violently interrupted when Dahli leaned forward and screamed into her face.

"DAHLI SANDINITI!" shouted Duone Alsayers.

Dahli stood up. "I know, I know, FINE! I'll go sit in the Bad Dahli Box in the office."

"And you're going to rewrite that report in a language native to this planet and our current plane of existence!"

"FINE!"

****

The day ended eventually. Dahli slogged home, wondering where her life had gone wrong. The only bright spot was when Diza caught up with her, taking her arm.

"Dahli where have you been?! And what was with you today?" She laughed. "I can't believe you screamed at Atania."

Dahli laughed. "It wasn't my fault, honest. I'm not sure what made me do it, but it was a lot of fun."

Diza looked her over. "So… is that it? Is that THE coat?"

"The one and only. This is his shirt and hat, too. This coat weighs a hundred tons."

"Well it's probably soaked."

Dahli shook her head. "It's not. It's some kind of hair. It's really soft but the rain just rolls right off it. I'm completely dry."

"Well why is it so heavy then?"

"I don't know, but my period started with a vengeance while sitting in the office and I am NOT giving this back to Draephus with a big red spot in the middle of it!"

Diza's eyes grew enormous. "Do you think…?"

"Oh I hope not but I have a horrible feeling I did."

They reached Dahli's house, going inside and heading up for Dahli's room. Dahli dumped the coat onto the bed and ran for the bathroom, while Diza examined the inner lining. After a few minutes Dahli returned, wearing a clean pair of pants.

"Well?"

"We're going to have to find a way to wash it," said Diza.

"I don't know," said Dahli worriedly. "Draephus doesn't wash it, there's gotta be a reason."

"Well do you want to give it back to him with *that* in the middle of it?"

"No." She sighed, and examined the coat. "Hey, look the lining comes out. We can wash the liner and not touch the outer shell."

"Too bad," said Diza. "I've had fantasies about washing this coat."

Dahli giggled. "Yeah me too, and every other Gryphons fan on the planet. C'mon, help me with it."

They found the snaps that attached the inner lining to the outer shell, slowly pulling it off. Beneath it was a second lining, of what material, Dahli didn't know. It was a cream colour, very thick and very soft, and also dotted with blood. Like the outer lining it was held in with snaps, and the two girls pulled it out as well.

They gaped in complete astonishment at what they found. Guns, drugs, several forms of currency, ammunition, sterile bandages, sealed rations, gold, gems, some medical instruments, keys stitched individually to the fabric in a row, and a vial of something nameless. All were firmly fixed into a sort of leather harness attached to the second inner lining. The infamous "iron dildo" that she and Straif had been joking about was a sawed off night stalker gun.

Dahli and Diza just stared, jaws hanging. Dahli reached out to touch one of the bands of ammunition.

"That's why he never takes it off," Dahli said softly. "That's the whole secret of the coat. If the Kryphisians come back... he doesn't want to be taken unawares. This is his safety net. It has everything he needs to survive for days. Why would he loan it to me? Why would he trust me with something so important? This is his lifeline! He just... sent me out the door this morning wearing his chance of survival like it was no big deal."

"Well," said Diza quietly, "I think he's saying you're pretty

513

important to him." She glanced at her, and said; "Look it's none of my business, Dahli, but I'm hearing some things at school about…your friendship…"

"I know," said Dahli. "I know it must look pretty strange to other people. But it's not like that. He's not my boyfriend, I'm not his girlfriend. There's no unspoken longing or any of that garbage. I know that from the outside our friendship must make no sense at all, and I'm not sure I understand it myself, but… I can sit beside him and say nothing and understand everything he's thinking. I don't know why we're friends. We just are." She ran a hand over the sealed packets of gemstones, then stood up. "C'mon. Let's take out this harness and set it aside, then wash the rest."

"Okay," said Diza, "But if we ruin it and have to go on the run then I want the little gun with the blue inlaid handle."

"Fine. But I get to keep the hat."

Dahli carefully hung the leather harness of ammunition on a chair, then she and Diza set about cleaning the coat.

"So did you say you got a job?" asked Diza as she and Dahli watched the most famous garment in Sferkkaan history get washed.

"Sort of," said Dahli. "I really want to go to the Year End Festival, so Draephus hired me to run around and do all the small jobs, like making sure there's always water available and getting stuff for the techs and swapping cables and watering the amp-plants and all that stuff. It's not hard but there's never a second to sit down. Then I decided to help myself to the stuff in Mars' glass and the next thing I know it's today, and Teirra is going to be so mad I'll never see the outside of this house again. I'm such a mess. Teirra thinks it's all Draephus' fault, but it's not. He just… inadvertently provides the opportunities for me to make things worse."

"I must admit," said Diza, "he really does not seem to understand why some of the things he does are bad."

"Yeah well he grew up in a jungle with drug-smugglers and faelins, that's bound to make anybody a little unclear on right and wrong." Dahli sighed. "I just want to go to the festival…."

"Me too. Maybe if I get a job too and pool our money… assuming Dad lets me go."

"We'll figure something out," said Dahli. "Hey, if I can steal a dead body, bust out of jail and firewalk through Avalair, I can get us to the festival."

"Well I hope it doesn't come to that," said Diza. "What are you getting paid to run errands?"

"I dunno, I forgot to ask. Great. Well... I have The Coat, and I have The Hat. I can hold them ransom."

The door of the house opened, and a voice called "Dahli?"

"Czamki! Come on in! We're watching the laundry."

"Ooooh, exciting. I brought a friend."

Czamkiar walked into the open area behind the house where the washer was kept, leading Gemma by the hand.

"Heia!" she said. "I am learned language!"

"You am learned better than the last time we had a shaumaus," said Dahli.

"Actually I have," said Gemma, smiling.

"Oh very tricky," said Dahli. "You should have let us go on thinking you were not that good yet!"

"I thought about it," said Gemma. "But I didn't want to get caught playing games. Anyway, I knew I had to get better for the festival. So what are we doing?"

"Watching the most famous coat in Sferkkaan history take a bath and hoping it survives," said Dahli.

"The coat?" said Czamkiar. "As in... THAT coat?!"

"Yup," said Dahli. "As in THAT coat. I kinda got a big red spot on it."

"How big?" asked Czamkiar.

"Big enough that I couldn't pass it off as a nose bleed," she said.

Gemma stared at Dahli. "I can't believe you would admit something like that!"

"Admit what?" asked Dahli. "That I menstruate? I'm a girl, we do that."

"I just can't believe you discussed it in front of a boy."

Dahli looked at Czamkiar. "Are you traumatized by my biology?"

"Deeply," he said. "I may never recover. Were there vaginas involved?"

"Yes," said Dahli gravely.

"Alas," he said. "I am traumatized. Oh, speaking of biology – I have some scrap fabric, did you want me to bring it over and you can make it into menstrual towels?"

"Definitely," said Dahli. "The ones I have don't really wash clean anymore."

Gemma blinked at the trio. "You have to make your own… protection?"

"What do you want me to do?" asked Dahli. "Leave little festive red dots wherever I go?"

"You can't go to the store and buy them?"

"Sometimes, but it depends on if the makers can find the proper fabric," said Dahli.

"Oh my god," said Gemma. "If I had to make my own pads – my life would totally be ruined."

"Oh, mine too," said Czamkiar dryly.

Gemma sighed, and reached into her coat pocket, pulling out a handful of brightly-wrapped squares and gave them to Dahli. "Here. A gift from a friend. Super-absorbent maxi-pads."

"Great!" said Dahli. "I'll go sacrifice one to the vaginal gods while chanting the holy prayer-song."

"What song would that be?" Diza called after her as Dahli headed to the bathroom.

"Let it Bleed by the Rolling Stones," called Dahli.

Gemma groaned. "You people are *way* too comfortable with each other."

"We are," said Czamkiar. "My life is ruined. So much so I may have to share the kiska nuts I brought."

"Kiska nuts?" said Diza. "Where did you get kiska nuts?!"

"Behind my house!" he said. "You know that old twisted tree with the white bark? It decided to bloom this year, and it turned out to be a kiska tree! Dad's thrilled, we've been trading them for all sorts of things. We're not going to starve *this* winter, I tell you."

"So your life is completely ruined," said Diza.

"Absolutely."

He drew out a bag of the nuts, and opened it, sharing it with his friends. After a few minutes, Dahli returned from the bathroom and reached in to take out a small handful as well, setting them in her lap and carefully opening one.

"Oh they look like little rose buds inside!" said Gemma. "They're all pink and green!"

"Pink and green and crispy and delicious!" said Diza. "I love these little morsels!"

The group paused as they heard a tap on the door.

"I really hope that's not Draephus," said Dahli.

"COME IN IF YOU'RE NOT KRYPHISIAN!" called Diza.

They heard the door open, then close, and the light step of a boy in high heels. Dahli smiled widely as she saw the familiar long brown hair and big green eyes.

"I swear I am not Kryphisian," Straif said

"Straif! Come in, sit down! Here…" She scurried to make an acceptable place for him. "You can sit next to Czamki. He doesn't bite and he doesn't smell too bad. Why are you here?"

Straif seated himself carefully beside Czamkiar, who looked to Dahli.

"Exactly how many famous musicians do you know?" he asked.

"They multiply," said Dahli. "When you know one you know a bunch. Straif this is Diza, Czamkiar, and Gemma. She's from Earth but that's okay, we forgive her."

"We've met," said Gemma, sulking. "I asked him to take me out and he said no."

"I was in *pain*," said Straif, clearly annoyed.

Gemma rolled her eyes. "Whatever, for a planet with so few women, you guys are sure picky."

Dahli decided to change the subject. "Straif why are you here? The last I saw you, you were working with Raski…"

He sighed. "Yeah, I was with Raski. Then Sivil walked into the studio…"

"Sivil Marden?" said Dahli.

"Yeah," said Straif. "Our brave and fearless lead vocalist. He interrupts me and Raski Jervyas to inform me that my pregnancy is interfering with band business so as of right now I am cut from Vortex. So then I did a Pete Townsend impression with my quinticord until I started cramping, whereupon Draephus and Khandi told me to go to Draephus' castle and take a nap and a bath."

"And you naturally mistook my house for Draephus' castle," said Dahli.

He smiled. "I just didn't want to be alone. I was *so angry*. The only reason anyone listens to Vortex is because of me, and they threw me away in the rudest, most humiliating way possible."

"Now you're free to find a real band," said Dahli. "Straif…

you're one of the greatest musicians alive. Once word gets out that you're available… let me put it this way, Sivil Marden is easily as smart as he is talented. He'll swirl down into obscurity and you will end up with a real band. Okay?"

"I know all that, it just made me angry. And I do not need to be angry right now. So! What are we doing?"

"Eating kiska nuts and watching Draephus' coat go 'round in the wash," said Diza.

"It's a vigil," said Czamkiar.

Straif's green eyes were enormous. "You're washing THE COAT?!"

"I had to," said Dahli. "I menstruated all over it."

Gemma had some sort of silent fit over Dahli mentioning her period to males. Straif helped himself to some nuts and tossed back his long hair.

"Ugh, don't talk to me about menstruating, I did nothing *but* for weeks after I got my implant. Cramping, bleeding, crying…"

"So it hurt," said Czamkiar.

"They had me on pure mushroom resin the first week," said Straif. "Most of the pain is from when they grind your pelvic basin larger to accommodate the fetus…"

There were howls of pain from all sides. Straif merrily continued.

"Not to mention the mesh they have to attach to your abdominal muscles to stop them from tearing, and then properly anchoring the implant to your…"

"WHY?" wailed Czamkiar. "WHY would you DO THAT to yourself?!"

"I want a family," said Straif. "And due to certain conditions, if I want one then I have to do things fast. And soon as I was healed and I had found a male with the traits I wanted, I was pregnant."

"So you *are* pregnant," said Diza. "Draephus didn't seem to want to talk about it."

"He's a bit superstitious," said Straif. "If you talk about an unborn baby to a stranger before the mother begins to show then something bad can happen. But yes, I am pregnant."

"Can I touch the baby?" asked Czamkiar.

"Well there is not much there to touch yet, but if you like."

"Eeeeeyyyyeeeewwww…." said Gemma as Czamkiar

cautiously reached out one gloved hand to touch Straif's stomach.

"Okay," said Dahli, "crazy Earth girls need to be quiet when pretty boys are touching each other."

"Mean Sferkkaan girls need to be nice to crazy Earth girls, or I won't take photos," said Gemma.

"What's it feel like?" asked Diza.

"Feels like a stomach," said Czamkiar.

"I'm only four weeks," said Straif. "Sorry. Not much baby there to feel yet. Oh! Czamkiar. You have to kiss me."

"I do? I mean not that I mind but… I do?"

Straif's green eyes gleamed. "Yes. You need to kiss me, Gemma needs to photograph it, and Dahli needs to post it to the Abyssal Plane."

"Isn't that the Vortex fan site?" asked Diza.

"Ooooh I smell payback cooking," said Dahli. "Czamki, you need to kiss the pretty musician, and not just because I will cherish the image for the rest of my life."

Czamkiar shrugged, then looked to Straif, who draped his arms around Czamkiar's neck and lay back on the old couch, drawing Czamkiar down on top of himself. Straif wrapped his long legs around Czamkiar, crossing his ankles. Gemma snapped several photos, then handed her phone to Dahli.

"Okay, Straif, what do I do now?"

Straif released Czamkiar, the pair sitting up looking rather rumpled. Straif pushed his long hair back, then said; "Post it to the site with the caption *'Straif Mannechek celebrates both his departure from Vortex to explore new musical territory, as well as the fourth week of his pregnancy, with a friend'*. Unless Czamkiar wants his name in there."

"Yes," said Czamkiar. "Yes I very much want people to think there is a chance I put a baby in Straif Mannechek. I can't wait to see Atania Nightwing implode at the idea."

"I thought you were straight," said Gemma dryly.

"Never too straight to make annoying people crazy," said Czamkiar.

Dahli posted the photo to the site, then read aloud the caption she added. *"Straif Mannechek celebrates both his departure from Vortex to explore new musical territory, as well as the fourth week of his pregnancy, with companion Czamkiar Sletkkaa."*

"Love it," said Straif. "Now let's see how long it takes for the walls of the Cylinder to split."

Six minutes later, Straif's telecom rang. He drew it out. "Heia? Oh heia Sivil. Oh you saw the photo. And....? What was that? I....? Oh šukat you."

"What did he say?" asked Dahli as Straif put his phone away.

"He says I'm still in Vortex, they never released me. That is not true and Raski can back me up. Raski may be high strung but he's not stupid."

"I wonder if the Vortex fans are having fits?" asked Diza.

Gemma drew out her phone to check the Vortex fan site, then handed the phone to Straif. He accepted it, and looked at the screen.

"Any good comments?" asked Diza.

"Well this one is pretty good," said Straif. "'*How could you let Straif Mannechek go? He's the only reason anyone listens to your clart.*' And here is another good one – '*Straif left?! Who is he playing for now?!*' And then there is this one – '*Well if Straif is gone there's no reason for me to buy the next cylinder.*' Oh, and this one – '*Is that the daddy of Straif's baby? Gonna be a very pretty kid.*' Czamkiar I believe the fans approve of your genes."

"Well I am High Northerner, we do make the prettiest babies."

There came a tap on the door.

"Come on in!" Dahli called as she began loading the linings of Draephus' coat into the dryer. The outer portion was virtually dry, so Dahli hung it up. Finally clean, it was a soft pearl grey. She hoped he wasn't angry that she had washed it.

Again she heard the light tappity-tap of high heels, and moments later Khandid Stracona appeared in the doorway.

"Donsa Mannechek, did we not tell you to get some rest?"

Straif made a show of looking around the laundry room. "Hey this isn't Draephus' castle!"

"How did you know he was here?" asked Dahli.

"I saw your little post on the Abyssal Plane and knew this was not Draephus' castle. So the only other likely place he would head was here. Why are we all in the laundry room?"

"I have a better question," said Dahli. "Why is it my house has no back wall at all, but people go to the front door and knock?"

Khandid did not answer. He was staring at something hanging from the door, blue eyes huge. "YOU WASHED THE COAT?!"

"YES," said Dahli. "I WASHED THE COAT."

"WHY?!"

"I got something all over the linings and I didn't want to give it back looking like I'd used it for a menstrual rag. Only don't say 'menstrual' in front of Gemma, it makes her cringe. Is he going to be mad?"

"I honestly do not know," said Khandid. "But I do think you had a valid reason for tossing it into the wash. I mean I would have. Just... make sure you put it back together."

Dahli nodded. "I will."

She finished drying it, then took the coat and the two liners upstairs, followed by Khandid. As Dahli spread the great pale grey coat out on the bed, Khandid gazed at the leather harness that held the guns, gems, drugs, ammunition, and other items.

"I knew it had to be something like this," said Khandid softly.

"I can't believe he let me walk out of the studio this morning with it on my back," said Dahli. "This is his survival kit."

"Well he's been through a lot lately," said Khandid. "Maybe he was just feeling protective."

Dahli took the leather harness and began carefully clipping it back into place. "He's an odd sort. One moment he's the sweetest man who ever lived, the next... I can see the man who fought in the Cylinder. I can't understand him. He's like two entirely different people."

"Draephus CZimcocious is what happens when you take a man who was born with an incredibly gentle spirit," said Khandid, "and smash him like a calurchi with a hammer."

Dahli finished putting in the harness, then added the heavy liner that kept the harness from weighing too heavily on the wearer's shoulders, then put in the outer lining.

"Done," she said. "Clean and intact. Hope he's not angry."

She gave the coat to Khandid, as well as the hat, then they went downstairs, where Straif was seated in a chair, looking rather weary.

"Are we ready to go now?" asked Khandid.

Straif nodded. "Yeah. I'm tired."

"Have you eaten?"

"Oh Khandid I'm not hungry, really."

"You need to eat, that's why they give expectant mothers extra rations."

Dahli walked over to him, taking his hand and helping him to his feet. She smiled as she realized he was the same height she was, but only with his heels on.

"Eat something," she said.

"After a nap," he said quietly. "Sleep first, then food. Will I see you at the studio later?"

"I don't know, my sister is pretty mad at me for being gone so long."

"Then I'll come by and steal you."

"Okay," she said softly, smiling.

She squeezed his hands, feeling light-headed and giggly and… really not like herself. There was something about him that made her so happy, and he seemed to feel just the same. Then she leaned forward and kissed him.

Ooooooooohhhhh….. yeah. She could get used to this…

She held him close and kissed him several times, reluctant to let Straif go, and he equally reluctant to leave. But then Khandid gently tugged him away.

"Come on, Straif, you need to rest."

"Yeah I do," Straif admitted. He smiled at Dahli. "I'll be back later, after a nap and after Khandid makes me eat something."

"I'll be here," she said.

She watched Straif leave with Khandid, then drifted back to the laundry room on a cloud of little hearts and pink bubbles.

"Awww…." said Diza. "Dahli's in looove…"

"Dahli is," admitted Dahli.

"That's so cute!" said Gemma.

"Yeah!" said Czamkiar. "Now we get to see Dahli tell her sister that her boyfriend is pregnant!"

Suddenly the cloud of hearts and bubbles was gone with a loud 'pop'!

"Clart," said Dahli.

Chapter Twenty-Three

Straif did not return that night; Draephus called her in the evening to let her know that he was simply too exhausted.

"So... uh... you cleaned my coat," he said.

"I'm so sorry, Draephus, I had to! I couldn't give it back to you after I made a mess on it! I really wasn't trying to pry into your private business, I just..."

"It's okay, Dahli. Khandid explained. I'm not angry. I'm just glad your sister let you live."

"Yeah well my life is still negotiable. But I really want the job and I really want to go to the Festival."

He laughed quietly. "I'll see what I can do. But you have another eight months. And I think Straif would like you to come."

"I'd love to go with him," she said. "Teirra and I had a huge fight tonight. She was so mad, Draephus. She was furious about me being gone and me getting into all that stuff at the studio, and then when I told her Straif was pregnant I thought she was going to blow up. She's so upset. I don't know what to tell her. She's just really scared for me. I keep trying to tell her I'm really not doing anything too bad, but... well we lost Dad, we lost our older brother, and then one day our mother just walked away and never came back. Some soldiers found her, and came to tell us, but... I couldn't hear it. I really could not. I kept screaming about how she wasn't dead, she wasn't. She just didn't want to be a mom anymore, and ran away to Charlendine. And she was the most beautiful woman there and everyone wanted to dance with her."

"Was she a dancer?"

"Not professionally, but she *did* dance. I know she was invited to the Cylinder once to a party with a lot of Kryphisian officers, and she danced for them. They didn't hurt her, I know that. When she came back she was just glowing. Said she met someone and he was wonderful. I don't know who. She died not long after that, and I just could not bear it. So I made up a story about how my mother was so beautiful she ran away with her Kryphisian lover and was having glamourous adventures."

"Was he Kryphisian?" asked Draephus.

"I don't know, I never saw him. He could have been anyone. Anyway, after we lost Mom... Teirra's been really scared of losing me too."

"Dahli, eventually you *are* going to grow up."

"I know. I think she's just terrified I'm going to do it sometime this week. But after everything I've done... I can't just go back to being a kid, either. It's such a frustrating place to be. And with Straif's pregnancy..."

"It *is* a huge responsibility," said Draephus.

"Yeah. But he's not asking me to move in and help him raise it. It's another ten months before the baby is even here, maybe by then we won't like each other. Maybe by then we will have decided we just want to be friends. Maybe by then he'll have married the Emperor! Who knows how this could all go?"

"Just give her a chance to calm down and adjust," said Draephus. Then he laughed quietly. "And maybe cut out some of the crazy stuff for a while. In the meantime, Straif is going to be staying with me for few weeks, and helping on the new tracks. Raski is going to be taking some time off."

"Is he okay?"

"He's fine. Well... actually he fell down and cracked his wrist. But he'll be fine. So while he's healing, we will use Straif."

"But Straif plays quinticord. Raski plays sepulchord."

"Straif can play sepulchord. He just plays it at light speed. It'll be fun watching Khandi and Yuri keep up with him. We could all use a kick in the butt to keep us from getting complacent. Look, don't worry about the festival too much, okay Fearless? There's plenty to do around the studio, we can genuinely use someone to run around like a crazy person and help out, and even if Straif doesn't want to take you, I will."

"Need someone to hit you with a door down there, huh?"

"Nah. I figure every teen girl needs a big brother with no common sense."

She felt her throat go tight, and her eyes began to burn with tears. Before she knew it, she was crying in a way she hadn't since she was little, and Draephus was sighing loudly.

"I can't šukating say anything to you *or* Raski, can I?"

Dahli managed a breath, snuffling loudly. "I love you too!"

She could almost hear him roll his eyes and slap a hand over his face. "Fine. Cry. See if I care."

****

Dahli met Czamkiar and Diza on the corner the next morning. It could have been any fall day of any year, but so much had happened. Still, Dahli was grateful that nothing had changed too much. She still had her two best friends, and some new ones she loved. And she now had a potential boyfriend. It was as if no time had passed at all, yet so much had.

"So how long until Teirra forgives you?" asked Diza.

"She wants me to quit my job at the studio and stay home. No way. Draephus may be my friend now but I'm *still* a Gryphons fan. Oh – you know that terrible fan site, the Gryphon's Roost? Be *very* careful what you post. Khandid and Raski practically live there."

Diza's eyes bulged. "You didn't tell them my on-line name, did you?!"

"No, don't worry Diza, I would never humiliate you like that. Just keep in mind that Raski and Khandid are there daily. They've offered me a reward if I can find out who is writing that horrible awful story where Raski is the whip-waving crazy man."

"Oh I love that one!" said Diza. "It's so awful it's hilarious!"

"Atania," said Czamkiar.

Dahli and Diza stopped, staring at him. Czamkiar gazed back through his make-up.

"Atania," he said. "She sits with me sometimes when we're supposed to be studying and works on it."

"Atania Nightwing?!" said Dahli. "She hates the Gryphons! She's a Vortex fan!"

"Doesn't stop her from writing clart about them," said Czamkiar.

"Are you going to tell Raski?" asked Diza.

"Absolutely," said Dahli. "Unless you want to make her life miserable first."

"Absolutely," said Diza.

They paused as they heard footsteps running up behind them. They turned, and saw a form in black and red, his white hair loose and wild, his blue eyes staring at Czamkiar. He looked as if someone had stabbed him in the guts; there was no other way to describe the expression on his face; as if his whole world was crumbling to dust. Czamkiar seemed to read his thoughts.

"You saw that picture of me with Straif."

Lyrellyn was shaking. He did not seem to be able to form words, and Dahli could not help but worry he may either faint or be sick.

"I'm not the father of Straif's baby," said Czamkiar "I never had sex with him, it was just a posed photo to annoy some people. And… at the risk of being cruel…. It's not your business what I do."

"I know. I know it's not. And I know I'm making a complete joke of myself and if my father knew he'd be horrified, but please… give me one more chance to win you. Tonight."

Czamkiar shifted, looking uncomfortable. "Lyrellyn… I really think it's not right for me to keep giving you chances. I hate the idea that I'm playing with your emotions."

Lyrellyn shook his head, hair and feathers swaying as he made a dismissive gesture with his hand. "No. It's completely self-inflicted, I know that. It hurts like everything I've ever experienced in my life and it's all my own fault but please, just once more."

"I don't think I should," said Czamkiar. "Lyrellyn… I really like you. I do. You're funny, you're smart, you're the only guy on the planet I know who can shoot water out his nostril to kill flies…"

"Oooh, and your daddy is an Imperial Bird of Prey," said Dahli. "Bet he's thrilled."

"As long as I don't do it in front of the Emperor, I can shoot anything I like with my nose," said Lyrellyn. "Czamki… please. One more. And… if you still feel the same… I'll stop. I swear."

Czamkiar seemed confused and uncomfortable. Finally he looked to Dahli and Diza.

"What do you two think?"

Dahli shrugged. "Why not? What can it hurt?"

"Says the girl who stole the dead body," said Czamkiar.

"Czamki, the guy is beautiful and he loves you," said Diza. "If he liked girls I'd take him myself."

"Awww….!" said Lyrellyn. "Really?"

Diza nodded, and Lyrellyn grinned. Czamkiar sighed.

"Okay. One last date. But if it doesn't work then don't ask me out anymore, I can't stand the guilt."

"I promise," said Lyrellyn. "So… you really are not…?"

"I am not the father of Straif's baby," said Czamkiar. "We just posed for that photo to make someone angry."

"Oh. Did it work?"

"Brilliantly," said Czamkiar.

"Let's get going," said Dahli. "I'm in enough trouble without being late for school. Are you going to walk with us, Lyrellyn?"

"All right," he said quietly.

****

As Dahli and her friends were walking to school, Draephus was carefully going through his castle, slowly but meticulously removing any and all traces of Vesper.

He was surprised there was so little.

He found traces of all his friends all over his house; bits and pieces of who they were and what they did for a living, such as the occasional glove or misplaced quinticord string or stray piece of jewelry. He found the notepad Mars used to track song ideas, and even found a sock he was pretty sure belonged to Dahli.

But nothing of Vesper's.

Of course, given that the entire relationship had been a farce, Draephus did not think that was too strange. But he needed something, anything, that belonged to the man he had loved. Vesper. Not the other bastard. Not the murderer. He needed something that proved some piece of Vesper had been real, but there was nothing. When Vesper had left, he had not planned on returning. He'd taken everything that he needed and wanted, and evaporated from Draephus' life. All he found was an old laser print in a frame, tossed into a drawer. Vesper had torn it in half, leaving the image of Draephus, and taking only the half with himself in it.

No. Not Vesper. That other guy. The murderer. The fraud. The lie.

Draephus burned the laser print, and put the now-empty frame in a drawer. At least now he knew why the spells had not been working.

He went to his telecom and phoned J'Vanni. Draephus smiled as he heard the slightly mechanized sounding accent, and the hawk screaming in the background.

"Heia?"

"Heia J'Vanni," said Draephus. "How are you?"

"I am well. Would you like a hawk? This one is too noisy."

Draephus grinned. "What's he doing?"

"He seems to be of the opinion that he should be the one getting eggs for breakfast, not proper hawk food. Even though eggs make him sick."

"The eggs probably taste better."

"Well he did not get the nickname "Picky" by accident. He is a naughty bird. Oh! I have news. They will be able to restore partial sight to my right eye."

Draephus felt genuine excitement for his friend, and suddenly Vesper's betrayal seemed further away and less important. The little bastard hadn't won, not in the least.

"That's fantastic!"

"Yes I think so. I like being able to see a little better than not at all. They will operate next week, and soon I will have two big blue eyes instead of holes in my face."

"Blue," said Draephus, feeling his joy deflate somewhat. "Not grey."

"I just want to be safe, Draephus. That is all."

"It's not fair," said Draephus.

"No. It is not. But as my lovely Delaes put it; we did not fight for *our* side, we fought for *your* side. And your side did not include Grey Boy monsters and half-breed freaks. We need to look to our own safety."

"I wish I could make it better," said Draephus.

"You did," said J'Vanni. "You made it better than ever we could have hoped, and we love you for it. But not everyone shares your perspective on things."

"How is Delaes?"

"He and the hawk are a package deal. Would you like them both?"

Draephus clamped a hand over his mouth to keep from laughing as he heard the familiar endless sentence in the background.

"I absolutely did-too hear that you big meanie honestly I get a little hormonal and I cry a few times and everybody starts treating me like glass and then I get frustrated and suddenly I'm an unsuitable spouse well you listen to me Donsa Pretty Boy…"

"So he's fine," said Draephus.

"He's beautiful," said J'Vanni affectionately.

"It's not a compliment if you are blind!" said Delaes hotly.

"Who needs eyes for such beauty?"

"YUCK!" screamed the hawk.

"I can't wait to see what your household looks like with a baby added to it," said Draephus.

"Yes about the baby," said J'Vanni. "Our plan to go to the South Continent seems to be off. And people are beginning to ask questions. We're a little frightened."

Draephus looked up as he heard the sound of Straif Mannechek coming down the stairs, singing to himself. And an idea came to mind.

"Straif! How would you like to participate in fraudulent activity for the greater good?"

"Does it involve cookies? Because I seriously need a cookie. Like now."

"What kind?"

"Those ones with crushed kiska nuts in them they sell at the little shop in the merchant district."

"Absolutely," said Draephus.

"Okay. What do you need?"

"Copies of your medical records for your implant."

"For cookies – I will do it. Who are they for?"

"Oh, uh… you don't know him."

"In that case you're gonna need a bigger cookie."

"We still need a doctor to sign the papers," said J'Vanni. "Dr. Arang is going to know he did not give Delaes an implant."

"It's fine, I have it covered. So just relax and heal while Straif and I commit fraud and forgery in the name of babies everywhere."

"Babies who are two-thirds Kryphisian, one-third Faelin," said J'Vanni. "We are hoping the eyes will be green, not grey."

"Like my hair is turning," said Draephus. "Okay. Now if you two can stay out of trouble for five minutes, I'll go break the law."

"Of course. Thank you, Draephus. We owe you so much more than we could ever repay…"

"Just rest. I'll call you later."

Draephus hung up, then turned to see Straif standing before him.

"Cookies. NOW."

"Fine. Just drag your hormones out to the conni and we'll go get cookies. What do we do if the shop is closed because it couldn't get supplies this week?"

"Cry."

Draephus sighed loudly. "Scruffin' lovely."

****

It took hours, but eventually Draephus had all the things he needed as well as the required falsified signatures and faked stamps. The folder of papers was then taken directly to J'Vanni and Delaes by Draephus personally, who then returned home. By the time he was stumbling back into the door of his castle, he was exhausted and in agony. All he wanted was to take some resin and fall into the bath and...

Draephus bumped into Raski on the stairs, and smiled.

"Heia, beautiful."

"Heia." Raski slipped his arms around Draephus' neck and kissed him, his right wrist encased in a cast. "Where have you been all day?"

"Out making the world safe for defected Grey Boys."

"A very noble cause." Raski kissed him again. "I have a present for you."

"Oh yeah? Does it involve you naked and covered in almaniki oil?"

"It does, but first... you have to follow me to the bedroom."

Draephus kissed him. "I love it already."

Raski led Draephus into the bedchamber and over to the bed. He sighed loudly as he saw the faelins had nibbled holes in the brightly-wrapped gift box.

"You have to tell them not to do that," said Draephus.

"You keep telling me how intelligent the little clart-blossoms are..."

"They are! But they are also very curious. You left a pretty box on the bed, so clearly it needs to be investigated."

Raski stared at Bacca and Czanda, who stared back.

"Your mother was a feralyke."

"ARF!"

"That's your excuse for everything."

"RARRAARARARARF!"

Raski looked to Draephus. "And Delaes is fifty percent one of these?"

Draephus sighed. "Yeah I don't like thinking about it either. At least it explains how he talks the way he does."

"Really?"

"Yeah faelins can draw air to make sound as well as exhale. That's how they make those incredibly long calls. When they run out of air they just start to inhale instead and they can make a continual sound. You and I have to stop and inhale to continue."

"And... this is a great survival trait... why?"

Draephus shrugged. "Don't know, I'm not a faelin. Hey did you two eat my box?"

"Arf!"

Draephus walked over to the bed and sat down on it, taking the brightly coloured box and opening it. Inside he found some brilliantly silvery chains, attached to rings and hoops. He held it up and gazed at it, puzzled.

"What is it?"

Raski took hold of the shiny device and gave it a light shake to straighten out the chains. He then began carefully fitting it onto Draephus' hand.

"Like this," he said softly. "It helps support the joints in your hands and wrists. It should stop some of the pain. It should slow some of the deterioration as well."

Draephus watched as Raski slipped the chain harnesses onto his hands and fastened them, then slowly flexed his fingers.

"How is it?" asked Raski.

"Bit restrictive. Where did you get these?"

"I went to Bonnikkaar and asked him about things to help slow the effects of the virus. I didn't tell him who it was for. I think he thinks they were for me, especially since I went to him with my wrist in a cast."

Draephus took Raski's hand in his own, running his fingers over the cast.

"Quite a pair, aren't we?"

"It could be worse," said Raski, smiling. He gazed at Draephus with luminous blue eyes. "I really wish you had told me."

"I knew it would just upset you."

"How bad is the decay? Do you know?"

"No," said Draephus. "Some days I feel fine, and some days I hurt so bad all I can do is lie in bed. I really haven't wanted to look into it too closely. They'll want me to just get into bed and stay there and I can't do that."

"I know. We'll figure something out, okay?" Raski kissed him gently. "I have an unpleasant question, though. Was our darling little Vesper working alone?"

"No," said Draephus. "Delaes said there were two others that he saw, and possibly a third as well. But with Vesper dead, their headquarters burned to dust, and their cover blown, they're not likely to be a problem for a while."

"They might be after you, now."

"I really doubt it. I think if I was meant to go, I would have gone when they shot J'Vanni."

"Just… be careful, okay?"

"I will. I promise. Now… why are you still dressed?"

Raski kissed him. "That's a very good question. You know… it's odd. I thought after we were together, I'd feel less intense towards you. But I don't."

"Well we haven't been together too long. But… I hope that doesn't fade anytime soon."

Raski began undressing, the rings on his fingers glittering in the firelight. "Speaking of implants…"

"Were we?"

"Well sort of. I thought since I couldn't play right now with my wrist in a cast, I thought I would get mine now. Then by the time the bone is set enough that I can play again, I'll be healed."

Draephus sighed. "Raski…"

"You promised."

"I did. And I mean to keep my promise. Just… isn't this a little soon?"

"Yes. But now is the best time. I'm just trying to be practical."

"Uh huh. I'm starting to think you broke your wrist on purpose."

"No," said Raski. "No I would never intentionally mess up *either* hand, not even for a family."

"Does this have anything to do with…?"

Raski kissed him. "You talk too much. And you're still

dressed."

"Shutting up and getting naked now, sir."

"Arf!"

Raski looked to Bacca. "And you are not invited."

"Pppppbbbbbrrrrrtttt…"

"And the same to you. Shoo."

Bacca and Czanda left. Raski gently pushed Draephus down to the bed. "And now…"

Draephus made a cry of pain. Raski sighed loudly.

"Fine. Mushrooms first, *then* sex."

"I love you."

****

Draephus lay on his back in the huge bed, his left arm around Raski, his right hand holding a cigarette. Outside the bedroom window, the rain pounded and lashed the trees. Inside the bedroom, John Lennon sang 'Mind Games'; the sound of the music filling the castle with haunting refrains.

"Imagine if we could have had John Lennon at the Festival," said Draephus.

"There's an awful pun in there somewhere," said Raski.

Draephus grinned. "Yeah. Just… makes me sick that Lennon is dead and we're left with… what? Vortex?"

"And Mickie Pastors, don't forget him."

"I'd like to," said Draephus. He drew on his cigarette. "I'd give a lot to see J'Vanni Dei Syncopius play live. There has to be a way to talk him into it."

"Yeah we'd have better luck inviting Donsa Lennon," said Raski. "For one thing, Lennon would probably be less nervous."

"There has to be a way," said Draephus.

"Would you?" asked Raski. "Knowing all the things J'Vanni has been through?"

"I don't know," said Draephus. "I mean look at everything Mars has been through, and he *loves* to perform live. I just think it would do J'Vanni good. I hate all that talent being locked away. Half the population of Sferkkaa thinks he's Delaes' alter-ego."

Raski nudged Draephus. "You're ignoring the esteemed Donsa Lennon."

"Why did he say?"

"We should make love, not war."

"Well I wasn't planning on starting a war, but it's still good advice…"

"He did have some very good ideas," said Raski, smiling as Draephus drew him close.

"And you're gonna help me get J'Vanni out on stage."

"He'll never do it," said Raski.

"Well let's try," said Draephus. "If he really won't go… well it's sad but it's his choice."

"I'll help," said Raski. "But if he says no, we have to respect that. I mean someone *did* try to blow his head off."

Draephus kissed him. "Fine. Now, in the meantime, let's do naughty things to each other."

****

The night passed, the storm raging to exhaustion. When Dahli woke the next day, the morning was bright and unseasonably warm. She did all the things she normally did; washing dressing, gathering her books, then heading downstairs to see if there was anything in the cupboards for breakfast. She braced herself for what seemed to be the latest ritual in her life; the daily disagreement with Teirra.

"Are you going to quit your job at the studio?" she asked sharply.

"No," said Dahli. "It was no yesterday, no today, and no tomorrow."

"I just want you to be safe!"

Dahli turned and gaped at her. "SAFE?! You want me to be SAFE?! No, you do not want me to be safe, you want me to be a little kid the rest of my life and stay in my room."

"That's not true."

"Then what is it?!" asked Dahli. "Because you seem to want to keep blaming Draephus for stuff that I did all on my own. He didn't make me steal the faelin; I did that. He didn't make me escape the center, he didn't make me fire-walk Avalair, and he did not make me get into the stuff at the studio, I did it all on my own. I'm sixteen, I am perfectly capable of making an idiot of myself without adult supervision. Teens do it all the time."

"You're running around with ex-revolutionaries, the boy you are seeing is pregnant…"

There was nothing in the cupboard. The markets were currently empty due to the storms, and it could be another day before there was anything more. At this time of the year, it could even be a few days. Dahli was hungry and depressed, and she did not understand what her sister wanted from her, other than to just hide in her room.

"Look, Teirra, tell ya what. I'll solve the whole issue for you. I'll pack my stuff and move out. There's an old brick house down the road, no one is living in it, I'll just go there and you won't have to worry about my friends or my ideas or my wanting to explore the world around me or anything. I'll be out of your life and Atterick won't have to be embarrassed by the fact that my friends are more famous than he is."

"You're not going anywhere," said Teirra.

"Yes, I am," said Dahli. "I used to love you, and you were always one of my closest friends. I could tell you anything. Now every time I see you I get a sick knot in my gut and the first thing I think is *'I wonder what she's mad about this time?'* I think I should go before I end up hating you."

"Dahli…"

"I'll pack when I get back from school."

"Can't we talk about this?" asked Teirra.

"NO!" yelled Dahli, slamming her books down on the table and startling her sister. "Because it won't be a talk! It will be you telling me I'm wrong and expecting me to apologize, and it's not happening. We're done. I'm leaving."

"I don't understand why you are being so hard about this!" said Teirra.

"Because nothing I do is good enough! I go to school, I do my homework, I help with the house, I let you know where I am, save for that one messed up incident which was totally my fault, I help with the garden, I go out and look for wild nuts and berries to help feed us when the shipments don't come in, I don't know what more you want!"

"Dahli…"

"See you after school. Bye."

Dahli left the house, shaking and frightened by her own

announcement. It was feasible, certainly. No one was using the brick house, and she had explored it enough that she knew she could block parts off to turn into a home. It was just a frightening concept to be well and truly on her own. But she couldn't stay. Teirra's constant fault-finding was wearing too hard on her. Maybe Teirra herself didn't know what the issue was. Dahli certainly didn't.

"Dahli!"

Dahli stopped in her tracks, and saw Diza running towards her.

"Wait up!"

"Sorry Diza," said Dahli. "Glad to see *you* at least still love me."

Diza ran up to her side, and the two continued on their way to school.

"Have another fight with Teirra?" asked Diza.

"Told her I was moving out."

Diza winced. "Oh Dahli…"

"I can't take it anymore. It makes me physically sick to see her now because it's just going to be another fight! I'm doing everything I can to make up for the things I've done but none of it is good enough. I don't know what she wants from me but I'm tired of trying to find out. I'm going to move into the brick house down the road. Honestly I'd rather stay home because if I move out I will be completely on my own, and that means digging up my own food and fuel as well as trying to get an education. Not to mention boiling my own water for cleaning and probably a thousand other things I can't even think of at the moment." Dahli sighed. "Will you still love me when I'm smelly and dirty and living in my own filth?"

"Of course I will. I'll just make you walk up-wind."

Both girls paused as they heard someone calling their names. Moments later Czamkiar joined them, looking somewhat nervous. His make-up was absolutely impeccable for once, and in his long, loose white hair was a gold clip shaped like a twisting serpent, sparkling with yellow stones. Instead of scales, it had slick fur, and golden wings on its back

"I am the worst person on the planet," he said.

Diza peered closely at Czamkiar's hair. "Czamki… is that the spiraled fur-snake that is on Lyrellyn's family crest?"

"Oh yes it is," he said, looking rather shaken.

Dahli and Diza looked to each other, then back to Czamkiar. "Czamki," said Diza, "what exactly did you do last night?"

"Well..." he said nervously, "there is a slight possibility that I spent the night at Lyrellyn's house doing things that this time yesterday I would have sworn I would never do."

Diza's jaw dropped.

"Czamki!" exclaimed Dahli, "what happened?!"

"I... I'm not sure. I'm really not. He..."

"Czamki," said Diza softly, "just calm down and tell us. It's okay."

Czamkiar drew a few steadying breaths, then began speaking.

"I went to his house last night. His father was on business with the emperor so it was just Lyrellyn and I and the housekeeper."

"Housekeeper?" queried Diza.

"Yeah," said Czamkiar. "Someone who tidies up and cooks meals and stuff."

"That's a thing?!" said Dahli. "They make those?!"

"Let the man talk," said Diza.

"Anyway," continued Czamkiar, "I went to his house and... and the housekeeper answers and leads me into the back sitting room. So I'm sitting there, and... there must be centuries of history in that room. Paintings, musical instruments, books, old furniture, art work...amazing stuff. And then the door opens and... and he walks in wearing this... I don't even know what it was! I've never seen anything like it in my life! This... yellow thing, made of velvet, with... I don't know, these little round things that sort of glowed. He said calurchi made them but I don't know how. They were sewn in strands all over it, and it had this long swath of scarlet fabric that was so fine I could see through it, like spider webs. It was like he had been turned into some kind of flower. And he played this... I don't know, I don't even have words for it; it really was like a picture out of another time, and I'm sure both that outfit and that instrument were at least four centuries old. And.... I started thinking. I started asking myself; why I was trying so hard to get this Earth girl to like me? Why? She has virtually *no* tolerance for my culture or point of view. Every single solitary thing that does not go flawlessly is a crisis of insurmountable magnitude. I'm pretty sure the only reason she likes me at all is because her mother is having fits over her dating a Sferkkaan boy, and yes, she *has* a mother. A live breathing mom and sisters and aunts and a house with all the walls and food whenever she's hungry and… and here's Lyrellyn breaking his heart just trying to get me to like him. And I thought; Am I out of my *mind*?! There's this beautiful boy with all this family history who could have anyone he wants, who will one day be an Imperial Bird of Prey in his own right with standing in the Empire… and I'm chasing this moron who will leave in a year! Who probably doesn't even really *like* me!"

"Wow," said Dahli.

"It was really humbling, I can tell you that," said Czamkiar. "It made me… I don't know. Rethink some of my own opinions. All right, I freely admit I would rather have a girlfriend than a boyfriend. But the girlfriend I have just sees me as a toy for right now, and the boyfriend I just acquired sees me as something special."

"So when did he give you the pretty hairpiece?" asked Diza.

Czamkiar flushed red. "When I left his house this morning. Told my uncle last night I was going to visit a friend and maybe do homework. Then the storm blew up and it was so bad outside that my uncle called and asked if I could stay. So I spent the night all right. We didn't get a lot of homework done but it was certainly educational. Now I have to tell Gemma that I found someone else."

"Well that should be exciting," said Diza.

"I'm not sure 'exciting' is the right word," said Czamkiar. "This is a girl who has a fit when her shirt gets a spot."

"Not much we can do about it now," said Dahli. She sighed heavily. "Well it's certainly been an exciting day, and it hasn't even begun yet."

****

Dahli came home directly from school, thinking she would have to pack quickly in order to move to the brick house before work. She smelled food, but ignored it; she didn't live here anymore. Any food she smelled belonged to Teirra.

"Dahli?" said a quiet voice.

"I'll be gone soon," Dahli snapped.

"Dahli," said Teirra, following her up the stairs, "I don't want you to move."

"Yeah well I'm sick of hearing what a problem I am," said Dahli. "And clearly, as long as I am here, no matter what I do, I will be a problem."

"I just want to be sure that you're all right," said Teirra. "I know you love Draephus and he's your friend, but I can't stop worrying that he's leading you into things you can't handle."

Dahli slammed her school books down onto the hall floor and turned on her sister, furious.

"When I was nine years old, which if you recall is when the war was still going, YOU took off for FIVE DAYS, and left me ALONE. I had NO food, NO water, NO lights, NOTHING. FOR FIVE DAYS. So you could chase Atterick, because the Empire knows there's a complete shortage of males around here. On the third night a wounded and bleeding Kryphisian officer crawled in through the opening in the back of the house and lay there for seven hours in agony until his friends found him and took him away. Fortunately they didn't notice me. I ate and drank the small amount of food and water they left behind. AND YOU ARE WORRIED THAT DRAEPHUS IS GETTING ME INTO THINGS I CAN'T HANDLE?! YOU NEVER EVEN APOLOGIZED OR ASKED HOW I WAS, YOU LEFT ME ALONE AND DIDN'T EVEN COME BACK WITH ANYTHING FOR ME TO EAT!"

"I'm sorry. I wasn't thinking. I was wrong and I would never do anything like that to you again. And I really didn't know that you were still angry about it."

"Why would I not be angry?" demanded Dahli. "I was hungry, and terrified, and you just came back in as if you hadn't been gone a minute. Well you know what? Draephus might not have the common sense of a feralyke, but he would never leave me alone in a burned out house for five days."

"I'm not saying he would," said Teirra quietly. "But he lives in a different world than you do, and those friends of his have all survived something very dark. The day he showed up with me at the Center he had two men with him that scared the life out of me. He has a very dark side to him…"

"Draephus CZimcocious wouldn't hurt anyone who didn't try to hurt him first," said Dahli.

"Is that what happened to your councillor?"

"People who try to bully girls into doing things against their will tend to make enemies," said Dahli.

"Yeah," said Teirra softly. "I guess they do. But I still want you to stay."

"I'll stay if you stop trying to blame Draephus for everything stupid in my life," said Dahli. "And if you stop getting angry at me for daring to breathe in your presence! Because I honestly don't know what the šukat you want but I'm getting *real* sick of wondering about it."

Teirra was clearly daunted. Dahli hoped it had finally sunk in just how tired she was of her sister's behaviour.

"Well maybe if I knew him better, I could relax," said Teirra.

Yeah that was a possible solution. Dahli really did not want to be on her own, she just wanted some peace from the relentless bickering.

"Would you like to watch me work for a while tonight?" asked Dahli. "Maybe see that I actually have a job? That I really do something other than steal drinks and get into trouble?"

"I don't know," said Teirra warily. "Am I going to be in the way?"

Dahli shook her head. "Just stay close. Let me put my books away and we'll go."

Chapter Twenty-Four

They drove down to the studio, pulling into the parking lot and entering the front doors. The first place Dahli went was to the common room, where the food would be. She put her books on the table, and immediately began tidying up, moving things around, stacking dishes, and setting assorted bags and bottles on shelves.

"How do you know what goes where in this mess?" asked Teirra.

"I sort of don't," said Dahli. "My job is to keep things neat enough that they can be located."

"Do they share the food with you?"

"Some of it. Depends on who it belongs to. Anything Draephus and Raski bring is for everyone. Anything for Mars will be laced with medications because pills make him throw up, so don't touch anything in a blue container."

"What does he have?" asked Teirra.

"I don't know, but it requires medication daily, and weekly examinations." Dahli opened the coldbox and gasped at what she saw inside. "WHOO! Bacca and Czanda caught a deer. Let's eat."

"Is it all right? How do you know where it came from?"

"Draephus is the only one who brings deer because his property is crawling with them."

Dahli sliced off some of the meat for herself and Teirra, eating ravenously. Then she picked up a bottle and read it before setting it in the cupboard. Next she found a pill bottle and read that label. She looked at the clock on the wall.

"Somebody little and cute needs his medication," she said, and walked out of the common room.

"Fearless!" shouted a voice.

"Heia Draephus!" Dahli ran to him and hugged him. "What's up?"

"Nothing much. Like the jewelry?"

Dahli looked at the silvery chains and rings on his hand. "That's really cool! And THANK YOU for the deer, I hadn't eaten in two days."

"Yeah I figured with the storms a few of us would be hungry.

I brought a deer, Khandi brought apples, and Straif brought nuts."

"Hey where *is* Straif? He has to take his pills in four minutes."

Draephus was saying nothing. He was, instead, staring at Teirra. That was when it occurred to Dahli that maybe sharing all the details with Draephus of her arguments with her sister was not a good idea. She sighed loudly.

"You are BOTH going to behave or I am moving into the Cylinder and becoming a mushroom breeder!"

Draephus perked up. "Cool!"

"You're a real comedian," said Dahli. "I am going to go give Straif his pills, you two are going to stay here and make friends, or I am going to move out and start listening to just the news."

Dahli went to find Straif, eventually locating him in the bathroom, throwing up. She sighed heavily.

"Did the doctor not tell you that if you don't take your pills, your supper will come back to haunt you?"

She gently drew back his long hair, looping it into a knot to stay out of his face. Straif breathed hard, fighting to control his stomach.

"It's not supper. It's Draephus. I love him but I can't handle that stink!"

Ah yes, the mysterious stink…

"Actually you don't smell that great either," said Straif.

"Well thanks, Straif, I think that's the most romantic thing you've ever said to me."

"Everything smells awful!" He threw up again.

"Well do you think you can stop smelling stuff long enough to take your pills?"

"No. I can't take the pills because I have to take them with food or get even sicker, and I can't eat because everything stinks."

Dahli rolled her eyes, then patted him on the back. "You wait here, I'll see if I can find you some food that doesn't smell."

He heaved and retched. "Oh kill me *noooowww…*" he moaned.

Dahli left the bathroom and returned to the common room, where Teirra and Draephus were talking. Well talking was better than killing each other. Dahli began looking through the cold box for food that would be fairly non-fragrant.

"Draephus do we have anything for Straif that doesn't have an odor?"

"We've got some apples. Is he sick?"

"Yeah," said Dahli, taking an apple and closing the coldbox door. "He's on the floor praying to the potty-gods to smite him."

Someone tapped her on the shoulder. She turned to see Diza blinking at her. It took a few moments to register, then she asked "Okay, what band are you with?"

"You stole my text book."

"I deny that I would ever steal a text book!"

Diza laughed. "For science."

"I deny I would steal one for that, either!"

"I let her in," said Draephus. "It's 'Annoy Dahli at Work Day'."

"It's so busy here!" said Teirra.

"Yes it is," said Dahli.

She pointed out the book for Diza, and began chopping an apple into small pieces. Once it was in bits, she returned to the bathroom with the apple. Straif was seated on the floor, looking positively grey, his long dark hair lank and damp.

"Straif I think you need to go lie down."

He nodded. "Soon. Just... let me catch my breath..."

Dahli began removing his boots. He was wobbly enough without them. She managed to get the pills and the apple pieces into him, then helped him to the quiet room with the beds. He was asleep almost before he lay down. Dahli kissed his face and covered him, then left him to sleep, heading back to the common room. Draephus had vanished, only to be replaced by Khandi, and, of all people, Gemma.

"Heia!" said Dahli. "What brings you here?"

"I *am* a professional musician, you know. I was hoping to get a look around the studio."

Dahli caught the expression on Khandid's face that implied Gemma wasn't getting on *any* of the tracks currently being laid down. Well well, it seemed *somebody* had an ego. Then Raski came bouncing into the room, hair flashing with white gems, an enormous grin on his face. Following after him was Mickie Pastors. Geeze who let him out without a leash?

"What is making you so happy?" asked Khandid.

Raski brandished a folder of papers. "Permission to do all the covers we requested at the festival."

Khandid sighed. "Remember when we just covered any Earth band we liked?"

"Remember when they had no idea we were up here covering them?"

"Well there is that," said Khandid.

"Doing any of mine?" asked Mickie.

"Let me check," said Raski, and began leafing through the papers. "Uh… Jethro Tull, Pink Floyd, Nirvana, Nine Inch Nails, Howlin Wolf… nope. I don't see Talentless Clart-blossom anywhere."

Gemma clamped her hands over her face in an unsuccessful attempt to stop a laugh. Dahli picked up her list of duties for the night, and stared at the next item on it. Then she began screaming and leaping around like an idiot.

"What?!" demanded Diza. "I know that outburst!"

"FEED TRILBY AND MIT-MIT!"

Diza began leaping around and screaming as well, while Gemma and Mickie just stared in confusion.

"Spot the Gryphon fans," said Raski dryly to Khandid.

"Who are Trilby and Mit-Mit?" asked Gemma warily, "and why can't they feed themselves?"

Dahli looked to Raski. "Are they allowed to have visitors?" she asked.

"Sure, if Gemma and Mickie want to see them. Just keep your voices down, okay? They *are* big enough that they can hurt you without meaning to."

"Dare I ask what they are?" asked Teirra.

"You'll see," said Dahli.

She led Diza, Gemma, Teirra and Mickie down the hall to the far side of the sprawling complex that was Gryphon Studios. A more apt name would have been "Five Overgrown Kids with More Trinta than Brains", but that was beside the point. The Gryphons had built their version of the ultimate musical playground, and it held everything a serious Sferkkaan musician could want.

They reached a pair of glass doors that led into a damp, dimly-lit room. A soft mist filled the air, and a warm fragrance like cream and apples. Diza stepped in first, trying hard to suppress her excited squeaks. Dahli waited until the others were in as well.

"Dark in here," said Gemma. "What's moving?"

"My boner," said Mickie.

Dahli reached out for a knob on the wall, and slowly turned up the lights. Things began to rustle in the rising light, and soon the room was bright enough to show its inhabitants.

Most of the plants were eight or nine feet tall, comfortably settled in large pots on rolling platforms. They had enormous ragged leaves of deep green that slowly waved and twitched like aerial fish, swaying gently. They bore small flowers of blue and deep orange, and both leaves and blossoms seemed as if they were trying to catch the mist.

"Oh cool," said Mickie, his voice heavy with sarcasm. "It's a nursery!"

"What are these?" asked Gemma.

"Amplifier plants," said Dahli. "Electricity is fine but in an outdoor venue in the rain it's dangerous. You'll be working with these little guys at the festival."

"How do they work?" asked Gemma.

"Just talk to it," said Dahli.

Gemma walked over to the closest plant, and said "Hi pretty plant!"

The leaves snapped in her direction, and reflected the sound back at her with perfect clarity, at easily twice the volume. Gemma backed up, and looked to Dahli, her eyes questioning.

"There's all kinds of energy," said Dahli. "Plants in the northern reaches rely on light, but the South Continent, especially in the deep jungles, is too dark. So some plants eat meat, and some plants, like these ones, use sound energy. And the reason they reflect it is because if everybody in the garden gets lots of energy, then everyone gets to grow and reproduce. I have no idea how they do it, but it works."

Gemma carefully touched the plant. "So which ones are Trilby and Mit-Mit?"

Dahli grinned. She was enjoying this far too much. "These plants right here are called valley song, because they live in valleys and sing. Trilby and Mit-Mit are a very rare type of amp plant called mountain dragon. And they are behind you."

Gemma slowly turned, Dahli positively giggling as she watched the gigantic plant slowly dip its "head" to investigate her.

Gemma made a terrified squeak. Trilby was nearly fifty feet tall, and boasted brilliant leaves of red, yellow and black that looked more like bird feathers than anything a plant may have. The pseudo-head that now carefully investigated Gemma was a deep, intense green, streaked with yellow and black to form what very much resembled a dragon's head, complete with eyes. Gemma looked as if she may faint, and Mickie appeared to be giving serious thought to wetting himself and sucking his thumb. Diza walked up to the gigantic thing and lightly pet it.

"Hi Trilby," she said. "Nice to meet you!"

Trilby turned to nudge Diza, as Gemma stood rigid in terror. "Is it going to eat us?" she managed to ask.

"No," said Dahli. "They're plants, they just mimic animals to avoid being eaten in the wild. They are very good at acting like a thinking animal, and they may be smarter than we give them credit for, but they're plants. These two are nearly as famous as the Gryphons themselves. This one is Trilby, and Mit-Mit is… escaping. Hey! Plant! Get back here."

Dahli began walking after the massive plant, which was using its leaves to slowly pull itself along, heading for the huge windows of the nursery with the sort of noise one would expect from a fifty foot tall plant in a stone pot on rollers.

"Determined, isn't it?" said Teirra.

"Yeah," said Dahli. "At live shows they have to chain her pot to the floor."

The gigantic plant reached a place that seemed to please it, and it unfurled its mighty leaves, settling into a pose that gave it greater access to the falling mist, and also completing the illusion of being a feathered dragon. Dahli went for the plant food, returning with a fragrant bucket of ground fish guts and destri droppings. Somehow sensing the presence of food, Trilby began slowly grinding along the floor to where Mit-Mit sat. Gemma took out her phone to record the deliberate, dignified march of the giant.

"Yes you get some too," said Dahli as Trilby nudged at her. "Here. Yummy. Clart and guts. I am so glad I am not a plant. There's a good boy…"

"How do you know it's a boy?" asked Gemma.

"Mit-Mit gets flowers on her," said Dahli. "Trilby gets big pods that harden and then burst open and shoot pollen in all directions."

"Kinky," said Gemma.

"Last year Mit-Mit made two little baby mountain dragons," said Dahli. "It was all over the news. They went to go live with an organization on the South Continent that's helping to rebuild the eco system down there. Trilby and Mit-Mit are the only two known mountain dragons old enough to reproduce. There may be some left in the jungles but so far all they have found is a few little spouts. Trilby and Mit-Mit were sitting in the ruins of Draephus' castle in what was left of a royal nursery, feeling very sad for themselves. No one knows how they managed to live up here unattended and in the cold all that time, but they are probably a hundred years old."

"Did he name them too?" asked Gemma.

"Someone else did, a century ago," said Dahli. "They found name plates on the boxes. Someone found them in the jungle, brought them up here, put them in a nursery, and then died. Anyway they seem happy enough. Probably just glad to be warm. They're going to the festival but that will be their last tour. They're retiring from the music industry, and Mit-Mit will be able to do all the scooting she likes."

Dahli gave each of the gigantic plants an equal helping of food, watching as they used thin, agile, finger-like roots to dig it into the earth. Then Mit-Mit settled to get down to the business of being a plant. Trilby however seemed restless. He fluttered his leaves rapidly, knocking one loose. It fluttered down, and Diza caught it before it hit the floor.

"Aw... is this for me? Thank you, Trilby!"

"Why would you want it?" asked Mickie. "It's all yellow and shit."

"It's from Trilby," said Diza.

"Oh fuck that, rip off a nice one. I'll climb up and get a red one!"

"Mickie!" said Dahli sharply. "If you climb on him and start ripping off leaves, he *will* defend himself! He will throw you right through that window and we'll be looking for chunks in Avalair!"

Mickie seemed to be about to tell her to get lost, but then changed his mind and backed away. Trilby meanwhile continued to be restless, and Dahli watched the huge plant with concern as it moved its enormous pseudo-head back and forth, as if sniffing the ground.

"What's he doing?" asked Teirra.

"I have no idea," said Dahli.

Trilby "sniffed", clearly working up to doing something. Then, as Dahli and her companions watched, one gigantic root slithered out of the pot and began reaching for the ground. Moments later, a second root did the same. Then, with a loud, resounding boom, Trilby knocked over his pot and broke it. Moments later, he was wandering free across the floor.

"Your plant is running away," said Diza.

Dahli stared in horror at the mess Trilby had made – broken bits of pot, dirt, and worse – the remains of his evening meal, all scattered freely around the room. Trilby then proceeded to go to the smaller plants and check to see if their pots were any better than the one he just smashed. With perfect ease he pulled another plant up by the roots and dropped it aside. Dahli fled the room in search of Raski, finding him preparing to leave, his wrist bound in a cast.

"Trilby escaped! He smashed his pot and now he's wandering around pulling up the other plants!"

"Oh," he said, eyes large. "Um… I think we need to fix that."

"Does he have another pot?"

"No, not right now. Just start heaping dirt into a big pile on the floor and let him settle into that. I'll start contacting people about getting him a bigger pot. Actually Mit-Mit is probably going to want one too. Okay, you dig, I'll call."

Dahli ran back to the nursery and began looking for where the dirt would be stored, while Trilby systematically pulled up every single plant in the room save for Mit-Mit, who would likely use her club-like head to smack him across the room if he tried. After a few moments of frantic seeking, Dahli found a chute that was used for filling the massive pots the plants sat in. She began spilling a huge quantity of dirt on the floor. Sensing fresh earth, Trilby crept to the heap, investigating it. Deeming it suitable, he settled into it, managing to throw a fair quantity of earth in all directions, adding more as he fluttered his leaves prior to settling down. When his brief adventure was over, twenty plants were uprooted, five pots, including his own, were smashed, and every single person in the room was covered in a layer of grime. Dahli was whimpering as she distastefully picked bits of what could only be destri droppings out of her hair, when a large man she knew as Badger walked up to her, and slapped her on the shoulder. He was the Gryphons' head roadie.

"Congratulations, Fearless. You're now officially a member of the team."

He handed her a t-shirt and walked over to the fallen valley song plants. Dahli held up the shirt and looked at it. On the front were emblazoned the words MORTIFIED GRYPHONS ROAD CREW. The back read "FEARLESS". Beneath that, the phrase "I actually asked for this job."

"Yay me," said Dahli weakly.

Raski walked into the room to survey the mess, looking around. Then he looked to Trilby and asked sternly; "Who is a naughty boy?"

Trilby just sat and looked smug, while Mit-Mit crept free of her own pot to come sit beside Trilby. Together the two plants happily scooped dirt around themselves and each other, making an already huge mess enormous.

"So… Dahli…" said Gemma carefully. "Do you know why Czamkiar hasn't answered any of my calls today?"

"No," said Dahli, although she suspected she knew why. She removed her old shirt to put on her new one, and heard Gemma draw a loud squeaking gasp.

"DAHLI! There are guys all over!"

Dahli rolled her eyes. "Yes I have noticed that too."

"Well you can't just be taking your clothes off in public!"

Dahli paused. Her eyes shifted to Raski, Teirra, and Diza. They then shifted back to Gemma.

"I'm not taking my clothes off. I'm changing my shirt. If I was ripping my pants off and waving them over my head that may be a different story."

"But there are guys here and you're a girl!"

"Yes, I've noticed that. I'm sure they have as well."

"But…"

"Gemma I like you but will you please keep your hysterics to yourself? Honestly your ideas about bodies are even more bizarre than some of the thoughts the Kryphisians had, and I truly did not think that was possible." She wriggled into her shirt.

"Can't be," said Raski.

"No?" said Dahli. "Ask her about her period."

"DAHLI!"

"See?"

Raski rolled his eyes. "Well I'm off, I have things to get done. Dahli if you need a shower, feel free."

"Anything you need doing specifically?"

"Just keep an eye out for Anazampini, they're going to be using our studio to start laying some tracks and they're bringing in some of their own equipment. Do *not* let the lead vocalist carry anything, she will want to but do not let her. She has a broken vertebra in her back she's supposed to be letting heal."

"Well why are any of them hauling their own stuff? I mean they're girls. Shouldn't the guys be doing it for them?" asked Gemma.

"BEING A GIRL IS NOT A DISABILITY!" shouted Dahli.

Gemma backed up. "I didn't say that!"

"Yes you did, about a million times! Girls can't do this, girls can't do that, girls should never do the other! Well if YOU want to blame everything on two tits and a hole then be my guest but some of us have lives to live and wars to win." She looked to Raski. "How long should we wait?"

"If they're not here by the time Khandi is ready to go, then lock up and head out. It's going to get very busy in the next few days; we have people coming in from all over to use the studio who don't have a place to record where they live, so we will be hiring a few more hands to help with…"

"ME!" yelled Diza.

"…the lifting and carrying and other tasks." Raski looked at Diza. Are you sure you want to do this? Because…"

"If you think for one second that Dahli is going to the Year End Festival without me then you haven't been paying attention," said Diza.

"Fine, but if a faelin dies around here then just let it lay, don't steal it."

"GRIM!"

Dahli nudged Diza. "Come on, let's find some shovels and help bury the equipment."

"I'll help," said Gemma. "I like gardening."

Teirra reached out to touch Dahli's shoulder. "I have to get going, I have things to get done. Are you… coming home tonight?"

"Yeah," said Dahli. "I might be late. There are a lot of plants to bury."

Teirra nodded. "All right. So long as I know where you are."

Teirra left, and Dahli felt the weight of the world leave her shoulders. At least for now things seemed better. They stepped out of the nursery, and stopped as something spooked in the hallway. Dahli froze, and beside her Diza uttered a tiny squeak as before her stood the unrequited love of her life, Yuri Stracona. Dahli carefully took Diza's arm and said softly into her ear; "He's a Breed, don't get close."

Diza of course knew Yuri was a Breed, but Dahli's warning let her know he was a particularly nervous type of Breed. She smiled at him.

"Heia. I'm… one of your biggest fans."

He was looking at Dahli as if not sure if he'd met her before. Then Gemma stepped forward.

"Hi Yuri! Remember me? We met at…"

Dahli yanked her out of the way as Yuri aimed a random kick in her general direction and fled. Gemma sat on the floor, hand over her heart, staring at Dahli.

"What the hell was that for?!"

Dahli helped her up. "He doesn't mean anything by it," said Dahli. "I'll explain it to you while we're getting the shovels and stuff."

Diza squeaked. "He's so beautiful!"

"He tried to kill me!" said Gemma, indignant.

"He didn't, really," said Dahli. "He just… has a really nervous disposition."

"He's so pretty!" squealed Diza.

"Dahli!" called a voice from down the hall. "Did my husband just try to kick your head off?"

"No, Khandi," said Dahli. "He tried to kick off Gemma's for daring to say 'heia' to him."

"Yuri, do *not* make me get the sock puppets."

Yuri kicked something. The trio of girls continued in their quest for shovels.

"What's wrong with him?" asked Gemma.

"Nothing," said Dahli. "He's a Breed."

"What's a Breed?" asked Gemma.

"It's when they take a little baby Sferkkaan boy and spend

551

twenty years re-engineering him into something pretty that a Kryphisian general will pay millions of trinta for in order to keep as a pet," said Dahli. "Yuri kicks because part of his DNA is now combined with that of numerous animals, some Sferkkaan, some Kryphisian, to make him delicate, pretty, graceful, and, occasionally in random instances, very, very, dangerous. He doesn't want to hurt you. He just has all these instincts in his head that make him react the way a wild animal would."

"That's so sad!" said Gemma. But he *is* pretty."

"I love you!" gushed Diza.

"Oh great!" said Dahli. "Now there's two of them!"

"You're just jealous because your Gryphon looks like he fell under a bus," said Diza.

"And you're just jealous because I saw Yuri Stracona with no make-up and got to see his animal patterns," said Dahli.

"DIE!"

"EVENTUALLY DUE TO NATURAL CAUSES!"

They located the shovels, brooms, pans, and other things they would need to replant the nursery, then returned to the large room. As Dahli opened the door, something tiny raced across the floor.

"What was that?" asked Diza.

Dahli reached for the knob on the wall that controlled the light, and slowly illuminated the room. She stared at roughly eighteen baby mountain dragons scuttling across the floor in search of a place to put down roots.

"Okay," said Dahli. "Everybody watch where they step. Let's just slowly catch them and put them in Mit-Mit's pot. There aren't that…"

Mit-Mit shook her leaves, releasing a veritable flock of tiny scuttling seedlings.

"…many."

"Are you done?" Diza asked the gigantic plant.

Mit-Mit shook loose a few last stragglers, then settled down next to Trilby, looking perfectly happy. Dahli sighed.

"Okay, one of us chases babies while two of us repot the plants."

"You chase," said Diza. "Gemma and I will start putting things in pots. Just nobody open the…"

The door was yanked open. "Hey what are you doing?"

Mickie asked, and roughly three hundred seedlings stampeded towards the light.

"...door."

"DON'T MOVE!" Dahli roared at him.

Unaccustomed to being bellowed at, he froze. Dahli walked over to the intercom, and pressed a button.

"If anybody has two free hands, Mit-Mit would like some help catching the three hundred babies she just cut loose that are now charging down the hallway!"

Mars peered out of a room, and watched the impossibly tiny and leafy stampede race by.

"Well," he said. "How adorable. I just love nature when it goes running down the halls of my recording studio and tries to take root in the mixing board."

"They're so cute!" squealed Gemma. "I'm totally gonna upload this video to my Facebook page."

"Yeah that's real helpful," said Dahli. She sighed. "Okay, let's get down to plant-herding."

Chapter Twenty-Five

Days past, then weeks, slowly becoming months. Other ships arrived from Earth, this time bearing journalists, documentary film crews, scientists, and some stupidly wealthy individuals who wanted to say they saw the Festival in person. One of the new arrivals seemed to have some sort of an idea in his head about some Earth-Sferkkaan venture he was sure the Emperor would love to hear. He went straight to the Imperial palace, barged in, walked into Mordrett's office, and informed the Emperor that he had come to bring something to Sferkkaa and he wasn't going to take no for an answer.

Mordrett had the man thrown out a second story window into the garden below. Hours later in the hospital he was informed that the Sferkkaan people had endured quite enough from bullies over the last eight centuries, and anyone who did not want to hear the word NO was going to have it jammed down their throats.

The Earth Ambassador had her work cut out for her, but she had to admit she loved having a tiny pretty male in high heels to sit on her desk and take notes.

In Dahli's tiny corner of the universe, life was a strange frantic dance. There was school by day, and in the evenings she was at the studio, working as well as learning. Her close friendship with Draephus didn't get her out of anything, and in some ways he was harder on her than anyone. It took some time before she realized it was because he believed she had real talent. At first she believed he just didn't want anyone to think he was favouring her. It wasn't until he presented her with a genuine hand-carved South Continental drum of her very own that she realized how much he believed in her. His own set remained off limits. At least, it did when he was in the building. Straif would do look-out, alerting her if he saw the familiar grey conni pulling into the parking lot.

Straif had become a fixture in her life, as had Gemma. Dahli was genuinely dreading the day Gemma had to return to Earth. Dahli was very glad that the break-up between Gemma and Czamkiar had been somewhat mutual. Of course Gemma may have been less calm about matters if she had known that Czamkiar and Lyrellyn were already together. As it was, no one saw any reason to raise the issue and cause a retroactive explosion. Things were currently nice and calm.

Straif's pregnancy was advancing nicely. He was beginning to look like a stick with something stuck on it, but every time Dahli saw him, he was dressed to perfection and still in his heels. She saw him daily at the studio, playing sepulchord. Raski Jervyas had been absent for a very long time, and Dahli was getting worried about him. However when she asked Draephus about it, she just got gentle assurances.

"He's fine, Fearless, he's just taking his time getting better."

Dahli didn't know much about broken bones, but she did know it shouldn't take nearly three months to recover from a cracked wrist. And the two times she had been up to the castle, she had seen him curled up in a chair looking grey, dull and miserable. The gleam had gone out of his pale blue eyes, and even his hair had lost its sheen. He was clearly sick and in pain, but Draephus wouldn't let her talk about it.

"Raski, is he holding you against your will?" she asked.

"No," said Raski. "Whenever he holds me, it is definitely not against my will."

Dahli turned to Draephus. "As a fan, I demand to know what you did to him."

"Absolutely nothing he didn't ask me to," was all Draephus would say as he gently but firmly escorted her out of the castle.

"Oooh, kinky!"

"Brat."

"No but seriously, is he okay?"

Draephus laughed quietly. "He's fine. He really is. He had a small operation and he's just taking a while to get over it, and he doesn't want people thinking he's dying. It does look like this will be the first ever Gryphons album without him, though. I was hoping he'd be well by now."

Dahli was worried, but there wasn't much she could do about the situation. Besides, she had her own problems. It was now the middle of winter, and like many other Sferkkaan families, she, Teirra and Atterick were starving. Storms had sunk freighters loaded with food, and many of the land transports simply could not reach that far north because of the terrain. Highways were being dug, but were taking inordinately long times to create because of hidden antipersonnel devices, as well as tiny pockets of forest that were carefully avoided. If a highway absolutely did have to go through any sort of natural habitat, then work was done by hand. Nothing was wantonly hacked down, and if it was at all possible, it was moved.

Mordrett kept his second story office window open as a warning to anyone who came in with fabulous money-saving ideas to speed up the highway. Money they could find. Fruiting trees and bushes, edible plants, and fertile soil were far more rare and valuable.

Dahli mainly ate at the studio, but even there she was not likely to get a meal this late in the year. The only person eating regularly was Straif, and even he was not getting enough for two. If there was food, Dahli never took more than a few bites. Usually it was deer from Draephus' property, and, when Mars had them to spare, edible aquatic plants. No one had much, but everyone contributed what they could. Dahli still recalled the magical day Straif showed up clutching n entire armload of ghost-weed and put it on the table in the common room, proudly displaying his prize.

"Where did you get this?!" Dahli asked, staring at the enormous heap of silvery-green plants.

"There was an old man living in a little house on the far side of Draephus' property," said Straif. "He died in the fall. His son came to get his animals and his few belongings, but I guess he didn't realize the old man had this growing behind his house. I took what I could and brought it here. And there is other stuff in my conni!"

"You sit here, I'll get it!"

Dahli and Straif spent the next two hours doing something Sferkkaans rarely had a chance to do – cook. They scavenged ingredients from everywhere they could, and by the time they were finished, they had breads and stew and hot steamed ghost-weed on a platter. Recording was done for the day – there was eating to be done. And when her shift was over, there were leftovers to bring home. For a few days, at least, there were full bellies, and work proceeded at a more lively pace. Despite food shortages, Dahli could not be happier.

****

Draephus found he also had little to complain about besides an empty belly. Other than a boyfriend with an agenda he wasn't sharing and poor health. Raski Jervyas was not going to appear on the latest album, that much was certain. Dr. Arang had done the surgery to put in the implant, and Raski then proceeded to become as sick as he possibly could. Persistent wound leakage, infections, and fevers were tearing him apart, and Draephus found himself in an uncomfortably familiar situation; caring for a very sick, possibly dying, lover. The fan sites, of course, were losing their minds, and people with little else to look forward to were demanding to know where Raski was. Draephus finally decided to take matters into his own hands and took a short video of Raski in bed with the faelins. It was short, it was adorable, it calmed a lot of hysterical rumours that he was dead, and most people were satisfied that Raski was alive, if unwell.

Rumours however would persist for decades that he actually had died and the Raski that appeared on future albums was a clone.

"Some people need a post-natal abortion, I swear," grumbled Draephus, checking the fan sites. He cast a glance to his lover, and softened. "How ya feelin', Raski?"

A black hand reached up to pet Bacca. "You know that feeling when someone splits you open, shoves an artificial uterus into you, then carves your pelvic basin bigger so you can have a baby?"

"No."

"Man I wish I didn't."

"And whose idea was all this?" gently teased Draephus.

"Bacca's."

"Riff?"

"Yeah, it was yours, you made me do it."

"Bff."

Raski pet the elegant red creature, then closed his eyes. "Oh Draephus I'm such an idiot. How did Straif get through all this?"

Draephus left the computer and walked over to the bed, carefully lying down on it to face Raski.

"Baby when Straif got his, he was sixteen. You're a little older. So it takes longer to recover."

"Uh huh. And what about the bleeding and infections? Is that age, too?"

"Raski some guys have a harder time with this. It's a risky operation, we were warned about that. You rearranged your body in order to make it do something it was never intended to do."

"But the babies from the tanks have so many problems," said Raski. "I want our babies to be normal."

Normal. Right. In this house, the kid's first words would either be "arf" or "werp". "Can't we just get another faelin?"

"BARK!"

"See? Bacca likes the idea."

Raski burst into tears, and Draephus felt himself slowly wither up and turn into something closely related to a maggot. "Oh come on, Raski, I was just teasing…."

Draephus had no idea what Raski said in response; most of it was squeaking and hiccupping and sobbing. Draephus drew him close and held him tightly.

"I'm sorry."

Raski aimed a very controlled jab of the fist at Draephus' gut; just hard enough to hurt. Draephus winced, then grinned.

"I'm sorry. I really am. I just want you better. Come on, what can I do to make it better?"

"I don't know, anything! Even a bath would do wonders! I stink like rotting meat."

Yeah Raski had definitely smelled better. It had to be pretty demoralizing lying in pain and reeking of old pus.

"Okay," said Draephus. "We'll have a bath."

Raski raised his head, half-hopeful. "Really?"

"I'll call Dr. Arang and get something arranged. Just stay there."

So Draephus called Dr. Arang, who sent out an intern to tend to Raski. The young man was only in his early twenties, and clearly ecstatic to be in charge of Raski Jervyas' infections. Draephus grinned and watched his beloved breathe hate and fire at the kid. Raski did not like doctors, or interns, or people in hospital robes in general. The young man examined the wound carefully.

"I think I may have found the cause of the ongoing infections."

"What is it?" asked Draephus.

"Well most hospital sutures are made from the fibers of a type of plant that grows near sources of fresh water called duck's fort. They're very strong, sterilize easily and don't allow bacteria to grow. But… in this case… I think the sutures themselves are the cause of the infection. Donsa Jervyas, are you allergic to duck's fort?"

"I have no idea."

"I think you are. Well congratulations, that makes you very

special. Less than one percent of the population is. Probably why Dr. Arang didn't think of it. I'll draw these out, clean the area, put on a watertight dressing and you can have your bath. I'm willing to bet you will be feeling better within a few days, if not hours."

"Tell Dr. Arang I hate him and I know he did this on purpose," said Raski.

The young man departed, and Draephus poured Raski a bath. He then helped him to the bathroom. That was a new and exciting experience; Raski with his painful infected sores and Draephus with arthritis eating his joints.

"This was a really bad idea, Rask," said Draephus.

"Just don't limp faster than me."

Bacca and Czanda padded after them, clearly not convinced the pair could make it all the way by themselves. Draephus did not go to the bathroom he normally used with the deep tub. Instead he went to the bathroom that Dahli had enjoyed on her visit. There was much more room, and it was easier for the pair to get into. No sooner were they settled in the hot, soothing water than Draephus heard the sound of high heels rapidly heading up the stairs. He sighed heavily as Straif came tearing into the bathroom, still perched in his five inch heels, and clearly six months pregnant. He paused and looked at the pair.

"Hey you're both naked."

"There is often an element of nudity in having a bath," said Draephus.

"You're skinny. I always thought you were big and brawny under that coat but you're just bones!"

"Yes," said Draephus. "I am skinny and naked. Next you are going to point out I am also wet."

"Well you are."

"Straif do you have anything to actually say or do you just like to watch people take a bath?"

"Oh!" He deftly seated himself on the edge of the tub, crossing his long legs as he passed Draephus a rather legal-looking document. "I'm in a band again. Delaes and Rysta are reforming Bad Influence and want me to join. We still need a drummer but I'd rather say I was in Bad Influence than Vortex any day."

Draephus took the document and read it over. Yeah, they were formally asking Straif to join the ranks of one of Sferkkaa's very few metal bands all right.

"I thought Delaes was taking some time off," said Draephus.

Straif shrugged. "Changed his mind, I guess. You know Delaes, he can't sit still for five minutes. Anyway I can't wait to get into a real band and start playing real music."

"Why did you stay so long?" asked Raski.

"Well I did *form* Vortex. I stayed around trying to fix it but you can't fix "stupid" no matter how hard you try. I shall now go try to get some rest. I've been up all night trying to play Black Metal around a bulge. Poor kid will probably come out clutching a pair of ear phones."

"I expect that baby to be playing faster than you within a year," said Raski.

"I'll have a word with it about that when I meet it."

"Is it a boy or a girl?" asked Raski.

"Don't know. Because of the special circumstances involved they are just letting the baby develop naturally instead of giving it little genetic prods to be a girl. I'm too delicate to poke."

"Apparently the father didn't think so," said Raski.

"Very classy, Raski," said Straif. "I'm going to go have a nap now."

Straif departed. Draephus reached over the edge of the tub to find his telecom in his pile of clothes on the floor. Locating it, he drew it out and called a number.

"Heia?"

"J'Vanni it's Draephus."

"Oh. So nice to hear from you."

"How's Delaes?"

J'Vanni cleared his throat. "He's… recovering."

Draephus felt his heart break into pieces. "He lost it."

J'Vanni was managing to hold himself together very well, but it was clear how emotional he was. "It was all the stress. There was the attack, and then the time in the pipes and up the tree, the fear of being found out and wondering if any of Vesper's little friends were still watching… it was too much for him. He just… collapsed. He's not dealing with it very well. He just wants to get back to making music and trying to put all of this behind him. Vesper should be very proud of himself. He murdered an infant. Such a great and powerful enemy."

"J'Vanni I am so very sorry."

"As am I, for all of us, for many reasons. But we have the documents you were kind enough to give us. Perhaps one day there will be another baby. We would like a family. For now, however, we will simply try to put our lives back together."

"Yeah," said Draephus. "I'll come up to visit the first chance I get."

"Thank you, Draephus, we would like that."

Draephus hung up, and looked to Raski. "Well now we know why Delaes is putting Bad Influence back together."

"I wish Vesper was still alive so we could kill him all over again."

"So do I but all we can do is support Delaes while he recovers. Support and protect."

"I still can't shake the idea they may want to hurt you at some point."

Draephus sighed. "Yeah, maybe. I just don't find it very likely."

He reached for his cigarettes, putting one between his lips and lighting it. Raski just stared at him.

"How can you smoke in the bath?"

"Talent."

The pair froze as they heard a screech down the hallway. Leaping out of the bath and charging to the rescue was not currently an option for either Raski or Draephus, so they had to simply wait until Straif came tearing back on his own.

"They found a city!" he blurted out.

Draephus and Raski stared back. "That's nice," said Draephus.

"No you don't understand! Off the coast of our own island! An entire underwater city! It's thousands of years old and almost completely intact! They think it was once part of this island but broke off and sank, and then with the Grey Boys running around blowing up stuff…"

"We forgot it was down there," said Raski.

"It's about two miles off-shore," said Straif. "Earth was already sending us some scientists and equipment to help us recover what we've lost so they're going to be sending down dive teams to explore it and camera crews to help us document it!"

There came a knock at the door, and Straif tore off to see who was there, followed by a pair of barking faelins. Draephus turned his head to look at Raski.

"You want *five* of those."

Raski indicated his incisions. "I'm not going through all of this to back out now."

They heard a lot of gleeful screeching and greetings, then a veritable herd of feet heading up the stairs. Draephus and Raski watched Straif go tearing by the bathroom door, chased by Gemma, Czamkiar, Diza, and of course Dahli. Apparently the nap had been called off due to invasion.

"Heia Draephus, heia Raski!" Dahli paused, then looked into the bathroom. "Hey you two are naked."

"That happens in the bath," said Draephus.

He watched sourly as Dahli borrowed Gemma's camera and took a photo, then closed the door, giggling.

"Five of them," said Draephus. "You want five."

"Five."

"Did you, or did you not, just see that mob that ran by, took a picture of us in the bath, and kept going?"

"You're the one who wanted Straif to have friends his own age, my darling one. Your wish has been granted."

"Yeah," said Draephus. He touched Raski's face. "How are you feeling?"

"Better," said Raski softly.

Draephus leaned forward, meaning to kiss Raski, when the bathroom door blew open and Straif charged in to throw up, followed by his entourage. That was when Draephus ran out of patience.

"All right, if everybody is not out of my bath in five seconds, I'M STANDING UP!"

Shrieking teenagers fled in all directions, including Straif when he finally stopped being sick. The door was closed, and just to make sure it would not be opened again, Draephus went to lock the door.

"You *are* a bit on the thin side, my lover," said Raski.

"We all are," said Draephus. "Can't wait for spring to come. Only three more months before the Festival, too."

"I can't wait to see Straif on stage nine months pregnant," said Raski.

"And in heels."

"If he can do a four hour set in four inch heels at nine months pregnant, I vote we make him Emperor," said Raski.

"Can't," said Draephus, getting back into the bath with Raski. "The one we have now will have to move in with Khandi and stop throwing people out second storey windows."

****

It was very late, and silent. Draephus slowly rose from the bed, wincing and shivering in pain. He'd been trying desperately hard to hold off on the resin with Raski so sick, but he wasn't going to get any peace without it. He could barely walk.

He took only a tiny amount, then waited to see how much of the pain subsided. Then he took a tiny bit more, and closed his eyes in pure bliss, able to draw a full breath for the first time in days. He leaned down to kiss Raski's face, smiling at him, then touched his brow, trying to determine how hot he was. The fever seemed to be down. Draephus hoped he was getting better. He was done with death and loss.

Draephus dressed, then carefully walked down the hall to Straif's room. He grinned at the pile of kids on the mighty bed that had once held an Empress. Draephus had no idea how long Straif was planning on remaining, but he wasn't about to do anything to discourage the kid from staying around. This castle could use a little laughter and joy after all the things it had seen. A smile touched his lips.

"Well," he said softly. "I see the kids are all right."

He went downstairs to his box of shaman items, taking out his bag and stick and dagger, then silently left the castle, heading into the torrential winter rains to the clearing. He sighed as he saw a miserable blue bird sitting in the cage on the stump. The door was wide open, and Draephus knew for a fact he had released it months ago. But the message was clear; the bird was cold, wet, hungry, and this was the only place it thought it could get warmth and food. He sighed and gently picked the sodden thing up.

"And what if I hadn't come back until spring?" he asked it.

He wrapped it carefully in a bit of cloth, and held it close, feeling the way it trembled. It was cold, and most likely ravenous. Well he could probably dig up something for one little silly long-beaked blue bird.

Draephus looked to the sapling that the carn-crow had given him, and saw it was flourishing. In the spring it would flower and bear fruit, bringing good health to the family it now guarded. Draephus looked down at the little shivering bird.

"You did try," said Draephus. "You tried to work the magic, but you couldn't, because everything was a lie. Come on, let's get you inside and dry, and feed you. No reason for all of us to starve. What sort of an ohwendai man lets little birds go hungry?"

He carried the bird into the castle and into the kitchen, putting the damp, rumpled creature on the table. He gave it some seeds and a slice of almaniki, and watched as the bird ate ravenously. He ate the rest of the fruit, wasting nothing, as he stood in contemplation. Did Vesper's compatriots intend to hurt him? Draephus doubted it. People like Delaes and J'Vanni were easier meat; they had secrets to hide, and not many people would show them any compassion, especially not J'Vanni. Draephus sighed as he noticed a pair of green eyes peer over the edge of the table, followed by a second pair. Both were fixed on the bird.

"That is not a snack," he warned.

Czanda gave up almost immediately. Bacca continued to stare, transfixed. Draephus sighed and shooed the faelin out of the kitchen, then returned to his thoughts. Maybe it was time to give serious consideration to laying down some protection magicks. He looked once more to the little blue bird. It was a Dusty Nightsinger, not one of the more powerful protection symbols, but a good little friend nonetheless. They were said to be a messenger to the more powerful guardian spirits. So even if the little bird could do nothing on its own, it would certainly know creatures that could, like that daeha out in the long grass.

Draephus went to fetch Raski's blue eye shadow, and gave the feasting bird the tiniest dusting of it, just enough to help it see its way to the spirit world. Then, with a small brush, he drew on the bird's back with pearl-grey pigments ground from the inner shells of calurchi. It was not easy to draw the symbols; the bird kept looking over its shoulder to see what its host was doing. But finally all was accomplished. The bird was full and rested and dry, and Draephus had drawn the tiny delicate symbols needed to convey his message on the shoulders of the little bird. Then, as daylight chased the last of the shadows away, Draephus opened the window and let the bird go. It flew a few feet away to a sapling and landed on a branch, then looked back. Draephus locked the larger, lower window, but then opened a small portal window, much higher up, used many years ago to release the heat of kitchen fires. He had to stand on a chair to reach it, and braced it open so the bird could return any time it wanted. He was just getting off the chair when he felt a pair of arms slip around him from behind.

"Were you up all night casting magic?" Raski asked.

"Well not intentionally, but yeah," said Draephus.

"You need your rest as much as I do," said Raski.

Draephus turned to look into the white-blue eyes, and kissed him. "How are you feeling?"

"Better. Much, much better. I think it *was* the sutures making me ill. I actually feel like eating. Do we have anything?"

"No, but we will. You make tea, I'll go get breakfast."

Draephus kissed him again, then walked to the door of the castle and took down a pair of collars with silver bells on them. He gave them a shake.

"*T'niski!*"

Bacca and Czanda shot down from the upper floor, barking, and tore out the door as Draephus held it for them. He then walked into the cold winter day, glad to see the rain was little more than the faintest mist, and the cloud cover was thin and high. It made him feel hopeful.

****

The weeks flew by in a blur. The festival was closing fast. Equipment was being shipped to Charlendine, as well as Trilby and Mit-Mit. The enormous mountain dragon plants were to be loaded carefully into their own container and anchored solidly to avoid any breakage. Both had made similar journeys many times, and likely had no idea what all the fuss was about as the usual Sferkkaan journalists, as well as a veritable herd of reporters, biologists, and photographers from Earth, came for a look. Included in the crowd were a few sight-seers. Gemma could not resist bringing some of her friends to look at the plants.

"You know that scene in Jurassic Park, where the Brachiosaurus comes to look at the people in the tree?" said K-Shot.

"Good thing plants don't sneeze," said Mystique.

Trilby was rustling his leaves in the late winter air, likely thinking he didn't care for it much. His pot was anchored, and his portion of the container was closed off. Next came Mit-Mit, craning her pseudo-head as if sensing the crowd.

"She's so pretty!" said Mystique. "Oh I'd love to have one."

"No you wouldn't," said Gemma. "Trust me. It's all fun and games until somebody busts open a pot and shakes babies all over the room."

"Hate when that happens," said K-Shot. Mystique elbowed him gently in the ribs.

The men hauling the huge plant paused for a breather, and Mit-Mit dipped her head to graciously meet her public, allowing herself to be petted. Then, once she realized she was colder than she liked, she calmly and with great dignity dragged her own pot into the container, much to the amusement of the on-lookers. She huddled down, shaking her leaves, then, once she was still, she too was anchored into place and closed in.

"So that's a sound system," said K-Shot.

"It is if you live here," said Gemma.

"I'm not sure I can get used to that," said K-Shot. "Is that what we'll be using at the festival?"

"Just think of them as a really big wireless speaker," said Gemma.

"Yeah but how do they know what to do?" asked K-Shot. "How do they know how loud to make one thing over another?"

"Staging," said Gemma. "The musicians closer to the plant are louder than the ones further away. K-Shot you should know all this by now. That's why the Gryphons opened up their studios to us, so we could learn how to handle things like giant leafy amplifiers."

Mystique gave him a gentle nudge. "She's right, you know."

"The fewer electrical devices the better," said Gemma. "That's why they use the plants for the outdoor venues. A plant is less likely to shock you."

"Yeah can't say I like the idea of being fried like an egg," said K-Shot. "I just can't warm up to the idea of getting back-up vocals from a house plant capable of running me over."

There was a glimpse of white and green, and Gemma pointed. "Hey there's Straif. HEIA! STRAIF!"

He turned to see who was calling his name, clad in a flowing outfit of green and white, then smiled and began approaching. Mystique and K-Shot just stared.

"That boy is *pregnant*," said Mystique.

"Yeah, you knew he was!" said Gemma.

"Yeah but there is a difference between knowing it and seeing it," she said.

"Seven and a half months," said Gemma. "Another three and a half to go. Takes eleven months to make a baby Sferkkaan."

"And still in the heels," said Mystique. "If I was seven and a half months pregnant I'd be in flats and a wheelchair. Just hand me the pickles and ice cream and roll my butt over to the TV!"

Gemma laughed. Straif walked up to her and gave her a hug, then seated himself on the edge of a low decorative wall.

"You're huge," said Gemma.

"Well thanks," said Straif. "I'm starting to think I may not make the festival. Between the bloating and the cramping and the crying and everything else I'm not so sure I want to be on stage. I may have to insist on something to sit on, and then arm extensions to reach my quinticord."

"At the very least get some different shoes," said Mystique.

"Never! Do you know how hard I worked to earn these blades?" He deftly flipped his long brown hair over one shoulder, pretending not to notice the trio of photographers creeping up on him. Gemma just smiled at him.

"You're so pretty."

"Yes I am. Seen Dahli?"

"I believe she's helping pack some of the equipment. She shouldn't be too much longer, they're nearly done with all the stuff that's going to Charlendine. Hey are you coming over to watch the visual tonight?"

"Would *not* miss it!" said Straif.

"Why?" asked Mystique. "What's on tonight?"

"Underwater exploration of the city they found, broadcast live," said Straif. "Oh I can't wait to see!"

"That does sound pretty cool," said Mystique.

"We're making a party of it," said Gemma. "Starts when it gets dark."

"Why are they going down in the dark?" asked K-Shot.

"Day or night, doesn't matter. We have excellent night-vision equipment," said Straif. "Well that's war for you. There's not a thing to eat but hey we can film in the dark!"

He finally deigned to notice the photographers, who were peering at him nervously; three artfully-scruffy men who were probably more used to filming wars than aliens.

"Hi," said one. "I'm David Cooper. Do you mind if...?"

Straif began ticking items off on his fingers. "Yes I'm male, yes I'm pregnant, no it's not natural, it's an implant, the father would prefer to be left alone, I don't know if it is a boy or a girl, I want to be surprised, I am due in three and a half months..."

Dahli ran up just then, throwing her arms around him and kissing him. "I'm done! We finally loaded up the last of it so I am free!"

"...and this is my girlfriend Dahli, because who I am sleeping with seems to fascinate you people," finished Straif.

"Yeah what is it with you people and genitalia?" asked Dahli. "You need another hobby."

"Like bodysnatching?" teased David.

She made a face at him, then looked to Straif. "Ready to go?"

He nodded, and Dahli helped him to stand up.

"This is going to be so much fun," said Gemma, taking Straif's free arm. "My first alien sleepover!"

"And we get to argue about who the alien is!" said Dahli. "Straif are you okay?"

"I haven't decided yet." He thought for a few moments, then said "No, I'm definitely gonna puke."

Dahli rolled her eyes as he staggered over to a bush to vomit behind it. "Our kind and benevolent Emperor does not give you extra rations to feed the dirt!"

"WHAT IS THAT ŠUKATING STENCH?!" he demanded angrily.

The four friends sniffed, first themselves, then each other, then finally located the source of the smell. They looked to the photographers, and one in particular.

"Hey this is very expensive cologne!" he said.

"It's upsetting a National Treasure, so can you and your very expensive feralyke urine please go stink someplace else?" said Dahli.

The man left. Gemma just giggled.

"Dahli you are so mean!"

"Oh like you would be any different if it was your boyfriend who was pregnant by some guy you didn't know," she said. She walked over to Straif and carefully helped him up. "Better?"

"Little woozy. I think.... Yeah I'm gonna faint."

Dahli managed to catch him before he hit the ground. She

carefully placed him down, then looked to Gemma.

"I need to get him someplace cool and quiet."

"We could just take him back to our place," said Gemma. "It's cool, and with the air-conditioning he won't be smelling things. He can have a nap and he won't have to go anywhere when the show starts."

"That sounds good," said Dahli. "Now how do we get him to the conni?"

K-Shot suddenly found himself beset by three pairs of big wet eyes.

"No! Oh no! I am a big mean scary tough rap artist. I do *not* carry around little pretty boys wearing five pounds of make-up and fifty pounds of baby."

"Oh come on, K-Shot!" pleaded Gemma. "You're all big and strong, and he's… passed out on the ground."

K-Shot ground his teeth, likely knowing a picture of this was going to crop up somewhere. And it was not as if he could just toss Straif over his shoulder like a bag of potatoes. Not in Straif's current condition. He knelt down and carefully gathered the small Sferkkaan into his arms. He rose to his feet and straightened, just in time to see Gemma and her camera.

"Don't you dare!" he warned.

She took his picture anyway. K-Shot ground his teeth.

"But you look so cute!" she gushed.

"Just carry him into the studio and put him in the common room until he gets his bearings," said Dahli. "We'll see if you can escape the studio with your reputation intact."

"I worked damned hard on my rep! Then I come here and it's like…. the ANTI-hood. Everybody's nice, everybody's considerate, no one's robbing anybody. And nobody's ugly! I demand to know where all the ugly Sferkkaans are at."

"We're very sorry," said Dahli. "Really. Truly we are."

"Uh huh. Don't lie to me, you're no good at it. Where do I put him? He's heavy."

Dahli indicated a couch, and K-Shot put Straif down on the cool smooth surface. Gemma did not like the way Straif was staying limp, and she could tell Dahli didn't either.

"Is he all right?" she asked.

Dahli crouched beside the limp form, stroking the long hair. "Straif?"

"I'm okay," he said softly, almost chagrinned.

"You want to just lie here for a while?"

He nodded.

"Okay. You just relax."

Dahli kissed Straif's face. Gemma glanced at Mystique and K-Shot, seeing the concern in their eyes. They knew exactly how delicate Straif was, and it was hard to watch him struggle this way. Gemma was about to suggest they leave Straif alone to rest, when she noticed a tall rangy figure come up behind K-Shot, slip his arms around him, and rest his face against the rapper's shoulder. Mystique giggled, as K-Shot looked over his shoulder at Draephus.

"Excuse me but I believe you have mistaken me for someone else."

Draephus raised his head and looked at K-Shot. "You're right. Sorry." He pointedly looked at Dahli and Gemma. "I haven't been sleeping much."

"I'm sorry," said Gemma, "who was up with us at stupid o'clock showing us how Bacca can run up walls?"

"Who is the *reason* I was up at stupid o'clock?" asked Draephus.

Gemma pointed at Dahli.

"Oh sure, blame me," said Dahli.

Raski walked into the room, looking rather weak and shaky himself, and stared at Draephus.

"Is there any particular reason that you are cuddling K-Shot?"

Draephus smiled and moved over to Raski to embrace him. "He said he was cold. I was keeping him warm."

"Uh-huh."

"I mean it! How could I trade away anything as beautiful as you? No one could ever compare."

They held each other, kissing. K-Shot, Gemma, Mystique and Dahli left the room, letting Raski and Draephus have a few moments alone.

"I am both confused and insulted," declared K-Shot. "I'm just as pretty as he is!"

"You need more blue eye shadow," said Mystique.

"And sparkly things in your hair," said Gemma.

"Well maybe I'll try it!" he said.

"Uh… not a good idea," said Dahli.

"Why not?" asked Mystique.

"The blue eye shadow is made from the shell of this little underwater snail," said Dahli. "You have to dive to catch it. A creature that lives in a hidden world within a hidden world is very big ohwendai magic. And the white jewels deflect evil magicks."

"So Raski is some sort of shaman?" asked Gemma.

Dahli shrugged. "I don't know what the word for it is. Neither of them says much about it, not even to me. It's a very old way of life. Draephus and Raski both learned slightly different versions of it on the South Continent."

"So he just doesn't wear all the blue and the white because it looks amazing on him," said Gemma.

"Very little that people wear here is just for show," said Dahli.

"What's the blue eye shadow do?" asked Mystique.

"I don't know," said Dahli. "Like I said they don't talk about it much. I do know there are reasons Raski wears it and Draephus doesn't. Every line and colour people wear here has significance. You can't just put on blue eye shadow and white gems and not have someone call you on it."

"What colours should I wear?" he asked.

"I don't know," said Dahli. "If you like I can bring my make-up kit when I come over tonight and you can tell me who you are. You can show everyone who you are when you go on stage at the festival."

"And me?" asked Mystique. "Or is all that stuff just for boys?"

"No we can paint you too! If you have a life and a story, you have colours," said Dahli.

"Wish I could wear my gold eye shadow," moaned Gemma.

"Oh poor Gemma," said Dahli. "Maybe if we look hard we can… find…"

Her words slowed to a halt. The four stared at something sitting on the table in the common room, noisily gnawing an animal bone. It had the red hide and hair of a faelin, but it also bore large, strangely streaky-splotchy black markings. It was missing an eye, and had horrible scars on one side of its face. It ignored the intruders as it chewed and cracked its bone.

"Wow," said Gemma. "That is the ugliest faelin I've ever seen."

Dahli looked at her, smiling. "Is it ruining your life?"

"GAWD you people! Let it lie!"

"I see you've met Seija," said a voice. Gemma looked up as

571

Draephus walked into the room, followed by Raski.

"That is the ugliest faelin I have ever seen," Gemma repeated.

"Is it ruining your life?" asked Raski.

Gemma made a loud noise of exasperation. "If I hear that joke one more time I am walking home to Earth!"

"I'd like to see that," said Dahli. "That would be really impressive. But yeah what's with the ugly faelin that's ruining Gemma's life?"

Gemma mimed strangling her. Draephus walked over to the creature. It made a series of noises at him, but none sounded especially hostile. Draephus stroked the long hair.

"Well I hope you don't think he's too ugly," said Draephus. He looked to Dahli. "He's yours."

Gemma looked to Dahli, watching the absolutely astounded look on her face. "Mine?"

"Good jungle-raised arboreal faelin. He needs a home."

Dahli slowly walked forward to approach the creature, reaching a hand out to touch him. "Where did he come from?" she asked.

"He used to belong… to a very good friend of mine," said Draephus softly, and Gemma did not miss the way his voice broke ever so slightly. "But she died, and now Seija needs a home. Be a shame to just leave a good faelin like that alone to get into trouble."

"But… if he belonged to your friend… why are you giving him to me?" Dahli asked.

"I already have two," said Draephus. "And… Seija doesn't get along with them."

Gemma smiled at the way Dahli was visibly tearing up over her gift, touching the soft red hair. "You're all spotty, silly thing."

Seija turned his head briefly to look at her, then continued chewing his bone.

"Is he supposed to be spotty?" asked Gemma. "He almost looks like he was rolling in something."

"He was," said Draephus. "When he was a little faelin. He found a patch of scribe's weed and had a good roll in it. Just one thing – it's absolutely permanent. That's why it's all streaks and splotches. He rolled all over a patch, and now he's spotty. There's an old myth about how the people of the South Continent were once all white like the Northerners, but fell into a vat of full of scribe's weed."

"We didn't fall, we were pushed," said Raski.

Draephus kissed him. "You're beautiful."

"When are you two going to formally announce you're a couple?" asked Dahli.

"Ask Raski, he's the one plotting to mortify me in public," said Draephus.

"Well the name of the band *is* 'Mortified Gryphons'," said Raski.

"That's a name, not an open invitation." Draephus looked to Dahli. "So do you like him?"

She nodded, holding his leash in her hands, visibly in tears. "He's the most wonderful thing I've ever seen. Are you going to teach me to hunt with him?"

"Not much to it," said Draephus. "Point him at what you want and say "*fetch it*". If he can catch it, he will. The only thing you must never forget is to give him his own cut; he did the work, he deserves a portion. If you don't share, he won't trust you, and he won't hunt for you."

"What parts do I give him?" asked Dahli.

"Best parts are the liver, kidneys, and heart. He will want those more than the other bits."

"Oh good, he'll eat all the bits I *don't* want." Dahli smiled, petting the faelin, then turned to Draephus and hugged him tightly. "Thank you! He'll be loved and cuddled and adored."

"Yeah well I figured you were someone I could entrust him with. I mean if you were willing to steal a dead one…"

"And would do it again," said Dahli. "And would gladly break into a lab and do it again only this time not *tell* anyone…"

He grinned. "That's the spirit, Fearless."

A tiny form with a great deal of pink-streaked hair walked into the room, looking rather displeased.

"Draephus you may wish to have a very sharp word with those people from Earth you gave permission to camp on your property."

"Why?" asked Draephus.

"Well they don't seem to be respecting your rules. I found this in your drive."

Khandid handed Draephus a tiny bundle wrapped in a bit of cloth. Draephus accepted it and unwrapped it, freezing as he saw what lay in his hand.

"Oh the poor tiny thing!" said Gemma. "Why would anyone

hurt something so small?"

"Not cool," said K-Shot. "That is just not cool."

Draephus stared at the little blue bird in his hands, carefully examining it. He moved aside some of the feathers and found a hole in the center of the bird's back.

"The people from Earth didn't do this. Look. The wound is burned. Earth weapons don't do that."

"Why would anyone hurt such a little bird?" asked Mystique. "Hurt it and then…. Did someone draw on it? There are markings…"

Draephus rewrapped the bird, saying something to it in a dialect Gemma did not know. He then gave Dahli a kiss on the top of her head.

"Have fun at the party tonight, Fearless."

He and Raski quickly walked away, departing from the studio. Dahli looked to Khandid.

"Why would someone shoot a Dusty Nightsinger?"

"I have no idea," said Khandid softly. "But I have the oddest feeling that Raski and Draephus do."

Chapter Twenty-Six

"So what do Earth people do at a slumber party?" asked Dahli as she helped Gemma get things set up.

"Well there's not usually a lot of sleeping," said Gemma, dragging pillows over to a place before the TV. "Mostly there's a lot of goofing around and eating too much and pillow fights and talking about boys and stuff."

"So pretty much what Diza and I do every other night, except for the eating part." Dahli watched Seija settle on the pillows, looking pleased with himself.

"And what boys are you discussing?" asked Straif, seated on one of the leather sofas, watching Dahli and Gemma get set up.

"Well it used to be the endless fight about why Draephus was so much cuter than Yuri," said Dahli. "But that one's gotten kinda strange since Draephus has decided he and I are related, and now you're my boyfriend, and most of the other musicians I used to gush over I now know at least enough to say 'Heia' to."

Straif stared at her. "Draephus? As in Draephus CZimcocious?"

"Yes as in Draephus CZimcocious," said Dahli. "Why?"

"Well he's...not exactly cute."

"HE'S ADORABLE, YOU TAKE THAT BACK!"

"Or what?" asked Straif, grinning.

"I start telling people that the father of your baby is Mickie Pastors."

"Oooh," winced Gemma. "Evil."

"Everyone picks on Draephus and says he's not cute but the man is šukating adorable and I won't hear otherwise."

"Well aren't I cute?" pouted Straif.

Dahli rolled her eyes. "Straif we've been over this. You're adorable, and I love you."

"But you'd love me more if I smelled like a mushroom den."

"Mushrooms?" asked Gemma as Dahli went to cuddle Straif. "Is that what that smell is?"

"South Continent Spined Mushrooms, yes," said Dahli quietly.

"Is that bad?" asked Gemma.

Dahli didn't look like she wanted to talk about it. Straif was the one who spoke up.

"If he's taking enough that we can smell it, then it only means two things. He's either an addict or he's in so much pain he's shooting pure resin. Likely at this point in his life he's both."

"Oh," said Gemma softly. "Wow. That kind of explains why Mars flipped on me."

"The Gryphons are really protective of each other," said Straif. "Even if Mars doesn't know *why* Draephus is taking it any more than we do, he would likely know the reasons can't be good."

"Thought he was going to tear my head off," said Gemma.

"Any one of them could," said Straif. "But Khandi is the one most likely to. Then Yuri. And now that I have been sitting for fifteen minutes, guess what I have to do."

Dahli rolled her eyes and helped him to his feet. "Are we going to end up having the party in the bathroom?"

"It may come to that," he said.

"I hope not," said Gemma. "None of the bathrooms are big enough."

Dahli and Gemma finished setting up for the party. They were planning on being in front of the TV for the better part of the night, so they had made a sort of enormous nest of blankets and pillows on the floor and dubbed it the Pillow Pit. Low tables were brought to hold snacks and drinks, and Straif had a place of honour with quilts to pad his extra weight. Then Gemma turned on the TV, just to make sure it was working properly, and was promptly treated to a shot of the inside of Gryphon Studios.

"Oh this ought to be good," said Dahli.

"What is it?" asked Gemma.

"Just a short programme about the coming festival," said Dahli. "Clips of the different musicians involved and stuff. Look, there's me in the background restringing Straif's sepulchord while Straif throws up in the bathroom."

"Such a romantic moment between you two," said Gemma.

"I like it," said Dahli, grinning.

As Dahli worked on the sepulchord in the background, in the foreground a telecom rang and Mars answered it.

"Gryphon Studios, home of the two-for-one kaisa sale, who the šukat are you?"

"Scruffin' lovely, Mars," said Khandid.

Mars stood listening for so long the other Gryphons became curious. Finally he shook his head and said "I'm sorry, you...wish to photograph us nude, is that what you're saying? I believe the appropriate response is 'you first'." He listened for a while longer, then said "I think you should talk to our band manager."

Mars passed the telecom to Raski, who took it.

"Raski here." He listened. "Nude. As in naked. Really."

Khandid briefly snatched the telecom. "No one wants to see Draephus naked, including Draephus."

Raski took it back and listened a while longer, then said "No. I don't care who you are or what publishing house you represent, we're a music group, not prostitutes."

"I was," said Khandid.

"Okay Khandid was for a while briefly but..." Raski listened. "No I'm sorry, naked is not happening." He listened again. "Let me ask the band." He looked to his four bandmates. "How do you feel about semi-nude?"

"I demand to know why we have to be naked or semi-naked in this," said Mars.

Raski listened to the person on the other end of the telecom, then looked to Mars. "She says she's willing to come down and show us her work if that will help."

The scene on the TV shifted, and Gemma realized they were not watching the documentary at all, they were actually watching a talk show which was being broadcast from the second ship that had arrived.

"Oh hey," said Gemma. "That's Barry Winfield, he has a talk show back home. The woman with him is Maria Solis, she's a really famous photographer."

"Is she the one trying to get Mars to take his clothes off?" asked Dahli.

"Probably. Her photos have hung in galleries all over my world, she does beautiful work. I wonder how they worked this? It's a day and a half delay for a signal to reach Earth. Unless Barry recorded his questions and Maria recorded her answers and they combined the images." Gemma studied the pair on the TV. "I think that's what they did."

On the TV, Barry and Maria talked.

"So they really did not trust you," he said.

"No," said Maria. "And you have to be careful because these are

577

not pampered celebrities, they're retired partisans and guerrilla fighters, and a couple of them are quite edgy away from their friends. But I did manage to photograph a number of bands for my upcoming book, not just Arucadda Dannatti, but they *are* the big deal up here. So here are some of the photos I managed to get of them…"

The screen switched to a photo of Khandid Stracona in full make up and heels, white hair streaked pink and blue, wearing only his boots, pants, and a pair of gloves he seldom wore, with blades emerging from the back. He stared out of the photo with bright blue eyes that somehow managed to say "Yes I'm cute, and heavily armed."

"Now…" said Barry, "this is Khandid, am I right? What did he do in the war?"

"He did both espionage and assassinations. Also pit-fighting for entertainment of enemy soldiers. I've got a few of him in motion with a training dummy…"

Gemma noticed Dahli sitting down to gaze at the photos of Khandid in full flight, his hair blowing.

"He's so *pretty*!" Dahli said. "These photos are beautiful!"

"Told you she's good," said Gemma, seating herself beside her.

"She is! She really is!" Dahli laughed. "He's gorgeous!"

"About the heels," said Barry. "Now… maybe I'm thinking in terms of fighting arts such as kung fu or tae-kwan-do, but those boot blades make no sense to me."

"If you look close," said Maria, "You can see the razors down the back. He can cut your throat with those. I did a frame-by-frame of the strike to show you how it works. It's not like our martial arts at all, it's very different…"

Gemma and Dahli watched as, frame by frame, Khandid leapt up, kicking out with the boot-blades first to puncture the lower abdomen and anchor himself on his opponent, then drove the blades on his gloves straight down, one into the skull, one into the clavicle, and used them to hold himself as he ripped the boot blades out with a savage tearing of the abdomen. The Earth audience could be heard reacting to the disturbing sight.

"That is *not* self-defence," said Barry.

"No," said Maria. "It's survival in a war zone; shock and awe as it were. The blow expends an enormous amount of energy, whereas our martial arts are about the conservation of energy. One opponent is blown apart in a blur of hair and fabric, and that usually buys the Whip enough time to escape if there is more than one opponent, or kills the single target so fast there is no time to sound an alarm. The whole thing takes just over a second, and you are either dead or incapacitated and on the way to death. Many of the men up here wear heels, but not all carry razors. I'm not sure yet what the significance of the heels *is,* but a good rule of thumb to follow is if he's wearing heels higher than yours, just don't annoy him."

Dahli squeaked in glee as the next photo came up on the screen. Gemma rolled her eyes. "Dahli you are such a Draephus groupie. And the man is not cute."

"He's adorable," said Dahli. "But he *is* skinnier than he was when I first met him."

The photo was of Draephus wearing pants, which were slightly loose on his bony frame. He had on his boots, hat and shades as per usual, and also per usual he had a lit cigarette in his mouth. Lounging at his feet were Bacca and Czanda, elegantly posed like something on an Egyptian temple. Straif returned from the bathroom as Barry and Maria were discussing the faelins, showing several photos of Draephus interacting with his beloved pets, including one where he actually smiled.

"The fans will never believe that one hasn't been tampered with," said Straif. Dahli grinned and gave him a nudge.

They watched the show, enjoying the photos, Dahli gently petting Seija as they listened to Maria discuss the photos and the people in them.

"And this I think is the most controversial one," said Maria, and Dahli and Straif both became excited at the next photo. It was of themselves, cuddling with obvious affection. Dahli was fully dressed, but Straif was in little more than shorts, his protruding belly on full display.

"This is Straif Mannechek, and his girlfriend, Dahli Sandiniti," said Maria.

"He's the boy who had the operation to enable himself to have a baby," said Barry.

"Yes and a lot of people are quite up in arms about this, certainly some religious leaders are saying the fact that *Straif* is pregnant and not his girlfriend is proof of how decadent Sferkkaan culture is, and even proof that this is what happens when you let women have rights. What they won't listen to is that this is a planet where the female population is so decimated that his chances of meeting a girl, and we won't even get into his odds of finding a girl who can bear children, are virtually non-existent. They also need to understand that he was pregnant when she met him."

"So his pregnancy is not her fault," said Barry. Some people in the audience giggled.

"Definitely is not," said Dahli, smiling.

"What people need to understand," said Maria, "is this is not a religious issue or a women's issue, this is a survival issue. On Sferkkaa there are far more men than women, and of the women remaining there only one in three can actually have children. We have people on Earth acting like this is some personal insult to them, when it's about survival of the species. And these two children you see in this photo are not likely to survive into their thirties. Straif has roughly five years to live, and Dahli has viral issues of the liver, so they have to take matters into their own hands at a young age. This is a planet that has survived atrocities on the scale of the largest disasters of Earth, and now they want to have the same things we do - families and a future. Personally I think the fact that the Sferkkaan men are willing to do this is fantastic. If we had to do this on Earth, then by the time people stopped fighting about the religious and moral consequences, we'd be extinct."

Gemma found herself staring at Dahli, her eyes enormous. "Dahli…?"

"Later, I'm looking at the photos. I wonder if we get a copy of the book?"

"She said everyone who was in it gets a copy," said Straif. I can't wait… aaaaand there is our beloved Emperor. Scruffin' lovely."

Gemma gaped at the photo of the Sferkkaan Emperor, then burst out laughing. He was posed in his best Mighty Conquering Hero pose, clad only in some strategically-placed folds of cloth, holding a leash that went to the collar around his long-suffering husband's neck. The husband looked like he was giving serious consideration to calling a divorce lawyer. Behind them was none other than Lyrellyn CZim-Relyn's father, trying very much to look as if there was nothing particularly odd about any of this. Clinging to Mordrett's right leg, staring up adoringly, was Khandid.

"Dare I even ask?" said Barry. "What music group is this?"

"It's not, it's the Emperor and his family."

"This is the Imperial family."

"Yes."

Barry tried very hard to look as if he was not on the verge of cracking up. "These are the people in charge of the planet."

"Well the naked guy holding the leash is the Emperor Mordrett Stratavarus, and the fellow with the white hair is of course Khandid Stracona, who is his cousin. And the fellow at the other end of the leash is Mordrett's husband."

"He looks like he's planning a coup."

Sofia laughed. "No he was having fun, the whole photo was planned."

"And who is the dramatic fellow with all the plumage?"

There came a knock at the door. Dahli ran off to let their friends in, while Gemma got up to ensure the party set-up was acceptable. She glanced to Straif.

"Are you comfortable?"

"I'm fine, really. But I may need a few more pillows to brace me up. Believe me, I will need help standing."

Gemma handed him a few more pillows, then looked at Seija, splayed across as much of the pillow-pit as possible. "It doesn't matter the planet or the species, does it? Pets always have to steal the whole bed."

Straif smiled. "Proves we are all more closely related than we care to admit. But I can't wait to get my book. There are so few books, and this one of the people I love will be very special."

"But you have posters, I've seen them," said Gemma.

"Yes but the materials we use for them must come out of unusable scraps, bits of things that have no other real use that can be ground down and turned into paper. Posters are not essential to life. Sadly at this point, books are not really, either. Not when we have people living in rubble heaps and houses missing walls. We cherish the ones we have kept, and there will be a day when there are more books printed, because they *are* important and what we have been through needs to be documented. But right now there are very few books being printed. Most of what we have, we scavenged. You forget we have so little because we have toys, but those are spoils of war. We have the right to play with them, but they are not important when we are struggling to feed and shelter ourselves." Straif pointed to the napping faelin. "Draephus did not give Seija to Dahli on a whim. An arboreal faelin is a lethal hunter. He can feed her, her family, and a few of the neighbours."

"Yeah I keep forgetting about that," she said softly. "I keep forgetting how incredibly lucky I am here on my little floating corner of Earth." Then she smiled. "Hey, you know what you and I need to do? We need to have a cultural exchange. Ever had chocolate?"

"Just Touskanian."

Gemma ran off to her room and found an opened box of chocolates, the last of several that she had brought with her. She returned to the pillow-pit in time to see Dahli coming up the stairs with Diza, Czamkiar and Lyrellyn. Oh yay. She wondered how much trouble she would be in if she pushed Lyrellyn right off his fancy boot-blades and down the stairs, the miserable boyfriend-snatching trollop. Just to make things perfect, Mickie showed up.

"What's going on here?" he asked.

"Slumber party," said Gemma. "Disgusting pigs not invited."

"Oh I just thought since you were all gonna be in bed you might want a man who knows what to do with a girl."

Lyrellyn made a spectacular threat display, leaping up, feathers and blades flying. Mickie ran for his life, while Lyrellyn stared after him with obvious dislike.

Okay so maybe Lyrellyn wasn't a total loss.

"I've decided it's time to introduce all of you to chocolate," said Gemma. "And not the chocolate that has been through Touskania to be perverted into a hallucinogen."

"That's what you get for eating things on the Emperor's desk," said Dahli.

"It wasn't the Emperor's, it was in the fridge at the studio."

"That's what you get for stealing candy from the Emperor's cousin," said Dahli.

Gemma opened the box and presented it to their friends, then sighed as Straif promptly grabbed up one of his ever-present army of vomit bags and was sick.

"Straif you must be a lot of fun at dinner parties," said Gemma as he slunk off to the bathroom.

"Wish he'd stop that," said Dahli. "He's skinny enough. He's supposed to be eating for two and I'm not sure he's even eating enough for one."

"Don't they have medicine for the vomiting?" asked Gemma.

"They can't give it to him," said Dahli. "With his particular virus, he has to be incredibly careful what sort of medicines he takes. He's... *really* delicate. Anyway, what is this brown lumpy stuff you're trying to poison us with?"

"Try one!"

Dahli did, nibbling carefully, her friends watching intently.

"How is it?" asked Diza.

Dahli ate the chocolate, then she and her friends waited for a reaction. Gemma had a funny feeling this was not the first time they had experimented with eating strange things. After a few moments, Dahli gave her report.

"Yup. Straif was right." She then ran off to be sick.

"Well that's it," said Gemma. "You're doomed as a species."

"Maybe it's the way you process it," said Czamkiar.

Diza picked up one and ate it, then looked at Lyrellyn and Czamkiar. Moments later she was grabbing one of Straif's vomit bags.

"I don't think Sferkkaans are meant to eat this stuff," said Diza.

Gemma closed the box and returned it to her room. This time she picked up a bag of peanut brittle and brought it out.

"Well let's see how this goes over."

She opened the bag. This time Czamkiar opted to be the subject of the experiment. He delicately bit one corner, and chewed, looking thoughtful. After a few moments, he looked to Lyrellyn.

"It's very tasty."

Lyrellyn touched noses with him, clearly so stupidly in love with Czamkiar it made her teeth hurt.

"Well I have one last thing to bring out," she said, and hurried off to her room to get her last box of ginger snap cookies; a treat she prized above all others, especially with strong tea. Her friends at home referred to it as her "granny snack", but she didn't care. She liked it. She found the cookies, then turned to leave, and froze, seeing Mickie standing in the doorway. He was staring at her in a way she didn't like at all, holding a pair of her panties, idly playing with them as he spoke.

"You know, you think you're all protected with guys like K-

Shot, and that fag in the chicken feathers, but one day there're not gonna be here, and I am. Stuck-up bitch."

He threw her panties at her, and left. Gemma stared after him, suddenly realizing he was right. One day she was going to end up alone in a room with him, and not because she wanted to, but because he was determined to make it happen. And regardless of what happened to him afterwards, it wouldn't make up for what he did to her. Not even in story books and movies did the hero always show up in time to save the damsel in distress.

She walked out to the common room, where there was already a reasonably large crowd of people wanting to see the mysterious sunken city. Gemma seated herself in the pillow pit, and looked to Lyrellyn.

"Hey, Lyrellyn…"

He looked up in surprise at hearing her say his name. "Yes?"

"Do you think you could show me some of what you do? The… fighting style?"

"I could," he said. "Did you want to learn the actual combat style, or the display style?"

She blushed. "Bit of both, actually."

"All right. How about we have our first lesson tomorrow?"

"I'd like that. Thanks Lyrellyn."

Well he may be a boyfriend-snatching asshole, but at least he had some use. Other than stealing her boyfriend. Now just to settle down and…

"I have to get up," said Straif.

"I knew it," said Czamkiar, "we're going to end up watching this in the bathroom."

"How long until you have your baby, hon?" asked Mystique.

"Three and a half months. I can't *wait* until this is over with. This seemed like a really great idea seven and a half months ago."

"Yeah I bet it's gonna be the biggest shit of your life," said Corey. "What sign is it gonna be? A Crap-with-corn?"

Straif glared at him, but said nothing, heading to the bathroom. Corey just chuckled to himself. Straif returned after a few minutes with Sigge and Vidar. They helped him over to Dahli, easing him down to the pillows.

"We is findings dis on da halls floor," said Sigge.

Dahli made a sound of distress. "Straif…"

"I'm fine, really. I just need to eat something that doesn't smell."

"Well dat is easy," said Vidar. "takes a bit of somet'ing dat nots makes you sick, puts da scent on a cloth an' puts da cloth overs you nose. You nots smells t'ings dat makes you sick."

The room fell silent as everyone stared at Vidar. Vidar blinked back.

"What? I is nots beings *completes* idiot, you know."

"Of course nots," said Sigge.

Corey stared in disgust as the two metal-heads dripped little black hearts and dead roses on each other. "Where are all these damn faggots coming from?"

Sigge nibbled Vidar fondly. "Dis faggot is comings from Sweden."

"I's comings from my Mor," said Vidar. "You betters havings word wit' all da straight ladies havings gay babies. Hey Sigge, while we is beings here, maybe we has operation to has a baby like Straif. Hey Straif? What is likes having operation?"

"Before or after they use a grinder to carve your pelvic basin bigger?"

Nearly everyone in the room winced and flinched. "Maybe we is adopting," said Vidar.

"Ja I'm t'inking we is," said Sigge.

"Faggots everywhere," growled Corey. Gemma noticed he had become far more vocal in his dislikes as of late. "Don't any of you like girls up here? Or is that why you killed them all?"

"*We* didn't kill them," growled Lyrellyn.

"I like girls," said Czamkiar, trying to keep a fight from breaking out. "There's just almost none around. This one girl in my class I liked a lot but she transferred to another class because she said I was too white."

"Now that's cold," said K-Shot, chuckling. "Hey Straif, what about some oatmeal? That's what my mama always gave me. And it doesn't have much of a smell."

"Just let me rest a while," said Straif.

He settled down on the pillows, closing his eyes, Dahli's hand in his long hair. The crowd gathered in the room fell silent as they watched the programme, fascinated by the clear water and small creatures.

"What sort of fish do you guys have?" asked Billy.

"No idea," said Dahli. "It's very hard to do research in a war. Oooh! Look at that! What's that thing?"

They watched as an enormous creature, which looked like the result of an unfortunate mating between a frog and an eel, stared directly into the underwater camera. It opened its mouth to explore the camera, giving everyone an excellent view of its throat. They could hear the sigh of an exasperated scientist.

"I did not fly all this way to see fish tonsils. Is there a way to shoo it away from the camera?"

A view from another camera gave them a look at the beast as a scuba diver approached. It ceased mouthing the camera to look at the approaching man, who proved to be slightly smaller than the fish before him. The pair considered each other, then the fish attempted to demonstrate its superiority with a veritable explosion of fins and facial expressions, its mouth expanding to a truly remarkable height and showing a myriad of flashing colours. It may have daunted another fish, but the humans were laughing fit to be tied.

Regardless of the attempts to chase it off, the enormous creature insisted on hanging around, adjusting camera angles, following submersibles, and looking over the shoulders of divers. It seemed harmless, but the snoopy giant was clearly a bit intimidating for the divers. However once the actual city came into view, everyone seemed to forget about the big fish. The room became silent as they stared in wonder at the city, sunken and silent for centuries. Streets where once people walked now formed avenues for fish, and strange creatures climbed up the walls and explored the plants that grew on the stonework. Shops, houses, statues, theatres, mills... all stood in darkness and silence, some hardly scathed, some so ruined it was difficult to tell what it had once been.

The group sat in silence for hours, watching the slow methodical exploration of the city, gazing at art and pottery and beautiful stonework that had been lost for centuries. Gradually, however, it grew late, and people began to drift away, sleep winning over curiosity. Soon it was only Gemma and her friends awake, apart from Straif, watching the dive teams take turns exploring the area, sometimes the city, sometimes the fish. At one point something truly gigantic loomed out of the darkness; a stature that had to be seventy feet tall of a rearing gryphon. Closer inspection showed that, even though its colours had been eradicated by sea water, the gems it had for eyes still burned in defiance.

"Wow!" said Gemma. "Lookit him! And mostly in one piece! How come something so big didn't smash apart?"

Dahli shrugged. "Maybe it has something to do with how the island sank. They said it didn't go down all at once. Some parts sank really slowly – slow enough that there wouldn't be enough of a jolt to damage something so delicate. Some parts crashed down so hard there's nothing left."

Diza leaned forward to peer at the screen. "Hey is that a cemetery?"

"If it is, it would be the Imperial graveyard," said Lyrellyn. "I've probably got some ancestors buried there."

"I think Straif may too," said Czamkiar, yawning.

Dahli looked at him, eyes large. "My Straif? Really?"

"Mannechek *is* one of the family names traced back to some of the royal houses," said Lyrellyn. "He can't wear the gold because we have no idea if it's the same family, but yeah it's possible."

Gemma looked down at the bundle curled up on the pillows and quilts, eyes closed, blankets wrapped around him. Dahli checked the time.

"I've got to wake him up, he has pills to take." She reached out to put a hand on his shoulder, and froze. She seemed to be wondering what she had felt, then carefully drew back the covers, carefully examining him, as if not quite believing what she was feeling. Then she looked up at Diza.

"He's cold."

Gemma felt her stomach tie up in knots. "What do you mean he's cold?"

Lyrellyn felt Straif's shoulder and arm, while Czamkiar dove for the phone. "He's stiff too."

Lyrellyn reached for his own phone, while Dahli just sat and stared at the body wrapped in quilts. She was starting to shake violently, as if the implications were beginning to catch up with her. Diza put an arm around her. Gemma just sat and tried to think what to do, but Lyrellyn and Czamkiar seemed to be handling things.

"Why are they calling for an ambulance?" Gemma quietly asked Diza.

"Depending on when he died, the device might still be

functioning and keeping the baby alive." Diza looked at Dahli. "Are you okay?"

"How can he be dead?" she whispered. "He was fine! He was... perfectly all right..."

It wasn't long before the common room filled up with people. The medics came to examine Straif, and not far behind them were Raski and Draephus. Other people came as well, some friends of Straif, some ship-mates of Gemma's. Then Mystique appeared and took her by the hand.

"Come on, baby-girl," she said quietly. "Nothing we can do here. Let people do their job."

Gemma watched as Dahli ran over to Draephus, throwing her arms around his neck and breaking down in sobs.

"Yeah," she said quietly. "I guess you're right."

****

Dahli did not go home. Teirra and Atterick believed her to be at Gemma's place all night, and so had gone to see some bands in Avalair. Dahli sat in the back of Draephus' conni, holding Seija tight in her arms, shaking and crying. Dead. Straif was dead. Her first real love was cold and stiff and unmoving. He would never play again, never ask her to help him up, never snuggle close... she would never touch or kiss or hold him again. He had just quietly lain down to die, and no one had even noticed.

They pulled up in the driveway, parking the conni by the bridge. It wasn't until she looked up that Dahli realized the yard was full of vehicles. Of course it would be; Straif had dozens of friends. Since this is where he had been living in his final days, this is where everyone would meet for his funeral party. Dahli forced herself to release her hold on Seija and slowly got out of the conni, feeling as if she was floating above her own body. She let Draephus lead her into the castle and into the main hall. It was like some strange scene out of the past, as if all the ghosts had risen to pay homage to their fallen friend. Delaes was there, and the other three Gryphons, as well as some people she didn't know. She found a chair and sank into it, trying to process what she had been through. Dead. He was dead. One minute he was there, the next he wasn't.

"Heia, Dahli," said a voice. She looked up to see a pair of

blood-shot blue eyes staring at her. "You should get some rest."

She stared back at Draephus. "Do *you* feel like resting?"

He sighed quietly. "No. I can't say I do."

"What happens now?" she asked.

"Well they're going to find out what happened, after they see if they can save the baby. Then, after that's all done, he'll be brought here for his funeral party, after which he will go into the catacombs under the castle."

She managed a faint smile. "He'd like that. Sometimes he and I would dare each other to look into your catacombs. I never got any further than a few feet."

"Would you like to see it?"

"Now?"

He nodded. "It's a good place, Dahli. It might make you feel a little better to see it. It's just people. Nothing terrible."

She thought about that, then nodded. "I think I would."

The telecom rang, and Raski quickly snatched it up. "Heia?"

The room was silent as Raski listened. After a long time, he spoke. "Thanks Dr. Arang. I'll tell everyone."

He set the receiver in its cradle, then looked to the sad gathering in the room.

"What happened?" asked Delaes.

Raski looked tired and grey and broken. "When he went in to be examined for the artificial uterus, they naturally checked him out very thoroughly. He was perfectly healthy and the virus was dormant. So they gave him the operation, which stressed his body. He was scarcely healed before he got pregnant, which stressed his body more. The pregnancy made it hard for him to eat, so that was even more stress. Then, about two days ago, the baby died for undetermined reasons, and that just pushed his physical limits too far and the virus woke up."

"Did he know the baby had died?" asked Khandid.

"Dr. Arang said Straif had some concerns and was going to go in to have the baby checked, but... no I don't think he knew it had died." Raski walked over to a chair and sat down heavily. "What it all comes down to is he worked himself too hard trying to get the things he wanted in life. If he'd gone a little more slowly... Anyway he's coming home soon and I need a šukating drink."

"Dahli and I were going to look at the catacomb where he'll

be staying," said Draephus. "Anybody want to come with us?"

"I do," said Delaes.

"Yeah me too," said Mars.

Dahli noticed that Anthony was not in the room. That was odd – she would have sworn he and Mars were still seeing each other. Maybe Mars just hadn't wanted to wake him up with news like this.

"We'll get to work up here," said Khandid.

Work? What work? What were they going to do? Then she realized no one had said the word "dead" in regards to Straif. Raski had said the baby had died, but there was no using of that word to describe Straif; no dead, died, departed, deceased or any euphemisms associated with the word. They had used terms like "coming home", and "where he'll be staying". But maybe that was the way of old warriors. Maybe they didn't use that word at times like this. Dahli decided that she wouldn't either. She really didn't want to anyway.

She got to her feet, and followed after Draephus, Mars and Delaes, remembering when something like exploring the house with the three of them would have been the stuff of dreams. Of course, in her fantasies, no one was dead.

There was a hidden door behind the stairs that led to the upper levels, covered by an old tapestry. Dahli noticed the faelins didn't go past the tapestry, and instead sat and waited, making small unhappy noises, Seija included.

"They don't come down here?" asked Mars.

"No," said Draephus quietly, but did not expound further.

They descended the stone steps, Dahli thinking about all the times she and Straif would make it to the halfway point, then flee giggling to the top stair. There Bacca and Czanda would bark at them, as if telling them not to be so silly, going down to where the dead lay. Would Straif want to be buried here? He really hadn't discussed dying with her very much. Babies had been mostly on his mind; toys, diapers, clothes, bedding, early education, and how old the kid should be before Mommy stuck a quinticord in his/her little hand.

"Mommy?" queried Dahli as they lounged on the huge bed in Draephus' guest room.

"If I'm the one pushing this baby out then I can call myself Empress Mizulda if I want."

He had wanted that baby so badly. He would have been absolutely shattered if he had known it died.

They reached the bottom of the steps and looked into a long stone tunnel that smelled of cold. It was dry and surprisingly clean.

"Who dusts?" asked Mars, echoing the question in Dahli's mind.

"These little guys," said Draephus, pointing at something on the wall. They had to strain to see the well-camouflaged little animals. Dahli gasped as she suddenly realized she was looking into a pair of deep brown eyes. No sooner had she seen the animal than it rapidly scurried off, galloping along the walls and into the depths of the catacombs.

"What are they?" asked Mars.

"I call them wall-dusters."

"Very creative. What do they eat down here?"

"Bugs, mostly. Lichens, mosses, mushrooms, other things that grow in tunnels. They eat the invasive bugs and plants, run up the walls to clear cobwebs, though probably not intentionally, make little nests in the alcoves, and occasionally, just to really irritate me, invade the kitchen and make the faelins go crazy at stupid o'clock in the šukating morning."

"Do the faelins eat them?" asked Mars.

"Yup. Sit right on the bed and crunch them in my ear. Then I have to get up and pick little bits of fur and bone off the covers."

"Yummy," said Dahli.

They walked down the hall, passing frescoes and carvings and statues, Draephus lighting torches as he walked along. The catacombs seemed just as dark after the torches were lit, the only difference being now there were shadows everywhere, flickering and dancing mindlessly, heedless of the living.

"And this doesn't give you nightmares?" asked Mars, reaching out to take Draephus' hand.

"Why would it? They're just people. Khandid's been down here plenty of times. So have you for that matter."

"Yeah but I always went to the Crypt of Names," said Mars.

"What's that?" asked Dahli.

"It's a large room you enter through a crypt that stands outside," said Mars. "That's where all the books and personal possessions are. I go there at times and read the books that can still be handled."

"We're just going to look at Straif's bed," said Draephus.

There it was again – not crypt or slab or anything like that, but bed. No references to death at all. As she pondered this, she heard Draephus speak once more.

"Here it is. It was carved about five centuries ago for one of the daughters of the current emperor. I don't know why she's not here, but Straif liked it."

"So he did choose to be here," she said, carefully avoiding any mention of death.

"Well you know Straif," said Draephus, "he was nothing if not organized. But yeah, he liked this one. I like it too, actually."

They walked into the enormous alcove, moving quietly, as if afraid to awaken someone. In the center of the alcove was a great slab of carved stone, made to look like a bed, complete with draping sheets and a pillow. It looked so realistic that Dahli had to touch it to make certain it really was stone and not fabric at all. On four sides stood great braziers to hold ceremonial offerings to the dead of fragrant wood chips soaked in perfumed oils, which would be lit to release the scents into the air. In the three walls were carved shelves and drawers, to hold the treasured belongings of the person who would occupy the slab.

"I'm going to hate seeing Straif's white quinticord down here," said Mars.

"He's not taking the white one," said Draephus. "He's taking the deep purple one with the flecks of white gem in it. The white quinticord goes to Dahli."

Dahli stared at him, her green eyes enormous. "ME?! What am I going to do with it? I'm not good enough to own something like that!"

"I think the idea is that you would someday be good enough," said Draephus. "He was crazy about you."

"I felt the same way," she said. "But if he'd mentioned giving me the Legri I'd have questioned his sanity. But, well, if he was crazy about me than I guess that would explain his giving it to me."

"He was very specific about what he wanted you to have," said Draephus.

"Why did he mention none of this to me?"

"I think he was afraid of upsetting you."

Dahli said nothing. It was so hard to take all of this in. He was gone. He wasn't coming back. He wasn't going to have his baby, and take her to the festival, and make that album with J'Vanni Dei Syncopius he wanted to so badly….

She burst into tears once more, and Draephus led her out of the catacombs, back up to the world of the living. She paused in surprise at the transformation of the main hall, looking around at the small crowd of people. The ancient and enormous stone vases that normally sat in a storage room had been brought out and filled with flowers, and the room smelled of late spring. Tables had been brought out, and everyone had contributed something from their gardens. At this late point in the year it was mostly nuts, some fruits, and baked goods, although somebody had been industrious and brought an entire deer which was now roasting over the fire in one of the two gigantic fire places. Then, of course, there was the array of alcohols, some illegal, holding reign on a banquet table. There was light and music and warmth, even if there was also a great deal of sadness.

"Dahli," said a voice, and she looked in the direction of whoever had called her name. It was Diza, followed closely by Czamkiar, Lyrellyn and Gemma. She walked over to her friends and tried to hug all of them at once.

"What are you guys doing here?" she asked.

"We followed you," said Gemma. "He was our friend too. And some of the people from the ship wanted to come say good-bye, too."

Dahli looked up at Draephus. "You don't mind, do you?"

He shrugged. "This is for Straif, so anyone who cared about him is welcome. You want a drink, Fearless?"

"Yeah, thanks," she said, and watched as he walked away.

"Fearless?" queried Gemma.

"It's what my name translates into in East Continental dialect," said Dahli, "'Fearless'. I keep telling them it's not strictly accurate, but they call me that anyway. Oh, uh… I'm not sure why, but no one is mentioning dead or death or any euphemisms that go with it. So maybe we shouldn't either."

"So what should we say about that?" asked Diza very softly, indicating the upper landing.

Dahli looked in the direction Diza indicated, and felt her jaw drop. They froze, not daring to move, as they stared up at the landing, seeing the slender figure there, his long brown hair hanging loose, green eyes focused on the crowd below. He was leaning over the railing, watching his friends, still clearly pregnant, with a facial expression that implied he didn't understand why everyone seemed so sad. Other people noticed as well, rising to their feet to look. An eerie silence fell, as if those gathered were afraid to frighten the specter away. Then Draephus spoke softly.

"Straif? Are you coming home to stay?"

He looked to Draephus, as if considering the offer, then faded away. There was silence, then Delaes looked to Draephus.

"All right I realize this is a very silly question but did you *see* that because I'm pretty sure it was Straif on the upper landing."

"It was Straif," said Draephus. "Delaes I keep telling you these things exist."

"I know you keep telling me they exist but I've never seen a ghost manifest in the middle of a…" He stopped talking and sat down. After a few moments he burst into tears. Khandid sat beside him to comfort him, just as the flash of headlights briefly shone through the enormous stained glass windows.

"Straif's home," said Raski quietly.

Chapter Twenty-Seven

Dahli awoke. Or rather, she managed to claw herself out of whatever blackened pit she had fallen into the night before. Things had gone rather dark after a certain point, and the next thing she knew she was rolled up in a ball under a pile of clothing on one of the great couches in the hall. Slowly she sat up, pushing aside various articles of clothing, and looked around. Her eyes became very large, and her jaw slowly dropped, simply falling open as if she had lost control if the muscles operating it.

"Oh. Wow," was all she managed to say.

As a fan, Dahli had certainly read about some of the parties thrown by the Gryphons, but to actually *see* it was something else entirely. She had no idea what had happened after she passed out, but she sincerely hoped someone got pictures.

She pushed the clothes off, and carefully stood up. There was no floor. It was thoroughly hidden by bodies, faelins, articles of clothing, and what looked like the start of a funeral pyre. She approached the pile of wood and... what was that? She reached in and carefully picked up the item, realizing belatedly that it was a sex toy of truly impressive length and girth. With a small noise of disgust, she tossed in back onto the pile, then located something else. It turned out to be some sort of enormous and rather ugly fish, covered extensively in mud. There were also several tins of beans in there, which had somehow been exploded. A glance up at the ceiling showed the delicate paintings liberally coated in cold dripping beans.

"There's a conni in the moat," said a voice. Dahli glanced over to see Diza standing by the window.

"Hope there's nobody in it," said Dahli. "Not sure I could do this twice in a week. What did we *do* last night?"

"*You* drank like a warrior," said Diza primly. "Gemma and I took pictures because we're still considered children and could only have tea. Then Draephus remembered I had asked him to help me do a proper fire walk."

"Is that where the pyre comes in?"

"Well they didn't think it would be a good idea to put me in the fireplace. Then Mars said we should have pyrotechnics and that was where the beans came in."

"So you blew up several tins of perfectly good beans at the end of winter when the transports are having trouble getting here."

"It seemed like a good idea at the time."

"Did you do your fire walk?"

"No I got partway through and then the beans blew up. It doesn't count if the beans blow up before you finish."

"I call clart-muffins on that one," said Dahli. "I think it should count as double."

There was a rustle of clothing, and Delaes Randerick emerged from the debris like some sort of strange monster. Someone had beaten him absolutely bloody, and his face, chest and back bore signs of having been struck repeatedly with some sort of blunt weapon.

"What happened to you?!" asked Dahli.

Delaes uttered the shortest sentence of his life. "Not sure."

"You left for a few hours then came back looking like that," said Diza. "Are you okay?"

"I think I am or at the very least I appear to be but at one point I woke up in a dumpster and now I can't think how I got there." He sneezed violently, producing an odd combination of snot, ashes and ants. Before Dahli could think about it too much, the telecom rang. By some miracle, she found it.

"CZimcocious residence, don't ask *me* what we were doing last night, I'm just the roadie."

It was Anthony, Mars' current squeeze. "Heia, Dahli? Is Mars there?"

"I don't know," she said, looking around. She then called tentatively; "Mars? Send up a flare if you're conscious."

To her absolutely horror, the shroud covering the ceremonial table that only last night held Straif's body moved, and Mars sat up.

"Kill me, please," he said.

"Where's Straif?!" she demanded.

Mars seemed to ponder the question, then looked around. "I don't know."

Dahli tossed him the telecom and began sorting under the mess in search of Straif. Diza began helping her. By now, bodies were beginning to climb out of the wreckage; strange zombies in a most unconventional cemetery. Khandid rose to his feet and looked around blearily.

"What happened last night?" he demanded of no one in particular.

"No idea," said Dahli. "But you're naked and someone painted you orange."

Khandid looked down at himself. "Why do they do that to me? They *know* how hard it is to get the stain off white skin. What are you looking for?"

"Straif," said Dahli.

"Check the fireplace."

She straightened abruptly and looked at him. "Why would he be in the fireplace?!"

"Tradition," said Khandid. "He would come here, get drunk, then go curl up in the ashes in the fireplace."

Dahli checked one of the two huge fireplaces, finding a body curled up as if asleep on the grate. Dahli burst into tears again, stroking the long hair. As she wept, the great door of the castle opened, and Draephus slogged in, soaking wet and muddy, dragging some sort of enormous aquatic monstrosity with him.

"Where's Vidar? You can *too* fish with a conni, the bastard owes me five trinta."

****

They got Straif out of the fireplace. He was cleaned, dressed in his favourite tour outfit, at least the parts that still fit him, and had his long hair brushed out. He was covered with a traditional death blanket made of white linen, and then Dahli painted his lines for him one last time, tracing the notable moments of his life, telling all who came after them who their friend had been. Then they carried him down to his alcove to lay him on his slab. They placed him in the position in which he died; on his side, slightly curled, one hand under his small face.

They stood there for a while, uncertain what to do with themselves, and reluctant to leave him there alone in the darkness. Finally, one by one, they drifted away, heading back into the main hall. Listlessly they picked at the mess, because there was nothing else to do. Khandid took the two enormous fish, cleaned them, and turned them into something resembling breakfast, while Raski sat on one of the great couches and quietly played his quinticord. Everything seemed so grey and empty now, as if tomorrow could never follow today.

"What will you do now?" Raski asked Delaes.

Delaes drew on a cigarette, looking sallow and drawn. "I really don't know I mean the new drummer we had picked out said he would only join if we could guarantee *Straif* would be there so no Straif no drummer which makes Rysta and I the most messed up version of Simon and Garfunkel ever."

"The problem is not many bands on Sferkkaa play metal," said Raski.

"And certainly not the type of metal Bad Influence does," agreed Delaes.

"Ever think about playing something other than metal?" asked Khandid.

"I don't take music advice from naked orange people."

"I'm not naked."

Draephus opened a window and began throwing wood from the pyre out of it. Delaes looked at him, raising one eyebrow.

"Why do I have the feeling that you and your fancy hand-jewelry have an opinion?"

"You don't want to hear my opinion." He threw out a scorched piece of wood.

"I might if it means I don't end up retiring from music."

"Look, there are many, many forms of metal music. There's thrash, black, harmonic, death, heavy, folk…"

"Yes thank you for the recital of things I already know but…"

"BUT," interrupted Draephus, "those all originate from Earth. It's not *our* form of metal. Maybe what you need to do is start thinking about a form of metal music that is distinctly Sferkkaan. Instead of going for an established sound we've all heard before, go for something that can *only* be Bad Influence when people hear it. Like Brian May's guitar. There's only one guitar with *that* sound. Like the Moody Blues and the mellotron. Like Anazampini and that nine string sepulchord."

"And you guys and those South Continental drums," said Delaes. He sighed. "I can think of names I would love to add to the band but we would have to drag them out of the Cylinder mushroom dens well anyone other than dear My'shlyin Achania did anyone other than me notice the little darling failed to show for the funeral of the mother of his child and the child itself?"

"No, we noticed," said Raski.

"Did he know Straif…?" asked Diza.

"Oh he knew," said Khandi. "Even if we hadn't told him, and we did, right now the only thing on the news is Straif."

"He's the first post-war loss of one of our little group of friends," said Raski.

"Maybe we should call My'shlyin," said Mars. "Maybe he didn't think he'd be welcome. He's not really a part of our clique."

Khandid picked up the telecom and called a number. "Is My'shlyin Achania there? Oh! Heia! It's Khandi Stracona. I was just wondering, did you know Straif's wake was last night? Actually make that Straif and your unborn child. No, the baby did *not* survive, why would you wait until someone called you to bother finding that out? Oh. Well. Yes I can certainly see your point."

Khandid set the telecom down and turned to face his friends. "Donsa My'shlyin did not come because he didn't think it had anything to do with him, and he finds the death of his child unfortunate, but no one asked him if he wanted to be a father anyway. He may have wanted it if it was a girl, but he doesn't really care, since he has a real live breathing woman in his life and he doesn't want her upset by sordid things like dead unwanted offspring."

There was a very long and very cold silence. Then Draephus snatched up a length of firewood and left the castle, followed by a veritable herd of painted and hungover warriors. The door slammed, and they listened as a number of connis started their engines and drove away. After a few moments, Vidar and Sigge emerged from the mess.

"I's thinkings somebodies gettingks his ass kicks," said Vidar.

Diza looked to Dahli. "Why didn't you go with them?"

"Wasn't sure I'd be able to get past all the other people to get in a good punch," said Dahli.

She continued working on the mess, because it kept her from thinking. Others joined in to help, and the cleaning went on in silence. Then there came a knock at the door, and the faelins began barking wildly. Dahli sighed.

"I'll get it."

She walked down the stairs, moving aside the barking faelins, and opening the door. She stared at the man she saw before her and burst into tears. She felt herself being hugged close.

"There now, skinny woman," said Harli softly. "I'm here."

****

It was late at night, and Dahli was sitting in the room where, so long ago, Draephus had dumped her after her warrior bash at the Contempo. Teirra and Atterick were still not home yet, and she really did not want to be alone. Not far away, resting in its stand, was Straif's white quinticord, glittering softly in the dim light as if enchanted. Its strings and pickups were czilbein, and glowed with a sort of inner light. The lacquered finish was infused with white gem dust and polished flecks of luminous pale blue shell. It looked exactly like what it was – a priceless and absolutely one of a kind custom instrument meant for a professional musician who knew how to best use the tools of his trade.

She couldn't imagine for one second why Straif had wanted her to have it.

She got off the bed and slowly approached it, as if afraid it would bite. A Legri Ice Storm, custom built for the fastest player their world had to offer. Why hadn't he given it to Vidar, or Sigge, or to Raski, or to somebody who could actually *play* it?

She picked it up carefully, astonished at how heavy it was. She hung the mighty weight around her neck, then slid her fingers down the elegant neck to turn it on. She turned the volume down very low, then carefully tried a few notes. The sound was distinctly Straif, but the playing style was definitely not. Dahli winced as she tortured the poor thing.

More practice was needed. Much more.

She shut it off and set it down, then returned to her seat on the bed and stared into the darkness. Dead. Straif was dead. One minute he was there, the next he wasn't, without so much as a sigh. It was frightening to think how a life could end so easily...

Dahli sighed heavily and got off the bed. She grabbed up her pillow, and shuffled out of the room, and down the hall to Draephus' chamber. Without ceremony, she dropped the pillow down onto his bed and climbed under the covers, scooting back until she felt Draephus' back against her own. Draephus didn't move an inch, but Raski raised his head to look at her.

"I think you need more practice," he said.

"No I don't. It's not me, it's the quinticord. It only knows three chords."

Raski rolled his eyes and put his head back down. A comfortable silence enveloped them. Dahli was finally drifting toward sleep when she felt Draephus shift his position and roll onto his side, facing her. A large hand came to rest on her head and give her a skritch.

"Good Bacca," said Draephus drowsily before sinking back into sleep.

"Arf," she mumbled.

Raski snorted with amusement. Dahli closed her eyes and willed herself to fall asleep, convinced she could hear just the faintest sound of a quinticord being played very, very fast.

****

Despite their grief over losing Straif, life went on, whether his friends liked it or not. For Dahli there was school, work at the studio, homework, and still trying to make time for her friends. There was also watching Atterick sulk and give her Legri longing glances, but Dahli was firm – no one touched it but her, and maybe the Gryphons.

Maybe.

The weeks were flying by now. There had only been six weeks left to the festival when Straif died, and now she was helping to pack equipment, wearing her shirt that proclaimed her to be a member of the crew. She was getting muscles in places she'd never thought about before, and did not hesitate to pitch in and help wrangle some of the heaviest pieces. She found she really liked the work and the people she was working with, and she found it incredibly satisfying that she would not merely be attending the festival; she was part of it.

"Dahli you're getting muscles all over!" exclaimed Gemma, dismayed. "You look like a boy!"

"*I* do?!" said Dahli. "Who here is running around in high heels and make up?!"

She picked up a sound board, and paused as she heard Raski in the next room, clearly on the verge of hysteria.

"What do you mean you lost Metallica?! How do you lose…?

IN THE CYLINDER?! YOU LOST METALLICA IN THE CYLINDER, DURING A FOOD SHORTAGE, KNOWING THERE ARE THINGS IN THERE THAT EAT PEOPLE?! I DON'T CARE IF THEY WANTED TO SEE IT! NOBODY WANTS TO COME TO A FESTIVAL TO WATCH SOME *VARADASAI* LIE ON THE STAGE AND DIGEST JAMES HETFIELD!"

"I think the real question here is – will the fans like it?" said Khandid.

Raski snatched up Mars' hat and began beating Khandid with it, shouting into the telecom as he did so.

"YOU SEARCH THE PLACE AND YOU FIND THEM AND YOU MAKE SURE THEY ARE UNEATEN OR I SWEAR BY WHATEVER GODS WE HAD BEFORE THE KRYPHISIANS SHOT THEM THAT I WILL HURT YOU!" Raski closed the phone, then screamed; "DRAEPHUS!"

"You bellowed, my darling one?"

"Delaes lost Metallica in the Cylinder."

"I heard. It's okay, I'll go get them."

"Do you need a weapon?" asked Raski.

"No, I have a sawed off Night Stalker in the conni, it'll be fine."

"Is your life ruined?" Dahli asked Raski as she walked past him.

Raski fixed her with a look that implied now was not the time for jokes. Dahli shrugged and carried the board out to the transport, trailed by Gemma.

"When did Metallica get here?" asked Gemma.

"About a week ago. They and some other bands were on the last ship from Earth. It should have been here sooner but the engine broke down and the ship kinda floated around for a few weeks until it got repaired. So they're late but they're here."

"Are there really things in the Cylinder that will eat you?" asked Gemma.

"Yup," said Dahli, handing the sound board up to another roadie. "I've seen them. They're pretty frightening. Not sure what they were bred for but now they scavenge up anything dead from the streets."

"I wonder if they would eat Mickie?" Gemma mused.

"They'll eat anything, but why Mickie in particular?"

Gemma looked uncomfortable, trailing after Dahli as she went back into the studio to see if anything else needed to be taken to the transport.

"He's following me around and getting really aggressive," said Gemma.

"Have you told anyone?" asked Dahli.

"I don't want to cause any trouble…"

Dahli sighed. What was *with* this girl? "No of course not, it's much better to let him maul you and then speak up and try to explain why you never said anything beforehand, when we could have stopped him. Incidentally, does little Mickie know what the penalty for rape is here?"

"No," said Gemma.

Dahli walked into the studio and looked around. Spying a box, she picked it up and began carrying it to the transport.

"They weight the rapist's arms and legs with heavy stones or bricks, cut his clothes off, tie a wire around the thing that got him in trouble and throw him out the window, just high enough to cause brutal and irreparable damage to it, but not high enough to kill him when he hits ground. Then they leave him there. If he manages to get out of the bricks and wire, he's earned his right at a second chance to live."

Gemma's jaw dropped. "Would they do that to Mickie?"

"Absolutely, and walk away from him screaming on the ground and not think anything of it. It was the common punishment before the invasion. Then during the war, with no time to properly try criminals, we just took up the practice once more."

"What do you do with child molesters?"

"Same thing. Then after three days if it looks like they may survive, we shoot them."

"That's… kinda harsh."

Dahli reached the transport and handed up the box. "We do not have the time, or the room, or the resources, for parasites. And if Mickie is scaring you then you need to report him, now."

"Will you throw him out the window?"

"I dunno, has he hurt you?"

"No."

"Then probably not. But I'm not sure he's smart enough to take a warning seriously."

"I don't want to get him into any trouble if he hasn't really done anything…" she said weakly.

Dahli walked back into the studio, and into the common room where Raski, Khandid and Mars were overseeing the packing and moving. Dahli drew a deep breath and did her best Delaes Randerick impersonation.

"Gemma's getting harassed by Mickie and she's scared he's going to get her alone and do something unforgiveable but she doesn't want to get him into trouble because of stupid reasons."

"Oh good, let's throw him out the window," said Khandid.

Mars looked at Khandid. "What is it with your family and windows?"

"We just like them."

Raski was going through an inventory sheet. "Does the little monster know what we do to rapists here?" he asked.

"No, but I'm not sure he'd care if he did," said Gemma. "He'd think he was above punishment."

"He's not," said Mars. "Has he said anything to make you think he will hurt you?"

"He said I know I think I'm safe with people like K-Shot and Lyrellyn around me, but one day he's going to get me alone."

"Sounds like a threat to me," said Mars.

"Me too," said Dahli.

"And me," said Raski, "so we have to report his behaviour now and get him monitored before he hurts someone. Once he's on the ship and headed back to Earth there is not much we can do to keep an eye on him, but if he's actively threatening and following people and announcing he has plans to hurt them then we're legally obligated to let someone know."

"He's going to have a fit," said Gemma. "So will his mother. She's the one who taught him he's too perfect to punish."

"I look forward to the hate mail," said Raski. He looked up as Badger appeared. The old roadie was tired and exasperated.

"What is it?" asked Raski warily.

"Four words," said Badger. "Dave Grohl Touskanian Chocolate."

"Did he *know* it was Touskanian Chocolate?" demanded Raski.

"He knew, but I think he was a little unclear as to what that meant. He's currently barking at the Gryphon statue in the lobby, and having a sniff-a-thon with Bacca."

Raski slapped his hands over his face. "By all the gods that were… okay, Badger, keep an eye on him. Your sole duty right now is to make sure he's safe." Raski dropped his hands and watched as a roadie slowly and carefully pushed a large cart holding a massive black drum case. "Is that Draephus'?"

The man nodded. "Last drum. Everything else is on the transport."

Raski nodded. "Right, load it up, I'll get our things on board."

"So we'll see you in Charlendine," said Mars.

"You and Draephus are leaving now?" asked Dahli.

Raski nodded. "Once those drums get loaded, we go too. Sadly there are people in this world stupid enough to try to take one or two, and those South Continental drums are one of a kind. If we lose them, that's our signature sound gone with them. It's not like we could replace them, unlike Khandi."

"You love me and you know it," said Khandid.

Raski did a passable impression of Sigge's heavy accent. "Likes da crotch-crabs I do."

The telecom rang, and Raski pounced on it. "Heia? Oh that's SUCH a relief! Where did you find them?" Raski listened, a look of utter disbelief slowly creeping over his face. "Say that again?"

He listened, then looked to his companions. "Metallica were on the fifth basement level of the Cylinder jamming with six defected Kryphisian soldiers who didn't know the war was over. Side note – the Kryphisians don't speak Earth, and Metallica don't speak Kryphisian."

"Wait – the war is over?" said Khandid.

Raski ignored him. "Delaes call Draephus, he's on his way over. We don't know how they got down there but we can't trust to dumb luck twice. Then tell him the drums are loaded and he and I need to go. Okay, later."

Raski closed the telecom then looked around, as if making sure they had packed everything. "So I will see you guys in a few days in Charlendine."

Khandid stood up to hug him, as did Mars. Dahli and Gemma joined in, as did a passing roadie. Finally it was time to release him, and he departed, heading for the transport.

"Well I guess I better get home and pack too," said Dahli.

"Are you going with the rest of the crew?" asked Khandi.

"Well… yeah," said Dahli. "I mean I *am* part of the road crew, that's what the shirt says."

"Just remember that we need those men to drag our stuff around, so don't hurt them," said Mars.

"Hey, they take their chances the same as the rest of you. Just remember that if Diza's dad calls – we went with Czamkiar. If he thought we were on the transport with the rest of the crew he'd probably split in half and die, thinking it was going to sink and drag us all to the bottom of the ocean."

"Well… transports *do* sink," said Gemma.

"The ones up from the South Continent do," said Mars. "The waters between here and Charlendine are much safer. And this late in winter, nearly all the storms are done with."

Gemma turned her head to look out the window at the torrential rain. "Okay…"

"Well," said Dahli. "See you guys in Charlendine."

Chapter Twenty-Eight

"Mars you really are a basket full of special," grumbled Draephus as he carried him through the hall of the hotel. Anthony trailed anxiously after them with the bags.

"Oh like you never fell off your heels," said Mars. "I've seen you trip on invisible animals."

"I just don't want to see you on stage in eight days on crutches."

"Just find me a big strong man and I can sit on his shoulders. Or a big strong woman. I could definitely go for that."

"You do realize I'm back here, right?" asked Anthony.

Mars let his head fall back so he could look beyond Draephus' arm. "Hi handsome."

"Uh huh. Someone's asking for a spanking. Here's our room."

Anthony unlocked the door, and they entered the small chamber, smelling the newness of it. It was not a particularly large room, but it was nice, decorated in soft pale golds that gave it a warm, inviting feel. It had two soft couches, a large bed, a desk, visual, a bathroom, and a tiny food preparation area, complete with coldbox. There was even a sliding glass door that led to a little balcony. A hotel on Earth perhaps may have been more grand, but Draephus liked this room immediately.

"They built this hotel just for the festival," said Mars. "They based it on an Earth design to make our visitors feel comfortable."

"Clean sheets? Four walls? Solid floor?" Draephus shook his head. "I dunno, not sure I trust it…"

"We could kick some holes in the wall and set the drapes on fire," said Mars. "Make it more homey…"

"Not sure the management would approve," said Anthony.

Draephus carefully set Mars down on one of the two pale gold couches in the room, then, as Anthony put away their belongings, Draephus began carefully removing Mars' boot.

"How does it look?" asked Mars.

"Not bad," said Draephus. "I don't think it's sprained, or at least not badly. I think with a bit of rest…"

Mars chose this moment to sneeze. It would have been a

wholly forgettable act, save for the violent spray of blood that shot out of his nostrils and bathed his hands in scarlet. It dripped down between his fingers to stain the carpet, and both Mars and Draephus froze, staring at each other. Draephus knew that if this sneeze meant the virus living in Mars' blood had become active, he was already infected and his life had just become a matter of days. But there was nothing he could do about that. He focussed on reassuring Mars.

"Okay, just… don't get upset. Anthony, lock the door, I'll…"

Draephus looked up as they heard the sliding glass door that lead to the balcony open, then close. Anthony had clearly opted to save his own skin.

"Did you tell him?" asked Draephus.

Mars nodded. "Yeah. I told him."

"So he knows this was a possibility."

"Yes. And… he was instructed on what to do if…" Mars stared at Anthony, his expression conveying a hurt that went to the bone. "He swore he'd stay beside me…"

"Yeah, well, we'll deal with him afterwards. Let's just… call the medics."

"Draephus…"

"Mars it's okay, I'm not leaving you."

"You… probably should stand on the balcony too…"

"Mars I was right at your feet when you sneezed, that means there is absolutely no point in my going to stand on the balcony."

Mars began to shake violently, green eyes welling with tears. Draephus went into the bathroom to get a cloth and dampen it with hot water, then brought it to Mars. He handed it to his friend, then drew out his 'com to call Raski.

"Heia Rask? Um… we've had a bit of an incident, and… well we're not sure who to call. Yeah well Mars just sneezed blood across…. Raski *PLEASE* don't do this! Raski? Raski! Šukat. Fine. Cry. See if I care."

Raski finally went to determine who to contact about the situation. Draephus sat beside Mars on the couch with his arm around him, trying to comfort his friend as best as he was able. He knew they were both dying if the virus was active, and they would never leave this room again. It could not be risked – an A-class virus could kill thousands. They could live out what was left of their life in the hotel room, or they could opt to just be shot and burned now.

After about an hour, the door was unlocked, and in stepped two men in bio-hazard suits. Mars began to cry in earnest, while Draephus held him tight, ignoring the blood that drenched the front of his coat.

"Heia," Draephus said weakly to the men.

"Heia," said the man closest to them. "I'm Dr. Baltain, and this is Major Manorne."

"Where's your pistol?" asked Mars. Draephus had seen Mars in a lot of dangerous situations – it broke his heart now to see him so clearly frightened now.

"We don't do it that way anymore," said the Major. "With luck we won't be doing it now."

"Can we have the groutnoll on the balcony shot for cowardice?" Draephus asked, rather loudly.

"We'll worry about him later," said Dr. Baltain. He knelt on the floor, smiling up into Mars' green eyes. "First thing we have to do is give you a shot, okay?"

"What for?" asked Draephus as Mars buried his face against his shoulder. Draephus noticed that Major Manorne walked to the glass door and locked it, then pulled the curtains so nothing Anthony did could further upset Mars.

"Well he's bled quite a bit," said Dr. Baltain. "And he seems to still be bleeding a little. This will help boost his immune system to keep him from getting an infection. It will also relax him. We have to perform a full five tests to be absolutely sure of what we are dealing with, and the last two are a bit painful. It's easier for the patient if he's sleepy."

Mars stared at the green needle with the smiling blue wiggle-worm on the side. Dr. Baltain smiled sheepishly.

"I have children. They tend to put the supplies from my paediatric kit in here to make people feel better."

"Maybe if you're good, you'll get a sweetie," said Draephus.

"Just so you know," said Mars, "If it's the virus I plan on having a tantrum before Major Manorne over there puts me to sleep."

"Understood," said the doctor, administering the shot. Draephus watched as Mars' eyes glazed over.

"Feeling better?" asked Draephus.

"Your coat is fuzzy."

"That would be a yes."

609

Draephus watched as the doctor analysed some of the blood running from Mars' nose, dreading he would say there was no need for further tests. He felt his stomach clench as the doctor drew some blood to check, then felt it clench further as he moved on to a third test. The fourth and fifth involved checking actual minute pieces of Mars' flesh, and Draephus opted not to watch those two. He was ready to vomit from the tension and wished they would just get it over with.

"Well," said the doctor, "he certainly does have A1-2, but it's not dormant. I'm… really not certain exactly *what* it's doing. I've never seen a virus behave this way."

"It's not affecting him?" asked the Major.

"It's…. well it looks like it hasn't the first idea what it *should* be doing. See for yourself."

The Major came to sit beside the doctor. Both watched the virus do whatever it was doing. Finally the doctor asked a question.

"What sort of drugs do you take?"

"Drugs? Us?" asked Mars and Draephus in perfect unity.

The doctor stared at them. Draephus wilted visibly.

"You're not going to shoot us then take our stash, are you?"

"No, but I need to know what your little Mars there is putting in his body, because something he is eating or shooting or snorting on a regular basis is greatly interfering with the virus' ability to function. I wouldn't say this virus is truly dormant. I would say it's responding to something it finds incredibly toxic and debilitating."

Draephus gently placed Mars down on the couch, then went to get the small green bag he knew would be in Mars' luggage. Mars simply lay on his side, blinking sleepily. The doctor removed his mask, and then the major, and Draephus felt his stomach unclench at last. They were okay. They would be fine. He forced himself not to collapse, although he was trembling visibly, almost violently. He returned to the spot where Mars was lying on the couch, blinking sleepily, looking small and vulnerable. He raised an eyebrow as he noticed the way Major Manorne was smiling at Mars, as if he would have liked to touch him. The Major was a very handsome boy, and clearly not a coward. Unlike some people Draephus could think of.

"You know, he was just dumped by his boyfriend if you'd like to ask him out," said Draephus, passing the bag to the doctor.

Major Manorne smiled. "I think I will wait until he's not

drugged out of his mind first."

"You don't have to wait," said Mars, his voice small, eyes staring at nothing. Draephus and Manorne gave each other a significant look, then Manorne turned back to Mars once more.

"In that case I will call in the morning and ask properly. Do you like children?"

"What flavour?"

Manorne grimaced, then looked up at Draephus. "I have six."

"Adopted, or is your husband inordinately fit?" asked Draephus.

"Neither. In Charlendine we do things a little differently – I actually had a female life partner."

"Nonsense," said Draephus. "Women are a myth. Like the sun."

"Well I better tell my four daughters, then. I'm not sure they'd believe you."

Draephus did not ask where their mother was; too often the answer was the same. And the Major didn't say.

"Well, Mars is fine," said the doctor. "At the very least he's not a danger to anyone else and the virus qualifies as "inactive". So I will just take samples of your... uh..." The doctor stared into the depths of the bag. "You are *very* bad boys."

"Show him the blue jar, too," said Mars sleepily.

Draephus rummaged through the bag until he located a very old ceramic jar. "This? It's tea."

"I make it myself," said Mars. "I grow and grind and mix the ingredients. I've been drinking it for years."

"So it's unique," said the doctor. "Not something someone could purchase in a shop."

"No," said Mars in a small voice. "My grandama taught me a little song to sing while I mixed, too..."

"He's exhausted," said Draephus. "I'd really like to get him settled in bed and let him rest while I tear his former boyfriend a new orifice."

The doctor nodded. "Just let me gather these samples, and... did he hurt his ankle?"

"Yeah, fell off his shoes."

"Bladed?" asked the major.

"I haven't earned my blades yet," said Mars.

Anthony pounded on the window. "Let me in!"

Draephus ignored him. Manorne began taping Mars' ankle as the doctor carefully labelled samples of Mars' stash as well as the tea. Once this was done, he handed Draephus a bottle of pills.

"His virus is not active, but he does have a very bad sinus infection. I have no idea how he's functioning. He *should* be miserable. Keep him warm, make sure he takes one of these every six hours, and let him sleep. To be honest I don't think he should be performing at the festival, but I know that's not going to happen. Just explain to the audience that if he sneezes blood in all directions it's just a sinus infection. Now I have no idea what plans you five had for your first night in town, but Mars needs to look after himself. He's fragile. He's got a bad infection and a dormant virus that could potentially wake up if he weakens enough. My advice is no drinking, no drugging, and no contact with anyone who could upset him."

Fragile. Yeah. Like Straif when he just silently fell asleep, never to wake again. Draephus knelt down beside Mars and looked into the glazed green eyes, feeling fiercely protective. "Mars? What do you want me to do with Anthony?"

Mars raised his head, still bloodied and looking very small and sad. "I don't know yet, what does Anthony have to say for himself? If he crawls in here on all fours and swears he'll never abandon me again I might forgive him."

Draephus walked over to the sliding glass doors, drawing the drapes and opening the doors. He stared at Anthony, wanting nothing more than to break his neck.

"Mars wants you to say you're sorry. I want you to go kill yourself."

"I want you to get out of our room."

Mars slowly sat up, looking at Anthony, who gazed back. Mars was still covered in his own blood. It was everywhere. After a moment, Anthony lowered his eyes and skulked over to his bag, picking it up and quietly leaving. Mars bit his lower lip and tried very hard not to cry, and succeeded for the most part.

"Come on," said Draephus softly. "We'll get someone to help clean up this mess."

"I really want a bath," said Mars.

"Not alone you don't," said the doctor.

Mars looked to Draephus. "I want a bath and you're helping."

"Fine. Then after you are taking a nap."

"Fine." Mars looked to Major Manorne. "Heia. I'm Mars David."

The man smiled. "Major Windsoar Manorne. Just like General Stratavarus' second in command."

"I think I love you."

"Let's wait until you're not quite so heavily sedated and see how you feel then. I'll see you in the morning, around tenhour?"

Mars nodded. Windsoar and Dr. Baltain departed, and Draephus began helping Mars get ready for his bath.

"I really liked Anthony…" said Mars sadly. He drew a shivering breath. "We talked about this so many times! We discussed what to do. I really thought he was okay with it, and then he just… left me…"

"Some people can't handle things like this," said Draephus. "They think they can, and then when it stands staring them in the face, they just can't. Do you think you might… forgive him?"

"No. How can I? If this is what he does when it's only a sinus infection, then what will he do when I'm really sick? Lock me in a room alone to die? What if you hadn't been here?"

"He didn't know it was only a sinus infection," said Draephus.

"He didn't bother to find out, either, did he?"

No, that was the truth. There was no shame in fleeing something fatal; the shame was because not once did Anthony ask how Mars was, or even if he was going to survive. Anthony's concern had been for Anthony alone.

"I'll pour you a bath. Man you are just covered in blood. How could your nose be this bad and you not know it?"

"How am I supposed to look up my own nose?"

Draephus removed his coat and hung it up, then began running Mars a bath. He heard the sound of Mars blowing his nose. Draephus was just about to suggest that may not be a good idea, when he heard Mars' voice.

"Oh, that is just… disgusting." Pause. "I think there's a piece of mucus membrane on the…"

"Mars I seriously do not wish to hear about whatever it is you left on that… whatever you blew your nose on."

"It's Anthony's lucky scarf, the one he wears on stage. He forgot it."

"In that case, don't wash it."

"Wash it? I don't even want it in the same room with me." Mars was silent for a bit, then said "I...really want to hurt him. I feel so betrayed..."

"Mars once word gets out that he ran out on you when you needed him, there's not a Gryphon fan alive who won't be yowling for his blood. All you have to do is sit back and look sad."

"Well that won't be hard. I am. I loved him. I would have been happy with an apology. But he couldn't even look me in the eye and do that. I can't..."

"Mars, I realize this is a dumb thing to say to you after everything you went through in the last couple hours, but you are not supposed to be getting upset. You need to be calm."

"Or I could end up like poor little Straif, I know," said Mars. "I wish the sedative the doctor had given me was a bit more powerful, it seems to be wearing off rather quickly."

Draephus drew out his telecom and called Raski. "Heia beautiful."

"THIS BETTER NOT BE MY GOODBYE CALL!"

"It's not," Draephus gently assured him. "We're both okay. You can come up now. Maybe bring up my kit, too."

"For who? Mars?"

"Yeah."

"Draephus you can't give him straight mushroom resin, you'll kill him."

"I am not planning on giving him any. Just bring it up. I missed you."

Draephus closed his 'com and put it away, watched by Mars.

"Why did you want your kit?"

"I have some dried ground kerry-root in it. If that doesn't put your lights out for the night, nothing will."

Mars made a face. "I hate Kerry-root. Tastes the way destri clart smells."

Within minutes, the other three Gryphons barrelled into the room like an outtake from a bad comedy movie. Bacca and Czanda were bringing up the rear, and proceeded to bark their heads off at the stink of blood. Draephus walked out of the bathroom and silenced the faelins with a glare. He then looked to Raski, Khandid and Yuri.

"In the words of the doctor – he's fragile. I think after what happened to Straif, those two words should be of enough significance to convince you that he needs quiet, and security."

"Wow," said Khandid. "Mars gets sick and Draephus turns into a grandmother."

Raski hurried over to Draephus and threw his arms around Draephus' neck. "I was so scared…"

"Yeah I think we all were," said Draephus, holding him. "It's okay, Raski, we're both fine…"

"Except the bath is about to overflow!" said Khandid, darting past the pair to shut off the water.

Draephus kissed Raski, stroking the black hair. Finally he released him. "I promised Mars I'd help him clean up."

Raski nodded. "All right. You look after Mars. You might want to clean yourself up as well. I'll call housekeeping and explain…"

There came a knock on the door, and Raski walked over to it, opening it to see one of the housekeeping staff. He looked like he had just been in the fight of his life, and he was grinning like an idiot.

"Heia! Heard from the management that there might be a bit of a mess up here."

Raski, Draephus, Khandi and Yuri stared at him. Mars was still trying to figure out how to stand up. Bacca and Czanda cocked their heads at the man, whose grin became somewhat sheepish.

"Actually my shift was over but I heard it was Mars David's room so I beat the clart out of three other guys to come up here."

"Lucky you," said Raski. He stepped aside and allowed the man to look into the room at the catastrophic aftermath of Mars' nosebleed. He sighed.

"Well serves me right for punching my brother in the face I suppose."

"Come on," said Raski. "We'll help."

Draephus walked by the housekeeper and over to Mars, picking him up. "Say heia to the man who beat up his brother to meet you, Mars, then we'll get you clean."

"Heia," said Mars weakly.

"Heia. I'm Archris. Saw you live in Trae Dae Mu, you were fabulous."

"Thank you. Now if you don't mind this big strange man is going to give me a bath."

Draephus could tell Archris was dying to ask if he could help. Draephus just smiled, and carried Mars into the bathroom, closing the door and setting Mars down on the floor before locking it.

"How are you holding up, Mars?"

"I want a bath and some hot soup and then I want to cry. I have never been that afraid in my life."

"Can you undress? Do you need help?"

Mars nodded. Draephus opened the door a crack and said to Archris "I'm taking his clothes off now."

"You're a big mean man!"

Draephus closed the door and locked it once more, then sat on the floor to face Mars. He began helping him to undress.

"You'll be okay. We'll get the room cleaned up and let you rest."

"I don't want you guys to leave. I don't want to be alone after what just happened."

"We're not going anywhere. We're here all night."

Draephus helped Mars into the bath, horrified by the sheer volume of blood. It seemed to be everywhere. Draephus used the wash cloth to run some water over Mars' hair, then squinted at what he found.

"Hey you've got a few little grey hairs…"

Mars' eyes became enormous. "WHAT DO YOU MEAN I'M GOING GREY?! I CAN'T BE GOING GREY, I'M NOT EVEN THIRTY!"

"Oh Mars relax," said Khandid. "I've been grey for years."

"That's different, you're a Northerner!"

"Just go back to lying in the bath and slathering your nude body with imported oils while eating something phallic-shaped as Draephus pleasures you sexually."

"You're all evil!" said Archris.

"Hey where is Anthony in all this?" asked Raski. "Isn't giving you a bath *his* job?"

"We no longer say the A-word in this hotel room," said Draephus.

There was a very long pause, and then the sound of bodies departing quickly. There was a tap at the bathroom door.

"Um… Raski and Khandid just blew out of here like they had a purpose," said Archris.

Draephus sighed. "Scruffin' lovely. What else could go…?"

Archris screeched as Yuri levelled a kick at him, destroying a hotel room chair.

****

It was a long night for everyone except Mars. The kerry-root did its job beautifully, and he slept the night away in a contented little ball, while his four friends and two faelins tried to get comfortable. Khandid was small enough to sleep beside Mars without disturbing him, but Yuri was far too tall and ended up on the floor, while Raski and Draephus spent an uncomfortable night on the room's couches. Eventually the long night ended, and Mars announced he was awake with a quizzical squeak. Raski slowly sat up, looking ragged.

"Mars, I love you, but I cannot do another night on the couch."

"I'm sorry," Mars squeaked sleepily. He spooned up against Khandid, who also squeaked. Raski rolled his eyes.

"It's tenhour in the morning and someone needs to oil Mars and Khandid."

The pair squeaked in harmony.

"Shut up! No one needs that much 'adorable' this early in the morning," said Raski, pushing his messy black hair out of his face.

"Coffee," said Khandid.

"Coffee and food," said Mars.

"How is trade up here in Charlendine?" asked Raski.

Draephus shrugged. "I'll go ask."

He was about to head for the door, when there was a polite knock. Puzzled, Draephus walked over to the door and opened it. Standing before him was Major Windsoar Manorne, holding a rather large blue canvas bag. Standing behind Windsoar was Dahli.

"What are you doing here?" he asked.

"Oh that's nice," said Dahli. "You get all rich and famous and you forget me?"

"No that is not what I meant and you know it."

"It's okay, Dahli," called Raski. "I still love you, even if you are a talentless quint-flogger."

Dahli slipped into the room past Draephus and Windsoar. Draephus motioned the man into the room, wincing as he heard Dahli squeak.

"That is so *adorable*, I have to get a photo, it will completely ruin Gemma's life."

"I nearly died yesterday, you know," said Mars.

"Yeah so did your ex-boyfriend after he started running his mouth about how you scared him with your virus," said Dahli. "It's a good thing Titan isn't playing the festival because they just kicked Anthony out of the band. Speaking of Anthony, he sent me up here to get his lucky scarf."

"Really brave, isn't he?" said Raski.

"I don't think you're going to want to touch that scarf," said Mars. "It's in the trash after I blew my nose on it."

"Oh no, I'll bring it," said Dahli, sounding oddly happy. She pulled the entire bag out of the garbage, tied it up, and turned to Draephus, still holding the bag containing bloodied tissues and a crusty snot and blood soaked scarf. "Now – why is my faelin barking at the window?"

"Because he has never seen a glass window and he thinks the rain hitting it may be something scary," said Draephus.

"How do I get him to *not* bark at the window? Because I'm becoming very unpopular, especially late at night."

"You just have to show him the window is really there, and it's just a noise," said Draephus. "It helps if you put a bit of tape or something on the glass so he gets the idea that something is there."

"And why does he insist on breaking open Gemma's hand cream and rolling in it?"

"He's a faelin. And that is not the most bizarre thing he will ever do."

"Oh goody, I get to look forward *more* weird stuff. Last night he ate my makeup kit and barfed paisley on the rug."

"I'll replace your makeup kit," said Draephus. "If he's too much of a problem I could always him back."

"Try it and die," said Dahli. "Later."

Dahli left with the destroyed scarf. Windsoar approached the bed, and Mars raised his head, smiling.

"I remember you. Vaguely."

Khandid raised his head. "Oooh, hello sexy. What were you doing with our Mars?"

"He came to kill him," said Draephus.

Khandid covered Mars with the blanket and held him

protectively. "Mars isn't here. Go away."

"I brought coffee, and some nuts, dried fruit and dried fish…"

Khandi pulled the covers back down. "Mars is here."

Mars blinked sleepily at Windsoar, then slowly dragged himself into a seated position. "I didn't think you'd come back."

"Well I said I would," said Windsoar. He glanced at Raski. "Did you sleep on that couch all night? You can turn them into a bed, you know. It's much more comfortable that way."

"We're from Second City," said Raski. "We were impressed enough that the hotel room had four walls and a floor. I seem to recall we stayed in a few in *this* city that looked that way, too."

"Charlendine is fortunate," said Windsoar. "The poisoning missed us almost completely. We have trees, vegetation, fish, and minimal viral infections. So we're wealthier than other areas and we could rebuild faster. That's why they hold the Year End Festival here. I'm rather surprised you five never moved here. You could afford to."

"Too many ties to our home," said Draephus. "Besides, it would be too much like spitting on the ones who *can't* afford to move for us to leave it."

"Yeah I suppose it would be. Well I brought breakfast, help yourselves. How is the food shortage over there? The storms have hit the transports pretty hard."

"Let me put it this way," said Khandi, reaching for a piece of fruit. "The night before we came here, I had kaisa. And it was actually pretty good."

They ate, drank coffee and talked, watching Mars get acquainted with his new friend. Then the mighty Charlendine Bell tolled the hour with a slow gravity that made one not accustomed to hearing it think some monstrous invasion was on the way. The bell was over a thousand years old, carefully restored after the war and put back to work as the marker of the passing hours. Draephus was sure he could feel the floor shaking each time it tolled.

"Raski we have to get going," said Draephus.

"Going?" asked Khandid. "Going where?"

"We had plans to go up Mount Salefe for three nights," said Draephus.

"And you're not taking us?!" exclaimed Khandid, indignant.

"Hard to believe, I know," said Draephus. "Mars are you going to be okay?"

"We'll look after the poor fragile thing," said Khandid.

"It was just a nosebleed," grumped Mars.

"You heard the doctor," said Raski. "Rest. He doesn't even want you on stage in eight days."

"None of us do," said Khandid. "But there is nothing we can do about it."

"Groutnoll," muttered Mars.

There was an excited tapping on the door, and Draephus went to answer it. He found Dahli, and she stood on her toes to hug him before darting into the room and onto the bed.

"Well you're certainly invasively cheerful," said Khandid.

"We had a news crew from Earth checking out the stage before the first bands go on tomorrow," said Dahli. "So of course the first thing they go to check out are Trilby and Mit-Mit, and they tried playing some different music for them to see how they would react."

"I'm not sure I like where this is heading," said Mars. "Is that Gemma's phone?"

"Actually it's mine, she had her sister put one on the last ship for me. So now my life is totally ruined. Anyway…"

Dahli showed them the clips she had taken of the news crew trying to get Trilby and Mit-Mit's attention. Popular bands had very little effect, and when they played Mickie Pastors, Trilby began trying to escape. A clip of music by the Mortified Gryphons prompted no response at all.

"That's it," said Khandid, "time to get the axe."

"Keep watching," said Dahli, grinning.

The next piece of music was a bouncy happy piece none of the Gryphons, or Windsoar either, had ever heard before. The song was sung by a little girl, and, as those in the hotel room watched, first Trilby, then Mit-Mit, began to slowly bounce in time to the music.

"They're *dancing*!" said Raski. "They're actually *dancing*! What are we listening to?"

"It's a song from Earth, called *'I Want a Hippopotamus for Christmas'*. It's a children's song," said Dahli.

"What's a hip-po-pot-a-mus, besides hard to say?" asked Mars.

Dahli showed them a video of a hippo wallowing in the mud.

"Why would a child want one of these for a gift?" asked Khandid warily.

"Well I wanted a dragon bird for my birthday," said Dahli.

"Dragon birds are pretty," said Raski. "This thing is using its tail to fling clart as far as it possibly can."

"Maybe that's the whole point of the song," said Dahli. "It's a perfectly ridiculous thing for a child to want."

"And our plants love it," said Draephus. "Come on, Raski. We have to get out of here before the next thing Dahli shows us is a hippopotamus dancing to a Gryphons song. We will be back in three days in time for the festival to start. Mars, you are not to worry about anything or get upset."

"I won't," he said. "I promise to not leave this bed all day."

Draephus and Raski returned to their own room, packed a few things for their adventure, including the faelins, then got into Draephus' grey conni and began to drive.

"I was wondering why you brought the vehicle," said Raski, as Bacca sat on his lap and watched excitedly all the things they were passing.

"I had plans to get you alone for a while," said Draephus. "Maybe ask when we're going to make this relationship public."

Raski grinned. "Very, very, soon. Before we return to Second City."

"It's not because of something bad, is it? Your delaying…?"

"No. Now stop prying. You promised me this."

"I know, I'm just terrified as to what you may do to me."

"Nothing bad." Raski stroked Bacca's hair. "Right?"

"Arf!"

"There, see? Bacca agrees."

"Bacca agrees with anything that anybody says. Bacca! Was your mother a goat?"

"Arf!"

"Do you live in a tube of toothpaste?"

"Arf!"

"Do you eat old shoes?"

"Arf!"

"See?" said Draephus. "He agrees with everything."

"And yet you insist they're intelligent."

"They *are* intelligent."

"Need I remind you that these are the same faelins that ate a box?"

"They're the same faelins that tried to mate with a feralyke once, too. Doesn't mean they're not smart. They can light a lamp. They can turn on a tap. They can…"

"They can open a suitcase, leave something in it and close it again."

"Told you there were smart," said Draephus.

"And I had to clean it while you were dying one floor above me."

Draephus reached out one hand to take Raski's. "If it makes you feel any better, we were pretty damned scared, too. And poor Mars… he was devastated when Anthony went and hid on the balcony."

"I'm not sure I would not have done the same," said Raski.

"Would you have at least cared what was happening to me?"

"Draephus, if you could have seen me clawing the walls you would not have asked me that. I was sick. I was losing my whole world. It would have been my lover, one of my dearest friends, and my band all in one shot. I *cared*, Draephus. I cried on the faelins for hours I was so sick with worry."

"Is that when they made a mess in your suitcase?"

"Yeah I think they were a little annoyed with me by then."

"Arf!"

"Don't you 'arf' at me. I never made a mess in *your* stuff."

Bacca made a few noises, shaking his long red hair. Raski stroked his head.

"I think I understand what you see in these guys. They are very sweet." Raski peered out the window, looking up at the cloud cover. "We should have started earlier. It will be dark when we get there."

"That's okay. We'll have days to play. Hey have you checked out the full listing for the bands that will be appearing at the festval?"

"Not really. I get to the big black line through Vortex's name and can't stop giggling."

Draephus indicated a concert programme on the dash of his conni. "Check out Day Four, about fifteenhour."

Raski picked up the rather weighty item, flipping through pages of band listings. "Let's see… Cylindrical View… how do *they* qualify to be here? We could feed kaisa to the faelins and hear better music."

"Arf!"

"Just keep reading, Donsa Jervyas," said Draephus.

"Okay, let me look here… Bad…. *Bad Influence*?! Is this a *joke*?! The last time I talked to Delaes there *was* no Bad Influence."

"Same here," said Draephus. "But Delaes has always been resourceful. And apparently four weeks ago he contacted the organizers and asked if there was still room for him, and they said yes."

"Yeah but four weeks is not long enough to prepare for a major festival with even a seasoned band. What does he think he's doing?"

"He's Delaes, he doesn't *think*, he just rams forward like the little brainless half-faelin he is. That's where he gets it from, I swear. Never saw anything more determined than a faelin on a mission. Right guys?"

Bacca yawned widely, showing formidable canines. Czanda just huffed from the back seat.

"They're tired," said Raski.

"Yeah, I am too. We'll be there soon."

Chapter Twenty-Nine

Draephus finally pulled up before the small, mountaintop cabin, wishing he had set out earlier and booked more time. It was such a beautiful area. Maybe he and Raski could come back and spend a month or so, just relaxing and being together. Why had he never noticed the knot in his gut he had when he was with Vesper? Raski was so much easier to be with. Even with his nerves and his occasional crying jags and single-minded baby fixation. He could lie in bed with Raski and just talk. With Vesper everything had been a fight or a debate. Of course, knowing what he did now, it must have been rough to pretend to be in love with someone he likely couldn't stand.

Yeah. Poor little lying, murdering, back-biting piece of garbage.

Draephus put a cigarette in his mouth, lighting it, then looking up at the sky. Stars. That was why he had brought Raski. Mount Salefe was one of the very few places on Sferkkaa where the rain stopped entirely, and stars could sometimes be seen. Sometimes, even the sun, though the sky cleared most often at night. This was also one of the few places that got snow, and Draephus was hoping there would be a little. This late in the year there was a good chance, even though it would likely be brief.

Draephus looked down at Raski, who was sound asleep, Bacca still in his lap. They were both so tired. By the time the festival was over, they'd probably all want to sleep for a week.

Draephus moved the baggage into the small cabin, walking into a warm, well-lit room made of timber. The air smelled of fresh-cut flowers and bread, and the attendant within moved to help Draephus with the bags. She was an aged woman, and Draephus found it briefly startling to be in her presence. It was even more unbalancing when a younger woman came out of a back room to assist her.

"Everything is ready," said the old woman. "I'm Almista, this is my daughter Charla."

"Heia," said Draephus, "sorry we're so late."

"Oh not a problem," she said. "Supper is ready, the bed is

warmed, and… well heia! How are you?"

Czanda slunk into the cabin, moving on all fours and yawning. He did not acknowledge the woman; instead he hopped onto the nearest soft surface and curled up, blinking sleepily.

"He'll be a little more interactive tomorrow," said Draephus.

"Oh I love faelins," she gushed. "Is he clever?"

Czanda yawned mightily, while choosing that moment to fart explosively. Draephus sighed heavily.

"Yes, but you'd never know it to look at him."

Draephus returned to the conni, grinning as he saw that Raski and Bacca hadn't moved an inch. He opened the door to the vehicle, then knelt down, reaching out to touch Raski's shoulder.

"Raski. Come on, wake up. We're here."

Bacca yipped unhappily. Draephus picked him up and carried him into the cabin, putting him down beside Czanda. The pair squiggled and fussed to get comfortable, which led to a yapping debate about who got to sleep in what position. Draephus left them to sort themselves out while he returned to the vehicle to get Raski. He knelt on the grass once more to look at his dearest companion.

"Raski. Come on, you know I can't carry you."

One blue eye opened. "Are we here?"

"Yeah. Come on, supper's on the table, then we can fall into a warm bed and sleep."

Raski stretched. "Maybe we can wake up long enough to do something between eating and sleeping."

Draephus grinned. "You talked me into it. Come on, come see the stars."

Raski rubbed at his eyes, yawning. "Stars?"

"Yeah. Real stars, right over head."

Raski blinked at Draephus. "Stars? You did say 'stars'."

"I did. Come on out and look up."

Raski slowly eased out of the conni, and slithered down to the ground, staring up at the night sky. Draephus sat down beside him, as Raski stared up, trembling violently. Draephus held him, watching his friend nervously. Some Sferkkaans could never get enough of the night sky once they saw it in all its glory. Some Sferkkaans went insane with terror, feeling as if they were about to be sucked into the endless cold of space. Raski appeared to be giving very serious consideration to the latter.

"It's okay," said Draephus softly. "I have you."

Raski was shaking so hard Draephus could feel it, listening to his friend's breath come in terrified gasps as he stared at a satin-black sky scattered with stars and distant galaxies, many unnamed and unknown, since astronomy was not an easy science to practice on Sferkkaa.

"You're all right," said Draephus softly. "You're not going anywhere, even though I know it feels like you're about to be yanked right off the planet. I felt it too the first time I came here. But you're safe. We're safe. Look... see that distant green dot? That's Veridia. Centuries ago, monks believed it to be the gem in the crown of the goddess-warrior Avalarian. And over there, the nine stars that look like they're following the line of an animal's neck and back. That's Makkaria, steed of the gods, who pulls the clouds across the sky."

Raski was still shivering, but he seemed a little less terrified as Draephus spoke. "It's just frightening; it's like staring into a hole leading to nothing."

"You were a pilot. Didn't you ever go above the cloud cover?"

"No. We were warned against it because sometimes the pilots went insane. The ones who didn't swore they'd never seen anything so beautiful in their lives. A few became obsessed with the sight, and tried to fly into the sun. Their planes froze up and fell to the ground, killing them. Pilots were needed, and in short supply, so we were ordered to stay in or under the clouds, and I obeyed. I wanted to see it, but at the time it seemed more important to keep my mind on business. Now, however.... I might like to see it." He straightened up a little, less frightened and more curious now. "It's beautiful..."

Almista appeared in the doorway just then. "Did you wish to eat out here?"

Draephus looked to Raski, who was now craning his neck, his fear mostly forgotten. He then looked back to Almista.

"Yeah, I think we would."

****

It was cold, but they stayed outside and watched the stars, enjoying them until the cloud cover slowly drifted over them once more, and it was time to go inside. Almista and her daughter had returned to their quarters for the night. Bacca and Czanda were on the rug before the fire, and Raski and Draephus dragged themselves to bed. It was not quite Draephus' gigantic antique bed in his great castle, but it was awful nice. Raski pressed close, wanting to be held. Draephus was only too happy to accommodate him. Draephus was nearly asleep when Raski began to worry.

"Charla seems nice."

"Yeah, she does."

"Nice, strong, pretty…"

"Raski…"

"I was just noticing."

"I have no doubt you noticed there is a really attractive woman in this cabin. I noticed it too. But I'm in love with you and nobody else, and if you do not feel the same way then you are sleeping with the faelins."

"That's not fair, you know I love you. It's just such a complicated situation."

"No, it's *not* complicated," said Draephus. "You and I are in a relationship that we fought rather hard for, and one I don't ever want to leave. The fact that, left to our own devices without Kryphisian interference, we would likely have a female lover as opposed to a male is irrelevant. I love *you*. And if you're going to start pointing out every chance you get that we are in one of the very few places left on our world that has a population of women then I'm gonna start thinking all those promises we made to each other don't mean anything."

"You know that's not true."

"Then what is the problem? You've been off your nut for about six weeks now, since Straif died. Is that it? Are you worried I'll die?"

"That's part of it, I suppose."

"I am not dying. Or at least not very fast."

"I just…"

"I am going to get no peace tonight, am I?" asked Draephus, rolling over to draw Raski close.

"I worry! You should know that by now."

Draephus kissed him. "I do know that by now, but I'm exhausted and there seems to be only one way to get you to be quiet."

Raski wrapped his arms around Draephus' neck and kissed him hard. "Well you could have told me to shut the šukat up, but I

627

like this idea better."

"I thought you might." He reached down to run his hand over Raski's abdomen. "How's the implant feel?"

"Fine. It's felt fine for a couple months now. Pretty much ever since they took the sutures out. It really doesn't feel like much of anything anymore, to be perfectly honest."

"How about when we...?"

"Well, sadly, being artificial, it doesn't feel like much of anything *then*, either, but I know how to fix that."

"Oh yeah? How?"

Raski dumped Draephus onto his back, then pounced on top of him, kissing him hard.

"Yeah that works," said Draephus.

"I've never been on top of you before," Raski purred, kissing him.

'Yeah and if you hurt me the way Vesper used to, you never will be again,' thought Draephus, but he sincerely doubted Raski would, and realized almost immediately that the thought was unfair. But Vesper had put him through so much it was a little hard at times not to be affected by it.

"Hey," said Raski softly, and Draephus opened his eyes to stare into luminous blue orbs. "Stop thinking about dead enemies and start thinking about live lovers."

"Okay. Wanna wrestle to see who gets on top?"

Raski's eyes almost glittered. "Oooh, sounds fun!"

Draephus normally would have put up more of a fight, but he was sore, and the drugs were wearing off. Raski seemed to sense it, and the "rough sex" only counted as rough because that had been the general intention. Draephus let Raski win without too much of a struggle, finally relaxing beneath him and drawing him down to kiss. It was a far cry from their first encounter, only... how long? About a year, was it? No, he was deteriorating too fast. He didn't want to die so soon. There must be something he could to gain more strength. He needed to live a while yet...

"Hey," whispered Raski. "Out of the darkness and back to me."

"I'm always with you. Even in the darkness."

They paused and looked at each other, blinking.

"That's good, we have to write that line down," said Raski.

"Sex first."

"Always."

Raski kissed him, and Draephus responded by holding him tightly. Yeah this was nice, though on the whole he preferred to be on top himself. But then again, he could always wait for Raski to finish then take advantage of his weakened state…

"You're plotting," said Raski.

"You've known me too long."

****

They made the most of their brief getaway; sleeping, eating, making love, and occasionally venturing outside to enjoy the beauty of the area. On the evening of the second day, Draephus opened the door to be greeted by snow, and he immediately called Raski and the faelins. All three greeted the sight with suspicion and growling.

"What is this?" asked Raski warily, as Bacca and Czanda skulked into the house to hide.

"Snow," said Draephus. "Come see."

"No… I don't think I want to…"

"Come on, Raski, you'll love it!"

"No… I don't think so…"

"Raski, come on, please?"

Raski looked frightened, but allowed Draephus to put an arm around him and draw him out of the cabin. The whole world was pearl grey, and drifting from the sky were soft, silent flakes of frozen whiteness. He stepped out of the cabin cautiously, one slow step at a time, eyes large, expression wary, his black hair dotted with icy fluff. Draephus found himself grinning so widely it was almost painful.

"Do you have any idea how adorably beautiful you are right now?"

Raski picked his way through the snow. "I'm reasonably certain that I was not meant to endure this."

Draephus laughed. Raski came to his side and pressed close, looking warily up at the sky.

"You brought me here to scare me, didn't you?"

"I wanted to share something beautiful with you. Something I loved."

Raski looked up at Draephus, puzzled. "When were you

here?"

"Oh, long time ago," said Draephus. "Before I had the faelins, even. I was about sixteen. I came up from the South Continent because I needed to think, and I couldn't do it where I was living at the time because between the other drug runners and the night stalkers I couldn't find five minutes to breathe. So I came here for almost a few months."

"What were you thinking about?"

"What else? Girls. Or rather one girl in particular. I really liked her."

Raski stared at Draephus sourly. "That's great, Draephus, your brought your insecure boyfriend up the mountain to talk about your first love, that's just fabulous."

"She wasn't my first love. I mean I thought she was. I thought I loved her, even though I can't even recall her name. But… well… didn't take me long to realize what I had mistaken for love was manipulation. Her grandmother was dying of the same bone disease I have, so I was giving her mushrooms for her grandmother. Except… she was giving them to her boyfriend instead. Her *real* boyfriend, I should add. He would take the mushrooms and sell them. Anyway, when I found out, I began delivering them to the grandmother myself. In fact, I was the only person with her when she died. She gave me everything she had in the world; her shack, her pregnant faelin, and, so I believed at the time, the viral arthritis that killed her."

"It's not contagious? I thought it was."

"Only from certain plants to people, not from people to people. I talked to Dr. Arang about it, asked what the chances were that I could pass it to you. He looked at me like I was so stupid it was frightening."

"Well I thought it could be passed that way," said Raski.

"Apparently it's a very common misconception," said Draephus. "Dr. Arang just stared at me and asked me why I would be permitted to run around and share a debilitating illness. So… as the saying goes, even the ohwendai man can learn."

Raski laughed quietly and kissed him. Draephus just grinned.

"Anyway… I came to terms with a lot of changes in my life on this very spot. Only seemed fitting to come here once more with you."

"I am rather rearranging your life, aren't I?"

"I don't mind. It's been a positive change. You know, it's strange, Raski. I thought I loved Vesper. I really did. But maybe I was just tired of being alone."

"I'm starting to get a little worried," said Raski.

"Worried? Why?"

"Well you thought you loved that girl, you thought you loved Vesper… maybe you only think you love me."

Draephus stared down into the pale blue eyes, searching their depths. "No. No this is really love. I'm sure of it."

"And Vesper?"

"All right, I admit it, I loved him too. I was just so hurt by the betrayal. You know why he picked me, out of the two of us? He said you were too nervous, too suspicious. You would have figured him out before I did."

Raski shrugged. "Maybe. Who can tell? It doesn't matter now, he's dead. And you seem certain his little band of fanatics won't be after us."

"I don't see why they would be," said Draephus. "I'm of no further use."

"No, but maybe…"

"Raski, I love you but I don't want to hear it. I have had a long miserable year and the last thing I want to think about is Vesper and anyone he was involved with." He nuzzled his lover gently. "Maybe after the next tour you can pick out a room in the castle for a nursery. Assuming you want to move in with me."

"I do, I just need to find the right buyer for my house. I need to sell it to someone who will appreciate it for what it is. I did a lot of work restoring it."

"Khandi and Yuri may want it. Soon as you formally announce we're a couple."

Raski grinned. "Very soon, my lover. Very soon. Come on, let's go back inside. It's cold out here."

****

Draephus had only just managed to reach the bed in his hotel room after returning from his short trip when a tiny blur of white came up behind him. Khandid was livid with wrath and could barely articulate the words he had to say. The fact that he was screaming them in a Northern dialect that Draephus did not speak did not make things any easier.

"Khandi... speak a language we both know..."

Khandid obliged, but he didn't bother to go back and explain what he said initially, he simply continued.

"...and Dahli is in tears and who can blame her I mean we ALL were but..."

"KHANDID! What are you talking about? Turning into Delaes on me is not helping!"

Khandid drew a deep, steadying breath, and started over. "Corey Hillman had an interview with a programme running on Earth in which he stated in reference to the death of Straif and his unborn infant and I quote "It's always a good day when the Lord smites an Unnatural and its spawn" end quote."

Draephus let that sink in for a few moments, uncertain he was really understanding what Khandid had just said. "Wait... does that mean it was a good thing that Straif and the baby died?"

Khandid was on the verge of hysterics as he visibly teared up. "He was laughing about it! And the monster he was talking to was laughing as well! Is that what we invited here to be our friend? Monsters who take joy over the deaths of children?! I thought we were done with those!"

Draephus put his arms around him, drawing him close. "Did you call the concert promoters?"

"I called Mordrett!"

Whoops.

"What did Mordrett say?" asked Draephus warily.

"He just said to let him handle it, that they..."

"HEY!" A tall, lanky figure stormed into the room, none other than Donsa Hillman in person. "What was the idea getting me and my band pulled from the venue six hours before we were due to go on?!"

Khandid turned to face him, barely standing as high as Corey's chest even in his heels. "You monster, where do you get off laughing over the death of children?!"

"Children? *What* children?"

"Straif Mannechek!"

"Oh you mean the little faggot carrying the ass-baby."

Draephus stepped back and simply let Khandid rise up like the little phoenix he was. Within seconds there was a spray of blood across the walls, and Corey was screaming, clutching his face, his stomach ripped open. Draephus simply kept backing up, reluctant to get in the way of a fully trained veteran Whip and anything he wished to kill. Within moments there were people coming from all directions, and one of them was Dahli. Draephus grabbed her and dragged her out of the way before she was injured, and just held her protectively close as others tried to break up the fight. The fight ended suddenly when Corey fell to the floor and Khandid was dragged down with him, his hand blades caught in Corey's skull and collarbone respectively. Gemma arrived moments later, and Draephus dragged her away from the mess as well. She screamed when she finally figured out what she was looking at. He held them tightly as he backed away, keeping them out of the way of the mess as medical personnel arrived to sort out the wounded.

"Is that the guy who made those hateful comments about Straif?" Dahli asked. "I can't recognize him though all the blood…"

"Yeah that's him," said Draephus. "You two stay back here."

He stepped forward, coming to Khandid's side and kneeling beside him on the floor. He didn't think Khandid was hurt, but Corey definitely was, and badly. Someone handed him a scarf, and Draephus wrapped it around Khandid's eyes. He then began slowly and carefully unbuckling the formidable blades before Khandid started to thrash and turned Corey's brains into scrambled meat. Draephus managed to extract Khandid from the boot and glove blades and moved him away from Corey, placing him on the floor. He seemed unconscious, which was worrying. The fight had been so short and so fast…

A medic moved Draephus aside, examining Khandid. "Is he okay?" Draephus asked.

"Hard to tell, he's soaked in blood. I can't tell if any of it's his. Is he a Whip?"

"Yeah that's why I blindfolded him. He's got contacts in, but they may slip…"

They moved Khandid to the bed while the majority of the medics worked on Corey. He was taken away to the hospital, while Khandid tried to get himself sorted. He'd been struck a hard blow when Corey fell on him, but for the most part he seemed to be fine.

"Oh I am in so much trouble," said Khandid, as Draephus took a hot wash cloth to clean him off.

"This is the second time since we have been here I've had to wipe blood off someone," said Draephus. "And yeah I think when your cousin hears what you did, you're going to be in a *lot* of trouble."

"He can't talk about Straif that way. He can't talk about *any* of us that way! What does he know about everything we have been through, about everything we have lost? I wouldn't laugh if *his* child died!"

"We're not all like that," said Gemma quietly. "Please don't think we all are because of people like Corey and Mickie."

"We don't," said Dahli. "But why would he say something so hideous?"

"Because some people like Corey believe it's wrong for two men to fall in love or have a family or raise a baby," said Gemma. "They believe it's *so* wrong and *such* a bad thing that it is better for them to be dead. Corey saw Straif's death as a sign that God thinks so too."

"Is this the same God you were telling me about who loves all beings equally?" asked Dahli. "Because I don't think you and Corey are talking about the same God."

"Dahli," said Draephus wearily, "can you grab my bags? I'm gonna carry Khandi up to Mars' room and let housekeeping clean up this mess. I swear they are never going to let the Gryphons book a room here ever again."

"Sure," she said softly, wiping at one eye. "I just can't believe anyone would think that! I loved Straif! We all did!"

They went up to Mars' room, where they found Raski, the faelins, Yuri, Mars, and one highly annoyed Emperor.

"What did you think you were doing?" demanded Mordrett.

"I love you too!" snapped Khandid.

"That is entirely beside the point. Do you know how many people I now have screaming at me because some bigoted clartblossom is currently in surgery having *your* blades removed from his skull? You don't know these Earth people. Believe me, they can make a religious and political incident out of *anything*!"

"He made a remark about our dead friend, we retaliated," said Draephus.

"And he's lucky it wasn't me or he'd have been picking a lot more than Khandid's blades out of his head," said Dahli.

Mordrett looked at Dahli as if he thought he remembered her, but wasn't sure. "The donselle who wanted to discuss faelins, am I right?"

Dahli blushed. "Yeah that's me."

"Oh charming, *another* troublemaker. Donselle when I told you to find like-minded people and organize, I did *not* mean organize a break-in and get yourself arrested!"

"I know," said Dahli. "It just… seemed like a good idea at the time."

"I see." Mordrett looked to Khandid. "And you, my beloved cousin?"

"Seemed like a good idea at the time," said Khandid.

"Is that your official statement? Because I now have to go face a bunch of Earth people who all look like someone forced them to clart backwards."

"Look," said Raski, "Corey Hillman went on the visual and was openly delighted by the death of a seventeen year old boy and that boy's child. He then came to confront us about his band being pulled from the festival and called Straif a little faggot and referred to his child as an ass-baby. I'm not entirely clear on what exactly an ass-baby is, but it sounds to me an awful lot like the sort of thing that is going to find you on the floor with some Whip's blades in your skull. Tell them that."

Mordrett nodded. "I will. Not quite in those words, but you have a point. This man was revelling in the death of children, and regardless of what Donsa Hillman thinks of Straif being pregnant, that is something we will not tolerate. Now, do the lot of you swear to do nothing to get any more blood on this hotel? Mars, how is your nose?"

"Sore and crusty."

"Excellent, go sit in the bath, now. You're the best band on the planet, I'm not having you show up on stage sneezing out crusted blood and snot. Khandid are you all right?"

"Apart from having a large smelly man fall on me. I should accuse him of attempted rape."

"I don't think it counts as attempted rape if the reason he falls on you is because you stuck a knife in his brain," said Raski.

"Now are the rest of you fine as well?" asked Mordrett. "Because if I get one more call about your behaviour I am locking the bunch of you up in one room until show time."

"We promise to be good," said Draephus.

"You have no choice, I'm putting one of my best men in charge of monitoring your behaviour; Major Windsoar Manorne."

"You mean the guy that's been taking Mars for walks around the park?" said Khandid.

"I don't care what he's been doing with Mars so long as he keeps the six of you out of trouble." Mordrett pointed at Dahli. "Don't think I don't know that they have made you their minion."

"I'm a minion too," said Gemma. "And Diza. She's a minion."

"We have many minions," said Raski. "Small ones as well. Many mini minions."

Mordrett clearly failed to see the humour in the remark. "I want every one of you to stay on *this* floor, and if I hear otherwise there *will* be repercussions, trust me."

"Well," said Raski as Mordrett left in a swirl of black and red, "I believe we are officially in the Bad Gryphon Box."

Mars went to take a bath, while Khandid sat on the bed, looking a little dazed. Yuri sat beside him, nuzzling him affectionately, while Dahli began idly tidying up a room that really didn't need it.

"Are you okay?" Gemma asked.

"No," said Dahli. "Not particularly. I'm having a hard time digesting the idea that anyone would see the death of a baby as a good thing. Especially since Corey has a baby of his own."

"Yeah but his baby is normal. It has a mommy and a daddy who are married. So…"

"So his baby is more important?" said Dahli. "You know… I really wish right at this moment that I was sick enough inside to wish his own baby would die. But unfortunately I'm not quite that ugly."

"I'm sorry," said Gemma. "Please believe me. We're not all like that."

"We believe you, we're just not happy about the ones who *are* like that," said Dahli. She looked at Draephus, and he could tell by the expression in her eyes that she was beginning to understand him very well indeed. He found himself wishing she didn't. He was trying to think of something to say to her, when there was a knock on the door.

"I really hope that is not a thundering herd of Corey-supporters," said Khandid. "There is only one man I want on top of me and he's currently nibbling my neck."

Yuri took Khandid's hand, as Dahli approached the door and opened it. Draephus looked up as he heard Billy's voice.

"Hi. We just came to say we were sorry about what Corey said."

"Ja," said Sigge. "And we is bringings traditional Earth apologies gifts."

"And what would those be?" asked Raski, as a small group of people filed into the room.

"Well we decided to share an assortment of things from all over," said K-Shot, carrying a tray as he walked over to a low table. "I brought some Tennessee whiskey, Billy brought buffalo wings, Sigge and Vidar brought…"

"Before we accept your gifts," said Raski, "I think you should know that our little Khandid there put Corey in the hospital."

"Is he hurt bad?" asked Billy.

"He's having one of Khandid's blades surgically removed from his skull as we speak," said Draephus.

K-Shot stared at Draephus, then shifted his large brown eyes to Khandid. "That little itty bitty fluffball? I mean I saw him scratch Mickie up once, but…?"

Gemma held up her trusty phone, showing a clip of a news item.

"…and this just in, Corey Hillman of the very popular country band Hillman and the Hillbillies is in the hospital after a fight with the quinticord player of Arucadda Dannatti, Khandid Stracona. Mr. Hillman made some distasteful remarks about the death of Straif Mannechek, and it is believed that is what the fight was about. Hillman is currently in surgery, having five fighting blades extracted from the bones of his collarbone, ribs, and skull…"

"He had it coming," said Billy. "If that had been my friend and a baby, I'd have done the same. But I would have stuck one of those blades up his ass."

"It's still a line in the sand we didn't mean to draw, though," said Gemma.

"And Khandid made it wider," said Raski. He looked down at Khandid. "What are we going to do with you?"

"Feed me wine while Yuri scruffs my brains out?"

"It would take him a long time considering we're not sure you have any brains," said Raski.

"I wanna know how Khandid messed up Corey so badly!" said K-Shot.

"I ams wantings to see dat, too," said Sigge. Vidar looked like he would rather *not* know, and put Sigge between himself and the little Sferkkaan.

Khandid sighed and sat up. He pulled on a set of black gloves, bladeless, then pulled on a pair of boots that had heels, but also no blades. He then stood up and walked over to K-Shot.

"Now you are absolutely certain you wish to see me do this."

Mystique motioned to Gemma. "Start recording because this is gonna be good."

Gemma did. K-Shot looked down at Khandid, clearly determined to learn the secret to what had happened.

"Show me," said K-Shot. "Hit me just the way you hit Corey. I won't get mad, I promise. I won't hate you or nuthin'. I just wanna see."

"All right," said Khandid. "Say when."

"When."

There was an explosion of white, and suddenly K-Shot was on the floor, bleeding from the head and clutching his stomach. Mystique ran to his side, helping him to sit up.

"Oh baby are you all right?"

K-Shot was too stunned to reply. He shook his head, looking dazed and coughing.

"I'm an idiot," he finally managed to say.

"I am SO posting this to my Facebook page!" said Gemma.

Dahli sat down beside Draephus and said quietly; "Is it just me, or are all these people crazy?"

"No I'm pretty sure it's not you," he said. "How are you holding up?"

"Well I'm angry," she said. "I wish I could have hurt Corey. I really do. I mean I didn't know Straif as long as everybody else did, but he still meant a lot to me."

"I know," said Draephus. "He meant a lot to many people, and Corey is not going to get any sympathy here."

"Mordrett is pretty angry at Khandi, isn't he?"

"Yeah," said Draephus. "Things like this can escalate, and he doesn't want what was supposed to be a fun, happy, event to turn into a mess. The first band goes on stage very soon and I think Mordrett would prefer things go smoothly."

"Oh who is going on first?" asked Dahli.

"Carn-Crow."

"Never heard of them."

"That's why they're on first," said Draephus. "The concert listing goes from smallest to tallest. We go on last."

"Which only makes sense, since after *you* play there won't be a stage," said Dahli.

He grinned and put an arm around her, letting her snuggle close. He was debating having a drink when a leggy form in black leather walked into the room

"…absolutely no idea why anyone would say such a thing I really do not you would think some people would have better things to do than piss on the corpses of children oh heia Billy YES I BREATHE!"

"Through your ears!" said Billy.

"I do not don't be ridiculous if you can help it where's Mars?"

"In the bath," said Draephus. "Cleaning out his nose."

"Heia Mars!" called Billy. "Use a toilet brush!"

"Get naked and come here and show me!" Mars called back.

"Isn't that Anthony's job?" called Mystique.

"We don't say that word around here anymore," said Mars.

The bathroom door opened, and Mars walked out, smelling of soap and damp air, his long hair hanging loose, wearing only his pants. His shoulders, arms and chest were a mass of violent scars that made some people flinch visibly.

"I can breathe," he announced.

"That's great, now take your medication and get into bed," said Raski.

"Only if Billy comes with me," said Mars.

"Sorry," said Billy. "My girlfriend gets cranky when I crawl into bed with other men. Or other women. Or anyone who is not her."

"I hate sleeping alone," grumbled Mars.

"So what happened to the former boyfriend?" asked Mystique.

"He thought I was dying so he ran off to save his own ass," said Mars. "So if anyone here has been harbouring a secret desire to make mad passionate love to me, please by all means feel free to speak up."

"Oh Mars," said a soft, strongly-accented voice. "If only I heard you say that before I was married."

Draephus' head shot up, and he watched as a tall, elegant man with long white hair walked into the room. He now had one blue eye, and the left portion of his face was covered in a leather patch. In his right hand, he had a cane, and was leaning on it heavily. Perched on his gloved left hand was Piska, who was fluffed up and ready to tear a strip off anyone who got too close to his master. The room fell completely silent as the Sferkkaans just stared, and those from Earth simply wondered who had walked into the room.

"J'Vanni?" said Draephus, not quite believing his eyes.

The tall man nodded. "I decided that hiding was not working, so I let Delaes talk me into coming here. I even insisted on walking the length of the hall by myself."

"He's becoming absolutely impossible," said Delaes, walking over to J'Vanni and taking his arm.

Draephus stared, blinking, then abruptly got up, nearly tossing Dahli onto the floor. "Are you all right? I had no idea you would be here. Let me help…"

"I can do it myself," he said, moving slowly over to a seat, Delaes following closely. J'Vanni managed to sit down without assistance, Piska still on his arm, eyeing the strangers warily.

"Should we bow?" asked Billy.

"Sorry," said Draephus. "Uh, Billy, K-Shot, Mystique, Gemma, Sigge, Vidar, Brian…" He paused as he realized the crowd in the room was slowly growing. "…and the rest of the milling throng whose names I don't really know… this is J'Vanni Dei Syncopius, and his friend Piska."

Brian Taylor fell to his knees with an audible thump. "You wrote that… glorious piece, that… I can't even *pronounce* it but I love it!"

"I may have," said J'Vanni warily.

Brian dove for the guitar he had brought, picking it up and playing a melody. J'Vanni smiled and nodded. "Yes, that is me."

"I love you!"

"He's taken," said Delaes, as Piska hopped from J'Vanni's arm over to the table where the snacks were being laid out.

"Piska…" said J'Vanni warningly.

Clearly undaunted, Piska helped himself to a piece of sushi, then hopped onto a couch to eat it.

"He's *so* well trained," said Draephus sarcastically.

"He *is* well trained," said J'Vanni. "I'll show you. Piska!"

The bird looked. J'Vanni asked him something in a language that Draephus suspected was Kryphisian. Piska lowered his head and shook it, muttering something in a voice like a vexed old woman.

"That's so cute!" said Mystique. "Oh who is a clever birdie?"

"Piska!" said the hawk. "Piska is clever birdie."

"*That* deserves another piece of sushi," said Mystique, selecting him one. "What does the name mean?"

"My grandmother used to call me that," said J'Vanni. "It means "Little Bother". But she meant it with love. And it truly does suit the bird. That is who he is impersonating when he shakes his head like that. I ask him what I am going to do with him, and he shakes his head and says children today are such a bother, he does not know what to do."

"Different planet, same issues," said Mystique.

"We are none of us so very different," said J'Vanni. He looked to Brian, who was still on his knees. "Are you quite all right?"

"I'm sorry, I'm having a major fan-boy moment."

J'Vanni stared at him, then looked to Draephus, who looked to Gemma.

"It's a *good* thing," she said.

They heard music start in the festival grounds, and Delaes got up to go to the window, opening the curtains wide.

"Party is starting," he said. He cocked his head. "Is that Carn-Crow I hear?"

"That be them," said Raski. He listened. "Wait. Are those little brats actually opening the festival with Sgt. Pepper's Lonely Heart's Club Band?"

"Should be fine," said Khandid. "I haven't seen a single Blue Meanie all day."

"And we're stuck in the Bad Gryphon Box for beating up Corey instead of sitting in the front row, teasing these boys," said Raski. "And speaking of bands appearing live and on stage at this festival…."

"I am telling you nothing you will just have to wait and find out like everyone else what we do," said Delaes.

"Are you appearing?" Brian asked J'Vanni.

"I am, and before Donsa CZimcocious begins demanding answers… I am saying nothing."

"You're evil, you know that," said Draephus.

"I have heard that rumour. Now since we cannot go outside because Khandid was a bad boy, we may as well open the windows and enjoy the music."

Delaes opened the window. Mars finished dressing, then applied some make-up before sitting on the edge of the bed to lace up his blackest boots with the highest heels.

"Are you being bad?" asked Raski.

"Me? No not at all. I'm in bed, resting, like a good little Gryphon. *Ai sikate,* my lovelies."

They watched as Mars took a running leap out the window. Several people hurried to the window to see what had happened to him, only to find him several storeys below them, climbing down a decorative pole erected just outside the hotel.

"Fuck me!" said Billy. "Did he know that pole was there? Tell me he at least knew the pole was there. How did he *do* that?"

"Mars has had a lot of practice playing with poles," said Khandid.

"How much practice has he had playing with law enforcement?" asked K-Shot. "Because I'm pretty sure down there waiting is what we refer as the po-po."

"And he is not going to be doing much running in those killer stilettos," said Mystique.

Billy stuck his head out the window. "GO MARS!"

"I have a question," said Mystique, turning to face Khandid as Mars tried to avoid going to jail.

"Which is good because we're highly questionable," said Khandid. "Draephus since you are getting up anyway, bring me some of the sushi."

Draephus stopped in his slow quest to get his own sushi, turning to look at him.

"Well you're already up!" said Khandid.

Draephus growled, thinking Khandid could use a smack on the butt some days. As he put sushi on a small plate, he let Piska taste a few bits before bringing them over to Khandid, who looked at them.

"What is this?"

"Well you *are* second in line to the throne, so I let Piska taste it for poison."

"Oh poor Piska!" said Gemma.

"YUCK!" screamed Piska.

"Piska says you have twenty minutes to live," said Delaes.

"Thank thee a bunch," said Khandid, eating his hawk-nibbled sushi. "Now ask your question, Donselle, I give you Imperial permission to do so."

"Well you and Yuri are married," said Mystique.

"That's more of an observation than a question, but yes."

"And Delaes and J'Vanni are married."

"Yes."

"Well my question is – what's the marriage ceremony like?"

"Ceremony?" queried Khandid.

"Well yeah! Like… what do you wear, where do you have it, what's the cake like, who performs the ceremony…."

Mystique's voice trailed off as the Sferkkaans stared at her.

"Well…." said Khandid, "the emperor usually has a sort of a ceremony where he or she writes down their names in the Book of Lines to keep track of who is related to whom in order to avoid marrying close relations, but…"

"You don't have weddings?!" exclaimed Gemma. "Like…. none?!"

"We agree to be together and to be family," said Khandid. "It's a promise we take very seriously."

"That's not fair!" said Gemma. "Every little girl alive dreams of her wedding day! And the pretty dress and the carriage and the church and her father walking her down the aisle to give her away to her new husband and…"

"Give you away?" said Khandid. "Like… here, this is my child, *you* can have her now?"

"Well not quite like that," said Gemma, flustered. "But that's kinda how it started, was like…. an agreement between the girl's father and…"

"So on your world, every little girl dreams of the day she will be put in a pretty dress and handed off to another man by her father like an unwanted puppy?" said Khandid.

"You're totally missing the point," said Gemma. "It's about the ceremony, and starting your life with someone! It's about love and making a vow to be with them through the good times and bad times, and celebrating that with friends and family! Khandid, where did you and Yuri get married?"

"In a five hundred year old cistern under the streets, while Kryphisian soldiers fire-bombed our homes above us," said Khandid. "I'm sorry, we haven't had a great deal of time to think about how best to dress up our children and give them away to someone. Usually we are just glad to have them alive and safe. You people really do consider the strangest and most insignificant things important."

"It *is* important!" insisted Gemma. "It's how families are made!"

"Families are made with devotion, not ceremony," said Draephus.

"Oh come on!" said Mystique. "None of you want a big romantic service with flowers and friends and really pretty clothes and…."

Her voice trailed off. The Sferkkaans and humans stared at each other, while Dahli went through her phone. Finally she showed a picture to Khandid, who looked at the screen. Draephus leaned over to also stare at a photo of a woman wearing a gown comprised of endless rows of white lace that covered her from her neck to her feet. Covering her face was an enormous white veil.

"You know what that looks like," said Draephus, "it looks like the thick froth that gathers at the corners of a destri's mouth when it's really tired."

"Why is she dressed like that?" asked Khandid.

"In case she's ugly?" suggested Raski.

"Well if she's ugly we have to assume the person she's marrying already knows it," said Khandid. "I mean unless they're giving her to a total stranger, which I can't see happening…"

"Well actually," said Gemma. "In some Earth cultures…"

"That's it!" said Khandid with much drama. "I am calling my cousin and we are officially banning, on this planet, the dressing of men, women, and children up like a massive ball of white destri spit, putting bags over their heads, and giving them away to random men. This is just not something a civilized race should be engaging in."

"I think there is a slight cultural difference that is not translating here," said J'Vanni.

"Well what did you and Delaes do for your wedding?" asked Mystique.

"Go ahead darling tell them about the flaming whip and the black eel-skin pants," said Delaes. "And the bed of iron spikes."

Mystique just stared as Sigge and Vidar threw up the horns. J'Vanni smiled as Piska hopped over to him to share a piece of sushi.

"Oh thank you, Piska, raw fish with bird spit is my favourite."

"Piska is clever birdie," said Piska.

"How are things going with our little Mars?" asked Khandid.

Billy watched the scene unfold below. "Well let's just say Mars fought the law and the law won, mostly because I think Mars really wanted to get caught by the big guy with all the muscles." He cocked his head. "Hey guys? What's the penalty on this world for wrapping your legs around a cop and shoving your tongue down his throat?"

Raski slapped a hand over his face, while Draephus sighed heavily.

"They are never going to let us come here again."

Chapter Thirty

Confining the Gryphons to one floor of the hotel did not turn out to be quite the punishment Mordrett had intended, as well-wishers came and went, turning the entire floor into one big party. Doors were opened, the food and booze flowed, and the music could be heard all the way into the lobby. Then it somehow turned into an impromptu wake for Straif when J'Vanni began playing "Goodbye Stranger" by Supertramp on an electric keyboard, and others joined in. It had long been one of Straif's very favourite songs, and Dahli and Draephus found themselves both on the same fire escape to share a cigarette and get away from the music. It would be a very long time before either of them could hear that song without feeling overwhelmed by emotion.

"He wanted to play it at the festival," Dahli said, looking in the direction of the gigantic stage. The world's biggest party was in full swing, with lights and music and pyrotechnics, and for the moment it just seemed dull and depressing.

"Yeah I know," said Draephus. "Wish he had the chance."

He noticed she was in tears again, and put an arm around her shoulders. "It will be okay, Fearless. Somehow, someway, it always is."

She nodded. "I know. I just feel so guilty."

"Guilty?" asked Draephus. "Why guilty?"

"Because I loved him so hard, but I was so worried about when he would have his baby. I know *he* was ready to have a baby but trust me, I'm *not* and I know it. I have a whole long list of things I want to do before I start talking to someone about a family, if ever I do, and I was so worried we'd break up after he had it, and now…"

Draephus sighed heavily, then put his arms around her and held her tightly. "Look, I'm sure it would have worked out. So don't beat yourself up about it, okay?" He paused, a thought coming to mind. "What was he going to name his baby?"

"Mautzi," she said dryly.

Draephus thought about that. "Mautzi. Uh… are you sure about that?"

"It was our first and only fight. Mautzi."

"Why 'Mautzi'?"

"When he was a kid he had a pet sand-diver named that."

Draephus sighed heavily. "Well he *was* only seventeen."

"I'm a year younger and even *I* knew it was a dumb name."

"Well maybe he would have changed his mind after he saw the baby. What did he want?"

"Little boy. Someone he could teach to walk in heels and wear makeup and do guy-stuff with." Dahli looked up at Draephus. "I've never seen you with your lines on. Not even when we went to the Cylinder. Raski wore his…"

"Partisan drug-runners don't have lines."

She shook her head. "I don't believe that. Draephus you've done so much…"

He dipped his head to kiss her nose. "Sometimes it is best for things to remain unknown, Fearless."

"But you…"

"Wear my lines on the inside. And believe me, it's not because I am ashamed of a single thing I have done."

She stared into his eyes for a few moments, then nodded. "Okay. I believe you. But one day you are going to let me do your lines. Okay?"

"One day, Fearless. Come on, let's get back to the party. Raski will be coming unglued."

"He's been a little edgy lately, hasn't he? I mean even for him," said Dahli.

"It's just the festival," said Draephus. "And he's all wound up about announcing our relationship. I wish he would get it over with."

"He *is* making a big deal out of this," said Dahli. "Why would he not just let you say 'Heia we're together now.' It's kind of silly."

"He's Raski," said Draephus. "He's also scared we'll both each meet a woman and somehow fall out of love."

"Do you think that's possible?" asked Dahli.

"I think my chances of falling out of love with Raski are roughly the same as my chances of falling off a building and learning to fly before I hit the ground."

"Oh please don't try that. I'd be really sad." She looked at the spray of dried blood across his shoulder from Mars' nosebleed. "But just so you know, when you pass out drunk tonight, I'm washing that coat again."

"Understood."

"Or I could paint like… little flowers and things over the blood to make…"

"No."

"Okay."

They returned to the party, noticing that room doors were open, and now there were family and friends as well as other musicians, and a few unknown people who seemed to have managed to sneak in. They reached Khandid's room to find some sort of fight going on between a couple of Corey's friends, and Mars and Raski.

"Oh this can't be good," said Draephus. "Dahli, help J'Vanni get out of the way, I can't imagine his sight is all that good, and he's probably frightened out of his mind. Fights are really *not* his thing."

Dahli nodded and went over to the tall man, who did indeed look frightened. '*Great,*' thought Draephus. '*J'Vanni finally leaves his apartment after six years and at his very first party, there's a fight.*'

Draephus moved to stand beside Raski, keeping one eye on Dahli. She wasn't exactly known for backing down from a bad situation, and he couldn't imagine she would tolerate more hateful comments about her recently deceased boyfriend. Then Delaes appeared to collect J'Vanni from her, and Draephus winced. Let's see, they had a Whip, recently awarded his blades, a half-breed faelin, and… Dahli. This was going to end up like a scene straight out of the old days in a matter of seconds.

"All right, take it easy…" Draephus said, as Delaes gently guided J'Vanni out of the way.

Corey's guitar player, Andy, got straight to the point. "Your faggot quint player put our friend in the hospital!"

"Well maybe your idiot friend shouldn't be dancing on the graves of our dead," said Mars.

"Big deal," said Andy. "Some dead queer boy with a bad case of constipation pretending it's…"

Draephus loved a good fight as much as the next guy, but with a live performance within a few days and arthritis eating his bones, he dove for cover and dragged Raski with him as Mars leapt.

"Šukating Whips!" Draephus complained as he held Raski down, hearing the crunch of bone. The fight was over in moments, with Andy unconscious on the floor, and his companion fleeing as fast as he was able to through the crowds. Draephus could hear a few people calling to each other "Did you get it?!" and he assumed they meant video footage of the fight. What was *with* these people? They'd take video of the transport that was about to run them over, he'd swear.

Draephus looked to Mars, who was panting. A couple people Draephus didn't know came to help Andy get off the floor, while K-Shot walked over to Draephus.

"Man I would have thought *you* were gonna take him out! Then I see Mars just… jump up like a bird or something! That was fucking crazy!"

"Never mess with a little guy in heels," said Draephus. "At least not on this world. Mars, are you okay?"

"No I am NOT all right, I am so NOT all right I could *kill*! SO IF ANYBODY ELSE WOULD LIKE TO MAKE A SICK REMARK ABOUT OUR DEAD FRIEND THEN EITHER LINE UP IN FRONT OF ME OR GET YOUR ŠUKATING ASSES OUT OF OUR ROOM NOW!"

Mystique walked up and gently folded her arms around him. "Oh sweetie I'm so sorry, some people can't help it if they're just mean."

"Will you please stop hugging all these guys that stand at about boob-height?" said K-Shot.

"We don't mind," said Mars, his face between the aforementioned boobs.

"Well I know *you* don't!" said K-Shot.

"I don't mind either," said Mystique.

Raski nudged Draephus. "Not that *I* mind you on top of me, but… you're getting heavy."

Draephus kissed his nose, then got to his feet. He looked to Dahli, and noticed she was standing with a puzzled expression on her face, watching her fingers. Tiny drips of blood were falling from her face, and he nearly pounced on her, turning her around. He almost had a coronary at the sight of her bloodied face.

"Do I still have an eye?" she asked.

She did still have an eye. She also had the most incredible set of slashes to her face imaginable. They were almost art. One went in a straight line above her right eyebrow, and four more curved almost gracefully down her right cheek. Then Mars noticed the interaction, and gasped, stepping away from Mystique.

"Oh, Dahli! I am so sorry!"

"Okay, this is the third room we've bled in, we have to stop this now!" said Draephus, feeling his heart do strange things in his chest. He was almost hysterical.

"I'm dying, aren't I?" asked Dahli, looking at the expression on Draephus' face.

He giggled, sounding like he was having a breakdown. Šukat he *felt* like he was having a breakdown.

"No," he finally managed to say. "No you are definitely not dying. ŠUKAT, DAHLI, WHAT WERE YOU THINKING!?"

"I wasn't!" she said, sounding like the teenager she actually was for once. "Andy said something bad about Straif, I lunged, and Mars leapt. Either I hit him or he hit me. I didn't *feel* anything, I just suddenly had blood in my eyes."

Khandid stepped closer, his blue eyes enormous at the sight. "Oh my."

"Dahli I am so sorry," said Mars.

"It's not your fault I'm stupid enough to jump in front of a Whip," she said.

Mars took her hand and led her into the bathroom to clean up. Draephus was shaking, almost ready to collapse from the stress of seeing Dahli bearing the claw marks of a Whip across her face.

"C'mon, K-Shot," said Draephus, slipping an arm around Raski. "Allow me to introduce you to the wonders of mushroom distillate. I need a drink."

K-Shot's mind was still on the image of Mars hugging his girlfriend. "He better watch his short little ass, I don't care how cute any of y'all think that is. How would he like it if I went up and hugged *his* girlfriend?"

"Well actually Mars is practitioner of *Nari nuisse*."

"What's that?" asked K-Shot.

"On your planet, you would call him a slut," said Raski. "So if he caught you hugging his girlfriend he would probably demand to be let into the cuddle."

"Y'all need Jesus," K-Shot grumbled.

"Are you sure Jesus needs us?" asked Raski. "Anyway Mars is very… liquid, both in himself and in the people he is attracted to. He kind of melts into whatever form he feels like at the moment."

Raski paused as he heard a few strains of music coming from

the far end of the hall, then turned to kiss Draephus.

"That's Sound of Darkness, I'm dying to go say heia to them."

Draephus returned the kiss, touching the long black hair. "Have fun."

Raski hurried off in the direction of the music. Draephus felt his bones began to protest, and he looked down at his hands. He suddenly felt a cold shot of terror rush through himself as he noticed the beds of his fingernails were discoloured. So now he had a new problem; cut back on the mushroom resin that kept the pain at bay, or keep taking it and free fall down into addiction.

"Everything okay?" asked K-Shot.

"No," said Draephus quietly. "But there's really not much I can do to fix it. C'mon, let's have a drink."

"So what's with the heels?" asked K-Shot as Draephus walked to his room to get the mushroom distillate.

"What do you mean?"

"Why do some guys have them and some not?"

"The heels show he is either a trained Whip or learning the craft. If he has blades in his boots, he's mastered the skill. Mars just got his blades. Khandi has had his blades for about eight years now. Generally you have to be very small to do it right, but there are exceptions."

"Yuri, right? The seven foot tall guy with all the hair."

"It is *very* impressive when Yuri fights."

"What about you and Raski?"

"Raski was a pilot in the Imperial air force, a very good one, I should add."

"And you?"

"I did what I had to. Here's my room."

They stepped into the room, and paused as they saw a tiny blue bird sitting on the bed. It twittered, then flew to the window and vanished, seemingly going straight through the curtains and glass with ease. Something stirred, and growled very softly. Bacca and Czanda seemed unconcerned, but hearing Raski's voice in the distance they escaped the room to go play with all the visitors. Draephus breathed in the strange scent of old earth and spring grass, knowing what it meant.

"Why did you come?" he asked the room softly. "Not that you are not always welcome, great one…"

"Draephus?" asked K-Shot. "What… are you talking to? And where is it?"

"It's a friend of mine," said Draephus. "A friend who must be respected."

K-Shot chose that moment to throw something very close to a mini-tantrum. "That's not good enough! Damn, man, every time I talk to you, it's all mysteries and half-answers and riddles. I want to *know*!"

Draephus grinned and shook his head. "Why K-Shot, you just said the magic phrase. In that case, come in, sit down, and have a drink. We will talk."

"Are you going to tell me what that thing in your room is?"

"Never refer to a daeha as a thing. They are great friends. They are powerful and bloody enemies. But the company of a daeha is advanced ohwendai magic. We will start a little more simply."

K-Shot stared at the small container of blue eye shadow he was handed. "This is where my masculinity hits the toilet, isn't it?"

"That depends very much on the planet, and whether you wish to learn what I have to teach, or prefer to hang on to meaningless things."

K-Shot stared at the blue powder for a moment, then said "Fuck it. Teach me this shit. I want to know."

Draephus nodded, then went for his shaman items, walking carefully past the great creature that he could not see, but sensed its outline. He poured it some of the mushroom distillate in an offering-bowl, then returned to K-Shot with his knife and bag.

"The first thing we need to do," said Draephus, "Is prove to you that everything I am about to say is true. Put on the powder."

K-Shot did, then looked at Draephus, his expression implying he thought at least part of this was a joke. Then he blinked, and Draephus watched comprehension come to him, knowing exactly what K-Shot could now see. He glanced to the daeha drinking from its bowl, and the small bird on Draephus' shoulder, and a woman standing at the far side of the room. She was black like Raski, with the luminous blue eyes, and she was staring at K-Shot as if she could not understand why his eyes were brown.

"We are surrounded by spirits and spirit creatures all the time," said Draephus. "The first step to becoming an ohwendai man is understanding this."

"But I put on the blue powder once before, and… I didn't see any of this!"

"The difference," said Draephus, "Is now you wish to know."

****

Draephus and K-Shot did not talk long; certainly not as long as they wished to. The brief conversation left K-Shot with a great deal to think about, and he left to go to his own room to ponder what he had learned. Not long after he departed, Draephus stepped out of his room, and found Gemma standing in the hall. The girl was in tears, and she was shaking as she leaned against the wall, a hand up to her mouth. Draephus closed his door, then slowly walked over to her.

"Gemma? Are you all right?"

She looked up at Draephus with large dark eyes, her brown hair damp from her tears. She whispered the three words that Draephus heard, but they may as well have been a roar.

"Mickie killed Straif."

He took her by the arm and hurried her into his room, closing the door behind himself before turning to Gemma once more.

"What did you say?" he asked.

She was trembling visibly, and again she whispered the words. "Mickie killed Straif."

"What makes you think that?" he asked.

"The night Straif died, I shared some of my chocolates with everybody. Well they made Straif sick, and Dahli and Diza as well. I put them back in my room, and brought out a couple other things. Then at one point, I found Mickie in my room. I thought he came in *after* me, but… well I put the chocolates away, and then I sort of forgot about them. Tonight I opened the box, and… and I noticed the chocolate I picked up tasted really strange and I spit it out. So I began looking them over, and there were needle marks in the bottoms. Every single chocolate had been injected with something. And I think… I think Mickie had somehow unlocked the door and been in there earlier, tampering with my candy. And I think Straif…"

"You think maybe because he was already fragile that it was enough to kill him."

She nodded. "And the doctors here probably wouldn't know to look for it." She wiped at her eyes. "I don't know if you can check for the drugs, since he's been dead so long, but something needs to be done. He may not have intended to hurt Straif, but he did intend to hurt *someone*. And I know now he's not going to stop until someone makes him quit."

Draephus nodded. "Okay. Well, you…did the right thing."

"What will you do to him?" she asked.

"I'll…" he swallowed hard. "I'll talk to him. We will get this straightened out."

"You won't hurt him?"

"No."

"Promise me."

This was easier to say. "I swear to you, Gemma, that I will not hurt him."

She looked at him with wet brown eyes. "Dahli says you wouldn't lie."

"No. I wouldn't."

She smiled faintly. "Thanks Draephus. I knew that you would know what to do."

"I'll take care of the situation," said Draephus softly. "You go have a nice soak in the bath and relax."

"Maybe later. I think I'll go for a walk instead."

She left, and Draephus shut the door, sighing loudly. "Since when did I become the champion of lost Earth-Children?"

He happened to glance in the direction of the daeha. It was staring back at him with a very stern gaze.

"I did not lie. I will *talk* to Mickie. And he will take no injury from *my* hand."

It seemed satisfied. He watched it as it climbed onto the bed to nap, then quietly left. He did not ask it why it had followed him to Charlendine. That was not his business. What he did was take his telecom out of his pocket once he was in the hall and call a number. Moments later he heard Khandid pick up.

"Heia?"

"Heia Khandi? This is Draephus. How do you feel about sneaking out of the hotel together?"

"Are we doing something naughty?"

"Yes. Tell no one. We're gonna pay little Mickie Pastors a very nasty visit. I'll meet you in your room."

It was all such a familiar dance, executed quickly and with

elegance. It took Khandid only minutes to dress up as his alter ego; a woman of the North Continent in black and silver, a set of black metal wings in his hair for a clip, his eyes, lips and cheeks all accentuated with black. Then they slipped away; Khandid the assassin, Draephus the back-up in the event Khandid got into trouble, although Draephus doubted Mickie would give them much concern.

There were so many people at the party that no one seemed to notice either of them as they slipped away; heading to the fire escape and down the stairs. Draephus trailed after Khandid in the shadows as they hunted their mark, eventually locating Mickie by the stage. It took very little to lure him in the woods.

Draephus kept his word to Gemma. He never touched Mickie.

****

Dahli found herself somewhat alone; meaning there was no one in the milling throng of rock stars she knew. Everyone seemed to have vanished, so she was simply one lone little roadie in a crowd when she heard a loud female voice shout "WE FINALLY ŠUKATING MADE IT!"

Dahli had heard of Anazampini, and she had certainly bought more than her fair share of their music cylinders, but their lead vocalist Khymiria was half Southern and half Eastern and that meant she stood roughly seven feet tall. She strode into the room with a bottle in each hand, her long black hair hanging down her back, her intensely blue eyes seeming to glow. She was big and broad-shouldered and imposing, and behind her were her four band-mates, no less impressive in height and build. That included Comtess Rae, who wrote most of the band's songs, and, like Yuri Stracona, said little, along with Mira Belamia, Astrin Chamin, and Saulefey Quintora. They were greeted with the sort of enthusiasm that implied most people in the room knew them and liked them. Then Dahli found herself staring up at Khymiria.

"Heia!" Khymiria said to the terrified teen. "Never seen you before. Who are you?"

"Dahli," she said softly, "Dahli Sandiniti."

Khymiria stared at her, blinking, then set down the bottles and hugged her tightly.

"Oh hon I am so sorry about Straif. We all loved him so much.

You were there, weren't you?"

"Yeah," said Dahli, fighting back the tears. Funny how every time she thought she had dealt with his death…

"Who are you here with?"

Dahli sniffed, hating herself for falling apart like this. She was supposed to be stronger. "Well I was here with my friend Diza, but she went to bed, and my friend Gemma went for a walk, and my friend Czamkiar crept off with his boyfriend, and I have *no* idea where Draephus went…"

"Well you stick close to me. I want to hear all about Straif before he passed. Did he ever pick a name for his baby?"

"Mautzi."

Khymiria stared at her. "Please tell me you are joking."

"It was our first and only fight."

Khymiria sighed. "Well he *was* only seventeen…"

"I'm only sixteen and I would never name a baby 'Mautzi'!"

"Yeah but he was a boy and their brains don't work right. There is a reason that males don't get pregnant in nature, and names like 'Mautzi' top the list. We should go dig him up and yell at him."

Dahli swallowed hard. "We don't have to dig, he's in Draephus' cat….a…. combs…"

She fell apart, crying hard. Khymiria sat beside her, putting an arm around her, while others gathered close, concerned. Dahli fought to get herself together, hearing someone ask Khymiria who the kid was.

"Dahli Sandiniti, Straif's friend."

She felt someone sit down on her right side and offer her a drink. She accepted it, recognizing the man who gave it to her as the quinticord player from Rhaksault. She wished she remembered his name, he seemed nice.

"Heia," she said.

"Heia," he said in return. "I knew Straif too. We were all very sad when he died. What… what happened?"

Dahli told the story, recounting how they had been gathered in the common room on Gemma's ship, and how he had simply fallen asleep.

"Well there are worse ways to go," said Khymiria.

"Yeah," said Dahli quietly. "At least he never found out the baby had died two days previously."

"Yeah he didn't need to know that," agreed Khymiria. She lightly touched the bandages over Dahli's face. "What happened here?"

"Mars David and I tried to kill the same groutnoll at the same time. I caught his glove-blades."

"Ooooh... Whip-lines," said Khymiria. "Let me see."

Dahli said nothing as Khymiria carefully removed the bandages and gazed at the injury. "*That* is a work of šukating *art*. You should ink it."

"Ink...?"

"Add colour to the open injury before it heals. Wait! I have my kit, I'll be right back!"

Dahli watched the woman dart out of the room, then looked to the guy from Rhaksault.

"Should I be scared?"

"Yes," he said.

Scruffin' lovely.

Dahli squeaked in surprise as Khymiria suddenly re-appeared, kit in hand, and straddled Dahli's lap, sitting on her.

"Let's do a fire line!"

"The quint player and I took a vote and we're scared," said Dahli.

"Yeah but Kalryk's just jealous he won't look as cool as you when it's done."

"Is this permanent?"

"Abso-tively. Is that a problem?"

"Well my sister sort of blames everything stupid I do on a friend of mine..."

"No problem. I'll make sure she knows your friend had nothing to do with it. Now let's give you the most fabulous ink ever..."

Dahli didn't know if she really wanted the lines immortalized, but...well... when was she ever going to get line art done by Khymiria at a party full of rock stars ever again?

"I'd love to get video of this," she said.

Several individuals whipped out phones. Well maybe these Earth people were good for something after all. Dahli just let her head fall back, and closed her eyes as Khymiria got to work.

"This is a very old form of West Continent art, meant to

display a warrior's battles," said Khymiria.

"But I wasn't fighting Mars, I just got in his way," said Dahli.

"That's fine! Hey you know they say if you face down a Whip and survive then he becomes your true love."

"That's not the version I heard," said Kalryk.

"What did you hear?" asked Khymiria, carefully opening and cleaning the cuts to apply the colour.

"That if you face down a Whip and live you are marked for death."

Dahli opened one eye and looked at Khymiria. She could tell their expressions matched.

"I like your interpretation better," said Dahli to Khymiria.

"So do I. Eyes closed."

Dahli closed her eyes and relaxed, letting Khymiria work. It did not take too terribly long, but Khymiria's weight seemed to grow as she sat. At last she put her needles away and got off Dahli's lap.

"Go look!"

Dahli went into the bathroom, and blinked at herself in the mirror. The cuts were now transformed into vibrant art, starting off black at the base, slowly turning to heated burning red and yellow at the ends. It was beautiful and powerful, and made her different, but not in the way her time at the Centre had. Somehow the lines erased that inner darkness, blotting it out with one powerful, glorious swipe.

Dahli quietly locked the door, not wanting to be interrupted, and gazed at herself. She'd gone from fifteen to sixteen in one long, strange, circuitous route, gaining and losing so much, and just... sweeping everything into a kind of mental closet, not really ready or willing to look at it yet. But it had left its mark on her nonetheless, and would be there forever. Like this swipe.

Mars had accidentally given all that had transpired this year a symbol, and Khymiria had brought it to life. Dahli was changed, dramatically, in an undeniable way, and no longer the person she had been. She was wiser, more learned, and for once in her life understood just how much of a child she had been at the beginning of this adventure. Things were not always black or white, right or wrong, good or evil. There was a whole spectrum between, and learning to step back and see that before proceeding was what would get her through life.

She turned off the light, opened the door, and walked out to face Khymiria.

"I šukating *love* it," she said.

"Who's that skinny woman?" said a voice. "Do I know her?"

Dahli turned to see Harli, Also Not Steve perched on his shoulder, and she pounced on him, hugging him tight. He returned the hug, then stepped back to look at her.

"Now what have you been up to?"

"Stuff."

"Uh huh. What did you do to get a Whip mad at you?"

"I accidentally got in the way of somebody he wanted to hurt because I wanted to hurt him first."

Harli rolled his eyes. "I knew you were trouble the moment I saw you."

She sat down next to Kalryk, Khymiria sitting down as well as Harli eased himself into a chair facing them. Kalryk cleared his throat, then asked ever-so-casually; "So… what happened to Straif's Legri?"

Dahli managed a small smile. "You mean the Legri Ice Storm with the wraparound bridge and czilbein pick-ups? The one with the whitegem-infused lacquer finish, and the growler screwed right into the wood to give it that signature sound?"

"Yeah." He was practically salivating.

"I have it. Straif left it to me."

He slithered off of the couch to land on his knees before her. "What would you want for it?"

"You don't have that much," said Dahli.

"No, really, what do you…?"

"You do not have that much," Dahli enunciated. "Not in trinta, not even in blood. That is all I have left of Straif that truly is a piece of him, and even if I can't play it well yet, the only way it will leave my possession is when I die."

"But…"

Dahli pointed to the door. "You know what that is. Use it. That instrument goes nowhere, even if I don't have the first idea why Straif left it to me."

"CAN I JUST BORROW IT?!" He fell to the floor and onto his back, gazing up at her with large dark eyes. "Just for the concert!"

Dahli looked at Khymiria. "Did he just roll over and beg?"

"I think he did," said Khymiria. "In a moment he may even wet himself."

"I can do that!" he said. He took a drink and poured it over his chest. "There! I wet myself!"

Dahli sighed. "Well I may be talked into loaning it." She drew out her telecom and called a number. "Just let me get Raski to write up the terms."

Khymiria laughed. "You're kidding. Raski Jervyas. As in…"

"As in the sepulchord player for the Gryphons, I know them."

Those gathered exchanged glances, then Khymiria cleared her throat. "Are you the kid who beat the guts out of Draephus, stole his conni and broke into a school to steal a dead faelin?"

"And then broke out of a detention centre and firewalked through Avalair…"

"Forced me to take her in," said Harli.

"Yeah that's me," said Dahli.

Khymiria picked at the edge of Dahli's shirt. "And the best they could do is make you a roadie?"

"I *wanted* to be a roadie, I get to pet the plants this way."

She kicked off her boots and rested her feet on Kalryk's stomach. She giggled when he didn't protest, though he did check how clean her socks were. After a few minutes, Raski showed up, surprisingly sober. He crossed his arms and stared at her.

"Dahli, why are you using Kalryk for a foot warmer? Granted it's a job he certainly qualifies for…."

"Šukat you, Jervyas."

"He wants to borrow the Legri," said Dahli.

"Does that mean Khandid gets to borrow it after?" Raski asked hopefully.

Dahli sighed. "I am *not* opposed to letting its voice be heard, I am *very much* opposed to the idea of losing it. Straif really wanted to be at this festival, so I think it would be a great way to have him here to share the Legri, but if it vanished I would be physically ill the rest of my life."

"Right," said Raski. "Let me work something out…"

"First things first," said Harli. "Can you play it yet?"

Before Dahli could answer, Raski was off like a shot. He returned quickly with the Ice Storm, holding it like a religious artefact. Several people rose to their feet at the sight of it, and there was the flash of a number of cameras. The room became quiet, and Raski handed it to her. Once more Dahli was struck by the weight of it, wondering what strange construction accounted for it, and the sound. Dahli sheepishly looked around, and swallowed nervously.

"Before I start," she said, "I want to point out that it only knows three cords."

"Perfectly fine," said Raski, "Khandid's has the same problem."

Dahli felt a strange tingling in her hands, and her heart and stomach were at war. She drew a deep breath, then turned it on, feeling as if she could pass out any moment.

Thank all the gods that went before she'd been practicing. She closed her eyes, and started playing 'Hill of Fire', a piece by J'Vanni Dei Syncopius. It was fast, though nowhere near the speed Straif played at. It was, however, quite complex, and she knew if she opened her eyes, she'd make a mess of it.

If she let herself think about who was watching she'd probably fall to the floor and suck her thumb.

She was not perfect, but she got through it without either mangling the song or making a fool of herself, and when she opened her eyes, she saw Harli was grinning at her, shaking his head.

Later that night, someone she didn't know emailed her a photo of that moment, her holding the Legri, Harli facing her, both smiling. Her feet were still on Kalryk, and standing beside her was Raski. She cherished that picture the rest of her life.

By morning, Straif Mannechek's beloved white quinticord was on stage, being played by Kalryk of Rhaksault, while off to one side Mordrett Stratavarus' Imperial Bird of Prey held watch over it.

****

It was the fourth day of the Year End Festival. All the lesser-known bands had played their sets, save for Mickie Pastors, who was oddly absent. Now it was strictly the biggest and best bands until the show closed tomorrow evening, ending with the Gryphons. Dahli spent the better part of the day with Draephus, listening to the music and watching him pull at his fingers, as if they bothered him. She noticed his fingernails seemed to be turning black as well, and she was worried for him, but had no idea what to say or do. So instead she stayed beside him, watching the bands they wanted to see, taking off to do other things when the band wasn't one that interested them. At the moment, she and the Gryphons were perched like a row of crows on a large decorative arch. Dahli was looking down at how far the ground was.

"I'm not sure people were meant to be this high up," said Dahli.

"Then why did they invent aircraft?" asked Raski. "Besides, this is the best seat."

"Especially if one of us falls off," said Dahli. "We'll splat right on the stage and the people in the front will end up wearing us."

"Those people paid extra to get smacked with a broken bleeding body," said Khandid.

"Eeeeyeeeewwww…." said Dahli.

The first band of the day had been Anazampini, and they had kicked so much ass on stage that, by the time the set was over, the band from Earth that was to follow them didn't want to go out. Dahli could hear the man in charge of making sure the bands were all on time screaming halfway across the festival grounds.

"YOU TELL THOSE PRECIOUS ŠUKATING DAINTY GLASS STATUES TO GET THEIR BUTTS ON STAGE! WE DIDN'T PAY FOR THEM TO COME ALL THE WAY FROM EARTH JUST TO HIDE IN THEIR DRESSING ROOM AND CRY BECAUSE SOMEBODY WAS BETTER THAN THEM!"

Eventually, Knights of Blackness showed themselves, but clearly had their feelings hurt by getting their asses handed to them by a pack of Sferkkaan women. They played a short set, sulking all the while, and did not come back for an encore. When K-Shot followed after them, Mystique in place as back-up vocals, he announced that Knights of Blackness were back stage accepting their award for Biggest Babies in Rock.

The ensuing fight later that night between K-Shot and the lead vocalist of the Knights would be the stuff of legend for many years to come.

Currently, in order to make up for the large gap left in the programming by Knights of Blackness' poor sportsmanship, an Earth comedian named Erick Holly stepped out to keep people amused while Vidar and Sigge's band rushed to prepare to go on early. Erick had made himself wildly popular with his knowledge, understanding, and obvious affection for Sferkkaan culture and the people, and had been invited to the festival to act as Master of Ceremonies and to fill in any blank spots, such as the one left by a certain band. He was greeted with enthusiasm as he stepped out, then stopped in the middle of the stage and pointed right at the decorative arch.

"Anyone noticed these little birdies?"

People looked up. Mars waved coyly, as Draephus smoked, hat down low, shades firmly in place, as was the infamous coat. Erick tilted his head and looked at Draephus.

"Do those come off?"

"He has another set on underneath," said Khandid.

Erick considered Draephus, then looked to the teen girl beside him. "And you are....?"

"Dahli," she called.

Erick indicated Draephus. "Is he as mean as he looks?"

"No he's really very sweet!" she called, smiling.

"Really. What's that on his coat?"

Dahli looked then shrugged. "Just some blood. But he's a sweetie, really!"

"Uh huh. And you are...?"

"His sister."

"So in other words you *have* to say he's sweet because he knows where you live."

Dahli hugged Draephus, who continued to stare at Erick as if giving very serious thought to eating him. Dahli and the other Gryphons knew Draephus really did not care for being teased in public, so he could well have been. Raski leaned close to Draephus.

"Please don't kill the Earth-man, at least not on stage."

Draephus gave no indication he had heard, and Erick fortunately decided to leave off teasing him. Dahli suspected he too had seen the infamous broadcast where Draephus launched himself at Astellis Monct. Instead Erick looked to Mars.

"How do you plan on getting down from there? In *heels*, I have to add."

Mars immediately began to flirt. "Give me a reason to come down and I will show you."

Erick just stared, blinking, as if uncertain he'd heard right. "I'm sorry?"

"Give me a reason."

Erick continued to blink. "Give you a reason....?"

Mars nodded. Erick stared up and shook his head. "I'm sorry,

I just never had a major rock star try to pick me up in front of a crowd. Actually I never had one try to pick me up. You know what? What the hell, uh…. Late lunch in my room? Is that okay?"

Draephus did not react as Mars got to his feet, stepping onto Raski's shoulder and using him as a stair to get onto Draephus'. Perched delicately, clearly conscious of where the lethal blades on his boots were, he leapt forward, clearing roughly ten feet of open air to catch hold of a supporting wire that helped anchor the arch with his hands. He then managed to get his legs around it as he slid down the wire, descending swiftly, then releasing to drop gracefully to the stage. He fluffed his hair, then gave Erick a smouldering look from over his shoulder before walking off stage, his swaying body alive with invitation. Erick looked to the audience.

"I'm actually heterosexual, so….uh…. yeah. I have absolutely no idea what to do in this situation."

"It's all right!" shouted Raski. "He comes with a full set of instructions!"

"Thank you. Uh… yeah. I'll just say that to my girlfriend. *"It's okay, honey, he comes with instructions!"* I'm sure she'll love it."

"She might," called Raski. "He goes for women, too."

Erick played with the Gryphons for a little while longer, until Sigge let him know they were ready to take the stage. Mars remained absent for a couple hours, returning just as Sigge and Vidar were wrapping up their set. He scaled the arch easily, returning to his place and sitting down.

"How was he?" asked Raski.

"Depressingly nice and devoted to his girlfriend," said Mars. "We had lunch. I can't say I didn't try, but… well. No play-time for me."

"What about that fine-looking Major?" asked Khandid.

Mars sighed. "He already told me that he has six children and, in the event a relationship develops, he's not taking them to Second City. And I am not moving here and away from the only family I have. So… that's the end of that. I even called Anthony but he said he wasn't coming back. So! What band is up next?"

"Bad Influence," said Khandid. "The band that is apparently no longer in existence and has one member deceased. They wanted to have the last set of the day for some reason, but the final group wouldn't switch."

"I can't wait to see what they do," said Draephus.

The stage at the moment was empty save for instruments and a large screen behind them. Then on the screen appeared the image of the inside of one of the Gryphons' studios. There came a sound like a door being unlocked, and the audience fell silent, curious. There was the quick clip of heels on a wooden floor, and then Straif appeared on the screen, looking around as if checking to see if he was alone, unaware he was being taped. He was just as Dahli remembered; bright-eyed and playful, and he seated himself at an enormous brilliant white keyboard. He played a few notes, then let out a startled yell as Rysta's voice could suddenly be heard in the background.

"I thought you were sleeping!"

"I thought I was too," said Straif, "but someone's in the nap room farting like they're getting paid to do it."

The audience laughed. The laughter only increased with the next two words.

"Probably Mars."

"As soon as I die I'm going to hurt him," said Mars. On the screen, Straif looked to a person who could not be seen.

"Gonna play with me, Rysta?"

"Yeah, okay."

Rysta himself walked out on stage then, picking up his quinticord, as another person Dahli did not recognize took his place behind the drums. Then Straif began to play a song she knew far too well, as Delaes emerged to do the back-up vocals.

"Well," said Raski, "Delaes did say that Bad Influence would play the festival. And Straif did really want to do Goodbye Stranger."

"I do not fart," said Mars indignantly.

"Yeah you do," said Draephus. "You all right, Fearless?"

She nodded, feeling tears burn her eyes. "I'm fine. He wanted to play this festival with Bad Influence so badly. I'm glad he got to. He's barely showing there, isn't he?"

"Yeah I think this footage was taken not long after you met him," said Draephus.

"Is that Studio Three back at our place?" asked Khandid warily.

"Yes," said Draephus, grinning.

"And... do those cameras play all the time?"

"Every time someone opens the door and comes in," said Raski happily. "They're security cameras."

Khandid slowly turned his head to look at Yuri, who was returning the look with a matching facial expression. Dahli simply raised an eyebrow.

"Boy I sure am glad Straif and I changed our minds about fooling around in the studio."

"Where's the tape?" demanded Khandid.

"Could be anywhere, you know how these things get misplaced," said Draephus, grinning.

Raski began to snicker. "I just had no idea you could achieve that particular range of vocals. Falsetto, wouldn't you say, Draephus?"

He shook his head. "Nah. Definitely soprano."

"Yuri and I would just like you to know that we hate you both. And why would you watch it, anyway?!"

"Oh how could we not?" said Mars. "You're just over five feet and Yuri is almost seven, we've been dying to know how you two…"

"*Please* tell me no one else saw that."

Mars shook his head. "No one other than the audio tech who was behind the tinted glass at the time. But I have to say, leaving just the heels on was a really nice touch."

"I hate all of you, and so does Yuri. Don't you, Yuri?"

"Whatever you say," said Yuri.

"There, I hope you're happy, you've traumatized him," said Khandid indignantly.

"Did we ruin his life?" asked Dahli happily.

"Just watch the show," said Draephus, ignoring the fat grey bird that came to perch on him.

"I do not fart all night!" snapped Mars.

They watched as Straif Mannechek managed to live out his dream of appearing at the Year End Festival with Bad Influence, even if it was posthumously. They worked their way through four of the newest songs, Straif on screen switching from the keyboard to his coveted Legri, playing his heart out, keeping up with his three bandmates as he had in life. Clearly it would take more than death to slow him down. Then halfway through the fifth song, Dahli got to see exactly how hard Delaes and his bandmates had worked to keep Straif alive for one last show, when on the screen Straif shook his head and stopped playing.

"It's not right," he complained.

On stage, Delaes looked back to the figure on the screen. "What's not right?"

"This whole section, this progression, it's.... šukating awful."

Rysta looked to Straif. "Sweetie, you wrote it."

"It's not that bad," said Straif.

The audience laughed, and so did Dahli, losing herself in the act, pretending he was alive, if just for a little while. On the screen Straif looked to Delaes.

"It needs a millitron."

"Oh like that one over there," said Delaes, pointing to the far right of the stage, as an enormous white millitron was rolled out. Dahli and the Gryphons all drew a breath and sat up, recognizing it. On the screen, Straif looked to the instrument.

"Oh! Yes! Like that."

"And someone to play it," said Rysta.

"Yeah and someone to play it," conceded Straif. "I can't, it's too complicated."

Draephus actually leapt to his feet, which, considering the height he and his friends were currently at, could have had serious repercussions. He actually screamed with joy when he saw the tall figure with the long white hair appear on stage.

"GIA!"

J'Vanni went to the millitron and seated himself, not hearing Draephus over the roar of the crowd, clearly a little flustered at being in front of such a large gathering. He began to play, but something about the music sounded strange, and the other members of Bad Influence waited, clearly uncertain what they were hearing. J'Vanni paused, then gazed at his sheet music, as if noticing something. Flushing red visibly, he reached out to turn the music the correct way up. There was a tremendous roar of laughter, and Delaes went over to his husband to hug him.

"Poor J'Vanni," said Dahli, trying not to giggle.

"Not an auspicious start to his first ever live appearance," said Draephus.

"This is either going to be complete rubbish," said Mars, "or utterly mind-blowing."

"Will it ruin your life?" asked Raski.

Mars just laughed. On stage, J'Vanni Dei Syncopius drew a steadying breath and began to play. On cue, Straif joined in, then Rysta and the drummer. Moments later Delaes joined in. The Gryphons watched, exchanging meaningful glances.

"Way too šukating good," said Raski. "We may have to hurt them. And sit down before you fall, you're making me nervous."

Draephus did. Dahli took his arm, smiling at him, as overhead the clouds thinned to a soft white layer, and the world was dry for perhaps the only time in Dahli's life. On the screen Straif Mannechek played, and she let herself forget for just a little while that he wasn't beside her anymore.

The set slowly came to an end. As the final song played, Delaes set aside the microphone and walked away. Moments later, as the keyboards ended, J'Vanni gathered his music and walked away also, then the drummer. Finally Rysta's part ended, and he too set aside his instrument and silently left the stage, which left only Straif. Then, as if noticing he was alone, he looked up and around. He quickly became indignant.

"Heia Randerick don't even THINK about leaving without me!" He set aside his quinticord, and rose from his seat. "Oh sure! Real classy guys, leave the pregnant kid to pick up!"

He hurried off screen. Moments later, the light went off, and then there came the sound of a door closing.

For a long time, there was not a sound.

Chapter Thirty-One

"You were absolutely fantastic," Raski said to Delaes.

Outside in the festival grounds, people were drinking and laughing and playing music of their own. Fireworks were shot off at random intervals, and in the centre of the grounds, a great dragonbird made of fragrant twigs from a type of tree Dahli did not know burned strange colours, releasing a scent like rain and flowers. People danced as winter's last hours slipped away, and she thought she might like to join them as she watched out the fourth floor window, where the Gryphons were once again up to their ears in friends and revellers.

"Of course we were," said Rysta as he stood beside Delaes. "Although the band that had to follow after us had a few choice words to say about our performance."

"They should have just given you the final spot and been done with it," said Raski.

"They had some silly idea that they should be the closing act," said Rysta. "But we worked hard at that performance. Do you have any idea how hard it was to edit that tape into something we could actually use for a three hour set?"

"So this was tape taken over a long period of time," said Raski.

"During the time we were all jamming in the studio," said Rysta. Dahli's eyes widened and her blood ran cold as Rysta turned to her and said; "And you're becoming really good on those drums."

Dahli flushed red as Raski looked at her sharply.

"You were playing Draephus' drums?!"

"Just a little!" she said.

"There's a two hour set on one of the tapes," said Rysta. "With our little Straif playing look-out. When he wasn't jamming with her, that is."

"Please don't tell Draephus," said Dahli.

"Tell Draephus what?" asked Draephus as he approached the trio.

"That Dahli was playing your drums," said Raski.

Dahli hid behind her hands, awaiting the dressing-down of a lifetime. Draephus for the moment just seemed puzzled.

"The small set we keep at the studio," said Draephus. Raski gave him a kiss and hurried off on business of his own.

"Uh-uh," said Rysta. "The big set. The one you take on tour with all those fancy irreplaceable hand-made drums. That monster set that you play standing up because if you sat down, you couldn't reach all of them."

Dahli peered at Draephus from between her hands. He didn't look angry. He looked like Rysta had just declared himself to be a bipedal newt. Slowly he shifted his eyes from Rysta to Dahli.

"The *big* set," said Draephus, clearly not believing this girl he had adopted, who was significantly shorter than himself, could handle his drum set. "No. Do not believe it. That set is *huge*, even I have trouble setting it up so I can reach everything."

"She was playing it," said Rysta.

Dahli blinked at Draephus, who just stared back at her.

"Are you gonna hurt me?" asked Dahli warily.

"No, right now I am too busy not believing you can even reach half the drums I have."

"I have footage!" said Rysta.

"Go get it."

Rysta did. Dahli just looked at Draephus with enormous frightened eyes.

"Please don't be angry."

"I'm not angry. I am deeply confused."

"I would never do anything stupid to hurt them, you know that, I know how important they are…"

He stared at her, clearly torn between anger and something else. Rysta returned with a recording cylinder and plugged it into the visual. Dahli hid behind her hands as she heard Straif's voice coming out of the device.

"He's gone!"

Moments later, Dahli herself scooted into view, heading straight for the drums and positioning herself behind them, reaching for the sticks. She then pulled over a short padded stool and stood on it. Straif appeared beside her moments later, and Draephus stared in silence as Dahli and Straif proceeded to play "Rain Forest". Dahli peered from between her fingers to look at Draephus to see if he was about to throw her out a window.

"Admit it," said Rysta. "You're impressed. That is *not* an easy piece to play."

Draephus kept watching. Dahli was sick to her stomach, thinking her close friendship with this man she loved and admired had just come to an end. Certainly he did *not* look pleased. Others gathered to watch what was on the visual, while Dahli just kept her eyes on Draephus. Yeah. He was *not* amused. Those drums were priceless, and now that she owned Straif's quinticord, she truly understood just how large her transgression was. Slowly he turned to look at her.

"Dahli…"

"I will never touch them again, I swear. Never. Please don't eat me."

"I am not going to eat you. I am not even going to kill you," he said, his voice *far* too calm for her comfort. "But when we get home, I am sitting your little butt down in my hall, handing you a piece of wood, a chisel, and some animal skins, and you are going to start making your *own* drums so you will never be tempted to play *mine* again."

He probably thought it was the worst punishment he could dish out. Certainly most people would be dreading the process of hand-carving a South Continent style drum. Dahli however did not quite see it that way.

"REALLY?!" she squealed. She then let out a screech of delight that caused the faelins to start howling as she pounced on Draephus and hugged him. "THANK YOU THANK YOU THANK YOU THIS IS THE MOST WONDERFUL THING EVER I LOVE YOU!"

"Yeah *that* really showed her," said Rysta dryly.

Draephus looked down at Dahli, softening visibly. "Never again, okay Fearless?"

"Never again," she said softly. "I'm sorry."

"What would you have done if I walked into the studio?"

"Honestly? Probably dropped to the floor in a foetal position, sucked my thumb and wet myself."

"So it's not like you thought I would only be a little annoyed," said Draephus.

"Well," said Dahli, "I figured you would eventually forgive me, and I didn't think you'd be angry enough to throw me out of your life, but I knew you'd be really upset."

"So why did you do it?" he asked.

Dahli released him and cringed slightly. "Because I think I'm a drummer."

He stared at her for a long moment, then laughed very quietly, putting an arm around her shoulders.

"Yeah I think we share a similar affliction."

Just then Khymiria approached the pair, her arm around the waist of her sepulchord player, Saulefey Quintora.

"Hey Draephus, are you aware that Raski is in the bathroom, throwing up and crying?"

Draephus sighed. "Yeah he's always nervous before a show."

"Earlier he was eating a plate of steamed kaisa."

Draephus seemed to consider this. "He hates kaisa."

"We *all* hate kaisa," grumbled Dahli.

Khymiria and Saulefey stared at Draephus, as if waiting for him to catch the implication of what they were telling him.

"Draephus," said Saulefey, "Crying, eating kaisa, throwing up…"

"Well the crying and the throwing up he does before every show. Not sure I understand why he's eating kaisa, though. I've seen him roast a dead rat before eating a kaisa."

"He's also gaining weight," said Khymiria.

Draephus stared at the two women. They stared back. Then Khymiria leaned forward to give him a kiss and a pat on the shoulder.

"It's okay, we love you anyway."

They walked away. Draephus looked to Dahli, confused.

"Am I missing something?"

Dahli stared at him. The implications seemed pretty clear to *her*, though she had no idea if they were true. "Really? *Really*?"

"Well am I?"

"Oh yeah."

"Are you gonna tell me?"

"No."

"I hope you realize you just ruined my life."

Dahli giggled. Moments later, Gemma walked up to the pair.

"Hey have either of you seem Mickie?"

"No," said Dahli. "But we really were not looking for him, either."

"Well normally he's dogging my every step, but I haven't seen him since Day One. He didn't even show up for his set and that's not like him. I saw him leave the festival grounds with some tiny little pretty High Northern girl. I tried to tell her not to, but…"

"Was she wearing heels?" asked Draephus. Dahli thought there was something off about his tone – a bit too casual, but maybe he suspected something and didn't want to worry Gemma.

"Yeah, real killer ones, black with a silver blade straight up the back and onto the heel."

"Did she have a set of black wings in her hair?"

"Yeah, beautiful ones, made of some sort of shining black metal. Why? Do you know her?"

"No, but I know what she is, and I have a feeling Donsa Pastors is now a pile of meat feeding the wildlife. I'll look into it."

He left hastily. Gemma took Dahli's hand, looking at her.

"Who was that girl?" asked Gemma. "Who did Mickie leave with?"

"You know what a Whip is, right?" asked Dahli.

"Yeah I know it's a type of fighter from the North Continent, and Khandid is one. Mars too, I think. That's why they wear those heels." Gemma went pale. "The black heels and wings mean she's a female Whip, right?"

"Worse," said Dahli. "On the Eastern Continent we're pretty relaxed about who intermingles with whom, mostly because we got the worst of the poisonings and the population was so decimated that… things like that really became rather pointless. In some remote parts of the North Continent, however, where they were not affected by the poisonings, there are very complicated caste systems in place, and if Mickey tried some of his usual games with her…"

"Then he's now a pile of meat feeding the wildlife somewhere," said Gemma. "Oh Dahli I didn't like him but I'm not sure he deserved to die."

"Come on, let's see if we can find Diza, Czamki and Lyrellyn. Draephus will let us know when he finds Mickie."

Sometime before sunrise, Mickie Pastors dragged his broken bleeding body out of the woods near the festival grounds, his eyes pulled from his head, his hands broken and splintered, and his genitalia ripped from his body and shoved up his own anus. He was taken to a hospital, where doctors did their best to repair him, then sent him to Second City to recover in his own bed on the ship. He would never discuss what happened, and the rough set of wings carved into his back so deeply that it scarred the bone remained a mystery. It was an insignia no one had seen since the war.

****

Morning arrived. Dahli was awakened by Seija sitting on her bed, nosing her relentlessly, letting her know he needed to go out, and breakfast might be nice as well. She fell out of bed and dragged herself across the room to open the window of her second floor room to allow him to leap out and onto a tree, which he liked to scrabble up and down. While he played, she took a bath, then made breakfast for the both of them.

Day five. The last day. Tomorrow morning they started breaking everything down and packing up to leave. It was depressing. She'd loved being in Charlendine and a part of something so large. Soon it would be back to Second City, and work and school and… oh yeah. Drum-carving lessons. So maybe it wouldn't be so bad. At least she would have more time for her friends. But it also meant Gemma would be leaving soon, too.

Maybe she'd be back one day.

Breakfast over, Dahli left her room, Seija following along after her, his collar with its bells and little wooden wards making odd sounds. They walked from the hotel to the festival grounds, heading to the stage where Trilby and Mit-Mit would be waiting for water. She hopped onto the stage and walked over to Mit-Mit, inspecting the nose of her pseudo-head. People were asked not to pet the plants, but when the massive head-like limb descended into the audience, it was too much of a temptation to resist. Mit-Mit's nose was showing obvious wear from many hands touching her, so Dahli went to the supply shed to get a few things. Returning to Mit-Mit, she began carefully wrapping gauze around the great snout. She was going to miss Trilby and Mit-Mit. Tomorrow they would be taken to a mountain on the South Continent to help revive the Mountain Dragon population. She kissed the great nose as she worked.

"Gonna miss you," she said. "But I guess it's okay. You can get into as much mischief as you like down there. Hey you're covered in flowers, I guess you like the warm weather, huh? You smell pretty."

She wrapped the great nose, then soaked the gauze with a green fluid that would help heal the wear spots. With Mit-Mit now fit for duty, she walked over to Trilby, who had his own crowd of admirers. He was also absolutely covered with massive silvery-grey pods, just threatening to burst. Some unfortunate band was going to find themselves encompassed in a looming cloud of plant-pollen.

"You better not open those up when the Gryphons are on!" she warned. "Now let me see your nose. Figures yours would be an even bigger mess."

"Are they dangerous?" asked a voice.

Dahli turned her head to see a man standing behind her, dressed mostly in green, wearing a knit cap coloured green, yellow, and black. He was holding a baby girl dressed in similar colours, and the moment she saw the colourful lines on Dahli's face, she reached for them. Dahli deflected little hands from the still-painful cuts by taking hold of the tiny fingers.

She wondered briefly what Straif's baby would have looked like.

Dahli could tell they were from Earth by the accent alone. At least they spoke the language; Dahli would swear some people showed up and got offended that the whole planet didn't speak *their* language.

"Not unless you pull on their leaves," she answered. "They *will* defend themselves, but they're not aggressive."

A woman in a long green dress with hair like woven snakes came to stand by the man, looking up at Trilby. "They're amazing! What are they?"

"Mountain Dragons," said Dahli. "This is Trilby, and the other one over there wearing her new spring flowers is Mit-Mit."

She watched as the man stepped a little closer, Trilby lowering his gigantic pseudo-head. Dahli winced, knowing logically that Trilby was very unlikely to lash out, yet unable to shake the image of what that head, weighting hundreds of pounds and made of solid wood, could do to them. Trilby however was his usual gracious self as the baby reached her tiny hands for the head of the mighty creature, touching the worn snout. Nice little family. Very cute. Mommy, Daddy, Baby...

She never wanted to crawl off and cry so badly in her life.

"Are they plants?" asked the woman. Dahli swallowed down

the lump in her throat.

"Yeah, big silly plants that are really good at pretending to be animals. It's the last concert for these two, after today they are going to a sanctuary down south. We'll be sad to see them go, but they're too big and too old and too special to be dragging around anymore."

"Will you get a new pair?" asked the woman. "How long do they take to get this size?"

"Well these two are over a hundred years old, so probably not. In a hundred years the Mortified Gryphons won't be making music."

"Oh these belong to the Gryphons?" asked the woman, tentatively touching Trilby's nose. "Do you work for them?"

"I'm part of the road crew."

"Oh wow," said the woman. "But you're so young. I mean… you're just a child. Aren't there like… labour laws?"

"I asked for a job, they gave it to me."

"But should you be working at your age…?"

"Why not?"

"Well shouldn't you just enjoy being young…?"

"Are you *seeeeeeerious*?" Dahli mentally winced as she heard Diza's accent come out of her mouth. "I'm sixteen and I work with the greatest band on the planet! I'm at the Year End Festival in Charlendine! There is *nothing* I would rather be doing, except maybe playing the drums."

The woman laughed. "Yeah I suppose."

"Not out with your boyfriend?" teased the man.

All right, that was the line, right there. Dahli knew he meant no harm, but the raw spot she had inside was still large and painful. She turned to stare into his dark eyes.

"My boyfriend was Straif Mannechek. I was with him the night he died. My boyfriend and his unborn child are stone cold on a slab in a catacomb, so instead of judging how I live my life, why don't you go enjoy your living, breathing family. Some of us don't have that option."

She turned her back on them and began bandaging Trilby's nose. He nudged her, as if sensing her emotions. It was like a love tap from a mountain.

"Hey, careful, you," she whispered, fighting to get her emotions under control. "Don't send me home with broken ribs. Look at your pods, you are just going to burst any minute now, aren't you?

Look at this leaf, it needs to come off. Are you going to let me take it? No? Okay, it doesn't matter. Just don't be making clouds while people are playing."

"I'm... sorry," said the man awkwardly. "I didn't know."

Dahli swallowed hard, forcing herself to be polite. He wasn't trying to be mean. She turned to face him.

"I'm sorry too. It's just only been a few weeks since he died and…. It still hurts."

"Was he the kid on the screen?"

"Yeah," she said. "He really wanted to play here. It was the only way to give that to him."

Seija rose onto his back legs to sniff the baby, and allowed himself to be touched and inspected by the visitors. Dahli finished tending to the plants, then put the supplies away before checking to see if there was anything else that needed doing. By now the first band of the day was setting up, so Dahli took Seija hunting. She was free until the final show of the day, when the Gryphons played. In the meantime she just wanted to be alone.

It was Seija who spied the tail of the reed eel poking out of the reeds in an overgrown stream bed. Cautiously, Dahli crept toward it.

****

Dahli staggered back to the hotel, covered in blood, filthy, and grinning like a fool. Ahead of her pranced Seija, equally filthy, looking as if he had defeated all Kryphis by himself. Across Dahli's shoulders was a truly enormous reed eel; black and monstrous with great fangs showing in the huge mouth. She carried it down to the common room on the Gryphons' floor and dropped it onto a table.

"Final night of the show, and I'm having spicy hrabaccaus! Who's with me?!"

Mars was standing in the room, along with some other people Dahli did not know. He simply stared at her for a long moment, blinking, as she gleefully showed him the savage bites up and down her arms. He said nothing to her. Instead he pulled out his telecom and called Draephus.

"You know that girl you adopted? Yeah. She's crazy. Bring her a knife and some bandages, I'm sure she will tell you all about it."

Khymiria and her ink kit beat Draephus to the room, and she

decorated the most impressive eel-bites on Dahli's left hand with blues, yellows and greens. As Dahli was getting her second set of lines, Draephus showed up with a truly enormous knife of South Continental make, not so much for the eel as to let Dahli know he was getting fed up. The eel was cleaned and prepared, and soon the booze was flowing. Dahli then went to her room and into the bathroom to clean up while Seija gleefully gnawed the eel head. As she settled into the hot water of the bath, she heard a knock at the door.

"Stay out, I'm naked."

Draephus came in anyway.

"DRAEPHUS! NOT OKAY!"

"We'll worry about you being naked later. What were you thinking? That thing weighs twice as much as you do. They regularly *kill* people, you know."

She glared at him. "I was thinking how incredibly angry I was that some groutnoll from Earth would tease me about how I live my life after all I've been through in the past year. And if it makes you feel any better, I didn't know it was that big when I grabbed the tail."

His jaw dropped. "You waded into the river to grab some eel's tail?"

"Well if I'd seen the *head* I'd have known how big it was and I wouldn't have gone after it, would I?!"

"You're turning my hair grey!"

"That's not me, that's age!"

He stared at her for a long moment, then shouted; "*T'niski!*"

Dahli stared at him with enormous eyes as she heard the sound of three faelins heading toward them at top speed.

"You wouldn't!"

He just smiled. Moments later, Dahli had three thrashing, barking, squiggling faelins in the bath with her.

"I LIKED YOU BETTER ON THE POSTER!" she yelled. Then she heard Raski in the background, laughing as if he was losing his mind.

"What's the matter?" asked Draephus.

"Trilby just pollinated half the festival!"

"Whoops," said Dahli.

"Did he get anyone we care about?" asked Draephus.

"That goth group from Japan you liked. Oh look, the lead singer is waving hello at us with one finger. And the bass player is getting tackled by our road crew for trying to bash Trilby with a mic stand. Well there's *another* band who won't be accepting future invitations. Come on, Draephus, let's go rescue Trilby before he's either salad or a hammer for turning Japanese people into big messy spots on the stage."

"Right." Draephus turned to face Dahli once more. "No more wading in the rivers."

"You're no fun."

He left. Dahli hugged the bundle of soapy wet faelins. "Okay, when we get out of the bath, everybody go roll on Draephus' bed!"

"ARF!"

"Good faelin."

****

It was late afternoon, and Dahli was on the decorative arch once more, this time with Diza, Gemma, Czamkiar and Lyrellyn. She was so excited that her hands were numb, and her stomach felt like a live ball of electricity. Sitting with them were Seija, Bacca, and Czanda, all three equally excited, although they seemed to enjoy the flashing lights more than the music.

"Why do these faelins smell like that rose soap I gave you?" asked Gemma.

"Because Draephus thought it would be funny to put them in my bath," said Dahli. "I think we really *are* related, now. That or we've been spending too much time together."

"Did it ruin your life?" inquired Diza.

"Give it a rest, you guys!" said Gemma, exasperated. "I didn't come all the way to Sterkkaa to become a meme!"

"Hey there's Mars," said Czamkiar.

"Where?" asked Dahli.

"Behind Mit-Mit."

Dahli watched him check something behind the massive plant, then vanish once more. Then Erick Holly came out to keep the crowd happy while they were waiting for the Gryphons.

"We're running a bit late," he said. "Due to *somebody's* uncontainable enthusiasm for Japanese Goth music."

He looked significantly towards Trilby, who was settled low in his pot. If a plant could smile, he would. In fact someone had drawn one on his bandages, but even without it he would have looked pleased with himself. A burst pod dropped to the stage and slowly rolled away.

"Who's a naughty boy?" asked Erick. "Could it be you?"

Trilby shivered his leaves, sending delicate clouds of silvery pollen into the air. He did not appear repentant in the least. Moments later a highly annoyed-looking roadie came out to clear away the new piles of pollen on the stage. Erick skittered out of the way before he came to harm; the road crews had been clearing away the fine delicate grey substance for hours, now. They certainly didn't need Erick giving Trilby any excuses to shed more. Before Erick could make a comment, a diminutive form came across the stage. Dahli felt every single thought in her mind leave as she stared at Mars in tight black leather and stilettos, his long tinted hair hanging loose, body swaying in a manner that could not be anything other than suggestive.

"I just became a fan of androgyny," said Gemma, eyes large.

"What band is that?" asked Czamkiar.

Mars sidled up to Erick, who looked down at him.

"You could have had all this," said Mars.

"And a broken pelvis too when my girlfriend found out," said Erick.

Mars looked him up and down, then said "Honey if you'd come to bed with me it probably would have just end up broken by repeated pounding anyway."

Erick stared down at Mars. "Don't you have a boyfriend to intimidate? Or a Teamster or a mob hitman?"

Raski came out on stage just then, wearing the remains of what had once been a uniform. "Mars leave the poor man alone, he has enough to worry about."

Mars rolled his eyes and walked away, while Raski checked his sepulchord. In the background Dahli could see Draephus at his drums, while Khandid and Yuri strolled out to take their places. Normally there would be a great deal more impact to their taking the stage, and Dahli couldn't think why they were so casual this time.

"Why no dramatics?" she asked. "Raski never lets them just wander out on stage."

"Maybe the entrance they planned was ruined by Trilby's evil scheme to pollinate most of Charlendine in one go," said Gemma.

"Yeah maybe," said Dahli, uncertain.

She watched the Gryphons. They were clearly ready to go, except Raski wouldn't stop messing with his sepulchord. As the crowd watched, he popped open a panel on the instrument, and a mighty cloud of dust poured out. As a roadie ran to get him a replacement, Erick walked over to him.

"Heia," said Erick.

"Heia," said Raski, shaking pollen out of his sepulchord.

"Nice uniform."

"Thanks," said Raski. "I died in it."

"How many times?"

"Just once, but I made certain it was impressive."

Dahli watched Draephus as Raski and Erick clowned around. She winced as she saw him pulling at his hands again. Something was very not right with him.

"So how's it going?" asked Erick, as a roadie ran up to hand Raski a new sepulchord, this one without its electronics packed full of pollen.

"Good," said Raski, accepting the instrument and hanging it around his neck. "I'm pregnant."

"Whut?" said Diza, jaw hanging. "What did he just say?"

"What did he say?' said Gemma, slowly straightening up.

"*There* we go," said Dahli, "*there's* the drama. I had faith in you, Raski."

Most of the audience seemed to be second-guessing what they had heard as well, as did Erick. Dahli looked straight to the back of the stage, where Draephus was just staring as if he was doubting either his ears or his sanity; possibly both.

"*What* was that?" asked Erick.

"I'm pregnant," said Raski. "Nine weeks. I just thought I'd share that."

Erick backed up a few steps, clearly stunned, as most of the audience began cheering. When the noise died down at last after several minutes, Erick asked the question on everyone's mind.

"So who's the father?"

Raski, Yuri, Mars, and Khandid looked to the back of the stage, where Draephus still just sat and stared, blinking.

"That is the face of a man who truly had no idea this was coming," said Gemma.

"He does look a bit like Trilby just ran him over," said Diza, just as Khymiria came on stage and borrowed a microphone. She addressed the audience as she pointed to Draephus.

"What makes the look on this man's face even better, is the night before last I pointed out to him Raski was gaining weight, eating kaisa, getting sick, getting emotional… and he looked me square in the eye and said; *'He always gets nervous before a show'!*"

"But really makes the look on his face *extra* special," said Raski, "is he was with me when I went for the operation, looked after me while I healed, had sex with me, repeatedly, and let me tell you it was *fantastic…*"

Dahli watched Draephus slowly die by degrees from behind his drums, hiding behind his hands and shaking his head. Khymiria grinned.

"That good?"

"He can go all night like a Kryphisian wall-wrecker," said Raski.

"That's it," said Erick, "I'm walking back to Earth. Good night, folks!"

Gemma pulled out her phone as Erick slipped away. "Oh this is totally going on Facebook."

"And after *all that* he still had *no* idea there was the remotest chance you might possibly be pregnant," said Khymiria.

"None," said Raski.

"Poor Draephus," said Dahli, smiling with affection.

She watched as he got out from behind his drums and walked over to Raski, just staring at him.

"I really hate public displays," said Draephus.

"I know," said Raski.

He put his arms around Draephus' neck and kissed him, holding him tightly for a little while before letting him go. Draephus went back to his drums just as Mars moved up to Khymiria. Even in his heels he barely came up to her shoulder.

"Gonna stay and play a bit?"

"Oh I suppose I could," she said.

Dahli and Diza were screaming before even the first note of the song started.

"Spot the Gryphon fans," said Czamkiar dryly, as Mars and Khymiria joined their voices in one of the Gryphons' most iconic songs; The Storm is Worth It. Gemma took photos of Mars in his tight leather next to Khymiria in her flat soled boots and worn pants.

"They'd be a cute couple," said Gemma.

"If Khymiria liked boys they would be," said Lyrellyn.

"A Sferkkaan lesbian?" said Gemma. "They make those?"

"In *very* limited quantity," said Czamkiar. "Something of an endangered species."

"I'd totally do her," said Diza.

The five roared with laughter. Khymiria stayed for three songs, then departed, but not before giving Raski and Draephus each a hug. Khandid moved to the front to stand beside Mars.

"What do you think Raski and Draephus will have?" asked Khandid.

"I don't know," said Mars. "But it will be pretty and it will be mean."

"So," said Khandid, "Pretty mean."

"Yup."

"I know where you two live," said Raski.

"Yay! Now I can get a ride home!" said Khandid.

Diza looked at Dahli. "Remember back in the days of our innocence when we thought these moments of idiocy were staged?"

Dahli giggled, then screamed with appreciation as Mars and Khandid launched into 'Just Around Midnight'.

"I have to climb down," said Dahli. "I can't dance up here."

"I'll come with you," said Diza.

They climbed down from the arch and found a place to dance, and were soon joined by others. The faelins chose to stay on the arch, watching the people around them with obvious interest. On stage, Mars and Khandid tore through some of the most popular songs; ones that were fun to dance to, as well as the few cover songs they had chosen to play. The light-hearted mood went on through most of the set. But then, heading toward the end when the sun was low in the sky, they went into 'Storm Dancer', which was a welcome but unexpected treat. Storm Dancer was one of their older songs, and had a dark, cruel, blatantly sexual aspect to it. The song gave Mars a chance to really demonstrate what he was capable of as a singer, and he screamed out the lyrics as if he had the person he was talking about right in front of him. Given what Anthony had done to him recently, he may have had someone clearly in mind onto which he could vent his rage. Then, when the song ended, the stage abruptly went dark and silent, save for one light aimed directly at Draephus. Dahli and Diza clutched each other in anticipation. There was not a sound as Draephus picked up a fresh set of sticks, panting visibly, his hands bleeding.

Dahli wanted to scream in ecstasy as she heard the first soft notes of her favourite song, Rain Forest. Behind her the crowd was absolutely still. Dahli watched Draephus for signs of his earlier discomfort, but if he was in pain, he didn't show it. The only reaction Dahli saw was the faelins leaping down from the arch to the stage, prowling about on all fours, looking up at the sky as if awaiting something. With no prompting from anyone, Bacca, Czanda, and Seija positioned themselves on the stage and began to sway, reacting to something sensed but unseen. Slowly the jungle behind the stage became eerily alive, as if Draephus was working some sort of spell.

The other Gryphons held their places in the darkness, playing softly, accompanying the complex drum solo but never interfering as wild creatures arrived, hopping onto the stage. At one point three wild destri appeared, a stallion and two mares, showing their unique dapple-and-stripe pattern. They, like the faelins, seemed to be reacting to something unseen. They stayed a few moments, but when the stallion wandered into the pool of light focused on Draephus, he and the mares quickly departed for the jungle once more, spooked by the light. Strange moths gathered, and a few nocturnal birds swooped by, their day beginning just as the sun was setting. At one point, Dahli realized she had stopped breathing, afraid her breath would be enough to break the delicate magic.

The sound gathered in power, Draephus suddenly hitting his bass drum at one point with a sound like thunder overhead. It grew in intensity and strength, and no one in the audience was aware of the roadies silently and swiftly moving great mirrors onto the darkened parts of the stage. Dahli however recognized that the song was going on longer than was usual, and once more held her breath, wondering what Draephus was waiting for...

There was an exceptionally loud blast of music, just as the very last rays of the sun bounced off the snow of the mountains, and the stage was suddenly ablaze with the pinks and golds of a sunset reflecting off the mirrors; something almost no Sferkkaan had seen. The wild creatures scattered in a flurry of wings and tails, startled by the light and noise, while the crowd cried out in surprise and delight at the vibrant colours. Then slowly it all faded from view, and there was nothing but a soft rumble of thunder in the distance. Then it stopped. For what seemed like forever there was not a sound, then the audience roared in approval. The lights came up, and Dahli could see Draephus was spent. He was grey and shaking, and his hands were torn to bits. Then Mars stepped into the middle of the stage.

"Good night, Charlendine! We will do it all over again next year!"

He walked away, clearly exhausted as well, but not as much as Draephus. Within the crowd, Dahli heard a male voice speaking to someone in the darkness.

"*That* alone was worth the trip from Earth."

There was the loud crunch of something being torn off the stage, and the show was over for another year.

****

When Dahli reached the back of the stage, she could tell Draephus was in real distress. He was clearly sick, and he shook like a feralyke with the foaming rage. His skin was grey, and when a roadie tried to help him up, he cried out in pain. Raski was holding his hand, gazing into the blue eyes.

"It's okay, you just sit here as long as you like. I'll get your kit. I think that's the only way we are going to get you onto your feet."

"I have it with me," said Draephus weakly. He coughed, a small streak of blood appearing on his lips. Raski reached into the inner pocket of Draephus' coat and drew out the case that held the gold and glass needles. Each contained silvery-grey liquid.

"If they'd caught you with this on you, you'd be in jail, you know," said Raski.

"I know," said Draephus, "but I knew I'd need it."

Raski gave him the injection, then waited a few minutes for it to take effect. Slowly, carefully, they managed to get him onto his feet, but it was clear he couldn't do much more than stand. A little more of the mushroom resin enabled him to actually move, but he was still in too much pain to walk far. Eventually they simply ended up making use of a borrowed blanket to place him on. Then, with Raski and three roadies each holding a corner, they carried Draephus back to the hotel room and placed him on the bed, with Khandid, Yuri, Mars, and the three faelins following after.

"You are a mess," Dahli heard Raski say as she crept into the room after them.

"I think I broke something, Rask," said Draephus sleepily.

Mars stepped forward and managed to slip Draephus out of the coat, then stepped back and stared at him.

"I don't even have to touch you, I can *tell* that shoulder is dislocated. Draephus how do you manage these things?"

"Talent," he said drowsily.

"Hilarious," said Raski. "All right, I'll go in search of a doctor, do you think you three could help with the drums?"

"Mars and I will get it," said Khandid. "Yuri's too tired to help."

"I'll stay with Draephus," said Dahli.

"All right," said Raski, "let's get this night over with, I want a plate of kaisa and about fourteen hours of sleep."

They left, and Dahli settled herself on one of the couches to watch over Draephus. He was asleep within moments, and Dahli decided to simply lay down with a blanket, close at hand if he needed her.

Several times the door opened, and someone would creep in to see how Draephus was. The first well-wisher was Khymiria, then Billy Waters came by, leaving a bottle of something out of respect. Then Delaes stopped in to visit, and someone else after him. By now Dahli had stopped paying attention to the quiet click of the door opening and closing as someone came and went. Delaes returned after a while with J'Vanni and of course Piska, and the pair settled onto a couch and shared a bottle of something from the small coldbox in the room, talking softly. She was stunned to learn that, when in a quiet room with no stressful factors, Delaes Randerick could actually speak in sentences. She drifted to sleep, then later woke up briefly to see that Delaes and J'Vanni had settled down together on one of the pull-out beds. She got herself a drink of water from one of the bottles in the coldbox, then checked the time, wondering what was taking Raski so long. She then returned to the couch and closed her eyes once more.

****

She woke up abruptly with the feeling that something was very wrong. It was late; far too late, and Raski still was not back. She felt scared, and strangely heavy and sleepy, as if weighed down under mountains of warm blankets. It was hard to focus, and she reached out for the comforting warmth of Seija to steady herself. He too was awake, growling very softly. She motioned for him to be silent, then looked around the room. Bacca and Czanda had their heads up, listening, but Delaes, J'Vanni and Draephus were all still very soundly asleep.

Something was really wrong here. Why was it so hard to wake up?

The door opened, and Dahli put her head down, feigning sleep as she listened to the sound of someone cautiously entering. There were three men, and they were carrying something. Dahli felt Seija stiffen. The faelin clearly did not know who these people were, and didn't like them. Piska ruffled his feathers and made a quiet grumbling noise.

"Are they out?" whispered a voice.

A second voice responded, still quiet but a little more loudly, as if he was not worried about waking anyone up.

"Yeah Draephus is drugged, and I managed to get the drugs into the water for the freak and the Grey Boy, so all we have to do is…"

Dahli sat up and shouted; "FETCH!"

Delaes may have been drugged, but he sat up immediately as he heard her shout. At the same time three faelins launched themselves at the strangers, who clearly meant them harm. The ensuing chaos was loud enough to draw people from all over as the men screamed while the faelins tore them apart. Blood and small chunks of flesh sprayed in all directions, and Piska dove into the fray to remove the better portion of one man's face.

Piska did not care for strangers who came to hurt his family.

"What the šukat is going on?" demanded Delaes, clearly a little too addled to understand the situation.

One of the men broke free and fled into the hall, only to encounter a whirling ball of white. Khandid did not pull back, and he wasted no time turning the man into a ragged pile of blood and flesh on the floor. The second man was dead on the floor with his throat torn out and his face removed. The third was cowering in the corner as Czanda prepared to kill him as well, but Dahli stopped him.

"Watch," she said, and he did, though it was clear he would have much preferred to kill the man. By now even Draephus and J'Vanni were awake, though they looked a little too bleary to grasp what had just happened. Khandid appeared in the doorway, half-dressed and stained with blood.

"Where's Raski?"

"I don't know," said Dahli. "He never came back."

"I'll go look for him."

Then he was gone, leaving Dahli in the middle of the worst mess she'd ever seen.

"I think I'd like to go home now," she said.

****

Raski had been found not far from the hotel, lying on his side in an alley, cut and bleeding but still very much alive. The swaths of blood and pieces of entrails that were found around him had clearly not come from him, but his attacker was never found. All Raski knew was that something had come out of the jungle, something huge and unseen, and it mangled his assailant before dragging him, screaming, into the darkness. Speculation abounded as to what it may be, but only Raski and Draephus knew. And they were not saying.

From the one remaining conspirator they learned the story; the residual members of Vesper's group had sworn an oath to get rid of Draephus, Delaes, and J'Vanni. Raski had been included at the last minute when he announced he was pregnant by Draephus. They had not intended to kill Raski, but they *had* intended to kill the baby he carried, leaving no part of Draephus in existence. The fact that they had made such a botched and amateur job of it demonstrated that it truly had been Vesper who was the brains of the operation. For one thing Vesper would have known better than to attack Raski outside where unseen creatures would notice.

Chapter Thirty-Two

Raski and Draephus were sent to Second City hospital to be cared for, then to the castle to recover in their own bed. Dahli stayed behind to be with Trilby and Mit-Mit as they were carefully loaded onto a transport to the South Continent, to a place they had not been in a century. She could do little more than stand and cry as the leafy giants were shut into their containers, and it was a long time before she stopped. Somehow emotions seemed a little more overwhelming than they had before. Then, before the container was shut, Trilby gave himself a mighty shake to free himself of remaining empty pods. As Dahli watched, one pod flew right toward her, and she caught it, looking down at the round silvery object, split open with a trace of pollen inside. It, along with her new line art, was the perfect reminder of this festival.

Two days after returning to Second City, she caught a seedling lurking within a small hole in the wall of Gryphon Studios. It was tiny and sad and pale, but with proper feeding it would soon take on the brilliant colours of its kind. Fortunately for Dahli it would not become a giant for many years, but it did seem to enjoy living on her window sill with the small valley song amp-plant Dahli already owned. She named it Tril-Mit, after its parents.

Two weeks after she returned home, her book arrived, with all the beautiful photos of herself, her friends, and Straif. His own copy of the book had been sent to her as well. She kept his copy, and gave her own to Gemma.

Slowly, things returned to normal. Gemma boarded the ship to return to Earth, vowing to return the first chance she got. Draephus and Raski healed together in Draephus' castle, as Yuri and Khandid moved out of their apartment and into Raski's great estate. J'Vanni became an official member of Bad Influence, but retained his solo career, as well as his tendency to just stay in his apartment.

However, one infamous night roughly four weeks after the festival, Bad Influence appeared on the Astellis Monct show, complete with their two new members – drummer Bethlarynn Shafyre, and keybarr player J'Vanni Dei Syncopius.

"What do you suppose Delaes promised J'Vanni to get him on

stage?" asked Dahli as she sat on the floor near Draephus and Raski, who were lounging on their bed, relentlessly working at the huge lump of wood that would hopefully one day be a drum.

"I don't know but I bet it was pretty pornographic," said Raski.

"They do seem to have an interesting love life," said Draephus.

They performed their latest song, 'The Night Turns Around', which was the final evolution of the Bad Influence sound – an eerie mixture of metal and the haunting, ethereal other-worldly style of J'Vanni. People could not get enough of it, and the Gryphons found themselves in the strange position of having to share their lofty perch with another band. They had decided not to worry unless the audience began tearing Bad Influence's stages apart. Then it would be laxatives in the shaumaus and redhir turds in the snack bowls. In the meanwhile, Dahli, Raski and Draephus watched as Bad Influence ended their song and came to sit near the same desk that Draephus had once launched himself across in an attempt to kill Astellis Monct.

"Daghuwai bastard," growled Draephus.

Raski kissed him. On the Visual, Astellis Monct did the impossible and made himself even more unpopular with Draephus than he already was.

"So you're a Grey Boy," he said to J'Vanni, grinning as he anticipated the impending break-down of the famous composer.

"I'll kill him," said Draephus.

"I'll help," said Raski.

On stage, J'Vanni stared back at the man coldly. "I beg your pardon?"

"You're a Grey Boy, one of the invaders. You're a baby-poisoner."

Rysta managed to get an arm around Delaes' neck before he outed himself as half-faelin by landing on Monct and tearing his face off. J'Vanni Dei Syncopius stared down the man before him, even though Raski, Draephus and Dahli knew he had to be terrified. Confrontation was not natural to J'Vanni, but he did not back down in response to the insult.

"Yes, I am a Grey Boy, but I am no baby-poisoner," he snarled. He reached into his long coat and pulled out a stack of papers, slamming them onto the desk. "This is my citizenship, from the Emperor himself, declaring me to be a rightful inhabitant of this world." He slammed something else onto the desk. "*This* is my Order of the Shadow. There are only *three* of these in existence, given to Kryphisians who *defected* to help *your* side because what was happening was *wrong*, and the other holders are now *dead*. And *this*, little worm, is my Red Wing, I'm sure you have heard of this particular military decoration before. I earned it by standing with my back to a very rickety door in a crumbling earthen basement holding my breath, as well as a half-empty laser pistol, to defend, *successfully* I might add, over four dozen Sferkkaan children. Now. Please tell me. What did *you* do in the war, Donsa Monct? We are dying to know."

There was a long and very tense silence. Then Astellis Monct made a run for it, just as Delaes tore loose and raced after him. J'Vanni sighed as he rose from his chair, following his husband.

"Delaes! Do not eat that, it may have diseases."

On camera, Bethlarynn and Rysta looked at each other, then Bethlarynn went to sit in Monct's chair, reaching into a drawer in the desk to pull out a handful of blue cards.

"Next up, we have author Melari Khanin!" Bethlarynn looked to Rysta. "Wasn't he on that time Draephus CZimcocious tried to kill Monct?"

"He was," said Rysta.

Melari Khanin darted out onto the stage and sat down, eyes enormous.

"I am *never* coming on this programme again!"

"None of us are," said Rysta. "Tell us about the new book. We understand Raski Jervyas is a huge fan of yours."

"Groutnolls," grumbled Raski softly. "How's the wood-carving coming, Fearless?"

"I thought this was supposed to be punishment," said Dahli, working away with a hammer and chisel, slowly hollowing the wood out.

"For most people, it is," said Draephus as he lounged on the couch and watched her. "You, however, do not function like other people."

She glanced up at him. "How are you feeling?"

"I'm fine."

"You hurt yourself pretty badly at the Festival."

"I'm fine."

Dahli kept chipping at her piece of wood. "Hey I was at the library, researching illnesses for absolutely no reason whatsoever, and I found a description for this type of disease called viral arthritis…?"

"Dahli don't force me to get up and hurt you."

"…and they recently found that eating this type of plant can actually prolong bone density and integrity for years! It can also significantly reduce the amount of pain a patient is in. Isn't that amazing?"

Raski sat up abruptly. "What plant?" he asked.

"Better not be kaisa!" growled Draephus.

"No. It's scribe's weed."

"Are you kidding me?!" demanded Draephus, as Raski left the bed and ran off to do something or other that likely involved importing scribe's weed. "That plant was put here on this planet for the sole purpose of making a permanent mess on everything it touches."

"Yes it was," said Dahli. "But apparently once you boil the ink out of it, what you have left is a yummy gelatinous mass of a snot-like consistency that will ease your pain and reverse some of the damage."

"So not a cure," said Draephus.

"Unfortunately not," Dahli said quietly. "But you'll remain a Gryphon a few more years yet."

He watched her for a few minutes, then asked; "What tipped you off.?"

"The hand-pulling," she said. "And the way your nail-beds are turning black. Dislocating your shoulder was a huge indicator, too. I don't care how hard you were playing the drums that night; it wouldn't have happened unless there were other factors involved."

"HEY!" called Raski from another room. "I FOUND RECIPES!"

"Oh yay," said Draephus.

The door opened, and Khandid tore into the castle, shouting from the main hall. "RASKI!"

"WHAT?"

"WE HAVE TO CHECK OUT THE GRYPHONS' ROOST!"

"WHY?"

"NEW FAN FICTION! AND IT'S REALLY BAD!"

"AM I THE WHIP-WAVING MANIAC AGAIN?! BECAUSE I'M NOT READING IT IF I AM!"

"NO! I AM! YOU JUST WORK FOR ME!"
"WELL I BETTER BE GETTING PAID FOR IT!"
"I'LL START THE COFFEE!"

Draephus sighed heavily, then looked to the great clock standing in the hall, visible through the open door. "Come on, Fearless, it's getting late, let's get you home so Teirra doesn't eat me. How are you two getting along?"

"Better," said Dahli, setting aside her tools. "We're just… very different people, but at least we're learning to love each other for who we are."

"How did she react to the lines?"

"Better than I thought she would, but she still thinks you had something to do with it."

"Of course. How's… you know who?"

"Anthony?" asked Dahli, rising to her feet and dusting herself off. "I don't know. Atterick kicked him out of the band after Anthony started calling Mars all sorts of names. He almost started a bar fight. I feel sorry for him. He must be feeling pretty stupid for abandoning Mars."

"Yeah well it's his own fault," said Draephus. "Come on, let's get you home."

****

Another day, and just more of the same. Dahli walked to the corner just past Diza's house, where Czamkiar and Lyrellyn were waiting, and moments later were joined by Diza.

"I can't believe I'm still not allowed to talk to you!" said Dahli.

"Oh I can," said Diza. "Dad never gets over anything."

The four walked to school; smoking, talking, laughing. Then, just as they reached the final block before the school, they saw a shape standing before them. He was shaggy and skinny, with scars all over him. His long dark hair was tied into a messy knot, and the single black diagonal lightning bolt painted across his left eye told them he was a scavenger from the depths of the Cylinder. He was wet and dirty, and they could see the knives in a holder around his thigh that he would use for killing whatever he caught, or digging things out of the mud. He was a genuinely dangerous creature, and Lyrellyn stepped in front of his friends to defend them if the situation arose. But this particular scavenger was making no threatening moves. In fact he was just standing, as if waiting for someone to recognize him...

Dahli felt her jaw drop. "Shae?"

He grinned, and she ran to him, throwing her arms around his neck. "Shae I was so worried for you! I looked everywhere, I couldn't find you..."

"Yeah I probably should have mentioned I was living in the Cylinder," he admitted.

"Well it would have helped! Oh Shae I am so glad to see you again. What happened to you?"

"That's a very long story," he said, and laughed. "Who are your friends?"

"Come on, I'll introduce you," she said. "We've got a lot to catch up on."

Epilogue

"Whatever happened to Astellis Monct, anyway?" asked Diza.

"No idea," said Dahli. "But after that night he tried to upset J'Vanni, no one has seen him."

"Much like my bag of kiska nuts," said Czamkiar. "Gemma are you sitting on them?"

Gemma was staring at Shae with a pout on her face. "How come Dahli gets all the pretty boyfriends?"

"She gets Draephus to go catch them for her," said Lyrellyn.

"Nuh-uh," said Dahli. "I caught that one myself. Seija! What have you got? Oh a rat. Yummy. No I don't want to share! Eyew! You can have that one all by yourself."

It was good to have the whole group back together again, albeit with one new member. Dahli had moved on, but she had not forgotten Straif, nor did she miss him any less. She would still go to his alcove in the catacombs to visit a while, making sure he was undisturbed. But then it would be time for lessons or work or school, or time for friends, and she would have to leave him. Sometimes his spectre was seen in the castle; forever seventeen and pregnant with his child. It broke Dahli's heart, but she had to live her own life. And she knew Straif would not want her to cry endlessly by his corpse.

"So what are we doing?" asked Gemma.

"Whatever it is, we're sure it will ruin your life," said Shae, smiling.

"Oh goody, they taught you that too! For a moment I thought I had escaped it."

It was late winter. In two months it would be time for the Year End Festival in Charlendine again, and this time Atterick would be on stage with his own band. Granted he would be the first to appear, and that was hardly an auspicious position, but he would be there. That in itself was cause for celebration.

Bad Influence would appear second to last. The Mortified Gryphons still held their place of honour.

"So glad the ship from Earth to Sferkkaa only took six weeks this time," said Gemma. "Four months in space was way too long."

"Show is starting!" said Diza.

The six teenagers watched as Erick Holly walked onto the stage that Astellis Monct had once stood upon. He had since moved to Sferkkaa, finding he liked the lifestyle better. He tried to get the audience to be quiet, but it was a lost cause, especially when Raski Jervyas walked out, sepulchord around his neck.

"Holy shit but that man is *pregnant*," said Gemma. "Look at the fucking *size* of him! How far is he?"

"A week past due," intoned Dahli gravely. "Could be a really exciting live performance."

Erick Holly watched Raski with a rather wary expression on his face, as the other Gryphons came out and took their places. Dahli sighed as she noticed Draephus pulling at his hands, but lately the habit had become infrequent. It only showed up just often enough to remind them that Draephus was not well. Raski popped open a panel on his sepulchord by accident, then closed it.

"Checking for pollen?" inquired Erick.

"Don't joke," said Raski, "I'm still finding tiny random piles of it all over."

"So how are you feeling?" asked Erick.

"Great!" said Raski. "I'm in labour."

"*There* we go," said Dahli. "*There's* the drama. I had faith in you, Raski."

Diza watched Draephus fall into his drums and then scramble to his feet. "YOU'RE WHAT?!"

"Oh calm down, we have hours yet."

"I'm not helping!" said Khandid.

"I will!" said Mars. "Get the toilet plunger."

"I don't want to have either of you watching me scream in agony," said Raski.

Khandid looked to Mars. "Well now I'm torn."

"As will Raski soon be, I'm sure," said Mars.

Draephus proceeded to have some sort of panic-induced fit that clearly implied his first instinct was to get his husband someplace safe where he could be cared for. Yuri delicately stepped away from him, and Khandid ran to help Draephus sit up.

"So what are you going to have?" asked Erick.

"With luck, a baby," said Raski.

"No I meant do you know if it is a boy or a girl?"

"Nope," said Raski. "If it's a girl we are naming it Shaktra after a friend of Draephus', and if it's a boy we are naming it Straif."

"What if it's a triple-breasted snake headed goddess?" asked Khandid.

Raski sighed. "Khandi if you tell that story…"

Erick turned to the audience. "Ladies and gentlemen, I present the Mortifying Gryphons."

"That's 'mortified'," said Mars.

"Not from where I am standing," said Erick.

Erick went to sit behind the infamous desk, and the Gryphons played their latest song. They stayed to talk a while, then, because Draephus was clearly coming unglued over the prospect of being a father any minute, went backstage. The next guest out was the newly-elected Minister of Education, there to discuss the building of not only new schools, but libraries as well, and how new history books were being written, covering not only the Sferkkaan side of the war, but including information about how the war looked from the Kryphisian side. Dahli could not help but feel a smug satisfaction in her heart that the man Vesper had tried so hard to destroy, J'Vanni Dei Syncopius, was now a hero in his own right.

It was so much easier to get information out of Draephus when he was gooned out of his mind on his new, more helpful and less destructive medication.

As Erick and the minister were talking, Khandid Stracona walked out, coming to sit on the edge of Erick's desk, holding something wrapped in a towel. Erick gave Khandid a puzzled look.

"Heia," he said.

"Heia," said Khandid brightly in return.

"What have you got there?"

"Oh this?" said Khandid. "It's a four minute old baby Sferkkaan."

"What did he say?!" exclaimed Diza, as Dahli just stared, jaw hanging.

"Wow," said Gemma. "Oh I am *SOOOO* glad he did not deliver on stage."

Khandid had just enough time to let the camera get a quick glimpse of the tiny baby girl with the befuddled face, deep golden skin and blazing blue eyes, before a pair of faelins came out to make certain he promptly returned to the room backstage where the parents were. Diza then nudged Dahli.

"Come on, let's get to the castle, we can see the baby when Raski and Draephus arrive home."

They got into Lyrellyn's conni and drove to the castle, a grey conni appearing behind them at some point in the journey and following after them. Both vehicles pulled into the gravel drive before the castle, parking. Raski was out of the conni in a moment, bright eyed and excited to show off his infant.

"Where's Draephus?" asked Dahli.

Raski looked to the grey conni in time to see something fall out of the passenger side, hitting the ground and lying there in a lump.

"You *did* explain to him that babies are what happen after the being pregnant part, right?" said Dahli.

"Yeah," said Raski, smiling. "I just don't think he knew they arrived in such a big pile of 'ick'."

"There is definitely a certain amount of ick involved in childbirth," said Dahli. "I've seen videos."

"It wasn't the ick," said Draephus, hauling himself to his feet and staggering over to the small group of people, followed by his faelins. "It was when Bacca stole the placenta and ate it."

"Yeah that would do it to me too," said Gemma.

"ARF!"

Raski kissed Draephus softly. "Come on, old man," he said quietly. "Let's get Shaktra to bed. It's cold out here."

Discographies -

Mortified Gryphons

-Gryphons in Yer Basement. (Gryphon Music)

'I'd Rather Believe.' - Y. Stracona.
'Rain Forest' - D CZimcocious.
'Lost in the Cylinder.' - D. CZimcocious.
The Hill.' - M. David.
'Caught in the Light' - M. David/Y. Stracona.
'Strangeness.' – Y. Stracona.
'Carrion.' - D. CZimcocious/M. David.
Come Down the Stairs.' - K. Stracona.

-Nothing Wrong Here. (Gryphon Music)

'Nothing Wrong Here' - M. David.
'The Storm is Worth it' – M.David/Y. Stracona
'But If You Turn out the Light It Will Be Dark' - (instrumental) - R. Jervyas.
'Storm Dancer' - M. David.
'The Rock' - D. CZimcocious.
'If You Stayed' – Y. Stracona.
'The Void' - Y. Stracona.
'Ever the Rain.' - K. Stracona.

-Gryphons by Moonlight. (Gryphon Music)

'Nightfall' - M. David.
'Things to do With a Kaisa.' - M. David.
'Just Around Midnight' – M. David
'Not a Chance.' - R. Jervyas.
'River Song.' - M. David.
'Satellite.' - R. Jervyas.
'Avalair Underground.' - D. CZimcocious.
Mushrooms and Jam.' - K./Y. Stracona.

-Nice Knowin' Ya. (Gryphon Music)

'Feeling Lucky' - D. CZimcocious.
'Tempestivity' - R. Jervyas.
'Maniac in the Bushes.' - D. CZimcocious.
'Brain Dead' - D. CZimcocious.
'Time and Again' - M. David/Y. Stracona.
'Flying to the Afterlife' - K. Stracona.

-Gryphons Up Your Nose. (Bootleg. Released on S.Base.4 Recordings)

'Cough Cough Tiddly Oop' - K. Stracona/R. Jervyas.
'The Dancing Song' - Revised by K. Stracona.
'Shut Up and Sing' - M. David.
'It's a Shoe' (instrumental) - R. Jervyas/ Y. Stracona.
'Can't See a Hole in a Ladder' - K. Stracona/D. CZimcocious.
'I'm the Sepulchord Player' - R. Jervyas.

-Time Flies, Heat Rises. (Gryphon Music)

Ysith Beach' - R. Jervyas, performed by S. Mannechek.
'Hold the Door' (instrumental) - K. Stracona.
'If You Do That Again' - M. David.
'Ice in the Summer' - M. David.
'Nightfall' – M. David.
'Put Me to Bed with a Shovel' - R. Jervyas, performed by S. Mannechek.
'You Can't Light That in Here' (instrumental) - M. David/S. Mannechek.

Solo Albums.

-Raski Jervyas and a Few Odd Friends. (Gryphon Music)

-R. Jervyas, D. Randerick, S. Mannechek, J. Syncopius, S. Ferril

-Time and Space. (Lead Records)
-K. Stracona/Y. Stracona

-Secret Elders. (Revolution Music)
-M. David.

Other Recordings.

Interview Cylinder with previously unreleased cuts; 'Nearly Black' and 'Not to Blame.' **(Gryphon Music)**

<u>**Bad Influence**</u>

- Part of the Ashes. (Revolution Music)

'Just Too Precious.' - D. Randerick/R. Sylvinia.
'Feels A Lot Like Nowhere.' - D. Randerick.
'Quit This Place.' - M. Kai.
'Limrat.' - R. Sylvinia.
'Backwards and Dead.' - D. Randerick.
'Caught in the Rain.' - R. Sylvinia.
'Avalair Grey.' - D. Randerick.

- The Music to the Story. (Revolution Music)

'Catch This.' - D. Randerick.
'I Wouldn't Bother.' - D. Randerick.
'Mind Rot.' - R. Sylvinia.
'Sick and Forgotten.' - D. Randerick.
'Eating at the Contempo.' - M. Kai.
'Call Me The Hunter.' - D. Randerick.
'The Weird Places in my Mind.' - R. Sylvinia.
'Tight Rope.' - M. Kai.
'Nervous.' - D. Randerick.

-Don't Give Us Any More Bad Ideas. (Revolution Music)

'Bile in the Aisle' - D. Randerick.
'Sha-Bomp-Bomp.' - R. Sylvinia.
'Chronic.' - R. Sylvinia.
'Gone This Morning.' - M. Kai.
'I Won't if You Can't.' - R. Sylvinia.
'Pointless.' - D. Randerick.
'Just Can't Anymore.' - D. Randerick.
'Fly off a Bridge.' - M. Kai.
'Lurking in Your Mind.' - D. Randerick.

-I've Got a Big One. (Revolution Music)

'Draephus' Killer Ducks.' - D. Randerick\R. Sylvinia.
'Creeping Malaise' - M. Kai.
'So Who's to Blame?' - M. Kai.
'Sacred Bird.' **- (previously unreleased track)** R. Sylvinia \M. Kai.
'Banned.' - D. Randerick.
'I Saw It, I Hate It' - D. Randerick.
'You Never Could.' - D. Randerick.
The Dark.' - R. Sylvinia.
'A Compiled Composition Between Myself and Donsa Randerick.'   - D. Randerick. **(previously unreleased track with J'Vanni Dei Syncopius.)**

-Why Can't We? (Revolution Music)

'Clart in the Corner.' - M. Kai.
'No Class.' - R. Sylvinia.
'Shattered Glass.' - D. Randerick.
'Disrespect Intended.' - D. Randerick.
'Kind of a Grey Night.' - D. Randerick.
'I'll Give You What I Can.' - M. Kai.
'Another Town, Another Fight.' - D. Randerick.
'Too Much Fun.' - R. Sylvinia.
'Could You Think of Me and Smile?' - R. Sylvinia.

-Hold This for a Second. (Revolution Music)

'Relax.' - D. Randerick.\ S. Mannechek.
'Hold This for a Second.' - D. Randerick.\ S. Mannechek.
'What You had Before Me.' - D. Randerick.
'Oh I Never.' - R. Sylvinia.
'Cry.' - D. Randerick.
'The Night Turns Around' – D. Randerick \ J. Syncopius \ S. Mannechek
'Blood Excitement.' - R. Sylvinia.\ S. Mannechek.
'Your Vacant Eyes.' - D. Randerick.
'Not Even if You Asked.' - D. Randerick.\ R. Sylvinia.
'Guarded Treasure.' - R. Sylvinia.
'Not Much But Enough.' - D. Randerick.\ S. Mannechek.

J'Vanni Dei Syncopius

-My Songs All Have Really Long Titles, Therefore My Album Should Have One Too. (Revolution Music)

'Contemplation on the Colour Orange.'
'Ode to a Tangle-Bunny Sitting in a Leaf Before the Day has Sung its Fear.'
'Some People Who Haven't Deserve To.'
'Odyssey.'
'Oracle.'

-Bird Seed Tea. (Revolution Music)

'Thoughts That Wander.'
'Pensive Moments in the Fifth Hour.'
'Please Skip This Song.'
'Epitaph on a Small Insect that I Accidentally Stepped On.'
'The Garden No One Can See.'

-With a Few Friends. (Revolution Music)

'Of The Wide World I Stand Alone.'
'Whimsy'
'Meandering of the Early Morning Mind.'
'Upon Regarding a Sea Bird.'
'Experimental Electric Piece Composed for Keybarr.'
'I Didn't Want to Record This One – Khandid and Delaes Made Me.'

-Don't You Wish You Knew What I Looked Like? (Revolution   Music)

'Comic Short Piece.'
'Thoughts While Watching My Lover Sleep.'
'Incidental Work.'
'Short Poem set to Laser Keybarr.'
'It Was Never Mere Infatuation.'
'Progressive Composition.'
'Hill of Fire.'

-J'Vanni, or Someone Who Looks Like Him. (Revolution Music)

'The Daylight Hours.'
'You Could Teach Me to Dance, But is it Worth it?'
'Short Piece for Acoustic Sepulchord with Incidental Vocals.' (Not Mine.)
'I Love You For Your Patience.'

Anazampini

-Next. (Revolution Music)

'No Second Chance.' - C. Rae.
'You're Good, But He's Better.' - C. Rae.\S. Quintora.
'I Like You This Way.' - S. Quintora.
'Long-Muzzled Night Stalker Gun.' - M. Belamia.
'Forgot You.' - C. Rae.
'I Lost My Virginity So Why Don't You Come Over And Help Me Look For it?' - A. Chamin.
'The Visual's Broke and the Only Thing on the Receiver is Vortex.' - A. Chamin.
'I'll Show You Mine.' - S. Quintora.

-Fine Without You. (Revolution Music)

'I Wouldn't Care You're Gone But You Took The Feralyke.' - C. Rae.\ A. Chamin.
'Piston Broke.' - S. Quintora.
'Draephus CZimcocious' Coat.' - C. Rae.
'Smells That Remind Me Of You.' - C. Rae.
'I'm Free, Not Cheap.' – C. Rae.
'The Faelan Ate the Laser Print of You and Died.' - A. Chamin
'Your Stuff's on the Lawn.' - S. Quintora.
'Substance Abuse.' - C. Rae.

-I'm Okay, You're Questionable. (Revolution Music)

'No, You Can't Come In.' - C. Rae.
'Clart.' - S. Quintora.
'Worse Influence.' – C. Rae.
'Delaes, Deleather, Deboots.' - C. Rae.
'Life's Too Short And So Are You.' - M. Belamia.
'Five of Us, One of You, And I've Got a Knife.' - A. Chamin.
'My Garden.' - S. Quintora.
'Don't Wanna Be Your Friend.' C. Rae.

Pronunciation, definitions, and hopefully useful information.

The profane words that the Sferkkaans use are all of an earthly origin, though out-of-date and from various countries. 'Šukat' *(pr: SHOO-kat)* is Czech, and basically means 'fuck'. It replaces a more obscure word, 'sklook', which means pretty much the same thing, but I never really cared for. 'Conni' is short for 'conveyance', which basically means car. The only "alien" word I came up with that I truly liked was 'clart-blossom', which means 'fart'. 'Beaker' was a term a friend used, and I basically put it in because it made me laugh. One stupid person was a Beaker. More than one Beaker was a Unit, which averaged out to so many Beakers per square inch. If you found yourself in a Unit of Beakers then you should flee immediately.

Ai sikate *(pr: eye sick-AT)* – informal, "Later!"
Shi-dah? *(pr: she-DAH?)* – "Understand?"
Nai-nan. *(pr: NAY-nan)* – Formal. "Absolutely not."
Shi-Kha *(pr: she-CO)* – type of martial art.
Donselle *(pr: don-SELL)* - respectful term for a woman "M'lady."
Donsa *(pr: DON-sa)* - respectful term for a man. "Mister."
Šukat *(pr: Czech dialect, "Shoo-KAT")* - Fuck.
Groutnoll *(pr:GROAT-knoll)* – asshole, bastard.
Clart *(pr: like 'cart' but with an l)* – shit.
Destri/s *(pr: DES-tree/s)* – a type of large mammal, used for riding and other things.
Duone/s *(pr: DOO-own)* – respectful term for teacher, either gender.
Kuvon *(pr: KOO-von)* – Sferkkaan motorcycle.
*T'nisk/i *(pr: tin-ISSK/ee)* – baby/babies. South Continent dialect. Affectionate.
Hrabaccaus *(pr: her-ABBAC-cus)* – Traditional South Continental dish, served only at certain rites of passage.
Varadasai *(pr: VARA-dass-eye)* – a genetically modified creature that tends to live in dark, sparsely-habited areas. Prefers carrion but will quite literally eat anything. Bones are a particular favourite.
Nari nuisse *(pr: NAR-ee noo-EESE)* - The literal translation is "it happened somewhere else." The implied meaning; 'it happened

but there's no need to mention it to anyone else'. East Continent in origin.

Redhir *(pr: RED-heer)* – basically a Sferkkaan guinea pig.

Loamwai *(pr: LOAM-way)* - closely related to redhir, and easily as cute, but a loamwai weighs five times what its little cousins do.

Daeha *(pr: DAY-haw)* – form of guardian spirit, very powerful.

Ohwendai *(pr: oh-WHEN-day)* – a form of South Continental nature and spirit-based magic. There are many variations and there are no written records. Traditions are passed down from the priests and priestesses to the younger generation through demonstration and story-telling, and as a result no two people practice the exact same rites and rituals.

The capital CZ at the beginning of Draephus' surname denotes Imperial lineage, though in his case it's possible he's not related to the Imperial line at all. But the double capital CZ is pronounced as an 's', so Draephus' last name is Sim-COKE-ee-us. The capital C small z combination in Czamkiar's name does not denote Imperial lineage, and is pronounced as a 'z'. So his name is pronounced Zam-kee-AR. Then there is Khandid's name. In some languages, 'kh' is pronounced as an 'h' sound. In Sferkkaan, the kh is pronounced as a k, but it changes the 'a' following to a short 'o' sound, like in Honda. So his name is pronounced CON-did.

Enston Legri – creator of musical instruments, various sound monitoring devices.

32 Earth hours in a Sferkkaan day.

Sferkkaan week is nine days long.

Five weeks in a Sferkkaan month.

Takes 11 (Sferkkaan) months to make a Sferkkaan baby.

*Draephus insists the word means "Baby/Babies." Those who speak the South Continental dialects say it actually means "Idiot/s."